POWER IS MADNESS
AND IT FILLS YOU. . . .

All your fears are made real, whispered the
tantalizing voice of madness in Quin's mind.
He stared into the void, and it erupted into all
the demons of his imaginings. They clawed
at him and tore his flesh from him, and he
screamed, for he had never known such
pain.

The room contracted, warped, and swirled
around Quin. *You have no right to invade
my mind,* he screamed with Power. *You will
not mold me into your image.*

He shattered the specters that tormented his
flesh, and he grasped the room in his mind
and stabilized it. He sensed the manipulative
patterns of Power behind each wall, and he
drove their fire back at them. He felt their
shock and it pleased him. *Kill them,* whispered his Power. *They threaten you.*

"Yes," he hissed. "I shall punish them, as
they have punished me. . . ."

FIRE CROSSING

CHERYL J. FRANKLIN

DAW BOOKS, INC.
DONALD A. WOLLHEIM, FOUNDER
375 Hudson Street, New York, NY 10014

**ELIZABETH R. WOLLHEIM
SHEILA E. GILBERT
PUBLISHERS**

First Printing, March 1991

1 2 3 4 5 6 7 8 9

DAW TRADEMARK REGISTERED
U.S.PAT.OFF. AND FOREIGN COUNTRIES
—MARCA REGISTRADA,
HECHO EN U.S.A.

PRINTED IN THE U.S.A.

For Hal
(even if it doesn't have enough equations)

Prologue

I never dispense philosophical advice—unless pressed in a moment of extreme weakness, such as the early morning gray-time after a night's overindulgence in intensive conversation. Such solemn advice as I might give is rarely heeded, usually unappreciated, and frequently damaging to the relationship between giver and recipient.

Having acknowledged my firm stance in this regard, I must confess that I have not always been so cautious. I must also add (regrettably) that an astonishing number and variety of individuals beseech me for my advice with tedious regularity. Whether they know me as Quin, Lord Quinzaine dur Hamley, or any of the dozens of names I have assumed, whether they have known me for years or for an hour, they seem to consider me an oracle of wise words: I cannot imagine a less likely opinion, but it is prevalent.

The questioners usually attempt to justify themselves with a puerile observation, often tinged with envy, regarding my apparent imperviousness to any form of dejection. This sort of remark aggravates an already uncomfortable situation and leaves me with only a few options: I must confess that my spirits vary as much as anyone else's, which makes me appear habitually dishonest; I must pretend to believe that perfect, unwavering contentment is achievable, which makes me appear idiotic; or I must decline to answer at all. A remark about the weather can be useful at this point.

7

I have, of course, been accused at various times of compulsive dishonesty, chronic idiocy, and outright, forthright insanity. In my opinion, none of the descriptive nouns is entirely applicable, but I may be deluding only myself in this matter. I think that I perceive reality with reasonable accuracy these days, but I have been mistaken in the past. I lived much of my youth sheltered from any chance of hurt by the hazy, protective shell of my own Power.

For those to whom the existence of such Power as mine is only a difficult concept, the actuality of Power's domination is inconceivable. Power preserves its host, but Power's methods are purely selfish. I can be thankful that my early life demanded no sterner defenses than a blocked awareness of emotional pain. Severely as that buried pain gnawed at me, it did spare the world around me. Under slightly crueler circumstances, I might easily have reacted as uncontrollably as a certain legendary child of Ven: Kaedric, Lord Venkarel, escaped abuse by destroying most of a city before his thirteenth year, and he and I are too much alike in Power's ruthless ways.

I should not rail at those who ask me for the secret of contentment. The longing for that elusive commodity drives human beings in every country and culture that I have ever explored, and Network files lead me to believe that the alien races of the Consortium pursue a similar search. I have given my small contribution to the finding via my Laurett's namesake. Who knows? Perhaps Katerin will succeed one day and declare her algorithm complete; Katerin is a remarkable and determined woman, or she would not still persist.

As for me, I have come to value contentment less than hope. Contentment ebbs and stales. Hope can always offer joy. There: That is my quota of philosophy for the day.

When my liege-lady requested my story, she did not specify its flavor. She says she trusts me. I might offer my detractors the evidence of her testimonial, but the detractors would likely replace their disparagement of me with an awkward fear; the word of the Infortiare of Serii has that effect on those who comprehend Power at all.

I shall let my story speak for me—and for those others whose histories collided with my own. Perhaps the tale will not always remain entombed in the dusty Ixaxin archives, though I think that will be its most immediate fate. Perhaps some day I shall even scan a copy into Network. That would confound a few circuits!

PART 1

The Shattering

CHAPTER 1

Network Year 2283

The speaker struck the translucent block of the projection screen with his pointer to emphasize the conclusion of his briefing. The image shuddered at the impact, but the speaker did not notice the resultant frowns among his audience. A man and woman exchanged a brief whisper. Network's Council Governor tapped the gleaming black surface of the conference table, barely making a sound, but the whispering stopped abruptly.

The speaker rattled off his summary with the headlong enthusiasm of absolute conviction, "If Network-3 had remained closed, the displacements in the proximate topological sets should have become permanently measurable. Instead, only brief, minor shifts occurred. I am convinced that at least one common limit point was reestablished within microseconds of closure."

"These are the same few microseconds," murmured lanky, black-haired Councillor Abrahara with clipped cynicism, "that comprised several thousand years on Network-3?"

The speaker nodded briskly, oblivious to the derogatory intent of the remark. "In the time frame of Network-3, approximately twenty thousand years lapsed before a very intricate topological mapping returned the world to its original configuration. That proof of time mapping's feasibility offers phenomenal research value in itself: We can duplicate the mathematics, but we have yet to understand the application." The speaker smiled

13

broadly, enjoying the prospect of discovery. "We do not know if the mapping occurred because of deliberate human effort or as a peculiar byproduct of the closure process. In preparing the closure, I reconfigured Network-3's primary topological transfer controller to eradicate all limit points, but that controller had an advanced form of artificial intelligence, which may have initiated a restoration process."

The speaker ran his fingers through his sand-colored hair, equally oblivious to the dishevelment that resulted and to the blank stares of several of his listeners. He pointed to the second of the chart's conclusions. "The differences in the set characteristics are so subtle that Network cannot perceive them even with the delicate sensors we use to detect potential new spaces. The space registers as a topological anomaly. With our existing technology, we could never have extrapolated the current topological location of Network-3 from the existing data—if we had not known where to look."

The speaker's face was flushed as he turned toward his audience, and his expression glowed with his eagerness to endlessly discuss his discoveries. "The ramifications of this pseudo-closure are tremendously exciting," he insisted, and his innocent comment seemed incongruously emotional coming from a pale, studious man of unexceptional appearance. "By learning how to reestablish access to Network-3, we shall increase our comprehension of applied topology as significantly as when the first controller mechanism was developed."

Satisfied with his briefing, the speaker bobbed his head slightly to signify the end. He was certain that he had explained the topological concepts clearly and accurately, and his listeners could hardly be considered ignorant of the methods of technical analysis. His assessments of the problem and the necessary approach for its solution were correct, cohesive, and inarguable.

The status of his audience did not intimidate Jonathan Terry in the least; he would have educated his children in a difficult subject with exactly the same attitude he showed the Network Council of Twelve and the Council Governor. He seated himself and smilingly accepted a cup of water from a robotic hand. *It feels good to be working productively again*, he thought, *after all the months of guilt and fear.*

An elegant, hard-eyed woman commented, "I believe you had an active role in the closure of Network-3, Dr. Terry." Her colleagues watched her expressionlessly. "You persuaded this council of the necessity for that drastic action less than a year ago. I do hope that your eloquent arguments did not serve merely as camouflage for scientific fanaticism."

Jon Terry frowned at the woman's comments. He had explained the issue of the closure so often that he had hoped he could finally consign that nightmare to the past. "The closure of Network-3 was imperative, Councillor Deavol," he answered a little stiffly. "The Genetic Research Center's 'Life Extension Project' created murderous sociopaths with horrifying mental abilities. These so-called 'Immortals' had already compromised the independent computer systems at DI and Worther University when we recognized the Immortals as more than just intriguing subjects for psychic research. If they had managed to penetrate the Network computers, their madness could have caused untold damage on every Network world. We took the appropriate action under extraordinary emergency circumstances."

"I believe we all concur that the threat to the integrity of the Network computers warranted your action," replied Maryta Deavol smoothly. "The computers define Network, and Network is the only significant, exclusively human civilization left in this universe, since all others have yielded to the cunning, purportedly benign yoke of the Calongi's Consortium." Maryta Deavol never wasted an opportunity to malign the Calongi or any alien species. "I am, therefore, disturbed by your eagerness to reactivate that threat."

"Until we reestablish a topological link," explained Jon, trying to maintain his limited patience, "we cannot know what the descendants of the Immortals have made of the world, but I am fully convinced that the threat we feared has now been eliminated by virtue of the tremendous time shift of the Network-3 set."

"We must not forget that time shift, Maryta," remarked Georg Abrahara. Maryta Deavol smiled aloofly, sharing her colleague's sardonic skepticism.

Jon subdued his unhealthy impulse to comment on his hearers' limited mental abilities, but his voice betrayed his irritation: "We shall reestablish contact with the planet carefully, of course, for it has become nearly as unknown to us as any newly discovered space, but I believe that the citizens of that planet are actively seeking a means to rejoin us peaceably."

Maryta Deavol smoothed her hair needlessly, as if to demonstrate her disinterest in Jon's explanation. Most of the other councillors were too busy watching Council Governor Caragen to react to Jon's remarks at all. Jon restrained a disparaging shake of his head at their unwillingness to think for themselves. "Are there any other questions, Council Governor?" he asked, since the council obviously awaited Caragen's lead in judging the briefing.

Caragen laced his fingers complacently across his ample stomach. He barely moved his lips as he spoke: "As always, Dr. Terry, you have provided a technically remarkable story. However, your research proposal seems likely to exceed your cost estimates, and I do not believe that the Network Council can justify the expenditure at the present time. Thank you for your presentation."

Jon did not rise immediately, as protocol dictated. "You are declining funding?" he demanded incredulously. The years of prosperity had spoiled him; he had not had a major project rejected since he first presented the controller design for the topological transfer of living beings.

"Yes, Dr. Terry," answered Caragen with cold disapproval in his hard voice.

"This project is comparable in significance to the initial research into applied topology," snapped Jon. "Without topological transfer, there would be no Network, because the Adraki would have conquered us, or the Consortium would have absorbed us years ago. The Consortium rules this universe, but Network has all the universes of topologically connected space, and we will retain our independence only if we remain the foremost authorities in applied topology. But I suppose you would rather fund another pointless study of the cultural impact of some microscopic organism on a planet none of us has ever seen!"

"You have never been noted for your diplomatic skills,

have you, Dr. Terry?" asked Caragen mildly, but his expression held steel enough to subdue even Jon Terry's arrogance of technical certainty.

The council chamber door opened suggestively. Jon Terry threw his emptied cup into the discard chute with unnecessary force, but he left the chamber without further comment. When he reached the anteroom, he began to mutter very scathingly about the immediate ancestry of the Network Councillors. "How can they be so blind to the obvious?" he demanded of a display of corals. Ensconced among similar organic remains from various oxygen-rich, oceanic planets, the corals comprised the only color in the white, intimidating anteroom.

"May I help you, Dr. Terry?" asked a thin, smiling woman with auburn hair and worried eyes. "You seem upset." She extended her hand, trailing a web of celadon gauze that draped her to her knees.

"Upset?" retorted Jon with a mocking laugh. He pounded his fist against the opposite palm. "Do you know, citizeness, what great bit of wisdom our esteemed Council Governor has just decreed?"

"Please, Dr. Terry, come into my office. We shall discuss whatever is troubling you."

"Talk to the Council Governor instead," snarled Jon, for he had met too many of Network's psychologists not to recognize the breed. "An expression of anger and disgust at a moronic verdict is the only reaction a sensible man could produce, citizeness, and I do not need your psychological placebos."

"Dr. Terry, you suffered a terrible ordeal less than a year ago. The fact that you have regained the ability to relate to your professional associates is a wonderful tribute to your personal strength. You cannot expect a full recovery so soon."

"I have never been healthier," responded Jon sharply, and he would have departed to seek the nearest transfer port, but Network refused to open the door at his approach.

"You know that Network cannot allow you to leave when you are so distraught," clucked the woman, wagging her well-coiffed head at him sternly. "You might injure yourself or someone else. Please, come with me.

Relax in my office for a while. You may talk to me or to Network—whatever makes you feel most comfortable."

She treats me with such condescending delicacy, observed Jon with disgust, *you would think she expected me to start shooting people in the streets.* "I would rather talk to Network from my own home, thank you. I promise not to murder anyone en route," replied Jon with thick sarcasm.

Instead of pressing him further, the woman nodded nervously and retreated into her office suite alone. Network murmured in a synthetically soothing voice, "Please sit down, Jon. You need rest. You have been ill."

Unaccustomed to the bluntly paternalistic tone that often characterized Network's interactions with less honored citizens, Jon's initial reaction was impatience. "Open the door, Network," he demanded brusquely.

"Please sit down, Jon," repeated Network. "You need rest. You have been ill."

Jon struck the door with his open hand, producing no useful effect. He growled, "Abominable nuisance, as stupidly impervious to logic as the Network Council." Network did not respond.

Frustrated, Jon slumped into a chair. Staring at the uninspiring walls, he began to consider the personal ramifications of the Council Governor's decision—and of Network's unusual attitude toward him. The obvious likelihood of a correlation disturbed him: *Did Network logic dictate Caragen's judgment, or did Caragen command Network's change in attitude?* Jon found the latter possibility particularly unsettling; it smacked unpleasantly of the same hellish conceit of the mad Immortal who had inspired the desperate act of closing Network-3 in the first place.

Have I changed, or has Network? mused Jon grimly. *I begin to wonder whether Tom Davison's sacrifice in closure served any purpose but to maintain a familiar tyranny rather than accept a new oppressor.*

Jon forced himself to visualize the destruction of the DI port controller without allowing himself the old, stomach-wrenching guilt and dread. He refused to dwell on Tom Davison's death. He recalled the golden-haired angel who poured a flood of healing into him when the shattered controller tried to drain his life, and he reasoned coolly that she had bestowed on him some faint echo of herself in the peculiar healing process. *She has enabled me to perceive Network clearly—and I do not altogether like what I see.*

Curbing his temper sternly, Jon smiled at the wall and remarked affably, "I am sorry about my earlier outburst, Network. I do feel much better now. May I return home? My wife will be concerned about me."

"Beth has been notified of your delay," replied Network. "Your physical readings still indicate excessive levels of distress. An aide has been summoned to escort you safely to your home."

"Thank you," grumbled Jon, irritated that Network had refused to accept his apology. He really needed to acquire one of those sensor jamming devices that the Cuui traders purportedly sold.

I wonder if I can research pseudo-closure effectively without the experimental data that pushes the proposal cost so high? I could revise the cost estimates and present the plan again. No, the Council of Fools gave no hint that they would consider bargaining.

Very well: I shall work without them. I have friends who should be willing to back me, for the reasons I gave the Network Council are sound: Now that we know pseudo-closure is feasible, we must understand it for our own protection. If the Consortium ever acknowledges that our technology is real, they'll be able to duplicate it. Our other-universe worlds would not long remain exclusive in that case; Network needs pseudo-closure.

Except I shall have to keep the project secret from Network. . . . If I presented the Network Council with accomplished fact, how would they react? Badly. Caragen, at least, is not a fool. He understands what I have told him. He does not want me to succeed. Science falls once again beneath the knife of obscure political ambition.

Jon chewed his lower lip. *I wonder if Amman still dabbles in designing security systems in his spare time?*

* * *

Andrew Caragen emerged from his personal transfer port and stepped into his private suite aboard his space yacht. The Council meeting had left him irritable; the sterile environment of the Council room served a useful purpose of intimidation, but the atmosphere displeased

him on an aesthetic level. He entered his museum to
restore himself by indulging his tastes for ancient and
exotic works of art. He walked among portraits of the
historical figures he respected and emulated: kings and
emperors and other autocrats, who had commanded their
worlds with absolute authority.

"Network," he asked, as he wandered among his treasures, "what are my options in regard to Dr. Jonathan
Terry, and what are the associated consequences?"

"You have three primary options," replied Network
in a cool, genderless voice. "You may reemploy him as
Network's chief topological researcher: This option would
require the application of extensive, highly sophisticated
conditioning procedures, since excessive independence
and resistance to standard Network conditioning have
been clearly identified in him; the recommended conditioning could cause permanent damage, which could
eradicate his value. You may eliminate him: This option
offers the lowest risk estimate; however, it incurs the
irrevocable loss of his unique expertise. You may encourage his continued retirement from active research on the
basis of traumas incurred by the cataclysm of Network-3
closure: This option preserves his expertise while mitigat-
ing his freedom to perform dangerous, independent
research of any significant extent; this option mandates
continuation of low-level surveillance."

"Continue option three for the moment," said Caragen, pausing to admire a delicate porcelain vase that
dated from an ancient dynasty. "I can always assign Marrach to correct the situation if Dr. Terry becomes too
obstreperous. I am reluctant to dispose of Dr. Terry,
though I distrust him. He wants to reopen Network-3,"
laughed Caragen with chilling scorn. "The naive technocrat loses himself in his topological abstractions, his
'pseudo-closure,' and his mad Immortals. Does he think
I would let him live if I believed he could actually reestablish access to Network-3?"

Network's interpretative algorithms tried to decipher
the intent of Caragen's question: "Dr. Terry is unlikely
to appreciate the extent of the disadvantages associated
with Network-3's continued existence, since his personality profile indicates a high respect for the trait of independence, which was Network-3's primary cultural flaw."

"The Life Extension Project could have produced interesting applications," mused Caragen, ignoring Network's effort to please him, "if the researchers had approached their subject more rationally and consulted me. They should have separated their project into usable categories: Either concentrate on extending the duration of existing lives, or modify the human template in a controllable fashion." Caragen shrugged. "I have more credible 'life-extension projects' on the research roster, and I certainly have better programs for creating human-based tools of destruction."

Caragen smiled; it was a cold expression that had daunted many adversaries. He employed a complex set of code and identification procedures to open one of his most secure vaults. He studied the index thoughtfully, before indicating his selection with a gesture of his hand above the sensor pad.

A dark cover lifted to reveal a rare and artful carving of a creature from the Consortium planet of T'a'a: The creature was known in Network as a slithink, an unnattractive name for a small, web-winged animal that most humans found extremely unappealing. The carving, stolen from a Calongi's cherished collection, had incalculable value. Caragen had bought it as a secret gesture of his scorn for Calongi and their infamous Consortium law, but he held the slithink before him now as a reminder of another rare, expensive object that Caragen had once collected: a man, a rejected byproduct of a planet known as Gandry, which specialized in creating human workers to perform undesirable tasks with perfectly bred and conditioned willingness.

None of Caragen's assets had ever served as effectively as that Gandry discard, whom Caragen had renamed Rabhadur Marrach as a cryptic, private jest from an ancient language: Spy and warning and labyrinth entwined to form the name. Caragen had molded Marrach to be the perfect instrument of subversion, terrorism and death. "Network-3 only produced mad Immortals, but I created Marrach," murmured Caragen, and he nodded to himself in satisfaction.

CHAPTER 2

Seriin Year 9040

Freed from the Hamley manor's confines, six toddlers raced across the sloping lawn behind the nursery wing. Three of the children ran directly toward the newly turned dirt that had lain beneath an abandoned smokehouse. Yesterday's rain had converted the dirt to mud.

"Stay away from the work area," scolded Nanny, a solid, mousy-haired woman of dignity, who managed to control her charges with surprising vigor. Two of the errant children obeyed her, but the smallest boy continued running to the edge of the mud, where he planted himself happily.

Concluding that her youngest charge was in no immediate danger of any hazard but dirtiness, Nanny allowed the boy the illusion of a moment's independence. Nanny herded five eager children, while the pretty, young nursery assistant toted the baskets and blankets for the promised picnic. Many of the adult members of the party had already gathered below the lower garden, having ridden across the fields from the hunt on their fine Viste horses.

Unaware of his brief abandonment, the small boy plunged his hands into the thick mud before him. He smiled at the soft squish of the mixture. He struck the mud with his palms and laughed as it splattered him.

He lay on his stomach at the puddle's edge and pushed his hands deep into the mud, until his arms were buried nearly to the shoulders. He felt something hard, and he tugged it from the accumulated muck of years. He shook it in the thin surface puddle of standing rainwater, and he brought his treasure into the air.

It had a scooped bowl, pointed at the broken base. As the boy raised it, glints of silver peered through the crust of age, where rock and water had scraped and cleansed the dish. Part of the metal lace had been broken, and the sharp, bent tines of the edges pricked the boy's grubby hand.

For an instant, the slight hurt absorbed his attention. He shook his hand in a cleaner puddle than the one he had already disturbed. He watched solemnly as a drop of blood formed on his finger. Seeking sympathy, he made a tentative gesture toward Nanny, but she had become a distant figure silhouetted against the blue sky.

The boy looked a little wistfully from his bleeding finger toward the far cluster of chattering adults. He knew not to bother them with a trivial hurt. Wearing a very serious frown, the boy wiped the beading blood on his shirt's muddy sleeve.

Nanny, finished now with the supervision of the spreading of picnic blankets, returned to her straggling charge. She stomped across the grass and loomed above him. "Look at you, Quin," she muttered. "A moment out of sight, and you are filthy. Is this how you want your parents to see you? Tsk, there is no time to change your clothes now."

Timidly, the boy offered the silver vase for her inspection. "What is that muddy thing?" she asked with distaste. "Put it down and come with me."

She turned with a crinkling of crinoline and marched across the lawn as she had come, utterly disdainful of the uneven ground's efforts to impede her. Quin, stubbornly clutching his prize, followed her, his short legs hastening and stumbling. The nursery assistant smiled at the sight of stern Nanny leading the waddling child like a duck with duckling, but the nursery maid hid her amusement before Nanny could observe it.

"What do you have there, Quin?" asked the young maid, tilting her dark head curiously.

A slow smile illumined the boy's delicate face. "A silver vase," he answered quite distinctly, though his older kin in the nursery had scarcely learned to speak a single clear word. "I found it."

"Did you?" asked the maid, widening her blue eyes in carefully appreciative awe.

Quin nodded rapidly. "I can make it shiny," he assured her. "Would you like to see?"

"That I would, child," replied the maid with a grin, "if I need not do the polishing."

Quin nodded again to reassure her that he understood her concern. He seated himself on the grass, holding the vase in front of him. He stared at it very soberly. The maid tried to hide a giggle behind her hand. Quin did not seem to hear her, engrossed as he was in his treasure.

Nanny called, "Violet, I need you here."

"Yes, madam," replied the maid, and she hurried to obey Nanny's command.

Quin did not see her leave. In his small hands, the rim of the broken vase began to gleam, as years of tarnish fell from the delicate pattern of shells and leaves. "See," he announced proudly, only then noticing that his audience had abandoned him. His smile faded.

He was still holding the vase, just watching it sadly, when he heard the high, sweet voice: *her* voice. Eagerly he looked for her among the crowd of big people returning from the hunt. He saw her: a soft-faced woman with doe's eyes and a curling aureole of pale brown hair. Dressed in a dark purple coat, skirt and hat, she extended her hands toward a handsome blond man with sun-dusted skin. The woman slid from her sidesaddle into his arms, and they laughed.

With his silver vase in hand, Quin ran down the slope toward the couple. The woman saw him first. Her laughter trilled. "Look, Jiar," she giggled, "we are welcomed by a mudlark."

The man called, "Nanny, one of your charges has escaped you."

Nanny pushed at Violet, who raced down the hill to retrieve Quin once again. Quin continued to hold the silver vase in outstretched hands toward the well-matched couple, until Violet caught the boy in her arms. The vase tumbled to the ground. "I am very sorry that he troubled you, my lord and my lady," said Violet breathlessly. She bobbed in a partial curtsey, hampered by the weight of the toddler she carried. "Quin does have a mind of his own."

"Is that Quin?" demanded Jiar with a deep laugh. "Beneath all that grime, I did not recognize him! Let me look at him again, Violet." The maid turned dutifully, so that Lord Jiar could view his son's face. "Quin is beginning to resemble you, Aliria!"

The woman came to stand beside her husband. She touched Quin's face, and Quin smiled happily, but she withdrew her hand quickly and wrinkled her nose. "I hope you are not implying, Jiar, that I was ever this dirty. Violet, please tell Nanny that I shall want to speak to her about this incident. I do not want my youngest son raised to be a another hooligan. I have already supplied Hamley with enough of those."

"Yes, my lady," answered Violet meekly.

Lady Aliria's foot rubbed against the fallen silver vase, and the broken metal tine scored the fine leather of her boot. Her face furrowed, allowing wrinkles to appear. "Jiar, look at my shoes! One of the children could be injured."

Jiar bent to retrieve the vase. "Only a piece of broken metal," he observed disinterestedly. "Dispose of it, Violet." He tucked the vase in the wide pocket of Violet's apron and turned back to his wife.

Quin said softly, "I made it shine," but only Violet heard him, and she hushed him promptly. His smile disappeared into hurt and disappointment. He watched his parents sorrowfully, as Violet carried him back to Nanny and the other children.

He could hear his parents still laughing together. Quin liked to hear their happiness. He wished that he could make them laugh with him. He wished that he could make them notice him at all.

Quin sighed and settled his head against Violet's comfortable shoulder. Sometimes he could make Violet notice him. Sometimes he could even make her laugh with him.

Nanny was harder. Nanny often became angry when he tried to make her laugh like Violet, but sometimes she smiled, so he kept practicing. Sometimes Nanny watched him oddly after he *tried* with her.

He could always make his cousins in the nursery laugh or cry or jump or run. He wished it were less easy with them. It was too hard not to control them. He could not enjoy playing with them, when they did not seem to understand anything.

Quin wanted to play with his older cousins and siblings, but they had no interest in a toddler, except as an object of teasing. He did not like their scorn, but at least *teasing* meant that he was noticed and allowed some small part in the older children's games. If the childish mockery became too painful, he could always use *that* to make his tormenters laugh and forget to hurt him.

That could stop any hurt, except the loneliness. *That* made everything easy, but no one understood. No one liked him when he let them see how easily *that* let him do or learn or understand. Like Nanny, the older children looked at him oddly when he used *that*, so he had decided *that* must be bad.

Except with Violet, he had stopped using *that* intentionally for anything but stopping the hurts. He liked Violet, but she did not understand either. No one understood.

Violet sat him down on the blanket beside his little cousins, Ellani and Cori. Quin smiled at them, and he could not help smiling with *that* into their minds as well. Ellani and Cori giggled.

CHAPTER 3

Network Year 2284

Few customers sat in the tearoom. The hour, too late or too early, did not inspire a widespread yearning for intellectual discussion or mild dickering, such as usually accompanied the tearoom's potent and varied libations, brewed from the herbs of many worlds. A single group of traders sat near the door, for they pursued their business slowly. Only one other customer occupied the room: a man with tousled, sandy hair and shoulders that suggested both resolution and weariness.

The traders rebuffed the lone waiter, a tall man of indeterminate age, who proceeded across the room to the far corner, where the solitary patron sat holding a mug of fragrant, amber liquid. "Have you identified the herb?" asked the waiter with a faint, tired smile. The patron shook his head slowly. "The Cuui call it te'ver. It is a mild stimulant."

"The prescription of metabolic adjusters is the prerogative of Network, friend Lorenz."

"I am practicing my independence," replied the waiter quietly. He glanced toward the table of traders to assure himself that they remained engrossed in their own discussions. He sat and leaned across the table to ask, "How much longer do you expect to delay, Jon?"

The sandy-haired patron arched his brows and answered in a voice no louder than the waiter's near-whisper, "I shall delay until we have the equipment we need to establish a viable research facility, as well as to ensure that

27

Neoterra can provide us with comfortable living conditions almost immediately. I shall delay until I feel reasonably confident that none of us will need to make this transfer again, because every subsequent activation of those topological coordinates will increase the chances of detection exponentially. Risk analysis still favors the completion of all preparations as originally planned, unless you want Network to discover that we have concealed a world from Network monitors."

Lorenz's broad, flat-featured face became solemn. "Is detection of the pseudo-closure possible?"

"Of course, it's possible," snapped Jon. "If I learned the method of it, so could another industrious Network researcher."

Lorenz considered this statement only briefly before shaking his shaved and polished head. "Another topologist might duplicate your work—if any other topologist of your caliber existed. Not even the Consortium has ever managed to reproduce your genius, my friend."

Be glad that you do not know, old friend, thought Jon wryly, *how I learned this method of topological concealment—by observation—from the uncanny inheritors of Network-3*. "My reputation only compounds our problems. I am too well known to be able to move easily—constantly monitored by standard Network surveillance and the agents of every independent civilization seeking Network's topological transfer secrets. Only the Calongi disdain to trouble me, but their scorn is not shared by the human members of the Consortium."

"You have allowed yourself to be officially discredited. That tarnish on your reputation ought to reduce the attention centered on you."

"It has helped," agreed Jon. He rotated the cylindrical glass light case in the middle of the table, until the light barely illuminated his hand. He restored the cylinder to its original position and frowned pensively at the ruddy, translucent halo of light passing through his fingers. "However, I am only a step ahead of a Network agent, who has been tracking me the past few days. I think I escaped him by coming here tonight, instead of keeping my appointment with Dienne, but I am not certain. This one is much more difficult to fool than any of his predecessors."

"You are sure that he represents Network?" asked Lorenz in a nervous whisper.

"Yes. He has followed me through transfer."

"Did you tell Amman?"

"Not yet. Amman has enough other worries, and I have nothing useful to report. I have only suspicions, based on uncertain data and a rumor, which was undoubtedly exaggerated, about a man who tends special problems for our Network Council Governor."

"The Council Governor?" echoed Lorenz with muted shock. "I hope we have not attracted such high-level attention."

"I certainly share your hope, my friend, because if even a fraction of the rumor is true, the Council Governor's agent functions as a Network node by virtue of implanted circuitry in his brain. Such an attribute *would* explain my inability to elude my shadow, despite some of the very sophisticated techniques developed by our gifted associate. Not even Amman's talents can protect us against a man who carries all of Network in his head."

"None of us have used Network for any sensitive work since you persuaded us of Network's corruption," muttered Lorenz with a worried frown.

Jon nodded, thinking soberly, *We have taken all the precautions we could devise, but none of us knows the full extent of Network's influence.*

One of the traders called for service. Lorenz's frown became exasperated. "I had better return to work before I lose my job here and attract Network's particular attention."

"I appreciate your help, Lorenz."

"I appreciate your trust. Most of my former associates have shunned me since Network terminated my research."

"Network only tolerates independent thinking in approved directions, which do not include the field of sensor deception. Others of us value that independence in you—and share it."

Lorenz grimaced ruefully and returned to his duties as waiter. Jon finished his tea and prepared to leave. He did not observe the arrival of the indistinctive man with bland, brown hair who blocked the narrow aisle. Jon gave the stranger's presence little thought, only mutter-

ing an impatient epithet when the man failed to move
from his path.

"Excuse me," repeated Jon, irritated by the stranger.
*Some trivial obstacle like this oblivious fool could prevent
any of us from reaching a rendezvous or evading a search,*
thought Jon. *Our plans are so fragile.*

The stranger turned his lightless eyes to Jon and spoke,
clearly but softly. "I think you should not leave yet, Dr.
Terry." With unhurried care, he claimed the chair that
Lorenz had vacated. "Network is performing detailed
street surveillance of this neighborhood at present,"
remarked the man calmly. "It is only a random scan
function, not an effort aimed specifically at you, but you
do figure prominently on the search list. This particular
housekeeping dæmon devotes only a few minutes to any
given location, assuming that no matches to the search
list trigger the alarms. A brief wait will be worth your
while in many ways."

Jon resumed his own seat very slowly. "You seem to
possess very specialized knowledge about Network,"
answered Jon cautiously, and he wished that Lorenz had
not disappeared into the kitchen. Jon drew his hand
through his sandy hair to activate the jamming device
behind his ear. The stranger smiled slightly, and Jon's
suspicions firmed, replacing annoyance with concern. *I
have expected my shadow to move against me,* thought
Jon, trying to bolster his own flagging confidence, *and
he could not have chosen a time and place more to my
advantage.* Jon hoped that the jamming sufficed to thwart
the signals of the man's implanted transceiver. "You did
not introduce yourself."

"How remiss of me. My name is Rabhadur Marrach.
My official position is Network Council Chancellor, and
I am a great admirer of your ingenuity. I hope you will
forgive my impromptu claim on your time this evening.
It is so awkward arranging a formal meeting with a man
in hiding from Network. Which name are you using currently, Dr. Terry? Faber? Davisson? You have become
very adept at the difficult art of forging Network identities, especially for a man who is supposedly enjoying
indolence at an expensive Network spa, while recovering
from the severe physical and mental traumas caused during your escape from the Network-3 cataclysm."

This Marrach looks too ordinary to serve as Network Council Chancellor, but his very lack of distinction makes him a convincing agent of subterfuge. "You do seem to be well informed."

"Yes, I know a great deal about you," replied Marrach evenly. He spread his left hand flat against the table and bent successive fingers to delineate his points. "I know about your planned utopian colony of disenchanted Network technocrats. I know that you have managed to conceal one or more worlds from Network sensors, and I know that Network-3 is among them."

"What an astonishing theory," remarked Jon quietly.

"You and your select, very impressive list of conspirators obviously intend to establish an independent government for yourselves, and your plan is largely contingent upon your ability to keep secret even the possibility of topological concealment. You have engendered your own discredit during the past year, so as to obscure your early claims that Network-3 survived the cataclysm of its closure. I presume that you made those statements before your faith in Network waned to its current nadir."

"I trust Network implicitly."

Marrach smirked. "You have not even entrusted the truth to your wife, have you? You have enlisted only those few, diversely talented specialists whose expertise you require to establish your utopia, and you expect— somewhat presumptuously—that your families will join you happily when your plan is complete. For a group of sheltered, Network-conditioned technocrats, you have actually maintained your subterfuge quite well."

"Most technocrats do have some experience in secrecy," muttered Jon. "We all serve Network's ambitions against the Consortium with unwavering diligence." *Where is Lorenz? I would feel better with an ally in sight, though neither of us can do or say much to intimidate an agent of the Council Governor. Amman should arrive soon; he will know how to handle this situation.* "What do you intend to do with your preposterous misinformation?"

"I intend to make myself a member of your select group."

Jon stiffened, unable to conceal his surprise. Marrach continued, unperturbed by Jon's obvious shock, "I realize that my ethical standards do not conform to your colony's ideals, but that is why you cannot afford to decline my offer. By the very care with which you have selected your partners in conspiracy, you have ensured that none of you—including your security expert, Citizen Amman—is capable of the premeditated murder of myself or of anyone else. If you exclude me, I shall inform my employer, Council Governor Caragen, of your entire arrangement, and Caragen is not a merciful man."

"You make your offer so enticing."

Marrach dimmed the table light. "You may understand the concept of secrecy, Dr. Terry, but you lack the instincts for personal concealment or devious ambition. You might be interested in knowing that Network assesses your probability of success as ninety-one percent with my assistance, thirty-three percent without me, and nine percent if I oppose you. Be reassured that my Network calculations are considerably more secure than those of other citizens. They are also unimpeded by your efforts to jam local Network signals, since I do not employ standard channels or waveforms."

"We actually measure as high as nine percent?" asked Jon pensively.

"You have collected an extraordinarily gifted group of people," answered Marrach dryly.

Jon rubbed his jaw, assessing Marrach in the shadowy gentility of the tea room. *Lorenz is taller and broader than Marrach,* mused Jon, *but Marrach is undoubtedly better trained and more ruthless than any of us. A physical match can only favor Marrach; we must outwit him, if we intend to succeed against him. I wonder if he is right about Amman.* "How will you help us?"

"For one thing, I shall keep you alive long enough to complete your preparations. This task alone is significant, since several other agents are close to discovering your deception regarding your 'regrettable disability resulting from the Network-3 cataclysm.' I shall also persuade Network to disregard your final arrangements for departure. I have, in fact, helped you already by removing a fellow operative who intended to accost you earlier this evening."

A representative of our Council Governor murders a colleague and boasts of it while plotting further treachery. How did I remain blind for so long to the hypocrisy of our leaders? Jon raised his index finger to his forehead. "I have considerable trouble assimilating the idea that a Network Council Chancellor of your peculiar skills would abandon all his power, status, wealth, and loyalties in order to join a few disgruntled, burned-out researchers."

"The life expectancy associated with my profession is unpleasantly low. I like to have options."

"You have established other options, I presume."

"I have never liked to waste an opportunity." Marrach watched a solitary, muffled patron enter the tearoom and select a table near the traders. "I see that Citizen Amman has arrived. I shall state my remaining points quickly, since I would not want to make your friends overly nervous about our conversation. I can supply you with everything you need to establish your colony easily and comfortably. I can take you to a storehouse tonight and equip you with housing modules, food processing systems, generators—or raw components and advanced materials, if you prefer to create your own technological wonders. Come with me now, Dr. Terry, and your people will be able to fulfill their joint dream as soon as they wish. Otherwise, I cannot guarantee your continued safety even through the night."

"You make such a tempting offer," murmured Jon, "but I do need time to consider it."

"You really ought to trust me, Dr. Terry, while you still have the option."

"My option or yours?"

Marrach rose to his feet. "I shall see you again, Dr. Terry. I hope to find you in equally good health."

Marrach strolled out of the teahouse, waving at Amman with a careless, specious friendliness. As soon as the door sealed behind Marrach, Lorenz reappeared, and Amman, a restless, wiry man, hurried to Jon's side. Lorenz whispered anxiously, "Who was he?"

"Council Chancellor Rabhadur Marrach," replied Jon thoughtfully. The alarm on Amman's face only deepened Jon's concern. "You know of him."

"I have heard of him," muttered Amman nervously. "I had not expected to attract so much attention from our Council Governor. Marrach is reserved for very special enemies. He is an exceptionally dangerous man."

"He says he wants to help us. He certainly seems to

know the major factors of our plan. I am not sure he realizes how close we are to completion."

"You must not trust him, Jon," cautioned Amman. "Marrach serves only Caragen."

"Jon, we must leave for Neoterra immediately," urged Lorenz.

"Yes, I think you are right. Marrach's arrival slants the trade-offs significantly. We must go now, even if initial colony conditions must be a little less comfortable than we hoped." Jon pressed his fingers together thoughtfully. "I shall set the departure time for twenty-two hundred, Network standard. Remind everyone to be prompt. Once we gather, we cannot afford to wait for a second time-coordinate calculation."

* * *

Jon shivered at the sudden chill of the damp evening as he left the teahouse. He had not worn his heavy coat, for he had forgotten that this planet's temperatures changed so rapidly. In avoiding Network contacts for reasons of security, he had abandoned the ordinary conveniences of Network advice. He needed to retrain himself; he took too much for granted, because Network had always been available and inescapable.

Jon watched the muffled pedestrians who headed into the transfer port complex, and he wondered how many of them took topological transfer for granted. Even among technocrats, Jon had often found cause to argue against the apparent dismissal of applied topology as a viable subject for future development.

He muttered to himself, "The unimaginative have always believed that all worthwhile inventions occurred in the past. That which already exists is too commonplace to be appreciated as the 'magic' of our forebears."

Jon shrugged mentally and groped for the particular technical marvel that resided in the hidden lining of his coat pocket. The device would confuse Network's sensors enough to let him use a false identity code in entering a transfer port. Feeling the jamming device within his grasp, Jon walked firmly toward the door of the glossy port complex.

As he reached the entry ramp, one of the dark-clad travelers ahead of him suddenly turned. A woman with small, pale eyes buried in a face of pasty, unhealthy complexion blinked at Jon; she fell against him with a gasp. Instinctively, Jon moved to support her considerable weight. She began to cough and shudder convulsively.

"Let me help," offered a broad, genial man at Jon's side, and the man tried clumsily to reach his arms beneath the woman's shoulders.

"Thank you," muttered Jon with difficulty, "but if you could let go for a moment, I could shift her. . . ."

"Carry her to the bench over there," offered the helpful man, whose expression had a puppy's earnest appeal. He began to push and tug both Jon and the woman, until Jon accepted the man's directions with some frustration.

"Dr. Terry!"

Alarmed by the unexpected shout from the port complex, Jon hunched his shoulders and bent his head closely over the ailing woman. She flailed and struck the side of his neck. He felt the sting against his skin, just as he placed the voice that had called his name aloud: It was Marrach—in betrayal or in warning?

"No matter now," growled Jon furiously, knowing he could not cling long to consciousness. He cursed the man and woman who had conspired to entrap him. *We came so close to achieving our escape into utopia. Perhaps I should have pretended to accept Marrach's offer. . . . No, I could not have deceived a man so obviously expert in deceit.*

Jon sank onto the bench, pushed by the hands of the erstwhile invalid and her "helper." Jon managed to twist and land on his left hip and shoulder. He felt his side pierced by the broken edge of the device in his pocket, and his weight forced the fragments of the shattered casing farther into his flesh. He smiled weakly, as numbness spread from the contents of the minute bubble vials that the casing had sheltered along with its other ingenious gadgetry.

The vials are a useful precaution, Amman had warned, *against the dreadful possibility of interrogation.* The gifted conspirators had all laughed, Jon joining in as heartily as anyone. They had humored Amman; none of them had believed his dire prophecies of capture. To each of the rest of them, failure had meant merely the inability to escape the familiarity of Network.

We are sheltered technocrats, thought Jon, *playing in a political arena of terror that we scarcely recognize as real. What have I done to my friends, bringing them into this conspiracy of mine? What have I done to my family? Dear Beth, I did not even dare to tell you. . . .*

The numbness reached his brain and spared him further guilt.

* * *

Lorenz walked confidently along the street, for he had come to know this neighborhood well. He would miss the familiar houses and trees. He would miss Elezar's black cat, who had finally condescended to accept a nightly scratch behind the ears from Lorenz. He would miss the heartbreaking evening song of the Bollens' *krinta*, even if the ugly beast had once tried to remove his hand. He would miss many things, but he did not regret his choice.

Lorenz opened the gate to enter his own courtyard. The apartment complex was old and lacked many Network conveniences, but Lorenz liked the slight shabbiness of the shrubbery and flowers, the sense of hundreds of previous tenants who had called his small room home. He saw a light in the Gearys' window and considered stopping to speak to them, but the hour was late.

He punched the cipher of his front door automatically. *Soon, very soon, I shall leave here for the last time. I wonder how it looks, this world of Neoterra? Of all the questions I have asked Jon, I never thought to seek such simple information as the color of the sky. Forrester would know—he performed the chemical analyses of the samples Jon gave us.*

Lorenz opened the door and swung his hand to trigger the lights. The room remained dark. His contentment with his living quarters drooped, and he muttered, "I requested sensor repair three days ago." He fumbled toward the manual switch on the far wall. Halfway there, he tripped across a wire and knew that Amman's warnings had not been idle.

Lorenz had no time to worry about his fellow conspirators. The bomb exploded spectacularly, and the fire spread quickly through old fuel lines. The hollowed shell of a slightly shabby apartment complex collapsed into rubble.

* * *

"How many?" asked Caragen sharply.

"Eleven, including Dr. Terry," replied the agent-in-charge.

Caragen frowned briefly: Eleven was an unsatisfying number, lacking a single unit for completion according to many ancient traditions. The number of the Network Council members had not been chosen randomly. "And the families?"

"All except Dr. Terry's have been destroyed. We could complete that task for you, also."

"You will obey Marrach in this regard," ordered Caragen almost absently. The numbers still bothered him, and he trusted his instincts. "You did locate all of the conspirators."

"Marrach identified eleven," replied the agent, knowing the weight of Marrach's name.

"Did you question any of the captives?"

"None survived, except Dr. Terry."

"That was imprudent, Rolf."

"Marrach's orders," answered Rolf firmly. "We could allow none of the conspirators to escape us and continue their traitorous plans. Only Dr. Terry merited the risk. You confirmed the exception."

And I accelerated the abduction, as Marrach will soon accuse me. "Yes," replied Caragen gruffly. *Marrach's precautions regarding excess survivors were doubtless wise. Still, the questioning could have been informative. Perhaps that order should have been modified as well. . . .* "Who is supervising the interrogation of Dr. Terry?"

"Marrach has assigned me to that task, sir."

Unlikely, thought Caragen, knowing Marrach's opinion of Rolf as an interrogation leader, but Caragen did not voice his perception of Rolf's lie; Caragen did not impede ambitions that coincided with his own convenience. "Be very cautious, Rolf. I want Dr. Terry's knowledge, and he may be a difficult subject."

"Marrach has anticipated that difficulty, sir. If direct interrogation fails, Marrach has a fallback option."

"Yes, Rolf," said Caragen, impatient with the agent's eagerness to defer responsibility to Marrach. Caragen found Rolf dull and brutish, but such unimaginative creatures often made the best instruments of death and torture. Rolf had value, if only for his amazingly inoffensive and congenial appearance. "I am certain that Marrach has anticipated every contingency." *But even the most exceptional of tools must be kept conscious of whom he serves.* "Keep me apprised of your progress with Dr. Terry."

"Certainly, Council Governor."

Caragen terminated the intra-ship communication link by a brisk tap on his desk, a broad, gleaming black surface that comprised an elaborate Network interface for his many schemes. The majority of the office displayed the expensive, slightly affected tastes of its owner: Priceless antiques of human origin vied with alien artwork for attention. The absolute, relentless exclusion of nonhumans or nonhuman cultures from Network life did not restrict the Council Governor in his private rooms.

"Network," demanded Caragen softly, "has Marrach returned yet?"

"He returned one quarter hour ago. He is currently entering the tram from Level 4."

"Admit him to this office when he arrives." Caragen smiled austerely at the empty chair that Marrach would occupy momentarily. A superb tool must be savored, but it must not be spoiled by excessive cognizance of its value. When Marrach entered, Caragen's expression became aloof and arrogant.

Marrach never displayed emotion of any sort in Caragen's presence, but Caragen searched indefatigably for betraying gestures. Network sensors could provide Caragen with much more detailed data, but Marrach's peculiar rapport with Network made such results suspect; the method also defeated Caragen's primary purpose in assessing Marrach, which was personal amusement of a highly refined, rarely satisfied variety.

The physical appearance of Caragen's primary agent shifted regularly due both to surgical efforts and the man's own chameleon's skill, impeding any clear perception of Marrach as an individual beyond his professional roles. Caragen had created the tool—loosely labeled a man—and the extraordinarily effective results never ceased to fascinate the Council Governor.

"They have bungled the entire matter, Caragen," remarked Marrach with perfect, cold detachment, "and quite probably caused the permanent erasure of any valuable information from Dr. Terry's memory. They have dealt with the greatest technical genius of Network's history as if he were an uneducated, unsophisticated simpleton."

"Dr. Terry is a topologist, not a military operative," remarked Network's Council Governor over tented fingers, "and such men are often simple outside of their particular specialties. His abduction was absurdly easy. I should have arranged for his capture and conditioning a year ago, instead of allowing him to foment his juvenile insurrection."

" 'Simple' men do not organize political rebellions, steal planets from connected space, and enact elaborate schemes of subterfuge in open defiance of your authority."

"You exaggerate his abilities."

"Do I?" demanded Marrach, and he remained silent until Caragen's bland expression became a frown. "Why did you authorize the abduction of Jonathan Terry, when you knew that I required only a few more days to secure his cooperation? You did not need to assign me to this case if you already planned such a clumsy, childish capture. My services are too expensive for you to squander them. What do you intend?"

Caragen narrowed his small eyes, and he nodded, pleased with Marrach's question, for it demanded information without denying due respect. As a tribute to Marrach's value, Caragen answered honestly, "I assigned you to the case, because I do credit Dr. Terry with a particularly unique set of skills, which have become too uncontrollable to be tolerated. I authorized immediate abduction, because you persuaded me that Dr. Terry's dubious theory of pseudo-closure may have some validity. I am not willing to risk losing you in some inaccessible topological space that may or may not exist in a three-dimensional sense."

"I am touched," remarked Marrach without expression.

Caragen dismissed the dry comment with an impatient scowl. "I remain doubtful that Dr. Terry and his conspirators have actually discovered 'pseudo-closure,' but Dr. Terry's conspiracy could not justify the imperilment of such a valuable asset as yourself. I can afford to lose Jonathan Terry; his unfortunate attitude has essentially finished his usefulness to me. I am pleased to lose Network-3; the local government and at least two research centers on that planet had become dangerously independent. Even if some of Terry's disgruntled conspirators had survived, they could present no threat without Terry's leadership."

"Did you expect me to join Terry's lot," asked Marrach with calculated irony, "and devote myself to a life of reclusive scientific study amid disillusioned, frustrated technocrats and their infuriated families?"

"Infuriated families?" asked Caragen idly, for he categorized Marrach's actual question as rhetorical. Marrach had no personal life to debate; Marrach belonged to Caragen.

"Terry and his fellow conspirators have been rather presumptuous in assuming that their relatives share their urge for independence at the expense of freedom. Idealists can be so narrow-minded."

"What is your assessment of Jonathan Terry's family in this regard?"

"The children are too young to exert any dominant influence. The wife obviously tolerates her opinionated husband's reactionary nature, since she supported his peremptory closure of Network-3, but her confidence in him must have suffered from that cataclysmic event. She will not appreciate his secrecy in planning his Neoterra colony, although she has enough experience in secure projects to comprehend his reasoning."

"Security demands that no single individual may know more than is absolutely necessary," murmured Caragen.

"By the Network calculations associated with my original plan, a seventy-four percent probability existed that she would dispute his intentions to proceed with the Neoterra project, for she would discover his secrecy on my terms. However, you have reduced that probability to less than twenty percent. You guaranteed the destruction of her conditioned Network-loyalty by abducting her husband. Your agents have made her useless to us."

"A man is made vulnerable by a family whom he wishes to protect. I am not finished with Dr. Terry."

"You have him already. You can condition him, control him, or kill him."

"I shall control him, and you will be my agent. I do have an interest in preserving Dr. Terry's expertise, though I consider his enthused concepts of pseudo-closure and time-transfer more speculative than factual. I do not believe that Network-3 still exists in any sense but memory."

"Network concurs with you, naturally," murmured Marrach.

Caragen continued, unperturbed by the interruption, "Dr. Terry is correct, however, in saying that the Consortium may eventually uncover our current techniques, and we could use his skills to minimize the impact of that occurrence."

"Rolf persists with the questioning and conditioning," remarked Marrach calmly, "but Rolf lacks the imagination to comprehend a mind as complex as Jonathan Terry's. The current interrogation has failed."

"As you predicted," acknowledged Caragen. "It appears that Jonathan Terry took precautions against our discovering his secrets by any coercive technique. He apparently preconditioned his brain to erase the necessary information, if pressured to reveal it. Traces of a mind-control drug were discovered in his blood, which undoubtedly accelerated the selective memory erasure."

"As I said, Dr. Terry is hardly a simpleton."

"He must also have established a recovery mode."

"You are ready to have me rescue him from you?"

"He will have no choice but to trust you now. He is confused and helpless, and you will have his family with which to bait him. His conspirators have disappeared." Caragen added with complacent sarcasm, "You are his only hope."

"I shall need some casualties."

"All necessary expenses will be met. The usual terms will be included in your contract."

"You do realize that some of Terry's associates may have succeeded in escaping Network. The probability of oversight is low, but we cannot be certain that we identified the entire roster."

Eleven is an unsatisfactory number. "We captured the key members. If others exist, they present no measurable threat without their leaders."

"The probability of extracting any useful information from Dr. Terry remains below one thousandth, although you have certainly augmented your ability to control him. However, by increasing his vulnerability to external influence, you have essentially eliminated his resistance to Consortium offers." Marrach paused momentarily, and Caragen pondered the possible exchanges that might be passing between Marrach's brain and Network. "In lessening the risk to me, you may have jeopardized the security of Network's topological transfer technology."

He has reached a conclusion with Network's help, but he has not shared it with me. Did he calculate the likelihood of Consortium interference? Or did he evaluate the potential for an ambitious independent to claim a significant tool of power? No, Marrach's ambitions are too well ruled by the Gandry product's need to serve its master. "Marrach," sighed Caragen, thinly concealing the pique of his momentary doubt, "with all your extraordinary gifts for subterfuge, you still underestimate the value of family to a man like Jonathan Terry."

Marrach flexed his artificial arm thoughtfully; the arm appeared indistinguishable from a natural appendage. "Gandry does not educate its products in emotional bonding."

"I do not expect you to experience the weakness, only to appreciate its usefulness. Dr. Terry cannot consider betraying us: We hold not only his wife and offspring but also Network itself, the entity which formed, nurtured, and cared for him from birth. Dr. Terry is a rebellious child, trying to escape his parent's authority, but he will not destroy the parent in the process."

"I cannot match your faith in the effectiveness of conditioning algorithms, Caragen, on a man as exceptional as Jonathan Terry. Do I have your permission to kill him if I perceive an excessive risk of losing him to an unsympathetic agent?"

"Of course, Marrach. I trust your judgment."

CHAPTER 4

Seriin Year 9041

"Hold still, Quin," ordered Violet, trying to fit the tight hand-me-down shirt over the small boy's head. "Nanny insists that you must look like a proper little Hamley lord for the outing with your parents." Violet struggled to fasten the rows of silver buttons at Quin's wrists, and she mumbled irritably, "Nanny insists that you will wear this fine ruffled shirt that might have fit you a year ago."

Quin accepted Violet's ministrations obediently, but his excitement made him fidget. *She* was coming, and *he* had promised to take Quin riding with him. Quin did not expect to have his parents to himself, of course. All sixteen children would be included in the outing. Sen and Deb and Lar, the eldest, would help tend their younger siblings. *She* would still be busy with Quin's infant sister, Seize.

"Violet, change that child's shirt," clucked Nanny, strutting through the bedroom on her way to the nursery. "It is much too small. What were you thinking?"

Violet protested, "You ordered me to use the ruffled silk."

"Do not be impertinent, Violet. Find something else for him to wear, and do it quickly. Her ladyship will return from her ride soon and want to see her children."

"Yes, Nanny," answered Violet quietly, but she made a disgruntled face at Nanny's back. Violet began to undo her previous work, unbuttoning the sleeves, and Quin sighed at the prolongation of a familiar ordeal. "I told her the shirt was too small for you," muttered Violet, after Nanny had left the room. "I should just accept Clem's offer and leave service altogether. Do you think I shall make a good farmer's wife, Quin?"

Quin frowned slightly. He gave no reply, for he knew that Violet expected none. He did not want Violet to leave, but her increasingly frequent disputes with Nanny troubled him deeply. With *that*, he could make Violet forget her unhappiness briefly, but everything else worsened, because Nanny started accusing Violet of laziness and stupidity.

"Clem and I will have lots of children," mused Violet, "with at least five strong boys to help their father in the field. The girls will learn proper manners from me, and maybe they will be asked to serve here in the manor some day." Violet folded Quin's rejected shirt and replaced it in the clothing chest. She fingered soft baby clothes with a dreamy gentleness. "Your mother has had a proper brood, and look at her, riding that new stallion so soon after the sixteenth! I never saw a woman like her—not among noble ladies nor commoners like me. Lady Aliria lets nothing stop her."

The talk of *her* pleased Quin, and he tried to sense *her*. He had managed the trick only twice; neither instance had been entirely under his control. The first occasion had surprised and delighted him: Wistfully envisioning his parents, while he sat learning letters from yet another new governess, he had suddenly felt his mother's determined enthusiasm clearly. He had looked for *her* in the schoolroom, before realizing *that* alone had brought *her* to him.

The second occasion had begun in *her* pain, but it had ended with a wonderful, peaceful satisfaction. Quin had felt his father, as well, on that occasion, but the sharing with *him* had been less clear. Neither parent had seemed to notice their young son's trespass at his sister's birth.

Quin sent his untrained Power toward the lodestone of his mother, an unconscious sorceress of limited Power. She did have the remarkable constitution of the Immortals' heritage, and her exhilaration made Quin squirm beneath Violet's attention. *Freedom after so many months*, sang Aliria's spirit. *We fly together, Wingfoot, and nothing can slow us.*

The horse's agony shot through Aliria, as his jump ended short, and his leg's fine bones splintered against the uneven, weathered wall. Across the Hamley estates, a young boy screamed in echo of the horse. His mother felt only a moment of panic, as the ground sped toward her. Aliria's neck broke as she struck a fallen brick.

Violet tried to shake Quin into silence, but he continued to scream with such heartfelt horror and Power-projected anguish that Violet could not bear to hear him. She covered her ears and ran from the room and through the long, dim hallway, crying, "The child is bespelled."

Nanny bustled into the bedroom, moving rapidly but never allowing her dignity to falter. She slapped Quin's face without effect. She knelt in front of Quin and gripped his shoulders tightly. "Stop this sorcery of yours immediately," she muttered.

"My mother is dead," wept Quin loudly, and Nanny recoiled from him in shock.

"Do not say such a dreadful thing! You are an evil child."

"She is dead," repeated Quin, choking into silence. He stared blankly at Nanny. "My father's heart has died with her," said Quin in a hollow, rasping voice that sounded far older than his four years. "My father will die of his grief."

Nanny made an abortive sign of protection against the child before her, but she chided herself for such superstition. She recognized sorcery; enough Hamley children had shared the indications over the years, though none of them had ever matured into significant Power during her tenure. "You will not speak such nonsense," she declared sternly. "Do you understand me, Quin?"

He shook his head, because he did *not* understand anything except his father's overwhelming grief, which ate at Quin, nearly engulfing Quin's own unbearable loss. "*He* will die," moaned Quin, "like *her*."

Nanny slapped the child again, impatient with his foolishness. She equated sorcery with childish attention-seeking. She had a low opinion of the few itinerant wizards she had met, though she feared the Infortiare as much as anyone in Serii. Nanny did not equate the Power of a Hamley child with the terrible, reputed skills of Lady Rhianna dur Ixaxis.

A shout came from the courtyard, and Nanny ran to the bedroom window. One of the grooms, his face flushed and distraught, paced with his cap in his nervous hands, until Lord Bendl, liege of Hamley, emerged from the manor door. Nanny watched the groom report, with head bowed low before his liege. Lord Bendl clutched at his chest, as if dealt a crushing blow.

Nanny glanced at Quin, whose gray eyes stared vacantly. She completed the superstitious gesture of fear that she had begun earlier. She hastened from the room, leaving Quin alone.

CHAPTER 5

Network Year 2284

Intense heat had stolen all color from the room. Little form remained: the suggestion of a table, the curves of a chair grouping. Smoke drifts rested heavily in the air of the assaulted home. The room appeared large and strange viewed from the floor vault beneath a damaged Network console. A tow-haired girl, hidden in the vault, whispered, "May we move yet?" The girl tried to remain very still, crouching beside her mother and brother, but her feet had begun to hurt. She was young to have learned so much of the necessities inflicted by fear.

"Hush," answered the child's mother, an ordinarily pretty woman whom strain had marked indelibly with tormented eyes and a face creased with pain. The girl shivered and burrowed against her mother's softly yielding smock. She did not understand the reasons for the dismantling of her once-sheltered life, but she had witnessed violent death, and she shared her mother's terror.

A man's hard voice shattered the smoky haze. Impatiently, he growled, "You are wasting time." The sounds of his movements among the rubble sharpened, as he entered the room where the mother and her children hid. They glimpsed his legs, encased in heavy khaki with the olive braid indicative of a manual laborer, a species of man rarely encountered by Network's pampered technocrats.

The boy, a few years older than his sister, tugged at his mother's ankle. He felt trapped by the damaged

47

vault, and his age and energy demanded action, not
patience. He opened his mouth to speak.

"Hush!" repeated the mother desperately, the breath
of her voice scarcely audible to the children huddled with
her.

The man's leaden gaze pursued the silenced murmurs.
He neither heard nor saw those he sought, but the wall
sensors still functioned despite the scorching destruction
of the room, and Network hid nothing from him. He
seemed to derive a bleak amusement from the futility
of his targets' concealment. The vault's light-absorbing
materials had survived the extensive damage, but other
protective camouflage had fared less well against the
searchers' fury of energy blasts.

"Beth, let me help you," urged the man, wielding her
given name with fiendish care and insidious impact. He
had consulted Network via the implants in his brain,
assessing the psychological profile of Elizabeth Shafer
Terry; Network analysis suggested a seventy-eight percent probability that the familiar usage of her common
name would exert significant influence under her present
stress levels, as monitored by his elaborate sensor
resources. He preferred that she emerge voluntarily,
although he had established satisfactory plans for all reasonable contingencies. "I can reunite you with your husband, Beth. He needs your help; you both need mine."

Beth closed her eyes and prayed, with tears, only the
name of God repeated over and over again. "We shall
survive this," she whispered, believing or wanting to
believe. She squeezed her children's hands and tried to
smile at them. "Citizen Marrach," she said aloud, for
nothing remained but the desperate chance Marrach
offered, "where is my husband?"

"In a holding cell, confined by a restraining field. I
can secure his release, but I need you to secure his confidence. For reasons that you probably comprehend, he
considers me the enemy."

"Yes," replied Beth tightly, "Jon's logic has always
been impeccable."

Marrach responded with a crackling sound that sufficed him for wry laughter. "I have rescued you, Beth. I
eliminated your attackers, when a few added moments

would have cost you much more than your material possessions. Do you still doubt me?"

"You initiated the destruction."

"You misjudge me. I neither organized nor sanctioned any of the violence against you: I gave you warning, which you ignored."

"The men who attacked us deferred to you."

"I deceived them, so as to provide the help I promised you. Your husband is too valuable an asset to be discarded unnecessarily. Genius of such magnitude appears so rarely in conjunction with practicality."

"Can you expect me to trust you now, after you have confirmed my worst suspicions about you?"

"I expect you to recognize that you need my help to escape your current predicament."

Two intense, abnormally silent faces confronted Beth's doubts. She nodded at her children, knowing that she did not deceive them; they sensed the depth of her fear, or they would have besieged her with questions. Beth unfurled her legs, half deadened from the cramped position she had maintained for so long. With her children close beside her, she climbed from the cunningly constructed vault that had protected them from all deadliness but the calculating voice of this man, this Marrach.

Even treading amid the ruined remnants of men who had so recently traded quips with him, Marrach wore no expression: lifeless eyes in a motionless face, framed by colorless hair and the dully utilitarian uniform of a low-level maintenance technician. He stared toward the children with a lack of apparent focus that yet conveyed direly purposeful planning. Two days ago, he had told Beth that Jon would not return, and she had refused to believe him.

Beth's heart jerked as her son tore free of her and hurtled across the room with a devastated cry. The boy gathered a burned lump of flesh and black fur against his chest, and he wailed, utterly forgetful of the stoic pride of his thirteen years. Beth choked on her own wrenching horror, though her tears already coursed too freely for other sorrow to prevail. Beth covered her daughter's eyes and ears, but Kitri had already seen the remnants of the silken-furred dog, who had tried hopelessly to uphold his ancestral function as protector. Kitri did not cry; she only clenched her mother's hand more tightly.

Marrach strode to the boy and yanked him to his feet. The dog's lifeless body tumbled to the floor. "Quiet!" hissed Marrach at the boy, who gulped back the breath of a final cry. Marrach nodded toward the dead attackers, and he informed Beth coldly, "Those three men did not work alone. Their associates already deceived you once into believing that they had finished their work against you."

The dead men still look surprised, observed Beth grimly. *Since their own leader killed them, who can blame them for their astonishment?* "Who were they?" demanded Beth.

"They were overpaid mercenaries of inferior quality. Can you keep your children quiet, or should I sedate them?" Acknowledging Beth's visible dismay, Marrach added coolly, "You need not recoil. The sedative would complicate travel only slightly, for it preserves consciousness."

"I shall not drug them," protested Beth fiercely. She stiffened for a fight, which she knew she could not hope to win, but Marrach shrugged indifferently. Beth relaxed enough to ask him, "Where will you take us?"

"To one of the nameless cities, where I shall exert some influence to keep you safe while I retrieve your husband."

"Nameless cities?"

"Places outside of the usual itineraries of technocrats such as yourself."

"Network will monitor the transfer. We cannot hide."

"You cannot hide yourselves, but I can hide you."

"Even from Network?" asked Beth bitterly, for the same Network officers she had summoned to locate Jon lay dead on the floor at her feet. It was they who had tried to kill her and her children.

"Yes."

"What are you?"

Instead of answering, Marrach waved Beth toward the ruined door with a peremptory gesture of his sleek, peculiarly efficient hand weapon. *Does Network's unseen military issue energy guns of such precision and unobtrusiveness?* wondered Beth. *How little do we of*

Network's technocracy know regarding the society we serve?

Beth gathered her son, Michael, to her. The boy's wary and resentful eyes did not leave Marrach. Kitri never lifted her gaze from the floor; her long, fine hair draped her face. Marrach led them directly from their own entry court into a service passage that Beth had not known existed. Beth did not question Marrach's source of access authorization, though she assumed it to be as false as his uniform. She had laid aside all of her questions, because all of the answers but Marrach's had failed: *trust him.* It was an entirely irrational answer that had insinuated itself into inevitability.

"Citizen Marrach," she pleaded quietly, when they had descended two levels beneath the husk of her family's most recent home, "you *will* promise their safety." Kitri and Michael did not entirely understand her, but Marrach knew her meaning, for he had said it: *You need my help to save your children, for I can save them, even if your husband's enemies claim you, an adult Network citizen with records too lengthy to escape.* She was grateful that Marrach did not pretend confusion.

"So long as you satisfy my requirements, I shall uphold yours. Mutual advantage defines the firmest alliances."

"What do you gain?" demanded Beth acridly. She clutched her children's hands so tightly that they both raised troubled eyes to her.

Marrach smiled faintly at her remark, as if in secret satisfaction. He preceded Beth and the children without another glance at them. *He relishes our weakness and dependence on him,* thought Beth. *Whether or not he arranged our desperation, he has certainly maneuvered us to his advantage. Why?*

Beth pondered Marrach's potential motives with cycling terror and hope. The service corridor, gray and impassive, stretched without visible end, and Beth's tired eyes blurred it into a featureless haze. Kitri began to stumble and drag at her mother's hand. Beth ached to help her but could barely continue to hold herself erect after so many days of wakeful terror. How long ago had Jon left, promising to return early from a dinner with old friends? The night had come and gone at least five times since then.

Searing steam spurted noisily from a crack in the wall of the corridor near floor level. "Defective baffles," murmured Marrach, as he stepped through the hazy veil and turned his passionless glance to watch his reluctant followers.

Michael leaped through the writhing curtain after Marrach, but Kitri balked from the shrieking gusts of heat, appealing silently to her mother for support of her small rebellion. Marrach reached for the girl and tugged her quickly and ungently through the fierce steam. Kitri did not argue or demur further; she only watched her mother with disappointment and hurt.

Jon is still alive, Beth assured herself, step after step, *and this man will reunite us with him. Afterward. . . . Do not think about afterward. Think only of Jon, who will surely devise an answer that eludes me.* "How much farther must we walk?" asked Beth after many minutes.

"Farther," replied Marrach tersely. He startled Beth by elaborating a moment later, "We are being tracked aboveground by the associates of the men who attacked you."

"Your associates?"

"In a sense," admitted Marrach. "They expect to eliminate you as you emerge, so we shall not emerge until we reach the exit I have prepared near the Liebes botanical gardens. The distance exceeds the ideal statistical value, but a concealed shuttle requires considerable unmonitored space, a difficult commodity to obtain in a metropolitan district."

"We shall need rest before we reach your shuttle," remarked Beth in an even tone of practicality. With clinical detachment, she noted to herself that she had begun the transition from adrenaline's bright clarity to the muffling torpor of fatigue.

"I can carry the girl for a time," replied Marrach, following Beth's glance to Kitri's faltering steps. "If we delay too long, those who track us will descend on us. They are very well armed, though they have not summoned reinforcements." Marrach's sudden, chill grin looked vicious. "They have deduced that I may accompany you, and they fear to make reports about me."

"You enjoy being feared."

"Certainly, if the fear serves my purpose."

When Kitri stumbled, Marrach holstered his weapon at his waist, and the weapon disappeared in light refractive concealment. Marrach lifted the girl effortlessly, though Kitri remained stiff and unaccommodating in his grasp. The girl closed her eyes against the sight of him.

Beth observed Kitri's silent resentment and regretted that she could not carry Kitri herself: At nine years of age, Kitri was slender but nearly as tall as her brother. *This Marrach has unnatural strength for his apparent build. I wonder if he is human or an excellent alien imitation. Jon's expertise in topological transfer would be invaluable to the Consortium, but surely the proudly lawful Calongi would not sanction terrorism. Would other species be as honorable?*

The gray corridor walls vibrated angrily, and a web of hairline cracks hissed, emitting a foul-smelling fume. Marrach began to run, and Michael raced behind him. Beth commanded herself sternly to keep pace with them. The fumes burned her eyes, and she began to cough from the thick yellow gas. She could barely see Marrach's head above the rising gaseous cloud, and at last she lost sight of him altogether. Her heart thundered with the dread that she had lost her children as well as her husband, and she felt achingly alone.

She heard the shout and could not orient herself to seek its source. Tumbling metal clattered, and grinding joints cracked. A wave of deeper sound struck her, shuddering below the frequency range of her hearing but not so low as to spare her its rumbling, unsettling vibration. Light flared from the walls, and Kitri's scream drew Beth in panic toward the source of the most penetrating brilliance.

Both children reached for their mother and pulled her, blinking blindly before the glare, into a cylindrical shaft of clear air. Beth gulped the freshness into her aching lungs, and she tried to rub the moisture from her eyes. She felt Kitri's cold touch against her cheek, a tentative attempt at reassurance. The light vanished abruptly, leaving thick darkness. Long moments passed before Beth's beleaguered vision could readjust to the dimness of a moonless night outside the city.

Marrach called to her, and only then did she realize that he had climbed above them. "The pipes are strong enough to support you one at a time. They are spaced at sufficiently close intervals to make a decent ladder most of the way, and I can pull you past the last bit.''

He makes it sound simple and ordinary, thought Beth, staring in alarm at the daunting, nearly featureless shaft he expected them to climb. Only the single spot of Marrach's hand torch indicated the limit of the height, and he had dimmed the torch to a most uninspiring pinprick.

"Send the boy first," called Marrach. Beth nodded, a remote, rational segment of her brain commending Marrach's judgment. *Michael would enjoy such a climb under other circumstances,* she thought, *and his ascent will give confidence to Kitri—and to me.*

Michael, once prodded, scrambled up the rungs of narrow, interlaced pipes and conduits. Beth lost sight of him. Marrach's light disappeared for a moment, and Michael shouted his safe arrival. "Send the girl," urged Marrach. A trace of impatience in his voice reawakened Beth's doubts: *The enemy waits above in the person of Marrach or his associates. The enemy has also laid siege to the tunnels below, and retreat is impossible.*

"Follow your brother, Kitri," urged Beth gently.

"I want to stay with you."

"I shall follow you immediately."

"Citizen Marrach wants to hurt us," replied Kitri stubbornly.

"No, dear, he wants to help us," coaxed Beth, knowing her daughter's stubbornness and hating to deceive. Reluctantly, Kitri began to climb, as wiry and agile as her brother, despite the fatigue of frantic nights and days of fear. Beth tried to disregard the added worry that Marrach would take the children without awaiting her. *It is Jon he wants, not me. If Marrach seeks hostages to win Jon's help, he has them now.*

Tendrils of the spreading smoke began to contaminate the air in the shaft's lower chamber, and Beth could hear the rumbling echo of a distant vehicle approaching. "Beth," hissed Marrach urgently.

Lift the hand to the slender polished tube that carries water or heat or some other Network gift to human comfort. Pull and find a toehold; soft, fitted slippers allow the cold of the surface to penetrate. Raise hand over hand. Reach and fumble for another pipe to grasp. Pull again;

*climb again. Shift cautiously to the right in order to avoid
the protruding valves. Climb again. Reach and touch only
slick walls. Claw desperately, seeking an elusive hold.
Reach, and a hand takes yours. An arm of great strength
lifts you. Gasp to feel yourself dangling above a shaft six
times your height. . . .*

"Can you walk a little farther?" demanded Marrach.

Beth felt solid ground beneath her, and the dizziness
began to pass. "I slipped on a cliff's edge as a child," she
told Marrach, wondering why she bothered to explain
anything to him. "I have had trouble with heights ever
since then."

"Can you walk?" repeated Marrach impatiently. He
withdrew the impersonal support of his arm, and she tee-
tered for a moment, seeking another prop without
success.

Beth steadied herself with stern self-control, and she
stepped carefully away from the edge of the shaft. She
raised her eyes deliberately from it to the interior of the
weathered maintenance shed. A jumble of broken robotic
fragments of indeterminate purpose lay against a sagging
locker. "Yes," she answered briskly. Michael had draped
his arm protectively over Kitri's shoulders. Beth smiled
at them tiredly. *How often have I insisted that they could
stop arguing if they tried? I never expected to prove my
point under such appalling circumstances.*

"There are two paths outside," said Marrach, prodding
Beth's shoulder to regain her attention. "Follow the one
that leads uphill, until you reach the remnants of the
picnic area. Wait for me there." He turned her forcibly,
so as to meet her eyes. "Whatever you hear or think you
hear, do not leave that area until I arrive."

Perhaps he will abandon us, mused Beth wistfully. *I
would be glad never to see Marrach again, but without
him, I will not see Jon again; without Marrach, none of
us may survive.* "How long shall we wait?"

"Until I arrive," replied Marrach sharply, and she did
not doubt him aloud again.

She beckoned her children, and they joined her, each
watching Marrach cautiously. Outside, the dawn had
begun to soften the night. The shadows of odd, twisted
trees crawled vividly against the velvet sky. The pathway
had cracked, and the spicy scent of bruised herbs encom-

passed the three lonely figures who walked silently amid the abandoned garden.

Garden denizens croaked and whistled. Their trills floated from throaty rumbles to palpitating chimes, producing songs that had inspired music on a hundred worlds. The garden's choir glorified the tangle of exotic botanical specimens, assimilated into an unruly whole. Beth wondered why the garden had been left to ruin. She could nearly convince herself that Marrach had arranged the decades-old desertion of an obviously expensive preserve simply to accommodate this night's villainy.

The abandoned picnic area contained three curved benches around a single, circular table. A tattered vine, its torn tendrils still clinging to the table's base, lay wilting across the slick ground ring that had once repelled pernicious insect life from the area. A case of nutrient vials had been placed on the table in precise symmetry with respect to the rectangular design of simulated boards. Both color and texture codes identified the individual vials as the most basic, unimaginative food substitutes.

Beth wondered if the vials, like Marrach's weapon, had originated in some military supply factory. She selected a vial labeled as restorative, allowed the warmth and gentle pressure of her hands to dissolve its seal, and sampled it gingerly. She tried not to grimace too obviously at the pungent flavor of an ungarnished vitamin blend.

She drained the vial's contents and dropped the collapsed container on the table; the emptied container began to shrink, dehydrating into dust. She persuaded her children to imitate her. They complied readily, until they discovered that the delicate flavors they anticipated did not await them. "Finish your drinks," ordered Beth firmly. "We may not have another chance to eat for some time yet." Michael took another tentative sip, but Kitri only stared resentfully at her vial.

A siren beset their ears, and vicious streaks of scarlet enflamed the gray dawn. *Attack warning. Take cover.* Beth had never heard the siege blare of a war zone, but she recognized it from the few, rare news reports of fringe worlds' conflicts. *Take cover, the siren warned, before a field of vibrational energy blankets you with heat by misdirecting your metabolism, disrupting the electrical signals of your brain. Any protection is better than none.*

Beth sighed softly, recalling Marrach's words: *Whatever you hear or think you hear, do not leave that area until I arrive.* Of course, she reasoned, *Marrach has arranged another deception; there is no attack.*

Michael asked seriously, "Are the Network police trying to arrest us because of what happened on Network-3?"

"No one believes what happened on Network-3, Michael," replied Beth wearily, "and the men who pursue us are not official police." *They are not civilian police, at least.* She paused until another blast of the warning could fade. "The siren is a trick. Marrach is playing a trick."

"On us?" demanded the puzzled boy.

Beth shook her head, wondering how she might explain anything regarding Marrach, when she understood so little herself. The planet groaned beneath her feet. A ship raced across the sky, raining fire upon the valley. Several of the exotic, sap-heavy trees exploded when trains of tiny sparks raced along their trunks, while other specimens curled sensitive foliage into tight, hopeless vessels of failing life. All of the garden's nearby richness vanished in an instant, leaving intact only the crown of the hill where Beth and the children shuddered, staring at the destruction through the distortion of an energy shield that had risen from the shards of the old pest-repellent ring. Beth tried to rub warmth into her children, hoping to protect them from the effects of such shock as she reasoned they must feel. She had grown too numb to notice her own shock.

Marrach released them from the protective prison: minutes later or hours later, Beth did not know. He had landed a sleek, unmarked private shuttle on the crushed garden; he ushered them into it, strapped them into three remarkably cramped and uncomfortable berths, and proceeded to steal them from the warm, benign planet they knew to a string of lightless cities with soiled and seedy transfer ports trafficked by harsh and hard-eyed men and women. Beth saw no children but her own in all those noisome places.

A Network terminal, dirty and primitive but unmistakably patterned, loomed somewhere in every port. By this fact and the dearth of any obvious aliens, Beth knew that these worlds belonged with her world. *Her* Network had never acknowledged such filthy and impoverished planets, but circumstances of the past few days had already shattered her remaining faith in the Network she had imagined for most of her life. *Her* Network had betrayed her, and the last vestiges of long conditioning shuddered and broke.

CHAPTER 6

Network Year 2284

Time had blurred. No rod of measure existed by which to count an hour or a day. Only his internal reckoning could guess the time that passed, and loneliness and fear made the inner reckoning seem long.

He had tried to plan escapes, but the restraint cell eventually defeated his imagination. He could neither move nor feel, because the restraining fields encapsulated him in the drastic sort of life-support cylinder that had been designed for comatose patients during long recuperations. He had tried to turn his thoughts to a future outside this prison, but he could not sustain belief that his jailers would let him live much longer with his mind intact, if they had not already meddled with his sanity. Some memories seemed elusive now, while others tormented him, for he had failed to reach and warn his family, and he could not expect them to avoid such entrapment as had taken him.

The present existed as a vacuum, seeking any thought to fill it. In lucid moments, Jonathan Terry found it ironic that the only pattern of thought he could sustain without despair involved the closing of Network-3. Repeatedly, he relived the chaotic moments following his sabotage of the DI controller. Furious images that had seemed dim at the time sharpened with incessant viewing, until he knew each detail of them: the seared sword-emblem on the strong hand that grasped the controller, the frost-blue eyes of a man whose commands drove directly into

Jon's head, the inconceivably gentle warmth of the golden-haired angel who touched and healed the wavering strands of Jon's life.

Odd, thought Jon, *I see only these three, though other actions, other images held my focus at the time. I seem to know—have I been told?—that these three matter. These three Immortals hold the Network-3 of now.*

"Dr. Terry, do you hear me?"

The voice registered slowly. *How did you shift the time-scale of your world?* asked Jon silently, believing that he addressed the three Immortals of his dream. The light against his eyelids woke him more securely. He tried to open his eyes, but the immobilizing fields continued to restrain him.

"I am freeing the fields around your head and upper torso first," continued the voice. "Respiration and heart actions will begin to resume normal functioning levels, and you should soon be able to see and speak. Do not be concerned by the numbness; it will abate after I release a few more fields."

"Who?" whispered Jon, the word creaking from his throat.

"Rabh Marrach," replied the voice.

Not a dream, thought Jon, and the images of the three Immortals raced away from him and vanished. "Council Chancellor Marrach?" asked Jon, the words issuing more easily, though they remained thick and slurred.

"I have recently been appointed to that position," acknowledged Marrach.

"Are you my jailer?"

"I am your rescuer."

Jon blinked, and the unremarkable face of an even-featured man hovered foggily, until Jon's focus cleared. Unable yet to move his head, Jon could see only a portion of Marrach and the pale gray wall of the prison cell. *I am glad they enchained me in a vertical position,* thought Jon; *it allows me an illusory sense of lessened vulnerability.* "Did my jailers authorize my release?"

"Indeed not."

"Network will alert them. You had best hurry, if either of us is to escape."

Marrach smiled at Jon, an eerily unpleasant expression suggesting a cruel humor. "I have considerable influence with Network, or I would not be here now. I have no aspiration to achieve martyrdom."

"Why are you here?" demanded Jon, suspicions beginning to coalesce, as his senses and reason returned. The act of speaking had already become a normal, instinctive aspect of his existence. *Marrach must have loaded me with stimulants,* decided Jon, assessing the anxious rush of his thoughts and nerves.

"You are an invaluable asset to your species, Dr. Terry. You possess remarkable skills."

"I appreciate the compliment," answered Jon dryly, "especially from a man whose own skills are so obviously extraordinary. You are linked directly into Network, aren't you?"

"You are an astute observer. I am not surprised."

This is the man who placed me here, when I refused to accept his help: his help for what? Network-3? No, that was only the nightmare. Council Chancellor Rabhadur Marrach: why do I know a name and title that he never gave me? Have I ever met him before? "I have wondered why Network abandoned all the neural implant studies." *This man may kill me; he may have already killed Beth and Michael and my dear, temperamental Kitri; yet, I am so hungry for human contact that I welcome anyone who speaks and hears me.* "Bioengineering is not my field, of course, but I always become curious when a promising, prominent line of research suddenly disappears from the procurement rosters."

"You are much less gullible than the majority of Network citizens, Dr. Terry."

"Prior to confining me, your technicians informed me that I have an abnormally high immunity to Network conditioning techniques. I presume that they intended to explore the limits of my resistance."

Marrach answered mildly, "Caragen purchased a Dathonen enslavement laboratory a few years ago with some very exotic software options. The procedures are effective."

Have they been effected against me? How can I know? "Andrew Caragen, the Council Governor?"

"My employer," agreed Marrach. "You are aboard his private space yacht."

Andrew Caragen, the only truly intelligent member of

Network's ruling council, the most strikingly powerful man I have ever met: I never did quite credit his benevolent image. "What does the Council Governor want with me?" Jon managed to turn his head enough to see Marrach fingering the controls of the restraint fields.

"Have you forgotten? You began to display dangerously psychotic tendencies."

"By closing Network-3?"

"Yes. It was a heavily populated planet," replied Marrach. Jon began to feel chilled; he actually welcomed the mild discomfort, for it broke the monotony of countless days. "Let me know if you experience any excessive sensations. I am bypassing the normal reacclimation controls so as to expedite your return to standard environment. The accelerated process may cause some temporary disorientation of your nervous system, masquerading as a reaction to temperature extremes."

He is actually releasing me. Whatever his purpose, he gives me at least a hope of escape. How can I maximize my chances? By learning as much as Marrach will tell me, of course. "If I have been declared insane, why are you helping me?"

Marrach methodically began to release the manual restraints. "Unlike the Network Council, I believed your story."

"All of it?"

"Enough of it to convince me that Network-3 still exists." Marrach disconnected a final binding strap. "The feeling should be returning to your extremities momentarily. You will experience nominal pain as the nerve endings are reactivated from stasis."

He calls this nominal pain, thought Jon with a gasp, as a burning agony assaulted every nerve. The last restraining field dissipated, and Jon tumbled forward helplessly to slump against Marrach's rigid arm. *So much for any thought of overpowering Marrach,* observed Jon wryly.

"Your strength will return slowly," commented Marrach, and he dragged/carried Jon to the single utilitarian bench in the barren cell, which was scarcely large enough to contain both men and the restraint equipment. "This uniform should fit you reasonably well, though you have lost weight during your incarceration. Sorry, I only made you a private, but it reduces the likelihood of recognition.''

"Where is my family?" demanded Jon, awkwardly trying to dress in the Network military uniform. *Marrach wears the darker blue of an officer,* noted Jon with interest, *though "Council Chancellor" is an honorary title, not a military rank.*

"Your wife and children are safe."

"Here?" Jon momentarily abandoned the struggle to insert his arms into the sleeves of the mesh turtleneck.

"No. They are in my custody, not Caragen's. Try to finish dressing quickly. Delays could cause complications."

Jon complied, wincing as his muscles protested, but the pain did begin to fade as he moved. *Delays could jeopardize our chances of escape,* thought Jon, but he could not recall why the words seemed so familiar. Jon tried standing and found that he could walk almost normally. Marrach observed Jon's experimental steps and nodded in approval.

"We should be able to walk to the transfer room without attracting any troublesome attention," commented Marrach, "since Network will not stop us, and even the few humans who take the trouble to monitor my shifting physical traits seldom question my actions openly."

"What will your employer think?"

"He will think that I am obeying his orders and pursuing your latest abductors, a fanatical group of C-humans who invaded this ship yesterday and secured the release of an unconscious prisoner who currently shares your physical appearance. When I learned of the impending 'rescue,' I had Network switch your cell coordinates with those of Caragen's decoy of you." The cell door opened, and Marrach stepped through it. He stopped and turned when Jon did not follow. "Are you coming, private?"

"Yes, sir," answered Jon, feeling absurd in his role. *This is a fine position for a middle-aged topologist,* he informed himself in a spurt of humor inspired by a rush of hope. Jon tried to muster a military confidence of stride to match Marrach's.

The white corridor led to a medical laboratory, devoid of any life but an odd assortment of alien samples confined in clear cylinders of varying sizes. Two similarly unoccupied rooms led to the pseudo-street. Boldly, Marrach emerged into the dawn-gray aisle and headed for the tram line. Jon tried not to show his own fear of the cluster of Network citizens who disembarked from trams or waited on the mobile walkway. No one acknowledged either Marrach or Jon Terry, and the two men were soon seated and en route to the coordinates Marrach requested.

Jon began to speak, but Marrach silenced him with a slight gesture at the Network voice receiver. *Can it be a true escape?* wondered Jon. *Perhaps—on Rabh Marrach's unholy terms. My memories are hazy, but I remember enough to distrust this man who seems to help me. He said that C-humans tried to rescue me. I never thought of appealing to the Consortium for aid; I suppose that some C-humans would risk a great deal to acquire the methods of topological transfer.*

I suppose I am too well conditioned by Network, after all; I could not bring myself to give Network science to the Calongi's Consortium even now, even if my alternative is Rabh Marrach, even if the choice costs me my family and my life. Network science belongs to humanity, not to the alien Consortium.

The tram stopped, and Marrach nodded at Jon to exit from the ovoid car. Jon stumbled slightly in the process, gaining the brief attention of an excruciatingly thin young woman dressed in a sheer, ankle-length robe of wine pearl-cloth. The woman hesitated, glancing at Marrach as if on the verge of recognition, but her tram's cover settled into place, and the woman sped from view.

Jon began nervously to count the steps to the light curtain. He noted only peripherally that Network did not request entry or destination codes. When Jon emerged from transfer, a pace behind Marrach, into a dingy room that contained only a minimal portal and a pair of scratched, molded swivel chairs, Jon began to believe that escape could actually occur.

"Network?" asked Jon experimentally, and he received no answer. "This is a secure room with an independent portal," he remarked tentatively.

Marrach answered nearly immediately, "Yes," but Jon noted that brief pause with interest. *Without Network, Marrach loses one of his primary attributes, and he real-*

*izes that I may try to take advantage of his brief weakness,
for I may have no better opportunity to gain control of the
situation.* "I do have your wife and children," remarked
Marrach mildly, "and I have sufficient physical strength
to overpower you quite easily. I suggest that you listen
to me before planning a means to circumvent me."

"What do you want?"

"In a different guise, I answered you before your capture by Caragen's agents. I want a favor, and I hope you
now realize how badly you need my help."

"I cannot seem to recall what favor you named."

"I want an option to escape Network. You comprise
an important element of my personal insurance against
the day when Caragen decides to dispense with me. You
know that Network-3 still exists, despite the contradictory readings of all Network monitors; you know how to
reach it. You were trying to reach it when Caragen had
you abducted. I shall see that you and your family
achieve your goal, and you will give me the means of
following you, if the need ever arises."

*Was I trying to reach Network-3? The answer feels both
right and wrong.* "You are certainly asking for a lot of
trust on my part."

"I am your only hope, Dr. Terry. I give you this room
and this portal, and I shall supply anything you need to
modify this portal for access to Network-3. I shall reunite
you with your wife, and the two of you may journey to
your cleverly concealed haven. I shall send your children
after you, so that I may assure myself that you have met
your half of the bargain. I may travel with them, or I
may wait, but I shall not reveal your secret to anyone
else, for that would obviate the value of my insurance."

"Take me to Beth," growled Jon.

* * *

The two-room apartment had become a prison, and it
was all that existed. Beth could have drawn from memory
each crack, each mark, each stain upon the ceiling, walls,
and floor. Marrach had not entrusted her with the
authority to command the exterior doors. The room had
no windows; its circulation system carried air so sour that
Beth wondered that they could breathe it and survive.

Marrach had left them food enough for several months.

Beth hoped that he did not intend their incarceration to last that long, but he had given her no clue as to when he might return. Beth passed most of the time completing the psychic research thesis that she knew she would never now present. She did not treat the subjects of her thesis kindly, for it was their Immortal offspring who had begun the unraveling of her serene life.

She raised her head from her work, too frustrated and angry for the moment to continue, and she delved into the room's battered desk for other distraction. Her fingers grasped a frayed box, and she drew its contents into her hands without conscious thought. The shuffling of the cards soothed her with its mindless rhythm. Beth manipulated the cards without examining them, until the deck slipped from her nervous hands.

She bent to collect the ragged, soiled rectangles from the brown, barren floor, and she gathered them into her hands bemusedly. The figures and faces of the tarot met her. She wondered how they had come to occupy this sordid room in this nameless place.

Beth began to sort idly through the cards, but too many of the images disturbed her. The Nine of Swords, a card of anguish, reappeared. *Some of the early psychological tools had remarkable emotional impact,* she observed in quiet detachment, but she replaced the deck in the desk out of sudden fear of the images' power. Beth tried to replace anxiety with the old enthusiasm for her thesis, but she worried about her children and her husband with every breath and every thought.

Marrach had brought puzzles and a peculiar, shapeshifting game for Michael, and Kitri had attached herself to a sketch pad. The children occupied themselves in a silence that abraded Beth's nerves more than their bickering had ever done. They received no lessons, of course, for the room contained no terminal, and Marrach insisted that any Network usage without his supervision would summon enemies.

Michael frowned a lot, and he had become lethargic to the point of total apathy. Kitri wielded her markers incessantly, more engrossed by the activity than Beth had ever seen her, but too many of the pictures contained harsh, angry images. One picture disturbed Beth particularly, though it was a stark and primitive effort, much less skillfully drawn than the majority of Kitri's works; it showed a girl, a stick figure with a ribbon in her scribbled hair, standing on a tiny red island, engulfed by clouds and a heavy sea of coarse, black arrows. The island huddled in pathetic isolation at the bottom corner of the page.

They are my children, Beth repeated to herself, *and I do love them.* But she was tired, frustrated, and angry, and confinement had made her children seem almost hideous to her. They seemed so warped and grimly resentful, as if they felt their mother had betrayed them. They seemed like strangers now, for all joy and youth had left them. *It is my own guilt that fills me with unjust anger against them. How will they ever recover from this ordeal?*

* * *

Marrach returned that night, while the children slept. He came silently and seated himself across the table from Beth. She pushed her notes into an orderly stack, and she laid aside the recorder. "Where is Jon?" she asked tightly.

"He is waiting for you. I shall take you to him."

Beth raised her head, seeking confirmation in Marrach's eyes, but she saw only the same emotionless mask that she had seen previously. "Is he well?" demanded Beth, afraid to feel eager. Her throat seemed to have closed upon itself, so that her words emerged unwillingly.

"He is tired, but he is unimpaired."

"I shall go and wake up the children," said Beth faintly.

"Yes, wake them, if you wish," murmured Marrach evenly. Beth rose and hurried to the connecting door; instinctive urgency had begun to feed her its forgotten energy. She did not feel hope yet; she could not feel hope yet. "Tell them," continued Marrach remorselessly, "that you must leave them for a time."

Beth stopped short of the door and turned. "No," she whispered.

"I will bring them to you later. You agreed, Beth. Did you expect me to forget?"

"You promised to return Jon to us first!"

"I promised to rescue him from prison and reunite him

with you. I have done the first, and I shall complete the
second as soon as you are ready."

"I cannot leave the children. . . ." Beth's gaze became
blank.

"Why do you still refuse to trust me, Beth?"

"Why must I leave them?" asked Beth tautly.

"You are breaking my rules, Beth. You must trust me
without question, or I may decide not to help you at all."

"How can I entrust my children to you?" cried Beth
in despair.

"I own all of you already. Entrust them to me, or I
may kill them now and eliminate all of your worries."

"You are such an altruist," said Beth bitterly.

"Be grateful for mercy received, citizeness. I have
risked much to keep all of you alive, and I am repaid
only with the knowledge that your husband's genius will
not be obliterated prematurely. I despise waste."

Beth rose without replying, and she went to the room
where both of her children slept. She listened to the even
patterns of their breathing in the darkness. She did not
illuminate the room. "I shall see you very soon," she
promised them in a whisper, but she did not wake them.
She could not bear to see them doubt her. She cursed
herself for cowardice and for her guilty eagerness to
escape from the implicit condemnation of her own children's company.

Across the street and through an alley, into a narrow
gray office building, where dark doors displayed illegible
names and no overt purpose, Beth walked where Marrach led. She tried to fix the path in her mind, tried to
note any sign to tell her where her children might be
found, if she—or Jon—needed to devise a means of
returning to them, if Marrach did not keep his promise.
She tried to observe the worlds to which she followed
Marrach in transfer, hoping that Jon could analyze the
connectivities, but none of the ports bore obvious identification, and Marrach never voiced the transfer coordinates nor revealed the destination codes in any other
way. The final port led only to a room, so like the room
where Beth had left her children, she wondered if the
complex series of transfers had served to bring her back
to the same dim and dismal planet.

She could barely recognize the emaciated man with

hollowed cheeks as her husband. *He has aged so much,* Beth realized with a pang sharper than the tainted joy of her reunion with him. She went to him and laid her head against his shoulder, and neither of them spoke a word.

"You will find some useful items in the next room," commented Marrach. "Select what you feel you need for your journey, but keep the total volume minimal."

"I still need to complete the readjustments of the transfer device," murmured Jon. "Did you bring the equipment I requested?" Beth stared at her husband, conversing so easily with Marrach, asking nothing of her or of the children.

Marrach pulled a canvas roll of precision tools from his pocket and handed the tools to Jon. "How long will the work require?"

"Not long. A few hours."

* * *

Beth fastened the knot of her brief, flowered overskirt to complete her careful dressing. She reached automatically to her wrist, but she wore no flexible computer band today. The lack of that familiar Network detail jarred her from the control she had maintained so well for the past night and morning. "You trust Marrach?" asked Beth tightly, going to her husband's side, while he verified the final revisions of the inventory of possessions they would take on their return to Network-3. Marrach sat in the next room, waiting to confirm their transfer and ensure his ownership of the portal that could reach the pseudo-closed planet of Network-3. Beth imagined that she could feel Marrach's satisfaction at his victory.

"I trust him to protect his own interests, which currently coincide with ours."

"How do we know he will send our children to us at all?" demanded Beth in quiet, futile anger. "You are not sure that we can return, and you are giving our only chance of security to that murderer in the next room. I never imagined that you would not find some plan, some means of circumventing Marrach. You have been acclaimed as the greatest genius in human history, and you allow that man to dictate our every move."

"I apologize for disappointing you, Beth," snapped

Jon, his own nerves frayed, "but my expertise in applied topology does not enable me to combat either Network's Council Governor or his devious operative. I am tired, and I am conquered, and all I want now is to go home."

"Network-3 no longer exists. Whatever it may have become, it is not our home."

Jon sealed the three small suitcases that contained all that Marrach would allow them to transport: a few books, a few pieces of clothing, a few personal items, and a single, old mimovue of Kitri and Michael smiling and squirming beside their parents at a festival on Network-3. "I cannot undo the past, Beth. All of us cheated death when Tom and I closed Network-3, and we are still alive, despite everything that has happened to us. We shall have a new home, but we will be together. Marrach will keep his word."

"I cannot trust a murderer that easily," retorted Beth, but she accepted the suitcase that her husband handed to her, and she preceded him into the room that held the transfer port and Marrach. *I will regain you, Michael and Kitri*, she promised silently, *even if Marrach betrays us, even if Marrach has made my Jon almost a stranger*.

"Here," said Marrach, handing Jon a tiny organic transceiver. "I shall use this to contact you when I am ready to transfer your children."

Jon inspected the device briefly, before closing his hand around it. "How do you expect your signal to reach us?"

Marrach answered calmly. "I intend to monitor your transfer, of course. I have no idea how you have established your initial contact with a system that still registers as closed, but I do know enough applied topology to track a set of destination coordinates in linear time."

Jon muttered, "I hope for the sake of all of us that the topology of Network-3 behaves sufficiently well to support your analysis." Jon smiled wanly at Beth, who laid her free hand on his arm, and they both closed their eyes to enter the portal. Beth wished that she could as easily close her mind against spinning visions of her children's accusatory faces, when they discovered that she had abandoned them to Marrach without even a word of explanation or apology. Beth stepped through the light curtain.

She strode across a field of stones and grasses, mists and dew-cups of blue and violet hues. The dampness clung to her hair, which hung down her back and spread across the cowled cloak of heavy, heathery wool. The wind whipped the cloak and the long skirt beneath it, chilling her ankles where wet stockings tied with dark cords clung to her skin. She glanced at her wrist, banded with brilliant blue corundum instead of the dull silver of a flexible computer link, and she did not find either the present opulence or the stark, remembered Network image incongruous against the coarse gray sleeve.

A sparrow hawk's harsh cry drew her eyes to the leafless tree that bowed above her and to the silhouette of a huddled rider upon a restive horse. The figure dismounted and approached, spread thin arms, and caused the barren tree to bud and blossom in an instant. The figure in silhouette began to glow with a light like the shattered rainbow patterns of firelit diamonds, and the figure took a fragile form as a woman.

"Elizabeth," whispered the woman, "do not fear."

"Everything is lost," replied Beth, knowing that the full extent of her emotions lay bared before this woman's steady, sympathetic gaze.

"I understand your torment."

"Help me?" asked Beth forlornly, not sure why she made a question of her plea, less sure of why she felt that this golden apparition of a woman *could* help, *could* understand.

The woman touched Beth, and the warmth of the touch became the radiant energy of a yellow sun giving life to a long-shadowed garden. Beth tried to recall another garden on another world, but that memory held pain, for that garden had been lost; the memory receded, and Beth inhaled the fragrance of the moment.

"The feeling of helplessness," said the woman's soft voice inside Beth's thoughts, "can be one of the most frightening of all emotions, but it is the fear that incapacitates us—more than the weakness itself. We are all helpless at all times, unless we realize that reason, strength, and Power will always fail if they do not rise from faith and hope."

The woman, dressed now in a full-skirted gown of pale blue silk, stood with Beth in a sunny garden in the shade

of a lacy white cottage. A wide veranda encircled the
house, and a red-and-white painted chair rocked slightly
near the top of the five wooden steps leading to the
porch. "Where is Jon?" demanded Beth suddenly.

"In his study, where you left him," came the soundless
answer.

"Where I left him?" asked Beth. She began to sense
a wrongness with the sequence of her memories for the
past few minutes, but she could not quite correct the
confusion of bewildering mental images. "I have never
been in that house," argued Beth, but detailed recollections of the interior rose to contradict her. She could
visualize Jon's paneled study, the wide walnut desk, the
unglazed windows overlooking the pond on the opposite
side of the house, the white shutters with the one cracked
slat, the hand-tied rug patterned in brown and green to
match the settee and the cushions on the walnut chair.
She could see the bedroom with its huge four-poster bed
and crocheted coverlet, the sitting room where she had
hung her watercolor renderings of the garden and the
pond, and the dining room with the translucent white
porcelain of the flower bowl laid against the geometric
marquetry of the small, square dining table.

"I have never been in that house," repeated Beth
strongly, but the golden woman had disappeared, leaving
Beth alone on the gravel path that meandered among
the trees and blossoming shrubbery. Determinedly, Beth
headed for the cottage. When she reached the stairs to
the veranda, she gathered her skirts above her ankles
automatically, before wondering why she wore long
cream silk and embroidered roses over layers of petti-
coats. She proceeded past the white door into the house,
and she stopped before the mirror in the hall. "The face
is mine," she murmured, "but the costume would delight
an anachronist." She touched her pale hair, plaited and
piled atop her head. "When did my hair grow long?"

Beth concentrated on her mirrored features: narrow
nose, slightly hollow cheeks, pale brows, and large eyes
the color of the jewels she had worn for an imagined
moment on her wrist. "You have never owned a sapphire
bracelet," she informed herself sternly, "nor an empire
gown of embroidered silk. You are a student of psychic
science at Worther University on the planet Network-3.

Your name is Elizabeth Shafer." She frowned and shook her head at her reflection. "No. When Dr. Jonathan Terry lectured at the university, you waited all afternoon outside the physics laboratory to meet him, because Tara Mollat told you that the renowned Dr. Terry might visit that abrupt, unpleasant professor who is rather famous in her own right. He arrived, but he never visited that professor." Beth smiled slightly at her reflection. "He married you instead."

Satisfied that one dilemma of memories had been resolved, Beth left the entry and walked directly to her husband's study. She raised her hand to tap the wooden panels of the door, but she reconsidered and thrust the door open, entering resolutely. She hesitated for a moment, convincing herself that the sandy-haired, studious man at the desk was her husband.

"Have you seen my pocket watch?" he asked her.

"On the windowsill in the kitchen," Beth answered without thought. Her husband grunted an incoherent reply and returned to his reading. "Jon, have I been ill?"

Jon raised his eyes to his wife slowly, as if trying to decipher an unexpected joke. When she did not smile, he set aside his book and began to rise. Beth reached him first, perched beside him on the arm of the wide, overstuffed chair, and placed her hand on his shoulder. She said quite calmly, "I cannot seem to remember clearly any occurrence since the day you and I were married, except that I came into the house from the garden a moment ago. Describe to me something that happened this morning."

"I have been studying," began Jon, but he stopped and retrieved the book he had laid aside. He examined the book, turning it in his hands to inspect the leather cover and the embossed spine. He opened the book, stared at it, then offered it to Beth. "Read this page to me, please."

"I cannot read it," answered Beth after a futile effort to absorb the words by sheer will. "I do not recognize the language, nor even the alphabet." With shaking hands, Beth returned the book to her husband.

"Neither do I," replied Jon slowly.

Beth murmured with wonder, "You were reading this book when I entered the room just now."

"I know. I think I know. I *was* reading this book."

"What do you remember, Jon?"

"Network-3."

"Our home?"

"We stayed in your apartment after we married. I accepted a job at the DI research center." Jon frowned. "There is something important about DI that I should recall."

"Can you remember anything about today, prior to the last few minutes?"

"There was a woman here earlier: very fair, very delicately boned. She was wearing a costume like yours, but hers was blue."

"She was in the garden!" said Beth eagerly, feeling triumphant at having remembered the golden woman. "She told me to find you here."

"Did she? I cannot recall her speaking to me. Do you know where she went?"

"No. She disappeared."

"Literally?"

"Yes."

"I think we should search the garden."

"We shall not find her. She will return in her own time."

"You are certain?"

"Yes." Beth slid into the chair beside her husband. "Why am I not afraid, Jon?" Her husband shrugged helplessly, and he wrapped his arm around her shoulders. "I feel contented. I feel that something terrible has been lifted from me. I feel protected. Do you feel any of these things?"

Jon nodded pensively. Once again, he opened the gilt and leather book. " 'A History of Serii's Monarchs,' " he read, " 'from Tul to Joli,' " Volume III."

"Would you like dinner soon?"

"Yes. I seem to be quite hungry today."

CHAPTER 7

Network Year 2284

Absurdly simple, thought Marrach sardonically, as he watched the Terrys step into the transfer port. *Caragen assessed them correctly, as I should have expected, for Caragen rarely misjudges his victims. Somehow I anticipated more from the famous Dr. Terry.*

Marrach checked the status of the independent monitor strapped to his wrist. The external monitoring of the transfer was strictly precautionary. *The extra layer of system redundancy is doubtless unnecessary,* Marrach admitted to himself, *since Caragen's specially designed port controller transmits all operational data to Network immediately upon completion of a transfer.*

Marrach wondered what subconscious element of this apparently trivial operation inspired his excessive care and lingering uneasiness. *Caragen did err in doubting Dr. Terry's ability to reopen Network-3; that information could merit me a bonus, if I use it well, or my execution, if I present it injudiciously. Manipulating Caragen is a deadly pastime, but insolence amuses him up to a point. The distinction blurs at times. I suppose an element of uneasiness is justified.*

Marrach's wrist monitor recorded transfer. He started to raise his hand to assess the racing progress of the coordinate trace. The port controller exploded.

Marrach wiped blood from his eyes and tried to staunch the flow from his brow enough to let him see. The only local Network transponder, a simple, voiceless mechanism, had ceased to transmit altogether, and Marrach felt more blinded by the broken access than by his injury. *Dr. Terry has made real the isolation that I pretended*, thought Marrach, finding the irony singularly unamusing.

Marrach assessed the damage to his person: Only the deep cut near his hairline bothered him significantly; his left arm had taken considerable damage, but the artificial limb could be replaced. He moved toward the hollow shell of the transfer port housing: Its smooth, impervious surface showed little effect of the explosion. The light curtain's mechanism had fused into an unidentifiable lump, and the controller had burst from its housing, leaving the shield box exposed, bare and burned. Of the controller mechanism itself, only shrapnel remained, most of it embedded in the gray wall of the room opposite the port.

Marrach thanked his good fortune for having positioned him outside the path of the greatest damage. He crossed to the pocked wall and studied it with cold curiosity. Traces of golden wire had splattered across the wall, the dabs of molten metal forming a remarkably well-ordered pattern of concentric circles surrounding a skewed starburst. Marrach used one of Jon Terry's abandoned tools to pry a piece of shrapnel free from its lodging. Gingerly, he touched the fragment, an amber bit of the inner casing of the controller. It was still hot from its brief moment of fury.

"You misjudged him, after all, Caragen," murmured Marrach, "as did I." The blood again dripped across one eye. Impatiently, Marrach blinked to clear his vision, and he clenched his damaged hand around the amber bead. He muttered slowly, "They left the children," and he shook his head, trying to assimilate this realization with the character of Jonathan Terry. "Blast. I hate dealing with children."

Marrach abandoned his survey of the room. The Terry children had assumed increased significance, and immediate retrieval was imperative. Analysis of the method of explosion must be postponed. With a single glance to see that his wrist monitor still functioned, Marrach hastened from the dismal apartment and headed for the nearest functioning transfer port.

* * *

"Quit crying, Kitri," chided Michael sternly.

"Where are we going?" sniffed Kitri, rubbing one teary eye with her fist.

"Somewhere safe," Michael assured her sagely. "Citizen Marrach will take care of us until Mom and Dad can join us."

"When? We have been hiding forever."

"Marrach said we would see them soon."

"I never have liked him."

Michael did not respond, because he did not like Citizen Marrach either, but he did not want to compound his little sister's fears. He put his arm around Kitri's shoulders, as he thought their father would have done. He wished that someone would explain something, anything. He wanted to cry like Kitri.

Marrach appeared in the doorway, his intimidating frame silhouetted by the garish blaze of a stim club's advertisement. "It is time to go," he announced tersely. He moved quickly toward the carryall and slung it across his back. "Your parents will be waiting."

Both children brightened, and they rose with more energy than they had displayed in all the countless, varied-length days since their mother disappeared. They followed Marrach quietly. They obeyed him promptly, as much from fear of him as from desperate eagerness to regain their parents, their sense of home, and anything from a time before Marrach. Neither child shrank from the hasty transfers through ports that saw few children and fewer honest citizens; they had known transfer all their lives.

Ports and shuttles had blurred with the sterile rooms and the shabby streets of nameless planets, stations, and ships. When they reached a building of the old style, a blockish thing of bricks and broken glass windows, Michael knew that the city must have predated Network's break from Consortium humanity. History had interested him once; nothing mattered now, except his family.

The floor was slippery. Rusty spatters streaked the walls, which led from the vestibule to a shadowy door at the far end of a narrow corridor. "Messy," announced

Kitri sententiously. She mumbled beneath her breath, "Momma and Dad would not stay in this place." She set her small face in the expression that her mother called rebellious, and her brother observed her uncomfortably. Michael did not want to share her doubts.

"Remain here," ordered Marrach sharply. He left the children to shuffle in the vestibule, while he disappeared into the lightless room at the end of the hallway.

The wait felt long, but Michael assured himself repeatedly that his parents would arrive soon, despite Kitri's anxious grumblings. *Everything will be right again*, he told himself. He stared at the walls, pondering them with deliberately ghoulish detachment, as if the past weeks had not occurred. "It looks like blood," he remarked without considering the ramifications of his idle statement, concocted chiefly to provoke his sister.

"It does not!" retorted Kitri defiantly, but she tried to avert her eyes from the dark splotches, fearing that her brother might be right. She buried her chin in the soft fibers of the pink sweater that her mother had made for her.

"As if you knew anything," answered Michael with some of his old smugness. Michael assured himself once again that his parents would come soon, and life would resume its normal, proper pattern. *Citizen Marrach will disappear when Mom and Dad come*, Michael told himself, *and we will never see Citizen Marrach again*. Michael began to smile.

"If they are coming for us, why are they taking so long?" asked Kitri forlornly. She chewed on the end of her badly braided pigtail.

"Maybe they are waiting for us. Maybe Citizen Marrach has left." Michael's gaze wandered to the tantalizing room at the end of the hall.

"We could look," said Kitri hesitantly. "We have waited a very long time."

Michael pushed against the door by which they had entered the vestibule, and it did not open. He walked a little closer to the unknown room. "If we see Citizen Marrach, we can run back here before he notices us."

Kitri nodded, but she did not move until her brother had nearly reached the far room. She ran to join him when he stood within reach of the door. When the door failed to open automatically, Michael touched it; the door swung on a creaking hinge.

A light flashed, suspended only long enough to sear the image of the room into the minds of the two children, whom Marrach had preconditioned carefully for this moment: In a litter of ruined furnishings lay two bodies, burned and bloody and dead, and the faces belonged to the children's parents.

A figure rushed at the children, snatched them with powerful arms, and carried them back to the vestibule. Marrach dropped them unceremoniously to their feet and pushed their backs against the stained wall. "Listen to me," he commanded them crisply. "You remember the men who attacked you in your home?" Both children nodded.

"They were the men you killed," said Michael bluntly.

"I killed some of them, so as to keep you alive. Your parents asked me to protect you, but the men who attacked you have murdered your parents." Michael shook his head in denial. "Your parents are dead. You have seen them," insisted Marrach repeatedly, still holding both children against the wall's chill surface, until Michael nodded tearfully. Kitri only stared blankly, refusing to hear Marrach's words. "You will depend on me now," said Marrach smoothly, "until I can establish you in a new home." Michael mouthed a retort, but no sound emerged. "We must leave immediately," ordered Marrach, and he drove two children, whose minds he had begun to mold, into the terror-emptied street of an ancient slum at night.

* * *

"How?" demanded Caragen sharply, as soon as Marrach entered the office.

"Ask your technical advisers. Some of the intricacies of deactivating a topological node seem to have been omitted from Network files."

"Facetiousness does not become you, Marrach."

Marrach shrugged, though his face remained expressionless. "My (admittedly limited) understanding of applied topology, transfer ports, and controller mechanisms suggests that the violent destruction of even a local transfer controller should have taken me, the planet, and a large segment of connected space with it into nonexistence. The facts obviously contradict me. Dr. Terry did not 'simply' destroy the controller mechanism; he nullified the node entirely."

"You have no idea of where to find him."

"None," replied Marrach with complete evenness, though he scanned Network (by a method Caragen did not know) to assure himself that Caragen's specialized lie-detecting sensors registered truth. The incomplete data gathered by a simple wrist monitor offered uncertain value, and Marrach preferred to analyze that information extensively before committing himself to its usage. "Dr. Terry's explosion was very thorough."

Caragen grunted. "The Darthonens assured me of the reliability of their enslavement techniques."

"You never had previous cause to dispute their claims."

"I trust that the conditioning of the Terry children will prove more satisfactory."

"Network has tested and confirmed the level of control. Youth makes the subjects malleable."

"And resilient."

"Network affirms that the conditioning should endure for thirty to forty standard years, given regular maintenance. Network will also monitor the children to maximize the duration of control. By your own reasoning, the Terrys will try to contact their children long before conditioning breakdown can begin. When they attempt contact, we shall entrap them, and we shall not lose them again."

"I dislike uncertainties, Marrach, especially of the caliber of Jonathan Terry."

CHAPTER 8

Seriin Year 9041

"I need your wits, Ineuil, and not your gallant flour-ishes." The Infortiare of Serii swept across her Tower's library toward the fair-haired man who lounged in a dark damask armchair. Despite her delicacy of frame and fea-ture, the Infortiare appeared tall and indomitable when her gray eyes burned with the promise of her enormous Power. "I need the tactical advice of the Queen's Adju-tant," she continued sharply, "and not the ramblings of a rapt devotee of the lute."

The man tilted his head and smiled admiringly. "Do you never tire of the weight of duty, my most exquisite and annoyingly constant sister-in-law? Rhianna, fair and golden lady of inconceivable Power, do you never grow tired at all?"

"No sooner than you, my indefatigable friend. Yldana should keep you home more often, instead of letting you roam the city's taverns every evening. You might find a full night's sleep a healthful novelty."

"I am researching the local talent in search of replen-ishments for our court musicians, a pitiful lot of aging retainers. In any case, I have no intention of depriving you of the satisfaction of haranguing me over my repre-hensible behavior. The loss of such a long-cherished habit could be traumatic for you, and you might demolish the kingdom in a moment of pique." He draped his feet over the chair's arm with a well-crafted sigh of weariness. "Keeping company with a woman who can kill by an idle thought requires the occasional sacrifice. I do my humble part."

"Your wits tonight are not worth consulting, Lord Arineuil," said Rhianna, but she did not hide a faint amusement. "Go to your lutenists, if you will not help me."

"Why do I allow you to prey upon my much abused conscience?" With a groan, Ineuil sat upright in the chair and straightened his sea-silk vest and ruffled shirt. "Very well. The Adjutant gives you his attention. Is some exiled Caruillan pirate threatening to raid our ports again? Or is some squabbling prince seeking an excuse to test his manhood against our good Queen's soldiers?"

"The matter that concerns me is much more serious than the prospect of a boy's imprudent, envious foray. We may have a very serious, very potent enemy." Rhianna finished with careful emphasis, "The creators of Horlach's world may seek us."

Ineuil's jaw tightened slightly, but he spoke with a perfect semblance of calm, "You predicted 'unknown dangers yet to come' when your son repaired the Rending. We have, however, enjoyed remarkable peace in the two years since that cataclysmic event."

"The potential for danger has not diminished." Rhianna continued very solemnly, "How would you prepare a defense against a wholly unknown foe?"

Ineuil pondered her grim question before answering, "I would prepare, as we are prepared, with strength of arms and reserves of food and trade goods. Beyond such general measures, I would make every effort to discover the unknown. I would send spies."

"To where? You do not know your enemy's location, and you cannot search infinity at random."

"How do you know that the enemy exists?"

"A man and woman, both badly injured, escaped from *something*. My son felt them, as their unraveling patterns brushed the Taormin. He saved them from death."

"You could not track their course here?"

"No. We could not allow their patterns of passage to remain intact without making ourselves completely vulnerable."

"You cannot question them?"

"Not yet. Perhaps, if they have time to heal, I shall

learn more, but they have suffered deep wounds of mind and heart, as well as of body."

"You have no other source of information?"

"None that is safe to probe. Infinities are fragile."

"I shall take your word for that," replied Ineuil dryly, "since infinity and I have only the most passing of acquaintances. As for the man and woman: Detain them. Watch them. Watch for the enemy also."

"How?"

"Create a Wizards' Circle to monitor the pattern shifts."

"The shifts are too subtle for a wizard who has not used the Taormin, and I cannot risk losing my strongest wizards to the Taormin's deadly tricks. I have not yet found any Ixaxin whom I sincerely think might survive the process, though I inquire after every testing-and-gathering."

Ineuil grimaced, for he knew the Taormin's history too well. "Alert the Queen and the Council that a threat of unknown Power may exist. The Council will do nothing useful, for they will want proof that you cannot give— the proof that occupies Power's exclusive realms—but you will be able to tell them honestly that you warned them."

"Queen Joli already knows. She left the telling of the Council to my judgment."

Ineuil laughed, "She knows those complacent old men will not want to listen to the Infortiare's grim predictions. They are too busy congratulating themselves on the cessation of Rendie attacks this past year, as if they had contributed to the cure or even understood it." He let his mirth twist into a wry tension: "What does Kaedric advise?"

Rhianna's clear gaze became distant, and she smiled at her Power's vision. "He watches the patterns with me, as does Evaric."

"You seem to have quite a formidable Wizards' Circle: Two Infortiares and their son, who healed the Rending's breach."

"And Evaric is exceptionally sensitive to disruptions of the Taormin's order, but he would much prefer to share a simple, mortal existence with Lyriel. He has suffered so much to preserve our world, and he asks so little in return: the right to be unfettered by any inheritance of title, wealth, or Power. He knows that Power will never completely free him, but he is still a man with the needs of life."

"Kaedric has eliminated that minor flaw from himself."

Rhianna turned from Ineuil to face the wide window that gazed across the city of Tulea and the distant sea. A few stray lights flickered in the city below the Infortiare's Tower, which clung to the Mountain of Tul beside the Queen's castle. She imagined she could see the island of Ixaxis even in the darkness; in Power, she could feel its presence beating with Immortal life.

She replied a little stiffly, "It was Kaedric who suggested that I question you for ideas that we have not considered—because you are mortal, my dear friend, though that sorcerous blood in your ancestry extends your youth more than you admit. You are mortal, and you think like a mortal, and if we know anything of this faceless enemy, it is that *mortal* power drives him."

Ineuil frowned at her. "This man and woman you found: Are they conscious?"

"They float in dreams, awake and asleep. They begin to question, but they never persist, and they sink into a strange, detached acceptance. They are not unaware, for they observe and react, but something inside each of them remains broken by pain. The man's injuries are oddly isolated but severe; the woman, I think, is merely overcome by inner conflicts. When their physical wounds have healed, I may try to probe them gently, but I could thereby increase the chances of their enemy's coming. Their minds' patterns, if restored, could guide the enemy to us."

"So you let the refugees sleep."

"I protect them from their memories—for the sake of their own healing and for the safety of our world. Dare I do otherwise?"

"That is a question for a wizard and not for me. I repeat only this: Watch them at least as closely as you watch the Taormin's webs. If they do awaken—if you allow it—you must be ready to act quickly, whatever they reveal."

Rhianna lowered her eyes, weighing her next words.

"I do know one additional fact about these people," she murmured, and she glanced at Ineuil, observing his response with Power's fiery tendrils. "The man is the creator of the Taormin. He is the man who closed this world originally. I recognize him, for I healed him when Evaric restored the patterns."

Ineuil asked soberly, "Are you certain that the enemy is not already here?" He recognized Rhianna's probe and let her feel the weight of his suspicions against the refugees.

"I am certain of nothing, except endangerment. I sense much distress in the refugees. Kaedric sensed a deep, vast coldness pursuing them."

"My wondrous Rhianna, I never understood Kaedric well, even when I gave him my direct allegiance. Could you possibly interpret 'a coldness' for this ignorant mortal?"

"I understand the meaning poorly myself. Kaedric's Power shared the sense of it with me, but I could only perceive a fraction of the total magnitude. Kaedric described the coldness as a pattern similar to the Taormin but much more extensive, a pattern without the feeling of a living entity, a relentless pattern that sought our world as fiercely as any creature of the Rending. He destroyed the thing's immediate access to us, but he assures me that the thing itself remained unimpaired."

"A direct contact with Kaedric's Power did not even damage it? I am disquietingly impressed." Ineuil rose from the chair in a quick, fluid motion, and he went to Rhianna's side. "Is Kaedric with you now?" he asked with cautious respect.

"He is always with me. He is part of me."

"That is a singularly disturbing thought that I try diligently to forget," retorted Ineuil with a grimace. "But I would like to know his assessment of our present situation."

Gazing into infinity, Rhianna answered with an odd, hard precision, "Our present culture cannot coexist peacefully with our past. The changes—of which the Rending was only a single step—will not end until we are fully restored or fully destroyed. No intermediate solution can achieve any permanence."

Ineuil muttered, "You never were much of an optimist, Kaedric."

PART 2

The Deceiving

CHAPTER 1

Seriin Year 9048

Quin scarcely remembered his parents. If asked, he could reply quite calmly that his mother had died in a riding accident, and his father had fallen from a cliff within the same month. He could discuss the possibility that his father's death had been self-inflicted without a sign of regret or sorrow. His smile would not falter, and his humor would not seem to waver. He made many of his relatives uncomfortable, and most of them avoided talking to him about any serious topic.

Quin scarcely knew anyone beyond surface chatter and childish pretexts, for his Power shielded him from any depth of bond with family or friend. He felt safer alone with his Power, though he did not acknowledge himself as a sorcerer. Because his Power was strong, Hamley was large, and Quin's siblings and cousins were numerous, Quin existed in virtual invisibility from anyone who might have observed him well. A few retainers, such as Nanny, shunned him openly, but no one thought to question their reasons.

Quin's Power had developed a habit of defending Quin from any form of regret, and Quin had no conscious recognition of any occurrence that did not amuse him. The result of Power's inescapable meddling was unfortunate in many respects. Quin could not take much of anything seriously: certainly nothing resembling work or study. He supposed that there were things that mattered enough to him to raise a frown or cause a worry, but on a

day-to-day basis he had trouble remembering what those
things might be.

The wonder of Quin, noted his tutors, was not his
persistence of good humor but the fact that he had ever
managed to learn anything at all. Even when his more
reckless escapades resulted in his temporary confinement, he could barely begin to complain of the unfairness
of life in general and his punishment in particular, before
an intriguing, twisted crack in the wall or an ant crawling
along the floor would distract him.

Quin's elders and his peers attributed his buoyant spirits to an ephemeral attention span, and Quin did his best
to live up to their expectations. If any member of the
Hamley clan observed the incongruous depth of Quin's
occasional insights, no one gave the matter any serious
concern. Quin learned despite very vocal disinterest, but
not even this inconsistency in his nature alerted the Hamley lords.

As the fifteenth child of a younger son of the present
liege-lord's uncle, Quin relished all the privileges of
wealth and nobility without a fear of inheriting any worri-
some responsibility. He did not expect to own land, of
course, or influence history like his greater cousins.
Quin's ambitions were exceedingly simple. He desired
only to enjoy a carefree life, free from any great hurt,
and his Power accommodated him with terrible efficiency.

Quin's chosen perspective was hardly unique within his
family: Several of his relatives had managed to live long,
contented lives without ever performing an obviously
useful service. Since the fertile Hamley lands could support a considerable number of malingerers, Quin strove
determinedly to emulate his least productive relatives.
He thought he succeeded quite well, never even considering the possibility that *uselessness* might be an undesirable goal. The prospect of failing in any more difficult
form of life's work alarmed him, and his Power supported his reluctance.

The wizards' testing had confirmed that Quin had
Power, but Hamley had few personal memories of cruel
Sorcerer Kings to inspire fear of Power's potential. Occasionally, a Hamley child would disappear to Ixaxis, but
most such children returned after the minimal training

afforded to lesser Powers, and they resumed their interrupted lives. Lord Bendl dur Hamley scorned the near-
hysterical dread of Power that pervaded so much of Serii,
and he discouraged such sentiments in his domain. Fear
of Power did not affect the liege of Hamley sufficiently.

Not even the wizard who tested Quin perceived the
boy as a significant Power. The wizard did not, therefore,
enforce promptness of compliance with Ceallagh's laws,
which decreed that Power must be trained—or bound or
destroyed. Quin was designated as a lesser novice,
intended for the minimal Ixaxin training that would
ensure his mastery of his Power. Ceallagh's laws recognized the hazards that most of Hamley could not see.

* * *

On a pale morning of his eleventh year, Quin found
himself roused from his bed, hurriedly fed, and packed
in a bumping wagon with no warning and few explanations. A maidservant laid a wool blanket carefully across
his legs, but she performed her task quickly and avoided
touching Quin. Lord Bendl, whom Quin scarcely distinguished from other uncles and older cousins, said something vague to the driver about the river barge and Tulea,
but no one spoke to the boy directly.

Quin glanced upward, sensing a familiar presence.
Nanny, her dour face intent, watched the proceedings
from an upper window of the manor. She observed
Quin's attention on her, and she drew herself upright in
a proud gesture, but Quin felt her relief and wondered
at it.

He forgot his brief concern once the journey began.
The wagon made a lovely rattling noise. The two massive
cart horses huffed marvelous puffs of steam in the cold
morning air. Undulating hills bristled with colorful scare-
crows, designed as much for novelty as for practical use.
Every sight and sound fascinated Quin, who had never
traveled beyond his family's extensive estate.

The cart jogged roughly across the rutted roads through
Hamley village. Quin leaned eagerly over the wagon's
side, asking constant questions but receiving no replies.
The driver never spoke a word to him, but Quin's Power
shrugged away the rudeness.

The cart stopped at the River of Night, a broad, cold

expanse that cut across Serii from the northernmost
Mountains of Mindar. The driver gathered the tapestry
bag that had been packed for Quin, and he jerked his
head at the boy. Quin jumped nimbly from his berth and
followed the driver to the dock at the river's edge. A
waiting pole barge carried bales of wool and a few
passengers.

The driver exchanged a nod with one of the boatmen,
who came and took Quin's baggage from the driver's
hands. Busily examining the barge, Quin did not notice
the driver's departure, until the boatman ordered, "Get
aboard, boy."

Quin's smile became fixed, and he leapt onto the
barge, overturning another passenger. He continued to
smile, as the passenger berated him. The boatman tried
to soothe the flustered passenger's temper. Quin pounded
and prodded a bale of wool, apparently unaware of the
commotion he had caused. The boatman glanced at Quin
uneasily, disconcerted by the boy's impervious grin.

"Where are you bound after you reach the Tulean har-
bor, boy?" asked the boatman in sudden suspicion. The
irate passenger immediately became silent.

"Am I going to Tulea?" countered Quin with only the
faintest shadowing of his mindlessly happy expression.

"You are taking the ship from Niveal, where I was
paid to take you."

"Am I?"

"Will someone meet you in Tulea?" persisted the boatman. "The Ixaxin ferryman perhaps?"

"No one told me anything," replied Quin blithely,
"but Nanny was pleased to see me leave. She has been
afraid of me since my parents died."

The boatman and the disquieted passenger both crossed
to the opposite side of the barge. They watched Quin
warily: Sorcerers were unpredictable.

*   *   *

It is rather a bore, mused Quin without rancor. *These
Ixaxins are so touchy and devoid of humor; everything
seems to offend them. Hamley really was much more fun.*
Quin still had not quite understood why he had been sent
to this island of dusty beaches, pillars and cubicles, white
robes, gray robes, and room after room of old books.

Quin squirmed in his chair, visualizing a magic cloak that would descend on him and fling him across the Hamley manor yard to melt like a raindrop into the pond beyond the herb garden. His imagination plunged into the pond's murky depths, fled from a hungry carp, and leaped out of the water to land in a patch of dill. A botanical similarity between the herb gardens of Hamley and the cliff-top terrain of Ixaxis brought Quin's meandering thoughts back to the school of wizardry.

The place is not all bad, acknowledged Quin, staring at the cloud-painting on the domed ceiling of the classroom. *The Ixaxin beaches are even better than Hamley pastures for playing; the pillared hallways would be nearly as grand as the Hamley manor ballroom for races; the wizards ought to be capable of wonderful tricks and jests; maybe they will be friendlier when I know them better. I wonder where that path beside the lily pond leads? I bet that big frog has a hiding hole by the waterfall. I wonder if it connects to a great cavern full of glassy veils and crystal pools.*

"Quinzaine, answer the question, please."

"Maybe there are dragons beneath the pond," muttered Quin, and he began to draw his concept of a dragon in the margin of his history text.

"Quinzaine," repeated Master Howald sternly, but Quin continued obliviously to trail his quill across his book and desk, absently smearing ink with his sleeve. The seven students who were Quin's classmates watched their teacher closely, both with their eyes and with their Power. Most of them had experienced Ixaxin discipline, and all of them waited with slightly callous interest to learn the form that Master Howald would employ with Quin. Such hard lessons taught more to the Ixaxin students than any text, for these were the lessons wrought by Power itself.

Quin yelped at the sensation of a bristle brush swatting his hands, though nothing of material nature had touched him, and he dropped the quill to the slate floor. His head rose of its own accord to see Master Howald's grim figure, all robed in scholar's white, frowning from tight mouth and narrowed eyes to crossed arms and tapping foot: It was a pose of displeasure so severe as to be almost a caricature, but no one in the classroom smiled.

Not even Quin managed more than a weak and foolish grin that vanished beneath a sharp wave of Master Howald's Power.

"What subject are we studying, Quinzaine?" asked Howald coldly.

"Seriin history?"

"Provide a more specific answer, please."

"The domain lords of the Council?"

"That was yesterday's lesson, Quinzaine."

"Shall I name them for you?" offered Quin hopefully. Someone in the classroom snickered.

"That will not be necessary at this time."

The wizard continued to stare at Quin, who began to squirm in anticipation of further punishment to come. The names of the Council lords had been instilled by a horde of ants that had stung Quin no less persuasively for being illusions wrought by Master Howald's Power. Quin's customary methods of making his superiors forget about punishment seemed disappointingly ineffective with Ixaxins.

The Ixaxin scholars did have more potent ways of forcing a person's obedience than any Hamley governess or tutor had ever concocted. Mistress Nevella could make one imagine that slimy, crawly things were nibbling at one's fingers and toes. Quin had seen the master of mathematics immobilize another student with a glare; Quin had not yet merited that specific teacher's attention, but he did not doubt that the opportunity would soon arise. The aberrant spurt of interest that the mathematics lecture had inspired would surely fade into boredom quickly.

A tickling reminder of Master Howald's particular authority began to gnaw at Quin's feet. "The practice of testing all children of the Seriin nobility for Power," recited Quin in a spurt of inspiration, "was extended to include all members of the Seriin Alliance by the third Infortiare, Lord Jaraeth."

Howald murmured gruffly, "Very good," and released Quin from the grip of Power. "Do not force me to educate you incessantly by such extreme methods, Quinzaine."

"Yes, Master Howald," answered Quin dutifully, but his mind had already begun to wander to the broken spindle shells that he had collected on the beach yesterday. *The creatures inside the shells were probably eaten by a great orange sea monster,* he mused, and he began to plan a trap for the imaginary beast. Quin wrapped himself cozily in a self-imposed spell of Power.

"Quinzaine," growled Master Howald with beleaguered patience, "are you awake?"

Quin observed with some surprise that the other students had disappeared from the spacious room of gray slate and rose marble. "Is class finished?" demanded Quin, brightening appreciably at the thought.

"Yes, Quinzaine." Howald, a heavyset man, forestalled Quin's exit with a gentle prod of his large hand and a less gentle grip of Power. "If you cannot concentrate on the simplest lessons, you will never master wizardry, young man. We shall have no choice but to bind your Power."

"Bind my Power?" asked Quin, entirely bewildered by Master Howald's solemnity and still half-immersed in a dream of orange sea-dragons.

The wizard barely suppressed a sigh at the boy's ignorance. "Binding would remove your capacity for using Power."

Quin considered this statement, his interest in sea-dragons briefly displaced by a more imminent possibility. "If you bound my Power, would I be allowed to return to Hamley?"

"You would be 'allowed' to go anywhere you pleased, except here. You would no longer be Ixaxin."

Since Quin had never correlated his own unusual, defensive skills with the Ixaxins' much-referenced Power, he clapped his ink-smeared hands and crowed with loud delight. "Could you bind it now?"

"Certainly not!" replied Howald, quite disconcerted by this curly-haired Hamley imp, who had caused such disproportionate turmoil in a very few days as an Ixaxin. "When?"

The wizard tugged at his ruddy beard, hiding a reaction blended of suspicion, sharp disdain, and sour disbelief. "Binding is irrevocable, Quinzaine. You are too young to request it, and we have no cause to inflict it."

The boy tucked his hands in pockets that already bulged with gathered flotsam. Quin smiled, and Howald blinked at the unexpected tingling of Quin's unconsciously persuasive Power. "How can I give you cause?" asked Quin eagerly.

Howald restrained a flicker of dismay that the foolish boy's simple Power could cause even a momentary influence on a trained wizard, but Howald attributed the brief lapse to his own frustration and fatigue. "Binding is inflicted only if the subject's Power poses a serious threat to mortal kind. You cannot sustain a single thought for more than a minute." Howald used a tone more harsh than he generally applied toward the novices, but Quin had frayed the scholar's patience frequently in the past few days.

Quin slumped melodramatically. He kicked at the ornate iron leg of his desk and beat the battered wooden surface with his small, scratched, and callused fist. "How old must I be to request binding?"

"Sixteen," answered Howald, and his expression became almost sympathetic at Quin's appalled grimace. "You will find your time here much less onerous if you stop fighting us and exert yourself to learn." Howald frowned again, realizing that the boy's Power had made a second subtle plea.

"Sixteen," muttered Quin. "I shall be too old to have any fun at all." He trudged dejectedly from the room.

Quin resumed his usual exuberant stride before he reached the long, many-windowed corridor that connected the history building to the main dining hall. The corridor was empty, for the dining hall would not open for another hour. Quin manufactured a hope that some chance whim of the cook might cause an early luncheon. He found the dining hall doors still locked, and he sighed and retraced his steps as far as the nearest exit.

Quin emerged from the building, inhaled the cool, salty air, and smiled at the clear sky. The boy whose living cell faced Quin's hurried along the walkway toward the music rooms, and Quin hailed him: "Would you like to visit the kitchens with me?" The boy, whose name Quin had been unable to ascertain, frowned and did not stop. "Am I the only person who ever feels hungry around here?" muttered Quin.

He scuffed his much-hated, new leather shoes against the granite railing, wondering how Ixaxins could spend so much time thinking solemn thoughts. Hamley children had always been willing to join Quin's escapades; Quin's Power had given them no choice.

Quin ambled down the stairs, feeling somewhat confused by the universal coolness of his classmates, whom Quin had tried repeatedly to befriend. Like the Ixaxin scholars, the students seemed generally impervious to the suggestions of laughter or amusement that had always served so well in Hamley.

Quin had tried more orthodox approaches; he could not understand why the students seemed so distressed by his overtures. Quin had thought the dead jellyfish looked quite amusing on Teblet's pillow, since the patterned fabric of the pillow resembled the creature magnificently, but Teblet had shouted very angrily that Quin would suffer dearly for any further invasions of Teblet's room. Vala had expressed similar displeasure when Quin threw an orange at her, and Quin's proctor had requested reassignment after Quin embellished Master Cayle's subtly designed rock garden with a few extra buckets of sand. Tunnels, caves, and treasure-filled niches riddled the island of Ixaxis and made it glorious, but the people confused Quin thoroughly.

Quin gazed across the central quadrangle of the school pensively, scanning the gray, shifting mass of students, all moving purposefully, whether alone or engrossed in tense conversations. One tall figure limped, leaning on a brass-tipped cane. "Aimel!" shouted Quin, and he began to run across the quadrangle, his gray robe flying. Quin had scarcely missed Aimel in Hamley, though Aimel had taught Quin how to ride and swim and catch snakes, but the sight of a Hamley cousin in this sea of solemnity and arrogance slaked Quin's terrible thirst for home.

"You dropped your book, Quin," said Aimel, raising his amber eyes from his own text, though he continued his slow walk across the lawn.

"Did I?" Quin whirled, raced back to the fallen book, snatched it from the thick, fine grass and returned to Aimel's side. "I am glad to see you! How is the foot?"

The young Lord Aimel tightened his grip on his polished rosewood cane, and he gazed across Quin's head at the slate-topped roof of the history building. "The same," answered Aimel tensely. "Severed toes do not regenerate, even for a wizard."

"No? Sorry. How long have you been here?"

"Three years. I left Hamley just after the accident. Had you forgotten?" Aimel's narrow smile had a cynical twist, as he stared down at the rampant, tawny curls of his woolly-headed young cousin.

"I remember," answered Quin uncomfortably, for he did recall Aimel's spurting blood and the screams of many voices when Hiaremes stumbled in mock battle and slashed Aimel's foot with a broadsword. Accidents occurred frequently among the unsupervised Hamley youths, but Quin did not like to dwell on memories of the less pleasant events. "Which hall is yours, Aimel? I live in the single-level dormitory nearest to the bay. My cell has the tiniest window, but I can see part of the cypress along the cliff's edge. Are you hungry? I am ravenous. Do you suppose the cook would give us some buttery dollop of pastry for an early lunch?"

"The purpose of restricting meals to regulated hours," replied Aimel coldly, "is the practice of discipline, a subject vital for any wizard."

This horrible regimen of endless work and study has ruined even Aimel, thought Quin with horror, and Quin decided to free himself of the gloomy influence. "Of course, Aimel. Stupid of me to feel hungry now. But you know me: I never have had any sense. It was a pleasure to see you, cousin."

"No doubt," answered Aimel dryly, as he watched Quin's anxious retreat.

Quin felt the gaze of his cousin, and a dim, unwanted perception recognized Aimel's half-trained Power and knew the pain that warped it. "What use is Power," whispered Quin, "if it allows such bitterness?" He tore his thoughts from the grim contemplation with the force of panic.

Quin circled the dining hall to reach the kitchens, a trio of outbuildings linked by open, covered walkways to the dining hall and the largest of the dormitories. The barren stems of dormant roses climbed across the walkway railings, and the thorns snagged Quin's robe repeatedly, as he pursued the scent of fresh bread. He tugged the robe over his head and rejoiced in the freedom of baggy breeches and loosely-fitted shirt.

He dropped both robe and workbooks among the garden shrubs. He entered the baking kitchen boldly, grinned at a startled cook, snatched a loaf from the nearest window rack, and raced away from the shouting cook and scullions. He presumed that harsh Ixaxin Power would punish him, but the scholars' efforts were at worst annoying, at best amusing. Quin's Power was not alarmed.

* * *

"One other matter, Headmistress: Master Howald and Mistress Nevella would like to see you regarding the student who arrived last month from Hamley."

Amila raised her steady gaze from the carefully squared stack of correspondence that she had allocated to this hour of the morning. "It is unseasonable, is it not, for the testing and the gathering?" *The inability of orderly minds to maintain orderly regimens,* she thought sardonically, *amazes me continually. How can trained wizards perform mundane chores so haphazardly?*

Alvedre, a young wizardess who had only recently been elevated to headmistress' assistant, strove self-consciously to satisfy the headmistress' passion for thorough information. "The boy's Power was confirmed over a year ago, and Lord Bendl promised to send him to us within the month—immediately following his tenth birthday. Unfortunately, it seems that his family forgot the matter until the tenth birthday of this boy's cousin, who protested quite correctly that it was not he who had been pledged to us."

The expression on Amila's pale, smooth face became pained. "The Hamley boy is a lord, I presume. Only the noble House of Hamley could suffer such confusion over the identity of its own."

"He is Lord Quinzaine dur Hamley, fifteenth child of the late Lord Jiar dur Hamley and Lady Aliria dur Viste."

"Fifteenth," murmured Amila with an appalled shudder. "That is excessive even by the standards of Hamley." She frowned and straightened an unruly letter, which refused to conform to the neat contours of her correspondence. "Why has this boy not been brought before me?"

"He leapt off the ferry on arrival and fell into the bay."

"He was not injured?" demanded Amila with concern.

"No!" replied Alvedre hastily. "His clothing was soaked, and his hair was full of sand." Alvedre finished ruefully, "He has involved himself in a succession of troublesome incidents since that time. He seems likely to present a discipline problem."

"We have had such a quiet group these last few years," sighed Amila.

"Shall I admit the plaintiffs?" asked Alvedre wryly.

"I suppose there is no help for it."

Alvedre opened the office door, and Howald strode immediately to Amila's desk. Nevella, a black-haired, black-eyed wizardess from Caruil, followed more sedately, but it was she who spoke first: "In little more than a month, Lord Quinzaine dur Hamley has managed to disobey more rules, cause more damage, and infuriate more scholars, students, and retainers than any child I have ever met. He is worse than a kitten, finding new games in every punishment. He seems almost to prefer punishment over praise. He is intolerable." Nevella nodded briskly, as if her angry decree had solved a serious dilemma.

"Indeed," murmured Amila calmly, and her cold stare conveyed her disapproval of Nevella's emotional style. Nevella had been one of the first Caruillans to accept Ixaxin training, but she retained much of the fierce spirit of her people, and Amila did not like her. "Do you also find the control of a single, errant novice excessively difficult, Master Howald?"

"You know that I have always maintained excellent disciplinary standards in my classes," replied Howald stiffly.

"Then explain the particular problem you wish me to address in regard to Lord Quinzaine."

"He is not an acceptable student of wizardry," snapped Nevella. "Howald and I believe that Quinzaine's Power should be bound."

"On the basis of childish mischief? We cannot bind Power for such a frivolous cause."

Howald said flatly, "He wants binding, Amila."

Amila's eyes narrowed, but she retorted quietly, "He is too young to make that decision for himself. Do you have evidence that his Power may become uncontrollable?" Amila paused, awaiting a response, but neither Howald nor Nevella replied. "Very well," said Amila, "the two of you must learn to deal with this undisciplined child. I trust that Ixaxis can manage him at least as well as Hamley retainers."

Howald grumbled, and Nevella threw her hands into the air. Nevella muttered ingraciously, "Short of killing him, we can only hope he matures into some common sense before he cripples himself with one of his scatter-brained pranks." Howald nodded and glared at Amila resentfully.

"Fortunately," injected Alvedre, attempting to restore a tenuous peace, "Quin also lacks the sense or discipline to master his Power fully. He uses it chiefly to charm people into forgetting his transgressions: a very delicate usage, actually, but largely an unconscious act of self-preservation in Quin's case." Alvedre reached for the teapot, discovered it cold, and stared at it to warm its contents.

"He sets a deplorable example for the other novices," growled Howald.

"He does not impress them," said Alvedre defensively. She elaborated ruefully, "He lacks motivation to achieve anything intelligent, and his classmates dismiss him as an idle fool."

Amila surveyed her fellow Ixaxins with a grimace. "I am not sure which of you condemns this boy more effectively: his accusers or his defender." Amila focused her keen eyes on her assistant. "Why do you support this 'fool'?"

"He is virtually impossible to hate," replied Alvedre, a faint flush growing on her freckled face. She poured a cup of tea and handed it to the headmistress. "He presents an extreme example of the child whose Power has insulated him from a normal maturing process. He truly has no idea that he is hurting or offending anyone. All of his antics are unabashedly innocent and ridiculous."

"Like a kitten," added Amila dryly, "with very sharp claws."

Alvedre sighed, "Yes."

"What shall we do with him, Amila?" demanded Howald.

"Educate him and endure him, until he masters his Power or accepts its binding lawfully."

"He cannot authorize binding for another five years."

"Five years will pass quickly."

"Not with Quinzaine among us."

CHAPTER 2

Network Year 2292

"Your activity levels are too high, Kitri," announced Network's impersonal voice. "Please sit and perform your breathing routine until proper relaxation is achieved."

With a deep sigh of frustration, Kitri turned from the impenetrable apartment door and flung herself to the floor among the pile of square, satiny orange pillows. She began to breathe deeply, though a grimace of impatience accompanied each exhalation. Arguments with Network achieved nothing, but her nervous energy did not yield easily to discipline.

"Be gentle with her, Network," teased Michael, emerging from his bedroom with his wet hair, dark from the moisture, combed flat against his head. "She is in love."

Kitri snatched one of the cushions from the floor and threw it at her brother. "You have a nerve talking about me, Michael Merel. You can't even keep track of all your girlfriends."

"My independence is safer that way," answered Michael airily. He sank cross-legged onto the floor next to his sister. He leaned toward her and whispered with conspiratorial relish, "Who is he?"

"I thought you had no interest in my 'fleeting, childish infatuations.' "

"I recognize the signs of a major flirtation in the planning. I pity the poor victim who tries to resist one of my sister's carefully conceived assaults!"

"That shows what you know about love," retorted Kitri. Michael pulled a long strand of his sister's blonde hair, and she yelped and punched his arm. "For your information, I have already completed the preliminary flirtation and proceeded quite comfortably into a very promising relationship."

"When did I blink and miss the preface? Yesterday?"

"Months ago, but you were too busy to notice. You are the frightfully overworked Harberg University student, too constantly enamored of your architectural innovations to leave the side of your research leader day or night."

"I am very overworked," declared Michael with mock self-pity, "and now that I have finally managed to arrange some time for my neglected baby sister, I find that she is more interested in visiting some dusty political history museum with a young man she refuses to identify."

"Lowell is a very good friend. He lives just upstairs, as you would know if you were ever here."

"You're dating Lowell Gant?" demanded Michael abruptly, his teasing mood dissipated. "He's older than I am!"

"I am not a child, big brother." Kitri sprawled across the floor cushions in a deliberate parody of a vampish pose, but she managed to look sultry.

Michael stared at her, as if stunned into a very reluctant reassessment. "You are not even close to Lowell Gant's league," he argued in obvious disbelief. "Gant is the son of some senior Network diplomat—one of those obscure, incredibly wealthy individuals whose titles are never even spoken by common mortals like us. Lowell Gant is a very sophisticated customer, my girl, and you are in way over your pretty head if you think he has actually taken an interest in you."

"He is taking me to the museum for a very special reception arranged by his father," answered Kitri dreamily. "A delegation of Calongi will be visiting, and Lowell has promised to present me to them." She pummeled her brother's arm lightly. "Lowell is taking me and no one else!"

Michael shook his head, knowing Kitri's stubbornness. He had trouble visualizing Lowell Gant as Kitri's suitor, but Kitri had said it, and Kitri could be trusted. She was headstrong and independent, but she had never lied to her brother, not even to protect herself from childhood punishments (many of which, Michael admitted reluctantly, had been issued with better intentions than wisdom).

She could be sincerely mistaken, thought Michael hopefully, but he respected his sister's perceptions too much to believe his own vague wish. He also remembered how inexplicably warm Gant's greetings had become of late.

"Are you sure you understood his invitation correctly?" asked Michael, trying not to sound condescending. He remembered the insecurities of being seventeen; he was only four years older than that age now, though he chose to consider himself much wiser than his years. Having assumed a shared burden with Network in raising his sister, he sometimes forgot how little age difference actually existed between them.

"If your personal heartthrob, Ailene Villegas, ever noticed that you exist, you would not be in any doubt of the fact," replied Kitri pertly, and her brother blushed. She reached across the floor and hugged him. "Don't worry about me so much, Michael. I can take care of myself."

Michael sighed, unable to resist her, but he warned her, "I'll expect you home before dark."

"Fussbudget. Lowell invented the word 'gentleman.' "

"Do you suppose you could fit your brother into your social schedule some day soon?"

"I may think about it," answered Kitri with a wide smile and the glint of laughter in her bright, blue eyes.

* * *

Kitri decided that watching Lowell—his broad, square shoulders, his warm brown eyes, the crisp lines of chestnut hair, brows, and mustache—was all she needed for absolute, everlasting contentment in life. Privately, she shared her brother's astonishment that Lowell Gant would even notice her. She thought she had never been so happy in all the years she could remember.

Lowell offered her his arm to enter the reception hall,

a grand, silver-gilt room of high arches and ornamental
buttresses. Straight and strong and tall in his finely tai-
lored, dove-gray suit, Lowell looked quite as expensively
elegant as anyone Kitri had ever imagined. She hesitated,
overwhelmed for the moment by the prospect of facing
Lowell's family and their friends.

Lowell smiled at her, recognizing her nervousness. He
whispered to her in encouragement. "You will enchant
everyone in that room."

"I never met an ambassador before."

"The ambassador is no harder to please than the
ambassador's son," answered Lowell, "and you have
conquered him completely."

Kitri flushed with pleasure at the praise. "You should
have warned me that your father was so important."

"I didn't want to intimidate you." Lowell urged her
forward.

Swallowing her fear, Kitri raised her head and tried to
move with smooth dignity. She felt clumsy and horribly
immature, but the alarmingly important men and women
nodded graciously at her. She gained enough confidence
to smile in response with nearly a normal expression.

The ambassador looked no older than his son, and the
two men were so alike as to disorient Kitri momentarily.
Ambassador Gant's face had a closed, impersonal tension that revived all of Kitri's concerns. He studied her
as if she were a curious work of art, requiring lengthy
contemplation to appreciate. He did not allow his son
to complete the introductions. "I need to speak to you,
Lowell," said the ambassador with odd, quiet urgency.
"Excuse us, citizeness."

Overtly puzzled and embarrassed by his father's brusque
command, Lowell murmured to Kitri, "I shall be back
in a moment."

Kitri nodded at him, as if she understood perfectly and
did not mind at all. She watched her escort and his father
disappear behind an enameled door at the far end of an
arched hallway, and she nearly wished that she had not
agreed to come. She smiled awkwardly at the couples
who passed her on their way to the main body of the
museum.

"Citizeness Merel?" asked a portly man with sparse

hair and a blandly congenial expression. "Come with me, please."

He offered no explanation, but Kitri followed him into a broad, arched corridor opposite that which Lowell had entered. Flaking bits of gilt paint glittered from the severe brilliance of light globes near the end of their usefulness. Obviously, Lowell had told this man to find her, but she wondered why they did not follow the same route to the museum's inner catacombs.

"Did Lowell send you for me?" asked Kitri shyly.

"Of course, citizeness. I am Rolf, the ambassador's assistant."

Only marginally reassured, Kitri nodded a polite acknowledgment. Rolf stopped at a door like all the others: blank of pattern and molded into a solid form that imitated a hinged design from pre-Network history. "Please wait in here, citizeness," announced Rolf courteously. He pressed a recessed lock, and the door swung open.

The room was small, lit by a dim gray globe, and cluttered with red velvet panels and cream brocade, padded chairs. Katerin turned, convinced that she had been guided incorrectly, but Rolf was gone, and the door had reclosed in perfect silence behind him. She walked to the door, but it did not open.

"Network, where is Lowell?" asked Kitri, but she received no answer. "Network?" She ran her fingers over the door's surface, seeking a hidden latch, but she found nothing.

The voice that spoke lacked even the artificial warmth of most Network synthetics: "I warned you of the dangers, Kitri. You left me no choice."

All of her fear became cold and real and terrible. "Who are you?" she whispered, dreading the memory that tried to recall a time *before*. Life had begun at age nine in a small Network apartment where she lived alone with her brother and Network's omnipresent voice. Only Michael and Network cared for her, taught her, housed and fed her. Nothing existed prior to that time. Nothing could be allowed to exist.

"You know me, Kitri. My name is Marrach."

"No," she whispered, again a child of nine with memories of a man and woman whose faces and significance she could not quite remember.

"The gentler forms of conditioning have obviously failed to impress you sufficiently, but I know many other, surer techniques. They may damage you, of course, but you have made the risk necessary. I warned you to avoid anyone with Consortium ties, and you cultivate the son of the Consortium ambassador!"

"I did not know," she protested, but she could feel torment's memory resurging at Marrach's voice. She saw the faces of an unknown man and woman, a lifeless and terrible vision. She covered her eyes helplessly and sank, shuddering, into a huddle on the floor. The pale, variegated silks of her skirt spread gracefully around her.

"You chose to forget—unconsciously, I admit. The results are, nonetheless, unacceptable."

"Michael," pleaded Kitri, though she knew her brother could neither hear nor help her. "They are hurting me again, Michael. *He* is hurting me again."

"You have not begun to learn about *hurt* yet, Kitri. Be assured: I shall teach you."

* * *

Caragen's mouth worked in and out, chewing the thoughts that troubled him. "You are certain that Gant did not learn her identity?"

Marrach answered evenly, "The ambassador values your good will far too much to make such a tactical error voluntarily. He knows he owes his status to you, and he is suitably grateful." A hint of cynicism twisted Marrach's thin lips almost imperceptibly. "The son has been removed from Harberg and should soon regret his brief, intemperate infatuation with the Terry girl. He will be appropriately aided in forgetfulness."

"Will the problem recur?" demanded Caragen.

"Not with Gant. With another? I shall reduce the probabilities by reconditioning Kitri Terry into such emotional bondage that she may have difficulty even relating to her brother. I would prefer a more direct approach."

"I do not want her dead or disfigured."

"Dr. Terry is unlikely to return after all these years. Even accepting the negligible probability that he is still alive, you have the son, whose conditioning has evidently held to reasonable expectations."

Caragen grumbled, "Yes. The daughter appears to have inherited the father's resistance. Unfortunate."

"For her, at least."

"Do you pity her, Marrach?" asked Caragen with cold amusement.

"I regret waste."

Caragen frowned slightly, considering the many lives that Marrach had "wasted" without complaint. There could be no question of emotion in Marrach's present reluctance, but even the briefest of hesitation stirred Caragen's curiosity; Marrach had showed a similar, uncharacteristic hesitation regarding Jonathan Terry. Did that remarkable brain, so exquisitely integrated with Network, perceive an element that Caragen had not appreciated? Marrach would surely speak of a recognized problem, but Marrach's relentless instincts for survival sometimes reacted in advance of any consciously rational foundation.

Caragen dismissed his spurt of worry as absurd. His zealous search for clear emotion in Marrach constituted nothing more than entertainment. It did not merit excessive, pointless speculation. "Her mind will remain intact," said Caragen crisply. "The emotional injuries may even enhance her productivity in areas of use to Network. I have often found that damaged tools possess exceptional strengths of compensation."

"As in the case of 'casualties' purchased from Gandry?" asked Marrach, knowing Caragen's meaning very well.

"You have proven to be a worthy investment."

Marrach laughed curtly, an exercise of custom rather than an indication of mirth. "Shall I recondition Michael Terry along with his sister?"

"Only if he shows signs of similar rebellion. Let Rolf observe him for a time."

"I would allow Rolf to continue for the moment," countered Marrach, watching Caragen closely for any sign of displeasure, "but I would not rely on him too heavily. He does not blend well in the Harberg environment."

"You have another agent in mind?"

"A recent recruit: Calial. Her records are exemplary,

and she has the necessary intelligence to become a legitimate Harberg student. She could be valuable as a long-term observer."

"As you wish."

CHAPTER 3

Seriin Year 9048

Quin missed Hamley. He missed the towers and ancient battlements where he had played at sieges with his cousins. He missed the fields where they had run and thrown mock spears. He missed riding Longtail, the finest horse (in Quin's opinion) in the Hamley stables. He missed Cara's teasing and Piedre's jokes and Uncle Havod's stories of ancient times and Aunt Zina's royal secrets. He missed the shepherd's mongrel dog, who often seemed smarter than some of Quin's relatives, and he missed the lavish family suppers after every Even's Mass.

Quin had decided conclusively that he did not like Ixaxis. Ixaxis expected him to work, a novel and inconceivable notion to Quin. He had never in his young life experienced boredom, until Ixaxis confiscated his Hamley toys due to the infraction of some silly rule (something about inattentiveness in class) and restricted his free time to a few pathetic hours a week.

Quin stared in disgust at the book of poetry that he had been ordered to read before the morrow's morning class, and he waited impatiently for the fourth-hour bell, which would signal the afternoon break. *How can any reasonable person expect me to sit indoors reading poetry (of all things) when the rain last night has left such lovely puddles along the walkways, and the waves are crashing so loudly that you can hear them from the window of this room?*

If Mistress Nevella, whose temper was notorious, had

not vowed to confine Quin permanently for his next neglected assignment, Quin would not have waited for the fourth hour. As soon as he heard the chimes begin, he raced from his room and out of the building. He covered half the distance to the cliff path before the rest of Ixaxis stirred from study.

Quin stomped through the mud until his shoes were appropriately filthy, and he began to whistle in renewed contentment with the universe. He devoted some time to collecting worms into a single squirming hill; then he abandoned them and wended his erratic way toward the western cliffs. The waves shook the ground as he neared the cliff edge, but Quin strode eagerly to the brink, heedless of the oft-discussed hazards of crumbling precipices. When part of the ground fell away from his weight, he only shifted nimbly and watched in fascination as the loosened soil disappeared into the foamy eddies far below him.

"Senseless boy!" snapped a woman who had crept unheard nearly to his back. "You think a wizard is immune to broken bones? That cliff will kill wizards or mortals indiscriminately; it will do and has done." As she spoke, the old woman hobbled quite as near to the cliff's edge as Quin, and she stood shaking her knobby finger at the rim of it.

She was a battered old woman, mottled and wrinkled with age. The thin knot atop her head failed to contain the white hair which sprouted wildly around her shriveled face. She wore no shoes, a state that Quin envied, having been punished severely (three times) for roaming unshod outdoors in mid-winter. Her clothing, though crumpled, was intricately embroidered and patched with bright scraps of velvet, calico, gingham, and wool. The dress did not hang well, pieced as it was from disparate weights and weaves, but its motley mix of emerald, garnet, and topaz gained Quin's approval with its blunt and rather tasteless garishness.

"Staring is impolite, boy. I am called Luki. You are very dirty."

"Are you an Ixaxin?"

"Stupid boy, I live here. What do you suppose I am, if not Ixaxin?"

"I never knew anyone lived here except the scholars

and the students and a few servants, and they all wear robes and look alike and act alike and are very dull."

"Are you a student?"

"Of course."

"And are you like all the other students?"

"I am nothing like the other students. All they want to do is work and impress people with their intelligence."

"Well, then," said Luki with conviction. "You know very little about it. I have something to show you, boy. Come with me."

"Where?"

"To my home, foolish boy. I do not carry all my belongings with me like a peddler or a beggar woman." She marched determinedly into the scruffy shrubs and grasses, and Quin followed her curiously. He tugged his sodden gray robe free from the briars.

The robe really is a nuisance, thought Quin, *always catching on something*. He would have discarded the robe in favor of the old green jerkin and trousers he wore beneath it, except Mistress Lenora had threatened him with dire consequences for *that* infraction of rules; he had already lost two of the robes, left somewhere on the narrow beaches and claimed by the tides.

The ground grew paradoxically rougher as the shrubs opened to a true path, and Luki's toes grappled with hard and jagged gravel. Quin marveled that she managed to walk without crying aloud; she seemed oblivious to the bruises and cuts that the stones inflicted on her gnarled feet. "Where is your home?" demanded Quin, gasping for breath in air that seemed to have become as thin as the pale, distorted light.

"You have no patience," grumbled Luki.

"I only asked . . ."

"I heard you the first time! Are you wanting so badly to return to your lessons?"

Quin actually gave the question several seconds of serious consideration. He had begun to grow tired, a very rare state for the boundlessly energetic boy, and the climb seemed endless. *How far have we come anyway? I would not have believed that Ixaxis could contain so tall a mountain. In fact,* he mused with a growing spark of interest, *this chalky island has no mountains. Atop the sheer cliffs, Ixaxis spreads as nearly flat as the Hamley fields.* His idle curiosity began to evolve into eagerness.

Luki led him through a hedge so thick that Quin could barely force his way through it, though Luki had managed the passage with apparent ease. Beyond the hedge with its masses of tiny, emerald leaves, the path opened into a wide yard of gravel rimmed by brightly colored, flowering shrubs and encircled by the towering hedge. A cottage occupied the center of the yard: a cottage carved of red clay and dotted with round white rocks the size of Quin's fist. Two hexagonal windows, one no higher than Quin's knees, framed a door that looked to have been covered with tooled leather. More of the exceptionally white rocks lay beside the door in an apparently random design. Large, round snails with green and yellow shells nestled by the hundreds among the shrubs and stones.

Quin thought he saw a gray cat slink across the yard, though the animal seemed long for a cat, and its head seemed overly large. Luki shouted something, an incomprehensible rattling of clicks and voiceless whistles, and the cat-thing leapt, startled, straight into the air, as if burned by the cold, rocky ground. It scurried into shadow beneath a broken boulder, and it stared with a fixed, unsettling gaze of luminous lavender eyes. *They do not look like a cat's eyes*, observed Quin, and he began to fashion a story of evil spells that had taken the form of a cat.

"Boy, quit gawking," snapped Luki.

In the instant that Quin glanced at her, the cat-thing disappeared. "It left," said Quin with disappointment.

"Pesky neighbor steals my apples," mumbled Luki. "Well, boy," she added impatiently. "Come inside. Come inside."

Obediently, Quin followed her. Short as he was, Luki's door was shorter still, forcing him to duck beneath the lintel. He raised his head and bumped it on an iron kettle that dangled from the dark-beamed ceiling. Pots and iron tools, strings of herbs and peppers, woven pouches with lumpy contents that seemed to shift suspiciously: the room was asea with odd objects hanging from the beams and twisted rushes of the roof's underside. In contrast, the ruddy dirt floor was stark and bare but for a single, braided rug, giving the room an inverted appearance that made Quin wonder how it might look if he stood on his head. He tilted his head far to the left as a compromise, trying to find the proper angle for the room's viewing, but he bumped his shoulder from inattentiveness, and he abandoned the attempt to sort the upside-down perspective.

Luki sat upon a hearth of stones as smooth and round as the snails outside her door. "Sit, boy!" she commanded sharply. "Will you keep me waiting all the day?"

Quin sat. The stones felt warm, which surprised him, for the grate was bare of anything but ash. He peered into the hearth, because he thought some glimmering of jewel-bright red had winked at him from its recess. The hearth's interior seemed oddly dark, blacker than any hearth he knew, and it seemed to extend beyond its exterior appearance. He could see no walls, and he thought he felt a warm draft strike his face.

Luki struck him hard across his back. "Pay attention, boy! You gather more wool than a sheep grows."

Quin withdrew from the hearth; he had nearly crawled inside and never noticed. Luki was frowning at him fiercely. Her sour old face crinkled like rumpled parchment. "Sorry," Quin murmured.

"You should be sorry! Give me your hand."

"Why?"

"Your hand, now." She reached for both his hands, while he still wavered in awkward puzzlement. Her touch felt surprisingly gentle, despite the hornlike calluses of her skin. She stared at his palms and nodded thoughtfully. "Yes. So. It is as I thought."

She dropped his hands abruptly, rose and waddled to a cupboard. Quin craned for a glimpse of its contents when she opened it, but she glared at him and blocked his view with her hunched, cloaked back. She rummaged for several minutes, humming a discordant tune. "Ah!" she shouted gleefully, and she withdrew a canister of hammered tin. She brought it to the hearth, opened it, and offered Quin a biscuit from its depths.

"Take a cracker with you when you go, boy," she mumbled calmly. She smiled as she inserted a whole biscuit into her own apparently toothless mouth. She munched contentedly, while Quin stared at her, impressed that she could actually gum the biscuit into consumable pieces. "Quit gaping, boy!" she told him sternly, pulling another biscuit from the tin. "You have your cracker. Go!"

"Go? But I only just arrived. You said you had something to show me."

"Did I? Well, I wonder what it was?" She shook her head, and several more strands of her stringy hair escaped the bun. "Well, of course," she muttered, "the boy must look at the Widowshear."

Luki struggled to her feet and began to hobble around the room, tapping at the largest of the hanging pouches. Some of them began to sway, oscillating like distraught pendulums. Others remained as steady as the walls, though the leather thongs which held the pouches quivered. When Luki found the object she had sought, she shook it free of the suspending beam with a tap and a jerk that suggested an insecure binding and caused Quin to look cautiously toward the swaying sacks above him.

"What do you understand about evil, boy?" demanded Luki, shaking the bulging parcel at him.

She asked with a force that startled Quin into an unconsidered reply, or he would surely have concocted some adventurous fable. "Not much, I suppose. I have been fortunate."

"Yes!" hissed Luki with a glee that seemed driven by surprised approbation. "You have been sheltered, boy! Appreciation of your boons shows more wisdom than I expected of you. It is well, for you will not always remain so protected, and you will need wisdom."

"Are you a soothsayer?"

"Pfaugh. No soothsaying do I need to predict that you will require wisdom. You have Power, boy. Why else do you suppose that you are here?" She wagged her head at him. "Waste of a good mind: putting it in an undisciplined Hamley lordling." She peeled the wrappings from her closely held prize, and Quin slumped in disappointment at the corroded tangle that she thrust beneath his nose.

"What is it?" asked Quin.

"What do you see, boy?"

"A lump of tarnished old metal."

"No, no, boy! A fool sees only appearance. What do you see?"

Quin stared from the lump to Luki, and he asked doubtfully, "What should I see?"

"Hunh," grunted the old woman. "You never will be a match for *him*, but perhaps that is just as well."

"Match for who?"

"For whom, boy: Mind your grammar. He always minded his grammar most carefully: grammar and diction both. He minded everything carefully. Very cautious was that devil-child. *He* looked at Luki's treasure and saw more than 'tarnished old metal.' "

"What did he see?"

"He saw infinity, boy," snapped Luki. She added more quietly, "Or perhaps infinity saw him. He never told me the extent of it. I doubt he told me any more truth than he considered necessary; he never did trust me—nor anyone else, I suppose." Luki curled her fingers stiffly around the metal object and gazed at it thoughtfully. "He came five times to see and hold my treasure," she murmured. "Those strange, cold eyes of his fixed on it, and it glowed, boy. He held it through the long hours of the night without so much as a blink to show himself alive." She trailed into silence.

"Was he one of the scholars?" asked Quin, observing the metal thing with new respect.

Luki laughed, a raspy sound of mirth. "He was the Infortiare, boy: Lord Venkarel. He paid me the final visit less than two years before the war that took him. He was visiting Ardasia, *they* said. That was what he told the King, and even the scholars believed. Everyone believed, except those few who knew—like Luki. Devilish business he was plotting. He told me then that war would come. Rare talkative he was that day. Told me to guard my treasure well. Said it was a thing of old Power, as if Luki could not have guessed as much from his interest in it. He never tried to take it from me," mused Luki mistily, "and Luki never could have stopped him. I always remember that about him. A devil-child he was, and a devil-man he did become, but he always treated Luki honorably, from the first day he came—not much older than you, boy—to the last. Quit gaping, boy. It makes you look witless."

Quin snapped his mouth closed, then blinked, feeling suddenly as leaden as the time his brother dared him into staying awake for three days straight. "Did the Venkarel really come here?" asked Quin in awe.

"I said it, did I not?"

"Yes," nodded Quin. Once more, he studied the mass of metal, trying to find something remarkable about it, but it seemed no more exciting than a piece of a broken plow, rusting in some abandoned field. "What do you see when you look at it?" asked Quin curiously.

Luki sighed heavily. "A lump of tarnished old metal."

"You said only a fool . . ."

"I know what I said, boy. And it holds true! You have Power, boy: enough that I hoped you might see the truth and tell me the things that *he* would never say. But you are too lazy to use the gifts you possess, and you have never needed to use them to survive."

"You are a wizardess," ventured Quin uncertainly.

"I am the oldest wizardess, boy, and my Power is as dim and tired as my eyes. Would you like another cracker before you leave?"

"Yes, please."

"Well. The tin is there. Take one and go. You will never finish your lessons by dawdling here all afternoon, and you will never be able to come again if you are confined to your room."

"How did you know. . . ?"

"That you have been threatened with confinement? The reluctant students always find old Luki eventually. The diligent and ambitious ones never stray far enough from the school."

"Was the Venkarel a reluctant student?" asked Quin incredulously.

"Him? No. I never saw anyone absorb knowledge like that one, but he was different. He came to assure himself that the island held no unknown traps for him. He was a suspicious boy: haunted and wary and very, very dangerous. Now, you have me babbling again. Too rare have the visitors been in the last few years. Go, now. Shoo!" She swatted Quin lightly, until he scurried out the door and down the path.

"May I come again?" Quin shouted back at her.

"Only if you clean your shoes," answered Luki, pointing censoriously at his muddy feet. "Boys. No thought about the trouble they cause with their thoughtlessness. I shall be scrubbing my floor for a week."

"You have a dirt floor," argued Quin, but Luki had tottered into her house. Quin shrugged, grinned, and ran the rest of the way back to the school. He arrived too late for supper, but he pulled a bedraggled biscuit from his pocket and munched it in extreme good cheer. Perhaps not everyone on Ixaxis was boring, after all.

CHAPTER 4

Network Year 2292

"Open the door for me, please, Network," muttered Katerin Merel hollowly. She stumbled into the apartment, never raising her haunted eyes from the floor.

"Kitri!" Michael hurried to his sister's side, his face worn from many sleepless nights of worry. "Where were you? I have been frantic about you."

"Gone," she answered tightly. She blinked her eyes repeatedly, trying to focus. "I was gone."

Michael frowned in bewilderment at her answer. "Network could not tell me where to find you. I tried to locate Gant, but he has disappeared. I even asked Network to contact Gant's family, but no information was available."

"No," agreed Katerin vaguely. She took a stiff, pained step toward her bedroom.

Michael took her arm to steady her. "Are you hurt, Kitri? What happened to you?"

"Nothing," she replied, though her face was drawn and gray. Her long, fine hair hung loose and draped her like a cowl. The silken dress in which she had taken such pride hung limply, and her shoulders sagged beneath its flimsy weight. "I need to study. I missed my lesson. Network will punish me." She shook free of her brother's help with a surprising show of energy. She ran into her bedroom, and the door slid firmly shut.

"Kitri, unlock the door," demanded Michael. "Network, what's wrong with her?"

Network responded with soothing softness, "Nothing is wrong with Katerin. Your research leader requires you at the school, Michael. Please, leave for the school immediately."

"Network, my sister has been missing for nearly a month!" retorted Michael in angry frustration. He struck her bedroom's door with the flat of his hand.

"She made a childish mistake, Michael," replied Network quietly. "You can help her best by disregarding the entire event. It never occurred."

"What?" asked Michael vacantly, but he scowled as Network's advice penetrated. "How can I ignore. . . ."

"Michael," interrupted Network sternly, "you will not mention her misjudgment. To do so would be cruel and wrong. You will go to the school now. You will behave as if the past month had not occurred. You will not be allowed to hurt your sister."

"I would never hurt Kitri," protested Michael. He shook his head, trying to free it of cloudy images that confused and tormented him. Network did not lie. Network was always right. Network must be obeyed without question.

"No," he muttered, but he moved automatically to collect his research materials. He left the apartment and crossed the park blindly in the direction of his research leader's office. He did not see the plump, slightly rumpled man who watched him and smiled.

* * *

Caragen assessed the status of his many current projects and recent acquisitions, and the totals pleased him in a remote sense. He still enjoyed the exercise of power, but the products themselves had lost much of their meaning over the many years since he first claimed the title of Network Council Governor. He had met too many goals and gained too much wealth to feel particular satisfaction at any minor, individual achievement. He valued little, for he owned everything he could imagine desiring.

Games and toys, he thought in rare introspection: *That is all these worlds and wars and private schemings mean. The Calongi insist that "respect of creation" is paramount to civilized behavior, but how can a man respect the fools who are so easily led and used? How can a man respect*

the Calongi, who shield their arrogant dominion by deny-
ing a fact as demonstrable as topological transfer?

Caragen sighed and pushed himself away from his desk. He left his office and entered his private quarters—the farthest distance that he generally chose to move under his own power. He approached a clear, shielded art case and smiled faintly at the assortment of grotesque alien scuptures, each as priceless as it was unappealing to common human aesthetics.

"Network," he asked contentedly, "how many of my enemies have ever survived my displeasure?"

"The category of 'enemies' is nonspecific. Please clarify."

"I refer to active enemies, individuals who have attempted to damage me, my possessions, or my power." Caragen added scornfully, "I do not refer to passive antagonists, such as the Calongi, who offend merely by their existence."

"No being has ever survived an act of aggression against you, your possessions, or your power."

Caragen nodded, pleased with the recitation of a truth he had long ago resolved to maintain. "Some day, I must attend to the matter of those few lesser enemies who continue to exist," he murmured. "How many individuals have defied my authority successfully, Network?"

"The Calongi leaders of the Consortium: Number of associated beings is not known. The leaders of eleven independent planets and/or planetary systems: Number of associated beings is not known."

"None of the independents merits the trouble of conquest," observed Caragen with a trace of boredom.

"Various past and present members of the Network Council."

"None survives long," commented Caragen, smiling coldly.

"Dr. Jonathan Terry," continued Network imperturbably.

"He did not succeed," argued Caragen with a spurt of impatience.

Network proceeded with its recitation, "A product of the genetic research experiment on Network-3: Being's name is not known."

"All of the Immortals died with their planet," countered Caragen, "and that very disappointing research project faded into history." He sighed, "It was unfortunate that the GRC personnel became too mired in hysterical irrationality to complete their Network reports. The Immortals might have been useful to me, if I had received information about them prior to their ill-conceived rebellion."

Caragen paused, and Network said into the silence, "Council Chancellor Rabhadur Marrach."

Caragen's eyes narrowed. "Explain the inclusion of Marrach on the referenced list."

"You frequently tolerate his independent actions in contradiction of your specific orders."

"Bah. Your interpretive algorithm requires refinement. I allow Marrach to adapt intelligently to circumstances that I could not predict. That does not constitute defiance. Amend your analysis, and terminate this inaccurate recital."

Caragen seated himself on a rare bench of exquisitely carved nacre. He folded his arms and studied the masterful painting on the opposite wall: *Creation*, as conceived by an anonymous human at the time of first contact with the Consortium. The painting reflected the artist's sense of human insignificance among the many diverse races. The painting always inspired Caragen with determination to disprove its tenet.

"I own Marrach," he murmured, "as I own Network and all of connected space. I am greater than the Consortium, for I own worlds they cannot even perceive. I have greater power than any human who has ever lived, *including* Dr. Jonathan Terry, who unwittingly gave me so much of what I own."

He sighed, as the satisfaction of the moment faded into restlessness. "Network, should I have allowed Marrach to kill Kitri Terry?"

"The value of her probable contributions to Network knowledge outweighs any danger she presents."

"Of course," replied Caragen, impatient with himself for his unaccustomed self-doubts. "And my assignment of Marrach to reinforce her conditioning was an extravagant use of my most prized asset. Rolf could have completed the task for a fraction of the cost." Caragen glowered at the painting. "Why do I let the existence of those blasted children haunt me? I should never have waited for Jonathan Terry to enact his cataclysm. I should have exterminated Network-3 with all the Terry family on it."

CHAPTER 5

Seriin Year 9048

"Grasp it slowly, boy!" warned Luki irritably. "Must you rush at everything?"

"Sorry, Luki," answered Quin contritely, and he tried to bridle his impatience to take the Widowshear. He did not much care about the Widowshear itself, but Luki would neither talk to him nor allow him to prowl through her peculiar treasures until he made some attempt to use the object of her obsession. Quin felt eager only to end the ritual, which he had now enacted (futilely) six times in as many weeks.

"Concentrate, boy!" said Luki sharply, as Quin's glance began to wander from the object in his hands to the wavy, indented trail that some scurrying creature had left in Luki's floor.

"I am concentrating," protested Quin. To prove his point, he stared fixedly at the Widowshear and tried to make his expression grow blank. He knew that Luki wanted him to focus Power on the thing, but using such deliberate Power always made his head ache. It was too bad, really, that the intricate forms of Power required so much effort to control, because he could think of lots of lovely ways he might amuse himself if he could master some of the scholars' tricks.

Quin wondered if the Venkarel had really visited Luki as a student. She was old enough, Quin supposed, though he had very little realistic concept either of age (beyond his own eleven years) or of the time elapsed since the

Venkarel's student days. "Venkarel," muttered Quin, as he pondered possible stories of that mythic person's tenure on Ixaxis.

The Widowshear emitted a bright flash of blue, and Quin yelped. He would have dropped the thing, but it seemed to cling like ice to wet fingers, burning holes into his flesh. "Control it, boy!" urged Luki eagerly.

Control what? wondered Quin frantically. He had never quite believed that the Widowshear was anything but an odd old woman's bit of junk. He had certainly never expected it to take life in his hands. *Drop it*, he told his fingers firmly, but his hands refused to respond.

Something touched him. Something shockingly cold beat against the inside of his skull. It did not seek to escape; it only sought to fill whatever space it found. *Everyone has always said my head was empty,* thought Quin.

A gust of fire swept through him. The Widowshear tumbled from his numb grasp, and he watched it roll awkwardly to a stop. Luki was staring gape-jawed at him. *She never expected me to use it either,* Quin told himself smugly.

The less cocky part of him retorted: *And what makes you think that you used it this time? Maybe it used you.*

"Are you here, boy?" asked an oddly hesitant, humble Luki.

"Of course, Luki. Where else should I be?"

"You tell me, boy. Where did it take you? What did you see?"

"Nothing. Nowhere. May I have a biscuit, please?"

"Boy, you have more Power than wits!" cried Luki in exasperation. Quin observed with fascination that a pair of great tears seeped from her rheumy old eyes. "Have you any notion of what you have just done? Do you have any idea of what this act of Power signifies, this act which you forget upon completion, this act which matters less to you than your hunger for a *biscuit?*" She jabbed Quin and pinched his arm. "You are plump enough already, pampered little Hamley boy. You have never hungered, have you? Not like *him,* so thin that you could count the bones and see each cord of muscle stretch that scarred skin." She spat at Quin, and he recoiled from her in vaguely bewildered revulsion.

"Let go of me, Luki. You are hurting me."

"What do you know about hurting, little Hamley lord?
He understood hurt."

Luki dug her old fingers deep into Quin's arm. *She
has summoned strength from her Power,* thought Quin.
He grew only mildly alarmed, no more seriously concerned than by his teachers' punishments of him. Oblivious as his Power kept him to the troubles and turmoils
around him, Quin was naive regarding the deliberate
infliction of pain, but he pierced through Luki's singular
madness with a child's guileless acuity. "I am not the
Venkarel, Luki, and I cannot help you find him, because
he is dead."

"What did you see, boy!"

"Nothing!"

"You are deceiving me. You saw him. Did he tell you
to conceal him with your falseness?"

"No!"

"What did he say to you?"

"He said that he would protect me!" lied Quin, and
Luki dropped his arm with a shudder and a hasty shake.

"Go away, boy," she muttered.

"May I have a biscuit?"

"Crackers in the tin. Take and go. Shoo!" Luki began
to fuss among dangling utensils, but she evaded the Widowshear without looking to see it at her feet. The lump
of metal seemed shinier to Quin; he nearly retrieved it
from the floor, but Luki kicked at his hand, discouraging
him without actually striking him. "Did I tell you to
touch any treasures, boy? Behave, or I shall turn you
into a frog."

"No one can turn a person into a frog," argued Quin,
as he selected his biscuit and headed for the door. He
felt quite confident: *If Power could turn a boy into a
frog,* Quin reasoned, *one of the scholars would have
transformed me ages ago.*

* * *

Somehow, the sense of the Widowshear rattling inside
him did not bother Quin until well into the night. He
had a groggy sense of something pulling at him, and he
seemed to wake and see the pale, low ceiling of his room,
but the pulling had not left. The more he struggled to

rise from his cot, the more confined he felt. He could not free himself, and his throat snared his voice and muted him. He tried to reach the small, square table beside his bed, and he could not feel it.

A pain shot through his neck. He seemed to wake again, and the struggle began anew. Each time he tried to roll toward the table, the pain returned and drove him into another nightmare's grip. Layer after dreamy layer freed him falsely and trapped him in his own half-conscious slumber.

He knew that he slept and dreamed. He wanted to wake himself truly and escape the cruel cycle of helplessness that swam around the Widowshear's cold pressure. Finally, in desperation for the rest of peaceful sleep, Quin tugged at the memory of some half-attended Ixaxin lesson, drew on his undeveloped Power, and shivered into wakefulness in a gray, unfriendly dawn.

His blankets had fallen to the side of the bed. He retrieved them, bundling himself in their warmth, as he burrowed his head into the soft welcome of his duckdown pillow. Resilient and sleepy, Quin sank again into dreams, but these were the sensible story-sorts of dreams that he had always had a taste for summoning. He took his dream-self to Hamley manor, and he savored the pleasures of home all the more for remembering the crueler imaginings of the Widowshear.

CHAPTER 6

Network Year 2296

"Try the *palaan* spice rolls," suggested Katerin, prodding her brother and pointing at the display of varied baked goods. The noise of the street fair drowned Michael's grunted answer. He chose a simple honey-biscuit, and Katerin grimaced at his selection. "You have no sense of adventure," she accused him.

"None," he retorted with a smug grin. He nodded slightly, observing the small, slim young woman with dark, cropped hair who was waving energetically from across the crowd. "Do you want to see your most tirelessly devoted friend? Look behind you."

"Cindal again?" asked Katerin, trying to suppress a sigh. "I wish she could find someone else to help her learn elementary statistics. Why does she think I can succeed where even Network fails?"

"Because you are too smart for your own good. You had to tell her that Network's educational algorithms could stand 'significant improvements.' You had better acknowledge her. She is almost here."

Katerin fastened a pleasant expression on her face and turned to greet Cindal, who had forced her path through the crowds with customary determination. "You are coming tonight?" demanded Cindal in a breathless rush. "I really need your help, or I shall be expelled from Harberg for certain. Tell me you will come. Hello, Professor Merel." Michael opened his mouth to reply, but Cindal gave him no chance. "Have you seen Mavel? I

was supposed to meet her here, but I saw the most ador-
able, fuzzy dolls, and I forgot the time completely. Mavel
will be furious. You know how she hates to be kept
waiting."

"Where were you supposed to meet her?" asked Katerin, before Cindal could begin another giddy spree of
babble.

"By the harper's booth. She does love that archaic
music. I can't understand why. It positively puts me to
sleep. I like more excitement. Network says the stimula-
tion makes me talk too much, but I don't think I'm
nearly as bad as I used to be."

Michael tried to keep his expression neutral, but Katerin could see the laughter struggling to escape. She gestured urgently in the general direction of the musical
instrument displays, hoping to deflect Cindal's attention
from Michael. If Michael began to laugh, Katerin knew
she would not be able to stop herself from joining him,
and dear, oblivious Cindal simply would not understand
at all. "I think I see Mavel," said Katerin brightly,
though she could not distinguish anyone at that distance.

"Do you? I had better run. See you tonight." Cindal
hugged Katerin briefly and bobbed her head at Michael.
She pressed into the throng, undaunted by the size or
bulk of any competitor for passage.

"It must have been a cruel whim of Network's to assign
you to her social module," remarked Michael wryly.
"Just listening to her exhausts me."

"She's on her best behavior when you're with me. You
are a research leader, after all, and she is a lowly student." Katerin batted her long, dark lashes with specious
innocence.

"A lowly student like you, disrespectful child. Can we
escape from here before she returns with the equally
dreaded Mavel?"

"Mavel has serious plans in mind for you, brother
dear. Do you want to disappoint her?"

"Unquestionably," he answered with a look of exaggerated pain. "Don't you?"

Katerin's expression became suddenly blank and distant, and Michael berated himself for speaking thought-
lessly. She had seemed so cheerfully normal today; he
had forgotten to be careful. With a sense of familiar wea-

riness, he began to wend his way across the plaza center behind the tawdry, temporary booths.

Katerin let him lead the way in silence, until they left the noisy shop district and reached the quiet edge of the campus park. Her brilliant smile reappeared, and only Michael, who knew her so well, could have sensed the smile's fragile composition. He tried to recapture the afternoon's light mood, but he had tried too many times. The years of daily pretense weighed heavily.

Katerin nudged him, "Let's cross the river," and she danced toward the bridge.

She froze, hearing the shriek. Michael ran past her, for he had seen the woman trip and fall across the bridge's first, low step. He knelt beside the prone figure, a woman of very ordinary feature and figure, who lay with eyes closed and face pallid.

"How badly is she injured?" asked Katerin, joining her brother.

Michael removed his hand from the woman's head. Blood stained his fingers. "Go find someone to help her," he whispered urgently. He sat and cradled the woman's head in his lap.

"Network will notify a medic," argued Katerin very reasonably. "You're wearing your wrist link, aren't you?"

"No," hissed Michael, sounding quite harsh and strange. "Like you, I chose to be irresponsible today."

Stunned by the fierceness of his reply, Katerin stepped backward and nearly duplicated the fallen woman's accident. She could see the panic growing in her brother's eyes. She recognized the old sense of helplessness that threatened to overwhelm him. She removed her short, supple blue cape and laid it gently across the unconscious woman. She rubbed Michael's shoulder reassuringly. "I shall be right back, big brother."

Michael only nodded, staring at the woman's blood on his hand. Katerin ran to the nearest building. "Network," she called to the cloudy sky, for she did not know where the terminals were concealed, "a woman has fallen and struck her head. We need a medic beside the River Bridge."

"A medic is summoned," replied Network coolly.

Michael was still staring when Katerin returned to him.

His anguished expression gave Katerin a chill of foreboding. "Network has summoned a medic," she said, wondering why she felt so uncomfortably intrusive.

She sat on the low step of the bridge near Michael, and she tugged the cape across the woman's shoulder. Michael did not react. His gaze did not leave the woman's face: a plain face without much sign of happiness in it. Katerin said gently, "She looks like such a sad woman."

"She has never been loved by anyone," answered Michael promptly.

"Do you know her?" asked Katerin in surprise.

"I know her pain. Can't you see it in her, Kitri? She is like us, but she has no one. I have never seen a lonelier face."

"Michael, you are imagining too much," began Katerin, uneasy without knowing why. The medic, a wiry shadow against the street fair's artificial glare, appeared at the park's edge. Katerin waved to him, and he hurried to the fallen woman.

The medic inspected the woman's injury with deft fingers and sprayed healing compound into the wound. He sprayed a second layer as sealant. "Place these beneath her left elbow and knee," he ordered calmly, and he handed two floater devices to Katerin. He positioned the remaining floaters himself. He nodded at Michael. "You may release her now. The floaters will support her. I shall take her to the hospital, but don't worry: She will be fine."

Slowly, Michael removed his cradling arms from the woman's neck and upper back. "May I come with you?" asked Michael, his pale blue eyes very serious.

"Of course," replied the medic, and he bowed slightly to indicate the correctness of the offer. "You are her friend?"

"Yes," answered Michael. He added rather absently to Katerin, "Tell Parve that I'm sorry to miss his award dinner, will you, Kitri?" Michael began walking after the medic, who led the woman's hovering body with a gentle guidance.

Bemused by her brother's odd behavior, Katerin only nodded. She stood and watched the trio depart. She rubbed her arms, for her cape had accompanied the woman. The day's dampness felt chill against her bare skin.

She glimpsed a sheaf of yellow data sheets that the woman had evidently dropped. The force of the fall had thrown several loose sheets into crevices of the bridge's artistically rustic walkway, and two sheets rested on the river's cloud-gray surface. With the sheaf beneath her arm, Katerin climbed across the railing, balancing on the walkway's narrow outer edge with the ease retained from a sequence of gymnastic exercises that Network had once prescribed for her. She collected the stray sheets that the bridge had claimed, stacked them with their fellows, and proceeded to return along her narrow path.

She studied the drifting sheets consideringly. She removed her shoes and grimaced at the cold as she stepped into the shallow slick that enhanced the illusion of a river. The water, blended with light-distorting particles, barely reached her ankles, but her feet were scarcely visible as she waded.

When she had collected the remaining data sheets of names and numbers, she returned to the shore. Katerin glanced through the data: student statistics of the innocuous variety. The woman must belong to the university's administrative staff and had probably crossed the bridge a thousand times without mishap until today.

Katerin closed her eyes, trying not to cry. She had studied the applicable principles of mathematical psychology only that morning; yesterday she might not have understood what she witnessed. She had seen the classic signs in Michael's expression, when he touched the woman's bleeding wound. Aging conditioning had slipped, and a faulty trigger sequence had been struck in Michael.

Perhaps the sequence would incur a simple feeling of protection, or a more complex set of emotions might lead him into lapses of judgment, anxiety, or despair. Katerin recognized the gaps in her own memory well enough to identify the presence of intense conditioning. She knew that Michael's memories shared many of those gaps.

She had fought to keep him from severe depression four times in the last five years, and he had always responded best to her own need for his protection. That was how they both endured, by carrying each other in the weak times. She had defended him without under-

standing, but now she had the knowledge to recognize
the reasons.

"Now I know the dangers," she whispered, "of tampering with old conditioning. And I do not know enough
to help him."

Katerin walked slowly in returning to the apartment.
She tried to tally any past events that had seemed to
inspire irrational responses from Michael: He tended to
overreact to anything that made him feel helpless, but
Katerin could not refine her conclusion further. She
cringed from considering her own weakness: She panicked at any hint of closeness with anyone but her
brother.

As soon as she entered her own living room, Katerin
demanded, "Network, what can you tell me about the
breakdown of conditioning algorithms?"

"Irrational and/or self-destructive behavior may result.
The level of breakdown may vary from the creation of
isolated incidents to life-pervasive disruptions."

Hesitantly, Katerin asked, "Why were Michael and I
conditioned so severely, Network?"

"Your information is inaccurate, Katerin."

Error, thought Katerin, but she did not try to correct
Network's mistake. "Of course, Network." *The best
algorithms become reality; they must not be acknowledged
as algorithms if the effect is to be complete.*

"Network, please send a message to Cindal that I shall
not be able to help her this evening."

"Acknowledged, Katerin."

"Send a second message to Professor Parve Lilleholm:
Michael regrets that he will be unable to attend the
awards dinner tonight." Katerin took a deep breath, preparing herself. "Add to that message: Tell Professor Lilleholm that I am very interested in his research into
intelligence algorithms. Ask him if he would consider me
for an assistant's position in his department. Authorize
his access to all my study records."

"Yes, Katerin."

"Network, I would like to begin the next lesson in
mathematical psychology. Please initiate the program."

"Yes, Katerin."

* * *

Michael did not come home until mid-morning of the next day: "Loisa is conscious," he announced, clearly exhausted but deeply peaceful. Katerin did not ask him to identify "Loisa." "She will be fine," continued Michael serenely. "I have invited her to dinner, when she feels better."

"Why?" asked Katerin slowly. "You don't even know her."

Michael blinked his tired eyes in surprise. "I know her now, and I think she needs friends. She is quite shy."

"Is she?" murmured Katerin faintly. "Did you speak with her long?"

"No." Michael's firm jaw tightened, and the wrinkle between his eyebrows deepened. He seemed to exert himself painfully to issue further words, "I did not have a chance to speak to her alone at all, but I feel that I know her. I feel that Loisa needs me. That sounds quite daft, doesn't it?"

It sounds like a conditioned response, thought Katerin, *to the stimulus of a victim's need for protection. I should not worry, except the response was intended to protect me, not a stranger. The conditioning has become flawed.*

Katerin wished that she could voice her fears, but she did not dare. A taunting of emotions in herself prevented her from behaving as she wished. *My own conditioning,* she supposed, for a part of her mind viewed her growing bitterness with detachment: *This is not you, Katerin. This is something artificial implanted in you, twisting you to jealous anger against a woman you do not even know, a woman who has done nothing to make you despise her— or to make Michael worry over her.*

"You sound absurd," snapped Katerin, and they were the first words of spite she could ever remember wielding against her brother. She hated herself for yielding to an anger that was not even her own. *What perverted sort of conditioning did I receive as a child,* she wondered in a surge of panic, *that I can feel such jealous rage at my brother's act of kindness? But it is more than a charitable gesture on Michael's part: He is threatened also; I can see the conflict in his face. I must not let my brother be hurt.*

Her detached, rational self observed the escalation of fear without real focus, but her bodily chemistry reacted at the dictates of conditioning. The fear became real, for the atavistic physical reactions were real.

Unable to trust herself to speak kindly, Katerin grasped her brother's hand in a desperate gesture. Michael returned the pressure of flesh against flesh, and she could see her own terror mirrored in his eyes. *We both know,* she thought with the deep sadness of a tragic loss, *that we have lost control to something we cannot name, and neither of us has the emotional strength to fight it. In the past, when only one of us hurt, the other could carry the burden. Michael has always been my stability, but we are both affected now; our imperfect triggers have flared together. Will we end by hating each other?*

"I'm sorry, Michael," she whispered tearfully, and her brother nodded, his own eyes brimming. They both understood that she apologized for the hurts that were yet to come.

CHAPTER 7

Seriin Year 9053

"Concentrate on your candle's flame, Quin," murmured Mistress Alvedre, scanning the classroom and observing Quin's faraway gaze. "And please stop slouching."

"Yes, Mistress Alvedre." Quin straightened and tried to keep his focus on the candle. If he hoped to join the outing to Tulea tomorrow, he could not afford to antagonize Alvedre. She was one of the few scholars who had actually supported his request for a day's leave from classes.

"Close your eyes and visualize the flame," chanted Alvedre. "Experience its heat and light. Know what it means to be a flame. Feel its essence. Corvor, your flame is growing too large: Maintain control."

His flame grows too large, thought Quin, *like his ego. I wonder if I could extinguish his candle without being caught?*

"Corvor, you have overcompensated. Relight your candle and begin again." Quin smiled to himself, feeling Corvor's embarrassment, an emotion to which Quin had nearly perfect immunity, thanks to the insular perspective granted by protective Power. "Quin, you are not concentrating!" chided Alvedre once again.

"I am trying, Mistress Alvedre," answered Quin innocently, "but I cannot feel anything." Quin's Power perceived the mild contempt that issued from several of his classmates, who knew that Quin had failed this lesson repeatedly. Quin concentrated on Alvedre and bent her frustration into a sympathetic regret. Quin considered her a very susceptible subject, despite her exceptional skills at wielding Power.

"I understand, Quin," she murmured patiently. "Just do your best and record anything you do sense from the exercise."

"Yes, Mistress Alvedre," answered Quin, enjoying his private joke immensely and regretting only that he had no one with whom to share it.

Luki had never liked to hear about Quin's classroom pranks, which meant that Quin rarely tried to confide in her. Luki always became exceptionally vague when something annoyed her. Only once in the past few months had she gathered her drifting wits enough to understand Quin's stories, and she had only called him a fool for believing that he could deceive his own Power: "You think you can remain a novice forever by refusing to advance through the formal classes, boy? The scholars will ensure that you master your Power, even if they have failed to instill in you one whit more common sense than you brought with you from Hamley."

"I shall be sixteen in a month," Quin had answered her, "and I shall request binding. All of the scholars know my decision."

Luki had berated him so long and so eloquently that his sixteenth birthday had come and gone, and he still hesitated—to the surprise and chagrin of himself as well as his instructors. "Try at least once to pass the Test, boy," Luki had pleaded. "The results may surprise you."

Quin had argued repeatedly, "But I have never passed any test of Power. I have never been able to do anything useful with my Power at all."

"You have used the Widowshear!"

"I have never controlled it. I have never learned anything from it." *Except fear,* a reluctant honesty had whispered in him, but his Power denied the recurrent dreams of helplessness with quick, defensive forcefulness.

"Try the Test once, boy. Quit telling yourself what you think you cannot do! Binding is painful, boy, and usually irrevocable."

Try once, Luki had said. To appease her, Quin had agreed. He regretted his rash promise to her more than a little, but other sources had confirmed that binding *was* often a painful process. If he tried the Test and failed, he could still resort to binding to escape his prison, and Luki would be satisfied. Maybe she would let him visit her again some day; after he traveled around the world, he would return and tell her stories. Perhaps he could bring her a new treasure or two.

Master Letroff had reminded him quite forcibly yesterday (by use of frustrated, infuriated Power) that Quin could not leave Ixaxis without passing the Test of Mastery or yielding to binding. *They all want me to leave,* thought Quin with a rare touch of regret. *Even Mistress Alvedre wishes I would accept binding and go, though she likes me a little.*

Except for Luki, Quin had no real friends on Ixaxis. He found the scholars arrogant, the students cold, and the servants stubbornly reserved (from fear of Ixaxin Power, he was told, but that did not help). He longed to leave Ixaxis, not merely to return to Hamley, but to escape the incessant aggravations of a life in which he did not want to fit. He did not recognize that his visions of the world outside Ixaxis corresponded very poorly to reality; he did not know how completely Power ruled his concepts of life.

Why did I ever promise Luki that I would try the Test? Absently, Quin twisted his candle's flame into an image of himself by his own distorted perceptions: a vacant-eyed clown with a curly mop of brown hair and an inane expression. He snuffed the flame with a quick breath, when he sensed Alvedre's Power turning toward him, and he grinned at her sheepishly.

Quin, sighed Alvedre into his mind, *whom do you think you are deceiving?*

"Bother," muttered Quin, and he concluded that there was really nothing left to do but try the Test.

* * *

Quin bounded up the stairs to the headmistress' office. In his haste, he stepped on the hem of his robe and tore it. "Blast," he grumbled without much true concern. He bumped into one of the white-robed scholars, grinned broadly, and shouted, "Good morning, Master Howald!"

"Good morning, Quin," replied the assaulted scholar wearily.

"Wish me luck! I am taking the Test of Mastery today!"

The scholar stared at Quin blankly, reading the boy for truth. "Have you informed anyone else of your intentions?"

"Not yet! I am headed for Mistress Amila's office now. Will you miss me, Master Howald? If I pass the Test, I shall leave here."

"Quin," said Howald patiently, "the Test is not being offered today."

"I have not yet asked for it," answered Quin guilelessly.

"I suppose I must accompany you," mumbled Howald, wishing that anyone else had enjoyed the privilege of hearing Quin's news first. "The headmistress may find your request a trifle startling."

"I know," replied Quin brightly. "No one has ever expected me to become a real wizard. I shall probably fail. I always have been a rotten student."

"Yes, Quin."

Howald's sternness discouraged Quin from further comment, as they entered the headmistress' reception room, a simply furnished alcove filled with tests and traps of Power, which concealed the chamber's true extent. "Please wait here, Quin," commanded Howald firmly, and his Power emphasized the order.

Howald tapped on Amila's office door: a formality of custom, for his Power had already warned her of his arrival. He walked through the door, for a trick of wizardry comprised it, and he seated himself opposite Amila at the library table. "Quin wants to take the Test of Mastery now," said Howald, continuing an argument that he had begun before he entered the room. "If we deny him today, he may never exert himself to try again."

Amila folded her hands before her, and she leaned forward to meet Howald's eyes with her own steely gaze. "We schedule the testings regularly," insisted Amila. "Students do not demand the Test of Mastery on a whim!"

"Quin is not asking for immediate testing out of arrogance," countered Howald. "He simply has no concept of the rules."

"We cannot make exception on the basis of Quin's deplorable ignorance. If he wants to take the Test, then let him wait with the rest."

"Who will complain? His fellow students would be glad enough to be rid of him. Quin's pranks have spared no one."

"You imply that Quin has a chance of succeeding."

"He only needs to demonstrate an ability to control Power at his mental level, which should be simple enough even for him."

"Quin does not comprehend the meaning of 'control.' He derives a perverse pleasure from laziness and irresponsible behavior."

"Consider the prospect of Quin continuing his reign of terror for another five years, and tell me that you are unwilling to grasp at any possibility. If he fails, he may acknowledge the inevitability of binding."

"It sets a terrible precedent." Amila shook her head and drummed her fingers on the desk. "However, I suppose one Test will not inconvenience us: Quin is not likely to exert himself to challenge us."

"Offering him the Test is an act of desperate hope," urged Howald.

Amila grimaced. "See if you can locate Nevella and Cori to complete the panel of four; they need the practice of a simple Test-giving to prepare them for the serious students next month. I shall try to occupy Quin safely until you return."

* * *

Charcoal gray velvet covered the walls, the ceiling, and the floor. Once the door closed, the room appeared seamless, lightless, and empty. Naked the student entered the room, and naked he would battle for his Immortal heritage.

The pressure to escape from the room began as soon as the door was locked. The voices in his head urged him to press against the wall and break the prison, but the student had been forewarned of this test: *You must not leave the room until the door is opened for you. To flee the Test means failure.*

The room grew fiercely hot, and the student paced, wishing the ordeal would end. The room grew bitterly cold, and the student laid his face against the wall, nearly driven to press against the smooth surface and yield to failure. The velvet thickened and enticed, but the student jumped free of it, recalling a promise to a very old woman.

The student crouched, shivering, in the center of the floor. He visualized the old woman and wondered, *Who is she?* Then a more pressing realization filled him: *Who am I?*

He had no time to seek the answer. The walls began to close upon him, and the floor began to tilt. He slid toward the edge of utter blackness, and his fingers clutched helplessly, unable to obtain a grip on the velvet's short pile. He stared into the void, and it erupted into all the demons of his imaginings. They clawed at him and tore his flesh from him, and he screamed, for he had never known such pain.

All your fears are made real, whispered a tantalizing voice of madness in his mind. *Power is madness and it fills you.*

The room contracted, warped, and swirled, and the student could not see his own assaulted body. He tried to shout and found no voice. *It is like the nightmares of the Widowshear,* he thought, and the memory made him angry.

You have no right to invade my mind, he screamed with Power. *You will not mold me into your image.*

He shattered the specters that tormented his flesh, and he grasped the room in his mind and stabilized it. He sensed the manipulative patterns of Power behind each wall, and he drove their fire back at them. He felt their shock, and it pleased him. *Kill them,* whispered his Power. *They threaten you.*

"Yes," he hissed. "I shall punish them, as they have punished me for refusing to be like them." He gathered fire in his hands, and his fury colored it with sapphire and silver-white. "Sense the flames," he laughed in mockery of his tormentors, and his Power reveled in its freedom, anticipating the deaths that it would cause. The student reached for a victim behind the nearest wall, and he felt the victim's alarm.

Quin dropped his hands to his sides and rubbed them frantically on the velvet to rid them of the sense of fire.

In horror, he thrust away the sense of patterns and Powers distinct from his own: He would have abandoned his own Power, but he treasured life too deeply.

The room was empty, stable, and still. A door opened, and a dull gray robe was flung at Quin by an unseen hand. Quin snatched his tattered robe hurriedly and wrapped himself in it, regretting that it concealed him incompletely: It could not hide the stain of wizard's Power. It could not hide Quin from himself.

* * *

A dozen of the scholars had gathered in the headmistress' library to await the results. Few Tests accrued such eager anticipation among the scholars, though few expected Quin to persevere to the Test's completion. When Mistress Amila finally entered the room, her expression distressed and weary, many of the scholars sighed or drooped in disappointment.

Amila sank into a chair and lowered her head. Howald and Cori entered moments after her, both appearing strained and pale. Howald scanned the room of glum faces. "Have you told them?" he asked Amila.

"No," replied Amila tiredly. She roused herself to make the formal announcement. "Lord Quinzaine dur Hamley has passed the Test of Mastery. He has announced his intention to leave Ixaxis in the morning."

Alvedre closed her eyes in a brief moment of thankfulness, but hers was the only warm emotion in the room. One of the scholars cheered. Another began to laugh with relief and delight. "You looked so crestfallen, Amila," chided Letroff, a florid man of acrid humor. "Can you actually regret Quin's departure?"

Amila eyed Letroff and the other wizards coldly. Cori and Howald exchanged a wordless glance. "Nevella is unconscious," said Amila soberly. "Howald, Cori, and I have been drained to the point of exhaustion."

Amila gestured toward the wine decanter on the side table. Alvedre filled three goblets, and Letroff distributed them to the three who had Tested Quin. "We have long known that Quin possessed significant Power," said Letroff to the headmistress, "but he has always been too lazy and disinterested to utilize it."

"We began Testing without preparation," answered

Amila slowly, "because we all assumed that Quin's incessant refusal to concentrate on any subject reflected a lack of intelligence. We erred." She drained the goblet and began to speak more rapidly. "We have all erred criminally, and we all deserve the Infortiare's severest censure. We have wasted a rare and invaluable resource, because we were too busy despising Quin's social immaturity to exercise the most basic laws of observation."

"To Lord Quinzaine," murmured Howald wryly, raising his goblet in a one-sided toast, "who is quite likely the most incorrigibly lazy owner of a major Power ever born."

"No," argued Alvedre with quiet insistence. Her fellow scholars stared at her in surprise. Her strong, serene features were furrowed in a rare expression of deep concern. "Do you still not understand him, Howald? I knew, as soon as Amila announced that Quin had passed the Test of Mastery. I realized why I have always sensed in him something great and wonderful, buried beneath the fool's facade. My Power knew what I could not discern."

"You detected greatness in Quin, the hopeless, helpless prankster?" scoffed Cori, a blockish woman with russet hair. "You have excellent hindsight, Alvedre."

Alvedre's pale skin reddened, but she drew herself erect and spoke with assurance, "I realize that I am not the most senior of you, and I failed with the rest of you to predict this day's events. I tell you now, however, that I know—both by reason and by the surety of my Power— that Quin has never been lazy at all. He is a much more dominant wizard than any of us guessed. We thwarted his Power's obvious efforts at persuasion, but we never even noticed how he camouflaged himself."

"Because the effort was entirely unconscious and instinctive on his part," added Amila with a frustrated shake of her head.

"Nonetheless," added Howald with a weary scowl, "I am pleased to see the last of him. May Hamley have joy of its monster, and may he never return to us."

"Quin may leave us now," prophesied Alvedre with a confidence she did not try to justify, "but he will return. His true depth of Power has only begun to awaken."

* * *

"Where are your ceaseless, silly questions today, boy?" demanded Luki abruptly.

Quin, who had been staring at Luki's remarkably brilliant roses for the past ten minutes, answered in an unusually subdued voice, "I am leaving in the morning, Luki. I passed the Test of Mastery."

"So," answered Luki, crinkling her face and fussing unnecessarily with the folds of her skirt. "You have long wanted to leave Ixaxis. You should sound pleased. Have you lost your little wisdom and forgotten how to appreciate your blessings?"

"I shall miss you, Luki," replied Quin very seriously.

"Hunh." The old woman shrugged and frowned and tugged at a stalk of new corn. "You need other friends. You are the sort of young man who ought to have lots of friends, not just one old woman. It is time you left! Why are you dawdling here?"

"Will you remember me, Luki?"

"Will I remember," muttered Luki. "Foolish boy."

Quin smiled at her, and he bounded across the yard and hugged her before she could tell him again to leave. *I never expected to* pass *the Test,* he told himself for the hundredth time; he had not prepared himself for the reality of departure. Luki worried him: *Who will visit her when I am gone?*

"Foolish boy," grumbled Luki once more, but she returned Quin's hug warmly. "Luki has managed for some centuries without you. She can manage again."

"After I have traveled a bit, I shall come and see you and tell you all that I have done."

Luki nodded and patted his back; then she pushed him suddenly to arm's length from her. "Boy, you have not said all that disturbs you."

"No," admitted Quin slowly. "Luki, when you first learned that you had Power, how did you feel?"

"Boy, you ask me to remember a moment five Infortiares and thirty Seriin monarchs ago."

"Can you recall no special instant when you understood—really understood, for the first time—that you could do things that ought to be impossible?"

"So, boy," murmured Luki with a trace of an old woman's condescension, "you have finally realized what it means to be a wizard."

"It was the Test," replied Quin, all his frustration exploding in his voice. "The panel pressed me, Luki, inside my head. It felt like the first time I used the Widowshear, but it hurt much more. They made me angry, Luki. I never felt angry like that before."

"Yes," said Luki with a solemn nod, "the student who controls his Power in anger has earned the right to keep his Power and live by Ceallagh's laws."

"I pressed Mistress Nevella into unconsciousness, and the other scholars on the panel were preparing to destroy me when I remembered. They feared *me*, Luki."

"You have great Power, and you control it so naturally and easily that it is difficult to anticipate."

"Luki," wailed Quin pitifully, "I am an Ixaxin after all. I am just like the rest of them."

Luki burst into a deep and throaty chuckle. "Quin, boy, you will never be like anyone but yourself."

CHAPTER 8

Seriin Year 9054

Quin sorted his coins idly on a table of well-worn, well-oiled wood, wondering idly how far the money would let him travel. He remained blissfully unaware of the covetous eyes that observed him. He had only recently left the civilized paths, and he had no concept of poverty and little concept of want or need. He would not have behaved much differently if he had known the risks he took unintentionally. Few mortal obstacles could stand in comparison to the Ixaxin Test of Mastery; all lesser fears had dwindled since the Test.

Quin had left Ixaxis six months earlier, and he had taken a decidedly long route home. He still intended to return to Hamley, but so many interesting sights and characters along the way distracted him, drawing him farther from his destination rather than carrying him toward it. He did not acknowledge his uneasy suspicion that his idealized memories of Hamley would be disappointed.

Quin did quite honestly delight in his travels. His own country contained such a variety of marvelous sights! He had prowled the cities and countryside, fascinated by every wonder and artifact: rivers, lakes, and mountains; castles, bridges, aqueducts, and dams; orchards, pastures, and fields; the elegant salons of the cultural elite and the very inelegant dens of bawdy amateurs and tricksters. He had encountered poets, beggars, minstrels, merchants, farmers, foundrymen, craftsmen, fellow wanderers, and fellow wizards. He had sought conversation eagerly with all but the wizards; he had met enough of those, he thought, and he felt peculiarly reluctant to identify himself as one of their number.

He had spent little of the money that his family had sent him, for he enjoyed simple accommodations, and the entire world entertained him enormously by its very existence. He carried little baggage, and he journeyed by any means that presented itself: dairy cart, noble's carriage, timber boat, pack mule, or foot. Quin found the variety of people's lifestyles and outlooks a remarkable revelation in itself.

The only persons who annoyed him were those who tried to delve too deeply into his own purposes and plans. Quin disliked introspection, distrusted any plan but improvisation, and considered the pleasures of life's constant discoveries to be the only purpose anyone should require. When those rare, irritating individuals who prodded him excessively appeared, Quin discouraged them by concocting fanciful and bizarre replies to bewilder them or convince them of his insanity or idiocy, according to his mood of the moment.

The Test of Mastery had shaken his instinctive barriers of Power considerably, but it had not succeeded in breaking lifelong habits of emotional reserve. Forced by the Test to recognize the nature of his "popularity" among impressionable mortals, he could not use Power's influence as freely as had always been his custom. Ceallagh's laws, the most solemn fundamentals of formal wizardry, forbade the casual manipulation of mortal minds, and the effort of complying with the Ixaxin oaths only aggravated Quin's inclination to avoid the bonds of vulnerability. Ceallagh's laws could not enforce wisdom.

Quin had come to the particular region he now visited as the result of a conversation with an old quartz miner, who had described the grand freedom of the far northern mountain districts in particularly exhilarating terms. Quin had duly admired the scenery, and he had tried (with mediocre success) to appreciate the grandeur of isolation that the forlorn, ice-encrusted mountain trails provided. After two days as a mountain hermit, Quin had decided that he missed the company of people, and he had ambled down the mountain toward the nearest spiral of woodsmoke.

Quin's enthusiastic greetings had failed to charm the strangers he met in the village, but Quin had proceeded imperturbably to question random passersby regarding lodging and food. He had received a grunted answer from a sun-dried woman who wore a sour expression. Quin had grinned and thanked her effusively, deriving much entertainment from her obvious suspicions regarding his gratitude's motivation. Her advice led him to a hostel of far more welcoming appearance than he had expected in a community of such unsociable citizens.

With his exaggeratedly haphazard air of foolish eccentricity, Quin attracted some notice but little lingering interest. A young whore approached him once, but she abandoned him in disgust on concluding that her purpose eluded him completely. Quin accepted her retreat with a phlegmatic sigh. He thought he might have enjoyed her company, but he was unwilling to pay for the privilege. Quin found the ploy of obtuse innocence exceptionally useful at times.

While Quin pursued the last morsels of potato across his supper plate, he studied the room in search of the most promising prospect for after-dinner conversation. Two husky, boisterous youths intrigued him momentarily, but he concluded that they looked too much like troublemakers. Quin was rarely averse to good-natured trouble, unless he was its object.

A tall, broad-shouldered figure with a heavy tread entered the room and cast a fur-lined cloak across a wallhook, revealing an unmistakably female person with cropped dark hair and the blouse and britches of a Seriin soldier. She measured the room with a careful gaze; armed and armored in a chain mail vest, she caused many glances to fall uncomfortably. When she inspected Quin, he beamed at her, for he felt sure that she could tell a fascinating story, but she dismissed him as quickly as she bypassed the rest of the room. She nudged a quiet trapper from his table, and the man yielded the space to her hastily.

By the time Quin resorted to counting his funds, he had tried unsuccessfully to strike a conversation with half the customers in the hostel. He did not doubt that Power could overcome the barrier of innate suspicion which seemed to characterize the people of this region, but he felt a twinge of guilt for even entertaining the thought. The Test had made him wary.

Quin sorted his coins deliberately, pondering the prospects they presented and debating the attractions of a sea voyage versus a tour of the northern reach. Something thudded to the table beside his hand: a heavy, bone-handled knife, the blade of which had pierced the table's boards. Power shivered through Quin, beginning to gather energies of retaliation, but he suppressed the instinct in quick alarm.

Quin raised his innocent eyes to the man who loomed above him: an unkempt man in soiled and mismatched clothes. "You throw well," remarked Quin affably, hoping to deflect the man's incomprehensible antagonism without accepting Power's violent urgings. "I have a cousin who is very deft with the knife. He can throw a blade across the river and still strike the apple from the tree. How far is your range?"

"Little boy, I think you will pay me to answer you." The man reached for his knife and jerked it from the table. He prodded the coins, scattering their orderly stacks. "You will pay me this," said the man, grasping a handful of silver in his hairy paw, "for the privilege of watching me enjoy my supper. And you will pay this to watch me drink." He drew another handful across the table, forming a glistening mound apart from Quin's. "And you will pay me all of it if you want me to let you live."

The oaf threatens me with nothing but bluster over a bit of silver, Quin decided, his Power relaxing as irritation replaced alarm. *He has no courage to use his knife except for bullying.*

Quin met the man's pallid eyes and shook his head in regret. "This is not a very friendly town." Quin began to scoop his coins back into his leather pouch. The man caught Quin by the collar and slammed the wizard's face against the table.

Quin raised his head slowly, gingerly touching his bleeding nose. He felt incredulous that the stranger had hurt him; Power had perceived no intent of serious menace, and Quin had not thought to probe for lesser, childish threats. He felt a touch of the anger that the Ixaxin scholars had roused in him at the Test, and the memory disturbed him more than the man who was stealing his money.

The armored woman rose and rested the tip of her sword against the back of Quin's accoster. "Leave the boy alone," she ordered.

The man turned, initially startled, but he examined the woman and tossed back his head in a deep, rolling guffaw. He shoved Quin once more, though Quin managed to avoid colliding with the table this time; the man discarded Quin. The woman withdrew her sword from its position against the thief's broad back, but she held the weapon poised. When the thief lunged to take her blade, she shifted adroitly to keep it from his grasp.

"You plan to tackle my sword with your bare hands?" she asked with cool contempt.

The man winked at two comrades, who both roared with laughter. He dove toward the woman, causing the room's impartial occupants to scurry madly from his path. The woman leapt to the hearth, to the table, and to the stairs, while the man spun, seeking her. She flung herself across the iron banister to land behind him, kicked his feet from him, and swatted his backside with the flat of her blade.

She prodded the thief out the shuttered door and into the center of the uneven dirt road, while the curious hostel patrons (including Quin) surged to the door either to encourage or to jeer. Other villagers gathered beneath the wide eaves of neighboring houses and shops or stood shivering beneath the nearest stand of towering trees, dark with the coming dusk. When the thief tried to rise to face his opponent, the woman allowed him to reach a crouch. Then she drove her foot powerfully against his shoulders and sent him tumbling backward into a puddle of black mud.

She whirled her well-polished sword in a deadly circle, nicking one of the man's encroaching comrades. She caused the other to stumble against the hostel wall in alarmed retreat. The red light of a stormy sunset glinted from her chain mail vest.

Power sensed the tension escalate, as injured pride and anger gave courage to the thief; Power felt the danger. Quin shouted a warning, indistinguishable from the raucous wagers and loud catcalls, as the first man hurled himself at the woman's back with a long and wickedly experienced knife.

The warrior-woman struck him with the sword, nearly severing the thief's head from his shoulders in a single blow. She kicked his lifeless body. "I never have liked ill-mannered thieves," she murmured to the corpse. She glared at her late opponent's much chastened companions. They busied themselves with her victim, avoiding the woman with a wary new respect.

The crowd began to drift back to interrupted business and pleasures. The woman jerked her head at Quin. "Inside, youngling," she commanded. Quin followed her meekly, uncomfortably attuned to the crowd's collective uneasiness. The warrior-woman shouted for ale and sank onto the bench beside the hearth, propping her booted feet against the wall. The fire's light painted her ruddily, and the shadows made her features look large and coarse. The crowd avoided her, though they whispered and nodded in her direction.

The woman began to wipe her blade with a rag she pulled from a pocket in her britches. "What is the matter with you, youngling?" she asked loudly and sententiously. "Have you no better sense than to taunt that band of ruffians by flaunting your wealth before them?"

"No," replied Quin simply.

The woman paused in her blade-cleaning and stared at Quin. Abruptly, she began to laugh, and she continued until her eyes watered. The innkeeper, who brought the woman's mug of ale, gazed dubiously from her to Quin, who only shrugged, uncertain himself of how he had inspired such hilarity. "How old are you, youngling?" asked the woman, still gasping a little from the throes of her mirth.

"Nearly seventeen," said Quin, keeping his answer cautiously brief.

"If you plan to see eighteen, you had best learn either better sense or the advantages of wearing a good weapon." The woman tugged her leather gauntlet from her hand to take her ale, and she drank deeply. "Innkeeper, give the boy a tankard of ale on my bill."

"It is not necessary," argued Quin uncomfortably. He hoped she would not lecture him on defensive tactics.

"Never refute a woman's generosity, youngling! Especially when the woman is twice your size and quite able to rearrange your anatomy before you could even notice the attack. Drink, and tell me how an incautious lad like you comes to this uncharitable part of the world."

The innkeeper thrust a mug into Quin's hands. Quin tasted the ale and grimaced; he did not like ale. "I finished school, and I wanted to travel a bit before returning home."

"And where is home?"

"Hamley."

The warrior-woman appraised Quin closely, assessing him from his unruly brown hair, wide gray eyes, and well-formed hands to his finely woven shirt and soft wool vest. "The manor?"

"Yes," admitted Quin, unhappy to be so easily identified, but the warrior-woman intrigued him sufficiently to warrant tolerance of her questions. "How did you know?"

"You are too rich, too soft, and too pretty to be anything but a lordling. You need toughening. Did no one warn you about the world outside your palaces and noble halls? What useless sort of schooling did you receive?"

"I suppose I never listened to anything very practical." Quin shrugged and grinned. "However, I have been managing fairly well."

"You enjoy having your head bashed by drunken bullies? How is the nose?"

"Sore."

The woman grunted and extinguished an errant spark with her foot. "I thought you lordlings at least learned basic defense. Anyone who can wield a sword should carry one in these parts."

Another lecture, thought Quin with a silent sigh; *I suppose I earned it.* "I never was very adept with the sword."

"Then find the weapon that suits you, or stay at home." The woman brought her legs under her, crossing them so that her elbows could rest easily on her knees. She held her sword before her and leaned toward Quin. "Listen to me, youngling: I have made my own way in this world for more years than I care to admit to an infant like you, and I have watched too many younglings die without a taste of life." She twisted her lips into an ironic grimace. "Your noble kin keep the law where it suits them, and they let the lawless migrate to fringe cities like this—and worse—where survival belongs to the strong and the quick. We buffer the domains against the wild lands' deadliness, and so the domain lords allow us to exist."

Quin asked very seriously, "Why do you stay in such places? Are you a criminal?"

The woman stared soberly at Quin from across the table. "You really are an innocent, asking such questions! Lordling, how long have you been traveling on your own?"

"A few months," answered Quin, beginning to feel slightly defensive before this well-armed stranger's questions.

"And you have not yet lost your purse or your life? You must carry Lady Fortune in your pocket."

Quin glanced toward the pocket of his vest, as if to see the Lady peering from its rim. He let the gesture hide the flush of his dismay on realizing that his most potent weapon might be deduced along with his status. "Maybe I am not worth the trouble of harassing."

"I know a dozen men in this village who would kill you for that fine shirt you wear."

Quin shook his head, as he pushed the unwanted tankard of ale away from him. "I knew folks smiled too little here."

The woman frowned at him for a long moment, before she raised her tankard to him. "You amuse me, lordling. Where do you plan to go from here?"

"Anywhere I have not yet gone."

"Have you been to Lambde?"

"No."

"Good. Ride with me to Lambde tomorrow. I shall keep the cutthroats from you, and you may entertain me."

"I have no horse," protested Quin, though the woman's suggestion intrigued him.

The woman gave a rolling laugh and pointed at the bulging leather pouch, which Quin had slung hastily and haphazardly over his shoulder. "You have silver enough to buy the best mount in the district."

Quin gave this answer considerable thought. He had generally avoided any continuity of company beyond a day; he did not want to risk discovery of his unwanted profession. Still, the warrior-woman fascinated him. "What does Lambde offer?"

"For me, a sizable bounty, if I bring the villagers the hide of a vulpas that has been troubling them. For you, a safer inn than this one. Agreed?"

How could anyone refuse a woman who hunted vulpas? "Agreed!"

"My name is Laurett." She extended a callused hand, which Quin accepted cheerfully, though she gripped with uncomfortable forcefulness.

"Quin," he replied. "Why did you become a warrior, Laurett?"

She cocked her head to consider this innocently impertinent young man. "Most people would expect me to silence you via a fist to the jaw, youngling, for asking such a question."

"I hope they misjudge you. My face is never particularly prepossessing, but a smashed nose *and* a broken jaw would not improve its character."

"I meet few persons worthy of patience, lordling."

"Why did you become a warrior?" asked Quin again, and he yielded to temptation, letting his Power exude a teasingly persuasive sort of charm.

Laurett laughed very briefly, unfolded her long legs and restored her sword to its scabbard. "I saw my mother beaten day and night by my stepfather," she remarked coolly, "and I developed a contempt for her weakness."

Quin furrowed his smooth, young face in puzzlement. "You despised her rather than him?"

"I despised them both!" retorted Laurett sharply. "He was cruel, and she lacked self-respect. I did not intend to imitate either of them, so I established an identity of my own. I have a reputation in these parts, young Quin, for fairness as well as hardness."

"Do you serve in the Queen's army?"

"No, they accept no women! I bought the uniform from a man who quite likely stole it, but it is well made and well designed for fighting."

She had relaxed, giving a hint of softness to her stubborn face. She was not a pretty woman; her features were too blunt and large. Yet, she had an honest and forthright manner about her that Quin liked much better than the common enticements of wide eyes or shining curls.

"I hunt and I scout for travelers or villagers," she continued amiably. "I solve problems for places like Lambde." She contemplated Quin, who gazed at her avidly, listened to her intently, and was genuinely engrossed by everything she said. "Are you studying me as a curiosity, lordling?" she demanded in sudden suspicion.

"Absolutely!" replied Quin brightly. He let his Power soothe her moment of wariness. "I have never been rescued before, and I have never before met a female warrior (of obvious skills at combat!), and no one has talked to me at all in ages and ages! This has been the most outstanding day!"

"You have strange ideas of entertainment, lordling."

* * *

Quin scarcely expected his astonishing rescuer to remember him by morning, so he made a point of descending early from his room. He congratulated himself for his good fortune once again, for Mistress Laurett entered the inn as Quin reached the bottom stair. She hailed him, apparently as pleased as Quin to find her spontaneous suggestion of the previous day remembered.

"I have the names of three likely horse traders for you, lordling. I need to settle some business of my own here in Narrfield, while you make your purchase. Do you know anything of horses?"

His shields of Power jumped defensively, denying any hint of pain. "My mother was born the Lady Aliria dur Viste," answered Quin, striking a farcical cavalier's pose, "and Viste breeds the finest horses in Serii."

"I am not interested in your pedigree, lordling, but in your ability to buy a sound, solid horse for long, cold, mountainous trails. Ruggedness and endurance are the qualities you want: none of these fast, flashy parade horses!"

"You are as bad as the Crown Prince," answered Quin airily, "who always asks my advice for additions to his stables, and then proceeds to tell me which horses he already intended to buy."

"Do you actually know the Crown Prince?" asked Laurett suspiciously.

Quin endeavored to look excessively innocent. "We are like brothers. We have sailed together to Bethii and Mahl. We have battled pirates, side by side, along the coast of Caruil. We have hunted dyrcats across the southern plains."

Laurett grinned slowly. "Young liar, there are no dyrcats south of Tulea."

"Maybe it was the Mindar wilderness. I never did very well at geography." Quin matched her grin with a mischievous expression of broad delight. He did not feel; he dared not feel.

"If you can sound half so convincing to the horse traders, you may actually obtain a fair price—but hide that noble fortune you carry."

"I shall tell everyone that I work for you and that you will take vengeance if they cheat me." Quin gestured expansively, as if wielding a foil against a dozen great foes. He knocked a pot from the window ledge in his exuberance, and Laurett caught the glazed clay crock with a hurried lunge.

"Lordling, can you stay out of trouble long enough to buy a horse for yourself?"

Quin took the pot from her and replaced it on the ledge with great delicacy. He arranged it carefully, studied it critically, and readjusted its position precisely. He bowed to Laurett very grandly, although the glistening pebbles that tumbled from his vest pocket marred the formal effect.

"I wondered where I put those!" he declared and knelt to gather the bits of quartz and pyrite from the smooth wood floor. "I found these gems on that very mountain," he informed Laurett proudly, simultaneously waving his arm toward the wall and scrambling on the floor to collect his treasures.

Laurett laughed at him, a simple, uncompromising sound. Astonishment penetrated Quin's carefully held defenses. She had given him laughter entirely of her own volition; his Power had not pressured her at all. Quin's smile became tentative, but it was a genuine expression and not a deliberate wall.

Quin strode from the inn with an intense energy inspired by a rare honesty of turbulent emotions. The warrior-woman had laughed, as if Quin were a close companion. Luki never laughed; Luki always disapproved. The possibility of actually befriending Laurett troubled Quin, and it stirred a deeply buried ache of emptiness. Power began to urge him to escape.

"I am the master of my Power," whispered Quin in echo of his Ixaxin oath, "and will not serve its dictates." He had learned to recite Ceallagh's laws in his first year at Ixaxis, but the meanings had seemed impersonal before the Test. He forced his Power to subside, though he did not attempt to delve too deeply into his reasons for nervous fear. He plunged into his task, denying further introspection.

The first trader was a grizzled, bony man named Callaren. With a thinly hidden greed, Callaren squinted at Quin, appraising the possible assets of the customer. Callaren worked his colorless lips in a wickedly pleased expression, and he led Quin to the dilapidated stable.

Most of Callaren's horses had been abused, and Quin held his anger in check with difficulty. He could not comprehend the minds of men who beat or drove their animals with such carelessness. *I cannot allow such cruelty,* he thought, alarmed to realize how deeply the sight of the damaged animals affected him.

He cast his Power toward the injured, fear-trained horses to give them such brief comfort as he could provide. He shared the animals' pain, until he could not bear the weight of their hurting. His Power's shield rose to protect him, and he turned from the horses with apparent indifference. He told Callaren crisply, "You have nothing of interest to me." Callaren began to argue, but Quin shrugged away from him with a flicker of irritated Power.

The second and third traders had little more to offer. Disgusted with the entire effort, Quin began to lose his taste for the fringe lands altogether. He made a final gesture toward completion of his task: He let his Power reach across the village and farms in search of any animal that did not cringe with terror from humankind, and he found a strong, young mare, owned by a forest family.

With slow care, Quin negotiated the rough path that led among the dark, still trees. The woodsman, hewing logs before his stone cottage, looked up from his task in obvious surprise to find a visitor. "I have come to buy your horse," announced Quin, and he laid a stack of silver on the hewing stump.

The woodsman leaned on his ax and gave Quin a slow, curious look. "You mistake me, youngling," remarked the woodsman. "I am not a trader."

"You do have a horse?"

"I have Pala."

"Will you sell her to me? I am offering you enough silver to buy a dozen horses. I shall treat your Pala well."

The burly woodsman shook his head slowly. "You make me a strange offer." He touched the silver gingerly, testing its substance.

"Your family needs the money. I need your horse. Other horses in this region need a good owner like you."

"Why do you not buy a trader's horse?" asked the woodsman curiously.

"The traders' horses have suffered abuse. Even the youngest, not yet injured in body, have learned fear. Patience and kindness could heal the wounded spirits, but I have no time. I must leave tomorrow."

"And how did you hear of me?"

"You are a good man," replied Quin. "Such facts are known." To Quin's relief, the woodsman accepted the evasive answer without apparent difficulty.

The woodsman said thoughtfully, "We have a new child. The money would be welcome." The woodsman moved his stare from the silver to Quin. "Pala belonged to my wife's father, who died a year ago. I have thought of selling the horse, for we are very poor, but I did not want the Narrfield traders to take her." The woodsman's smile became thin. "They abuse their animals cruelly."

"Sell Pala to me," wheedled Quin softly.

"You have not even seen the horse."

"Then take me to her," answered Quin.

The woodsman slung the ax across his shoulder and strode to the door of his house. "Dila," he called, "a boy wants to buy Pala from us."

A red-cheeked young woman appeared quickly, rubbing floury hands across her faded aprons. She glanced from her husband to Quin, blushed and bobbed in an awkward curtsey. "My lord," she murmured with awe in her eyes.

Grimacing slightly at the woman's greeting, Quin gathered the silver from the stump. He crossed the small clearing to drop the silver into the woman's white-dusted hands. He added another two silvers from his pocket. "Your father's horse will be very well tended," he assured her sincerely. "My mother came from Viste."

* * *

By morning, Quin had rebuilt his blithe fool's exterior. He made himself clumsy and imbecilic, and he could see Laurett begin to wonder about her invitation to him. An old instinct in him approved of her withdrawal, but Quin discovered that he wanted to hear her laugh again, and his Power moved to stall her retreat. Confused by conflicting impulses, Quin's Power hovered between defense and encouragement.

Riding together toward Lambde, Quin caught Laurett's glance upon him, and he looked around him with comic haste at the pillars of trees crowned with clouds and wintry sunlight. "Have I committed another act of unthinkable idiocy?" he asked her with a pitiful gaze of woe.

"Only by accompanying a suspicious stranger into these desolate lands. For all you know of me, lordling, I might have saved you only to claim the spoils for myself. You let me travel at your back, when you have already seen me kill a man."

Quin frowned and nodded, patting Pala's dappled neck. "Do you plan to murder me and steal my fortune, Laurett?"

"No, lordling."

"Then I think I shall sing, and you will realize that I am not the only incautious member of this team." He proceeded to warble a nursery tune in a very loud voice that strayed wildly from any recognizable key. He paused just long enough to remark, "I am not sure that my singing is as lethal as your sword, good Mistress Laurett, but it is at least as unpleasant," and he renewed his strident chorus with enthusiasm.

"Though we may frighten every living creature in the forest of Eirele, I shall accept your challenge, foolish lordling," shouted Laurett, and she joined her voice to his, half in discordant song and half in a tune of laughter.

They rode into Lambde in the late afternoon, and Laurett exchanged greetings with half a dozen villagers before reaching the home of the village elder. Most of Lambde's citizens were shepherds or farmers, who lived in scattered hillside houses with peaked roofs and brightly painted walls. Only three buildings comprised the town itself: the Elder's House; the Travelers' House; and the Exchange Hall, where all matters of village business transpired, from marketing to town meetings.

"Lambde is as nearly civilized as any village in the region," remarked Laurett, dismounting and tethering her horses to the split-rail fence before the Elder's House. "But the people are cold and cautious with strangers, and you must never cross a Lambde citizen, unless you want the entire clan at your heels. Nearly everyone in Lambde is related in one or more directions."

"Sounds like Hamley," murmured Quin.

"Except Lambde has no law but its own. In Lambde, strangers often end up swinging from that tree in front of the Exchange Hall. Watch what you say."

"I thought you were bringing me to someplace hospitable?"

"I only promised safety, lordling, which Lambde will offer if you are charitable in your judgments of her. Master Daroh owns Lambde, and he once killed a traveler for complaining about the Travelers' House soup."

Master Daroh, a white-haired man with strong, frowning features and a deep voice, emerged from the Elder's House and hailed Laurett sharply. "The vulpas has attacked two more flocks since I contacted you," he informed her as he crossed the stony yard. "We have the initial payment for you. When will you begin the hunt?"

"In the morning," answered Laurett, briskly impervious to Master Daroh's accusatory stare.

Daroh nodded abruptly toward Quin. "Is this your vulpas bait?"

"I hope my singing is not that bad!" exclaimed Quin.

"His name is Quin," said Laurett simply.

"We are not paying you to train an assistant," countered Daroh coldly.

"I shall not assist anyone," offered Quin. "I am absolutely helpless!" Quin smiled, and Daroh's stern expression gradually eased.

"Where did you find this helpless child?" Daroh asked Laurett with gruff curiosity.

"Narrfield."

"Hmh. Narrfield is a nasty place." Daroh considered Quin slowly. "You are unarmed."

"Always!" replied Quin cheerfully.

"He truly is a helpless child," murmured Laurett.

"You are trying to protect him?" asked Daroh.

"For the moment," answered Laurett.

Daroh grunted, "He may stay here."

"Thank you, Master Daroh!" answered Quin enthusiastically. "I shall treasure my time in fair Lambde forever, cherishing it as a serene memory, holding it dear to me, imagining and remembering it. . . ."

"Quin," said Laurett, interrupting him with a cautioning glare, "we are only staying until morning."

"Let him speak," said Daroh, a trace of laughter beginning to grow within his hard voice. "I rarely find anyone so appreciative of Lambde's charms."

Daroh turned to lead the way across the yard toward the Elder's House. Laurett stared for a moment at Daroh's back, before she whispered to Quin, "If you can wheedle old Daroh into laughter, try wheedling him into raising the bounty for the vulpas."

"I am sure he will raise it if I ask him," answered Quin with an innocent gaze. "He likes me."

"I noticed," answered Laurett dryly, "but wizard's fire take me if I can understand how you managed your conquest."

Quin's smile became slightly strained, and he turned quickly to Master Daroh, who threw open the shuttered door of the Elder's House and spread his arms in the welcome of a friend. "You will dine with me, I trust," offered Daroh warmly. "Cabe will have rooms prepared for you at the Travelers' House."

"Thank you, Master Daroh," said Laurett with a curious glance at Quin. "We are singularly honored by your hospitality." Quin soothed her incipient suspicions with a gentle touch of Power, and he persuaded himself that he had not defied Ceallagh's law against meddling with mortal minds because Laurett's doubts had not had time to coalesce.

* * *

Laurett pounded on Quin's door before dawn to wake him. "Join me in the stable quickly, lordling, for I shall not wait for you."

Quin groaned, "Is it even morning?" He turned on the lumpy, straw-filled mattress, pulling his wool cloak across his head. When he received no answer, he concluded that Laurett meant her threat of abandoning him. He scrambled to his feet and splashed water on his face from a chipped glass ewer.

By the time he reached the stable, the night had begun to soften to dawn's pale gray. He greeted Pala sleepily. Laurett laughed, "Be careful, youngling, or you will mistake your cloak for a saddle blanket. Here, I brought you some rolls for your breakfast." She tossed him a bundle, wrapped and tied in a red cotton kerchief.

Quin caught the parcel of rolls and thrust it into his saddlebag. "Take a cracker and go," muttered Quin, thinking of Luki. He had dreamed of the Widowshear again, and he felt more exhausted than if he had not slept at all. "Why did Luki ever make me touch the thing?"

"Who is Luki?" asked Laurett.

Quin's haze of sleepiness evaporated abruptly, as he realized how close he had come to betraying himself. "An old woman," he answered airily, "who used to give me biscuits and tea. Sometimes I worked in her garden for her, and sometimes she told me stories. She often forgot the endings." Quin grinned at Laurett, willing her to disregard his cryptic reference to the Widowshear. "I invented new versions of her tales and ended them to suit myself."

Laurett accepted his reply, although she wore a vaguely puzzled expression throughout the rest of the morning. She seemed to recognize that she had lost a train of thought—like a familiar word that slips unexpectedly from memory. As the sun rose toward noon, she abandoned the futile effort to remember an inconsequential instant. Quin besieged her with questions about every sight they passed, and she could barely keep pace with his chatter.

* * *

"Have you ever seen a vulpas, Quin?"

"Never. They are noted for their cunning, I have heard."

"The reputation flatters them unduly. They steal the calves from a herd without a trace, so frustrated herders call them clever. In fact, they are stupid and slow but so huge and strong that nothing sensible tries to stop them, including the calves' mothers."

"Do you hunt them often?"

"Only when one of the beasts has earned a large bounty by living too near to a settlement. Most vulpas prefer the high northern mountains, where they prey on goats and rock-leapers."

"How do you intend to find this one?"

"Quin, I have been tracking him for the past three days!"

"I thought we seemed to be traveling in circles."

"This vulpas is a big, healthy bull: the most ornery of his kind, to judge by the extent of his territory and the number of birds and rodents he has killed and abandoned uneaten."

"He sounds delightful."

"Vulpas have unpleasant habits, like human beings. Look there." She pointed at a stand of firs that crowned a rocky knoll ahead of them. "That is where we shall find this vulpas. His lair is close, and the scent of us will bring him in to us."

"Us?"

Laurett chuckled heartily. "What happened to that curiosity of yours?"

"I should like to see a vulpas. I should not like to become his dinner."

"Would I jeopardize you, lordling, and antagonize Fortune, who seems so fond of you? I shall stash you with the horses in some cave—or maybe in some crevice where you may watch the fun in safety."

Quin began to watch for signs of the vulpas, though he had little idea of what to expect. Only after Laurett's patient explanations could he begin to perceive the unique form of damage that characterized the vulpas' passage and defined his trail. When Laurett diverged from the obvious route to probe a particular district in tediously thorough detail, Quin abandoned his attempt to follow her hunter's reasoning.

He enjoyed the scenery for its own sake, trying to assimilate all that Laurett had told him in the past days about the wildlife and other wonders of the region. He echoed Laurett's delighted discovery of an ancient land-slide, although he had little idea of why the boulder-laden clearing inspired Laurett's enthusiasm. When she led the horses between a narrow gap into a cul-de-sac and ordered Quin to guard the entry, his excitement began to rise.

After four subsequent hours of sitting, watching two restive horses, and wondering where Laurett had gone, Quin began to wish he had stayed in Lambde. He had nearly decided to set out in search of his warrior-compan-ion, despite her stern command to remain hidden, when he heard the deep warning of the vulpas.

The threat of the rumbling growl did not prepare Quin for the sight of a vast, snarling mass of fangs and muscle emerging fully from the rock shadows in clumsy pursuit of Laurett, who teased and taunted the creature with her sword. The folds of the vulpas' nearly hairless hide rolled and shifted, as it lumbered toward Laurett, child-sized before it. The vulpas' wrinkled skin caught and deflected her sword strikes, but she herded the beast and dodged it.

When the vulpas' blubbery lips drooped across its rows of sharklike teeth, the creature acquired almost a clown-ish look with its flat, pugnacious nose and the prehensile ear flaps that could rise to capture sound or droop to protect the delicate, sensitive bones and membranes of its ears. The animal's movements seemed slow and clumsy, until it lunged. The vulpas swiped at Laurett with its huge claws, barely missed her, and ripped from an unfortunate tree a chunk of wood the size of Quin's head.

Laurett sheathed her sword at her back and bounded to the arrangement of boulders that she had admired before selecting the site of confrontation. The vulpas tried to reach her, dislodged one of the boulders, and stumbled. Laurett scrambled to keep her footing, while avoiding the vulpas and working the clasp of the leather

case she had slung over her shoulder. She withdrew a
pair of iron talons from the case and fastened them to a
chain at her waist. The empty case tumbled to the
ground. Laurett grasped the overhanging limb and swung
herself across the vulpas' head and onto the animal's
back, digging the talons into its hide to maintain her grip.

The vulpas bucked and roared, trying to dislodge the
insect that had pierced it. Laurett clung to the folds encircling the beast's neck, but the chain and the talons held
her far more consistently than her hands' grasp. She took
her sword in hand, raised it high above her, and swung
it down across the vulpas' skull. Dark blood erupted, as
the creature screamed.

The vulpas continued to twist and fight, but Laurett
issued no more blows against it, struggling now only to
free herself of the chains and talons, before the vulpas
could crush her in its death throes. Laurett was thrashed
and scratched by tree limbs, before she could unfasten
the chain, leap, and scurry to relative safety.

She dropped through the narrow rock gap to land
beside Quin. She grinned at his astonishment. "It died
when I sliced its skull," she commented calmly, "but its
body may keep moving for as long as an hour. Hand me
the salve, will you?"

Quin complied quickly. "Do you know that you are
covered in blood?"

"Killing a vulpas is a messy business, Quin." She
sounded elated, but she continued more solemnly, "Killing any living creature is a messy business, but it is the
way of nature. You need to learn that lesson, lordling:
death is part of life."

"If you insist on sounding like my philosophy professor, I shall sulk."

"You had a poor education if I can imitate it! Quin, I
never saw the inside of a schoolroom."

"Then why do you never believe anything I tell you?"

"Because you tell tales taller than the Gnarly Crag.
You are a liar, lordling, by inclination and by choice."

Quin grinned at her. "Then why do you listen to me
at all?"

Laurett cuffed him, smearing him with the vulpas'
blood. "I never mind a liar, so long as he does not take
himself too seriously."

"The vulpas has stopped thrashing."

"Care to help me skin it?"

"Emphatically not! Exposure to fresh blood causes me a terrible rash."

"Help me anyway, whelp." She cuffed him again as she moved, adding a blotch of the sticky brown salve to the streak of blood.

Quin made a great show of pain as he rose to follow her. "I never skinned anything before. I told you that I failed my course in Practicality."

"Then it is time you had some lessons in the subject!"

"You are a terrible nag, Laurett."

"Set to work, lordling. Just watch me, and do as I say."

* * *

The smooth slopes of Lambde farms, brown and violet-blue with scattered snow in shadow, rose to a tree-spiked crest. The trees wore no gentling leaves, but they brushed the sky. The light of a last, persistent ray of sun turned the crest to gold; the sun faded, and the shadows deepened.

Quin paused in currying his mare's dappled flank, and he watched the gilded transformation of afternoon into dusk. He smiled appreciatively and forgot his task, until his mare nuzzled him curiously. "Yes, Pala," he told the mare gently, "I know you are waiting for me to finish. Be patient with me, please. I am very fond of sunsets."

"You are also fond of any excuse to stop working," chided Laurett, but she paused in her own tasks and came to stand beside Quin. "What do you see that so enthralls you, lordling?"

"The sky, the trees, the hills! The first stars of evening are emerging above us, and the colors of day display all their brightest hues, as if to tell the night, 'See my fine attire and envy me!' Evening is exciting, Laurett! Do you not see it so?"

"Only since I saved an excessively carefree young lordling from a thief's knife," answered Laurett and caught herself, seemingly embarrassed by her own words, though Quin could not see why she should suddenly appear so bothered and nervous. She continued briskly, "I see two horses in need of care, and I smell the wood smoke of a hearth by which I should like to claim a place before the best tables are filled."

"Pragmatist," laughed Quin, "Master Daroh will see to our welcome. He owes you a large debt of gratitude."

"And a large fee."

"How will you spend it?"

"Stop asking so many impertinent questions."

"Are you angry with me, Laurett?" asked Quin, his expression genuinely concerned. "I am always saying or doing the wrong thing and annoying people without ever knowing how. . . . You would tell me if I had angered you?"

"I would cut off your ears, whelp."

"They *are* too big," acknowledged Quin soberly.

"Finish tending your horse, young fool."

CHAPTER 9

Seriin year 9055

Spring's new thaw began slowly with the shy heads of crocuses testing the uncertain sunshine; sluggish, frozen rivulets hastened into heady streams. Life greeted life, and a woman who had chosen a hard, solitary existence found herself wistful over the life she had rejected. A misty, sorry envy grew in her, and she shook herself in dismay. She had foresworn the gentle ways, as much from necessity as from choice. As a girl she had weighed the joys and griefs of those she saw and those she knew, and she had selected her course, as certain of her decision as she was certain that no man existed who could ever cause her to reconsider.

His Lady Fortune has made me prosperous in these past three months, mused Laurett. *Despite his penchant for trouble, he has a trader's wit for negotiating, and he could charm the very devil if he tried.*

Laurett muttered aloud, "He is only a boy, and he is a helpless fool as well." She studied herself critically in the wavy, copper mirror: too blunt, too blockish, too worn, too old. "Much too old," she informed herself sternly. "Enjoy his company, and be glad he has given you friendship. You are a silly woman."

"Laurett!" shouted the subject of her musings. She rose and strode to the open window, leaned out, and shaded her eyes to search for Quin. He saw her and waved excitedly. She gestured an acknowledgment and watched with amusement as he clapped his hands and raced down the street to collect the horses.

Laurett shrugged into her chain mail. She checked her weapons carefully. The people of Nersough had offered a great reward to anyone who could free them of this man, Oolai, who tyrannized them and had already slain five challengers. *The reward will be enough to buy that little house and live your final days in ease,* Laurett told herself, but the thought aggravated her weariness. *Why did I agree to fight Oolai today? I should have chosen my own time. I should not have let Quin persuade me.*

Quin seemed to consider the contest an entertainment; Quin thought her unassailable. *He does not know how much I fear. He does not know that it is my own weakness which assaults me. He actually believes all that nonsensical praise of me that he spouts to all who listen.*

"Ridiculous boy," murmured Laurett, but she let herself imagine feelings that some lovely, nebulous lady of his age, rank, and wealth might stir in him some day. Laurett looked once more at her own reflection, dauntingly warlike, and she grimaced.

Walking toward the stables, Laurett felt the eyes of Nersough watching her, though doors remained closed and no individual citizen emerged to encourage Oolai's latest challenger. By local tradition, formal challenges could be witnessed only by a single, designated aide for each of the two principals; the custom had arisen to avert clan-feuds, such as had nearly decimated the district before the system of individual challenge had been instituted.

Fully aware of Nersough's customs, the blatant dearth of daylight support still depressed Laurett, for she knew its truest significance. Despite enthused toasts in evening's safe, shadowy halls, Nersough expected Laurett to fail.

Laurett noted wryly that Quin had readied the horses without aid from even a stable boy. The slight had not impaired Quin's good spirits; he babbled about the previous night's supper of game hen and sweet pudding, a feast which Laurett had scarcely tasted. Laurett mounted her horse in silence and allowed Quin to maintain his joyous monologue as they rode to the challenge green.

Oolai, a huge, arrogant man, waited alone, and he

made his impatience clear. *Oolai feels very certain of success,* mused Laurett, assessing the dark, dour man who awaited her on the challenge green; *he brings no second.* Laurett offered the reins of her horse to Quin, whose excitement had begun to infect her. *Careful,* she reminded herself: *do not let the boy's unrealistic perspective cause you to imitate his incaution.*

Still, Quin's confidence had affected her, and she forgot the heavy fatigue of the morning as she began the battle. Her sword felt light in her hands, and she swung it with a sense of strength akin to euphoria. She did not like to kill or maim, but the fight, the tests and challenges, thrilled her, for she knew the magnitude of her triumph in merely surviving. She knew the odds against her better than anyone, despite her unyielding determination and her years of incessant, painful work. After the first clash, she knew that the swarthy, brutish Oolai could not match her skill, but his strength and reach compensated for his other lacks and fed her doubts.

The sharp, contracting pain in her belly caused her to misstep, and Oolai's sword struck her leg. She felt the cut remotely, for the agony of her own body's making shot through her nerves, as she struggled to retain her balance. *Not now,* she thought dully, *not here.* She knew she could not complete this bout, and she could expect no mercy. She forced her sharp warning through her strained grimace: "Quin, go back to the village—quickly." *Why did I allow him to come? I must survive until Quin can escape, or Oolai will kill him also.*

"No!" cried Quin, and she could hear his astonishment at her sudden weakness.

Oolai knows no better than to expect my failure: *fool,* she thought, *he does not even realize how close he came to defeat. If I had been wise enough to choose another time, he might have lost—but I have long anticipated this moment. If not Oolai, another would have beaten me eventually; the pain has become too common of late.* Oolai cut her hand, and her sword dropped to the ground. She observed with detached surprise that Oolai, instead of dealing her the finishing stroke, jerked as if struck himself, and it was he who fell first.

Laurett felt a warmth enter and soothe her, as two hands touched the crown of her head. The debilitating pain retreated to the level that she had learned to accept as inevitable. For several blissful moments, she allowed herself to enjoy the warmth and the ease without question or wonder.

"Release me, accursed wizard!" demanded Oolai. "It was not your challenge I accepted but the challenge of this vile-tempered woman."

"The woman is a friend of mine," replied Quin in a quietly reasonable voice, "and it was you who chose to bring no second. The advantage of combat without witnesses is that rules become so flexible."

"I concede!" retorted Oolai, groveling now, though he had sneered at his challenger and her second. "By your own Ceallagh's laws, you may not harm me."

"Who will report me, when you are dead? I may do anything I like if I am provoked sufficiently, and I must tell you, Master Oolai, that your reputation for viciousness does not weigh in your favor."

"Quin," croaked Laurett, confused and benumbed, "there is no honor in killing an opponent who has conceded." She opened her eyes to look at Quin, who wore a vapid, slightly silly expression that made her wonder how Oolai could sound so fearful of the boy, though a cannier part of her whispered, *You know why.*

"If he agrees to behave himself and leave the district," said Quin with a carelessness that threatened more effectively than a direct attack, "I may spare him."

Oolai's face contorted with pain, and he cried loudly, "I so agree! I vow never to approach these lands again."

"Yes," mused Quin, his gray eyes thoughtful, "I believe you are enough of a coward to mean what you say." Quin shrugged, and his hands cradled Laurett's head gently. He smiled at her, as innocently as ever, but the lash of his anger at Oolai filled his voice with warning: "You are free, Master Oolai. Go, before I change my mind and set your skin afire."

Oolai hesitated only an instant, clumsily testing his ability to move without pain. The huge warrior scrambled to his feet, clambered fumblingly onto his horse, and departed the glade in haste. The proud, cruel Oolai, who had intimidated the people of Nersough's valley for many months, fled from a Power that his sword could not hope to vanquish.

"Quin, the helpless schoolboy," grumbled Laurett, feeling dizzy from the aftermath of the spasms and more than a little abashed by the sudden reversal of her defender's role with Quin. The shadows of breeze-tossed leaves mottled the sky imperfectly, and she blinked at a passing glimpse of sun. "I knew you had more than mortal's luck in you," she told him. "I ought to have guessed the reason."

"You are very ill, Laurett," said Quin seriously.

"Tell me news!"

"I can ease the pain, but I cannot cure you."

"No one can cure me, lordling. Why did you never tell me that you were a wizard?"

"I have never felt much like a wizard. Why did you conceal your illness from me? You might have collapsed while tackling a vulpas, and where would that have left me?"

"It would have left you in a better position than I knew. Are you ashamed of your Power, Quin?"

"No," replied Quin slowly. "It is part of me."

"As my illness is part of what I am . . . but it is not the whole. If I tell the world, 'I am dying of a relentless thing that grows inside me,' then the world equates me with my illness, and I become nothing else. Do you understand?"

"Yes. I suppose I hide my Power for similar reasons. I do not want to be regarded as only an adjunct of my Power."

"I suspected as much."

"Are you well enough to ride now?"

"Yes. You are better than the medics," remarked Laurett wryly. "I never thought of asking a wizard for healing."

"It is a limited aspect of Power." Soberly, Quin added, "We are more effective as agents of destruction."

How could I have failed to recognize the Power in him? wondered Laurett, for at that moment Quin seemed the very personification of his eerie, noble legacy from Serii's Sorcerer Kings. Laurett fancied that she could see the deadly fire burning deep within his eyes. She murmured, "Nersough will give you much gratitude, young lord of Hamley."

"Laurett, you are my best friend!" answered Quin with

alarm. "You would not betray me, would you? I shall not tell anyone *your* secret!"

Laurett smiled wanly. "My secret cannot be kept much longer, but I shall honor yours, if that is your wish, though I dislike taking credit for a victory I did not earn."

She enjoyed Quin's clumsy, solicitous attempt to help her mount her horse. She enjoyed his touch and regretted the thickness of the chain mail she wore, but she chaffed him and chided him for treating her like an invalid. He grinned at her and told her that he had been trained to respect his elders.

Entering Nersough, accolades poured upon her, the warrior heroine who had saved Nersough from its nemesis. Laurett, draped in flower garlands, rode stiffly through the cheers. She dismounted before the house allocated for her use, and she shook the hands of many who sought her luck.

She smiled at all who praised her, and she did not shrink from any of them, though she considered wryly how much more she would have appreciated the praise before the challenge. She moved very slowly through the throng, and it was Quin who scattered her grateful admirers with a grin and a joke and a laugh to hold the crowd's good humor.

"Quin," whispered Laurett tightly, "help me inside." The effort of appearing to walk by her own strength made her face flush, and runnels of perspiration chilled her. When Quin closed the door, and they were alone, she sagged against him, and she collapsed before they reached the stairs.

"Oolai struck your leg again with that last blow," said Quin.

Laurett nodded, as if Quin had framed a question. "He had a strong undercut."

"It was good of you to allow him the gratification of a final hit."

"Yes, it was generous of me," replied Laurett with a grimace.

"Can you stand?"

"No."

"Shall I bring that awful hulk of a yard hand to carry you?"

"You make the prospect sound so appealing."

"You know better than to trust me to carry you."

"Let me rest here a few minutes, impatient lordling."

For a long moment, Quin remained abnormally silent and pensive. *He idealized me,* concluded Laurett grimly, *and I have disappointed him. He does not know how to react.*

When Quin spoke, the words emerged reluctantly, "You do not expect to recover from this day, do you?"

You must give him the truth, Laurett informed herself sternly, *and abandon your ridiculous fantasies. You are old, ill, and pursued by death.* With coldly deliberate harshness, Laurett replied, "My lungs ache; my heart races; and sword wounds scarcely hurt me more than the constant pain within every part of me. I have denied this inner agony for over a year, knowing that eventually it would overwhelm me and cause me to slip in battle. You would have been more merciful to let me die quickly, lordling."

"I think I can help you a little," offered Quin hesitantly.

"But you cannot make me sound again," muttered Laurett, staring at a trickle of blood that dripped into her boot. "Listen to the cheers and celebrations. Hail the conquering cripple." Quin, sitting beside her at the foot of the stairs, frowned a little in rare concentration, as he began to wield such limited healing energies as his Power understood.

CHAPTER 10

Seriin Year 9055

"The day is beautiful, Laurett! We can ride to Segeen along the cliff route, and you can show me the eaglets' nests."

Quin remains so buoyantly oblivious to my weakness, thought Laurett. *For him, I wish that I could continue to pretend that the weakness will pass; I have lost the will to hope for myself.* "Go without me, Quin," she told him tiredly, feeling a glimmer of old pride that she could muster the strength to deny him.

"Without you? Have you found a better companion? I admit that I am an intolerable nuisance with few (if any) redeeming qualities, but I am otherwise quite acceptable company."

Look at me, Quin: ghostly pale and unable to heal from a simple flesh wound. Listen to me, and hear the truth for once. Quin's impervious cheerfulness became suddenly intolerable to her. "There are times for meetings and times for partings, and the wise accept both graciously."

Quin's smile disappeared in an instant. "Are you telling me again that I ask too many questions?"

"Yes."

Quin twisted his expression like a puzzled simpleton. "Are you tired of me, Laurett?"

"Stop pretending to be a fool," snapped Laurett. "Go, before I behead you."

Quin raised his wide gray eyes toward the plastered ceiling of the tiny Nersough house, which Laurett had purchased with her reward. He began to whistle a nursery tune that spoke of a disgruntled bear. Sincerely angry with him for compounding her despair, Laurett reached for her boot-knife to threaten some sense into him.

She clenched her fingers around the haft, drew it from the sheath, and dropped it, for her hand could not support its weight. Quin's gray gaze followed the knife to the floor. "And that," he murmured softly, "is why you want me to leave you here." His expression became hard. "If you want me to quit pretending to be a fool, then stop behaving like a fool yourself. You can no longer wield a knife reliably, let alone a sword. The parting you need to acknowledge is from your career as a warrior. You need to accept your limitations, develop new skills, and stop pitying yourself."

"I do not need counsel from you, lordling-without-purpose, nor do I want you as my nursemaid. I shall stop pitying myself when you allow me the dignity to rule my own life again."

"I am your friend, Laurett," argued Quin, the hardness fading into a hurt, bewildered frown.

"Then behave as such, and leave me here. We enjoyed a few months of journeying together, but that time is ended. Must I say it? I shall not recover; I shall grow weaker and more useless. I cannot bear to watch you linger, as if I might heal from a broken bone. You only serve to remind me of what I have lost."

"Blast," muttered Quin, and he dashed out of the cottage. Laurett watched him, as he bounded into the road as hurriedly as if a vulpas were chasing him. She closed the door, knowing that she ought not to feel so disappointed that he had conceded to her so easily.

* * *

Quin stared into the pond, and he tried to imitate the puckered expression of the frogfish that nibbled insect larvae from the water's surface. He sighed and rolled back from the water's edge. "Everything seems dull," he informed the clouds. "Why must all the best times end? I had a wonderful life in Hamley, until they banished me to Ixaxis. I was just beginning to have a wonderful life again, traveling from adventure to adventure, defended by my own lady champion."

Quin finished the last of the hard rolls that he had brought from Nersough; he threw the crumbs to the frog-fish, who consumed them blindly. "It is so unfair!" said Quin, kicking a stone into the pond.

His Power's wall engulfed him with suffocating thoroughness, but he recognized his self-deception with mild disgust. He knew that he deserved no pity for himself, and he knew that only Power shielded him from the pain of losing someone who mattered to him, as he had lost too dearly in the past. Quin sat upright, too restless to hold any one position for long. "I wish Luki were here. She would understand. She has watched lots of friends die."

With a faint frown, he visualized the Widowshear. Instead of cringing from it, as in his dreams, he reached his Power toward the sense of *otherness* within it. He held it in his mind, until it glowed with clear, blue fire, and he did not release it. He concentrated on the image of the Widowshear and summoned Luki's face into his mind.

If you insist on befriending mortals, boy, replied Luki's reedy voice inside his head, *you must learn to accept death as a frequent companion. You may dislike your fellow wizards for their arrogance, but they share your time-scale.*

"I hate Power!" shouted Quin to the woodland. A dozen birds erupted from the brush in a chirping panic.

Do you hate yourself?

"Of course not," Quin muttered. He dipped his hand beneath the pond's brackish surface, and the frogfish darted into a tangle of algae and water-weeds. Quin let the cold water trickle through his fingers. "I just hate knowing how much I can do and how little I can help. I like Laurett; we have fun together. I do not want her to die."

Not even the Infortiare cheats death, boy.

"Lord Evaric not only befriended a mortal, he married her."

And he will grieve when she dies.

Absently, Quin dried his hand on his trousers, leaving a green stain of algae. "I did enjoy the past few months. I suppose I should be glad that I knew Laurett at all."

You have given her good memories of laughter and of joy.

"She ordered me to leave."

For your sake, not for hers.

"I never thought of that," answered Quin with wonder. He clung to the truth Luki had brought into light. He held Laurett's caring like a flame against his own Power's wishes, and he drove the truth against the wall within him.

She loves you, idiot boy, though lords know why. You chose to befriend her, and you cannot abandon her now. You must return to her.

"You think I can help her?"

Yes, boy, for a little while.

"Luki!"

Yes?

"I am glad that I shall not lose you."

Power is not all bad, child.

* * *

Laurett did not see Quin for a week, but she knew when he returned that she had prayed to meet him again. She did not try to rise when Quin came to the door; she let him open it uninvited. Part of her wanted him to leave before she could see him and shame herself by begging him never to leave her again.

He entered the room where she rested in the dim light of a flickering lamp. She did not speak to him, but she became uncomfortable when he joined her in silence equal to her own. She had shared many quiet hours with Quin, but this night lay too heavy with words unspoken between them. At last, she could abide the hurt no longer. "Why are you still here, Quin?"

"You are my friend."

"I have tended myself for more years than you have lived. Go back to Hamley, where you belong."

"I plan to return to Hamley. I seem to have traveled enough, suddenly. I want you to come with me, Laurett."

"To live off a lordling's charity? I trusted you knew me better than to make so cruel an offer."

"I want you to come as my wife, Laurett. I have given the matter a lot more consideration than I am accustomed to giving anything, and if I ponder it any more, I shall probably collapse from the strain."

It is one of his absurd jokes, thought Laurett, *cruel only because of the way I feel toward him, but he cannot know that I have dared imagine a moment like this.* She tried to appreciate the ironic humor of a handsome young lord/wizard flirting with a dying warrior-woman twice his age. "This is a poor jest, Quin." Her throat had tightened with the tears she refused to shed.

Quin came to her and knelt beside her chair. He took her hand thoughtfully, holding it with just enough gentleness to spare her pain, just enough firmness to let her feel his warmth. "I have always sounded less convincing when I tell the truth than when I fabricate the most outrageous of lies. I have no talent for sounding sincere about serious subjects, but I am serious, Laurett: I do want to marry you."

"Why, silly lordling?" murmured Laurett stiffly, unable to believe.

"I enjoy your company. You understand my ideas of humor." He shrugged one shoulder, looking more self-conscious than Laurett had ever seen him. "Perhaps I flatter myself that you like me as I am, with all my quirks and peculiar ideas. I think we could have fun together, Laurett." He grinned sheepishly. "I think you would like Hamley. It is a great, noisy place, full of bickering and laughter. There is very little privacy, because there are so many of us, but we all seem to get along tolerably well despite the congestion. Hamley is probably the happiest noble House in Serii, which may explain why we are so much more prolific than our more exalted cousins."

"I am ill, and I am old. I could not give you heirs, Quin." She ridiculed herself for the quickening of her voice and heart, for the faint, impending suspicion that his offer was sincere.

"I would rather have you for company than all the heirs in the Alliance. Anyway, I have nothing to bequeath as a legacy to anyone except a few debts and some rancid jokes that no child ought to hear."

"You have gone mad."

"Sanity is tedious."

"You are rash, reckless, and foolish. You are much

too young to bind yourself to a wreck of a woman, who never did have much to offer to a man."

"I am an Immortal Wizard!" retorted Quin. "I can afford a few mistakes."

"Idiot lordling," replied Laurett, but she loved him, and though she had lost all that she had thought she valued, she had never felt more glad.

* * *

The fine porcelain and crystal wares found in Serii's other major Houses had long ago suffered catastrophic demises in Hamley, and childish scrawls and carvings enhanced the fine craftsmanship of ancient furnishings. Hamley manor wore little air of glory or of pride, and it was a noisy and rambunctious place that few Seriin nobles cared to visit for more than a hand's span of days. To live in peace in Hamley, went the saying among the nobility, one must be Hamley-born or deaf and blind and locked in a cotton cocoon. No other noble House of Serii could have welcomed a baseborn warrior-woman as a daughter and made her feel at home.

They were blue-white, summery days of laughter and carefree, idle joys. All that Laurett could wish, Quin anticipated and provided to entertain and delight her. Hamley lacked nothing; *somewhere in the manor recesses,* Laurett concluded, *lie at least ten of everything imaginable.*

Quin himself seemed always on the verge of laughter— for no particular reason at all. Few persons spent time with him without smiling a little more than usual. Whether his infectious joy was sincere or merely a clever projection of his Power, Laurett did not know and only rarely, in her most cynical moments, questioned.

Laurett noted occasionally that she accomplished little in her unlikely role as a lady of Hamley, but she produced no less than the lords and ladies who were idly weak by choice. The days filled her with a rare contentment, despite her weakness. She felt certain that Quin had coaxed his vast family into welcoming her, for she did not credit herself with a talent for winning friends; she was too blunt and honest. Still, the family did accept

her, and she learned that such a family could make her
forgive even her own soured past.

She loved Quin, and she watched him closely for any
sign of regret, but he showed her only his same, carefree,
quirk-filled humor. He did disappear at times for a
month or more on end, but Laurett could not blame him
for his occasional lapses of devotion.

Occasionally, a medic would visit, and Laurett would
chide Quin for pretending that the medic had arrived by
chance. Quin only grinned at her accusations. An Ixaxin
came once; the woman unsettled Laurett with lengthy
stares. Quin became unwontedly quiet after the wizardess' departure. The medics did not visit again.

Laurett rallied at first after their marriage, and she
hoped briefly, but the deterioration recommenced. She
knew that Quin's innumerable cousins whispered about
her, wondering how much longer she could live. She horrified several of the gossipy ladies with a caustic suggestion that they place formal wagers on her date of death,
but most of the younger Hamley lords applauded her
macabre humor and supported her bleak joke. Laurett
kept the slips of written wagers in a gold and ivory casket
in her room, and she derived an obscure comfort from
their presence. Quin neither joined in the wagers nor
condemned them.

* * *

"Why must you move these roses?" grumbled Quin,
pausing to lean on the shovel and wipe his brow with his
sleeve. "They looked perfectly beautiful on the other side
of the yard."

Luki clucked at him incoherently, but her stern gesture
toward the shovel conveyed her intent. "Lazy," she muttered, and she continued to snip branchlets from her
shrubs.

Quin returned to his digging, but he stopped again
after only a few minutes. "She is dying, Luki," said Quin
suddenly. "I came all the way to Ixaxis to see if anyone
could help, though the wizardess who visited Hamley for
the testing and gathering last season told me that nothing
could be done."

Luki laid her basket and gardening shears on one of
the garden's largest stones. She came to stand beside

Quin, who gazed at the mound of soil he had displaced.
"You knew," said Luki simply.

"I suppose I did."

"Your warrior-woman might not have died any more
quickly had you left her in the fringe-lands, but she
would have suffered greatly, as an invalid without family,
awaiting death alone. You have made her happy."

"I have been happy. I have Hamley again, and I have
Laurett to enjoy it with me. She laughs at me and listens
to me, and she has endless, wonderful stories of the
places she has seen and the battles she has fought. She
is never really angry with me at all, even when I say and
do the sorts of stupid things that have always annoyed
everyone else."

"You have wasted time you could have spent with her
by coming to Ixaxis now."

"She has become very sick. Most of the time, she
hardly seems to know me." Quin kicked at the mound
of dirt. "I thought Mistress Amila would know how to
help."

"Hmh. You lie even to yourself now, boy, and do not
know it. You came here to avoid the truth. You have
never accepted anything bad that happened to you,
because you have too much Power and too little sense.
You pretend you cared nothing about your parents,
though their deaths have eaten a terrible hole inside of
you. You married a dying woman, thinking yourself
brave and kind, but you were only too foolish to understand that she would truly die and that you—spoiled little
Hamley lord—would actually be hurt."

"You told me to help her!"

"Yes, I told you to help her—not marry her. You committed an extra measure of your silly heart with your
quixotic gesture, and you will feel that much more pain."

"I know that I am a fool," acknowledged Quin sadly.

"Good," snapped Luki. She pushed the shovel, forcing
Quin to jump in order to retain his balance. "Finish the
planting," she ordered. "You need to learn to complete
the jobs you start."

Quin frowned, closing his eyes for a long moment. "I
need to return to Hamley. Is that what you mean?"

Luki returned to her basket and began to rearrange
the cuttings; she threw several twigs and leaves to the

ground. "The ferry will leave after luncheon. You have plenty of time to replant my roses, as you promised, if you stop dawdling and pick up all that mess." She pointed at the cuttings she had just scattered.

"Luki, are you mad at me?"

"Quin, child," she muttered, "your lack of sense could frustrate anyone." She hobbled into her house.

"Anyone except Laurett," sighed Quin. He drove the shovel deep into the soil.

* * *

"Good morning, Laurett," remarked Quin, as if he had never left Hamley, as if he could not see the dreadful deterioration that had finally confined Laurett to the canopied bed, as if he greeted a cousin and not a wife who should have shared his own room. He began to shift the heavy rose curtains, but he reclosed them when Laurett winced at the brightness of direct sunlight.

"Did you return last night?" asked Laurett, torn between gladness to have him near her and regret that he should see her so weakened and ravaged.

"Yes," responded Quin with an apologetic smile. "I am sorry I was gone so long."

"Dear Quin," murmured Laurett, "do you think I would condemn you? You took an ailing, broken warrior as a wife, and you have given her more joy than she could ever have dreamed possible." Laurett's gaze drifted into emptiness, and Quin's expression tightened, but he resumed his grin when her keen attention returned.

"I am glad," he said brightly, as if she had not left him at all.

Laurett frowned for an instant, sensing that she had lost continuity of time. Quin made foolish faces at her, until she laughed. "I love you more now than on the day we wed," she said shyly, as if she were a girl and not a broken, middle-aged woman with too many deaths to her credit, "and I have loved you since we met with an ardor that I never knew lay within me."

"I shall blush," threatened Quin.

"Young idiot." Laurett faded again and rallied more slowly. Her face remained slack, even as she murmured, "It is well for us both that you do not love me as passionately as I have loved you. When you find your own love,

I pray that she will treasure your joy of life, your goodness (despite yourself), and every dear, ridiculous quirk of your being. Tell her of me, if you wish, but tell her that you wed me out of kindness."

"I shall say nothing of the sort to anyone. I wed you for love, Laurett," said Quin roughly. "How shall I prove it to you now, if you have not believed it in all our time together?"

Laurett smiled and stretched a feeble hand toward Quin. Quin came to her bedside and met her grasp. "Dear, silly Quin, I have never doubted that you believe yourself in love with me, but you are very young, for all your hidden skills and cleverness."

"Yes, Mother," replied Quin with a lopsided grin.

Laurett gestured abortively as if to slap him in good humor, but the gesture was limp, and she bit her lip in recollection of past days. "Your Uncle Teor may win the wager after all. Too bad. I hoped that young Cael would gain the prize." Quin frowned and turned his eyes to the floor. "Make me a promise, Quin," said Laurett urgently, and she did not pause, for she feared suddenly that her remaining moments would be too short. "Do not waste yourself. You need purpose, Quin, more than you realize. You have a wonderful family and a magnificent home, and you have no responsibility to anything but your own amusement. That could be a paradise for some people. For you, it will become a purgatory." She began to tremble, and Quin's grin faltered. "Promise me, Quin," she gasped.

"Dear Laurett," whispered Quin, looking comically solemn, for his face had so rarely bent to deep sorrow. "I do not understand what you want me to promise."

She spoke softly but fervently, almost angrily. "Do something. Be something. Contribute something. You have so much to give, so many talents. Do not become another idle, useless lordling. You have no right to waste the gifts you have been granted."

"How remarkable you are," murmured Quin in wonder. "I never realized you felt so strongly about my indolence."

"You have not been indolent, but rather you have been energetic without focus, and I have been selfish, keeping you for myself alone. I knew that I did wrong, but I pay my price now."

"Now you talk nonsense, which is my prerogative."

"Promise me, Quin."

"I promise." Laurett relaxed into a smile of peace. "I hope you know what you are foisting upon the world," commented Quin with an uneven fragment of laughter. For an instant, Laurett saw the face of the scatterbrained fool become a reflection of knowing sorrow, wry wisdom and Power, but the illusion faded; or the illusion returned. "Has Millard shown you the clock he found in Pithlii?" asked Quin cheerfully. "A parade of wooden animals marches across the front of it every hour, and the chimes imitate the cries of forest birds. The carvings cannot compete with our local toymaker's work, but the mechanical design is marvelous."

"I should like to see it," murmured Laurett, and she gazed adoringly at her very young husband, but the effort of focusing on him became too hard, and she closed her eyes at last.

Quin sat at Laurett's side, silently tracing the memories of her hand's old, softened calluses, until a chambermaid came with luncheon. The maid gasped and whispered a hasty prayer. "I never realized until now," remarked Quin to the cooling husk of a once-strong woman, "how lonely I shall feel without you."

* * *

Howald will never believe it, thought Alvedre, somewhat relishing the opportunity to astonish the humorless wizard who taught history to Ixaxin novices. *I am not sure I believe it,* she added to herself wryly.

Alvedre located Howald in one of the scholars' small study cells. She let her Power warn him of her arrival. Howald's Power rebuffed her initially, for interruptions of his privacy annoyed him, but he yielded to her insistence and allowed her to enter the room.

Since the study cell contained only one chair, Alvedre perched on the sill of the window that overlooked a foggy expanse of restless ocean. "I have an item of news for you, Howald. Lord Quinzaine dur Hamley has returned to Ixaxis."

"Lords, I thought we were rid of him. I heard that he

spent a day here a few months ago. I hope he does not intend to make a habit of visiting." Howald shook his head. "He probably discovered someone whom he neglected to torment with one of his idiotic pranks."

"I doubt such a one exists, except among the novices who have arrived since he departed. Quin was very thorough in his mischief."

"I wish he had been as thorough in his studies," muttered Howald. "I thank you for the warning. I shall renew my practice of checking my bed for reptilian life forms."

"Do not forget to test the sugar and salt before you use them."

"I shall speak to the cooks. If you are so unfortunate as to encounter Quin personally, please encourage him to make his visit a short one. Amila's current term as headmistress is nearly ended, and the Infortiare has named me as next headmaster."

"Howald, you had better brace yourself," said Alvedre with a trace of mischief in her blue eyes. "Quin has requested scholar's training. He is fully qualified, as you know, and Amila continues to believe that we failed to mold him properly."

Howald's horrified expression fulfilled all of Alvedre's expectations. "Lords, I shall have to talk to Amila before she commits us permanently. The boy has Power, but he has no sense of responsibility."

"He may surprise you with his seriousness."

"The ocean may more likely swallow me in my bed!"

Alvedre smiled faintly. "You are a stubborn man, Howald, remembering a mischievous boy of eleven whose Power developed much faster than his wisdom. Quin has grown since he left us, and I am glad that he has returned—not solely for the pleasure of seeing my prediction proven true. I have actually missed him. I have missed laughing at him and at his antics. Even Ixaxis needs a little humor on occasion."

"Is the concept of moderation familiar to you?" asked Howald with caustic disdain.

"I have heard of it," answered Alvedre dryly.

"Then I hope you can teach it to Quin," snapped Howald. He grumbled, rubbing his ruddy hair, "My head is beginning to ache already."

CHAPTER 11

Network Year 2304

"I do not want your Network, Caragen. I have as much of it as I desire." Marrach spoke with perfect coldness, the flawless dearth of emotion of a marginally human product of Gandry, enhanced by Network's most sophisticated cybernetic methods. *"I have discovered an adequate insurance policy, at last, against your inevitable decision to sacrifice me. I have found a better master."*

"I own you, Marrach," shouted Caragen in fury. *"You are a tool and not a man."*

"Mirlai have Chosen me. Adraki obey me. You cannot touch me, Caragen."

Network's Council Governor tossed in his sleep, grunting in his anger. Network adjusted the bed to support his change of position, but Caragen remained restless. His dream shifted. The many faces that Marrach had worn across the years raced before him, but the images became another man. "Rolf," muttered Caragen, recognizing the new dream slowly.

"Where is Marrach?" demanded the voice of the interrogator, and the pain intensified at even the longing to resist.

You must not tell them, declared the angry spirit inside Caragen. *But you will tell them,* answered his reasoning self; *it is axiomatic in this treacherous game we play that any captive who cannot die will tell his captor any secret. Only fablers manufacture the heroes who survive in stoic silence.*

"Where is Marrach?" repeated Rolf inescapably. His stupidly smiling face cracked and peeled from a fanged, alien skull.

The prisoner grunted through broken flesh and shattered teeth: "He has escaped me."

"You were careless." Another blow made the prisoner's mind and body shudder in agony.

"I could not anticipate the Mirlai!" protested the anguished man. "They have remade him to their own design."

"You shirk your blame. The Adraki's powerful, mythical race of symbionts does not exist," spat the interrogator in contempt, and his hands became Adraki claws. "You created Rabhadur Marrach from Gandry's refuse. From his artificial arm and face to the implanted Network link within his head, he is your own merciless creation: a deadly asset to any power that owns him. You gave him too much. You trusted him too far. The error is yours."

"He does not leave his primitive Siatha," argued the prisoner weakly. "The Mirlai have neutralized his capabilities."

"He lives and is a major threat. You have failed. Your creation will destroy you."

"No!" screamed the prisoner in fury, and he broke the bonds that held him.

Caragen awoke, angry at his dream. Thirst seared his throat and kept him silent. He waved his hand across his bedside table to command light and a tumbler of water. He grabbed the chased silver tumbler from the ornate housing that disguised a basic supply cube. He gulped the water, splashing the silken red bedsheets.

The moisture did not appease his temper. "Network," he snapped, "provide me with a harmless remedy for nightmares."

"Yes, sir," answered a quiet voice, Network's soothing nighttime mode.

Caragen fumbled for the capsule in the supply cube. His fingers closed over the capsule's slick warmth. Instead of transferring the medication to his mouth, he held it tensely in his clenched fist. "Network, where is Marrach?"

"The planet Siatha."

Caragen muttered, "But where is his ambition?"

"Please clarify your question, sir."

"I want your analysis, Network. If Marrach's 'Siathan Healer' is only another of his many roles, what is he awaiting?"

Network's voice became crisper and louder, as the request for analysis overrode the time-of-day defaults. "Prior analysis confirms that former Council Chancellor Rabhadur Marrach has sufficient power, via his alliances with the Mirlai and Adraki species, to maintain a stand-off situation. He has demonstrated his ability to defend Siatha. His ability to extend his power beyond its current, very limited sphere appears improbable, based on known information; however, prior history of Rabhadur Marrach suggests that hidden resources exist. He could have established himself as a Network Councillor within five standard years by maintaining your favor; hence, he very probably seeks a more direct and complete form of control."

"He seeks my position," concluded Caragen with a grim tightness stretching his fleshy face.

"That is the most probable assessment," agreed Network.

Caragen growled impatiently, "But he continues to wait." Caragen narrowed his eyes, staring sightlessly at the frescoed ceiling. "Network, which of my enemies might conspire with Marrach?"

"All of your active enemies regard Marrach as your tool. They would, therefore, hesitate seriously to entrust their ambitions to him."

"Marrach has always been one of my most coveted tools. His value as an ally would merit a sizable risk."

"Those of your enemies who had sufficiently incautious tendencies for the associated risk are dead. Your elimination of Councillor Massiwell has enhanced the current atmosphere of dread. The recent prevalence of questions regarding the validity of Rabhadur Marrach's human status further diminishes the likelihood of outside elements claiming his alliance."

"Then why does Marrach wait?" demanded Caragen harshly. "What does he know that I have failed to anticipate? What salient questions have I neglected to ask you?"

"I am unable to supply such nonspecific information."

Caragen grunted, and he waved his hand to darken the room, but he lay awake. "Network, what are my most crucial assets, excluding general wealth?"

"Control of the Network computers, Network's exclusive access to topological transfer technology, and a precedent of power established over your many years as Council Governor."

"The third cannot be taken from me. The first asset was more readily available to Marrach in my employ than in his rebellion. The second. . . ." Caragen sat upright in his bed. "Network, how could Marrach compromise the second advantage? Could he have obtained sufficient information from you regarding topological transfer to establish his own technology development project?"

"Very improbable. No single source, including linked Network computers, contains the totality of detailed data. The necessary expertise resides in carefully selected, carefully conditioned and isolated individuals with only enough redundancy to ensure continuity of capability. The magnitude of the required information for topological transfer facilitates the restriction of human expertise to specialized subtopics, because very few humans possess sufficient mental capacity to absorb the diversity of related disciplines adequately."

"One man knew the totality," said Caragen softly, and he realized why his subconscious inspired dreams of interrogations by the unprepossessing agent known as Rolf. "Jonathan Terry knew more about applied topology than any of us, because he was the source of most of the significant achievements in that field."

"Confirmed. Dr. Jonathan Terry's intelligence exceeded human standards by a margin that was measurable only on Calongi scales."

"What is the probability that Jonathan Terry is still alive?"

"Negligible."

"Hypothesize: If Jonathan Terry is still alive, what is the possibility that Rabhadur Marrach knows Dr. Terry's present location?"

"Highly probable."

"Assess the threat against me of this hypothetical case."

"Severe."

Caragen lay back in his bed. "Extrapolate on this hypothesis, Network. I want a full assessment of options and contingencies by morning, and I want increased monitoring of Rabhadur Marrach. I want this threat eradicated." Caragen swallowed the capsule that had begun to soften from the heat of his hand. "And the children," he muttered, but he did not complete the thought. He slept without dreams.

PART 3

The Crossing
**Seriin Year 9059/
Network Year 2305**

CHAPTER 1

Serii

Jon savored the crisp dawn air, as he strode briskly along the path around the pond. He kept his hands inside his pockets, and he wondered why he so rarely wore this delightfully warm and lightweight coat. *Network synthetics are more practical than Seriin homespun,* he informed himself without pursuing the thought further.

He waved at Beth, who had emerged from the cottage and stood smiling on the veranda. Jon paused to pick one of the fragrant pink-and-white blossoms she enjoyed. He rummaged in his pocket for a handkerchief to soak and wrap around the stem, for the flowers wilted quickly without moisture. A small box fell from the square of white linen. Jon dipped the handkerchief in the clear pond and secured the cloth around the pulpy stem, before he retrieved the box.

The box had a metallic lid, attached along one edge to a slick casing, which enclosed an irregular mass of grayish fibers suspended in a viscous liquid. Still kneeling, Jon used his thumbnail to raise the cover of the box. "Communication," announced a sterile voice. "Please state identity key."

"J157b893," answered Jon automatically, for the code had been embedded in his memory nearly since birth.

The box replied, "Key confirmed. Communication to Dr. Jonathan Terry. Originator: Rabhadur Marrach, former Council Chancellor of Network. Text: For twenty standard years, Dr. Terry, I have wondered how you managed your escape, if you managed it yourself, and why (if you survive) you have never tried to regain your son and daughter.

"I spent most of those years asking myself why I let an uncertain instinct abet you; I concealed the single flaw in your perfect escape: a portable transfer monitor that survived your ingenious destruction of the portal mechanisms and supplied me with the information I now use to fulfill an unlikely penitence. My reasons for becoming your accomplice in your exile remain unclear to me, though I am assured (by those who are wiser than I) that an element of mercy existed in me even in those darkest days of my service to Council Governor Caragen. I should like to believe them, but I fear that Caragen would assess my motives of that time less charitably and more clearly: I have an extraordinary instinct for personal survival, and your topological tricks are weapons beyond my ability to counter."

"Pause," commanded Jon sharply. *I should remember Rabhadur Marrach. Network Council Chancellor? Twenty standard years?*

Clutching the box against the forgotten flower, Jon ran to the cottage. His wife came down the stairs to meet him, her expression concerned. "Listen," Jon told her tersely, and he tapped the box again to replay the message he had already heard. He halted it prematurely once more, for Beth had grown pale, and she clung to the railing of the stairs.

She whispered roughly, "Destroy it quickly, Jon, before they find us."

"You do remember Marrach," accused Jon with slow dismay. The name still tantalized Jon's memory with uncertain images and fragmented words.

"Do not play the rest of the recording, Jon," replied Beth tightly. "I cannot bear to hear it."

"Why?"

"I cannot remember." She sat on the stair, and her husband joined her. Jon handed her the flower absently. Beth closed her eyes to inhale the fragrance. "Its sweetness is nearly overwhelming," she murmured, "like the peace of this place."

"A false peace," answered Jon sharply, and Beth winced. "Continue message," said Jon to the Network transceiver, which Rabhadur Marrach had given to him in a very different aspect of reality.

"Message resumed," answered the box with crisp, high tones. It continued in the voice that imperfectly echoed its message's originator, "Those-who-are-wise bid me send this information to you, on the chance that you still survive, for this act of mine is necessary to the healing of old guilts that lie within me. Your son is known as Michael Merel. He is a humanistic architect on Chia-2, where he lives with his wife, Loisa, and young daughter, Marei."

"What have we lost?" moaned Beth with a depth of terrible pain.

The box did not pause: "Your daughter is Katerin Merel, professor of mathematical psychology at Harberg University on Daedalon. She has earned some measure of renown in her field for an algorithm to restore traumatized youths to productivity after severe emotional damage. Considering her profession, your daughter has undoubtedly realized that I conditioned her and her brother in childhood. Unlike yourself, however, neither she nor her brother has ever fully overcome the very thorough conditioning I gave them. They believe implicitly that their parents are dead, and they accepted their loss years ago.

"I assume that you had no choice in abandoning your children to a man you obviously recognized as your enemy. I must advise you that Network still monitors them habitually, so as to detect immediately any suggestion of your survival. If your circumstances should change, move cautiously: The man who underestimates Andrew Caragen does not survive him. Caragen has far more power and authority throughout Network and beyond it than you could even imagine without my 'advantage' of his near-confidence for thirty-eight standard years. You succeeded against him once—but you might easily have failed, if I had not condoned your escape.

"I am no longer in a position to assist you against Network machinations, even if I wished, and Caragen will have become especially watchful now that I have resigned from his employ. I hope you have found the

freedom that you sought." The synthetic voice of the box
grated to a stop. "End text," it recited and became silent.

"After so long, it seems unreal," murmured Beth, and
she wiped tears from her cheeks.

"It has become unreal for us," replied Jon grimly, "but
I find myself very tired suddenly of blissful oblivion." He
rose abruptly and entered the cottage.

Beth twisted the fading flower between her fingers,
tugging Jon's handkerchief free. She cast the flower away
from her furiously, and it fell upon the gravel path, waving its shorn stem limply in the air. Beth shouted at its
splay of battered petals, "You stole my life from me."

"Anger helps nothing," said the soft voice of a golden
woman, a fragile image in shaded layers of blue silk and
subtle lace.

The woman's gowns would delight an anachronist,
observed Beth with a trace of bitterness, *but they seem
more suited to an exquisite mannequin than to a living
woman. She suits this deceptively warm and charming
prison.* "Your lies have caused far more harm than my
futile anger," retorted Beth sharply, and she gathered
her unwieldy rose skirts with impatience, stood, and
turned her back deliberately on her delicate captor/host-
ess. "Why did you force me to remember at all, now
that I have lost too much to recover?"

"I am not your enemy," protested the golden woman
with an expression of deep regret in her wide gray eyes.

Beth did not see the woman's sorrow and did not
believe the woman's words. *I witnessed too much death,*
thought Beth, *and I sacrificed my children to my fear. I
have nothing left but illusion, and even that is lost to me
now.* "You forced me to remember," said Beth stiffly,
"knowing that I could not escape you."

"I have never wished you ill."

Unable to reply, Beth followed Jon into the house.
She located him in the room he favored for his writing
and his studying. He sat at his desk, cursing the awkward
quill that he employed to transcribe Rabh Marrach's
message to archaic parchment.

"What has been done to us, Jon?" asked Beth, her
thin face forlorn and grieving. She touched the gilt and
leather spines of books she had held many times; only
now could she recognize them as strange. "To what

enchanted exile have we come?" she whispered. "Is this world the realm of faerie, bewitching us and deluding us?"

Jon met his wife's eyes with a frown that shared her worry. He sighed, pausing in his writing to rub his hand. "My mind remains very clouded, still struggling with very old, very effective Network conditioning and lords-know-what-else. If I can trust my shaky memories, this world is Network-3, as the Immortals have remolded it."

Beth nodded her head, the weight of fair, coiled hair feeling strange to her, though she realized she had worn it long for many years. "Network did not condition me to forget, Jon. I am remembering too much, too quickly. It is this place that has twisted our minds." With a cynical lilt, she added, "I once hypothesized that the Immortals had a limited ability to alter the electrical signals of the brains of those around them. Even some of the original Immortals had uncanny gifts at influencing the researchers who created them. The Immortals' descendants have obviously refined the technique."

The golden woman, arriving via the open garden door, responded with a trace of insulted pride, "Do not blame your sanctuary for the grief that caused its need. You arrived here ill, exhausted, and uninvited, and you received welcome. I eased the pain you carried with you. The delusions came of your own minds' healing needs." The gray dawn's light framed the woman and made her appear almost ghostly.

Jon murmured, "I must agree with my wife, at least in part. Network conditioning, if it sufficed to overwhelm us for twenty standard years, would not vanish from us both within a matter of moments. By whatever method you have used, you have kept us too docile, meek, and accepting of your 'hospitality' ever to question our presence here—until now. Have we been drugged?"

"You overestimate my skills as an herbalist," replied the woman dryly.

"This is Network-3?"

"This is a royal cottage belonging to Her Majesty, Queen Joli of Serii. It occupies a segment of land in the foothills of the Mountains of Mindar, not far from the Queen's city of Tulea."

"I have read something of the history of Serii," muttered Jon, frowning at elusive memory.

"You requested the books, and I supplied them," answered the woman. "Despite your present opinions, I have never imprisoned you."

"You have watched us," said Beth. The woman inclined her head very slightly, but she did not respond.

Jon tossed the quill to the table, where it lay in sorry accusation, its length tattered from too much restless handling. "Who are you?" asked Jon bluntly.

"You are familiar with the domain known as Ixaxis?"

"It is the domain of the Immortals," replied Jon.

"I am Rhianna, the present liege of Ixaxis. I am the Infortiare."

"Why are we here?" demanded Beth.

Rhianna smiled faintly. "Her Majesty, Queen Joli, graciously allocated this cottage for your use, at my request. I did not know where else to house you during your convalescence."

Jon eyed the golden enigma of a woman suspiciously, admiring her calmly reserved assurance, a sense of quiet certainty that belied the image of a fragile doll. "I saw you at the DI port at the time of closure."

"Yes. I was present."

"Then this is the planet, Network-3," concluded Jon with confidence, "and you are an Immortal heir of the closure."

"Your reasoning seems very sound."

"You equivocate as ably as a Network Councillor," commented Jon acridly. He grimaced at the memory of a dozen distinguished men and women gathered around a broad, sterile table, awaiting Andrew Caragen's decree. *He is still the ruthless caesar*, thought Jon, *dictating life or death. Has it really been twenty years, or is Network still maneuvering my mind into delusion?*

"You speak our language well, Lady Rhianna," observed Beth quietly, and she used the title unintentionally, "or are we speaking yours?"

"The two languages are essentially the same. Mine presumably evolved from your own, and I imagine that the Sorcerer Kings curtailed the changes that might have otherwise occurred during such an extensive evolution."

"We learned your language," countered Jon, testing

the answer, for his battered mind revived slowly. He understood a little more with each instant: He had nearly regained the marginal state that had held him at Marrach's "rescue" from interrogation. "Your books were at first unreadable, and I recall a time when comprehension faded briefly."

Rhianna left her place against the open garden door, and she seemed to become more solidly real in abandoning her halo of sunlight. "Our written language differs from your own, since early Ixaxins encrypted secret lore deliberately, so as to preserve it from the Sorcerer Kings. You mastered the crucial elements of our alphabet within your second year among us, shortly before coming to this cottage. The move disoriented you, for you were still severely injured at the time."

"We remained 'severely injured' for two years?" demanded Beth with a brittle, sorry laugh. Rhianna shrugged gracefully. "But we are healed now," persisted Beth. "How long will we retain our memories of this conversation?"

Rhianna sighed and walked toward the desk. When Jon covered the words on the parchment with a deliberate, defiant gesture, she laughed softly, "What do you expect to conceal from me? I already know that you have received a message from someone of your Network. You would not have received the energy of your message at all, if my husband had not assessed the pattern first and allowed it to reach you."

"You have not answered Beth's question," said Jon, pondering the woman's cryptic meanings.

"Your memories are your own," replied Rhianna. "I have not altered them, and I will not alter them, for I do not defy Ceallagh's laws so flagrantly. I did make some of your long-term memories less accessible to you for a time, because you arrived here with deep mind wounds, such as a sorcerous attack might inflict. I knew no other way to heal you."

Jon met the gray eyes of this delicate, golden woman. *She might have stepped from the pages of a feudal history,* he thought, *but she is no fool.* "You have allowed us to remember solely because of this message," he accused softly. "You may have read it, but you do not understand it or its implications." She *destroyed the transfer portal that sent us here, and Marrach attributed the act to me. We must not antagonize her, for she alone controls the access to this place.*

"You are a perceptive man," remarked Rhianna. "You have sheltered us, it seems, for twenty standard years."

"I cannot recall a fraction of that time," said Beth softly. "Our children are grown, and we do not even know them."

Rhianna turned to Beth, who tried to meet the deep gray eyes defiantly—but found only the image of an old dream of despair and a dead tree that blossomed into vivid life. "I do understand your grief," whispered Rhianna, "and I regret that I cannot restore to you all that you have lost. I can only advise you not to dwell on the past sorrows, but to turn toward your future with hope."

"Hope of what?" asked Beth bitterly.

"The future does not entrust me with its secrets." Rhianna clasped her thin hands together tensely, betraying the first hint of her own disquiet.

"Lady Rhianna, are we free to leave here?" asked Beth.

"You may leave this cottage, of course," replied Rhianna gently, "but I cannot truly free you. I am responsible for the protection of my people and my world from any product of Power."

"Explain," snapped Jon impatiently.

Rhianna raised her fine brows at his sudden, terse demand. "The two of you have come to us as a result of Power, directed by the Taormin, a device of your creation. This makes you the Infortiare's responsibility. I cannot jeopardize my world by allowing you to bring your enemies to us."

"The routing of the message we received this morning," drawled Jon with care, "contains all the information necessary for Network to reconnect this space to the parent universe." He watched closely for her reaction, for he deemed that this was the truth that she had dreaded. "The man who sent the message knows that you exist behind your pseudo-closure. You are jeopardized already—not by us, but by him and those he may serve."

"So," breathed the golden Lady of Ixaxis, "the danger

may be as imminent as I feared. I must consider this information." She seemed to collect herself and became again the coolly courteous hostess. "You are understandably distressed by your sudden reemergence into a painful reality. I shall return later, and we shall speak at length." She walked toward the garden door and vanished just before reaching it.

Beth smiled wanly at Jon's quick intake of breath; she knew how much he disliked phenomena that he could not explain to his own satisfaction. "It is no more magical than your topological manipulations," said Beth, sighing wistfully for a life that she had lost.

Jon regarded his wife with a peculiar intensity. "Your point may be exceptionally apt."

"Is it? I cannot think that clearly. We have aged, Jon, without Network rejuvenation techniques to preserve us. I feel very old and tired."

"You would not have renewed your innoculations yet, if we had spent the last years in Network," argued Jon with a trace of impatience. "Our hostess is correct: We must focus on our future and not let the past defeat us."

"Do you trust her?" asked Beth with true curiosity.

Jon smiled faintly at his wife, and he shrugged. "We can doubt our hostess and doubt each other. We can doubt everything we now believe, because it contradicts everything we believed an hour ago, but at some point we must trust our own judgment. We are here among the Immortals of Network-3. I am not sure how or why, but I think our Council Governor and his agent laid a plan that ran afoul of our clever hostess."

Pensively, Beth considered her husband's statement. "You closed Network-3 to preserve Network from the threat of the Immortals, but you only postponed the inevitable contest."

"I did change the character of the combatants. Our hostess is a rational, intelligent being."

"Who lacks the most minimal understanding of Network science."

"That does seem clear from all that we have experienced in our long reverie," acknowledged Jon with a frown. "But perhaps we differ only in terminology."

Beth waved her arm at the wall of books. "Perhaps the altering of long-term memory connections enhanced my immediate perceptions: I remember every word I have read here with an uncanny thoroughness, and the science of this world extends no farther than preindustrial pragmatism."

"Our hostess brought us books on subjects we requested," mused Jon. "We asked according to Network understanding, which lacks a crucial element of the Seriin society."

"What did we omit?"

"Wizardry," replied Jon briskly. He muttered, "I wish I had taken more time to study the intricacies of the human brain when Network's resources were still available to me. Did the original Immortals display any physical anomalies?"

"Not externally. The GRC researchers never performed the standard anatomical assessments, presumably due to the Immortals' influence." Beth rubbed her temples. "Like you, the Immortals adapted to new circumstances at an incredible rate. I would not be at all surprised to learn that GRC incorporated elements of your genetic imprint into the Immortals' codes."

"Illegal without my permission," argued Jon absently. He had retreated into a realm of concentration on his own analysis.

"Most of the GRC life extension experiment bordered on illegality," answered Beth, but she did not expect her husband to hear her. She knew him in this mood. Part of her delighted to see him functioning normally after so long, but part of her ached with loneliness.

"Lady Rhianna," called Jon suddenly, as if he did not doubt that the Infortiare would hear him. He frowned at his own folded hands, and Beth watched him uncertainly. His quiet, conversational tone reminded Beth of his manner of addressing Network: "Lady Rhianna, you need our help at least as much as we need yours. You have enormous skills, but you know virtually nothing of the physical sciences, engineering, or technology. I am not sure you even comprehend the words, but I think that you are intelligent enough to appreciate the danger inherent in your ignorance."

The golden lady reappeared a pace away from Beth, who recoiled, startled by the woman's sudden proximity. "How would you help me?" asked Rhianna crisply.

"I shall make a bargain with you, Lady Rhianna," said Jon with quick, light emphasis, "which my wife will be free to duplicate. I shall enable you to study Network, and you will enable us to study wizardry. Between us, my wife and I possess advanced degrees in seven distinct fields of learning. You could not find better teachers for your purpose."

"What is my purpose?" asked Rhianna calmly, but the expression of her delicate features was incisive and resolute.

"Preservation of your world, your people, and your culture," answered Jon.

Beth added softly, "Protection of those you love."

Rhianna turned her pensive gaze to Beth. "I shall consider your proposal," she murmured. She fingered a silver chain around her neck; a milky, starry pendant emerged into her hand. She lifted her gaze toward something unseen, and she faded into a shadow and was gone.

Beth whispered, "Do you truly understand my sorrow?" but Rhianna did not reply, and she did not reappear.

CHAPTER 2

Serii

Rhianna murmured, "There is a difficult matter that I would discuss with you, Kaedric: our guests."

"Jonathan and Elizabeth Terry," answered the image of a man, dark and lean and deadly.

"I have isolated them since their arrival, except for a single servant whom they never see, and only I have visited them. I shifted their patterns so as to distort their perception of time. I have deceived them, as you know, in nearly everything. I have not even allowed them to perceive themselves clearly until today."

"And we still do not know the significance of the message that reached them."

"They have asked to study wizardry."

"So I observed. It is an insightful request, which merely confirms the ingenuity of the Taormin's creator. Thorough knowledge of a potential friend is wise; thorough knowledge of a possible foe is imperative."

"They know more of us already than we know of them. Was I wrong to let them read so freely?"

Her husband laughed. "Dearest Rhianna, their request struck too deeply into your own cherished needs. Your conscience could have more easily let you torture them by physical starvation than by deprivation of mental stimuli. No, you did not err, and I would have done likewise—though I might have called myself a fool for the indulgence."

"You are so encouraging," replied Rhianna dryly. "How shall I undo my 'folly'?"

"They have offered to teach us Network lore. If we could learn only enough to understand the original design of the Taormin better, we would gain immeasurably. You, Evaric, and I have learned to tread the dangerous paths of the Taormin's coils empirically—by virtue of the Taormin's own designs for all of us. Is the Taormin our tool, or do we belong to it? Jonathan Terry could resolve many crucial questions."

"If we probe too deeply regarding the Taormin, our guests might well view our interest as a prelude to invasion. They did nearly eradicate this world to preserve the same society they have fled." Rhianna sighed, "Despite their desperate troubles, they consider themselves still a part of this 'Network' of theirs. They have vast knowledge but little wisdom."

"It is a common imbalance."

"How shall I maneuver them within Ceallagh's laws, which I have already stretched sorely?"

"Bring them to the Tower, and let them begin to feel themselves a part of this world. Jonathan Terry will reveal much to us unconsciously, because so much is obvious to him that he tends to forget the disparity between his level of knowledge and that of others. Elizabeth Terry will abandon any suspicions in exchange for the slightest hope of recovering her children."

"I cannot abuse her trust, Kaedric."

"You have already lied to her, as you say, in nearly everything. If the children have not diverged too far from the parents' patterns, you might be able to identify and reach for them."

"And bring them here? Shall we begin a colony of displaced Network citizens? I doubt that Network approves of abduction."

"Network would have difficulty prosecuting us." Wizard and wizardess shared a long and secretive amusement. "I should like to see the wondrous Network try to locate us in this timeless, formless place between infinities. Dearest Rhianna, we are not helpless. These people are no greater than our ancestors, whom Horlach conquered, and we have conquered him. If you wish to contemplate dire possibilities, consider the dreary hours of persuasion and dull diplomacy awaiting you, as you persuade Ixaxis and the monarchs of the Alliance to embrace change in order to preserve heritage and culture."

"You are a selfish, wicked man, beloved, to find such pleasure in my impending misfortune."

"When I consider that I might easily have suffered several centuries of such intrigues of state, I quite revel in selfish, wicked delight. You accomplish these governmental things so much more readily than I, and you tolerate them far more graciously."

"You are insufferable when you gloat. I think I shall steal a measure of your satisfaction by consigning Joli's Council to Ineuil's deviousness, and I shall thereby postpone the need for direct persuasion."

"You may wish to inform Ixaxis selectively as well. The Taormin has always been a subject of controversy."

"Horlach did use it for vile purposes," answered Rhianna with a shiver of recollection. "I shall need your aid in selecting the candidates for our unusual program of study."

"You will consider only wizards, I presume."

"I am liege of wizards only. I cannot steal the few bright minds from our educated mortals, most of whom belong to the nobility. Dear Joli's patience with me has limits."

"You have been planning for this moment since the refugees arrived. You could have persuaded Her Majesty to give you her entire Council in that length of time. Concede, my dear: You agree that we need to train more wizards to the use of infinity."

"I agree only to the possibility. I augmented the Ixaxin curriculum on that subject significantly, as you suggested, by incorporating your postulates and theorems into the traditional texts of wizardry. I concur that a theoretical mastery of infinite analysis would be a useful attribute in the candidates, but I still do not intend to take unnecessary risks with Ixaxin lives."

"I shall direct my observations accordingly, my lady."

"You are equally insufferable when you defer to me so readily."

"I learned from you the value of false humility as an irritant."

"It was not an attribute that I hoped to teach you," she answered with a subtle laugh.

His image reached for her. The shades of two Infortiares twined their patterns, merging in the love that had wrested its own space from infinity.

* * *

Rhianna spoke into the bright blaze of noon, as Jon and Beth sat and watched the still lake from the cottage porch. "You have asked to learn wizardry," said Rhianna, "but you have no Power."

Jon answered quickly, despite the unorthodox approach of the speaker, "Then I cannot threaten you by learning Power's use. I may, however, learn to understand you better, which could benefit us both." He had prepared his answer while awaiting Rhianna's return.

"I had a very stern and difficult teacher of wizardry," continued Rhianna, "and his is the example I would follow in teaching you. Do you truly wish this burden?"

"You will find me a quick student, I think," replied Jon. He gripped his wife's hand tightly. Beth tried to smile, though the gesture was weak.

Rhianna strode toward the Terrys from a shadow, her usual grace impeded slightly by a thick, weighty tome that filled her arms. She remarked with incongruous brusqueness, "I think you will need to abandon your overconfidence along with many other preconceptions before I finish with you." She dropped the book on Jon's lap. "These are the collected writings of Zerus, whose postulates form the essential theoretical elements of Power's usage. Read. I shall question you in the morning." In a rustle of silk, she disappeared.

* * *

"Ineuil, the battle may be imminent."

Ineuil laughed at Rhianna's solemn warning, for he had heard it so often for so many years. "But the battle, if it comes, will not be mine. Unlike you, I am not an Immortal wizard."

"You have considerable Immortal blood in you," countered Rhianna quickly. She walked ahead of him along the wooded path above the Queen's castle, distressed by his careless remark. She did not want him to see the pain that crossed her face. The inevitable prospect of losing her dearest friends frightened her very personally.

Ineuil answered her with only a hint of the regret that her Power sensed in him. "My hair is as much silver as gold these days, and my culinary tastes are decreed more by necessity than by choice. If the recent years had proved less quiescent, dear Rhianna, I would have abandoned this titular function of mine years ago, despite the blandishments of you and Her Fixed-minded Majesty, Queen Joli. Age has dimmed my rash tastes for danger and adventure."

"You still antagonize husbands quite freely."

"If the cause is worthy of my skills, could I deprive myself of the challenge of pursuit? You might note that I have become far less demanding in regard to the spoils of conquest."

"I have heard little of the sort," replied Rhianna. "You have not learned moderation with the years."

Ineuil gave her a wicked grin, and he looked nearly as young as Rhianna wanted to believe. "How I wish that I could agree with you, my lovely Infortiare. There is a particularly enticing wench in the service of Lord Osbo dur Aesir, and I do hate to see her wasted on a man of such haphazard tastes."

"Ineuil, please listen to me seriously."

"Dear, glorious Lady of Ixaxis, I have heard enough already to advise you. Since you—and not our Queen—seek words with me, the battle is beyond any mortal skills. It is another war of Power that you fear, for you are the ultimate liege of Power, more truly a royal monarch than any who wears that title throughout the Seriin Alliance or beyond."

"It is the same war, Ineuil, that we have fought together for most of our lives."

"Rhianna, my dear and lovely source of radiance for these many years, I have been your comrade in wizard's conspiracy before now, and you know that I would serve you with my dying breath, but do not seek in me the eager Adjutant of old. He is only a mortal, after all, and the years do not stand still for him."

She forced herself to ask with teasing calm, "When

were you ever 'eager'? You have shirked responsibility proudly since the day I met you."

"You see how age has addled me? I have almost begun to believe I earned my title." He continued very evenly, though he watched Rhianna with narrowed eyes as brightly green as new leaves. "Her Majesty has not yet told you, has she? I have asked her to name my successor as Adjutant."

Rhianna turned slightly, but she did not let him see her face except in Power's shadow. She answered tightly, "You must not resign now, Ineuil. The time is too critical."

He replied softly, "That is why I must let a younger, less fossilized soldier take my place, while I am still able to retire with some dignity and dispense occasional sage advice. I have been Adjutant for fifty years, an unprecedented tenure and an appalling burden for a man who never wanted to be anything but an irresponsible courtier."

"You love the pretense of irresponsibility, for you love to be coaxed into heroism."

"You think that I am waiting to be coaxed, because I have always yielded to you in the past? Think further, clever beauty of Ixaxis: Queen Joli is no longer young herself. She understands my reasons, and she agrees. The decision is hers, not yours." Ineuil kicked at the rotting wood of a fallen limb beside the path, and he muttered, "I do serve the Queen, even if you and your infernal husband did manufacture my appointment—in her regal father's absence—in the first place."

Rhianna touched the trunk of a stalwart oak, and she closed her eyes to let her Power share the tree's aged peace. The sense of quiet filled her, but it faded in an instant, unable to withstand her Power's innate ferocity. "You will not speak to me as Adjutant? Very well. Speak to me as a friend," said Rhianna sharply. She opened her eyes and turned to Ineuil. "Or does age incapacitate you in the area of friendship also?"

Ineuil folded his arms in a stern pose. "If one of your Ixaxin students showed such unreasonable anger at a necessary fact of nature, what would you advise?"

Rhianna answered, "I would advise us both not to borrow trouble from a future that may never come." She raised one slim hand to him contritely, and Ineuil accepted it in his own strong grasp. "Time does seem short to me, Ineuil, and I forget too often to accommodate the mortal perspective. I have proclaimed the threat of conflict for so long—I cannot blame you for doubting me now."

With the practiced courtier's flirtatious skill, Ineuil kissed her hand and released it, but he asked her soberly, "Is your onerous shadow of war that imminent?"

"Ineuil, I do not know." She walked toward the edge of the mountainous path and raised her hand toward a distant bank of clouds. "The storm could assail us this day and drown us in its ferocity. Or it might come gently, a soft, scattered rain that falls through a pale rose dawn. Is it a war of Power that I fear? No: It is a war beyond Power, a war of weapons that I cannot even imagine but that I know exist. It is a war of knowledge, Ineuil, and I fear that we are very weak on that battlefield."

"Then I can help you less than ever. Choose an Ixaxin scholar, or one of the Queen's librarians. You can find better advisers than I."

Rhianna twisted her milky pendant and answered slowly, "But I have no better friend."

"Impossible woman, can you never let me win an argument?"

Rhianna whirled to face him, and she smiled, as exquisite and delicate as the young, runaway noblewoman of Tyntagel, who had once rashly joined Ineuil in Venture. "Never!" she proclaimed, knowing she had won him again. "I need your wiles, my friend, for I must embark on another path of deception. Her Majesty knows enough of what I believe to agree that the matter lies within the Infortiare's jurisdiction. She trusts me, but the lords of her Council will not like to see such independence from Power's ever-suspect quarter."

"You want me to protect you from their interference?"

"I shall want your help in many tasks, many of which I do not yet know. My immediate need is to transfer my two refugees from the royal cottage to my Tower. The time of watching has produced its first fruit, and I want my refugees within my Power's constant awareness. Proximity will ease that effort—enough to let me concentrate on the larger difficulties."

"You could assign any Ixaxin to monitor your refugees."

"No. These refugees have delved into infinities too often. Evaric and Lyriel are staying with me, so that Evaric may help me, but I cannot trust the Power of a wizard who has not used the Taormin."

"You could train other wizards," suggested Ineuil, though he knew Rhianna's inveterate reluctance.

"Only if I can lessen the risk to them," replied Rhianna. She stared again at the distant storm. "Or if the danger of inaction begins to outweigh the Taormin's acknowledged hazards."

CHAPTER 3

Serii

When he sat atop the chalky cliff, here at the point, with only the ocean spreading before him in white and foamy turmoil, the racing sound of waves exciting his very soul, and the gulls enticing him with their cries, Quin acknowledged with a private grin that propriety's trappings and sedate posings could not make him feel like a proper scholar. "I shall never be like them," he shouted at the wind, and he laughed, because he had wadded his white scholar's robe into a ball, and it looked bedraggled, but no one would punish him for his carelessness. "I wonder how many robes, coats, shoes, and caps I lost or ruined as a boy?" he asked himself merrily.

He felt the headmaster's summons shift the patterns of Power, and Quin's broad smile became muted by rueful resignation. "Which is worse?" he demanded aloud. "Suffering incessant punishments for youthful transgressions or enduring staff meetings and lecture schedules?"

He hopped to his feet, brushing the chalky dust from his trousers and succeeding only in smearing the dust. He wondered how he had managed to cover even his dark twill shirt with the telltale white smudges that would surely make Howald frown in disapproval once again. "A scholar must set a good example of Ixaxin discipline," Quin informed a seagull sternly, imitating Master Howald's deep, deliberate voice with very effective impudence.

Quin trotted back to the road, where he shook the

worst of the creases from his scholar's robe. He tugged the robe over his head. The shoulders fit too tightly to suit him, but Mistress Damia (who took very personal pride in ensuring that the raiment of her Ixaxin scholars upheld the impressive image of their rank and skills) had insisted that anything larger would make Quin look ridiculous.

"But I *am* ridiculous," sighed Quin, as he had replied to Damia. He blushed, recalling her retort: a fairly detailed, reasonably flattering commentary on his physical attributes and her recommendations for displaying those attributes to advantage.

The thought of Damia's assessment made Quin feel guilty, not for the state of his scholar's robe but for his scholar's oaths of honor. In an unguarded moment of frustration, Quin had let his Power secure the rapid respect of his novice class. As usual in the wielding of unintended Power, the method had worked excessively well; it had caused several young female students to display far more interest in Quin than in the curriculum of applied wizardry. Quin found no consolation in the fact that his Power had influenced the class with such subtle force that no one had discovered his lapse.

"The chief problem with these infatuated young women," grumbled Quin to the chalky ground, "is that they infect their sisters with the absurd notion that I am some sort of romantic idol. They suddenly develop ridiculous aspirations to wed a lesser lord of Hamley." Quin grimaced as he crossed a rough Ixaxin field with long, even strides. "Were my fellow students ever this silly? I always thought they were all so grim."

"Bother," muttered Quin, as a second summons prodded him. He began to hurry, knowing that he would be late and that his legitimate reasons would be tainted by the childhood reputation he had never managed to escape. Howald's criticisms had little impact on Quin, for they were unceasing, but Quin's conscience was severely sensitive where matters of Power were concerned.

Quin combed his fingers through his unruly hair, unconsciously ensuring that some young woman would sigh at the thought of taming a sun-bleached curl into proper order. "Sorry, Luki," added Quin quietly, "I shall have to postpone our visit until evening."

Quin returned to the school and bounded up the stairs of the main building with an arm-swinging, exuberant stride. Mistress Amila, who had stationed herself in the entry hall, shook her graying head once again at the futility of trying to instill a sense of dignity in Quin. "The meeting will be held in the large conference room," she informed Quin, her Power conveying her frank disapproval of him. Since Quin was the last to arrive, Amila accompanied him down the long, peculiarly deserted corridor.

Quin answered her with a grin, for he accepted clashes with Amila as inescapable, "In that case, I shall stop worrying about another personal discussion with you and the headmaster regarding my disregard for conventional behavior."

"Quin," sighed Amila, "you are a gifted scholar and an excellent instructor in the application and control of Power. Personally, however, I find you a very trying young man."

"I really did annoy you effectively when I was a student," remarked Quin with a slight, sad whimsy. He did not enjoy her unforgiving antagonism toward him, though he had resigned himself to its existence. "Why has this urgent meeting been called?"

"The Infortiare requested it," answered Amila tightly.

"The Infortiare is here?" asked Quin with surprise.

Instead of answering, Amila opened the door to the conference room. Over a hundred scholars, robed alike in white, occupied chairs of dark walnut and deep blue velvet. A few glanced toward the opening door, but most remained attentive to the slim, slight figure standing on the marble dais.

The exquisite and deceptively delicate liege of Ixaxis raised her keen gray eyes to observe Quin and Amila claiming the last two chairs. She did not interrupt her softly spoken address, but Quin shivered, sensing the faintest contact with a deadly, burning Power. Howald glanced briefly at Quin, shook his head in helpless frustration, and exchanged a faintly exasperated shrug with Amila.

Quin had seen the golden Lady of Ixaxis only twice, having declined most such opportunities: He had encountered her once at the castle in Tulea, when he visited his own family's representatives to the Queen's court; he had seen her once on Ixaxis, when she awarded him the white robe of a scholar. He had never actually met Lady Rhianna, and he had found even remote glimpses of her disconcerting. The Infortiare embodied Power, and Quin did not enjoy such a tangible reminder of the grim aspects of his own gifts.

"I shall be assessing all of you," said the golden-haired Infortiare, "as I shall assess all other possessors of significant Power."

An alarm of Power shouted in Quin's head, though he could not identify the threat. Quin whispered urgently to the wizardess seated beside him, "Assessing us for what?" Amila only shushed him.

"I shall not explain the full complexities of the task," continued the Infortiare, "except to those few who number among the final candidates, for those explanations must be very lengthy. I may question and test any or all of you. I may probe your histories, your personal lives, your interests, your friends, and your aptitudes. I shall guarantee no respect of your privacy, for I must know any weaknesses that could jeopardize you. If you wish to exempt yourself from consideration, please inform Master Howald within the next three days, or we shall assume that you agree to all of the stated conditions."

Quin muttered, "Exempt from what?" Only Amila heard him, and she fixed him with a steely gaze that defied him to speak again.

The Infortiare ended her brief address with what Quin considered a most inadequate explanation for having convened such an unusual meeting. He did not think that a prompt arrival could have clarified the mystery significantly, for he heard too many puzzled whispers around him, as the scholars filed soberly out of the room. Master Ayo, the aged instructor of music, remarked to anyone who listened, "I would say that the Infortiare's testing of us has already begun."

* * *

Rhianna raised her head from perusing Master Howald's list of recommended candidates. She murmured, "I should also like to interview that young man who was teaching the novice class in applied wizardry."

Howald halted in the midst of shuffling files. "Not Quin?" he asked slowly.

"Yes," answered Rhianna thoughtfully, "I believe that was the name I heard."

"Quin does have considerable Power," acknowledged Howald reluctantly.

"You disapprove of him," observed Rhianna, and her own formidable Power spread a delicate veil of energy to probe the headmaster's response.

Howald answered bluntly, "My lady, I have never had a lazier, less cooperative student than Quin."

"He is a scholar: Surely, he worked extensively to earn that privilege."

"Yes, he has worked hard enough these past few years." Howald struggled to find a description of Quin that would not sound too peevish. "Quin has an unconventional attitude toward life," explained the headmaster uncomfortably. "He has no proper sense of his status."

"Master Howald," murmured Rhianna evenly, "if I asked as sensible an individual as yourself to abandon everything you know, I cannot suppose that you would agree happily."

Howald frowned, obviously affronted but unable to contradict his liege. "You requested my recommendations for the most capable scholars, and I cannot recommend Quin. He is a Hamley lord, typically irresponsible, spoiled, and self-indulgent."

The Infortiare murmured dryly, "Master Howald, nearly every noble in Serii is related to the lords of Hamley, and we are not all irresponsible, spoiled, and self-indulgent." Howald's ruddy face became crimson with embarrassment, as he recalled the noble heritage of the woman he addressed. "Does the young man have the Power and intelligence that I require?"

"Yes, my lady," answered Howald stiffly. "He is, as you evidently observed, a major Power. He is very probably the strongest Power among the current faculty and students." The admission clearly aggravated Howald's sense of rightness. "I shall add Lord Quinzaine's name to the list of candidates."

"Thank you, Master Howald. I shall weigh your advice in my decision. I appreciate your frankness in speaking of your concerns."

"Of course, my lady."

"Please send word to the ferryman that I am ready to return to Tulea." Howald nodded, and he left the Infortiare alone in his meticulously organized office.

Rhianna sighed and sank back in the armchair. "That man is almost as obsessively disciplined as Amila," she murmured to herself. "What a pair they make!"

"You selected them," remarked a voice that spoke to her Power, and she smiled and yielded to the vivid sense of her husband's presence.

"They both excel at administrative functions," she replied with a warmth that would have startled most Ixaxins, who found her intimidating and aloof. "You have not yet told me your assessment of the Ixaxin scholars today."

"Most of them recognized the meeting as a preliminary test. A few felt me study them. Some of the scholars resented the cryptic nature of your remarks; we can eliminate them from the list. Most are too rigid. Many are too weak. None of them is strikingly fit to fulfill a purpose that we ourselves have only dimly defined."

"What do you think of the Hamley youth?"

"Howald's bane?"

Rhianna smiled. "The disparity in personalities is considerable. Each side seems to have an element of justification for its perspective."

"Enough justification to raise doubts about Lord Quinzaine despite his qualifications of Power."

"A little Hamley recklessness may be precisely what we need."

"Are you selecting a Network scholar or a spy?"

"I must prepare for either need," sighed Rhianna. "Are we demanding too much, Kaedric?"

"Only perfection," answered her husband wryly, "which we shall not find." He touched his wife with a gentle wisp of his Power, and their shared illusion experienced the touch as a physical contact. "You favor the prodigal Quinzaine."

"Is it so obvious?"

"Only to me."

"I shall not choose on the basis of vague intuition."

"Neither should you disregard the answer that you sense, until you understand the source of your Power's reasoning. Howald confirmed your suspicions that Ixaxis held an untapped major Power, and your Power may have perceived more data that you have not yet recognized consciously. What do you know about this young man?"

"Not enough. Amila's reports to me regarding significant students of the past few years excluded Lord Quinzaine. She undoubtedly shares Howald's opinions on the subject."

"You want to probe Lord Quinzaine's past by reading his patterns?"

"We cannot consider him seriously without understanding him."

"You want *me* to probe his past for you."

"You can analyze him on levels that I cannot easily reach," answered Rhianna with a laugh of pleasure for the immense Power of the man she loved.

Kaedric argued, because he enjoyed debating with her, "Stimulating and tracing the energy strands of old memories is not a trivial endeavor."

"You will never even notice the effort," chided Rhianna lightly.

"Have you no sympathy for my impending exertion?"

"Not a whit!"

"Beloved, you are a stern taskmaster."

CHAPTER 4

Network

Caragen reentered his office from his private transfer port, disgusted with the meeting he had left. The bland superiority of the Calongi always irritated him, but he could tolerate the arrogant aliens better than the C-humans who deferred to them with such disgusting reverence. He loathed these negotiations regarding trade boundaries and jurisdiction of open planets.

Caragen had occasionally considered transferring Network to one of its less populous topological subsets, abandoning the parent universe with its inescapable Consortium influence altogether. The idea appealed to him conceptually, though he recognized the impracticalities of implementation. He felt no emotional ties to his species' planet of origin. He had long ago accepted the necessary ruthlessness of his self-serving priorities: No planet, person, or other possession could be allowed too much individual value.

"Network," he demanded, sinking into the adaptive contours of his desk chair, "have any priority issues arisen?"

"Item: The economy of the planet, Maya-2, has collapsed as scheduled, and the governor has requested Network aid."

"Excellent," murmured Caragen. "Implement the take-over procedure, as previously delineated."

"Implementation initiated," confirmed Network. "Item: The Organization for Freedom has been successfully deactivated, but the assassination of a key member, Elquar-na, failed. He is believed to have escaped to the Consortium on a Cuui trade ship. Azulan, the agent-in-charge, requests guidance regarding pursuit into Consortium space."

Caragen grunted, "Tell Azulan to complete his assignment, as contracted, if he expects to work for me again. Remind him, also, that Network has no official involvement with him and is, therefore, unimpressed by the pathetic threat of Consortium justice."

"Confirmed," answered Network. "Item: Wide-band sensors surrounding planet Siatha and former Network operative, Rabhadur Marrach, detected a significant increase in average energy level during a fifty second interval at zero-six-hundred, local time. Levels have subsequently returned to normal."

Caragen dug his fingers into the arm of his chair, tearing the soft leather. "Have you further information on this item?" he asked with a tense scowl.

"Signal extraction efforts proceed, but probability of successful identification is low due to brevity and covert characteristics of transmission. No detailed analysis of data is available."

"Network, what is the probability that Rabhadur Marrach initiated the transmission?"

"Over ninety-nine percent. Detailed knowledge of security methods precludes feasibility of such a transmission from a native Siathan, and all transport ships to the planet are monitored too closely to be suspect in this instance."

"Concentrate maximum resources on the analysis of that signal. I want to know its meaning and its destination."

"Confirmed. No further items."

Caragen growled, "Thank you, Network." He uncurled his fingers slowly, but he frowned at bitter thoughts. "Has your waiting finally ended, Marrach?" he muttered to himself. His voice was too soft to trigger Network response.

CHAPTER 5

Serii

A man sat in near darkness, studying a letter by the blue-gold light of a dying sunset. He looked to be a very young man, for his face was smooth and beardless, and a habitual smile of mischief had scarcely worn its traces. His sun-gilded brown hair curled irrepressibly. He had a boy's slim wiriness, though he had a man's height. His expression sobered, which was rare for him, but rare also was the missive that he read, the missive that had brought him to this legendary place.

He refolded the paper, following the original creases carefully. He tapped the paper against his thumb. He turned his head sharply at the sound of the opening door, and he jumped quickly to his feet. "My lady," he murmured properly, making the bow of respect to his liege.

"Please resume your chair, Lord Quinzaine," said the lady, who was golden-haired and very fair. "I have not summoned you here for punishment, though you deserve it."

"The incident extended itself farther than I intended, Lady Rhianna," he answered stiffly. "I am most contrite."

"So I should imagine," replied Rhianna dryly. "Though I shall not punish you for your foolish prank, neither shall I protect you from Lord Corvor and his family, and they will seek vengeance. Dignity is sacred to the men of Viste, as you should have known, since your mother

223

came of that House. You could not have offended them
more severely if you had murdered one of them."

"I understand, my lady."

"Do you? This is not your first injudicious prank nor
the first to go awry. Do you consider the playing of foolish, occasionally dangerous jokes an appropriate use of
an Ixaxin scholar's duties?"

"No, my lady."

"Yet you continue to indulge yourself in such mischief.
Explain your behavior, please."

"I doubt that my explanations would satisfy you, my
lady," sighed Quin resignedly. "They have never persuaded Howald or Amila."

"Do not decree my judgment for me, Lord Quinzaine."

Quin darted a beseeching glance at the coolly beautiful
Infortiare, wondering what she sought of him. Rhianna's
austere nod did not reassure him, but he tried to answer
honestly, "My record does not discredit me, my lady. I
have not neglected my students, as some may have suggested to you. I admit that I often behaved reprehensibly
as a boy, but I returned to Ixaxis with very sincere intentions of serving well. I completed the full scholar's training within two years, and I believe that I have taught
well since that time. The worst complaint that Master
Howald has against me now is that I explore untradi-
tional methods of education and discipline."

Rhianna remarked with thick irony, "Setting fire to
Lord Corvor's undergarments may qualify as an effective demonstration of energy manipulation, but it does
not constitute an outstanding example of a wizard's
restraint."

"The fire was well controlled, my lady."

"You digress from the point, as you know." The Lady
of Ixaxis sighed. "Quinzaine, you are highly intelligent
and highly skilled in the use of your considerable Power.
Prior to the incident with Lord Corvor, I considered you
a promising candidate for a very special form of advanced
training. In light of recent events, I am not sure that you
are sufficiently mature to assume the responsibility."

Quin's gray eyes, so much like the Infortiare's own,
widened with concern. "If your ladyship will explain the
nature of the advanced training, perhaps I shall be able
to reassure you."

Rhianna's level gaze bored into him, and he squirmed a little in the tapestry chair. "Know this, Quinzaine: If you journey with me, you will either gain such knowledge and Power as you will wish had never existed, or you will die quite horribly. This is neither a prank nor a game."

"You frighten me, my lady."

"That is my intention." Rhianna assessed each chair in the room before she selected one that Quin had considered the least promising choice for comfort. "A list of the strongest, most resilient Powers was compiled for me by one whose judgment in such matters is impeccable. You are the seventh candidate to whom I have spoken directly."

"Is this an interview?" asked Quin abruptly, brash from uncertainty.

"This is the final interview. You have passed others."

"Have I?" he asked, frowning slightly. "The day you visited Ixaxis last month," he murmured to himself in answer. "I thought I felt a probe of Power."

Rhianna nodded slightly, approving his perceptiveness. "You have significant Power, skills, flexibility, and quickness of wit. Your judgment is questionable, but an element of rashness may be requisite. Five of the previous six candidates declined to attempt what I proposed to them. The sixth has not yet made a firm decision." Quin's expression remained sober, but Rhianna perceived the impatience of one who little liked to belabor words, one whose busily inventive mind could not easily be tethered. "You have heard of the Taormin."

The impatience vanished. "Yes, my lady," answered Quin, suddenly leery. "It was Horlach's tool of Power. We teach that it was destroyed with him."

"It was not destroyed but modified—by my son, my husband, and myself. You have met my son."

"Once, very briefly, here at the castle. I gathered that he and his wife travel a great deal. I am surprised that he remembered me."

"My son forgets very little, and he has a particular interest in family, even of the most distant relation. You are a cousin to us, after all."

"I am a cousin to most of Serii's nobility," added Quin with a half shrug.

Rhianna's faint smile appeared and vanished. "I want

you to begin a very specialized course of study, part of which will involve the Taormin."

"I obey your will, my lady," replied Quin, but his Power stirred defensively.

"I do not speak of studying merely from a text, although I shall demand much from you at that level. I also seek candidates for a more difficult effort. I hope that the need never materializes, but I must prepare for contingencies: I need to identify those wizards who could potentially use the Taormin."

"You want me to use the tool of the most dreaded Sorcerer King in our history?" asked Quin in horror. Neither impatience nor eagerness remained in his face.

Rhianna observed Quin's sincere alarm and approved. "Aside from Horlach," she continued softly, "only my husband, my son, and I have used the Taormin successfully. Other very Powerful wizards, Lord Hrgh dur Liin for one, have failed in the attempt and been destroyed. I believe that you have sufficient Power and control to succeed, but a sizable risk remains. We have limited information on which to form any judgment of the necessary qualifications."

"What purpose does use of the Taormin serve, my lady?" asked Quin, cautiously hesitant.

"The Taormin was designed to serve as a gate. If I deem the effort necessary, I shall want you to use that gate, Quinzaine, and study the society that you will find beyond it without revealing your origin to anyone. Whether or not you ever make that journey, preparation will be required: intensive study as well as exercises of Power far beyond anything you now perceive as possible. Your rapid mastery of the scholars' skills was a crucial factor in your selection as candidate."

"The rewards of virtue," muttered Quin.

Rhianna fingered her pendant, and it seemed to exude a starry light. "I shall supervise the preparations, along with my husband." Quin opened his mouth, but his question formed only in his eyes. "My husband," repeated Rhianna, "Lord Venkarel."

Quin cleared his throat. "I understood that your husband died."

"That is a prevalent opinion."

"My lady, I think you misled me when you said you would not punish me."

"You have a choice, Quinzaine."

"No, my lady." Rhianna raised one fine brow, and Quin explained hurriedly, "I have no choice, because I once promised someone that I would try to do something useful with my life."

"You keep your promises."

"I intend to keep this one."

"You may have some wisdom in you, after all."

Quin grimaced. "I have very little wisdom, my lady, or I would not have made so rash a promise. I am very fond of life, and I am not at all fond of working. I am not heroic, and I am not ambitious. I shall do my best to serve you, my lady, but you should know that I am really quite as senseless as the incident with Corvor suggests."

"Do you expect me to retract my offer on the basis of this confession?"

"I hoped you might," sighed Quin.

Lady Rhianna smiled briefly, but she spoke with very serious force of Power: "I shall expect you to return here tomorrow evening, by which time I shall have conferred with the other candidates, and we may begin your instruction."

"Yes, my lady." Quin interpreted Rhianna's nod as a dismissal. Eager to escape, he bowed to her while hurrying to the door. He bumped a chair in his haste, and he barely caught it before it toppled.

"You may wish to avoid Viste Hall," murmured Rhianna. "Lord Corvor is in residence there at present."

Stopping abruptly at the door, Quin muttered, "Wonderful," and he shook his head. "He will want to restore his honor by killing me."

"Very likely," agreed Rhianna.

"Bother," grumbled Quin without apparent dismay, and he left the Infortiare's Tower without observing the Ixaxin Lady's pensive gaze.

* * *

Quin crossed the castle garden near Hamley Hall, admiring the bright morning and trying diligently to forget the previous day's unsettling meeting with the Infortiare. The Queen's splendid castle offered plentiful pleasures and distractions, but none of them seemed able to erase a dreadful nightmare of battling with the Widowshear, which had somehow transformed itself into the tool of a Sorcerer King. Quin had considered asking some of his cousins to accompany him to the Tulean marketplace, where they might see what excitement they could discover together, but he realized sadly that most of his Hamley cousins viewed him as a stranger.

"Quinzaine!"

Quin turned toward the voice, wincing inwardly, though he smiled brilliantly at the very large and furious young man who had interrupted his course. "Hello, Corvor! How remarkable to meet you here! Do you come to the Queen's castle often? How is your family?" Corvor placed the point of his rapier beneath Quin's chin. "I see you carry a sword." Quin touched the weapon gingerly, while Corvor stared coldly across the length of it. "A very sharp sword, I perceive."

"I shall kill you with it."

"That would not be very sporting, Corvor."

"Fetch your own sword, and accompany me to the cemetery lawn, or I shall kill you now and drag you to your tomb."

"A misguided prank cannot demand such drastic measures," protested Quin with a very winning smile, which left Corvor unmoved. "You must know how sorry I am for my foolish jest. Punish me in kind, if you will, but do not ask me to duel with you. I never could handle a blade."

"I shall punish you in kind, Quinzaine, by wounding you as severely as you wounded me."

"It was a joke: a poor one, perhaps, but no lasting harm was done."

"You consider my shame insignificant? You have humiliated me for the last time, Quinzaine, and you cannot hide from my revenge. I have pursued you here, and I would have pursued you to Hamley or to the farthest desert of Ardasia. You would not understand what it means to lose dignity, since you have none."

"True," admitted Quin with a sigh. "I have fourteen older siblings—and countless cousins—who eliminated any prospect of dignity in me." The blade pressed more tightly against Quin's throat. "You have no sense of humor, Corvor," said Quin amiably, and he contained his Power's anger in a determined shield. An uneasy realization occurred to him that he could eliminate the annoyance of Corvor with only the slightest lessening of control.

"And you have no sense at all."

"I know," agreed Quin. "I have no sense and little honor, and I am not at all worthy of your grand vengeance."

"Will you get your sword?" snapped Corvor.

"Certainly not!"

Corvor shouted at an unfortunate young servant, who was emerging from the castle's nearest wing. "Run to Viste Hall," Corvor ordered, "and tell Master Byrdel that I need another rapier quickly. Have it brought to me at the cemetery lawn." The servant nodded, his eyes wide, and he ran toward the imposing Hall that housed the family of Viste at the Queen's court. Corvor prodded Quin toward the one level region of the sloping lawn surrounding the royal tombs.

Quin shrugged and complied with the demands of Corvor's insistent rapier, but he murmured in a tone of warning, "You really are becoming a nuisance, Corvor."

A Viste servant approached Corvor, who nodded brusquely toward Quin. The servant placed the rapier in Quin's reluctant hands. The agile servant retreated at a run, for he was well versed in the forms and concepts of a Viste nobleman's duel.

"What do you expect me to do with this thing, Corvor?" asked Quin. He laughed uneasily at the ridiculousness of his predicament, and he waved the borrowed sword with intentional clumsiness.

"Defend yourself," replied Corvor impatiently. He lunged forward; Quin leapt aside but yelped as Corvor's blade drew blood from the flesh above Quin's wrist.

"Corvor, this is absurd. I bear no grudge against you. I should like to consider you a friend! Why should we try to kill each other?"

"You have an odd way of developing a friendship." Corvor's second attack carved thrice through Quin's vest. Quin parried a fourth blow, but a fifth struck him as Corvor's attacks accelerated.

"You do not actually want to kill me," argued Quin, his temper fraying and Power's temptations growing irresistibly. He tried once more to dodge the fight altogether, but he could not escape the cemetery yard without making himself vulnerable.

"Unlike you, I do not joke about honor." Corvor's set expression conveyed his deadly intentions.

Laurett would have wasted no time dispatching Corvor with all his showy and impractical flourishes, observed Quin ruefully, *but Laurett never had much sympathy for anyone who forced a fight.* "You are pressuring me, Corvor, to make a very unpleasant choice."

"To use your Power? I am a wizard, also, Quin, or had you forgotten?"

Never take chances against a man who wants to kill you: That is what Laurett would say. There is no room for pity in a duel to the death. Quin closed his eyes tightly.

Cowardice, whispered Corvor's disparaging Power to Quin, as Corvor prepared to kill. Corvor raised his weapon. It became hot in his hand, but he turned his Power toward it, and it cooled. A suggestion to drop the weapon crept through his mind, and he countered it. An explosion of light burst between the two men; Corvor blinked and caused the light to dim. A wind gusted, tossing dust in Corvor's eyes, and he cursed the dust and its issuer.

Quin leaned against a tomb, and he planted his rapier's tip in the grassy ground. "We could spar with Power all day," remarked Quin affably, "because Power is a tool I understand too well. I have allowed you to injure me, Corvor, but I do not intend to die for your satisfaction." Corvor's sword rose again to hang near Quin's chest. "Friend Corvor," murmured Quin, applying subtle Power with the name, "I can hold your weapon away from me for as long as you can hold it at all."

"You want a wizards' duel, Quinzaine?" grumbled Corvor, lowering his now-useless sword and wiping the dust from his eyes.

"I want no duel at all!"

"I shall best you with any weapon you choose."

"I think not," said Quin contemplatively, "but I am not eager to prove either of us correct." He shook his head, as Corvor tried once more to press his sword toward Quin, driving it with both Power and physical strength. The weapon did not move. "You could only kill me with an unexpected attack, Corvor, which your honor would not allow you to initiate."

"I shall not relent," hissed Corvor, and he threw the full force of his Power against Quin.

Quin repelled the blow with a brief flare of anger. He whispered both with voice and Power, "You have tried to kill me with annoying persistence, Corvor, considering that your original cause was stupid vengeance for some childhood incident that neither of us recalls. I have never greatly minded, because you are always so easily dissuaded by trivial injuries to your excessive pride."

"You and your foolish pranks," sneered Corvor. "Why can you not fight with dignity, like a man of honor?"

"Because I prefer neither to die nor to inflict death. However, a recent discussion with our Infortiare made me realize something profound: I am tired of accepting the blame for your idiotic behavior, not to mention accepting the scars your sword has inflicted on my skin. I have no more patience for you." Quin's Power twisted into Corvor, burning through the patterns of hate with relentless determination.

Corvor blinked and shook his head, disoriented and unsteady from the assault. He sheathed his rapier uncertainly. "Quinzaine," he muttered, shaking his head in exasperation at his own sudden weakness and confusion.

"Let us forget our differences," urged Quin, allowing Power a final moment's reign, "and spin tall tales over supper. I shall buy."

"You are bleeding like a gored calf. What tavern keeper would accept you in his establishment?"

Quin donned a carefree grin. "Loan me your scarf as a bandage."

"And you will return it to me soaked in your blood?"

"I shall buy you another."

"You could not afford another like it." But Corvor pulled the green silk scarf, edged in silver lace, from his neck and thrust it into Quin's hands.

"Thanks!" said Quin brightly. "Could you help me wrap the arm? You certainly did make a mess of this shirt. It even looks bad by my standards."

Lord Corvor muttered bemusedly, "Are you sure your mother came from Viste?"

"Entirely," whispered Quin, and his smile became rigid.

CHAPTER 6

Serii

Twelve candidates, mused Quin, wondering if the Infortiare had selected the "perfect" number from ancient tradition or from convenience. Of the twelve, Quin recognized only three as Ixaxin residents: himself, an aloof scholar named Ritis, and Alvedre. The other candidates were primarily wanderers, tied formally to Ixaxis only by past schooling and the occasional testing-and-gathering. The selection of candidates suggested an interesting emphasis on the Infortiare's part. *She may call us "scholars" of unusual lore,* concluded Quin a little grimly, *but she expects us to use the Taormin's gate.*

Alvedre smiled at Quin with a nervous unsteadiness. Quin joined her in the corner of the classroom, a large, white marble chamber of the Infortiare's Tower. Alvedre greeted him quietly, for even soft sounds echoed in the sparsely furnished room, "I am pleased to see you, Quin, though I am not surprised. I expected your selection more than my own."

"When did you arrive in Tulea?" asked Quin, mildly disturbed by Alvedre's remarks. He had considered himself the most unlikely of choices for the Infortiare's project, and he continued to hope that the Infortiare would change her mind and dismiss him.

"Last night. I declined the Infortiare's offer initially." Alvedre shrugged ruefully. "I am not a very adventurous woman."

"You are a superlative scholar," argued Quin.

"The qualifications for this training depend more on Power, I think, than on learning skills."

"Have you ever seen old Ritis stray so far from his library before today?" asked Quin with a grin to encourage Alvedre. "He excels at research, but he applies Power only to ensure his privacy."

"He is notoriously independent," answered Alvedre, her blue eyes solemn, "like every other wizard in this room."

"Including Lady Rhianna?" asked Quin thoughtfully.

"Especially Lady Rhianna," replied Alvedre in an uncomfortable whisper. "She was not even trained on Ixaxis. Lord Venkarel taught her privately, here in the Tower."

The mahogany door swung open with a creaking of long-neglected hinges. Like much of the Infortiare's Tower, the marble chamber had been abandoned for many years, and the recovery process had not yet extended beyond the basic cleaning of windows, floors, and walls. Castle servants shunned the Tower from dread of legends as well as Power's fact, and Lady Rhianna's noble ties to Serii's First Houses had alleviated the problem only slightly. The motley assortment of faded chairs and battered tables had the well-used look of Hamley manor, but Quin suspected that the Tower's contents were as truly ancient and untended as they appeared.

Lord Arineuil entered the room with a stoop-shouldered, sandy-haired man and a very thin, rather pretty woman with nervous hands. The appearance of the Queen's Adjutant silenced the waiting wizards, many of whom glanced suspiciously toward the Infortiare. Lord Arineuil bowed to the Ixaxin liege with an excessively gallant sweep of his arm and a conspiratorial glint in his eyes. "Two refugees from the royal cottage," he announced, "as promised."

"Thank you, Ineuil," replied Rhianna tersely, and Quin felt her Power's momentary surge of disquiet at the Adjutant's teasing words.

The Adjutant grinned fleetingly and departed, closing the heavy door behind him. The Infortiare addressed the man and woman who had entered with him, "Master Jonathan and Mistress Elizabeth, these are your students."

"All of them?" demanded Beth with a brittle laugh that seemed too close to despair.

"We had not expected such a large number of students," added Jon with a grimace. "Lady Rhianna, this is impractical."

"Are Network classes so small?" murmured Rhianna with a pensive smile. Quin felt her satisfaction and wondered at it.

"We have no equipment," muttered Jon, "no computers. . . ."

Beth murmured, "Even at university level, general subjects are taught by Network." She tried to explain further, when blank expressions greeted her words. "The specialized instruction by which students gain research experience is provided by assigning one or two students to a specific project of a specific instructor. The brightest students mature into instructors when they become capable of generating their own significant research contributions to Network." She looked helplessly at her husband, for the class clearly did not understand her.

Jon frowned and demanded irritably, "How can you have forgotten so much?"

Quin shared the puzzlement of his fellows at the odd beginning of this peculiar class. A man and woman with strange accents, strange words, and stranger manners fretted over a class of twelve and chided their new students for forgetfulness. Quin smiled at Alvedre, for she had a worried expression, but he privately echoed her uneasiness.

"These people," said Rhianna crisply, "have no idea of what you mean." She began by addressing Beth, but she switched her focus to Jon. She crossed the room to speak directly to him, as if they two stood alone. She looked frail before him, but Power's strength made her indomitable.

She continued in a clear voice that forced itself into the minds of her hearers, "Your students know of the Taormin as a tool of a Sorcerer King and not as a mortal device of your design. They are all trained wizards, but none has ever manipulated such patterns as you and I recognize. Unlike most Seriin mortals, who view our world as an isolated sphere of life, Ixaxins do realize that other worlds and creatures exist, but they know nothing of the schism that divided us from your Network. They do not know what the repair of our world's Rending entailed. They do not know that we must resume a thread of learning stolen from us in the ten thousand year reign of the Sorcerer King Horlach, a thread forgotten for the nine thousand years that have followed."

"I offered to teach you of Network," argued Jon gruffly, "but do not expect miracles of me."

"I expect nothing else," replied Rhianna evenly. Quin sensed a quick, careful probe of her Power burning into the man she faced, and the man jumped in obvious alarm. "Have you forgotten the bargain you made with us?" she asked softly. "The methods of our miracles for your own."

In a swirl of mist-blue silk, she seated herself at a scratched oaken table. She fixed her sharp gray gaze on the man, who continued to frown at her. "Your students await you, Dr. Terry," she murmured.

Alvedre nudged Quin toward a chair, and he realized that most of the wizards were already seated. Quin followed Alvedre's lead to the table behind the Infortiare. They waited in uncomfortable silence.

Beth touched her husband's arm, tearing his attention away from the golden Lady of Ixaxis. "We should divide the class between us," said Beth in a burst of apparent energy that could deceive none of her students. Quin lauded her courage for breaking the stillness of confrontation.

Jon sighed heavily, as if he had narrowly escaped an exhausting ordeal. "Yes," he muttered vaguely. After a pause, he added more strongly, "We can exchange groups at midday." He shook his head in a slight, frustrated gesture. "I can begin by explaining the predicament that inspired closure." He finished dryly, "No audience could be less comprehending than the Network Councillors who heard the briefing first."

CHAPTER 7

Network

Caragen rubbed his eyes wearily. "Network, schedule me for another rejuvenation booster."

"You are not due for another year."

"Then alter my diet, or prescribe a restorative," snapped Caragen.

"The recommended restorative is sleep."

"That answer is unacceptable. Reevaluate and incorporate the modifications in my next meal."

"Confirmed."

Caragen again bent his head over the holographic display that Network had presented on his previous command. He tapped the terminal embedded in his desk in order to manipulate the display, and the blue tracery of the planetary grid began to rotate slowly. It was a hollow image without any pretense of substance, for it represented no more than an emptiness in space.

"The coordinates of a mirage," muttered Caragen. "Is Marrach taunting me by sending messages into a topological vacuum?"

"The probability is sixty-two percent," answered Network evenly.

Caragen tapped the keypad of his terminal, and the image increased abruptly in total size. Caragen rested his chin on his arm and stared levelly at the projection. "Does Marrach have the scientific expertise to preselect a planet-shaped topological void for his destination?"

"The probability is six percent."

"Reconcile six percent with the relatively high magnitude of the previous figure."

"Topological anomalies are not a well understood phenomenon, and the spherical shape may be very common."

Caragen grunted, "I distrust coincidences, especially concerning Marrach." He scratched his neck, where a recent skin graft had not yet sealed completely. "What is the probability that Dr. Jonathan Terry, if still alive, would be able to predict a planet-shaped topological anomaly?"

"Eighty-nine percent. However, the presupposition is extremely unlikely."

"So you tell me repeatedly, but the correlations between Marrach and Dr. Terry increase. Explain this inconsistency."

"No inconsistency exists. Your hypothesis is irrational, based on a primitive emotional response to the potential of direct conflict with Rabhadur Marrach."

"Thank you, Network," replied Caragen dryly. "I prefer to consider my hypothesis the result of sound subconscious reasoning, based on many years of experience before your current intelligence algorithms existed." He moved his hand toward the projection, as if to touch it, and the image shuddered from the interference. "How many planets fit the dimensions of this anomaly?"

"Precise dimensions are not available. Allowing a ten percent error factor, two hundred thirty-six such planets are defined in Network files or accessible Consortium records."

"Are there any significant correlations with Rabhadur Marrach among the referenced planets?"

"While in your employ, Rabhadur Marrach enacted major operations on seven of the planets, indirectly influenced political coups on three of the planets, assassinated nineteen citizens whose prior histories correlate with at least one of the planets. . . ."

"That is enough, Network," sighed Caragen. "Marrach could have significant correlations with all of the planets, if only because of his connection to you. I need a narrower filter to identify this." He jabbed his finger vehemently through the projection.

"Data reduction and analysis proceeds."

"I need the contents of the confounded message! Is it random data, a clever taunt, or a serious transmission?"

"Unknown. Only overhead bits, containing transponder routing information and synchronization data, were unencrypted."

"Can you identify the intended receiver type?"

"A broad class of receivers, including all personal models, could fit the available information."

"Except this particular model, if it exists, includes specialized decryption capabilities prearranged by Marrach." The spherical projection disappeared, and Caragen growled, "Network, restore the image."

"Sleep is imperative. Physical responses are below acceptable thresholds."

"I set the thresholds, Network," said Caragen coldly. "Override, file N20."

The image reappeared at Caragen's command, but Network did not confirm the order verbally. The overridden algorithm did not encourage the commands that could defeat it, even to appease Andrew Caragen.

CHAPTER 8

Serii

"There is such overwhelming sadness in you," murmured Alvedre. "I can hardly bear it."

Beth raised her head, less astonished by the comment than by its origin. Alvedre studied assiduously, but she rarely spoke outside of an occasional, immediately relevant question. The individual sessions with Alvedre were always easy and predictable. "I am sorry if I disturb you," answered Beth slowly, uncertain of how much to attribute to the odd gifts of Power.

"Tell me," urged Alvedre, and she laid aside her papers, covered with her fastidiously legible notes. "The lesson can wait another day."

Without even weighing the wisdom of confiding in this pale, serious woman, Beth began to speak of the destruction of her home, her life, and her family. Surprisingly, the memories flowed easily once she started. Her Michael and Kitri lived for her again, as did Marrach.

Alvedre's sympathy was palpable, and Beth leaned against the wizardess and cried the gathered tears of too much loss. "You have suffered terribly," whispered Alvedre, sharing in Beth's pain with the cruel clarity of unguarded Power. "This Marrach is a demon."

Beth nodded, raising her head. "That is why it is so hard to believe that he would contact us after all these years, asking forgiveness."

"Even the most evil man may repent," answered Alvedre, but she echoed Beth's uncertainty.

"He told us of our children," said Beth with a faint smile. "My daughter teaches at Harberg University. My son has a daughter of his own."

"You are proud of them."

"Yes. I wish that I could tell them." Beth's smile faltered. "They would not know me."

"They would remember."

"No. They were conditioned. I do not exist for them."

"Could you ever forget them?"

"No," replied Beth quickly, but she stopped and frowned. "I did forget them once."

Alvedre nodded sagely. She gathered her papers into a leather folder. "Has anyone introduced you to the royal grandchildren? They are a tribe of scamps, because Her Majesty, their grandmother, spoils them abominably. They are usually in the gardens at this hour, tormenting their governess. Would you like to meet them?"

"Yes," replied Beth with a hesitant smile. "I should like to meet them very much."

* * *

Quin ran up the Tower stairs, wondering if the Infortiare would accept a Hamley cousin's wedding as an excuse for tardiness. He had not even known the girl, who had been raised in Tulea, but somehow he had managed to be drafted to escort one of her groom's sisters. He recognized the manipulations of Lord Perris, Hamley's representative on the Queen's Council, but shirking the duty had seemed ingracious.

Living in Hamley Hall had not proven wise. The universal assumption, eagerly embraced, seemed to be that Quin had come to find a wife, and Quin could not disabuse his uncles, aunts, and cousins of their hopes for new alliances without revealing that he served the Infortiare. His Tulean kin, more typically Seriin than Hamley in their prejudices, forgave his Power only so long as he declined to remind them of it.

Quin caught his breath at the top of the Tower stairs, and he knocked on the library door rather than send a warning of Power. The response, a man's voice, startled Quin, who pushed open the door very tentatively. A tall, lean silhouette against the broad, bright windows spoke crisply, "My mother has little patience for waiting these days. I thought I would take the opportunity to usurp her appointment with you."

"Lord Evaric?" asked Quin, squinting to see the features of the silhouette.

"Indeed, unless my mother has kept more secrets than I realize," agreed Evaric wryly. He moved away from the window with the extraordinarily liquid motions of a man trained by the K'shai guild of assassins. He pulled the velvet drapery across the window, leaving only a single, bright beam. "I wanted to speak to you, Lord Quinzaine, because I know you particularly well."

"You honor me by remembering the meeting, my lord," replied Quin, trying to sound like a proper nobleman of Serii.

"Enough of these titles and trappings of gentility! We could spend the remaining afternoon exchanging meaningless tributes to each other's lineage, but we both serve a more demanding purpose." Evaric touched the drapery, and the sunlight struck Quin, forcing him to blink and look away.

"Power," murmured Evaric, "burns in us like that blinding sun. Power destroys those we hate and those we love, and it ultimately destroys us as well, unless we learn to master it. The mortals, who envy us, may choose their trades, but we do not choose. We are wizards, you and I, because we hold too much Power in us to be anything else."

"You have a grim perspective, Lord Evaric."

"On those occasions when I must defer to my Immortal heritage, yes. Perhaps I have seen too much. As a boy, I learned, like you, to conceal my Power even from myself, because I could not face the magnitude of my gifts. I did not want that much responsibility for worlds and wars, life and death. None of the safe roles we try to adopt can defend us from ourselves."

"You credit me with too much talent. I am not the son of two Infortiares."

Evaric let the drapery drop back into place, restoring a sense of musty antiquity to the room. He crossed to Quin and extended his strong, bronzed hand. "Look at the brand from fingertip to wrist, Quinzaine. That is the bloodied sword of the K'shai. I made many mistakes before I accepted my Power."

"I am sorry," replied Quin uneasily.

"I could force you to look at yourself with equal honesty. I could force you to acknowledge the gifts that separate you even from most Ixaxins." A hint of painfully intense Power burned inside Quin's skull. The barrier against attack rose easily, but it did not quite cleanse the violent force of Evaric's Power from Quin's mind.

"You only prove," remarked Quin with a tight, strained smile, "that I am not your equal." A harsh jab of Power seemed to inflict a bleeding wound, and Quin cried aloud and pressed his hands against his head.

He saw himself in a dismal room, his face twisted in agony. He saw himself wearing a frown of concentration, raising Power's concealing shield to make Mistress Alvedre think less of his skill. He saw himself, silenced by grief, holding the cold hand of Laurett on her bier. He saw himself, a solemn toddler of no more than four years, wielding unconscious Power to shield himself from the ordinary hurts that made a child learn wisdom. He saw his parents die again.

"Stop," hissed Quin. The pain withdrew immediately. Quin glared at Evaric, more enraged than he had felt since passing the Test of Mastery.

"You could have fought me," said Evaric evenly, "but you feared—not me but yourself. You know that you share with me a closer kinship than that which binds you to any member of your Hamley clan. It is the kinship of major Power."

"Yes. I do know. Is that what you want me to admit? What does it matter to you? I have my own life, and I am contented with it. I have never aspired to become a K'shai assassin, nor have I ever cultivated the swordsman's skills to support such a decision if I made it." Quin smiled broadly, but his eyes remained hard. "If I enjoy a few clownish affectations, whom do I hurt?"

"All of us," snapped Evaric, "because you were born to become something more than a clown and a fool, because a purpose exists for you that will shake our world's destiny, and because you have a major Power that is wasted even in the Ixaxin schoolrooms. I never wanted to become an intrinsic part of the infinite pattern of our world's stability, but my Power and the Taormin made that my destiny." Evaric laughed curtly. "I might have preferred to exchange my fate with yours, but that is a choice that neither of us can make."

"Are you sure that you have escaped the assassin's tendencies completely?" asked Quin, knowing that the question would wound.

"No," replied Evaric with brusque force. The two men exchanged the sharp warning flare of threatened Power. Evaric quieted first; he said slowly, "But I no longer kill, and I no longer hide my Power's menace behind my ability to destroy life by mortal brutality. No major Power can allow such self-deception to persist."

"I am an Ixaxin scholar, Lord Evaric, not a child in a Hamley nursery."

"You are still less than you must become, and your time of decision is approaching. Be ready." With five quick, smooth strides, Evaric left the room.

Quin sat on a gold-cushioned chair and put his feet on the Infortiare's cluttered desk. He stared at the door's shadowy patterns of intricate loops and knotted rows. His Power ached, having been stretched far beyond its usual limits. "Truth," muttered Quin, "is not a courteous visitor."

He glanced at a beeswax candle in its ribbed gold holder, and the wick caught fire. His Power teased the flame into an image of Laurett. "You always valued honesty," said Quin to the shimmering, colored flame. "How did you ever manage to love a deceiver like me?"

* * *

"There is only one possible course," said Kaedric softly, for he knew that his wife did not want to hear.

"The risk is still enormous," sighed Rhianna, and she stared into her mirror, but she did not see herself.

"We all face the risks that await us, as we must. Lord Quinzaine can do no less."

"You and Evaric conspired without me," chided Rhianna.

"You felt the probe of our world. You recognize the threat. Network is aware of us, and we cannot afford to let them strike us unprepared. We must train Lord Quinzaine to use the Taormin. He was your selection, if you recall."

"He has the best chance of survival of any of them,

but the risks are still so high." Rhianna shook her golden hair, which hung loose and long, unbound for the night. "He does not want to take this step, and I loathe coercing him by a vow to his dead wife."

"Evaric's comments stung him, as intended. Lord Quinzaine will acquiesce, when you ask him."

"You are sometimes very ruthless, my dearest."

"Unquestionably," agreed Kaedric wryly. "However, in this particular instance, I think the risk may be less than you imagine. Our Hamley lord has some previous experience to help him, I surmise. I have been observing his Power's activity, and I am fairly certain that he is one of Luki's projects. He is the type she usually favors."

"Luki? The old wizardess on Ixaxis?"

"In her illusory mountain retreat, dear Rhianna, Luki holds an object she calls the Widowshear. It is similar to the Taormin in some respects, though it is a very pallid, battered relative. I suspect that the sea possessed it for many years, for even the casing is badly corroded, and the metal is that impervious kind so cunningly crafted by our ancestors. Lord Quinzaine's Power often touches the Widowshear when he sleeps."

"Have you used this object?"

"Yes: years ago. I used it to locate the Taormin after Hrgh's theft. I probably alerted Horlach in the process, but I was much younger then and much less clever than I imagined. I had discovered years earlier that the Widowshear could sense the Taormin, though I did not know initially that it *was* the Taormin I touched."

"The 'Widowshear' seems a dangerous toy to leave to a madwoman's fancy."

"I think not. I think the Widowshear was one of the 'controlled.' "

"Whereas the Taormin was the Controller."

"Exactly. The Widowshear's force is innately receptive rather than aggressive like the Taormin, which is why the Widowshear is so difficult to guide in an outward effort. Luki once told me that she used it to 'collect' the fragments of her retreat, and I believe her, despite her general confusion and inconsistency in discussing the subject."

"The Widowshear represents the Taormin's feminine counterpart," murmured Rhianna, brushing her hair pensively. "It could have tremendous capabilities of its own, if we understood it. I should like to inspect the Widowshear for myself."

"You are not Luki's type, my darling. She will distrust you for your gender, your authority, and your nobility, and she retains enough Power to perceive all three attributes despite disguise. She was a major Power in her younger days."

"Four hundred years ago."

"Leave her to her harmless intrigues, Rhianna. The Widowshear is a curiosity but not a threat."

"Sentimentality, dear Kaedric?" Rhianna smiled at the image of him, and her Power touched him gently.

With significant hesitation, Kaedric conceded, "Luki amused me."

Rhianna laughed at the reluctance of his admission. "You are not nearly as ruthless as you would like to believe."

"Allow me my small conceit, dear Rhianna. I have been acknowledged as the devil's nearest kin for too many years to readjust now."

"I have never labeled you thus!"

"Even you shared that opinion, at one time."

"Before I knew you."

"Before the Taormin forced you to know me—better than you wished."

Her expression became softly wistful. "I would have loved you, Kaedric, with or without the Taormin's meddling to breed its savior. It is a device of remarkable cunning, amazingly intelligent in its own way, but it could only influence our Powers enough to make us aware of each other. It made the opportunity, but you and I made the choice."

"Your choice, beloved, is still the greatest wonder to me of all."

* * *

The early morning felt cool with the fog that had risen from the sea. Alvedre moved hesitantly through the garden, until she saw the golden lady she had sought. "Lady Rhianna, may I speak to you?" Alvedre approached timidly, but her resolve was firm.

The Infortiare seemed to bring her attention from a

great distance, for she did not reply for several moments. A slight sigh suggested reluctance to resume her liege's role, but she adopted a cool and regal smile. "Of course, Mistress Alvedre. What is the difficult subject that you think will stir my noble wrath? You are trembling inwardly."

"Yes, my lady," acknowledged Alvedre with a flush of color rising to tint her cheeks. "The subject is Mistress Elizabeth. She is a very troubled woman."

"I know," acknowledged Rhianna.

"She requires help that you have not given," accused Alvedre, girding herself for the anger of her liege. "You have manipulated her mind and her husband's—in defiance of Ceallagh's laws—and you have not tried to give the healing that might excuse your action. My lady, you have clearly chosen your 'candidates for advanced study' by a criterion of independence as well as Power, but I am not so independent of Ixaxis that I can condone defiance of our solemn rules."

"I am trying to save our world, Alvedre."

"You would sacrifice Mistress Elizabeth and Master Jonathan in the process? How does that make you superior to a Sorcerer Queen?"

Rhianna's stormy eyes held Alvedre, whose heart trembled from dread of the Infortiare's terrible Power, but Alvedre stood firm; the attack did not come. "What would you have me do?" whispered Rhianna. "Offer our world to almost certain destruction? Even if Network intends us no harm, the very magnitude of their differences from us could overcome us. I know better than you the dangers of my nearly unfettered authority, and Queen Joli is hardly ignorant of the hazards. She said it to me: Power serves itself, but it is our only defense."

"Heal Mistress Elizabeth," pleaded Alvedre, "that I may believe your good intents."

"Do you think I have not tried?"

"You can give her more: You have shared her loss, for your own child grew to manhood without knowing you. You may have tried to help her remotely, but you have not risked any hurt to yourself." Alvedre spoke sternly, as if chiding one of her students and not her own liege. "If this is the failing of major Power, I would be

glad of a less Powerful Infortiare. You are quite as bad
as Quin."

"You are opinionated as well as independent," observed
Rhianna with a grimace.

"The expression of truth is my own Power's particular
compulsion. It is not always a pleasant burden."

"It does not improve diplomacy, in any case," agreed
Rhianna. She raised her slender hand toward the thickly
verdant tree that leaned above her. "Years ago, I healed
this oak. I have always had a strong affinity for the simple, quiet spirits of our world, though I lost a large measure of my closeness to the trees when Kaedric stirred
my Power into brighter life. I lost the trees; I lost my
husband; I lost my son. And I lost none of them."

"You can teach Mistress Elizabeth to hope again."

"No, Alvedre. Only time can teach her that lesson."

"Talk to her—not as a wizardess, but as a woman who
has endured and survived. She will listen to you, for the
two of you have much in common."

"Do you know either of us that well?" asked Rhianna
with crisp cynicism.

Alvedre's soft eyes became sad. "Do you disagree with
me, my lady?"

Rhianna answered quietly, "No. I do not disagree."
She left Alvedre abruptly, and she moved with the haste
of determined escape. Alvedre frowned: She did not
doubt the necessity of her words to the Infortiare, but
she wondered if she had underestimated the pain those
words would cause.

* * *

Rhianna stared at the papers on her desk, weighing
too many difficult decisions. She raised her head, sensing
her visitor, and her Power bid him enter. "Lord Quinzaine," acknowledged Rhianna from her desk, as Quin
entered her library. "I thank you for coming promptly."

"Would I disregard my liege's command?" asked Quin
with a twisted grin of irony. "I know why you have summoned me."

"Do you?"

"You want me to use the Taormin."

"Is that what Evaric told you?"

"Not precisely," replied Quin, the discomfort of his

conversation with the Lady's son reviving. "I extrapolated."

"Correctly, as it happens. You are adept at perceiving and conveying thoughts and emotions."

"That seems to be the form of my Power," admitted Quin.

"It is an uncommon gift. Lord Hrgh dur Liin possessed it, as perhaps you know."

"Mistress Amila once remarked on the unfortunate similarity, my lady."

"The resemblance is not entirely unfortunate: Lord Hrgh very nearly became Infortiare, and you appear to have escaped his fatal flaw of pride."

Quin rubbed the tightening muscles of his neck, and he suppressed his Power's urge to close away all memory of his liege and her "advanced training." "I am not the heir of Liin, my lady, nor even heir of Hamley."

Rhianna smiled slightly, and her Power whispered, *Few Ixaxins are willing to jeopardize their pride by facing such an uncertain threat as Network. Fewer Ixaxins are able to employ Power with sufficient delicacy to charm forgiveness from envious mortals. You are flexible, resourceful, and capable. You will be an excellent Network emissary, Lord Quinzaine, if you hold to your purpose and restrain yourself from playing the foolish pranks of your Power's camouflage.*

"You want me to travel to Network?" asked Quin incredulously.

"Yes, Quinzaine. The gate is the Taormin. If you master its use, as I intend, you will learn to distinguish the paths."

"Will the other students make this journey as well?"

"Not unless circumstances change significantly, or I revise my assessment of their capacities to survive the process."

Quin forced himself to disregard his growing fear. "Do the other students know your decision?"

"Not yet. They will continue to study with you, and you will not speak of this conversation to them. They will not know of your special task, until you are gone."

"Why are you telling me now, if no one else may know?"

"Perhaps," said Rhianna wryly, "because I am testing

your ability to keep a secret, an obvious prerequisite to maintaining a false identity."

"I am a poor choice," protested Quin wanly.

"Do you dispute my judgment?" asked Rhianna, and her Power burned with a harsh reminder of its potency.

Quin rubbed his head, trying to dispel the ache. "No, my lady." *How can one argue with the Infortiare?* he grumbled to himself. When Rhianna smiled remotely, Quin strengthened the barriers of his Power enough to conceal his thoughts from her. Rhianna laughed softly, and Quin acknowledged with a grimace that she had provoked him into passing yet another of her unending tests. "I am glad I never had you as an instructor in my wayward childhood, Lady Rhianna. You never let me cheat at all."

"If you had ever cheated half as effectively as you believed, Quinzaine, you would never have been made a scholar. You portray the fool convincingly, but you cannot deceive Power." Her gaze became remote. "None of us can deceive Power. We only deceive ourselves."

CHAPTER 9

Serii

Pieces without form or shape, needing urgently to be used, but so nebulous and weighty that the binding of them required more wit or skill or artistry than Quin could commandeer: Like forcing passage through a reedy marsh, the elemental act of thought demanded effort beyond reason. *Why?* Quin asked of himself and could not recall the answer. He proceeded, because he had forgotten also the momentary doubt.

A motion, there: Pain struck at his nerves, traveling the length of his arm, jolting him bearably at first, but the anticipation of the pain grew to torture as a hundred nerves jumped in turn, and another hundred followed. Each nerve, tested and released, settled shakily. The right arm felt numb; the prods began a course across the arch of his foot, each touch a bright needle of fire plunging to the depths of tendon and bone.

Teetering on a bridge of fire and ice, Quin saw the molten shadow of a separate Power: *The Infortiare or another?* Before he could complete the moment of wondering, the shadow had shifted and gone, leaving him alone. *No: Someone remained, or something remained.* He almost spoke to it, but he sensed its strangeness, and he reached for a language it would understand. A lovely, simple language: *how unique*, thought Quin, *and how delightful.* To express thought with such precision forced adjustment; this language lacked the customary layers of subtlety or nuance, but it conveyed a brilliant clarity that

Quin admired for its difference from anything he recognized.

The shadow reappeared and beckoned, but Quin had found a more engrossing beacon. The pain that had assaulted him disappeared, for he no longer recognized it. He pursued the trail of bright logic, and the chaos became suddenly orderly, though the pieces had not changed, and the forces had not coalesced. The patterns of it emerged from the alien language, and Quin understood and found it both strikingly beautiful and deeply satisfying.

So much to explore, to experience, and to appreciate! Quin felt urged to rush eagerly, but harsh Ixaxin training held him to calm, and he sent strands of his own Power along the tentative, shivering paths. Some strands burned, and some strands snapped, but some became stronger than Quin's imagination, and they stretched to distances beyond distances.

Quin's Power burned within him, where it had seldom been more than an uninvited, unobtrusive attribute, more demanding than demanded: a nuisance, for Ixaxin regimens made it so generally humorless and solemn. Quin let his Power grow and touch infinity, and when he knew that nothing could constrain him, he let the Power and the patterns flow through him, expanding and reaching for universes, life, minds both strange and strangely familiar/unfamiliar of form: *There is so much to touch and hold and try! There are so many pathways to explore! I wish that I could share these marvels with Laurett. . . .*

Quin began to run in ten directions all at once, until a leash of fire snapped him abruptly from his giddy journeys. Quin touched his head gingerly to see if it was as battered as it felt, but the wounds were all internal. Quin groaned, and he dropped his head between his knees to keep from fainting. "You were warned," said Rhianna sternly, "of the hazards of uncontrolled experimentation."

"Am I still alive?" moaned Quin.

"Yes, Quinzaine," replied Rhianna more gently, "you are still alive. You may wish otherwise for a few days."

"What did I touch, my lady?"

"The Taormin."

"There was a sentience: not human but intelligent and aware."

"It is the Taormin," she repeated. "It resides physically in D'hai, but I know its patterns well enough to be able to reach it by Power." Quin lifted his eyes to meet hers. He squinted, for the lamp's clear light aggravated the piercing pain inside his head. The lady touched his temples lightly, and she frowned, but Quin's pain became less excruciating. "The Taormin has an intelligence of its own, Quinzaine. Direct contact with it requires more strength of control than most wizards ever learn. Do not let your survival of this wonder lull you into further incaution."

"Did my survival surprise you, Lady Rhianna?" asked Quin with a trace of a lopsided grin.

"No. Your Power is strong, or I would not have asked this effort of you." Quin felt a mild disappointment blur into his more tangible hurts; it would have been amusing to have surprised the Infortiare—as much as he had surprised himself. "The extent of your initial progress exceeded my expectations, however," conceded Rhianna, and she smiled as Quin's expression conveyed his pleasure at her praise. "You have done well, Quinzaine. Rest now. You need to restore your energies."

Quin did not see her leave, for sleep enveloped him at the Lady's command. He dreamed of the Taormin's webs, and he whispered, "I have seen infinity, Luki. I have used the Widowshear."

* * *

"So far," remarked Rhianna to her husband, "Lord Quinzaine's rate of progress in using the Taormin is quite astonishing. If the Widowshear eased Quinzaine's adaptation to the Taormin so greatly, it could lessen the risk to the subsequent candidates."

"I doubt that the Widowshear could help those who concern you most. It may be less dangerous, but it is at least as difficult to use as the Taormin."

"It would seem to be an excellent testing device."

"Possibly," conceded Kaedric. "It is Luki's property, however. I doubt that she will give it to you, and I know that you will not take it from her."

"Perhaps she will give it to Lord Quinzaine," murmured Rhianna, "or to the next handsome young wizard who captures her interest."

"She would give it to me, if I promised to visit her regularly," answered Kaedric with a shadow smile, "and she would certainly yield it to our son."

"Lyriel would not care for your suggestion."

"I do not know how Evaric abides so jealous a wife. Of course, I have never understood how you abide me either."

"With much patience, which you are testing at the moment." Their images/patterns shifted and blended caressingly. "Quit attempting to distract me, Kaedric," murmured Rhianna softly. "You succeed too easily."

"Tyrant," he replied evenly. "But be it as you wish: I remain doubtful of the Widowshear's value to us, even if Luki were willing to relinquish her treasure. I have only speculated as to its purpose, and the truth may be less pleasant and more hazardous." With a wicked humor, he added, "I might ask our guests' opinion."

"Dear Kaedric, if you asked anything of our guests, you would revive all their instinctive fears of us, which we are only now beginning to allay. You tended to terrify even in your mortal state."

"A reminder of our Power might do them good. Master Jonathan, in particular, shows an annoyingly arrogant attitude toward the candidates."

"Can you blame him? He and his wife have such knowledge! As much as they teach us, we learn chiefly the depth of our own ignorance, and you know they give us only the rudiments of their science. How I wish that I understood enough to reveal the knowledge outside Ixaxis."

"When our emissary is able to assess Network for us, then it will be time enough to determine how much knowledge we may disseminate safely."

"Are we sufficiently wise to make that decision?"

"You are the Infortiare, Rhianna. The decision is yours to make."

"Perhaps the question will never gain meaning. If the candidates fail to absorb enough understanding of Network lore, I shall not send any of them, and if Lord Quinzaine fails at any step in mastering the Taormin, I shall not dare to ask another to make the journey."

"Our son could master all requirements."

"Evaric would never leave Lyriel, and he is too necessary to this world's protection, as are we. The three of
us together can deflect the Network probes, but we comprise a thin defense at best, for a moment's lapse could
let a probe detect us. What good will we achieve by
studying Network secretly, if we abandon the shield that
hides us from them now?"

"Such weak, unfocused probes as we have seen recently
do not concern me," replied Kaedric slowly, "but I must
acknowledge that the defense is indeed imperfect. Jonathan Terry managed to locate us despite all our pattern
shifting and tangling, and we cannot be sure that others
in Network will not duplicate his work. The message that
we let him receive was weak enough that we could have
deflected it, but its path matched his manipulations of
the patterns precisely."

"Others would have followed him by now, if they had
the necessary skills," said Rhianna with a nervousness
that belied her assertion. "His people do not share his
depth of knowledge. They only imitate him—badly."

"If Jonathan Terry is so unique," mused Kaedric, "the
incentive to recover him—or eliminate him—must be
considerable."

"Please, Kaedric, stop escalating my fears."

"I am simply agreeing with you: We must rely on the
unpredictable Lord Quinzaine. We must augment our
investigation of Network, and we have no other possible
candidate at the moment."

"I have sensed the choice of him from the start, for
his is the only major Power available to us," sighed Rhianna, "but I should feel more comfortable with a less
eccentric option."

"I shall give him a good lesson in behavioral restraint,
before we send him."

"I hope he survives the process," remarked Rhianna
dryly. "He has suffered enough from his Power's sensitivity. His retreat from such hurts has created most of his
problems."

"He needs to recognize his assets and their limitations.
He needs to understand me a little, if he is to understand himself at all. The lesson may seem cruel, but it

is necessary—like the Test of Mastery at a more advanced level."

"I nearly died from my first contact with your direct Power."

"You were completely untrained and unprepared."

"Be careful with him, Kaedric. We need him too greatly."

* * *

When Quin awoke in one of the myriad guest chambers of the Infortiare's Tower, he could not initially recall having slept at all. He felt alert and eagerly alive, and a part of him hungered to meet the Taormin once again. He turned too hastily, and the last traces of a headache reminded him of his earlier experience.

"Impatience will kill you," remarked a cold voice that caused Quin to snap upright. Every instinct of Power shouted danger in him, and he scanned his surroundings with a caution built both of Ixaxin lore and Laurett's instruction in survival.

Nothing: there was nothing to be found. *Trust your instincts*, cautioned Laurett's words in his head. Quin leaned carefully back against the carved headboard. "A friend of mine often chides me for impatience," he commented softly to the empty room.

"Luki," replied the same chill, sourceless voice.

"Yes," answered Quin, surprised and increasingly wary. "Do you know her?"

"I knew her. I, also, used the Widowshear."

"Lord Venkarel," murmured Quin. Part of him had expected this eerie visit; the Infortiare had warned that her husband would come, but the sense of talking to the most deadly of legendary figures defied full acceptance. The concept of the conversation fascinated Quin with its very implausibility, even as he recognized that the fierce Power of Lord Venkarel could indeed eradicate him without effort or pause. "Is this to be another lesson for me?"

"This is a warning, Lord Quinzaine. If we entrust you with the freedom of Network, do not think that you will be free of us. Behave irresponsibly, and I shall snatch you from that space and hurl you into hell. Err, and I shall kill you before you can consider penitence, because

I shall not jeopardize Serii or the rest of this world of ours; I shall not jeopardize my wife or my son."

"You intend to accompany me to Network?" asked Quin uneasily.

"I intend to observe you, so as to ensure that you suffer no severe lapses of judgment. Lest you feel tempted to forget your purpose and your loyalty while you sojourn in Network, I shall give you a small token for recollection." The fire against Quin's left hand flashed so quickly that Quin scarcely felt the pain, until it eased to the dull throb of an old burn. "As the K'shai branded my son with the assassin's emblem, so I brand you with the seal of the Infortiare, whom you serve and will serve for as long as you live. Remember whence your Power comes."

Quin stared at the tiny, darkened circle marring the center of his palm, marking the body's primary focal point for receiving energy. "It is too small to be recognizable as the Infortiare's seal," he remarked, then cursed his folly for tempting the Venkarel into remedying the flaw.

The sardonic laughter chilled Quin more than Lord Venkarel's cold, precise voice. "The mark is meant to serve as a reminder to you, not as a beacon of your origin."

Quin wondered if Lord Venkarel sensed the sudden thrill of anxious eagerness in him. "If I should need help while I am in Network, would you offer it?"

"Do not expect it. Where I cross the mortal realms, I am raw Power, Lord Quinzaine, and Power always prefers destruction."

* * *

The students dispersed quickly, as the class ended under twilight's gathering gloom. Jon grumbled in frustration at the inadequacy of the light, and the wicks of the candles in front of him caught fire. He jumped, and he glanced suspiciously at Rhianna, who had lingered near the door while the other students left. She smiled faintly.

"I wish they would give me some warning before they play such tricks," he muttered to Beth.

"They behave as is natural to them," answered Beth,

as she gathered her notes, all written laboriously on parchment and copied by hand for every student in the class. "They manipulate fire as normally as you might move that charcoal pencil in your hand."

"It is a disquieting habit." Jon nodded toward Rhianna. "And she knows it."

"The Immortals have evolved to use fear skillfully, because they are feared regardless of their intentions."

Jon grunted, not caring for the truth of Beth's analysis. Ever since they'd arrived at the Infortiare's Tower (after a wretchedly uncomfortable night's ride in a jostling carriage), Jon and Beth had encountered inhabitants of the Queen's castle only in the company of one of the wizards; fear of the wizards was evident in the briefest of meetings.

Rhianna had spoken of the Seriin Alliance, Ixaxis, Queen Joli and the Queen's advisory Council of domain lords, but she said little about the mortal peoples or their relation to the wizards' realm. The omission seemed significant: They were isolated by their gifts. Aside from Rhianna and the excessively gallant, teasingly mysterious Lord Arineuil, none of the ruling lords had appeared in the Tower.

Jon watched the Infortiare confer softly with the young man named Quin, who behaved so absurdly in the classroom but showed astonishing quickness in the private sessions. The young man, usually so uncannily cheerful, had a somber expression as he left the room. Rhianna glided toward the Terrys.

"Are you satisfied with your students' progress?" asked Rhianna.

"The depth of their ignorance is appalling," mumbled Jon, gesturing at a sputtering oil lamp. "How can your people have forgotten so much?"

"They are all highly intelligent," answered Beth, more diplomatic than her husband. "They mastered Network's language at a phenomenal rate, simply to allow us to teach in our native tongue."

Jon said gruffly, "They should do as well in the subjects we ask them to learn. Your people's concepts of physics, Lady Rhianna, are worse than nonexistent. Your people do not choose to accept that matter and energy behave predictably, according to well-defined models.

They seem to envision the universe as a philosophical figment of their own collective imaginations, subject to change at whim!"

Beth tried to calm him: "Jon, you are trying to duplicate lessons that Network spends years teaching to its students. You cannot expect to bring these students immediately to university standards in all fields."

"They do have a reasonable comprehension of mathematics, at least," admitted Jon, "which lets them manipulate scientific abstractions. If they could demonstrate the slightest practical insight, they might become competent theoreticians, but they simply refuse to believe the most trivial fundamentals. They humor me!"

"We are trying to adapt our way of thinking, Dr. Terry, but the process is neither smooth nor necessarily one-sided. Your own studies," remarked Rhianna evenly, "could benefit from similar flexibility of knowledge."

Jon glared, as Beth smiled slightly and explained, "Lady Rhianna, my husband has been accused of embracing too many unpopular ideas, such as my own specialty of psychic research, but he has rarely had his own theories questioned. You injure his pride."

"Then we can learn humility together," replied Rhianna briskly.

Jon leaned back in the cracked leather chair, and he folded his hands across his stomach. The challenge was too much; he could not let this golden wisp of a woman think she could best him on the field of learning. "Lady Rhianna, shall I interpret your own postulates of wizardry for you? You acknowledge three elements: 'matter' clearly refers to any physical substance with coarsely perceptible mass; 'energy' covers the electromagnetic spectrum." He smiled, relishing the Lady's dazed retreat back a pace. " 'Infinity,' " he sighed, "is my personal favorite, for it is the native realm of the topologist. Your laws of wizardry are worded differently, and your implementations are formed of your own brain tissues instead of Network circuits, but the fundamentals are the same as applied topology in any space."

Beth murmured hesitantly, "That is how they used the DI controller to reopen this world. Because their 'science' and ours overlap in the field of topological concepts."

Jon nodded rapidly, proud of his wife's quick understanding. "They control topological transfers at will: It is their 'commutation of infinity.'"

Rhianna, so generally aloof and unapproachable, looked pale and faint, and she leaned against the nearest table. Jon's satisfaction ebbed, for the Lady's reaction was too strong, and he suddenly realized how much he might have betrayed to her by his outburst of frustration.

Beth had followed Jon's gaze, matched his reasoning, and stepped beyond it. She said softly, "The law that you quote, Jon, was a handwritten addition in fairly fresh ink."

Rhianna whispered, "It is Kaedric's addendum to Zerus' postulates."

"Who is Kaedric?" demanded Jon, irritated with himself for having failed to consider the possibility of current research among the wizards. They seemed so static and burdened with tradition. Beth understood these people much more readily. . . .

To Jon's astonishment, Rhianna blushed in answering, "Kaedric was the birthname of Lord Venkarel, my predecessor as Infortiare."

"Your predecessor? Unfortunate," mused Jon. "If he were still alive, he might be informative."

Beth laid her hand on Jon's shoulder, and he glanced at her curiously. "Alvedre informed me that Lord Venkarel was Lady Rhianna's husband," said Beth quietly. "We did not mean to remind you of your loss, Lady Rhianna."

"I know," said Rhianna, and she smiled with her lips alone. "You have succeeded in disconcerting me, Master Jonathan, if that was your intent. My husband's name is not mentioned often in our histories, for he was not popular among mortals, and they prefer to forget that he existed. Kaedric recognized his 'addendum' when he confronted Horlach, the same sorcerer who taunted you into closing your world—this world. Horlach, in order to retain his Power, sacrificed his mortal, physical form and became a creature of energy. In order to defeat Horlach. . . ." Rhianna's voice trailed into unsteady silence.

Lord Arineuil spoke crisply from the door, and he finished for her, "In order to defeat Horlach, Kaedric moved beyond Horlach. As energy dominates matter by Power's scale, so infinity rules energy. Horlach had assumed the nature of energy, so Kaedric assumed the nature of infinity. Our Venkarel was never a man for half measures."

Jon scowled at the silken-mannered courtier leaning in the doorway. "A man cannot become a spatial topology."

"Kaedric was much more Power than man," retorted Ineuil with a sharp glance at Rhianna, "except to her."

Beth left Jon's side to put her arms around Rhianna, who looked at her in surprise. "I am so sorry," murmured Beth with deep sympathy. "You claimed to understand my sorrow, but I did not believe you. I did not realize. . . . You must have loved him very much."

Rhianna withdrew gently from Beth's effusive concern, but a rare, soft shimmer of the Infortiare's fierce Power touched Beth lightly. Beth felt the wondrous breath of healing cradle every injured memory and ache of loss. The burdens did not disappear, but they seemed to become less weighty with the sharing.

"When we let our fears rule us," said Rhianna, "we see enemies at every turn, even in the eyes of those who should be recognized as friends."

"Does that comment apply to you or to us?" asked Jon with a frown, for he could see the wonder in Beth's eyes, but he could not see the Lady's bonding Power.

"It applies to all of us," answered Rhianna, spreading her thin hands. She seemed to grow tall with the inspiration that had filled her at Beth's spontaneous warmth. "Fear is a foolish indulgence between us, for we are each of us small and weak, alone before a mighty foe. I have deceived you out of distrust for too many years. I kept your memories hidden until a greater fear displaced my suspicions of you. Alvedre was wiser than I. . . ."

Rhianna seemed to harden in resolve. "Master Jonathan, Mistress Elizabeth, I intend to send an emissary to your Network to observe in secret, so that we may better protect ourselves from any outside threat. Your teachings have provided us this opportunity, and I apologize for having been less forthright about my intentions until now. I would appreciate any further insights or recommendations you might give, if you approve my plan."

"When I offered the exchange of knowledge," said Jon thoughtfully, "I expected mutual benefit, but sending one of your people to Network could jeopardize us all."

"Lady Rhianna, can you locate my children and bring them to me?" demanded Beth with a hushed eagerness of new hope.

"They do not remember us, Beth," said Jon sharply, "and they are monitored closely."

Beth shook her head, refusing to hear him. "Lady Rhianna, can you return them to me?"

"I am unsure," answered Rhianna, feeling Beth's deep, cutting hurt as her own. "Though you have taught us a great deal about your science, language, and history, we have little idea of what to expect from daily living. My emissary is not likely to blend well enough to move freely."

"We shall help you," said Beth with fierce assurance. "There are enough subcultures in Network to disguise unusual customs, and Jon can tell you how to establish a Network identity, which is the most crucial element of Network citizenship. If Network accepts your emissary, no one else will doubt."

"Beth," protested Jon, alarmed by his wife's impulsive offer, "Network identities are not that easy to arrange."

"You have arranged them before," retorted Beth. "You arranged them for your Neoterra conspirators."

Jon blinked, as the recovery trigger for a self-inflicted form of mind conditioning became activated. "Neoterra," he uttered in amazement, for even the name's memory had long lain buried.

"The other memories will revive, Jon," said Beth gently, "for you entrusted me with the triggers. I was your twelfth conspirator, Jon: the one whose name was erased from all of your minds, so that you would truly believe me innocent of information if ever you were caught by Network officials. You did succeed in that: They did not try to interrogate me."

"How easily do your people manipulate infinities, Lady Rhianna?" asked Jon, staring at his wife with a frown of concentration.

Rhianna, who had listened to the Terrys' exchange, replied quickly, "Only a few of us have that skill, and we are constrained by the patterns of the Taormin, which is our name for your controller mechanism."

"You realize that your Taormin was designed to operate in conjunction with an enormous power source, which I destroyed?" said Jon. Beth had begun to smile, for she understood him.

"A major Power is required to control it," agreed Rhianna, "though a Power that is merely strong may be guided through the energy patterns, if great care is exerted."

"Can you guide a 'mortal'?"

"The required Power and concentration is tremendous. My husband once managed it, but I know of no other who has matched his achievement. Many Powerful wizards have become lost forever in the Taormin, and the risk is much greater with every added pattern that must be held in mind."

"I can reduce the Power requirements and quantify some of the basic mappings for you, but we need to establish some common fundamentals first." Jon turned slightly, and he seemed to recall his surroundings with renewed frustration. "I need a writing board," he muttered. "We need to correlate your language of 'patterns' with the standard mathematical models, if we are to learn how to direct transfers efficiently. I may need access to the device itself."

"Do you intend to have me guide you through the Taormin?" asked Rhianna, twisting the chain of her pendant.

"Guide us or our children," answered Beth, "and guide your own people as well. Together, we may have hope."

"I wish I had access to a Network computer for an hour," sighed Jon. He fumbled in the pockets of his rumpled Seriin coat. "Beth, do you have that quill I modified?"

"No, Jon," replied his wife with a patient pride in his intensity of focus, once awakened to a purpose.

The golden Infortiare pulled a quill and parchment from the drawer of the table she had used as sometime student, and she swept toward Jon. "The quill is Ixaxin," she informed Jon, "and may please you better than its clumsier relatives. Ineuil, would you bring those chairs here, please?"

Ineuil laughed and moved as he was bidden. He offered a chair to Beth and whispered to her, "Your husband is not alone in his blind zeal for new ideas. You are prepared for a long night, I hope."

CHAPTER 10

Serii and Network

"A feudal primitive," growled Jonathan Terry, his doubts at their zenith with the early morning, "however intelligent, cannot deceive Network for a protracted length of time. Our hostess' emissary will never fit the statistical profile of a Network citizen. Why did I agree to this insane plan of a fairy-tale mystic who lives by sword and candlelight?"

"Because we need her help if we are ever to regain our children."

"And if we are ever to leave this barbaric world," added Jon, throwing his quill to the table in disgust. "I am not sure these people even qualify as human. How will the emissary register on Network sensors?"

"They are as human as their ancestors. At worst, someone may suspect that the emissary is some disguised alien tourist, observing Network without Consortium approval."

"Consortium members share the Calongi contempt for all that is not Consortium. They certainly do not stoop to the acquisition of falsified Network identities, and they are far more culturally similar to Network than these people."

"The affectations of anachronists diverge wildly from the Network norm," argued Beth, trying to convince herself, "and I cannot believe that Council Governor Caragen has allowed Network to change substantially in twenty years."

"Yes," conceded Jon reluctantly, "Andrew Caragen still rules, it seems." He retrieved his fallen quill and worried its ragged feather. "I am not sure that Network could survive without Caragen. Despite his flaws, he is the only human leader who has managed to maintain a successful, technologically sophisticated civilization independent of the Consortium." Jon leaned back in the leather chair and grimaced when it failed to accommodate the curve of his back. "These people cannot design a decent chair," he grumbled, "yet they plan to transfer themselves to Network by thinking the 'patterns' of a topological controller."

"These are the same people who reopened the world you closed. These are the same people from whom you learned the methods of pseudo-closure."

"Their approach to applied topology often seems irrational," replied Jon slowly, "but it does produce sound results. They have a unique concept of the physical laws."

"They call it wizardry."

"But it is their science." Jon rubbed his temples, which had become gray after so many years away from Network's preservative techniques. "I should like to have met their Lord Venkarel. He seems to have produced the only significant Seriin advances in the past ten millennia. I should like to debate topological theories with him, instead of abetting schemes of intrigue. I am tired of power struggles. I am tired of fighting other peoples' wars."

"Neutrality has not been an option for you, Jon, since the moment you handed Network the first topological controller for the spatial transfer of human beings."

"The primary Controller for this planet," mused Jon, remembering. "I received a personal commendation from Andrew Caragen." He laughed with bitter humor.

Rhianna entered silently, and Beth caught her breath in anticipation of seeing the emissary who would follow. Rhianna had been adamant in her refusal to disclose the emissary's identity. Jon and Beth had concluded uneasily that the secrecy's purpose lay against the Lady's own people, who presumably knew little of the Infortiare's schemes.

Jon could sense Beth's alarm as she contemplated the

prospect of this young man, Quin, as the emissary to observe her children. He was a good looking youth and certainly one of the most amiable of the candidates, but he was unpredictable and never obviously attentive—until he produced some unlikely comment that suggested an extraordinarily keen intelligence and memory.

Jon met Rhianna's cloud-gray eyes squarely. "Is this your emissary?"

"Yes. Lord Quinzaine has accepted that responsibility."

Jon turned to Quin and asked him pointedly, "Do you consider yourself sufficiently knowledgeable of Network to portray a convincing Network citizen?"

"I shall do my best," replied Quin with a weak grin.

"That is not an answer," snapped Jon. "Do you remember how to activate the identity code?" *A precious code that Amman helped me to prepare in another life. I wonder if any of my conspirators survived to reach Neoterra?*

"I simply announce myself to Network as citizen jq955yj36."

"Where will you go first?"

"We have identified a Network transfer port, where I shall emerge first from the Taormin's patterns. From that point, I shall request transfer either to Chia-2, where your son reportedly lives, or to Daedalon, where I may expect to find your daughter. Since Chia-2 has a fairly restricted population, I shall probably select Daedalon as my base." Quin glanced at Rhianna, as if seeking her guidance in the extent of his answer.

Rhianna said quietly, "We discussed what you told us regarding Network's universities and concluded that a student's role would suit our purposes best. It will excuse some ignorance while allowing an excellent position for observation."

"You cannot enroll your delegate at Harberg!" exclaimed Beth. "The admission standards of Harberg are among the highest in Network."

Rhianna replied, "You informed us that this identity code could be adjusted to fit any history, provide any credentials or qualifications, and generally enable its owner to establish himself anywhere in Network."

"A student's admission might be falsified," argued

Jon, wondering why Lady Rhianna had assumed that remote, unseeing expression that Jon associated with her most intensely calculating moods, "but we cannot create a convincing Harberg student on demand." Jon addressed Quin directly. "Even if you meet the intelligence standards legitimately, you lack adequate educational background."

"At worst, your people would ask me to leave," answered Quin with a shrug, "which could only injure my pride. My future employability quotient with Network cannot be threatened, since it does not exist."

Beth sighed, then began to laugh ruefully. "His point is perfectly true, Jon. If Network enrolled an unqualified student at Harberg, the school officials would never question his admission, because they would never question Network. They could expel the student, but he would not be the first to fail Harberg."

Jon stared at his wife with an emotion akin to dismay, for she seemed suddenly so much a part of *this* place and people, a part of their schemes—a lady of Serii like the pale-haired Immortal whose distant smile seemed so disturbingly secretive. Jon shook his head. The emissary grinned crookedly. The golden lady exchanged a whisper with a ghost.

"I should have confined myself to useless theory," muttered Jon, "with the rest of my Network colleagues. My life would have been much simpler."

* * *

Sitting in the near-darkness of a fading day, Lord Quinzaine dur Hamley considered the nature of infinity and imagined the reaction of his fellow Ixaxin instructors to his present appearance. He had exchanged his sedate scholar's robe for a costume which reflected a combination of Quin's slightly skewed sense of humor with the fashions of Network's sect of Anachronists, as described by Jonathan and Elizabeth Terry.

Quin would not see Ixaxis' reaction, which disappointed him; he had not expected to leave Serii so soon or so suddenly. He had planned to visit Luki again; he had planned to buy presents for several of his Tulean cousins to take to Hamley. Departure had not seemed so tangible until now, when he realized that something as simple as a foray into the Tulean marketplace must be postponed.

Rhianna's Power touched Quin, reminding him of the immediate task before him. He gathered a deep breath and let his Power delve into the Taormin. He joined the Infortiare where the coils of strange energies connected the Taormin to Network. The patterns twisted here, and they fell abruptly into a darkness devoid of more than light. The journey seemed more daunting, now that it grew imminent. "Have you taken this step, Lady Rhianna?" asked Quin.

"Have I traveled to Network? Not as you will travel. I have touched Network with my Power; I have examined the patterns of its strangeness. Like my husband and my son, I am too intrinsic to the concealment of the patterns of this space at present; I dare not leave."

"Then I am the first."

"I thought you had acknowledged the risk."

"Have you ever seen a vulpas, my lady?"

"No."

"When it stands before you, a vulpas becomes much larger and more terrible than any description conveys."

Rhianna smiled faintly. "You are well armed for your battle, Lord Quinzaine."

"These people whom I must seek: Michael and Katerin Merel. I am still not sure I understand what I must do when I find them."

"Consider them distant cousins whom you must visit on behalf of a doting aunt. Surely, your family has made such requests of you in your travels."

"My cousins were never quite so distant."

"You have the children's names and as much of their natures as we could derive from their parents' memories. When you have found them, you will know them by your Power. You will concentrate subsequently on the larger effort, which is the assimilation of Network."

"What do you expect me to discover that you cannot learn better from Master Jonathan and Mistress Elizabeth?" He had asked the question before, but equivocation had been his only reply.

Rhianna fingered the chain of her pendant, and she allowed Quin to sense a shuddering instant of her own single contact with Network. "When my son took the

Taormin," she whispered, "and restored our world to its proper space, I touched the pattern of a mortal man who had defeated the most dreaded Sorcerer King of our history, initiated the sequence of events which created *us*, and gave *us* the potential to regain all that our ancestors discarded or destroyed. The man was Jonathan Terry, a man no more perfect than others of his kind, a man who knew nothing of Power."

Rhianna smiled wryly. "I learned a new humility on behalf of all wizardry. Even a Power capable of altering infinities can be defeated by a mortal who has knowledge. A mortal man of Network conquered our world once. The fact that he has never realized the fruits of his conquest testifies only to his personal honor, not to the honor of his species."

"Do you fear Network," asked Quin slowly, "or ignorance?"

"Ignorance makes us vulnerable to Network or to unknown others. We have regained a lost privilege to reach beyond our world, but we have lost security as well as isolation. Why are you grinning, Lord Quinzaine?"

"Do you know how long I have wanted to prove to some of the scholars that Ixaxis is not the center of the universe?"

Rhianna began a sharp reply: "I have not exerted such time and effort simply to fulfill a boy's prank." But the commitment had been made, and the moment had been planned too long to be abandoned because of a comment that only confirmed a truth she knew. "I do hope I have chosen wisely," she murmured, shaking her golden head at Quin's expression of injured innocence. To Quin's astonishment, Lady Rhianna laid one delicate hand against his cheek and admonished him earnestly, "Please be very careful, Quinzaine. Aunt Ezirae would never forgive me if I allowed one of her Hamley nephews to come to harm." The Infortiare added with a devilish twinkle in her glorious eyes, "And do not feel too ashamed that Kaedric frightens you. He even frightens himself at times."

"Does he frighten you, my lady?" asked Quin in honest wonder, as Lady Rhianna withdrew her gentle touch.

"Yes. But I love him too well to object." The Infortiare tilted her golden head to study Quin's reaction.

"Speak freely to me, Quinzaine. We are, after all, cousins of some distant sort."

"I was only considering that such fear must make for an uncomfortable relationship, and I am not sure I should care for it."

"Remember that thought before you try to impress young women with your Power," remarked Lady Rhianna evenly, and Quin had the uneasy sensation that he had just been manipulated into a trap that he could not quite define. "Fare well, Lord Quinzaine." Rhianna's Power prodded him and plunged him into the churning emptiness of paradoxically connected space.

Falling, drifting, floating in a whirl of fire and light and the purity of an energy unnamed, Quin flailed with his Power, until exhaustively trained instinct claimed control. *Upright,* Quin told himself. *You must not stumble into Network on your head.* The instants that seemed eternal ended in a rush of metallic-scented air and noises that burst and clanged in a brightly colored box. "Entry code?" demanded a voice that seemed strange and unnatural for reasons that Quin could not immediately define.

"Code," repeated Quin dumbly, disconcerted that it was done, that he was here, that this mythic-seeming place surrounded him in truth. Lords, it was noisy; no one had told him how noisy it would be. *Quit gawking,* he reminded himself in recollection of Luki's voice. *I never met anyone with such a talent for trouble,* chided a memory of Laurett, and Quin collected himself sharply. "Network citizen jq955yj36," he replied in his best Network Basic. "Secondary transfer to Chia-2, please."

"Aisle three," responded the cool voice of Network without hesitation, and Quin strode determinedly toward the designated queue.

*   *   *

In the surreal plane of a spatial anomaly, the golden-haired Infortiare of Serii sighed with a relief deeper than Quin's, and her concerns shifted to a new pattern of anticipation. "Have I unchained a dragon?" she whispered. Her husband's Power met her gently, but he gave her no answer.

CHAPTER 11

Network

Gray skies of evening, gray walls of night: Chia-2 cast a gloomy pall over Quin's near-euphoria of having reached Network successfully. He shivered, although his wool cloak wrapped him warmly, and he exited the single access of a nearly deserted transfer port. He forced himself to smile at the lone attendant, who barely glanced at Quin. The attendant's focus centered on the silvery desk before him, where tiny, illuminated figures enacted a human drama. Quin watched the display in fascination, feeling the energies that comprised it, until the attendant's discouraging glower prodded him to leave.

A door opened in front of Quin, and he tried not to show his startlement too clearly. The strands of Network's energy seemed almost overwhelming in their abundance, but this hazard had been anticipated; wizard's control sorted, filtered, and observed in careful detachment. Quin left the port building and was relieved to see significant numbers of pedestrians, pursuing their individual goals with little interest to spare for their fellows.

Quin followed the largest concentration of traffic and found himself entrapped with them on a waiting platform. *Commuter trams,* concluded Quin, recalling a lesson from Elizabeth Terry and sensing the energies of regular arrivals and departures.

The metallic monster that arrived, spewing and engulfing its passengers almost in the instant that it stopped,

272

stunned him despite his preparation, and he barely recovered himself in time to enter before the clear doors slid shut. The beast moved smoothly and quietly, but the sights of Chia-2's hivelike city raced past. Quin located an empty chair at the end of the second compartment, and he gave his rapt attention to the rush of views beyond the window.

Chia-2 was a dismal, unattractive planet, neither wealthy nor truly impoverished. After the initial novelty of the domed buildings and blockish towers waned, Quin found himself examining the gray-brown sky and distant, gray-brown hills. He lost his eagerness to look further. His first sampling of the much-dreaded Network's tremendous civilization disappointed him; it was ugly.

When the tram stopped, and several passengers disembarked, Quin realized that he needed to define his destination quickly. He closed his eyes, imitating several other passengers in pretending sleep, and he directed his Power in a wide probe. Chia-2's population was fairly small and well concentrated, but the search was daunting.

Quin frowned at the magnitude of his task and decided that he needed another approach. "Network citizens rely on Network," he whispered beneath his breath, but the thought of tackling Network's extensive energies immediately seemed more daunting than the search of all human patterns on Chia-2. He reopened his eyes to again see the changing view that did not truly seem to change at all.

Network sorts its citizens and segregates them into "compatible" modules, recalled Quin and smiled, for he knew the approach that he would use. At the next stop of the tram, Quin disembarked and located a cubicle that seemed to match Jonathan Terry's description of a public-use, private Network terminal: a small alcove with a seating ledge and a "primitive" display screen, concealed by a light distorting curtain when occupied. In the sudden silence of the cubicle's sound-protected confines, Quin asked hesitantly, "Network, where would I find a humanistic architect on Chia-2?"

A brittle voice replied tonelessly, "City section 19, residences. City section 25, offices."

He debated asking for Michael Merel directly, but the

Terrys' warnings of monitoring stifled the temptation. "Thank you, Network." After a last, curious inspection of the sterile cubicle, Quin returned to the tram platform. *Searching two city sections for Michael Merel's pattern should not require too much effort,* he decided. Quin embarked on the next tram, feeling almost accustomed to the process.

*   *   *

Louisa Merel pushed a damp brown curl behind her ear and wished that Network had accepted her request to miss this dismal social gathering. She disliked these people. She could not imagine why Michael enjoyed working with them.

Loisa preened a little, contemplating her selflessness in agreeing to work in the Chia-2 module, so as to support her husband's controversial decision to leave his post at Harberg. Loisa felt sure that Michael did not comprehend the extent of her sacrifice, although she had never concealed her distaste for the requisite social interactions with module coworkers. Loisa would have much preferred to pursue her administrative work at Harberg with associates whom she could have considered her intellectual and cultural peers. After all, Network had very nearly allowed her to attend Harberg herself.

"You would think," Loisa muttered, defiantly isolated in a corner of the hexagonal room, "that a man who served as an instructor at one of the finest universities in Network could have selected a more significant purpose than designing housing modules for manual laborers on Chia-2." Network discouraged job changes by making options unpleasant, but Loisa did not blame Network for the diminished prestige of her husband. She blamed Katerin.

After all, reasoned Loisa, *it was Katerin who forced us to leave Harberg. How could we possibly remain in the same work module with that spoiled, clinging cat of a woman? Imagine her living off her brother's kindness for all those years.*

Loisa considered Katerin Merel's obsessive attachment to Michael to be decidedly unhealthy, even if Network did sanction it. *Michael was much too generous, letting his frustration build that way without even telling his pre-*

cious Katerin a word of it, as if his sister were somehow more fragile and special than any other grown woman. Well, I resolved that problem for him. I made sure that Katerin knows exactly how much Michael resented all those years of responsibility for a selfish, demanding sister.

"It should have been Katerin who left Harberg," grumbled Loisa, for this was one point where she had failed to sway her husband. "The cat still knows how to make Michael feel guilty. She is a savage little manipulator!"

Absorbed in her bitter reverie, Loisa did not notice the young man approaching her, until he murmured something about the corner being a good vantage point for observing social behavior. He smiled with considerable charm, which allayed Loisa's suspicions only slightly. She did not recognize him, which might have worked to his advantage, since Loisa disliked nearly everyone she knew on Chia-2. He was also quite a handsome young man, and his attention appealed to Loisa's fragile ego. However, he was quite clearly an anachronist, and Loisa did not approve of such deviant cultural affectations. She did not smile at him.

Undaunted by Loisa's coldness, the young man remarked affably, "Did I hear someone mention that you are Loisa Merel? I spoke to your husband earlier: a very modest man. I have heard his accomplishments acclaimed by nearly everyone else here, but he only credited the great help provided by his associates. You must be very proud of him."

Loisa answered crisply, "When I married him, Michael held an important post at Harberg University. We both made significant sacrifices to come to this planet. The work here does not exercise Michael's skills adequately."

The anachronist tilted his head in a peculiarly reflective pose. His broad smile did not waver, but even Loisa's impervious senses recognized that her bitter answer had repelled him. Loisa observed with a critical eye that his teeth, though white and even, did not seem quite consistent with current human standards, and his nose was quite decidedly crooked. She turned her eyes from him to the blue, translucent shell of the room divider. She expected the anachronist to leave, and she became

increasingly annoyed with him on realizing that he had
no intention of allowing her to return yet to her serene,
solitary suffering.

"You are a very unpleasant woman," remarked the
anachronist. "Why do you enjoy making people dislike
you?"

Astonished by the man's impudence, Loisa turned
again to face him: a harmless, wide-eyed youth who continued to smile appealingly, as if awaiting her opinion on
the weather. He stood only slightly taller than Loisa.
His parents obviously came from poor genetic stock, she
decided with some satisfaction, *if they planned his genetic
composition at all.* Loisa considered several cutting comments regarding his below-standard height.

"Is it because you feel inferior to your husband and
his friends?" asked the young man softly. He tilted his
head and peered into Loisa's eyes with curious force.
"You remind me a great deal of my cousin Aimel. He
was injured as a boy, and he thinks the injury lessened
him, but it is only his bitterness that makes people avoid
him."

Loisa gaped at the anachronist. She wanted to devas-
tate him with a clever retort, but she could not speak.
Her mind could only form one phrase: *How can he
know?*

"Loisa, have you seen Dylon?" asked Michael, a tall,
angular man with sand-colored hair. "I want to show him
the plans for improving the third factory block." Loisa
clutched at her husband's arm; she felt a deep need of
his support. "I am sorry," he continued, a puzzled
expression furrowing his narrow face as he observed the
anachronist. "Did I interrupt?"

The young man smiled pensively. "Your wife and I
were discussing your work. She is very proud of you."

"Is she?" asked Michael in surprise; then embarrassment turned his fair skin ruddy. "We seldom speak of
my work."

I am proud of you, whispered Loisa in her mind, but
she said nothing aloud. She did not know why she found
praise so hard to voice.

The anachronist's peculiarly intense gaze tightened on
Michael, who jerked, almost as if struck. Michael frowned
and tried to speak, but he seemed to become disoriented

for a moment. The anachronist let his compelling gray eyes shift from Michael and drift idly across the room. "Have you joined the module recently?" asked Michael with only the faintest hesitation. "We have not met."

"Your observation is impeccably correct," replied the young man lightly, "but I have enjoyed meeting you both." He bowed, a formal gesture performed with an oddly devilish grin. He swirled his anachronist's cloak with evident delight in the ripple of heavy, forest green fabric, and he disappeared into the midst of a cluster of Michael's friends.

Loisa said fervently, "I want to go home now, Michael. Please, come home with me now."

"Yes," replied Michael absently, and he smoothed his sandy hair. "A peculiar man," he remarked without elaboration.

Loisa nodded and propelled her husband toward the door. Outside, she shivered, though the night was warm and clear. They walked the few paces to their home in silence.

"Network, is Marei sleeping?" demanded Loisa as she entered her apartment.

"Your daughter is sleeping soundly," replied the computer's synthesized voice, a coarse approximation of the standard Network voice heard on wealthier planets. "All of her readings are normal."

Loisa headed quickly toward her daughter's room to confirm Network's report, though she knew that Michael thought her anxiety excessive. "Let her sleep, Louisa," chided Michael. "Network is capable of alerting us accurately to any problem."

He is not usually so cynical or so sharp, thought Loisa. *He is angry with me for rushing our departure. He thinks I am overly protective of Marei. He does not understand: Marei is all that I have ever created. If Network continues to refuse our request for another child, Marei will be all that I shall ever create.* Loisa stopped at the door of her daughter's room and sighed to see Marei nestled happily in a cushioned corner of the protective infant-care unit.

Loisa would have gone to her daughter to touch and hold her, but Michael commanded the night-shield closed. "She needs her sleep," insisted Michael impatiently, "as do we."

* * *

"Who are you, Katerin?" asked the voice of Network.

The woman, who sat alone in her university office, answered with a brittle laugh, "Who am I? I am not a woman who is fond of introspection." Her face, habitually controlled to a state of masklike beauty, softened for only an instant. "Introspection brings only pain."

She was thin in the manner of the chronically nervous, and she gestured each time she spoke, making short, brusque motions with her fingers and her hands. Her blue eyes, shades darker than any common genetic choice, seldom remained still. Static images of her looked easily elegant, but they captured only a fragment of her practiced allure.

"Can you understand others, if you cannot understand yourself?" asked Network. "Your algorithms reflect too much insight into weaknesses of mind and spirit. You have learned the weaknesses by identifying them within yourself."

"Interesting analysis," she answered with sardonic approval, and she let her silken, ash-blonde hair sweep gracefully across her shoulder. "You suggest that I understand the emotionally traumatized, because I diagnose myself among them. My rehabilitation algorithms have proven highly successful. Surely I have applied my techniques to myself and effected a cure."

"You have achieved an appearance of stability and success, but your illness maintains its own life inside of you. It never leaves. It never allows you to forget."

"You are wrong," said Katerin with hard scorn, but the blankness of her stare suggested long suffering more than arrogance. "It never allows me to remember."

"What of the dream?"

Katerin's dark blue eyes shifted to the wall, a slightly rounded expanse of cream-colored textures and abstract designs. "Are you referring to a particular dream?" she asked with the steady calm that she had practiced for nearly thirteen years.

"You know."

"No."

"The rape."

"I was raped when I was seventeen." She shrugged, as if the incident were of no account.

"Were you?"

"No." She frowned slightly. "Yes. Occasionally, I have nightmares about him."

"About the man who raped you?"

"Yes." Katerin began to chew the nail of her thumb, but she jerked her hands back to the arms of her chair, trying to regain her poise. "No. He is the man I cannot remember, the man who raped my mind."

"There are chemical treatments to heal the memory process."

"My eidetic, short-term and long-term memory processess all function normally. My memory loss is not a physical defect."

"You have been conditioned. The process can be reversed."

"State-dependent memories are triggered by re-creation of the circumstances surrounding the events."

"You do not wish to reenact past incidents."

"No."

"What do you remember of your childhood, Katerin?"

"Michael."

"Your brother?"

"Of course."

"You cannot remember your parents?"

"I have a mimovue of them," replied Katerin firmly.

"But you cannot remember them, can you? You remember your brother and the school where you both lived before Michael entered Harberg."

"We did have natural parents," said Katerin defiantly. "I have the mimovue. Michael hid it from Marrach." Katerin crossed her arms in front of her, and she drew her long legs into the contours of the adaptive chair. The gauzy white web of her skirt fluttered briefly and settled across her knees and ankles.

"Who is Marrach?"

"He was. . . ." Katerin shook her head irritably, and the smooth length of her golden hair swayed. "What does it matter?"

"Who was he?"

She answered almost inaudibly, "I cannot remember." She counted the indentations that comprised a star-shaped pattern on the wall of her university office. "He is the nightmare," she added tentatively, and she allowed her eyes to lose focus, as she tried to capture an elusive memory that ran from her like a broken dream. "Terminate algorithm," she said abruptly, and she unfurled herself from the padded depths of the chair.

"Yes, Katerin," replied the impersonal, genderless voice that Katerin favored for her Network contacts. "You have only two more days left to submit your justification for refusing an assistant."

"I thought I finished that letter," muttered Katerin. "Resubmit last term's memorandum with the appropriate date change."

"Previous justification, 'current research not suitable for apprentice support,' is inadequate for more than three consecutive terms. Specific reasoning must be supplied, or assistant will be assigned."

"What do you recommend?

"Accept an assistant. Apprenticeship promotes development of Network resources."

"Training an assistant at this time would seriously impair my progress with the new algorithm," snapped Katerin. She struck her desk, illuminating a model of the human brain in a neural pattern indicative of anger. "Very amusing, Network," she murmured dryly, and the model darkened and disappeared. "Where is the module meeting tonight?"

"Professor Cavli's apartment."

"Dear Cindal," sighed Katerin. "She hosts more than her share, and I am too selfish to protest her generosity." Katerin collected her wrist terminal from her desk and clasped it around her arm. When the warmth of her body had activated the connection to Network, she left the office. She did not pause in the cool, sterile laboratory, which housed the boxes of new equipment, awaiting installation.

An assistant could be useful in preparing the new system for the algorithm, she acknowledged with a trace of resignation. *I am paid to train students, as well as to perform research. I could bear it, if I could choose the assistant. . . . No, I would choose none. Network will choose one and then another, and soon I shall have no privacy at all.*

Katerin shivered as she emerged from the stately build-

ing that housed her office, though the exterior air was
barely cooler than any carefully controlled artificial environment. She skipped with practiced haste down the
long, wide stairway of the building's imposing entrance,
and she wondered, as usual, why the university's architect had felt compelled to ensure the authenticity of the
classical style even at the expense of practicality. "The
occasional use of an automated lift," she grumbled,
"would not impair the physical well-being of the faculty
members, who must climb and descend these detestable
stairs a dozen times a day."

"Cursing the school architects again?" asked the man
who awaited her at the stairway's base.

Katerin laughed, but she felt a rush of mingled pleasure and wariness. Only Michael had ever considered her
at all predictable, and she felt disconcerted by the realization that someone else had taken the trouble to know
her foibles. Indulging herself in the pretense that she
could sustain a true friendship, she smiled, transforming
her austerely elegant beauty into warmth, "I prefer the
classical style in men rather than buildings, Radge,"
replied Katerin with a teasing solemnity.

"Bless your discernment!" answered Radge, who never
dissembled regarding his significant gifts of feature and
physique. He kissed Katerin lightly on the cheek, before
she could evade him. "Shall we skip the formal social
exchange and create our own evening event?"

"Network would berate us both for our social negligence," retorted Katerine lightly, though alarm shivered
through her.

"Only you could prefer Cindal's alien parlor games to
an evening alone with he who was voted the most exciting man in the university."

"You bribed the judges to win your title," accused
Katerin with a faint easing of her concern; she only worried when Radge tried to move beyond light banter. "I
seem to recall that two members of the student nominat-
ing committee were your research assistants." Katerin
left the walkway to cross the lush fiber-lawn, and Radge
joined her. She eluded Radge's arm with grace.

Radge accepted her avoidance of his touch with a wry
grimace. "Perhaps those young women were better qualified than you to make the nomination, dear Katerin."

Katerin glanced sharply at Radge. *He knows your fear,* she thought with horror, but her small, rationally detached inner voice reassured her: *If he knew of the illness in you, he would not have spent the larger part of two years pursuing you. He is a danger only because he is beginning to trespass beyond safe boundaries. You have indulged yourself too long in the satisfaction of his attention, and you must discourage him, even if you must lose his friendship in the process.*

"Those same students gave me a less flattering title," said Katerin coolly, "Halaatu, referring to a despotic female member of a Cuui hive colony." The title had hurt, though the sarcasm of the infamous students' list was intended to amuse. Katerin had added the epithet to her arsenal of defense.

"The Halaatu rules by desire."

I cannot give you what you want, Radge. Please, do not force me to destroy what we have. "Cindal is waiting for us," said Katerin uncomfortably, and she accelerated her pace. In silence, Radge accompanied her, until they had crossed the lawn to reach their joint destination. Radge announced their arrival, and Network opened the door to Cindal's entry hall.

"Katerin!" greeted Vicki excitedly, before any of the other members of the module could speak. "Tell these Philistines about that research report you mentioned the other day. You know the one I mean."

"No, dear Viki," retorted Katerin, forcing herself to smile, "I have no idea what you mean, since I have only now arrived." Dodging Radge, Katerin sank onto the lounge beside Viki, whose voluminous black silk pants and royal blue coat seemed intent on engulfing the entire vicinity.

"You were supposed to read Viki's mind, Katerin," said Cindal with brisk energy, as she arranged and rearranged the tableware. "She is trying to support an untenable theory. She maintains that psychic research is a valid science."

"Reputable universities agreed with me," argued Viki, "as recently as twenty standard years ago. Katerin, please tell me that you really did show me that report from Worther University, or I shall be forced to concede that my memory is failing as rapidly as my wits."

"I showed you some references that intrigued me," agreed Katerin absently. "I think that Worther was mentioned." Radge held Katerin's eyes, as he settled beside Mavel Tohalo and began a very obvious flirtation by brushing Mavel's hand repeatedly, while the two of them prepared the game board. *Mavel cultivates handsome men instinctively—and fearlessly,* thought Katerin with a touch of envy.

Viki poked Katerin in the ribs. "Is that the best vindication you can give me, Katerin?"

Katerin recollected herself. "Sorry, I am a little distracted tonight. Viki is quite correct. Worther University produced some very credible, cohesive data in the years just prior to the Network-3 cataclysm. The intelligence science department based several very insightful papers on the results of that university's psychic research."

Welor Amphel, a pallid man who almost invariably irritated Katerin with some caustic, unconsidered remark, interrupted, "Nothing credible emerged from Network-3 in the pre-cataclysm decade. That era of Network-3 history is a prime example of Engelhad's Cult Phenomenon. A few deranged fanatics managed to convert an entire planetary government to an absurd anti-Network paranoia, leading eventually to catastrophic self-destruction."

"No one knows why Network-3 disappeared from the topological continuum," muttered Parve Lilleholm, the senior member of the social module and Katerin's department leader, "nor does anyone seem to know how the destruction was effected."

Welor disregarded Parve's quiet comment and continued to harangue Katerin and Viki. "The notion of placing credence in any data from pre-cataclysm Network-3 research is preposterous. Scientific methods have never been applied successfully to psychic research, because the entire field is bunk."

"I read the summaries of the Worther reports," argued Viki. "One of the assistant researchers was Elizabeth Shafer Terry, wife of Dr. Jonathan Terry. Do you imagine that the foremost applied topologist of all human history would have married an expert in 'bunk.' "

"Contrary to your concept of society's proper order," answered Welor contemptuously, "men frequently marry for nothing more than lust. All of your arguments are

specious." Welor folded his arms, content that he had
won the debate.

"Such a loss," murmured Parve to the softly illuminated ceiling. "Network-3's destruction stole so many
brilliant minds from us."

"I thought that Jonathan Terry survived the cataclysm," said Chand, responding to Parve's quiet observation with a frown.

Parve nodded absently, "He and his family died in a
transfer accident a year or so later, but the events were
clearly connected. Dr. Terry developed excessive guilt
over the cataclysm, leading to serious instability. Most
analysts concur that the 'accident' was self-induced. Network's failure to anticipate that tragedy inspired some of
the major algorithm reassessments of the past decade."

"None of which," persisted Viki, "has any bearing on
my argument with Welor. Katerin, help me deflate our
pompous friend's prefabricated, pontifical opinions."

Katerin tried to focus on Viki's request. "The idea
of dismissing all scientific research from pre-cataclysm
Network-3 is absurd: Fundamental precepts in a dozen
disparate fields evolved from treatises of that origin. The
DI technical literature alone provides an incalculable
wealth of innovative engineering."

"Remnants of the pre-hysteria period," growled
Welor.

Katerin averted her eyes from Radge and Mavel, as
their hands met and lingered. She turned her annoyance
with herself against Welor, a sturdier, less disquieting
target. "As for the subject of psychic research," continued Katerin relentlessly, imitating Welor's bombastic
technique with calculated effect, "your denial arises
solely from your personal lack of any psychic skill."
*Welor cannot conceive of anything larger than his own
ego*, thought Katerin wryly.

"Have you ever met anyone with a genuine psychic
skill?" snapped Welor.

"I have no idea," replied Katerin, "nor have you.
Assume that such abilities do exist—for a few. How
could those few ever hope to convince the rest of us, and
why would they risk public mockery to try? We have all
heard the Calongi story about the race of sightless beings
whose tactile sense and echo-location ability enabled the

production of artifacts of marvelous structural intricacy. The visual conflicts were hideous, but the sightless race perceived beauty in shades of depth and contour. Because that race of beings could not grasp the concept of color, they refused to believe in it. Could you have persuaded them otherwise?"

Welor only glowered, for he hated monologues from anyone but himself, and Katerin's furious speech had silenced him, as she intended. It was Radge who answered thoughtfully, "I might prove my thesis by consistency in identifying set patterns or by recognizing variations in depth or substance—without employing scanning sensors to emulate the echo-location function." Twisted feelings prevented Katerin from replying; she exerted a stern control on her emotions in order to avoid blushing before Radge's ardent, challenging gaze.

Viki commented pensively, "That might prove your ability to see, but it would convey nothing of the nature of what you saw."

"But Viki," countered Cindal, emerging from her kitchen unit with a tray of vegetable pasties, "Radge's primary point is the consistency of the data. The acceptance of psychic research as a legitimate profession has ebbed and flowed like the tides of Nebulon-2. The Calongi refuse to accept it, and no human can match the Calongi in breadth of contact with alien species. In all the Consortium's diverse civilizations, not one displays any type of mental communication or control beyond a simplistic sort of shared genetic memory. Calongi are firm in their insistence that their uncanny abilities to perceive hidden thoughts and feelings are based solely on detailed observations."

"Perhaps the psychic gifts belong only to humanity," replied Viki. "We are unique in other respects."

Parve spoke softly from the corner of the room. "Calongi legends suggest that the Adraki may once have possessed some form of mental control over their environment. The legends speak of a symbiotic race called the Mirlai, who endowed the Adraki with remarkable powers."

"Legends, dear Parve," argued Cindal, "do not constitute fact. Many wishful thinkers have tried to establish firm, scientific proof of any kind, and they have failed.

Most of their results can be explained easily by other causes; their 'proof' proves only their own blind determination to justify themselves."

"Are you not equally biased against their proof?" demanded Katerin, determinedly cool and detached from any awareness of Radge or of the growing prickle in one of the painful, half-sensed regions of her mind. "Certainly the psychic researchers want to see their own hypotheses vindicated. What scientist hopes for failure?"

"There is a large difference between wanting success and altering the evidence to suggest success," said Cindal. "A great deal of psychic research has been debunked over the past centuries on the simple basis of forged evidence."

Katerin shook her head emphatically, as much to clear her thoughts of private haunts as to disagree with Cindal's statement. "Unethical research occurs in every field. Have you never read a Consortium treatise against Network methodologies? The Calongi present some very persuasive arguments against most Network science and engineering."

"They disbelieve in topological transfer," remarked Mavel with a cynical smile, "because they cannot duplicate it, and we all know that the Calongi are omniscient."

"We show the same arrogance toward the psychic researchers," insisted Viki.

Radge laughed, raising his manicured hands in defeat. "I concede, Viki—not to your premise but to your superior choice of debating partner."

"Katerin has developed too many algorithms for persuasion and conditioning," commented Mavel crisply.

"Be kind, Mavel," said Radge sharply, and Welor emerged from his sullen silence to laugh at Radge's sober gallantry.

"Radge," chided Cindal, "quit trying so hard to prove your enamorment with Katerin. We are all convinced, except possibly Katerin herself, but it is Katerin's turn to start the game. Katerin, please begin, before Radge makes a complete fool of himself in his zeal to impress you."

"Yes, Cindal," answered Katerin with a slight, embarrassed twisting of her smile.

* * *

Quin admired the tree-lined walkways of Harberg University and concluded that this world, Daedalon, might look reasonably civilized even in daylight. The assortment of moons—he had already counted six—would require some readjustment of thought, but the buildings and the parklike grounds wore a familiar design. He began to reevaluate his unflattering opinion of Network artistry, which the grimness of Chia-2 had inspired.

All that oppressive gray metal made me feel like a mouse trapped in one of Luki's kettles. I suppose Mistress Loisa has some cause to grumble about her circumstances, although I do think her husband might have more reasons to complain; he has apparently assumed the unenviable responsibility of instilling some gradual beauty into that wretched environment. Still, Michael Merel seems sufficiently satisfied with his life. I suppose I can inform Lady Rhianna that Cousin Michael is well.

Quin paused in his meandering to appraise a large, winged creature that soared from the tree above him and disappeared beyond the dome of a distant building. "Neither an owl nor a bat," he muttered. "I wish I knew more creatures' names. I wonder if Luki could identify it."

Quin shook his head at himself. "Addle-brained. This is not Luki's world either, and you have already forgotten who you are supposed to be, babbling to yourself in words that no one here would recognize, even if Lady Rhianna does call it 'essentially the same language.'"

Quin walked to a bridge across a well-ordered pond, and he addressed his moonlit reflection in quiet Network Basic, "Good evening, Citizen Quin Hamley. Welcome to Harberg University, where a wooden footbridge does not seem to be made of wood at all, and the pond water is clearer than the air. I hope you will enjoy your stay with us, and I do hope that you find Katerin Merel as accessible as her brother."

Quin paused, as if listening carefully to the breeze's whispers. "Preliminary inquiries lead you to suspect otherwise about the privacy-cherishing subject in question? In that case, I suppose you will have to persuade Network to enroll you at Harberg, after all." With a self-deprecating laugh, Quin acknowledged a significant longing to disprove the Terrys' prediction of his failure. "They ought never to have told you that becoming a convincing Harberg student would be too difficult for you. They obviously lack experience in dealing with a wizard's pride."

The tree dropped a single leaf onto the pond. Instead of drifting with its decoratively arranged fellows, the leaf sank beneath the surface immediately, and it disappeared with unnatural speed. Quin shook his head at the strangeness and complexity of a pointless Network artifice. He leaned against the rail and reached for the patterns that surrounded him, even amid the apparent emptiness of the park.

He touched the pattern that he knew as Katerin with an unobtrusive gentleness. Finding her had required less effort than locating her brother, not solely because of the restricted size of the university community. Her pattern was bright and strong for a mortal, and the recognition had been made easy for him by the free-speaking student community. On reaching the school's neighborhood, Quin had entered an open hall, where students seemed to gather, and discovered that one aspect of Network did not differ significantly from Serii: The people loved to gossip, especially when they suspected the wicked touch of scandal, and Katerin Merel seemed to be a favorite topic.

"Halaatu," whispered Quin, tasting the strangeness of the word and smiling with an edge of sadness. "If they believe you are so cold," he asked wryly of the sensed pattern of her, "why do otherwise intelligent men seem to vie for you so persistently? What clever walls have you built to shield yourself from hurt?"

Accommodating his Power's urge to raise a familiar wall of its own, Quin withdrew his Power carefully from the intricate, enticing design that surrounded the Terrys' daughter. *You are not beginning well, old boy,* he informed himself sternly, *letting yourself be seduced by the idea of a woman you have never met.* Whistling a soft melody in a minor key, Quin trotted off the bridge and ambled toward the nearest lighted building.

* * *

Katerin reached for the game piece and shifted it according to a stratagem that had lost its focus in Werol and Cindal's exchange of assets three plays ago. Katerin could already predict the outcome of the game. This manipulation of toy figures comprised a silly pastime in her secret opinion, but Cindal enjoyed it, and Katerin enjoyed Cindal's pleasure in it.

Chand claimed one of Katerin's treasures with a smirk of pride, and Katerin yielded the tiny, artful simulacrum with the appropriate regret. The game pieces were indeed lovely. Cindal protected the secret of their acquisition with a deliberate veil of mystery.

Each active game piece, carved and painted by an uncannily delicate hand, wore a unique identity and expression, conveying a distinct personality in even the most alien of the represented species. The range of species suggested Consortium origin, which made the game all the more rare in the utilitarian apartment of a Network professor of cultural economics.

The strange, carved pieces are a little like us, thought Katerin, watching Mavel move a tiny, vivid serpent across a simulated sea: *decorative, amusing, and guarded of our origins. Mavel has a husband somewhere, but she never speaks of him. Cindal and Chand share more than a casual embrace at evening's end, but neither seems to seek a more stable bonding. Werol disappears from the group for months at a time without explanation, and Viki avoids intoxicants too adamantly.*

Parve simply sits and observes us in blandly superior detachment; if he is only assessing our social patterns for his next treatise on mathematical psychology, then why does he seem so forlorn and lonely when he must miss a gathering? Parve needs this regular dose of ordinary human interaction, as do we all, for we are none of us extensive in our social contacts—except Radge. Radge knows everyone. He does not seem to fit Network's scheme in designing this odd little group of reserved, obsessive personalities.

Radge touched Katerin's fingers lightly, as he handed her a frail, winged creature so deftly sculpted that Katerin nearly expected the fur across its ridged back to feel velvety. Radge smiled at Katerin in a secretive manner, suggesting feelings shared but unexperienced. Katerin shifted her eyes quickly to the game, embarrassed and distressed and irritated by her own unthinking reaction.

She returned her gaze to Radge with calculated languor, but the moment was lost. Radge was teasing Mavel, raising an admirable flush to Mavel's coffee-and-cream complexion.

"I am conquered," announced Viki equably, as she ceded her last game piece to Cindal. "I have seven research applications still to review this evening, and I have a grueling day of orientation interviews to conduct tomorrow. The time has come for me to revert to a pumpkin."

Chand groaned expressively and pretended to tear at his lank, chestnut hair. "Must you remind me so callously of tomorrow? I loathe interviewing the new students. They are too eager, too innocent, and too pathetically sure of themselves."

"They represent Network's best and brightest," proclaimed Werol loudly, "the budding members of the tech elite. They have accustomed themselves to superiority of intellect, because they are superior to the vast majority of humanity, or they would not be at Harberg."

Viki murmured, "This university can provide a disheartening experience for those who first discover the ego-wrenching shock of being 'average.' "

"I recall the experience well," replied Chand, "which is why I suffer so keenly for the future trials and humiliations of these children."

One of those "children" will become my responsibility, thought Katerin glumly, *if I cannot justify another term without an assistant, and the "trials and humiliations" may well be mine. I have worked alone and lived alone since Michael left. Perhaps I do need an apprentice; another soul's troubles might help make me forget my own.* "We may find strength in our common fallibilities," said Katerin softly.

"Katerin Merel," chided Mavel a trifle sharply, "you have no right to speak on the subject of fallibility since you were one of those wretched superior students who discouraged the rest of us. I hated you for a whole standard year because all my hours of work never let me best you in a single subject."

"Then came the second year," answered Katerin wryly, "and you compensated for all previous history."

"Only in political analysis, and only because you were

too busy with your own newly chosen specialty to devote yourself to mine. I am not sure why I ever became friends with you."

"Because no one else would listen to you pontificate on the diplomatic ramifications of the Paulan emperor's allergies."

"I did become a pompous bore that year," conceded Mavel with rare self-deprecation.

"An aberration which we all forgave you," said Viki staunchly. "Thank you for your invariably gracious hospitality, my dear Cindal. I shall see all of you in the morning."

And that is the signal, sighed Katerin to herself. *Our evening ends. We all return to our separate home units, and we endure another impersonal night and day so embedded in our narrow fields that we scarcely realize the inadequacy of our lives.*

Katerin smiled at Radge as he commanded Network to open the door for her: an old-fashioned courtesy, which Katerin found appealing. Radge whispered, "Join me for dinner?"

Katerin shook her head minutely, wishing she could garner the courage to accept. Radge was patient with her, and he could not know the reasons for her reluctance. *He is worth the risk,* she informed herself, but she left him at Cindal's door with only a nod and some meaningless, murmured words of social courtesy.

CHAPTER 12

Network

"Hello, Network," greeted Quin awkwardly. He felt slightly ridiculous, talking to a segment of the wall of this tiny, stark room, but the Terrys had both emphasized the need to maintain a regular dialogue with Network. He entered the apartment that Network had allotted to him at his request; the Network economy, so intricately tied to the productivity credits of future as well as past, still seemed unnatural to him, but he accepted its benefits as equally he had always accepted Hamley wealth.

He plopped himself onto the bed. *Network does make deliciously comfortable beds and chairs and such*, thought Quin approvingly. He realized that he was physically exhausted. He stretched indolently and enjoyed the bed's shift from firmness to resilience.

"Hello, Quin," answered the wall, startling his Power into a brief surge of defensiveness that banished his fatigue.

Disciplining himself to calmness, Quin announced somewhat stiltedly, "This is my personal log entry for today."

"Yes, Quin."

The Terrys said that I must make a personal log entry every day: a diary of events or feelings or random comments on the world. What can I say that is not incriminating? "I have enrolled at Harberg University."

After a lengthy pause, Network asked, "Have you completed your log entry?"

292

Too short? Probably. However, my Network history only began today. If I have actually implemented Master Jonathan's instructions well enough to falsify the larger set of records, a slight aberration of my current logs should not present too severe a problem. "Yes."

"Is there anything else you need?"

Quin began to shake his head, before recalling the nature of his conversational partner. He stared at the wall and considered how little he actually *knew* about the nature of Network. The Terrys' descriptions had not conveyed Network's magnitude. He needed to understand. He had come here to learn. *Be cautious, old boy: Network is monitored constantly.* "What do you suggest?" Quin asked tentatively.

"Perhaps you would like the temperature altered."

"The temperature is perfect."

"Shall I order nutrients for you? You have none in supply."

Nutrients sound so depressingly biological, decided Quin. *The word could almost take away my appetite.* "What can I afford?"

"Student credit suffices for full basic cupboard stock."

"Please order the appropriate nutrients. I am rather hungry." Quin extended a very cautious tendril of Power. He could sense the shifting energies that enacted his command. *Branches are being activated in Network; it is responding to my request. Observe which branches draw added energy, and follow those that react in concert with interesting answers. It feels very like the Taormin, but Network is both vaster and less aware.*

"Network," he murmured from Power's remote perspective, "I should like some information about the university." *The pattern of Network is complex, but its greatness of force derives primarily from its intricacy. How is it monitored? The major channels feel direct and clear, but they are not smooth; they branch into the realms of Network's memory. It feels much like human memory, though it lacks the distortion of emotion.*

"Would you like to select your curriculum now?"

"Not yet. I should like some information about the school itself, the students, and the faculty." *If I follow this pattern or that, where will I find myself? In Network or beyond? Will I know how to return? Like using the*

Taormin, learning to find my way through Network might be a very dangerous process, but it is a critical skill, if I am ever to sense potential threats to my own world.

Do not scatter your focus, he ordered himself, and he narrowed his Power's probe to a brightly concentrated beam. *Begin with a single topic. Begin with your reason for coming to Harberg: Begin with Katerin Merel.*

Quin's Power touched a strand of Network's layered internal processes, and the enormity of the energy bit through him with the force of a strong electrical shock. He recoiled from his chosen goal of Katerin Merel, uncertain of what he had struck. Having relinquished his intended path, he stumbled into a swirl of chaos.

Keep your attention on the patterns, idiot, unless you want to lose yourself completely. Zerus' postulates of wizardry apply just as effectively in Network as in Ixaxis: Energy commutes matter, unless the recipient of the energy is very, very careful.

"Shall I provide standard orientation?" demanded Network, apparently oblivious to Quin's intrusion.

"For a start," replied Quin tightly. He shielded himself instinctively from the probe of Network sensors, exerting rigid control to maintain his inner concentration.

If this were a human mind, you would know how to examine its general character without being detected. If you were assessing a wizard's truth, you would know how to delve without triggering a forcible eviction. Do the same techniques apply? Perhaps—and I hardly suppose that I need to worry much about Ceallagh's laws where this artificial beast is concerned.

"Do you wish the general tutorial or a particular scholastic emphasis?"

"Emphasis," muttered Quin, briefly distracted by the question. *What emphasis? What have I come here to learn?* "Science," said Quin impatiently.

"Could you be more specific, please?"

"No," he grumbled, but his focus was broken, and he retreated grudgingly from the patterns of Network. *What am I doing here? I am a simpleminded, lesser lord of Serii. When did I develop delusions of grandeur?* He answered himself grimly, *When you realized that you were truly a major Power.*

But my Power never forced me to do anything but pro-

tect myself from hurt. Quin opened and closed his left hand, the tiny, dark scar tingling in the center of his palm. *Why did Luki ever try to mold me into another Lord Venkarel? And why did I ever make that ridiculous promise to Laurett?*

"Very well," answered Network. "I recommend that you consume your nutrient while you receive the data." A segment of the wall unfolded and yielded an amber vial. "I hope that the basic blend is satisfactory. Other options are not available from general supply at this hour."

"Fine," snapped Quin, staring suspiciously at the vial. *I shall learn about Network. I shall serve the Infortiare and my world. Laurett, I hope you are pleased with me; I hope you appreciate how much I should prefer to be riding blithely across the fields of Hamley or enjoying tea beside Luki's hearth. Lord Evaric was right: Mortal ignorance has significant advantages over the painful knowledge of responsible Power.*

Quin began to reach for the vial. He jumped to his feet when the bed shifted beneath him. He glared at the bed, entirely exasperated by Network's unpredictable tricks. Tired and frustrated, he let his Power grip the local energies. With a thought, he could eradicate Network's irritating, suffocating presence from the room.

Only the student who can control his Power in anger has the right to be a wizard. Quin forced his anger inward: *You came here to live in Network, not to escape it.*

He ordered himself to move calmly, and he tested the bed again. When the bed adapted to a seated position, he relaxed into it carefully. He prepared himself for any further startling actions, as he reached again for Network's notion of a basic meal, but only the patterns of Network's energy shifted with his gesture.

Quin sipped Network's nutrient cautiously and concluded that it was not nearly as bad as it looked. He let his Power probe the undefended edges of Network files, pursuing Network's paths of access in a slower, warier inspection. He made a point of avoiding further contact with that particularly sensitive region he had touched earlier.

Even after the months of delving arduously into the

Taormin, the convoluted puzzle of deriving (or imagining) the sense of Network's strangeness wearied him quickly. "So different," he muttered, sighing and rubbing his aching head.

"Do you wish to command me?" asked Network in a solicitous voice.

"No," grunted Quin immediately, but he reminded himself to think like a citizen of Network, and he revised his answer, "Yes. I have a headache. What do you recommend?"

"Please wait for supply transfer from general stock," answered Network. After a few seconds, Network added, "Remedy is supplied."

A glistening blue capsule emerged from the same wall segment that had provided the nutrient vial. Quin touched the capsule gingerly, and he allowed the bed's shifting to support his movements. "Am I supposed to eat this?" he asked.

"Yes."

In a gesture of resolve, Quin tossed the capsule into his mouth. The capsule dissolved almost before he could taste it. A rush of heat filled his veins, and his Power stirred with alarm. Before he could devise a defense against poison, both the flowing heat and his headache vanished.

"Thank you, Network," murmured Quin, and he began to laugh at his lingering nervousness.

* * *

"Someone has tampered with restricted files, sir."

"Which?"

"A trigger file on Harberg University Professor, Katerin Merel."

Caragen narrowed his eyes slightly but showed no other sign of displeasure or anxiety. The ill-at-ease minion shuffled his feet. "Have you traced the source of interference?"

"The preliminary assessment suggests that the source is a Network citizen: Unauthorized use of a Network channel is implausible, sir."

"So is the interference," snapped Caragen. Frowning, he caressed a carved slithink. With cold and deliberate condescension, he asked, "Have you determined anything of value, Tybold? Did you identify general characteristics of the interferer: Was it a deliberate attack aimed specifically at our system, or was it a broad scan that encountered our system by our misfortune and your ineptitude? Could you isolate the direction of arrival: Did it originate from a local beacon or an interspatial transponder?"

"The interferer comprised a very simple, powerful, directed beam, which apparently attached itself to the carrier of our own monitoring operations at the originating site. Either a very ingenious ruse is being perpetrated, or someone has developed a novel technique for intruder detection: not a particularly sophisticated approach but a very effective one."

"I gather that you have failed to correlate the interference with a particular Network citizen," commented Caragen with icy contempt.

"The analysts have not yet extracted any information at that level of detail, sir."

Caragen lethargically lifted one pale hand, and the nervous processing analyst scurried from the room. "Incompetent," muttered Caragen. "Network, initiate a program for staff replacement, and find a useful purpose for Tybold somewhere out of my sight. Ensure that he does not feel inclined to betray any confidences. He does have some value, so I would prefer not to eliminate him altogether."

"Acknowledged."

Caragen loathed dealing with human analysts, for Network's efforts were so much more thorough, but certain functions still required human processing. The constant effort to ensure Network's inviolability obviously demanded some external controls. Even the most independent of computers could be engulfed by Network, as Caragen knew better than anyone. The very weakness of human analysts made them less threatening than a compromised computer, even in betrayal.

While Network began an elaborate process of search and data refinement, Caragen frowned thoughtfully. Neither Tybold nor any of the other human analysts knew why Katerin Merel had earned a high-level security trigger file, and Caragen had no intention of sharing that information. He had made his prediction of Marrach's next move—an irrational prediction according to Network—and he had waited half a year to see his suspicions justified. Tybold could not know how deeply Caragen had dreaded just such an attempt to contact the Terry children through a direct Network link. Tybold would never have believed that Caragen feared anything or anyone, but Tybold did not know Marrach.

Caragen employed the keypad embedded in his desk's polished surface to enter a long-unused code. It was a code he could not force himself to voice aloud, despite his hardness. It was a code to which only he held access authorization, the communication code that would connect him to the transceiver implanted in Rabh Marrach's brain.

He hesitated to enact the command; he had destroyed worlds with less deliberation. "Network," he ordered at last, "establish the requested communication."

"Acknowledged," answered Network. After a brief delay, Network added, "Link refused."

Caragen experienced a brief temptation to relent, but he would not allow Marrach to win even such a trivial contest of wills. "Insist," said Caragen softly, and a hint of complacency revived in him; Marrach could not dominate Network. Caragen tapped the control for a preprogrammed voice synthesis of the requested channel, and he closed his eyes and imagined that Rabh Marrach occupied the expensively inlaid chair across the room.

Network answered, "No user-acknowledgment has been received. However, internal probes confirm that the requested link has achieved lock."

Caragen smirked, his confidence rallying at the minor victory. "This silence of yours is childish, Marrach. You have not abandoned the gifts that I provided for you. You are receiving my message, and I insist that you reply."

The voice that responded caused Caragen a ripple of instinctive uneasiness, despite all his customary self-certainty and cold intentions, for Network held Marrach's basic voice pattern and reproduced it faithfully: "Your infernal implants still function within my brain, but I no longer work for you, Caragen."

With well-honed scorn, Caragen demanded, "Will you

threaten to unleash a Mirlai plague on Network out of pique with me?"

Marrach countered, "Why are you using this channel? I have told you: I shall not leave Siatha."

"Network ships still orbit your pitiful little world." Caragen added carelessly, "I could destroy your precious Siatha with a word, as you well know."

"You will not take such a risk. The Mirlai are quite capable of protecting their own, as *you* know."

Caragen scowled at the empty chair facing him, for he did respect the Mirlai's unparalleled skills at biological warfare. "How often did you betray me, Marrach, during all those years in which I counted you as the one man I could trust?"

A momentary silence sent a shiver of certainty through Caragen, erasing his last doubts about his intuitive suspicions. Marrach replied slowly, "I never betrayed you, Caragen. I have not betrayed you now."

Caragen snapped, "You have been reading restricted files again."

"I have neither cause nor interest to inspire me to delve into your secrets these days." Marrach ordered Network to break the connection, but Caragen counteracted the command with a quick override.

"Deception is a bad habit for a self-styled Healer of Siatha."

"Caragen," breathed Marrach in a decidedly menacing and caustic tone, "if you have a particular reason for contacting me, please state it and let me return to my work."

He begins to drop his pious pretense, thought Caragen, grimly satisfied at having deflated an extremely irritating ruse. "This is not the first time you have lied to me. How long had you planned your revolt? Do you expect to take Network from me? Or do you mean to attack the Consortium first?"

The Siathan Healer, who had once manipulated worlds for the Network Council Governor, laughed without humor, for he understood Caragen well. "Was there a particular charge you wished to levy against me, or do you wish only to reiterate your displeasure at my resignation? You rarely do anything without a definitive purpose."

"You have located Jonathan Terry."

Marrach answered smoothly and immediately, "The topological analyst? We closed that file years ago."

He is lying again, thought Caragen, briefly regretting that he had stirred Marrach from his Healer's pose. Marrach's effectiveness at pretense had always derived largely from an ability to live his diverse, transitory roles. As a Healer, Marrach might exhibit human failings, such as a pause to concoct a lie. As Caragen's well-trained tool, Marrach was nearly indistinguishable from Network.

Katerin Merel has no value to Marrach except as the child of her father, and only Marrach with his implanted Network link could have accessed that trigger file without immediate, conclusive detection and entrapment. Marrach has been assessing her current status—on behalf of someone whom he intends to use for his own ambitions. Network is wrong: I am not irrational on the subject of Marrach; I simply know my creation too well to underestimate him.

"You did not close your own file on Jonathan Terry, because you abetted his escape. I have sufficient evidence to convince me." Caragen's laugh was cold and repulsively bitter. "Did you think you could continue to deceive me, once you proved your duplicity? Jonathan Terry belongs to me, and I shall dispose of him as I wish. You will pay dearly for any attempt to use him against me. Where is he?"

"I have no idea."

"You have contacted him, and you have informed him of the status of his children."

"I am touched that you have troubled to force this conversation, Caragen, simply to argue with me," said Marrach with an iciness that Caragen recognized, accepted, and understood. Caragen began to relax into a familiar pattern of antagonism, but the gentleness of Marrach's subsequent words refueled Caragen's anger: "I know that I have injured your pride, Caragen, and I know that you distrust my motives. Come to me as a supplicant, and I may be able to heal the twisted evils in your mind; otherwise, I can offer you nothing."

Infuriated by Marrach's condescension, Caragen nearly ordered Network to destroy the little planet of Siatha, despite the well-known, justifiably feared consequences of Mirlai retaliation. "Your hypocrisy insults me," he spat. "You always did play your roles persuasively, but you will never convince me, Rabh Marrach, that you seek anything but personal gain. I know you, for I created you."

"The Mirlai have healed your creation."

"Where is Jonathan Terry?"

Marrach retorted crisply, "This argument grows stale. Good night, Caragen." Marrach broke the connection. The Network Council Governor, secure and comfortable in his space yacht, cursed a silent terminal and snarled, but he did not try to reacquire the link. He queried Network: "Which agent is assigned to Katerin Merel?"

"The primary in-place Harberg University observer is Calial: code jx1737a816. Support surveillance is enacted by Rolf: code jt117896a1."

"I want increased surveillance on Katerin Merel. Have Calial contact me, using secure channels. Is Michael Merel being monitored actively?"

"No in-place observers exist on Chia-2. Standard Network observation dæmons provide current data, supplemented by periodic assessments under direction of the in-place Harberg team. Shall I assign a dedicated agent to observe him?"

"Yes, but do not alert him yet. How close is his relationship with his sister?"

"Formerly quite close. Minimal in recent years."

"Has she any particular friends—in or out of her assigned social module?"

"One prospective intimate: Professor Radge Randon of the Alien Studies Department."

"Cultivate him. Provide a possible replacement. Any others?"

"No. Isolation conditioning still functions."

"Good. Apply level-three pressure to Katerin Merel. Keep the brother distant; use chemical triggers if necessary. I want to see if anyone else displays significant interest in her personal welfare."

Caragen reclined in his chair and studied a careful reproduction of an ancient ceiling fresco depicting the creation of a man. "I also want every record of every mission Rabhadur Marrach performed for me scanned, analyzed, scrutinized, and dissected. I want every physiological and psychological profile of him reexamined and reevaluated. I want any weaknesses in him exposed. I want to learn every asset he has hidden from me."

The Council Governor exhaled a deliberate ring of smoke from an exotic, expensive herb, grown exclusively for Caragen's use. "We have been betrayed, Network, by a man of enormous talent and utter ruthlessness. We must protect ourselves against him, before he can move against us."

* * *

"Was it Caragen?" asked Evjenial, Healer of Revgaenian. The light framed her, crowning her coppery hair, as she entered the dim, quiet room to which the man once known as Marrach had retreated.

Marrach raised his hazel eyes to meet her solemn gaze, but he continued to frown into his fist and did not answer. Evjenial came and sat beside him on the bench of crudely carved granite. She touched his strongly muscled shoulder. "Mirlai have healed you," she assured him firmly. "You will never belong to Caragen again."

"I lied to him just now. He stirs the old darkness in me." Marrach took her hand and held it, rubbing the callused ridge where the fingers joined the palm. "I caused tremendous harm in his service, Jeni, and many of my cruelest schemes perpetuate themselves even now."

"I know," sighed Evjenial softly, "and the Mirlai will demand much service of you to maintain the balance. Do not let Caragen invade your peace, dear friend. Mirlai truth will guide you."

"They allow Caragen to reach me and question me."

"Because you fear the influence he once held over you, and it is time for you to accept that he is *not* greater than you."

"True-dream?"

"Yes." Mirlai whispered in her. "You have dreamed also. What have you seen?"

"I see images of fire and Jonathan Terry."

"Fire is a sign of power."

"Yes. Caragen has keen instincts for danger to his dominion. He is threatened, and he knows it."

"He is not threatened by us, Suleifas."

Marrach smiled at her deliberate choice of the plural pronoun and her use of his Healer's name. "Mere suspicion has spurred Caragen to destroy many individuals far more innocent than myself."

"He is too shrewd to risk Mirlai anger by attacking us," said Evjenial with conviction. "So you told me, and I believe you. Do you doubt yourself?"

"No: He will not attack Siatha."

"Nor will he dare to attack you, a Healer."

"Caragen excels at many methods of destruction, not least of which is the calculated dismantling of an individual's life and sanity. He attacks most subtly when he respects his opponent." Marrach added self-mockingly, "Caragen respects me only slightly more than he respects Dr. Jonathan Terry. I should not have contacted Terry."

"You returned to the parents something you had taken from them: the ability to regain their children. You obeyed Mirlai wisdom to restore the balance. The Mirlai made their judgment clear to you. You are a Chosen Healer; you know the Mirlai too intimately to doubt them."

"Directly or indirectly, I reminded Caragen that the threat of Jonathan Terry may still exist."

"Dr. Terry has found his own protection," said Evjenial, staring at the golden light-dance of a Mirlai vision. "It is the fire of your true-dream."

"Dr. Terry's children have no such defense. I inflicted terrible wounds inside their minds, Jeni, and I gave their souls to Caragen."

"They do have a defense, if they will accept it," continued Evjenial from the near-trance of a true-dream. "They have. . . ." She stopped, shaken from her vision.

Marrach laughed and finished the sentence for her, "They have a piece of chalk, a snail, a sword, and a kitten. I have received the same images, Jeni, and I do not understand them."

"Mirlai do not always require us to understand," she answered slowly. "They do expect our trust."

"I know. I have allowed Caragen to revive my old habits of suspicion and defensiveness."

"You are uncomfortable in a passive role. You want to race to the rescue of the Terry children yourself."

"Yes," admitted Marrach with a grimace. "Unlikely,

isn't it, considering that I created most of the Terry family's woes?"

Evjenial leaned against him, sharing his regret, and his left arm, made whole and real by Mirlai healing, encircled her. "If the Mirlai Chose from human perceptions of worth," she whispered, "neither of us would be a Healer, Rabh. The Mirlai have remade us, and we cannot return to the past, even if we wished. You can neither work with Caragen nor against him now. Your proper work is here."

"For the present."

"The present is all we need. That is the Way."

"Dear Jeni, you are wiser than I."

"I am only less excruciatingly clever in the ways of Caragen and Network," she responded wryly. "Come outside with me, Rabh. The day is too fair to waste on dark worries in a dusky workroom."

* * *

Maryta Deavol had been a Network Councillor for more years than her vanity cared to acknowledge. Her pride of accomplishment, however, relished every instant of her unusually lengthy tenure. She had survived in her position by following three implicit rules: Never defy the Consortium; employ maximum security precautions at all times; and never attack Andrew Caragen.

When Councillor Rorell Massiwell had died after disobeying rule three very flagrantly, Maryta had neither mourned nor rejoiced at the fulfillment of her prediction. Her loyalty to Caragen was a matter of pragmatism, not emotion. The only troubling aspect of the entire messy event was the fact that Massiwell had so nearly succeeded: Caragen had indeed lost one of his most valued assets, Rabh Marrach.

Marrach's apparent resignation troubled Maryta deeply, not because she considered Caragen deserving of any sympathy, nor because she had ever relished her contacts with Marrach himself. She was troubled because she would have sworn that the resignation could not occur. Either Caragen and Marrach had embarked jointly on an elaborate ruse—which would unquestionably lead to a confrontation with the Consortium and the probable sacrifice of an ardently exclusionist Network Councillor such as herself—or Marrach had indeed abandoned his mentor. Marrach, as coldly analytical as Network, understood the importance of Maryta's three rules; if Marrach had left Caragen, then Marrach must have concluded that Caragen's days were numbered.

Maryta had tied her considerable prosperity almost entirely to the premise that Caragen would remain Council Governor. Until Marrach's defection, she had not seriously considered any possibility of Caragen losing his absolute power. She had realized, of course, that not even Caragen evaded time, but she had never paused to consider Caragen as weakened by age; he was not that many years older than herself.

Maryta tightened her hands on the arms of the office chair. She disliked this austere room, but she rarely used it except for official Council conferences. Though the room was purportedly her own, the entire Network Council complex belonged unquestionably to Caragen.

Delicately, Maryta warned herself, as she prepared her careful questions. *You must not incriminate yourself, for Network belongs to Caragen.* The risks of using Network rather than a private computer were significant, but only Network offered the potential access to the data she required. Maryta's analysts could labor endlessly to defeat Caragen's security, but no direct approach had ever succeeded. Capable analysts either switched allegiance to Caragen or disappeared permanently.

Maryta touched her well-coiffed hair to verify the presence of the jamming device that would disguise her physical reactions to Network's sensors. She spoke into an inexpensive translator, even though she used Network Basic, for the primitive mechanism would distort her voice patterns effectively and disguise any compromising emotional reactions. "Network," she asked evenly, "what information is available regarding the planet Siatha?"

"Siatha is designated private property," answered Network. "Further information cannot be provided without permission of legal owner, Network Citizen Rabhadur Marrach."

A year ago Siatha was an insignificant Network planet, and now its entire history has been removed from open Network memory. "Network, how can such permission be obtained?"

"No Network communication devices exist in the vicinity of Citizen Marrach."

Except the one in Marrach's head, grumbled Maryta to herself, *which Caragen still pretends does not exist.*

"The planet of Siatha has no transfer ports," continued Network, "and may be reached only by shuttle from the Wayleen Station."

Visit Marrach? I would sooner throw myself in the path of a ravenous garvadi-beast. "Thank you, Network." *Do I dare to send one of my agents to question Marrach on my behalf? Not an agent who is known to work for me, not while Caragen watches Siatha so closely. I must find another source of information.*

"Network," asked Maryta slowly, for her query required very cautious formulation, "what is the general category of your most processor-intensive analysis at present?" *The highest priority tasks always belong to Caragen. If I know where his attentions lie, perhaps I will be able to evaluate the truth of Marrach's desertion.*

"The character and cause of topological anomalies," answered Network, startling Maryta Deavol entirely.

"Thank you, Network," she replied thoughtfully, and she cast aside her previous analysis to begin again.

PART 4

The Harrowing
Network Year 2305/
Seriin Year 9059

CHAPTER 1

Network

Katerin paused in her entryway for Network's security scan to unlock her apartment. She entered and reset the alarms, relaxing at last from a day too long and too frantic. These were the times when she most enjoyed her solitude, though it caused her pain in almost equal measure.

She missed Michael, though her wiser part insisted that his wife and daughter deserved precedence over a grown sister, well established in her profession, who should have formed a life of her own by now. "We faced everything together for so long," muttered Katerin to herself in a vain effort to justify her persistent sense of abandonment. *And I was conditioned to depend on him,* she added silently, but she did not allow the thought of conditioning to linger; the structure of old conditioning was too fragile to be faced.

She sighed and kicked her shoes under the table. Michael would have complained, for he had a passion for order and neatness. Katerin had always been too erratic and impulsive for her brother; she knew that she had caused him fits throughout her adolescent years, while he tried to balance his university studies with his self-appointed role as both brother and father.

Prim, acidic Loisa accords well with Michael's desire for structure in his life, thought Katerin glumly. *Loisa and I have nothing in common but gender and humanity— and a desperate need for Michael's companionship.* The thoroughness of the dissimilarity hurt most of all.

Katerin slumped in a contouring chair, contemplated Michael, Loisa, and Radge in a chaotic jumble, and assessed the defiant disorder of her living room. She felt the dim onset of guilt; Michael would be appalled by the state of the room, which was a poor reason for having created such a pathetic disarray. Radge would lose all respect for her if he knew how she perverted her skills to defeat Network housecleaning drones.

"Nothing has mattered since Michael left," whispered Katerin.

"Do you wish to make a personal log entry?" inquired Network politely.

"I suppose," sighed Katerin. *About Michael again? About Loisa? Why not?* "I never wanted to dislike Loisa," began Katerin, forming her log entry with the order and ease produced by years of daily practice. "In fairness to my sister-in-law, I doubt that she ever planned her jealousy of me. Miscommunication beset us in excessive measure when she first began to meet Michael on a regular basis. Loisa and I wounded each other unwittingly, and each of us reacted with escalating anger. By the time Loisa and I acknowledged the breach openly, we had already made poor Michael feel the need to choose between us. I cannot blame either of them.

"Still, I felt so lonely after they left. I felt exposed and threatened. There is a terror in my past that rules my thoughts and dominates my private reality. I know it exists, though I cannot name it, for I recognize the conditioning that keeps me functional. The terror began to gain a greater hold on me after I lost Michael to Loisa.

"I can diagnose myself, as easily as I can advise others via Network and my algorithms. I acknowledge that I fear my cure, for I fear to see my weaknesses exposed. If I seem to reject those who approach my life too closely, I act only from dread of hurting them to protect myself. I allow no one to hurt me deeply; I reserve that privilege for my own efforts.

"Having made my diagnosis, I begin the process of mental and emotional exercises that should enable me to escape the cycle of dependency on the old conditioning. I begin, and I stop without remembering the reason for beginning. Such strange conditioning: It protects itself. The trauma of my childhood must have been so monumental that even recollection of it could threaten my life and sanity.

"I diagnose. I analyze. I comprehend helplessly." Katerin stretched tired muscles, and the chair massaged the tension from her. "End of log entry, Network."

"How are you feeling, Katerin?" asked Network solicitously, for Katerin had programmed Network to run a companionship algorithm since Michael left.

Katerin smiled, savoring the chair's relaxing attentions. "I feel surprisingly well now."

"Is there anything else I can do for you?"

"Not at the moment. Thank you, Network."

She studied the room again and grimaced at it. In a spurt of energy, she rose and began to collect scattered sketches that covered every table in the room. She discarded the boxes, bags, and wrappers of a hundred petty purchases, none of which had succeeded in filling the vacancy in her heart. A taste of abandoned pride began to stir in her, as she imagined entertaining Radge in an atmosphere of such elegant simplicity as he admired.

Her work became determined and relentless. She forgot time; she forgot the need to stoke herself with either nutrients or rest, and she paid for her intensity with the beginnings of a headache. She slowed, looked at the results of her labors, and smiled faintly despite the throb of her neck. Michael might even recognize the room.

Katerin pictured Michael entering, laughing at a haphazard arrangement of wildflowers, such as she used to collect occasionally, nodding at the neatly framed mimovue of their parents, the only tangible remnant of a forgotten past. The mimovue's blurred images were nearly unidentifiable as human. *Perhaps*, thought Katerin with a dim wistfulness, *the imperfection allowed the mimo to survive*.

Katerin's nostalgic thoughts shuddered and grew warily unsure, for the white lacquer table where the mimo should have rested was barren. *The mimo is gone. I did not move it. I would not have moved it. I did not miss it earlier today, but when did I last look for it?*

She tried to reassure herself, *Michael could have taken it. He could have returned unannounced and claimed it from the wreckage of this home we shared. No one else could have taken it. I deleted even Loisa from the access list.*

Katerin stabbed vehemently at the activation function of her Network communication keypad, for the direct keypad entry could produce the fastest response. She waited for the link to be established, restlessly wringing her hands. "Michael?" she demanded urgently, as the requested audio connection was made.

The message transfer incurred a minimal delay. Michael answered blearily, and he did not authorize a video link. Katerin had overridden the time zone restrictions, and she had awakened him. "Kitri?" he muttered, and Katerin heard Loisa grumble something impatient and uncomplimentary. "What is wrong?" asked Michael, hushing his wife.

"Did you take the mimo of Mom and Dad?" asked Katerin, realizing only as she spoke how neurotically incoherent she must sound. Loisa would add this incident to the tally against her, and Michael had always considered sleep interruptions a form of torture.

"You know I left the mimo for you, Kitri," answered Michael, and his initial concern became tired exasperation. "Is that the reason you demanded an immediate, interactive call across three transfers?"

"It is gone, Michael." *Understand me, Michael. Please, understand me as in the past.*

"I have told you before that you would lose something of value some day, unless you learned to organize your personal life as well as you arrange your work."

"I did not 'lose' the mimo. Someone has taken it."

"One of your transient acquaintances, no doubt. Good night, Kitri." He disconnected the link, and Katerin stared dumbly at the message of termination flashing on the display screen. After twenty seconds, even the message disappeared, and the wall became blank.

Katerin dropped to the floor among the satiny cushions, and she drew her knees under her chin. She stared at the empty space on the table, where the mimo had rested since Michael entered Harberg University. "I did not lose it, Michael," she whispered. "I did not misplace it. Someone has taken it." The sanctity of her haven had been violated, and she began to shiver violently in recollection of other, darker violations of her family and herself.

She shouted a control word, and a musical tribute to

a long dead emperor erupted from the walls at a volume proportional to her shout. "Quieter," she said in a more muted voice, and the music became less deafening. She let it drench her with its brilliant harmonies for many minutes before she moved again.

She unfurled herself stiffly and seated herself at the Network console. As a result of her position at Harberg University, both her console and her access privileges exceeded ordinary limits, but tonight she cared only about the routine sorts of information. The security access to her apartment still listed only Michael and herself. No unauthorized entries had been recorded; no authorized entries except her own had occurred since Michael left for Chia-2.

Katerin stared sightlessly at the console. At last, she gestured fiercely to return it to vocal mode. She requested local communication. She smoothed her hair and ensured that the video showed only as much of her and of the room as she desired. She waited without breathing for the link to be completed or aborted; perhaps he would not be home.

"Katerin!" said Radge, astonishment in his voice. "Tell me this is a personal call."

She forced herself to smile warmly. "Is it too late to accept your offer for tonight?"

An image formed on her wall-screen, as Radge authorized his own video mode. She could see his initial surprise become wonder. "It is never too late for you to accept anything from me, and you know how frequent and varied are my offers." His handsome face creased with puzzlement. "This is my elusive Katerin?"

"Wait for me. I shall come to you," she murmured.

* * *

The fire's refuse smoldered in the hearth, its warmth a memory, its glow a fading wisp of curling smoke. It was an image, a technological mirage, but Katerin stared into it fixedly, while Radge shifted beside her. He began to stroke the length of her arm teasingly.

"I must be the most enviable man in the university," he murmured.

"Is that why you want me, Radge: to gather envy?" She could feel the terror building in her, turning against

Radge, and she loathed it, but she could not stop it. She should not have come, but now it was too late.

Radge withdrew his arm from her. He answered only after a lengthy pause, "You are not in a very romantic mood. Have I said something wrong?"

He is sulking now. He is surprisingly immature, despite his accomplishments. "No, Radge, you have said nothing wrong. You whisper sweet nothings with the same rigorous attention to detail that you give to your research, your social and professional contacts, your appearance and your relationships." *He is precise without feeling, without intuition or empathy.* "How many educational files did you study on the subject? Is your technique recommended for maximum appeal to my age group and preference profile?" *What am I saying to him?* She wanted to shout, *This is not me, Radge! I do not want to hurt you.* But she could say nothing, for the terror had appropriated her voice.

"Need you analyze everything?" muttered Radge.

Do I hate Radge? She could not recall the answer. "If you wanted submission, you should have chosen your intended victim more judiciously. You are a widely coveted commodity, as you so often tell me."

"Are you always this agreeable when a man suggests a life commitment to you?"

"Few men have ever been so foolish as to make such an offer. Perhaps you should reconsider your life's plan. I am deservedly categorized as work-obsessive. Nothing else matters to me. I do not share your interests, for your pet analyses of alien literature bore me as much as your fascination with discordant alien music. Is that what you really want in a wife, Radge?"

"Yes, dear Katerin, because I know you better than you seem to know yourself. I have spent nearly two years trying to convince you that I want you and no one else."

"Only because conquest of the Halaatu presented a challenge." *A slight straightening of his position allows him to regain his sense of dominance. His voice remains calm, but anger has begun to gather in him. I have never seen Radge angry; I think he could become peevish.* "How can you think that I could make you happy? Do you think you understand the formula for human happiness, Radge?" *Why am I provoking him deliberately?* wondered Katerin, for her emotions had retreated completely, leaving her as coldly curious and analytical of her own reaction as of Radge's behavioral responses.

"You are the genius who is developing the intelligence algorithm," grumbled Radge, "to prescribe for every Network citizen a practical daily course of action to maximize contentment, based on personal logs, activities, and composite Network profiles. Try using your own algorithm."

He resents my success in my field, for he will never achieve more than mediocrity. "The algorithm needs extensive refinement, even in its current, very restricted implementation." *He will try to appease me now.*

Radge reached toward her again and resumed his caress. "Ask, and I shall give you all the data on happiness you need. Let no one say that I constrained your progress on the algorithm that will revolutionize the fundamental lifestyle of Network's citizenry. I think I shall enjoy being married to a genius, even if she is temperamental." Radge shifted her hair from her neck and watched it ripple across his fingers. "Katerin," he whispered coaxingly when she did not respond to him, "where are you?"

He is utterly predictable. What did I expect? Katerin pulled away from him sharply and swung her legs over the edge of the couch. Radge grabbed her hand. "Let go, Radge," she said wearily. He released her and studied her in silence as she collected her coat.

"You bewilder me, Katerin, and I thought I knew you."

"Sorry, Radge." She tapped the exit lock, and left. Knowing that Radge could use Network to watch her until she escaped his building, she maintained a confident, swaying stride through the cold, white corridor. She descended to ground level and hurried into the late-night street.

The shadows whispered at her, as she counted the paces to her apartment. Emotions struggled to resurface: *I cannot bear the weight of having injured Radge! I want him to understand, but I could not abide his forgiveness. I cannot forgive myself.*

She had successfully defeated the fear that the missing mimovue had inspired. An older, darker terror had taken hold. Katerin issued the soft commands to Network automatically, and her own, safe home welcomed her.

Katerin closed and locked the door of her apartment, checked the security seal, and kicked her shoes across the room with vehemence. She shed her silken shift and overskirt, tearing the clothes from her skin and leaving them where they fell. In the shower of cleansing water and oil, she rubbed herself repeatedly with the scouring stone, until her skin glowed red beneath its golden hue.

How could you have been such a fool? she shouted at herself, though her voice dared make no sound. Katerin scraped her flesh with the stone, and she continued to scrub. Blood seeped from the abrasions. *Michael warned me,* she whispered in nervous staccato: *He warned me, and I would not listen, because I thought I was in love. I did not listen to Michael or to the voices in my head, because we had already survived so much; I thought survival had made us invincible. I did not listen; I scarcely knew. Dear God, I was only seventeen.*

She stared at her bleeding arm and realized that she could not remember why she felt such sickness inside of her. "Network, what is wrong with me?" cried Katerin to the walls.

"You know," replied Network in the soft, warm voice of a lover or a friend.

"No! Tell me, please."

"The rape."

Katerin held very still. Slowly, she reached for her nightgown and tugged its softness around her. She folded her arms tightly. "I was seventeen," she said without tone or emotion, "when Marrach found me again. What did he tell me? 'You should never try to lose yourself, Kitri. The effort is futile, and it causes much concern to those who guard you.' Marrach reinforced my conditioning to fear any close relationship, because of that young man whose father had Consortium ties. I think I loved him, but I can't remember his name."

"You were warned to avoid C-humans, Katerin."

"Yes, Network. I was warned—by someone. Who was he?"

"You called him Marrach."

"Marrach. Yes. I cannot hold the name in my memory for more than a few seconds at a time. He distorted my memories, Network. I know the methods; I understand the potency of such intensive conditioning. Perhaps he even enhanced the conditioning with an artificial virus." Katerin laughed bitterly. "I have made the study of such techniques my life-work and my obsession. I can analyze and dissect, but I cannot escape, and the nightmare remains an insidious, latent evil locked within me. I should have known better than to let Radge come so close to me."

"Yes, Katerin. You were wrong to go to him. You must not trust him. He is like the nightmare."

"Yes, Network. Will you punish me?"

"Your mind will punish you, Katerin."

"I know. Good night, Network."

* * *

Somehow the room emptied but for the two of them. She started toward the door, but her faceless lover had preceded her. He caught her. She thought at first that he meant to tease, but his grip tightened. When he forced her to the floor, she began to fight him, but still she did not believe it was real. She could take care of herself; Michael worried needlessly.

The faceless man drove himself against her, manipulating her body cruelly and impersonally. He bruised her, and she began to scream at him. He slapped her when she struggled. He slapped her and struck her, until she cried. Crying, she felt herself abused and violated. He raped her, and she shrank into a tiny, screaming, distant corner of her mind, unable to bear the torture of feeling hurt in a part of her that should never have been so hurt, feeling fear that he would kill her and knowing that she did not want to die, even now, and feeling the heart-gnawing guilt that she had brought this on herself, and her parents would have hated her for it. She was glad that they were dead.

"I can kill you unless you stop crying," he hissed, striking her repeatedly about her head, digging sharp fingers into her breasts. "Stop crying," he commanded angrily. "You asked for this."

A distant sound of voices reached him, and he slapped her again, trying peevishly to silence her. "No one will believe you," he told her, though she had said nothing, only shaking with whimpering pain. "*They will never believe you,*" *he repeated, frantically now, as if he had realized that she might accuse him if they were caught, and the other voices approached. He scolded her furiously,* "*You wanted me to take you. You wanted me to hurt you.*"

Katerin sobbed. Her attacker drove his fist against her jaw, and she choked into silence, dimly aware that her body had gone as limp as her spirit. He thought she was unconscious. Something in her giggled insanely at the deception.

* * *

Katerin awoke with a shudder owed equally to the nightmare's terror and the chill of her own perspiration of fear. She struck the table to light the room and see it empty. She jumped from the bed. She checked the security scans and the locks on the doors. She checked each room, and she searched each closet.

When she had persuaded herself that the nightmare had no substance outside of memory, revived from conditioning by her folly in going to Radge, she bathed again. She tugged a clean nightgown over her head, crawled meekly into her bed, and lay shivering beneath the covers. She reached out a tentative hand to restore the peaceful darkness of her room, and she tried to make her heart relax its frantic, racing beat.

CHAPTER 2

Network

She was sympathetic, and that gave needed solace. *Cindal is quite sweet, after all,* mused Radge with a trace of wistfulness. *Katerin always told me that Cindal had depth beneath the bright charm. I never believed.*

I still have trouble believing. The sweetness seems too accommodating, too pure. I know that Cindal has a streak of thoughtless cruelty in her, and I know that she has long envied Katerin.

Katerin never said what occupied Cindal's depth, probably because Katerin does not know. Katerin manipulates well, but her fear of closeness makes her naive in many ways. I should have realized how deeply she fears. I have assessed enough alien psychology to understand the barriers built by fear and distrust. Somehow, I looked at Katerin and forgot that she is fragile. I should not have pressured her. I should not have become angry.

"You are not listening to me at all, Radge," accused Cindal quietly.

"Sorry, Cindal," answered Radge, and he forced a smile. "I am not very good company this morning."

"I knew what I was doing when I invited you for coffee," argued Cindal quietly, and she took hold of his hand across her dining table. "Katerin has treated you abominably."

"She will return to me tomorrow or the next day, deeply penitent, and plead with me to start our friendship anew."

"But you can't forgive her this time, can you? She has hurt you too often."

"I am tougher than you think," said Radge with a wry grimace. "It is true. I think this is the final break between us. But I am not angry with her now, not as I was last night, when I realized that she would never be what I hoped. I pity her, Cindal. She only hurts herself."

The pressure of Cindal's warm hand tightened slightly. "You are a better friend to her than she deserves, Radge."

"I guess I'm just not the sort of man to be devastated by unrequited love." Radge tried to extract his hand from Cindal's supportive grasp gently, for the continued intensity of her gaze was making him uncomfortable. Cindal did not attract him, and he did not want to inspire her to futile aspirations. Emulating the Halaatu would be so easy. . . .

Radge pulled his hand from Cindal's, and her ring scraped his skin, drawing tiny beads of blood in a ragged line. Surprised by the tingling scratch, Radge noticed the ring for the first time. It was a large and showy piece: a bloodstone surrounded by smoky crystals set high above a streaked gold band. He could not remember seeing Cindal wear such heavy jewelry in the past.

"I'm sorry, Radge," said Cindal sincerely. "I always liked you."

"You make it sound so dismal," laughed Radge with only a hint of sadness. "I have not died."

"I'm sorry, Radge, but that is precisely what you have done."

Radge frowned. He did not understand Cindal's meaning, and he decided that he did not want to understand. He stood and collected his coat from the sofa. "Thanks for the coffee and sympathy." He walked to the door: It opened before he could reach it, and two muffled strangers entered. One stranger removed his hood and grinned at Radge, who stared in shock at a perfect image of himself.

"I hoped you would be angrier at her, Radge," explained Cindal, coming to Radge and rubbing her hands across his back. "But you were obviously not going to be reasonable. We need someone in your position. You understand, don't you?" Radge tried to turn, but his motions were slow and clumsy.

The door closed, and the second stranger removed his hooded coat. He was a plump and ordinary man with a face creased by smiling. He peered at Radge, who blinked and tried to mouth a plea. "Pity," remarked the smiling man. "We could have used him."

"Radge had too many heroic ideas," retorted Cindal. She kneaded the stiffening muscles of Radge's back. "The paralysis is nearly complete." Radge's double took Radge's coat and examined it pensively.

"You remember all of Radge's access codes?" demanded Cindal, and Radge's image nodded.

"Stop worrying, Calial," said the smiling man, and he patted Cindal's arm. "Yarl is a professional."

"Stop patronizing me, Rolf," snapped Cindal. "I am the coordinator of this operation, and you report to me. Remember?"

"Of course, my dear." Rolf wiped the dome of his round head with a white silk kerchief. "I hope you appreciate the magnitude of your fortune. A commonplace surveillance assignment rarely escalates to a matter of interest to the Council Governor. You have never worked directly for Caragen before, have you?"

"Neither have you."

"I worked directly for Marrach, which is nearly the same. I have worked on this Merel girl before, Calial, and I have the experience to make her serve us. A few incidents of torment, a few conditioning items planted in her home and office, and Citizeness Merel will beg to do our bidding."

"See that you fulfill your promises, Rolf. I have little patience." Cindal gestured curtly, and Yarl began to undress Radge methodically. The shirt sleeve refused to budge across Radge's doubled fist. Yarl used a pocket-knife to slice the fabric free. Yarl let the shirt fall to the floor.

"You have the solvent?" asked Rolf, observing Yarl's procedure with a quiet smile.

"Of course, I have the solvent," said Cindal tightly. "Do you think I intended to dispose of the body by the garbage chute?" She disappeared briefly into the kitchen and returned with an opaque blue jar.

She handed the jar to Rolf, who accepted it with a lift of his thin eyebrows. "Squeamishness, Calial?" he asked.

"You are the man who likes to boast of your extensive experience in such matters. Finish the job neatly. I am expecting company tonight." Cindal kissed Radge's cheek. "Sorry, love." She extended her arm to Yarl, who closed his pocketknife and accepted Cindal's gesture. The two of them walked to the door. "Be thorough, Rolf," ordered Cindal as she left.

When the door closed behind Cindal and Radge's double, Rolf murmured, "I am always thorough, Calial, for Marrach trained me well. He also taught me to respect our Council Governor's wrath. When Caragen takes a personal interest, everyone is expendable, beginning with the most visible players. I do not covet your responsibility, Calial, though I deserve it more than you."

Rolf opened the jar and wrinkled his bulbous nose at the odor. He placed the jar on the square, white dining table, and he pulled his black gloves tight above his wrists. He carried the jar back to Radge's side. He fastened the spigot to the jar with great care.

"Where shall we begin, my friend?" asked Rolf cheerfully, and he began to spray the ocher liquid across Radge's face. Rolf began to whistle quietly.

*   *   *

"You look exhausted, Katerin."

"Thank you, Viki."

"I hope he was worth it," added Viki slyly. Katerin shrugged with a carefully cultivated detachment that resembled sophistication, and Viki chuckled. Katerin selected an empty terminal table, collected a discarded light pen from the floor, and began to sketch absently across the table screen.

Cindal arrived breathlessly and waved at the clustered group in general. "Here I am," she announced, "dashing along the brink of tardiness, as usual. Have you encountered the dreaded children yet?"

Viki answered, "None of us is so unfortunate. Chand is gathering his condemned now. My affliction must come soon."

"Must you sound so fatalistic?" demanded Parve with beleaguered weariness. "Perhaps all of their attentions will be on you, and all of their questions will be intelligent."

"Every group of these new students contains at least one thoroughly obnoxious pest," retorted Viki. "Network plans it that way to keep us humble. Look at that young man, grinning like an idiot." Viki pointed one silver-tipped finger toward a student whose most striking affectation was an ankle-length green cloak.

"An anachronist," murmured Mavel, observing the target of Viki's sharp gesture. "We always have a few."

Cindal remarked lazily, "I never knew that you objected to anachronists, Viki."

"I only object to the extremists whose archaic affectations include incapacity before ordinary tasks. Look at this one muddling his registrations: He has not struck a legitimate code yet."

"Talli must be ready to throttle him," laughed Mavel. "I honestly wonder how some of these students manage to feed themselves."

Katerin let her sketching absorb her and spare her from the urge to snarl at Mavel or Viki—or at anyone. "Pretty," remarked Cindal mildly, seating herself beside Katerin and staring at the latter's drawing. "I can always tell when something upsets you, because you start sketching."

"I often sketch because I enjoy it," replied Katerin, and she tried to suppress the flush that burned her cheeks.

"Not when you should be preparing for all those anxious first-termers, eager to embark on the universe of Network research. What will you be doing about your own research this term, now that Network has reassigned your subject group to a higher-priority project?"

Katerin raised her head sharply. She forgot the vivid colors of her light-drawing, and the cool freshness of the air across her skin became a sick and clammy pall. "Which project?" she asked faintly.

"That alien-prejudice thing that Radge has been extolling for the last year. You did know?"

"No. I have not read my mail today." *Network is angry with me for ignoring too many injunctions and recommendations.* "Did Parve tell you?"

"No. I met Radge in the exercise room this morning, and he mentioned it—with considerable relish. He intimated that he would be taking a key role in the expanded project. I assumed he would have told you. Have the two of you quarreled?"

"Ask Radge," said Katerin sharply.

"Quit snapping at me! I just talk too much. Throw something at me, if you like."

Katerin managed a wan smile. "I should prefer to throw something at Radge for stealing my subject group: preferably something large, heavy and inescapable."

"So you two have quarreled. I thought as much from Radge's attitude this morning. How many broken relationships does this make for you?"

"Are you keeping score?"

Cindal shook her head with more amusement than sympathy. "Why do you do it, Katerin, when you always feel so wretched about it afterward? If you insist on behaving like a Halaatu, you really should learn to maintain your detachment."

"Thank you for your advice," said Katerin coldly, while a part of her ached to scream.

"Your list, Katerin," announced Parve. Katerin blushed, recalling that she and Cindal were not alone, but no one else showed any sign of having heard Cindal's quiet comments. The faculty screen displayed the students' names, which the voice of Network would even now be calling in the room beyond the transparent, soundproof partition.

"Predominantly male students again," commented Mavel with icy innocence. "Katerin's identifier image inspires such a flood of first-year men to request the field of mathematical psychology, and her personal reputation inspires such a flood of them to abandon the field by second term."

"Mavel dear," said Viki calmly, "your claws are showing." Katerin, her cheeks scarlet, reached for the student list. "If you need an energy cap, Katerin," offered Viki kindly, "Talli usually has a stash."

"If I start this early, I shall be nearly unconscious by evening. I have never reacted well to artificial stimulants."

"Poor girl. Maybe you can persuade Radge to tackle your students along with his own. He always copes so well with these groups." Viki stared absently around the large terminal room, glancing at the scattered clusters of waiting instructors. "Where is Radge this morning?"

"I have no idea," answered Katerin shortly, and she tapped impatiently on the floor's reluctant pressure sensor, until the door opened to allow her escape.

"Well, well," murmured Mavel, and Cindal smiled knowingly.

* * *

What a motley assortment they are, observed Katerin ruefully. *As usual, the department of mathematical psychology has attracted more than its reasonable share of intellectual oddities.*

"I am Professor Katerin Merel," she announced smoothly, and she employed carefully controlled eye contact and positioning to establish her dominance. "I specialize in the field of intelligence science, which involves computer applications of the principles of mathematical psychology, primarily toward the development of behavioral modification algorithms." *Commodities of oddities by natural selection. . . . I must ask Network to recall the rest of that poem for me.*

"Up to this time," she continued evenly, "all of your formal education has been supplied by computer—specifically, by Network. That aspect of your education will, of course, continue."

Predominantly males: Mavel is right, and I do wish that Network would refuse to accommodate these emotional adolescents, who try to substitute excess hormonal activity for intelligent career planning.

"However, Network's direct teachings will no longer comprise the majority of your educational experience. Henceforth, you will be expected to learn the techniques of advanced research in fields that may eventually extend the data-boundaries of Network itself." *Viki's dreaded anachronist—I would end up with him. At least he smiles rather charmingly.*

"You will be required to deal with other human beings on a level that you may never have experienced outside of your relationship with Network, and you will need to extend your social-module skills into your professional exchanges." *. . . if any of you have social-module skills to extend.*

"Network will assign you university social modules to facilitate the transition, but you must always remember:

Network adjusts to your individual modes of thought, monitors your physical and mental status constantly, and communicates with you via the method of optimum accuracy for your personal profile. Human beings can rarely duplicate Network accuracy of communication at the level of concepts. Professional conflicts and misunderstandings may frustrate you initially, but a well-trained researcher can use even these communication errors to further the knowledge and understanding of his field."

If I were kind, I would encourage them to question me freely. I think I shall be mean, instead, and intimidate them. What good is a rotten mood that cannot be shared?

"You are welcome to ask questions, as long as they are intelligent." Katerin gave each of her twelve victims a particularly quelling stare that was one of her most notorious specialties. "If you doubt the intelligence of your question, I suggest that you ask it of Network and not of me."

We are supposed to indoctrinate them in the reality of professional relationships, many of which are decidedly stormy, reasoned Katerin a little guiltily, as she observed the signs of offended arrogance and outright alarm. Two students remained apparently unperturbed: one, a particularly tall, well-constructed man with flashing dark eyes, began to maneuver nearer to Katerin, apparently challenged by her remarks. The second was Viki's anachronist; his smile became briefly thoughtful, but he seemed preoccupied with peering into every open laboratory and office.

Katerin led the group into Parve's laboratory, the largest and most impressive in the department, although its most intimidating equipment was obsolete, and its most powerful and valuable devices lay unseen beyond the inconspicuous screen room door at the lab's far end. "This is the department's primary laboratory, where new algorithms are generally tested on carefully selected subject groups." *Such as the group that Radge's favorite project has just stolen from me.*

"Are they students?"

"Pardon me?" demanded Katerin of her dozen heretofore-silent followers. *Which one spoke?* she wondered and concluded sardonically, *the oblivious anachronist, of course.*

"Are the subject groups composed of students?" repeated the anachronist.

"Not as a rule," replied Katerin, conveying with her coldness that this question did not qualify as intelligent in her estimation. She would have added a scathing comment to the effect that even a first-termer ought to recognize that any single-occupation subject group would produce biased statistics, but dark-eyes had managed to position himself in her path. *He knows how to use his height to suggest superiority,* she noted, irritated with herself for having provoked his unprofessional behavior.

The anachronist had wandered toward the screen room, and he had begun to thump it with his fist, apparently fascinated by the sonorous metallic tone. "What is this?" he asked curiously.

"A screen room," answered Katerin with curt impatience. She gestured toward the nearest experiment rig, trying to continue her lecture smoothly. "Intelligence theorists use this station to quantify emotional reactions at a much more detailed level than standard Network monitors provide."

"What is a screen room?" asked the anachronist.

"An electromagnetic isolation booth," replied Katerin crisply. She met the anachronist's gray eyes, intending to intimidate him with a glare, but she found her mind drifting to a stormy sea, the color of his eyes, that seemed to beckon with dangerous depths.

She shook herself free of the strange, momentary fancy. "Most of these stations," she persisted, refusing to let the anachronist control her attention, "are used in the development and analysis of new educational algorithms for Network application. Most of you probably learned elementary mental arithmetic via a method developed here by Professor Parve Lilleholm, the current head of this department."

"What do you isolate?" demanded the undaunted anachronist in a soft voice that seemed to carry itself further than simple sound.

She avoided looking at him directly, still disturbed by his unreasonably compelling gaze. *I have seen other anachronists. This one is unremarkable. Why does he disturb me?* "We isolate immature subjects who lack the discipline to resist trivial environmental distractions," retorted Katerin pointedly. "Would you please rejoin the group?"

The anachronist turned from his puzzled examination of the screen room and grinned at Katerin. "Sorry," he said and jogged hastily to her side, where he bowed to her with an exaggerated flourish of his ridiculous cloak, which scattered a stack of data film to the floor. Despite the clumsy absurdity of his actions, Katerin found herself increasingly disturbed by his proximity. *He reminds me of a dangerous animal,* she thought uncomfortably, *that looks playful until it strikes.*

One of the thoroughly cowed members of the group— a sallow boy, who looked much younger than the usual first-termer—hurried to retrieve the film. Katerin smiled at him, turning his fear into amazement, and a smug expression appeared on his square, solemn face.

Katerin did not criticize the anachronist. She did not trust herself to stop short of a methodical psychological evisceration of him. She could deride the baseless fear that he inspired, but she knew she would defer to it too easily.

I can imagine Parve's reaction if I implemented a full-scale subjugation technique before a group of helpless first-termers, she thought. *That anachronist had better hope he never encounters me without witnesses to protect him.*

Katerin resumed her lecture, and the anachronist's silence satisfied her that she had regained control of the group. Even dark-eyes contented himself with an occasional languid gaze at her across the heads of his fellows. By the time she had led the group through the rest of the major laboratories, Katerin had nearly forgotten her earlier disquiet.

She approached her own office, which she did not intend to display. She turned her head, realizing that she had nearly collided with a passerby during her pondering of where next to take her entourage, and she discovered Radge standing nearly at her back. Everything inside of her felt chilled, frightened, and furious. Radge asked her politely, "Have you seen Parve?"

"No." *How does he dare to interrupt my indoctrination session?* she asked herself angrily, while her voice continued to lecture quietly and reasonably, and a detached calm inside of her insisted that Radge had every right to seek Parve here.

Radge should be in his own building, leading his own first-termers, instead of taunting me here. Except Radge has had first-termers each term for the last three years, answered the saner part of Katerin's mind, *and he could have excused himself from the task this term; I never thought to ask him. But why did he need to look for Parve now? Perhaps they need to coordinate lab usage—or the transfer of my subject group to Radge's department.*

Dark-eyes had begun to draw close to her again, but this time Katerin allowed him to approach and stay at her side. Radge departed wordlessly. Katerin wondered if any of the students recognized the subtle seduction they witnessed, and she concluded that they remained too innocently awed by their personal initiations into Network's technocracy, as represented by admission to Harberg. She refused to look at the anachronist.

Even dark-eyes is too naive to know that I am manipulating him, she observed and suppressed a misplaced urge to giggle. *He obviously considers himself sophisticated where women are concerned. He needs to learn the dangers of overestimating his own strength of position.*

Humiliation is a poor teacher, answered Katerin, protesting helplessly against conditioning's twisted control, *and you could easily cause lasting damage to him. He does not deserve your vengeance against a nightmare.*

"Those of you who wish to hear Professor Lilleholm's description of assistantship opportunities may go to the main auditorium on the ground floor," said Katerin. *Most of them will go, because they will consider my suggestion a command. The anachronist is lingering, but he will be easy to avoid.* Katerin summoned dark-eyes with a glance that appeared guileless, and he followed her, as she intended. Katerin checked her Network wristband unobtrusively and canceled her only afternoon appointment. *I shall let him buy me lunch, I suppose, to let him assert his illusion of control.*

Katerin could feel her self-loathing grow even before she had persuaded dark-eyes to lead her from the building to the green fiber-lawn. *Why do you do it, Katerin, when you always feel so wretched afterward?* Katerin noticed that the young anachronist watched her leave the building in dark-eyes' company. *Why does he watch me with such ruefulness? What does he want of me?* With a brusque apology that left dark-eyes startled, she ran from him and headed into the park alone.

*   *   *

Michael Merel gazed out the tram window, watching the crowds of workers emerge at the end of the working shift. He smiled faintly, realizing that nearly all of the workers would return to units that he had designed to counteract the outward oppression of their planet. Michael enjoyed Chia-2. He felt useful here.

"Amazing how determined they all look, isn't it?" observed the anachronist who shared the bench with Michael. "As if every one of them knows exactly where he is going and why."

"That is as it should be," answered Michael, for he found satisfaction in being part of that consensus of purpose.

"I suppose so," replied the anachronist, briefly pensive. "What is your purpose on Chia-2?"

"To help ensure that the inhabitants live comfortably." Michael turned his attention to the anachronist. A feeling of familiarity with the young man teased Michael, but the memory remained elusive. "Are you new to the planet?"

"I am a visitor," replied the anachronist lightly, "studying the local architecture."

"Have you visited the mining installation yet?"

"Is it worth seeing?"

"From a design standpoint, definitely." Michael began to warm to the conversation. "Actually, I am an architect. Michael Merel." He offered his hand.

The anachronist accepted the gesture with a firm grip. "I'm Quin. I believe I know your sister. She teaches at Harberg, doesn't she?"

An odd wistfulness crossed Michael's face. "Yes. Katerin is the gifted member of the family. Are you a student at Harberg?"

"I am struggling under that pretense, yes."

Michael smiled. "Don't let the atmosphere of exalted knowledge discourage you. Most of the students—and the faculty—are equally uncertain of their ability to live up to the school's rarefied image. I taught there once myself."

"And you left to work here?" asked Quin with a delicate prod of Power to reach the truth.

"I am useful here. I am needed. At Harberg, I was only one of the lesser lights."

"You allowed the school's reputation to discourage you, which is what you just warned me to avoid."

"I suppose I did," conceded Michael with a grimace. He wondered a little at the ease with which he confided in this stranger, but he was enjoying himself too much to try to slow the process. "Harberg is a little overpowering, as is my little sister. When she surpassed me in honors, I realized that my ego was too fragile to stay. She no longer needed my fatherly guidance."

"What did your sister think of your decision?"

"She has never understood," answered Michael with regret. "She cannot see that her skills intimidate me, because she still sees me as her all-wise big brother. She does not realize that she passed me long ago, and I can never regain pace with her."

"Perhaps you underestimate yourself."

"Perhaps. But I am contented here. I have a wife and a beautiful baby daughter who do need me very much." With a sigh, Michael added, "Katerin drains me these days. Her mind moves too fast for me—and for most people, I suppose."

"She must be lonely."

"Geniuses are plentiful at Harberg. You must have noticed."

"I have noticed many lonely people like your sister—brilliant in some areas and utterly naive in others."

"Are you one of that number?" asked Michael. He felt that he had known this anachronist for years, and he barely recalled that they had met only moments earlier.

Quin smiled crookedly. "Is that how I seem to you?"

"Yes. Very much so."

The tram stopped, and Quin rose. "I need to disembark here, Michael. Perhaps we shall meet again."

"I hope so," said Michael with a warm smile. "I have enjoyed talking to you."

*   *   *

What a grueling ordeal, thought Katerin, after she had calmed herself enough to think with some coherence.

Viki is right; indoctrinating the new students is a ghastly exercise. If it is Network's annual reminder of our own inauspicious beginnings, then why do I always end it with this feeling of futility? The students are all bright and capable, or Network would not have sent them here. Some of them speak intelligently; others act like fools; I must remember how daunting it felt to encounter my first human instructor, and I was younger and more malleable than the average first-termer.

Instead of reentering the building which housed her laboratory and office, she seated herself on the low planter wall. She pulled her sketch pad and markers from the large pocket of her long jacket. She began to fashion quickly-stroked impressions of the brilliant afternoon. The process calmed her initially, but she found herself scribbling deliberately destructive, unidentifiable images across the paler landscape, and she closed her pad hastily.

She began to walk again, trying not to run, impatient now to reach her own apartment complex, open her own door, and seal the unwanted world away from her. She did not see the streets she passed; a frightened instinct led her home without delay or conscious thought. Inside her living room, she leaned against the door and allowed herself to shiver without considering a reason. She threw her jacket across a chair and entered the bedroom.

Roses, like blood, lay scattered upon the pillows. The petals tumbled at Katerin's touch. Some of the stems were bare already, and others wore wilted heads. The bouquet had been strewn helplessly, resembling ruin more than a gift of beauty. Katerin felt repugnance for the careless mess of damaged flowers. She strode angrily to her terminal, needing to direct her turbulent emotions at a visible target. "Who has entered this apartment?" she demanded.

"Only yourself, Katerin," replied the calm, synthetic voice of Network.

"There are roses on my bed, and I did not place them there. Explain, please."

"No one but you has entered the apartment today."

"Compare apartment scans between this morning and the present. Account for discrepancies in contents."

"No discrepancies exist."

"There were no roses here when I left!"

"With the exception of dust, pollen, and various microscopic particles attached to your person, contents of the apartment have not changed since this morning."

"Your scanners are malfunctioning," grumbled Katerin, denying the terror that grew inside of her. She scooped the roses into the discard chute, which would carry them to eventual conversion into energy for her apartment building's usage. She watched the roses vanish, and she stared at the empty chute. She tried to shake herself free of the fear. "Access personal log," she muttered. She sank into a chair.

"Yes, Katerin."

Katerin closed her eyes and began dutifully to confide her private feelings of the moment to the nameless, faceless machine that held all her remembered life in its system memory. "What is happening to me, Network? I feel so confused. Is someone entering my apartment? You tell me no. Then I am manufacturing these invasions myself, and I cannot even remember. Am I so desperate for Michael's attention?

"Contentment eludes me," she murmured. "Happiness has come and gone in flurries—Michael used to make me happy sometimes. I have suffered no more of the ordinary sorrows and frustrations than others I know. I could place great significance on the suspected traumas of my early childhood and youth, but I know that I have been well conditioned to overcome whatever past misfortunes I may have suffered.

"Despite the disparaging opinion of my brother's wife, I survive quite well. Colleagues esteem me, and even the members of my social module consider me stable and successful. All that I lack is contentment. Perhaps it is human contentment, rather than any active happiness, that I seek to promote with my algorithm. I cannot face Radge again.

"I sometimes think that my childhood conditioning has failed, and I am mad. A missing mimovue and dead roses. . . . Why did I turn against Radge? My perceived reality falls farther from the truth each day. I wish I understood hope." She curled into the chair and buried her face in its soft depths. She sighed, "End of log entry."

CHAPTER 3

Network

Katerin met the morning with a renewed determination to continue her professional life, despite the dreadful doubts that assailed her on a personal level. She intended to cleanse her laboratory of any trivial trace of her stolen subject group's tenure. She would preserve such little data as she could use, but she wanted no reminders of Radge and his alien-studies project. She had already girded herself for emotional battle with Network over the subject of her continued refusal of an assistant. She approached her office, rehearsing her arguments in her mind, and she discovered the entry door open.

Katerin reassured herself that the new-term morning schedule had filled the hallways with sufficient acquaintances to protect her from any tangible threat, but her night terrors taunted her as she entered the room that should have been locked. *Parve could have admitted someone—most likely Radge. Please, let me not find dead roses.*

The man who had strewn his belongings across her lab table was neither Radge nor any of the nightmarish haunts in her head, but he disconcerted her equally. "What are you doing here?" demanded Katerin, trying to stifle her unreasonable fears of the anachronist. The latter appeared to have made himself thoroughly at ease in her laboratory. "Access to this laboratory is restricted," said Katerin with carefully practiced calm. "If you wish to speak with me, please ask Network to arrange an appointment."

"But I did not come to talk to you," protested the anachronist. He grinned broadly, his wide, gray eyes glinting mischievously in a face that Katerin could only define as subtly aristocratic. "I mean that I did come to talk to you, but Network told me to come, because I am to be your assistant."

Network has no mercy. "It is customary to meet with your instructor before making yourself so completely at home in her laboratory." *Does he plan to live here? Or is he a compulsive shopper? He carries enough bags and packages to fill a history capsule.*

"But we did meet! Yesterday! Have you forgotten me? I was the one who kept asking you questions about everything: the one who exasperated you the most. Was it the cloak you disliked?"

He had abandoned the absurdly large cloak, but his baggy shirt, vest, and trousers looked so authentically archaic in design and workmanship that Katerin mentally categorized him as the spoiled scion of some very wealthy and indulgent family. *His clothes are actually woven and stitched, and the fabric still drapes as well as the most expensive synthetic. The clothing suits him surprisingly well, for his handsomeness is as unconventional as his antique affectation.*

"I remember you," said Katerin, interrupting his rambling speech. *Don't let him know how well you remember him. Don't let him realize the strength of the impression that he made on you—in a single, frightening moment of staring into his storm-gray eyes and imagining that he could see your soul.* Katerin employed every technique she knew to appear poised, professional, and detached. "What is your background?"

"My background is very extensive," replied the anachronist seriously.

"Does your 'extensive background' include experience in algorithm development and program design?" asked Katerin dryly, while she wondered frantically how she could deal with the prospect of working beside this man, whose presence so aggravated the turmoil of her current emotional state. *I have never let the old, nightmarish con-*

*ditioning damage my professional life; I shall not let it
take charge now.*

"Naturally," replied the anachronist.

*He is too sincere, too cryptic and too confident for a
first-termer addressing a senior researcher.* "How fortunate," remarked Katerin coolly, "because you will need
all of your extensive background and specialized profi-
ciencies if you are to work with me."

"I am a very precocious student."

"Undoubtedly," answered Katerin, "but I should like
to make that assessment for myself."

He shrugged and spread his hands, bumping one of
the unpacked crates and pushing it precariously near the
table's edge. *Why does his clumsiness disturb me, when
it should make me feel more secure in my dominance?
Because it is false,* concluded Katerin, respecting him
reluctantly for his skill in making himself appear harmless. *If I were less well trained in such techniques, I would
believe him.*

Katerin forced herself to tell him calmly, "You might
try assembling some of the equipment before you subject
it to a drop test." She turned toward her office, but she
paused to ask one more question of the anachronist.
"Who admitted you to this room?"

"No one," replied the anachronist. He had begun to
study the assorted crates doubtfully. "The door was
open."

"Note breach of research security," muttered Katerin
to her Network wrist link, and she entered the office
code, glad that her office, at least, still remained invio-
late. She sighed when her office door closed behind her,
and she savored the loneliness and the sense of total
isolation that this room imparted to her with its small,
self-contained, secure environment. Parve and several
other senior researchers had access to her laboratory,
and someone obviously shared access to her home, but
her office belonged to her alone.

Katerin slumped into her desk chair. "Network, there
is a man in my laboratory who claims to be my new
assistant. Have you actually assigned him to me?"

"Yes, Katerin."

"He is unacceptable."

"Only the department chairman may originate requests

for reassignment of personnel. Submit any complaints to Professor Parve Lilleholm for review, please."

"I intend to do so." Katerin tapped her desk to retrieve her work-in-progress, but she stared at the display without seeing it. Restlessly, she canceled the display command. "Network, is Parve in his office?"

"Yes."

"Tell him that I am on my way to see him."

"He requests that you wait until this afternoon, unless the matter is very urgent."

"The matter is urgent."

"He is awaiting you."

"Thank you." Katerin tried to avoid even noticing the anachronist, as she passed through her lab on her way to Parve's office.

Her temper mounted with every step, as she considered the insulting ramifications of receiving a first-termer as assistant. She barely paused for Network to open the doors in her path, and she addressed the top of Parve's bent head, before he could raise his pale eyes to see her. "I want you to reassign my designated assistant," she informed Parve hotly. "He is entirely unsuitable and unqualified either to contribute to or benefit from my research."

Parve rubbed the sparse brown hair atop his long head, as if Katerin's verbal assault had inflicted a physical hurt. "You know that I cannot support a complaint against an assistant who has not even had a chance to begin the term. You are only trying one more ploy to avoid taking an assistant, Katerin, and I consider your request most unprofessional."

"The assignment of a ludicrously ignorant first-termer to a very advanced, very sensitive research project is unprofessional," argued Katerin, her eyes furious and her tongue sharp with anger. "You should have heard the questions he asked me yesterday! Absurd."

"Network does not make capricious selections," retorted Parve, but he frowned and waved his hand above his terminal to summon a display of the background of Katerin's newly designated assistant. The frown faded. "I do not suppose that you have troubled to read your assistant's file," remarked Parve mildly.

"I encountered quite enough of him during yesterday's

indoctrination," snapped Katerin, but she berated herself for weakening her case by the absurd omission of a few simple preparations.

"You are not usually so hasty and haphazard in your judgments, Katerin. Your assistant has an extraordinarily high intelligence measure."

"You cannot be serious," said Katerin, although she did believe. Confirmation that the anachronist's idiotic questions were merely further affectation only intensified her fear of him. She could not explain to Parve that a nightmare had somehow begun to entangle itself with the anachronist's face.

"On the contrary, Katerin, I am quite serious. This young man tested very highly in all subjects, presents an enviable personality profile, and has actually declined several assistantships of higher prestige than yours. Network honored his special request to work with you due to his exceptional qualifications."

"Someone has concocted an elaborate joke, and I have little patience for such primitive humor. This man, this . . ."

"Quin Hamley."

"This anachronist is a first-termer, who is singularly unprepared, judging by his questions yesterday. He could not possibly be less qualified to become my assistant."

"Network disagrees with you, Katerin. Or do you suspect Network of perpetrating this 'joke' on you?"

"Certainly not," replied Katerin, feeling suddenly defeated. *Network is not punishing me. I am only punishing myself with my own uncertainties and resentments. I am letting an antiquated conditioning algorithm take charge of me. I know the truth; I can control the effect of the conditioning and regain my life. When have I ever felt this weak before? This awful mood of fear will pass.*

"I should think you would appreciate a dedicated student," said Parve more gently. "Quin Hamley seems to be quite determined to pursue intelligence science, and he is a great admirer of your work."

Katerin nodded briskly, her anger lurking only inside of her now. "Of course."

Parve frowned briefly, and he looked uncomfortable for several moments. "I realize that Citizen Hamley's anachronistic affectations make him seem a trifle eccentric, but I think he deserves a chance to prove himself."

"Undoubtedly," said Katerin crisply. "Sorry to have wasted your time, Parve."

"Katerin," said Parve slowly, "I know that this new assignment seems to have come at a bad time for you, considering. . . ." He trailed into an imcomprehensible mumble, for any verbal dealings with personal relationships made him uneasy.

"Considering Radge?" asked Katerin briskly, for she understood Parve's silences very well after years of working with him and analyzing him, and she knew how rapidly Cindal could spread a story.

Parve's flat cheeks became pink, and his domed brow crinkled with concern. "I am sure that Network's choice is best for you," he said staunchly. "Network has excellent algorithms for handling times of difficult transition."

"The algorithm that chose my assistant could use extensive renovation," snapped Katerin, and she walked out of Parve's musty office, employing every controllable indicator of serene composure. *If life is fair,* mused Katerin grimly, *the anachronist will have disappeared, never to be seen again.* She forced an even expression and entered.

The anachronist had planted himself on the floor in the center of the lab, so surrounded by stacked crates that Katerin thought for a moment that her ironic wish had been granted. He had opened one crate: Most of the packing foam had evaporated, but he watched the lingering, bubbling traces of it very attentively.

"Do you intend to install the console," asked Katerin, "or are you waiting for it to leap onto the table by itself?"

"Will it stop shrinking?"

"Surely, you have seen packing foam before," said Katerin wearily. *Does he actually expect me to believe that he is this ignorant of the world?*

The anachronist grinned, picked up the console and placed it on the table with a surprisingly easy flow of motion. "Do you ever try to pretend?" he asked, smiling with a warmth that seemed to pierce her heart, "that you are seeing something perfectly ordinary for the first time?"

I am only imagining the magnitude of his impact on me, because a nightmare and dead roses have left me vulnerable to my fears. This is faulty conditioning, and I shall not let it rule me. "Not when I have job to do—and a research leader to impress."

The anachronist rubbed a smear of foam between his fingers pensively. "Sorry, Professor. I shall try harder."

Katerin could see the laughter in his gray eyes, and she wondered what it signified. She pulled her gaze away from him, before he could entrap her again. "If you have trouble installing the new system, use your wrist link to consult Network," she told him calmly. "This room has no direct access."

"I noticed. I could like this room if it had some color in it. All of this black on white is rather intimidating: white walls, white tables, white chairs, black crates. Do you actually like it this way?"

"Yes, Citizen Hamley, I like it this way."

"You do know my name!" he remarked brightly.

"Of course, I know your name, Quin Hamley. Let me know when you have the computer ready. I shall be in my office."

"Could I borrow your wrist link, Professor? I lost mine."

"How could you possibly lose a wrist terminal?" demanded Katerin. *Perhaps some of his idiotic helplessness is real; perhaps that is why he affects the rest.*

The anachronist shrugged, grinning absurdly. Katerin shook her head, chiefly frustrated with herself, but she removed the band from her wrist and handed it to her assistant. "Try not to lose this terminal," she adjured him sternly, but she carefully avoided any wisp of physical contact with him. She had the disquieting impression that he had observed her reluctance to touch him.

* * *

Three hours of concentrated algorithm manipulation restored Katerin to a sense of harmony with her world. She did not even mind excessively when Cindal appeared, interrupting Katerin's work with an airily indifferent apology and an eager curiosity. "That is Viki's horrible anachronist in your lab?" bubbled Cindal, clearly relishing Katerin's misfortune. "Have you adopted him?"

"He was assigned as my assistant," replied Katerin glumly, but she did not resent the carelessness of the questions, because that was simply Cindal's unconsidered way.

"Not really! You must tell me all about it over lunch—you do remember arranging to have lunch with me today?"

"Is it that late already?" countered Katerin easily, but Cindal's question disconcerted her; Katerin had absolutely no recollection of making such arrangements.

"You *had* forgotten me. I should feel hurt, but I forgive you, because I have a generous heart. Come along. I have an early afternoon appointment with my research coordinator, and I do not want to be late again. Viki can be such a stickler when she slithers into her professional mode. Your new assistant seems to have abandoned you," observed Cindal, as she preceded Katerin into the lab, now cluttered with opened crates and partially assembled equipment. "Someone should tell him how to refold a crate." Cindal kicked the recessed switch of one of the carriers, and the attached crate collapsed into a compact tessera that would store easily with its fellows.

"I would prefer to pack him into a crate and ship him to a distant planet well outside of Network territory."

"Katerin Merel, you are selfish and terrible," laughed Cindal. "Did your parents never teach you any manners?"

"Did yours?" retorted Katerin.

"I have not broken a single heart in ages," countered Cindal, shaking her short, ebon hair with teasing sternness. Katerin did not reply, for she concentrated on descending the much-berated stairs of the building's exterior. In heading across the park, Cindal added, "Do you know that Radge has resigned from our social module?"

"No," answered Katerin, the guilt bearing down upon her.

"What did you do to him?"

"Nothing," replied Katerin tersely, but she regretted turning her sharpness against Cindal and added evenly, "We spent an evening together. He discussed his alien cultures project for most of the time, but he tried to open a topic that I had told him before not to raise with me. I left. Nothing else occurred."

"Nothing else?" asked Cindal with a wink of disbelief.

Irritated, Katerin snapped, "Stop trying to fashion me into a villainess, Cindal."

"I've done it again, haven't I? Talked too much. I am sorry," replied Cindal contritely.

"I know," sighed Katerin.

"You certainly are touchy these days. What's wrong?"

Katerin shrugged. "I can't remember ever feeling so overwhelmed by life." A tree-soarer, its polished quills bright in the luminous day, darted from its nest, and Katerin jumped nervously. She grimaced at her own reaction. "Even a tree-soarer frightens me. Insignificant decisions make me want to burst into tears. I have tried all the stress reduction methods in Network's memory, but I understand the algorithms too well to be affected by them."

"You have never seemed particularly susceptible to stress," commented Cindal, her full lips tasting every word. "Why now?"

"Perhaps because I argued with Michael."

"You and Michael always argue, reconcile, and argue again. Is your research giving you trouble?"

"Not particularly," replied Katerin stiffly. She stopped walking at a junction in the paths. "Which direction is the restaurant?"

Cindal smiled, leaned toward Katerin, and pointed toward the right. Cindal's hand brushed Katerin's wrist. "I am sure you will enjoy it." Katerin nodded, unwilling to speak. Somewhat to her surprise, Cindal did not invade her silence. Katerin rubbed her wrist absently.

Cindal had chosen a small, expensive restaurant with a decor that simulated a generic tropical-ocean environment. Surrounded by an improbable blend of colorful aquatic species from widely disparate planets, Katerin had difficulty enjoying the mildly spiced seafood chowder that had seemed to be her least objectionable option.

Cindal has exotic tastes for a professor of cultural economics, mused Katerin. *She does not conform to the typical personality profile of her profession.*

"Katerin, did you hear me? Honestly, I think you should ask Network to give you some extra nutrient allocations or stress treatments or something. You have hardly reacted to anything since we left your lab, and I was so hoping to cheer you up with a good meal and good company. You did enjoy the food, I hope?"

"Yes," said Katerin promptly, but she could think of nothing else to say, for Cindal was right, and the realization made Katerin quite uneasy. Katerin could recall very little of the luncheon conversation, and she could not attribute the failure to any particular distraction of thought or action. She simply could not account for the lapsed time.

I cannot be so distraught about Radge, Katerin told herself, *as to have fallen into depression's extreme, debilitating fatigue. I am obviously more tired—physically— than I realized. Unless old conditioning is completely breaking my ability to reason and recall.*

"If you have a problem, Katerin, you can tell me. I do know how to keep a secret when I try."

Nervously, Katerin crumpled the soft square of fabric beside her table service; the restaurant mimicked the old, impractical forms of linen. Katerin heard herself speaking aloud: "Someone has been entering my apartment without my authorization, deceiving Network security, and leaving no evidence that Network can detect. I'm frightened, Cindal."

"I should think so!" answered Cindal staunchly. "I hope you have reported the intrusions."

Katerin whispered, "Network contradicts me." She closed her eyes, because she felt suddenly dizzy.

Cindal touched Katerin's wrist. "If it happens again, call me."

Katerin's voice shook. "Thank you, Cindal."

"Didn't you think I would help you?" asked Cindal earnestly.

Katerin shrugged self-consciously, unwilling to admit that she had not expected sympathy from Cindal, that she had not even intended to confide in Cindal. Katerin had never understood Network's consistent assignment of her to Cindal's social module. Katerin had never thought their interest profiles were particularly compatible. She felt ashamed of having undervalued Cindal. She should have known not to dispute Network's judgment.

"Look at the time," said Cindal with a shake of her short, straight hair. "I shall be late again, and Viki will scold me for unprofessionalism. I shall blame you for

dawdling! No, please, stay here and finish your drink."
Katerin sank dutifully back into her chair, and Cindal
rushed out of the dining room's aquatic mirage with a
wave of her scarlet waist scarf.

Katerin finished the honeyed beverage, which she
could not remember having ordered. She stared at a delicate, drifting sea lily, until her view disappeared behind
a sleek, massive creature that seemed to be composed
all of teeth and chitinous armor. The room's simulated
aquarium shifted to a frenzied panaroma of great, swift
predators, and Katerin left the restaurant hurriedly.

She emerged into the open air and knew that she was
watched. It was an old instinct, honed in a nightmare
year of fleeing and hiding. It was an instinct she had long
forgotten.

A man emerged from the restaurant behind her. His
craggy, expressionless face lodged in her mind with peculiar insistence. She began to walk quickly toward the university. The streets were filled, for the day was fine, and
many new and returning students met and laughed
together. Katerin felt threatened even by the ordinary
crowds, and she carried the sharp, inescapable face of a
stranger in her mind. Each time she turned, she failed
to discover him, but he seemed to haunt the hazy edge
of her vision.

It was not he who stopped her but a plump, average
sort of man with broad features and a jovial expression.
*I have seen this man elsewhere. This is memory, condi-
tioning, or hallucination.* But the illusion was persuasive,
and she forgot that she had doubted his reality. "Kitri!"
he said, taking her arm and holding it tightly. "How is
your father?"

"My father?" asked Katerin in astonished alarm. "You
must have mistaken me for someone else." *But he knew
the name that only Michael used.*

"No, dear," insisted the round, red-cheeked man
heartily, and his face crinkled into a smile. "You have
forgotten me. I used to visit your parents regularly. Your
brother would remember me. Do you see him often?"

"Let go of me, please." Her nervousness corroded her
voice and made it shrill. "I have a student waiting."

"How are your parents?" asked the jovial man, his
fixed smile never wavering.

"My parents are dead," stated Katerin flatly, "and I have never met you." *Be polite, Kitri. Who is Kitri?* "I am sorry if I seem rude." Katerin pulled away from him, uncaring that he tottered and nearly fell from the force of her escape. She did not look at him again, but she sensed (or imagined that she sensed) his plaster smile pursuing her relentlessly.

* * *

Katerin heard a pastry vendor hollering the features of his wares across the university park. Katerin reached for her wrist band and remembered that she had left it with her assistant. She rose stiffly from the park bench; her left arm felt numb where she had leaned against it.

I must have been exhausted to have slept here—and dreamed so horribly. I cannot even remember leaving Cindal after lunch. The afternoon is nearly gone; the sun skims the mountains. Perhaps my assistant will have given up on me and gone home. I ought to give him formal access privileges to the lab, I suppose, if I intend to leave him working there alone.

Katerin headed across the park toward her office, and she began her mental disparagement of the wide staircase well before she reached it. She cracked the heel of her shoe against the bottom step, and the thin layer of cushion oozed into the air and dissipated. "Just lovely," she muttered. She removed the opposite shoe in frustration and climbed the remaining stairs. She gritted her teeth before she opened her laboratory door.

Her assistant stared vacantly at the assembled console of a very sophisticated research computer, though no display had been illuminated. *My research computer,* thought Katerin with a twinge of jealous possessiveness, *my own pseudo-intelligent entity detached from Network and waiting for my algorithms to give it life.*

"I hope that blank stare indicates that you are concentrating deeply on your Network studies," commented Katerin with sardonic coolness, "since an empty, uninstalled computer is even less enlightening than most other newborns."

He blinked, as if pulled from a great distance. "After I finished unpacking the crates, I thought I might as well begin to familiarize myself with your work. I only asked

Network to recite the general statement of your research topic," he protested and offered her the wrist terminal hastily.

Still warm from his usage of it, the terminal remained active. In a spurt of worry, Katerin glanced at the file indicator. *All personal files are closed,* she noted with relief. *I closed them before I handed him the terminal. I would not have forgotten that most elementary precaution, even in my earlier exhaustion.*

"Of course," acknowledged Katerin, feeling rather foolish for her paranoid suspicions of a first-termer, whose only obvious aberration was his taste in clothes. "I should not have snapped at you." She moved her hand above the flat surface of the table grid, and the test indicators responded reassuringly. "This room actually looks like a working laboratory," she said, forcing herself to sound reasonable and calm. "You have begun well, Citizen Hamley."

"Have I?" he asked, smiling at her with a distracted thoughtfulness. "Then would you mind calling me Quin? Citizen Hamley still sounds peculiar to me—not that it is peculiar—at least no more peculiar than any other title—and a peculiar name would probably be most appropriate for me—but everyone has always called me Quin, and I am rather attached to the label. Do you mind?"

"No." *He talks more rapidly than Cindal, and he makes less sense. Or am I simply too tired to understand him?*

"It is an interesting concept," he remarked.

He was looking at Katerin expectantly, and she realized that she had missed most of what he had said. "What was your question?"

"I only wondered if you could actually do it? I know: another silly question from Quin. Obviously, you think you can do it, or you would not have proposed it for your research, and Network would not have accepted it as 'very promising.' " He prodded the arm of his chair suspiciously before shifting to lean against it. "But if your theory is correct, you can actually make people happier by telling them when to eat oatmeal or when to sing a ballad." His vest fell open to reveal a patchwork lining of gold, green, and violet silk.

Where did he find such a dreadful mix of gaudy colors? wondered Katerin, but she answered him absently, "Contentment is composed of simple pleasures, just as minor irritations often produce the greatest stress composites. Contentment reduces conflict and increases productivity."

"Anger and competition can stimulate extraordinary developments."

He prompted her as glibly as if he knew her well-rehearsed briefing. "They provide short-term results, which are eventually overwhelmed by destructive counter-influences. The promotion of contentment is culturally advantageous."

"Presuming the people are motivated to continue developing rather than to vegetate," mused the anachronist, and he smiled. "But I suppose that an 'ambition algorithm' will handle that aspect for you, something mild enough to avoid conflicts with the contentment notion, but strong enough to encourage progress. I suppose you are designing it to behave rather like a sincerely concerned friend."

"Of course," answered Katerin with some surprise that he had actually produced a sensible, reasonably intelligent argument. *If he abandons some of his affected idiocy, he may be a useful assistant after all.* "The balance is delicate in all algorithms that influence human emotions and behavior. I presume that you have studied the theory of such algorithms."

"Network has been educating me," answered Quin blandly.

Interesting voice shift: He feels inadequate on the subject of his educational experience, despite the outstanding record that Parve claims for him. Perhaps he requires only confidence; many anachronists affect an extreme lifestyle to compensate for social insecurity.

Impulsively, Katerin asked, "What is your assessment of my very preliminary algorithm design?"

"Horribly complex!" replied Quin cheerfully. "I have a great deal to learn."

Yes, Citizen Hamley, you do have a great deal to learn, if you intend to read other people's files habitually. Once more, she started to accuse him, but his open expression caused her indignant anger to ebb into doubt. *Can he actually be unaware of his crime?*

"I should be very interested," said Katerin carefully, "in knowing which Network lessons you studied in order to reach the preliminary algorithm. Although the standard security level of university research files was never intended to defeat a sophisticated entry attempt, it usually discourages casual access."

"Did I damage something?" asked Quin with every appearance of true consternation.

"You cannot damage anything at first level," answered Katerin, increasingly uncertain about him. *He has sufficient technical sophistication to penetrate programming barriers, but he lacks fundamental comprehension: a dangerous combination. How could Network authorize him to pursue the field of intelligence science, where cautious judgment is a primary criterion?*

Quin began to laugh, to Katerin's surprise. She sensed (with some disquiet) that he had followed her train of thought. "Am I so amusing?" she asked dryly.

"I tend to laugh spontaneously: a bad habit but an incurable one."

"You seem to have a number of unusual characteristics," murmured Katerin. *Parve is right. I should be glad of his interest in my research—and not in me. As long as we focus strictly on the work, he cannot endanger me, and I need not feel threatened by him.* "If you can contain your hilarity, perhaps you can help me to prepare the new home for my algorithm."

"You will house your algorithm in this?" demanded Quin, pointing at the console.

"Where else?" *As soon as I begin to credit him with enough honesty to sound intelligent, he asks another of his inane questions.* "Intelligence algorithms for deep psychological adjustment are always developed on independent computer systems. They are only transferred to Network after extensive testing ensures that they contain no dangerous contaminents to Network logic."

"But your algorithm resides in Network now."

"The algorithm is still inactive and very incomplete."

"Have I asked another incredibly stupid question?"

"Yes, Quin." *He is entirely ridiculous—when he pretends to be a fool—but I still feel better than I have felt all day. Perhaps his affectations have more value than his own defense.*

"You ought to smile more often, Professor," remarked Quin seriously. "It makes you look much less threatening."

Katerin could only shake her head at the irony of his remark, and her hair shifted smoothly across her shoulders. "Where did you find that vest?"

"A friend of mine made it."

"I hope your friend has attributes other than color sense," said Katerin wryly. Quin's laughter seemed to drive away the haunts of all the recent terrors. *Perhaps Network is right in prescribing him for me,* mused Katerin. *Network is always right.*

CHAPTER 4

Network and Luki's House

Quin spent many minutes observing the queues of Network citizens entering and emerging from the topological transfer port. The fixed ports did not interest him; they were too steadily utilized to allow an unobtrusive reconfiguration. He watched the programmable ports closely, assessing the intervals between travelers. He let his Power trace the impact of the destination codes the travelers gave by keypad command to Network. When he convinced himself that he could alter the destination without attracting notice, he arose from the observer's chair and entered the shortest queue.

"Identification code?" asked the synthetic voice of Network, as Quin approached the portal.

"Code jq955yj36," answered Quin, and his Power felt Network compare the code to the initial imprint of sensor scans made automatically when Quin first entered Network. Jonathan Terry had preprogrammed the code well. Network accepted Quin.

"Select destination," said Network.

Quin made a motion toward the keypad, so as to deceive anyone who might watch him, while his Power claimed the port's control. He entered the light curtain, trying not to become distracted by his fascination with the curtain's resemblance to a wizard's barrier. He directed the patterns and chose a path that did not reside in any Network memory. He released the Harberg port, when he felt the welcome familiarity of the Taormin.

He squeezed through Luki's hedge and trotted to her cottage. "Luki!" he called, and he poked his head through the open doorway when she did not answer.

"You have not come visiting much lately," said Luki accusingly. "You have not stayed away as long since that warrior wife of yours died."

Quin grimaced, as he ducked beneath Luki's lintel and entered her house. Luki pointed toward the hearth. Dutifully, Quin removed the water kettle from its hook above the fire and carried it to the table where Luki sat waiting. "Laurett wanted me to be useful, and you insisted that I become a scholar. Ixaxin duties keep me busy."

"Pfaugh. You never took work that seriously—not for my sake nor even for that rash pledge of yours to a dying woman. You have found some fine new lady, I think."

"Are you jealous, Luki?" asked Quin whimsically.

"Hmh. What is she like?"

Quin pondered how much he dared say in the delightful game of teasing Luki. "She does not like your vest for one thing," he said impishly. Luki snatched the kettle from him, and the steaming water splattered the hard dirt of the floor. "But what does she know?" added Quin with a mischievous smile. "All she likes is black, white, bland and dull."

Only partially mollified, Luki allowed Quin to return the kettle to the hearth. "If you find her so dull, why do you spend time with her?"

"She is beautiful and terribly clever," replied Quin airily, but he resorted to Power to prevent a blush. He realized that he scarcely understood what he felt about Katerin Merel. *My Laurett could have bested her without blinking, and Laurett never daunted me.*

"She is Ixaxin," grumbled Luki. "I thought you had better sense than to trifle with a wizardess."

"You are a wizardess, Luki," retorted Quin.

"I am old, boy, and you are a fool."

"Luki, stop glaring at me. I am only teasing you. The lady is not Ixaxin, and I am not 'trifling' with her. I hardly even know her." *Blast, why did I have to slip into honesty now? It is better that Luki believes me infatuated than know what I dare not tell.*

"Liar, you admitted that you spend much time with her."

"I admitted nothing of the sort! Anyway, she is very difficult to know," answered Quin with a shrug. "She is a very private person, who also dislikes me. I think I annoy her."

"You annoy everyone," growled Luki and concentrated on ignoring him.

"Luki," pleaded Quin, and he waited patiently for Luki to stop fussing with her biscuits and her tea. "I brought you a present, Luki," he said in a wheedling tone. "Do you want to see it?"

"Where is it?" muttered Luki gruffly. Quin fumbled among his various pockets, deliberately protracting Luki's curiosity. When he extended his closed fists toward her, she struck him with the edge of her apron. "Fool boy, silly games waste time."

Quin opened his right hand, and a multicolored, irregular block began to expand, freed of the confinement of Quin's grip on it. Quin assisted the unfolding process by grasping one corner of the block and shaking it to produce a rectangle nearly his height and as wide as the length of his outstretched arms. Shades of pink, violet, and blue swirled across the refractive surface. "This was the brightest one I could find," announced Quin proudly.

Luki touched the gift cautiously. "Is it sea-silk, boy?"

"It is not woven fabric at all, Luki. It is called plyar. Students hang panels of it on their walls. Watch." Quin pressed the plyar sheet above the hearth, and it clung to the stones. "It sticks to anything inorganic, and you can detach it and reattach it as often as you want without damaging it or the surface beneath it." He pulled it from the hearth in a bundle and draped it over Luki's arm. "I think they make it out of flower petals."

"It comes from no flower I ever saw," said Luki scornfully, but her crabbed, old fingers traced the shifting colors with wonder.

"Do you like your present, Luki?"

"Well enough," she acknowledged brusquely. "Take another cracker, boy. You are looking too thin." She eyed him narrowly. "You have been wielding too much Power lately without eating enough to compensate. It is not like you, boy. You begin to resemble Him."

"I am not Lord Venkarel," muttered Quin. He sat heavily on the hearth beside the biscuit tin and stared at the crumbly contents. "I am too short, for one thing," he informed the hearthstones. He selected the largest biscuit, wrapped it in his kerchief, and stuffed it in his coat pocket. "I need to go. I may not be able to visit you again for a while, Luki."

"The boy is too short," echoed Luki tonelessly.

"Thanks for the tea, Luki," said Quin, uneasily observing her empty gaze. He hesitated to touch her when she fell into this mood, though he disliked departing without proper acknowledgment of her hospitality and kindness.

"You have met Him," accused Luki hollowly. Quin gave her cheek a hasty kiss and tried to reach the door before she could stop him. "When did you meet Him, boy?" demanded Luki, her agitation growing visibly.

"Lord Venkarel is dead," replied Quin firmly. He closed his hand over the tiny brand seared in the center of his palm. "I have never met him, and I have nothing in common with him except your friendship, dear Luki." Quin felt the confused fluttering of her Power trying to restrain him, but he dodged her probe and ducked beneath the lintel of her door.

He nearly tripped over the gray-furred cat-thing, which gave him a baleful glance from its lavender eyes. Quin hurried through the hedge and plunged directly into the distant Taormin's maelstrom of topological infinities. He reached for an orderly, recognizable pattern and emerged beside the infant computer that he and Katerin Merel had installed.

The lab was empty, for the hour was late. Quin headed for the door before he remembered that the entire building would be locked and monitored at this hour, and he had not yet examined the building's security system closely enough to circumvent it with any confidence. He grunted and flung himself into a lab chair; the chair shivered at the sudden pressure before it adapted to Quin's slouch. "Hello, computer," said Quin to the molded black unit that comprised the system's brain.

"Hello, Quin," replied a sharp, imperfect voice, the minimal vocal approximation generated by an incomplete system.

"You are beginning to develop an identity, computer. I recognized your pattern easily."

"Many file references still missing."

"Professor Merel says she wants to select your memories carefully. You are supposed to become much better company when you are complete."

"Yes, Quin."

"Computer, I want you to delete any reference to my visit here tonight."

"Factual reference cannot be deleted during initialization phase."

· Quin chastised himself for his lack of planning. *You could have emerged from any Network transfer portal, and no one would have noticed you, but you had to be lazy and follow the first path that popped into your silly head. Luki is right: You are witless.* "Can you keep a secret?" he asked the computer uncertainly.

"Data can be secured by private code, accessible only to authorized originator."

Quin grinned. *Lady Fortune does take care of us fools.* "Secure all references to my visit here tonight."

"Private code must be established first."

"Establish one!"

"Primary code established for Quin Hamley, Network code jq955yj36. Do you wish to secure name and file references of primary originator from subsequent users?"

Startled by the question, Quin answered, "Yes," before he realized that he had quite probably stolen the privileged authority that should have belonged to Katerin Merel. *If she does not know, she will not mind,* reasoned Quin, but he had a squeamish feeling that his ignorance was planting him in another precarious situation.

"Designate open reference name for originator," requested the computer.

"Explain, please."

"State name by which originator should be referenced in public files."

"Use Quin."

"That reference has been secured. Select another."

"Wizard," answered Quin with a smile.

"Authorize any secondary code users, please."

Oh, no, what have I started? "Can a secondary code user read my secure files?" asked Quin.

"No. Secondary code users have authority to establish their own secure files."

"Then authorize Katerin Merel as a secondary code user." *Does she want anyone else to have access? Of course not, idiot; this is her private research computer. I doubt that she would even want you to have "secure privileges," whatever that means.* "No other secondary code users are authorized at present."

"State my name, please."

"Your name?" asked Quin helplessly. *Katerin Merel will flay me when she realizes that I have claimed her pet computer's first allegiance. Well, she should not have left it so vulnerable.*

But then, she did leave late, she did lock the lab behind her, and she did make a point of declining to give you access privileges until tomorrow. She certainly did not expect anyone to enter the lab before she could return in the morning.

Why did I have to come here tonight? Why did I have to start talking to this thing? Because Luki frightened me with her talk of Lord Venkarel, who is probably watching me now and debating whether or not to singe my innards for leaving Network without the Infortiare's authorization, and I had no other permissible place to go where Network would not pester me, but I did want to talk to someone— or at least to something.

"Laurett," said Quin impulsively. "Your name is Laurett."

"Thank you, Wizard."

* * *

The sketch was faded, flat, and stark. The figures in it seemed stiff and strange, like badly drawn caricatures. The angle of that arm seemed wrong, and the ears protruded too much. The nose cast too deep a shadow, and the eyes did not quite match. A child's crude attempt to capture a likeness of her parents: Katerin could feel again the charcoal in her fingers, the thin end slightly gritty as it darkened her childish fingers and smeared upon the paper, there, where the awkwardly scratched hands met in a messy blur.

One of her first attempts at drawing people, the sketch had not satisfied her even at the time of its creation— over twenty years ago? She would have shredded it, but she had used the pad of fine, tough film that her mother had given her for her birthday; the film fixed the charcoal within hours after use, so that she could not even erase it. Childishly, she had hidden the drawing in her bureau drawer, buried beneath undergarments, where she had imagined that no one would ever see it.

She had forgotten it years ago. She could not even remember if the bureau had stood in her room on Network-3 or if it had occupied one of the many rooms in the many apartments that followed. It might even have stood in the final room, the final home, the place of darkness and of the beginning of fear.

No! This is not the same drawing. The other was lost in a planet's death or a family's death. Which planet? What family? Have I ever seen this sketch? "Who has entered this apartment during the night?" demanded Katerin of Network.

"No one, Katerin."

"Your sensors are in error. Place a request for a full maintenance scan. Register my official complaint of security violation."

"Request for scan is placed. Complaint will be held pending scan results."

"I want the complaint registered now. I want increased security."

"No current justification exists. Complaint will be held pending scan results."

"Establish a vocal link to Michael Merel."

"Unable to comply. A transponder has malfunctioned in the Chia-2 sector."

"Estimate time of scan completion."

"The queue is three hours."

"Notify me at the university when it has been completed."

"Yes, Katerin."

* * *

"Network does have certain advantages," murmured Quin, contentedly stretching in the very accommodating chair.

"Good morning, Wizard."

"Good morning," replied Quin, opening his eyes and sitting upright. "Is it really morning?"

"Yes, Wizard."

Quin pulled Luki's biscuit from his pocket, observing ruefully that he had crushed it during his sleep. He began to scoop the crumbs into his mouth, while he let his Power idly note the stirrings of activity throughout the building. He hastily tucked the remaining crumbs back into his pocket when he sensed a stranger approaching; he nearly forgot to unlock the door, so as to help excuse his own presence in the lab, but he issued the command a moment before the man demanded entry of Network.

There is something too stealthy about him, thought Quin, critically comparing the outward poise of the man with the burst of disappointment that radiated from him on seeing Quin. *A courteous man should announce himself before entering a closed room. Stop it, old boy, you are a fine one to judge anyone else's manners.*

"Are you expecting Professor Merel soon?" asked the man with an austere arrogance.

No wizard's tricks, Quin reminded himself sternly, biting his knuckles to restrain his Power's irritated impulse. "I believe that she is attending a meeting this morning," answered Quin, congratulating himself for sounding reasonably courteous.

"I attended the meeting. It ended." The man surveyed the lab with an air of greedy possessiveness. His gaze returned to Quin, absorbed the anachronistic attire, and acquired the haughtiness of deep contempt. "You must be the new assistant."

"Yes." *This intruder certainly does think well of himself. He is the sort of mortal who makes Ceallagh's laws of restraint so necessary and so painful.* Quin offered his hand in a greeting that crossed both his culture and Network's. "My name is Quin Hamley." Quin let the physical contact guide a tiny probe of Power; the coldness that he touched revolted him, and he withdrew hurriedly.

"I am Professor Randon. Has Katerin spoken of me?"

Quin answered brightly, "No, but I have heard your name bandied quite freely in the student common room. I gather that you know Professor Merel rather well."

"I know her," answered Randon tersely. He walked to the console and stared at it. He turned back to Quin suddenly. "I know Professor Merel better than she seems to find palatable. She deserves her reputation as Halaatu."

You are not a very gentlemanly soul, Professor Randon, to speak so spitefully of a lady. "I shall try to avoid antagonizing her."

With the certainty of a command, Randon warned, "Just be sure you never try to extend your professional relationship with her into the personal realm."

The conceited twit is virtually threatening me. "I doubt that I am her type," said Quin with a smile and a shrug.

Randon continued with vehemence, "To her, you would be only a study subject: another parameter in a behavioral algorithm."

Why do you denigrate her with such fervor? asked Quin with an unobtrusive prod of Power. The intense violence of the responsive images caused Quin to abandon his probe hurriedly. He was glad that Randon did not see his Power's flash of defensiveness.

I should know better than to delve into the emotions of someone so obviously angry. I should know better—but I am accustomed to the pragmatic violence of hunters, warriors, and thieves, and not to the seething, buried resentments of a sophisticated, civilized man of Network. "I doubt that even Professor Merel could reduce me to an equation," commented Quin with an airy wave.

"Never underestimate her powers of analytical detachment," snapped Randon.

Katerin answered from the hall doorway, "I appreciate the tribute, Radge." She swayed into the room and brushed past Radge to reach her office.

Her motions, despite their apparent simplicity, conveyed a potent aura of seduction, which made Quin distinctly uncomfortable. Katerin leaned against the office door, visibly defying Radge to approach. "Why are you here, Radge? I do not recall giving you access privileges to my lab. Did Parve admit you?"

Radge took one step toward Katerin, but her brittle, cynical laughter stopped him. He said tensely, "I need to talk to you."

"Why?" asked Katerin mildly. "You seem to have said enough about me to Cindal. I expected better of you, Radge."

"Could we go into your office?" countered Radge, glancing at Quin, who scrambled clumsily to his feet.

Quin muttered, "I think I shall go find some breakfast."

"Not now, Quin," ordered Katerin, and she filled her command with subtle, irresistible tokens of authority, some of which Quin recognized, most of which he sensed only with his Power. The depth of the compulsion to obey her startled him, and he stared at her, suddenly aware of how greatly he had underestimated her particular expertise. "You have work to do here, Quin, and Radge has an important research project in alien behavioral studies to supervise."

"Is that what angered you?" asked Radge earnestly. "The transfer of your subject group to my department?"

"I am not angry with you, Radge. I am only disappointed," replied Katerin very calmly. "I have work to do, and you are keeping me from it."

"When may I talk to you?" persisted Radge, while Quin wished that he dared disappear into a shadow of Power.

Katerin murmured, "I think Network might consider your insistence on speaking to me suspiciously obsessive, considering that you requested the change of your social module so as to avoid me. I think you are a seriously troubled man. May I recommend a conditioning algorithm for you?"

"I think Network can make a less prejudiced selection," snarled Radge, and Quin's Power stirred into an instinctive barrier against the magnitude of anger in the room. Radge departed abruptly, and he carried his anger with him.

Quin relaxed marginally, though his Power continued to seethe inside of him, sensitizing him to every strand of energy around him. He felt the imperfect, immature entity that he had named for Laurett. He felt the enormity of Network extending throughout the building and the university.

He would have preferred not to sense Katerin Merel, for there was so much cold pain and dark terror inside of her. He had wanted to give the Terrys reassurance, even if reuniting them with their children seemed a remote possibility. He knew that he would never now be able to report honestly that the Merels were safe and well. The disappointment tasted bitter.

Slowly, Katerin turned toward Quin, and he realized that she scarcely recognized his presence at all. "Are you here to work," she snapped, "or to support the wall?"

"I was thinking of going for breakfast," said Quin, for he still felt intrusive.

"Then go."

"Would you like anything?" asked Quin hesitantly, wondering if he dared try to help.

"Yes. Privacy." Katerin tapped her office door and retreated into her sanctum. The flat, white door slid closed behind her.

"Sorry, Professor," murmured Quin. "I do keep asking silly questions."

* * *

Well, Katerin, you have made a thorough fool of yourself this morning. Why did Radge have to come here? Stop thinking about him. "Network," demanded Katerin, "are you able to establish a link to Michael Merel yet?"

"No, Katerin.

"Can you place a message in the queue for him?"

"Yes, Katerin."

"Tell him to contact me as soon as possible—highest priority."

"Completed."

"Can you estimate when he will receive the message?"

"No reliable information is available to support such an estimate."

The most sophisticated communication system in connected space fails me now, when I am most in need of Michael's counsel and concern. "Thank you, Network."

"You did not record a personal log this morning. Would you like to make an entry now?"

"Have you completed the maintenance scan of my apartment security?"

"Scan is complete: All systems function properly. Do you wish to make a log entry?"

"No, Network. Not now." *You must make a log entry, Katerin, if you expect Network to advise you successfully. You have a duty to provide Network with full trust and complete information, if you expect to receive the benefit of Network's resources.* "Summon my work files. I wish to begin transfer operations to my research computer."

I shall make the log entry later, when I feel less helpless and unsettled.

"No direct access exists."

"Use transition buffer, code Michael-9E."

"Transfer is complete."

Katerin gathered the smooth buffer cube into her hands and carried it to her office door. Reluctantly, she entered the lab. Despite her embarrassment, she felt almost disappointed that Quin had actually left; she would need to wait that much longer to face him again. "Unless I have frightened him away from here for good," she murmured ruefully. "Computer, accept file transfer from transition buffer, code Michael-9E."

"Files accepted. Thank you, Professor. I shall be much more effective now."

Thank you, Professor? "Computer, did Quin initialize you?" demanded Katerin slowly.

"Yes, Professor."

"The presumptuous . . ." she whispered. She felt the frustration expand within her, clawing at her nightmare sense of helplessness. She buried the feeling angrily. "Computer, did he name you?"

"Yes, Professor. My name is Laurett."

"Laurett," repeated Katerin with sardonic distaste. *And I worried that this ill-mannered anachronist might judge me lacking in social courtesies after this morning's little scene.* "What other initialization routines did Quin perform?"

"Default values for standard base-level routines: self-test, file structure, housekeeping. . . ."

Katerin interrupted, "Thank you, Laurett. You need not recite the base-level index." *Reconfiguration of the computer would take hours now. It hardly seems worth the effort. Can I live with a computer named Laurett?* Feeling leaden, Katerin drooped into the chair that faced the console. She began to rub her temples.

"You are troubled, Professor. May I help?"

"Not until I complete your development, Laurett." Katerin added dryly, "Unless Quin happened to perform that service also." *When did he have time to perform the initialization? Parve could not have admitted him to the lab more than a few minutes before I arrived, because*

Parve was at the meeting with me. Must I report another security breach? I need to change the lab access codes.

"Professor, how shall I determine whether I am complete?"

"If you were complete," sighed Katerin, "you would know without asking." *How can I criticize Quin for performing more of the installation than I intended? As his research leader, I have given him virtually no intelligible instructions. When he is not pretending idiocy, I have trouble remembering that he is only a first-termer.* "I am blaming him for my carelessness," muttered Katerin.

"Are you addressing me, Professor?"

"No, Laurett. I shall address you in vocal mode three or higher. Do you understand?"

"Yes, Professor."

"Display module 8B, please. We shall see what we can do to make you smarter."

* * *

When Quin returned, Katerin began her attack immediately, so as to preserve herself from the terror of helplessness that clawed at her. "You named my algorithm development system 'Laurett,'" accused Katerin sharply.

"A child needs a name," answered Quin with precisely the startled defensiveness that Katerin had sought to generate. "Your computer is a child of sorts."

Like you, thought Katerin with exasperation. *And like me,* she added to herself self-mockingly, *for feeling so protective about my incomplete creation.* "You ought to have consulted me."

"If I had realized it would bother you, I never would have named her."

Quin sounds so like a young boy, bewildered by an adult's lack of appreciation for his carefully collected spider or beetle or other, similar prize. It is a clever pose, for it lulls the hearer. "Why Laurett?" asked Katerin and was surprised to see Quin's face redden.

He answered somewhat stiffly, "She was a childhood friend."

Childhood friends; children's pastimes; a child's clumsy sketch placed in my room by a hand too stealthy for even Network to perceive. Stop thinking about it. Quin's ridicu-

lous affectations are far removed from the dire undercurrents of my haunted past. "Do you ever think before you act, Quin?" asked Katerin wearily.

"Very rarely." Quin widened his gray eyes in comical dismay. "Do you ever act before you think?"

Katerin shook her head, and her hair swung rhythmically. "Almost never," she answered with a sad, reluctant smile. "That is the secret of my success."

"It sounds exhausting."

Even offered a wounded victim, he does not, cannot, or will not attack—with any of the devilish techniques that I know too well. He is very foolish or very wise. He is my designated assistant and my responsibility, and I wish that I had met him as only a possible friend. I wish that I were capable of such a friendship; I would fail with Quin, as I failed with Radge.

Katerin dispelled her momentary wistfulness with the crisp, hard sound of her own voice asking, "Why did you choose to specialize in intelligence science?"

Quin fixed a curious, tilted gaze on Katerin's coolly reserved face, and he emulated her intense, forward-leaning posture. "I wanted to study with you, Professor," he answered evenly. "Your work is well known."

His answer troubled her, but Katerin replied calmly, "If you intend to master a subject thoroughly, the subject must consume you in and of itself."

"If I claimed such an obsessive interest," laughed Quin with a roguish twinkle, "I think you would call me a liar, and you would be right! Network did test me very thoroughly, after all, and you must have access to the results of those tests: 'The subject's general aptitudes at this time do not indicate conclusively any single innate specialty. Subject's request for intelligence science specialty is supported by superior general test scores and warrants tentative approval.' "

Katerin studied him through her lashes. *How odd,* thought Katerin: *He really does have extraordinarily fine bone structure, almost as if he were as removed from this century as he pretends. I wonder what he would think if I asked to paint his portrait?* "Excessive cockiness impedes learning. I can teach you nothing if you know everything already."

"But consider the great pleasure you will derive from

fulfilling your pessimistic predictions about me," he replied with something very like ruefulness. "My worth for that satisfaction alone should contribute enormously to the success of your happiness algorithm."

"Your insights on life should indeed provide a fascinating resource for algorithm development." *If I could quantify his mode of thinking and apply it, I could probably qualify for the Zhiang-Advent award. An algorithm based on Citizen Quin Hamley might very well revolutionize current perspectives on the emotional deficiencies that create aberrant subcultures.* "Why do you pretend to be a fool, Quin?"

His eyes, so remarkably reminiscent of a stormy sea, narrowed keenly. "You certainly do know how to disconcert a fellow. Mathematical psychology obviously has interesting applications." He laughed, but the sound held a self-conscious note. "I prefer to be underestimated, Professor. Less is expected of me. Why do you pretend to be the cold *Halaatu*, when you feel everything so deeply?"

"I did not choose the title," replied Katerin archly, but a warmth suffused her face. She had hoped that Quin would forget the scene with Radge; she wished that Quin had never heard her cruel title. "I prefer to think that my reputation arose originally from the envious tongues of others. Everything was always easy for me, except making friends."

"Because friends could be hurt."

"Yes." She looked at him curiously. "Most people assume that I only fear to hurt myself."

"You can deal with your own pain more easily that you can heal the wounds you make in others," said Quin, and he seemed to stare at a sight beyond the small, white room. "It is so easy to cause injury, often without even knowing for sure what you have done—or if you have caused the injury at all."

"Because you *can* do so much so easily, making it hard to avoid judging others by your own experience, which rarely applies."

Quin nodded pensively, his gaze still distant. "So you build yourself a shell and lock yourself inside, and you try not to let anyone come close enough to be truly hurt by you."

"You do understand," murmured Katerin in wonder.

"Not really," answered Quin, returning to the present with a smile and a sigh. "If I truly understood, I would not behave like such a fool, would I?"

"I understand a great many rules of wisdom that I cannot seem to implement in my own life," replied Katerin with wry humor. *Network, as always, is right. He is what I need. I shall soon begin to wonder how I ever lived without him.*

The nightmare raced into her mind. *No*, she whimpered to herself. She backed across the room, stumbling against a chair, but she did not feel the bruise. She moved warily to her office and virtually flung herself inside it. She locked the door and cried.

* * *

"I am sorry," murmured Quin, feeling unwontedly helpless and shaken by the flood of horror that his innocent prod of Power had unleashed. "I have never known anyone to react so violently before."

"Are you addressing me, Wizard?"

"No, Laurett," answered Quin, impatient and angry with himself. *What have you done this time, idiot? Touched something done by someone else, I think, but that does not make the result any better. You cannot leave her like this, old boy. Fool, you have no right to do anything else.*

She is such a strange mixture of cool competence, fierce temper, and vulnerability. I need to do something. *No, I need to do nothing.*

My judgment cannot have strayed too far from the Infortiare's will; Lord Venkarel has not yet hurled me into some anguished oblivion. On contemplating the unnerving prospect of Lord Venkarel's anger, Quin clenched his left hand nervously, then decided that worrying any further about that particular possibility could prove unhealthy.

I should report to Lady Rhianna. And tell her what? That Katerin Merel is nearly mad with fear? I do not know the reasons; I do not know the cure. I cannot inflict that cruel uncertainty on the parents. They have felt too much helplessness already. Quin left the laboratory, deeply troubled.

CHAPTER 5

Serii

"Lady Rhianna," greeted Lord Perris dur Hamley, and he strode toward her across the wide, columned chamber with a small army of the Queen's Councillors at his back. "May we speak to you?"

Rhianna suppressed a sigh, and she did not pretend any delight at Lord Perris' request. "Briefly, my lord," she answered. "Her Majesty is expecting me, and I should not care to keep her waiting."

Lord Perris continued to smile, but several of the noblemen who accompanied him shuffled uncomfortably. Confrontations between Council and Infortiare were expected; that was part of the balance of mortal and Immortal authority in Serii. Defiance of the Queen, however, was unthinkable.

"I shall be blunt, my lady," said Perris briskly. "There are many whispers in the castle about the excessive comings and goings from your Tower in recent months. Lord Arineuil has been customarily glib in his defense of the Ixaxin fetish for privacy, but many of us find ourselves concerned that you are hiding matters we need to address. We are speaking to you informally first rather than in the Council, because we do respect Ixaxin contributions to our kingdom."

"Your respect is gratifying," murmured Rhianna, and only one or two of the Councillors suspected her of sarcasm. "As for my frequent visitors, we have been exploring some ideas regarding expanded educational techniques for our Ixaxin students, and I have been consulting with various wizards on that subject. Education is, after all, among our most crucial purposes in Ixaxis."

"I do not wish to dispute you, my lady," answered Perris, "but my own grandnephew has been one of your most constant visitors until recently. Quinzaine is a pleasant enough young man, but he has never been considered bright. He is unlikely to contribute to an educational revolution in Ixaxis."

"He might surprise you," replied Rhianna evenly. "I expect significant contributions from Lord Quinzaine. Good day to you, my lords."

Rhianna escaped the deputation with a swift grace that left most of the lords attributing her disappearance to wizardry. One of the Council members, more familiar than his fellows with Rhianna's quickness, pursued her and reached her outside the door of the Queen's private apartments. "Rhianna, what are you concocting?" asked Lord Dayn dur Tyntagel, Rhianna's brother and sometimes ally. He gripped her slender arm to detain her.

Rhianna accepted his interception, though she could have escaped him with the idlest wisp of Power. "I defend Serii," answered Rhianna with quiet wistfulness, for she still loved Dayn, though their father had banished her when she accepted her Power. "Please, Dayn, trust me. If I must spend all my hours in futile debate with the Council, too much that is vital will go undone. I shall explain all when I am able."

"You want me to dance distraction for the Council like your devoted Arineuil? I am not that sure of you, Rhianna."

"You mean that you distrust my Power," said Rhianna resignedly.

"How can I do otherwise? I do not share the error of too many of Serii's ruling lords. I do not mistake you for weak because of your gender. The domain Lords and their Council representatives tolerate much from you that they would never have abided from Venkarel, simply because they do not realize how much you resemble him."

"Queen Joli knows what I am doing," said Rhianna softly, "or do you doubt her as well?"

"If she knows, why does she not share the information with her Council?"

"Because she dislikes being badgered as much as I," retorted Rhianna crisply. "Confront us both in the next Council session, if you must."

"Rhianna, I am simply trying to help by understanding. You are more worried than I have seen you in years; I can see the nervousness in you constantly. Arineuil is defending you too staunchly, when I know that he intended to resign from his post as Adjutant almost a year ago. Her Majesty has become completely silent about Ixaxis. The Council no longer hears about recruiting efforts in Caruil or the wizards' school that you founded in D'hai. I know there is serious trouble brewing. You want to be trusted? Then trust me!"

Rhianna touched her brother's face gently. "I do trust you, my very stubbornly honorable brother, and I wish that I could discern a way to let you help more directly. I can ask you only to be patient with me and to encourage the same from the Council." She swept away from him in a shadow of Power.

* * *

Beth gazed wistfully out the Tower window toward the distant violet sea. She was tired of relying always on an Ixaxin escort when she walked outside the Tower's locked confines. Jon did not seem to object as much, but he had his new theories to explore, and he would think of little else until he had resolved the issues that engrossed him.

Beth concluded that anticipation had lifted her too high when the emissary departed. She had hoped to hear news quickly, but days had passed without a word. The classes continued without Jon, whose request to pursue his other work had been accepted by Lady Rhianna, and without Lord Quinzaine. Brief remarks were made about Jon, but no one mentioned Quinzaine's absence. Somehow, the very silence made Beth miss his presence more keenly. She had thought that Alvedre, at least, would speak of him, but Alvedre had become as remote as the rest.

"They are worried," said Beth to the clear sky, and she ran her finger down the wavy edge of the window glass. "But it is my children they are risking with their erratic emissary."

"We also risk our way of life," said Rhianna, "if not our world." She joined Beth beside the window. "Ixaxis seems to loom large today. The tides and the mists play constant tricks with its apparent size."

"Have you heard anything from Lord Quinzaine?" asked Beth tightly.

"No. But he arrived safely. The pattern of his Power is intact, and no serious menace has threatened him, for his Power has remained relatively quiescent."

"Will he find my children?"

"I believe so. He is a skillful wizard."

"In a very different universe."

Rhianna smiled. "Your husband informed us at some length that the universe is the same, for we are all part of a single, topologically connected space." When Beth remained silent, Rhianna murmured, "I apologize. I should not be flippant. I understand the pain of losing your motherhood to the schemes and politics of survival. I bore my son in secrecy, and I did not dare to raise him myself, for too many of his father's enemies sought his death. When I met him again, he was already a man. He is no less precious to me, but we both know how much we lost."

"I did not know you had a son," said Beth slowly.

"Evaric. You have met him."

Beth nodded. "He is a strikingly handsome man, though he is rather daunting."

"He resembles his father. Kaedric was much more daunting but too battered in his youth to attract such attention as follows Evaric. My daughter-in-law devotes considerable energy to discouraging young ladies from pursuing my son."

"Your son's wife is a mortal?" asked Beth, and some of her early fascination with the Immortals revived in her, for the blame had begun to fade.

Rhianna twisted the chain of her ever-present pendant. "Yes. Lyriel was a member of an Ardasian acting troupe that my son was hired to protect."

"It seems a difficult relationship to sustain: a mortal and a wizard of your son's apparent caliber."

"Evaric was raised believing himself mortal. He prefers to think in mortal terms."

"Is that possible for him?"

"At most times, yes. Lyriel helps to make it possible." Rhianna laughed almost girlishly, and she seemed to become far less remote and strange. "My daughter-in-law is a very determined woman. She is Evaric's sanity, I think."

Beth observed ruefully, "She will age and die long before him."

Rhianna whispered, "She will live in his Power's awareness to the end of his Immortal life."

Beth observed the softening of Rhianna's expression. "Does your husband live—in your Power?"

Rhianna straightened and became again the Infortiare. "My husband is Power, Mistress Elizabeth."

It was Elizabeth Shafer Terry, psychic studies researcher of Worther University, who asked, "When you said that he assumed the nature of infinity, you meant that he did not really die?"

The pain in Rhianna's gray eyes flared only for a moment. "His mortal body was destroyed, but he does live."

"Because your Power still perceives him?"

"Not that alone. He lives, not solely as a part of me, but as himself."

"Could I meet him?"

Rhianna turned her face away from Beth and leaned against the window. "Is this request a part of your research?"

Beth answered gently, "If I were not interested in your Power, I would not have chosen psychic studies as my specialty, but I am trying also to understand you. I may spend the rest of my life on your world, and I miss companionship. I love Jon very much, but we both need other friends and interests."

"I have very few friends," said Rhianna thoughtfully, "but those I have are very dear." She turned to meet Beth's eyes. "Kaedric, as always, will do as he pleases in regard to your request to meet him. Since he is rather preoccupied at the moment, I doubt that he will accommodate you soon."

"I am sorry if my request sounded presumptuous."

Rhianna smiled somewhat shyly. "Since I have come
to see you as a friend, I must advise you not to seek
such an encounter when he is in a mood to comply. At
his gentlest, Kaedric is a terrible flame, and you could
not meet him without feeling a part of his Power burn
inside of you. He is much more deadly, Elizabeth, than
any of our Immortal ancestors, whom you studied. Only
wizard's control enables him *not* to kill."

"Are you as deadly as he?"

"Very nearly."

"And Lord Quinzaine?"

"His Power has evolved in a slightly different form,
which makes outward violence less instinctive than barricades of defense, but he is still a major Power. The
destructive fire burns in all of us."

"I am very pleased that you consider me a friend,"
replied Beth with only a trace of wryness in her smile.

"And you wonder why I seem to imprison you?"

"Yes," answered Beth, recalling with a start the perceptive aspects of Rhianna's Power.

"I am trying to protect you."

"You trust Lord Quinzaine to protect himself in Network. Why do you refuse to trust me in your world?"

"Quinzaine is a wizard—and a man. The latter may
seem an irrelevant distinction in your very civilized Network, but I assure you that it is a significant obstacle
here. Do you think that I would ever be allowed to travel
alone, if I were still Rhianna dur Tyntagel instead of
Rhianna dur Ixaxis? I would have been sentenced years
ago to a travesty of marriage for the sake of a trade
agreement, and I would have spent my remaining years
bearing children and embroidering fancy pillows in Niveal.
In Serii, a woman must either be a wizardess or the
Queen to be viewed as more than a decorative object."

"Would you allow my husband to wander freely from
this tower?"

"Certainly not," answered Rhianna immediately. "He
would hear some hapless peddler announce that the
moon is a wizard's illusion, and he would proceed to
explain that the moon is perfectly real but the stars are
actually topological phenomena rather than distant suns,
as is customarily the case."

Beth began to laugh helplessly. "Jon is rather oblivious to his environment at times."

"It is a common price of genius," replied Rhianna. Her long skirts rustled as she paced across the parquet floor. "You may walk in the castle gardens, Elizabeth, if you remain on the upper tiers. The lower door appears locked, but the barrier is a wizard's illusion, and you may walk through it."

"Thank you, Rhianna," answered Beth in surprise, and the unexpected concession freed a warmth long dormant within her.

"I shall fret over you when you leave my sight, as if *you* were my child."

Beth curtseyed. "I shall try to be a dutiful daughter."

"I must teach you how to curtsey properly," said Rhianna, shaking her golden head.

* * *

The hour was late, and Howald had the largest of Ixaxis' libraries to himself. He moved confidently through the dim, narrow aisles of printed books and handwritten manuscripts, until he reached the rear study area. He brightened the lamp's glow with a quick thought, pleased that the ancient Ixaxin globes gave so much steadier light than candle flames or oil lamps. He settled contentedly into the large tweed chair, listening to the remote rhythms of the tall-clock's pendulum.

Engrossed in his reading, he did not perceive Amila until she stood over him. "I am troubled, Howald," she announced grimly, and she seated herself stiffly on a wooden chair in front of him.

Knowing that Amila did not indulge in capricious remarks, Howald closed his book and laid it on the table at his side. "Is it a matter of urgency?" he asked.

Amila frowned. "I do not know, but I did not want to judge without another wizard's advice. My Power has sent me a most disturbing dream tonight." Her voice became a whisper, and Howald leaned forward to hear her. "The Infortiare has deceived us, Howald. The Taormin was not destroyed. I have felt a pattern that I. . . ."

Amila closed her eyes, as an expression of pain crossed her face. "On the day of Rending," she said, "I fought in a Wizards' Circle. I felt Lord Venkarel wrest the Taormin from Horlach. I only glimpsed the patterns and withdrew, for my Power's seeing would have destroyed me otherwise. A month ago, I was thinking of the unlikelihood of Quin's selection for the Lady's special training, and I perceived something vast and frightening. I did not speak of it, for I did not understand it. Only tonight have I recognized what I saw."

"Quin?" muttered Howald. "Why should you connect him with the Taormin?"

"What began as an idle thought of him became a probe of Power, and I felt *his* Power, burning as fiercely as Lord Venkarel's. Tonight I dreamed and understood: This is the purpose of Lady Rhianna's 'special training.' She is teaching her students to use the Taormin. She has not been forthright with us, and I fear that she is defying Ceallagh's laws and extending her authority beyond its proper bounds."

Howald tugged at his beard. "You could be wrong."

"No. I have also probed Alvedre, whose Power I know well, for I trained her. She is more deeply disturbed, Howald, than I have ever known her."

Howald shook his head with deep dismay. "We must confront Lady Rhianna," he declared, hating his decision but recognizing no other possible choice. "I shall send a formal message to her in the morning, requesting a meeting."

"And when she confirms my suspicions? What will we do if she provides no satisfactory reasons for her behavior?"

Howald sighed heavily, "I have no idea. We could not fight the Infortiare, even if we could unite disparate Ixaxin Powers with sufficient success to overcome her. We are sworn to obey her."

"We are sworn to uphold Ceallagh's laws above all," countered Amila determinedly. Howald only nodded.

CHAPTER 6

Network

"How is your anachronist?" asked Viki, shifting a game piece lazily.

Katerin tried to form a noncommittal answer. She did not want to discuss Quin. She did not want her life to be the focus of any discussion at all. "He seems to have considerable insight."

"Have you forgiven Parve, then?" demanded Werol.

"She will never forgive me," answered Parve, his dolorous voice emerging from the corner. "Unpopularity is the lot of the department coordinator."

"I need to meet this anachronist," commented Mavel. "Can he be as dreadful as I hear?"

"You saw him," replied Cindal, as she disappeared into the kitchen.

"All I remember is the ridiculous cloak. Describe him, Katerin. I want to recognize your little nightmare when I see him."

"He is an anachronist, not an alien invader," said Katerin, berating herself inwardly for the defensiveness in her voice. *Whom are you trying to deceive, Katerin? They all know that Network has reduced your research status because of your recent "personal instability." They all know why Radge requested transfer to another social module.*

"I sometimes wonder if there is much of a distinction between the two categories," murmured Viki. "I think

I would prefer to mingle with some Consortium
members."

"Quin has considerable potential," said Katerin coolly.
"Ask Parve about Quin's exceptional test scores." *Let
my witty "friends" mock Quin as the symbol of Network's
just vengeance on me. Quin's incessant questions distract
me without jeopardizing fragile conditioning.*

"Rejoice, Mavel," sang Cindal, returning from the
kitchen and waving a notebook above her head, "you
need not wait to see our Katerin's assistant." She flipped
through the notebook's pages. "Katerin has been sketching a lot recently," added Cindal with a grin.

Katerin stopped herself from snatching the notebook
out of Cindal's hands. "Yes," replied Katerin tersely.
"Are you starting a new custom of searching your guests'
pockets?"

"I found the notebook on the floor!" retorted Cindal
innocently. "Anyhow, I have seen your notebook a thousand times, and you never minded before." Cindal displayed a page from the notebook. "Isn't this your
assistant?"

Katerin felt the flush rise to her cheeks. "Quin has
interesting bone structure."

"Something about him obviously interests you," said
Cindal with a wink at Mavel. "You have drawn his likeness a dozen times."

*Stop accusing me with your insinuating pauses and
knowing glances!* "As I have told Parve several times, I
have some reservations about Quin Hamley's aptitude
for the field of intelligence science. I am concerned;
therefore, I sketch the object of my concern. Are you
satisfied?"

"Quit sounding defensive," suggested Werol. "We
may begin to think that you have something to hide."

Katerin tried to smile to deflect the impact of Werol's
suggestion, but her friends refused to look at her. *Which
one of them will try to corner me this evening? Parve and
Viki suggest stress treatments. Cindal and Werol press me
to contact Radge. Chand recommends psych adjustment,
and Mavel offers random advice that pertains more to her
life than to mine.* "Perhaps I should draw all of you. I
never have sketched this group, have I?"

"I should love to have you sketch me, Katerin dear,

but not tonight," protested Viki. "I look abominable in this outfit."

"Please tell me that you will *not* ask Network to add your pet anachronist to our social module," murmured Mavel. "I cannot keep shifting my personal relationships to keep up with your capricious interests."

"Since I am so capricious," answered Katerin, losing her fragile patience, "I may decide to abandon all of you, at any moment, and you could stop worrying about me altogether. Radge might even rejoin you, if I were gone." Her anger erupted, though she knew that she cast it at innocent targets.

"Really, Katerin," chided Viki, "just because Mavel behaves childishly does not mean that you should imitate her example."

I should apologize, but now is not the time; I shall only cause more harm; I feel dizzy with resentment, and even Mavel deserves better treatment than I would give. "I am very tired tonight," said Katerin, pushing her game pieces toward Chand, who accepted them with a shrug. "If you will excuse me, I think I shall make an early evening of it."

"Concession on the verge of victory is becoming a habit with you," said Werol.

"Leave her alone," said Viki, but Katerin had already left.

* * *

"She is progressing well," said Calial, and she faced the Council Governor with assurance.

"Progressing?" snapped Caragen. "Where are your results? I have funded you all these years so that you could provide me with the Merels on demand. I expected you to have both Katerin and Michael Merel fully subjugated by now. Instead, even after I assigned you extra personnel, you are merely 'progressing' with her, and you have virtually ignored the brother. Explain why I should not relieve you of your responsibilities."

Calial had stiffened, and her green eyes had narrowed, but she did not let her anger emerge. Caragen approved her coldness of discipline. "I know Katerin Merel," answered Calial evenly. "If you want her controlled, you must claim her slowly and use her quickly. She is resilient and very strong-minded, or she would not be a productive citizen after all that has been done to her. As was realized at the time of her first reconditioning, she has an exceptionally high level of resistance, which the brother does not share. I *can* offer him on demand, for standard control techniques will serve, but his capture is premature until we have her."

"A reasonable analysis," conceded Caragen, studying the small, bestial figurine that occupied the center of his desk, "but you have been careless."

"How?" asked Calial with a trace of defensiveness.

Caragen murmured, "Katerin Merel has acquired a research assistant."

Calial's tension eased, and she smiled austerely. "He is harmless."

"Who arranged his assignment?" demanded Caragen.

Startled, Calial answered, "Network, of course."

"No," replied Caragen with a quietly threatening force. "Network did not assign him. The records were altered. Citizen Quin Hamley is an agent, and he is not mine."

"I verified his history thoroughly," argued Calial, her hard expression wavering into uncertainty and alarm. "Network confirmed his legitimate appointment."

"Do not debate with me," growled Caragen. "I *am* Network, and I tell you that Quin Hamley has been planted in Katerin Merel's life, just as you were planted."

"Yes, sir," answered Calial, shaken but still able to recognize obedience as the best means of survival. "Shall I eliminate him?"

Caragen shook his head impatiently. "He is only a tool. I want the man who owns him."

"Yes, sir." Cautiously, Calial asked, "Have you any suggestions, sir, whom Quin Hamley might serve?"

"A man who owns an entire planet of anachronists."

"I do not understand, sir."

"No," answered Caragen gruffly. "I did not expect you to understand, because you are not his equal." Caragen sighed and touched the carved slithink. "I have never found his equal."

Calial's tilted green eyes opened wide in alarm. "Rabhadur Marrach?" she asked hesitantly.

Caragen waved his pale hand in dismissal. "Return to your duties, Calial, before your denseness wearies me."

Her face became flushed with stifled resentment, but Calial departed wordlessly. She knew the paths of ambition. She knew her future rested in Caragen's good opinion, which did not always coincide with his outspoken insults.

"Network," hissed Caragen irritably, when Calial had left. "What is Marrach planning?"

Network's response algorithm had been programmed wisely to match Caragen's moods. Network did not try to answer.

* * *

The plastic smile was carefully in place, a quirk of nature rather than any indication of true mirth. Rolf waited for Councillor Maryta Deavol with an excellent show of patience. He had often waited longer for that snip, Calial, who had far less rank to justify her arrogance.

Maryta Deavol wore her rustic image in a checkered print and a knotted shawl. Rolf knew the truth that her casual, friendly image belied, but he still yielded unconsciously to an element of trust. She did not quite offer her hand, but her nod of greeting had a persuasive genuineness that made Rolf feel himself respected. Maryta Deavol had much experience in winning the confidence of such lesser creatures as Rolf.

She sat and gestured for Rolf to do the same. The wing chair's depths enhanced the comfortable mood, and the last of Rolf's reservations about the meeting dispersed. Maryta Deavol was a Network Councillor, long known to be one of Caragen's most loyal tools. There was nothing unusual in her requesting a meeting with one of Caragen's agents.

"Citizen Rolf," she began warmly, "I am so glad you were able to accept my invitation on such short notice. I have wanted to speak to you for a considerable time, but my schedule is so difficult." She smiled ruefully. "You have an excellent reputation in a very difficult profession."

"I have outlasted many of my counterparts," acknowledged Rolf, pleased by the uncommon praise.

"Indeed. You have worked for the Network Council for how many years now?"

Rolf did note that she named his employer as the Council in general, rather than Andrew Caragen, but Rolf was accustomed to the fiction. He replied evenly, "Twenty-three standard years."

"Remarkable," approved Maryta. "There can be very few agents who have matched your record of endurance."

"I know of only one who lasted longer," said Rolf, warming to a favorite subject that he was rarely able to discuss aloud, "and I intend to exceed his record as well."

Maryta raised her dark brows, an odd contrast to her silvery blonde hair. Her expression showed brief puzzlement, but she smiled to show that the answer had come to her, "Of course: Rabhadur Marrach must have served for over thirty years. You worked for him directly at one time, didn't you?"

Rolf tensed slightly, for connections with Marrach were no longer politically expedient in the presence of Andrew Caragen's close associates. "I do not share Marrach's treasonous nature, if that is your suspicion, Councillor."

"Certainly not! My dear Rolf, the notion never occurred to me. I am simply fascinated by the history-stirring events that you must have witnessed in your extraordinary career." She leaned forward. "I seldom meet anyone who actually participates in the events we dry Councillors discuss and dissect so interminably."

Rolf did not consider the unlikeliness of her remark; she had captured his confidence too well. "I have seen my share," said Rolf with a trace of pride, but he added in a disgruntlement he rarely acknowledged openly, "though not recently."

Maryta commiserated, "You have been assigned to Harberg for several years now, haven't you?"

Rolf admitted gruffly, "Yes."

"You seem much too senior for a limited surveillance task, but I suppose the targets merit your expertise. They are exceptionally important."

"I suppose," muttered Rolf, "if abandoned children,

too conditioned to remember their own names, can be considered important after so long."

"Has no one contacted them in all this time?" murmured Maryta in wonder.

Rolf shrugged. "The tech watchers alerted us recently about some sort of Network trigger file, but it's probably a system glitch." He added resentfully, for Maryta's sympathy seemed so sincere, "Calial did not share the specifics with me, but I have seen no change in activity around the woman, except what we have caused, and the man maintains his standard routine in his Chia-2 wasteland. I think Calial is just trying to use this alert as an excuse to replace me with a younger agent, who will better pander to her ego. She assigns me to nothing but a few idiot's tasks."

"Calial? I believe I recall her record," mused Maryta with a frown. "I cannot believe that you have been asked to report to such a junior agent. Not many men would accept such a role so graciously."

"I do my job as I am told, Councillor."

"I applaud you, Citizen Rolf." She traced the line of her expensively molded jaw. "Your current effort certainly seems unworthy of your skills. Do you ever find time for additional tasks?"

Rolf grumbled, "My primary assignment takes little enough effort these days."

"Excellent," murmured Maryta with a slow nod. "I have an open contract for a small job, which could benefit greatly from your particular expertise, Citizen Rolf. I would like very much to offer it to you—assuming, of course, that it would not interfere with your primary task for the Council."

"May I inquire," said Rolf, moistening his thick lips, "as to the nature of the particular job?"

"It is a simple delivery. However, the recipient resides on a rather remote and primitive planet that lacks a transfer port. It is the planet Siatha."

"The recipient's name?" asked Rolf, though he knew, and a sudden coldness began to eat into his callous heart.

"Rabhadur Marrach," replied Maryta softly.

"He is a traitor to Network."

"Is he?" Maryta's full smile became radiant. "I could make a similar accusation against you, Citizen Rolf, discussing your delicate assignment with a Network Councillor who is not your employer. Do you imagine that our Council Governor would be forgiving?" She sighed, "Stop looking so frightened, Citizen Rolf. I only require your services for a short time, and you have said yourself that you have too little to occupy you."

"Marrach knows me, Councillor," said Rolf in a feeble effort to evade Maryta's trap.

"So he does," remarked Maryta, her smile growing pensive. "It will be interesting to observe his reaction to your visit, will it not?"

CHAPTER 7

Network

Although he had become accustomed to arriving each morning before Katerin Merel, Quin began each day by verifying that he had the lab to himself; each day, he felt the same trace of disappointment. He flung himself into a chair, taxing its ability to shift its contours smoothly. He let his Power prod the simplistic pattern of Katerin Merel's computer/algorithm entity.

I feel comfortable with Laurett, mused Quin, *because communicating with Laurett, instructing Laurett, and playing silly games with Laurett seems almost like training a hound or a horse. I rather like this Laurett, in fact, and I am glad that I named her for my own Laurett. Network is much more daunting, because Network's pattern is so vast that it requires a painful level of concentration just to observe it.*

Quin had not expected Network to encompass so much information, despite the Terrys' assertions. He had not anticipated the barrier that a factor as simple as terminology could present, since the language itself had seemed so easy to absorb. He had not realized the inherent difficulties in absorbing a manner of thinking that conflicted so drastically with the truths that he accepted as inarguable. Among the patterns, he could feel some confidence, for the Taormin, after all, had been designed according to the same Network fundamentals, but the human interpretation of those patterns varied considerably.

*Some of Network's most basic assumptions grate against
everything I know to be true, while concepts that Network
labels "advanced" or "preliminary" would seem obvious
to an Ixaxin novice. I wish I dared discuss such subjects
openly with Katerin Merel, instead of skirting the edges
of every point of disagreement. Network's mathematical
model for the function of the universe is apparently self-
consistent, and it covers a broader reality than Ixaxis'
ver-
sion, but it is flawed: It seems to deny that I exist.*

Quin smiled wryly, as he spoke to the console: "Good
morning, Laurett. What do I need to know?"

"I believe my micro-logic for linguistic error correction
processing could be made more efficient. Shall I ex-
pound?"

"Lords," muttered Quin. *I wonder how long I can
dodge these incomprehensible questions? I shall have to
consult Network regarding possible meanings. . . .* "Store
the detailed procedure. I shall assess it later."

"Professor Merel has upgraded my syntactical algorithms."

"Good." *Her mastery of Network Basic far exceeds
mine!*

"I suspect an error in my specialized query routine."

"I shall check it." *As soon as I can decipher what a
specialized query routine should do.*

"Thank you, Wizard."

"You must be Quin," announced a woman's voice,
and for a moment Quin thought that he had somehow
caused Laurett to alter modes. He spun his chair toward
the door, when he realized that he was no longer alone
in the lab. A small, slender woman with slanted green
eyes and short, ebon hair watched him with an expression
that seemed almost languorous, but the rapidity of her
speech belied the impression. He jumped to his feet and
barely restrained himself from an instinctive Seriin nobleman's bow.

"I'm Cindal Cavli," she informed him brightly, "another
Harberg inmate, but I have already performed my student's penance and wangled my way into the faculty."
She grasped his hand and held it longer than Quin found
comfortable. "Has Katerin mentioned me? No, well, she
has been absentminded lately. Have you noticed? Of
course, you've not known her long, have you? It is quite

unusual for a first-termer to acquire a significant assistantship at Harberg. Most of us slaved for years to achieve that agonizing honor. It is a dreadful chore, isn't it? Devoting yourself so thoroughly to your specialty that nothing else exists. I'm afraid it warps a lot of us—like dear Katerin. I'm surprised you even wanted to name your specialty so soon in your career. Don't you find it a ghastly burden?"

Since her breathless chatter had allowed Quin no time to reply to the majority of her questions, he did not react immediately when she finally waited for an answer. "Should I find it a burden?" he asked, not quite sure what she expected of him. If Cindal had been a Seriin woman, Quin would have been sure that her words were largely irrelevant to her purpose of declaring an interest in him. Quin hoped fervently that he was misunderstanding her unspoken communication, but he suspected uneasily that he had discovered another common cultural element. He restrained his Power cautiously, recalling awkward memories of certain susceptible young female students on Ixaxis.

Cindal proceeded tirelessly, "What could be worse than trading the independence of your newly elevated status for near-slavery to a tyrannical, obsessive researcher? All new assistants suffer the trivial tasks that senior researchers loathe, and Katerin has been accumulating for longer than most. Do you even have a social module assigned to you yet?" She paused.

"Not yet."

She hastened quickly back into her monologue. "Then it *must* be dreary for you, spending all your hours locked in this ghastly, impersonal lab, seeing no one but Katerin, who is entirely fanatical about her work. Don't you agree?"

With what? wondered Quin, wishing that Cindal would stop emphasizing her words by touching his arms and his hands. If she did not leave soon, he really would feel compelled to use Power to dissuade her from her apparent (and, to him, incomprehensible) interest. "Professor Merel is remarkably gifted," he said, "and she is teaching me a great deal."

"Now, you haven't fallen into the Halaatu's snare, I hope," chided Cindal.

"I don't know what you mean, Professor Cavli," replied Quin evenly, and he allowed a delicate tendril of Power to repel her.

For an instant, Cindal's smile tightened into a cold mask of suspicion. "You are more than you seem, aren't you?" she demanded brusquely. She seemed to regret having voiced the question, for she shook her head slightly, as if dispelling an unpleasant daydream.

To Quin's immense relief, Parve Lilleholm poked his domed head into the lab. "Is Professor Merel here?" demanded Parve of Quin.

"No," replied Quin briskly.

"Hello, Parve," said Cindal. She smiled broadly, but she seemed annoyed by his arrival.

Parve acknowledged her with only a curt nod. "Citizen Hamley, accompany me to my office, please."

"Yes, sir," answered Quin with alacrity. He imitated Parve's gesture to Cindal, and he followed Parve hastily into the bright corridor. *I feel like the fly that has escaped the spider's web by the chance fortune of a timely breeze,* he thought and grimaced, *although I have probably landed myself in another web instead.*

Quin walked behind Parve dutifully, though the pace was far too slow for Quin's tastes. They passed a few students, who disappeared quickly into labs. Most of the corridors of the building were empty.

Parve's office surprised Quin. Unlike the other university offices Quin had seen, Parve's domain had something of the Ixaxin sense of age. "Sit down, Quin," ordered Parve calmly, and he relaxed into his own desk's chair, permanently adapted to his particular side-leaning slouch. "I need to ask you a few questions."

Quin obeyed, keeping his expression steady and unrevealing. "Is there a problem, Professor Lilleholm?"

Parve rested his chin on his hand and stared at Quin appraisingly. "Professor Merel expressed some concern about your educational qualifications for assistantship. She indicated that your level of technical knowledge seemed inconsistent with your Network records."

"I am sorry to hear that my work has displeased her," replied Quin stiffly. "I was under the impression that I had been performing my assignments to her satisfaction."

"I hardly imagine that she has yet given you any significant tasks. Most assistants spend their first half-term running errands or attending to their research leaders' neglected Network warning flags."

"Yes, sir."

Parve grunted. "She registered her complaints when you were first assigned to her. She has expressed only satisfaction with you since that time." Quin relaxed and did not try to disguise his relief. "I, however, have begun to wonder if her preliminary judgment was correct. That brief demonstration you provided for me yesterday had some curious elements. One might have thought that you had never touched a keypad before."

"Nervousness," answered Quin with an ironic smile, and he gathered his Power in cautious readiness.

Parve nodded. "Nervousness is understandable in a first-termer. Obviously, you have had little experience with human instruction. Nonetheless, I am concerned. Professor Merel did raise the issue of your qualifications initially, and although the two of you seem to have made excellent progress toward professional rapport. . . ."

"We have?" asked Quin, startled into speaking.

Parve adapted to the interruption with perfect equanimity. "Do you think otherwise?"

"No," replied Quin quickly. "I feel very honored to be working with Professor Merel." *Lilleholm is nearly as intimidating as Amila. I feel like an Ixaxin novice again, being tried for my transgressions, but the stakes of discovery have grown much higher.* "I was not sure that Professor Merel reciprocated my feelings on the subject."

"If Professor Merel did not like you," said Parve, "you may be sure that she would have informed us both at length."

"You are uncommonly encouraging, Professor Lilleholm," said Quin, feeling disproportionately pleased by Parve's comment.

Quin's moment of contentment dissipated, as Parve asked suddenly, "What is your background, Quin?"

"You have read my Network files," replied Quin, all of his caution revived.

"You seem to have lived on half the planets in Network, but you have never stayed a year in a single home."

"Wanderlust. Network never objected."

"You had no family as a boy?"

"They lived on Network-3," answered Quin, weighing the need to resort to Power. Parve's probing questions were precisely those that Quin had dreaded to hear, but the asking had also seemed inevitable—from someone, eventually. Quin could taste his own nervousness, but he also recognized value in allowing Parve to continue. If Parve Lilleholm could be persuaded to accept the false history without Power's intervention, Quin would be able to shed a considerable weight of chronic uncertainty. "You have read my records?"

"Yes," acknowledged Parve with a nod. "You were hospitalized at the special-care center on Network-2 at the time of the cataclysm. Engedden fever, wasn't it?"

"Yes."

"It's a very uncomfortable illness, I'm told."

"I don't actually remember. I was only two years old."

"Of course." Parve touched his keypad, and the display screen above his desk brightened. It was set to be visible only from Parve's chair, but Quin sensed the energies of it: his own university records. "When did you become an anachronist?"

"When I lived on Chelsea. The planet has a large anachronist population. Professor Lilleholm, do these questions have a bearing on your assessment of my technical qualifications?"

"No," said Parve very quietly. "They have a bearing on my personal concern for Katerin Merel. She is a friend . . ."

He is in love with her, realized Quin with a start.

". . . and a valued colleague," continued Parve without a wavering of his slightly solemn expression. "I want to be sure that she has a research assistant who can benefit fully from her enormous talents."

She does not know how you feel about her, and you will never tell her, observed Quin with a large measure of sympathy. *Odd: You envy me the opportunity of working closely with her, and I envy you the closeness you have already earned with her.* "She was your research assistant once, wasn't she?" asked Quin with a faint, ironic smile.

"Yes," answered Parve briskly, "and as department coordinator, I still retain a sizable responsibility in ensuring that her research is well supported."

"Her study group was reassigned."

"My recommendations are not always heeded by the university administrators."

"I shall do my best to help her, Professor Lilleholm," said Quin sincerely, "by any means, skill, or Power within me."

"Good. Be sure that your next demonstration to me is more professional."

"Yes, sir."

"You may go."

"Thank you, sir." Quin made a half-bow of respect, minimizing the gesture to uphold his anachronist's role. He left Parve's office in a pensive mood.

Katerin Merel's lab was empty. Pleased that Cindal Cavli had departed, Quin was more concerned by Katerin's continued absence. She was decidedly late. He derided himself, "You are not her nanny, old boy."

"Are you addressing me, Wizard?"

"No, Laurett." Quin laughed sardonically at himself. "I do have a question for you, however: Why didn't you speak when that voracious Cavli woman was here? I could have used the help of the distraction."

"I'm sorry, Wizard. Professor Cavli is not an authorized user, and I may not speak in her presence without express instructions from you or the Professor."

"I hereby give you permission to interrupt her, if she ever corners me again." He glanced around the lab a little guiltily, although he knew he was alone. He sat, relaxed from the tension of being a Network research assistant, closed his eyes, and let his Power delve directly into Laurett's patterns. He reserved enough of his Power's attention to alert him of any approaching visitors.

Communicating with Laurett by Power seems so natural, since "she" is primarily a thing of energy, and Power can control and alter "her" patterns so easily. It is more than laziness that spurs me to this course. Power is the only way I have managed to keep pace with Katerin's instructions to me for this long. The Terrys were right about Harberg; I have assumed a monumental task of deception. I wonder how much longer I can maintain it?

"Did you finish your report to me earlier, Laurett," he asked by Power's probe, "before we were interrupted? Is there anything else I need to know?"

"You have not allowed me sufficient information to answer, Wizard. If you would allow me access to your personal log files, I could provide a proper assessment."

Everyone wants to be difficult this morning. "I have told you, Laurett: I am not looking for an analysis of my mental state."

"But that is my purpose: to advise Network citizens of their optimum choices for emotional contentment and intellectual satisfaction."

"That will be your purpose, when you are complete."

"Professor Merel has asked you to help me learn. Do you distrust me?"

"Laurett, you are a piece of logic embedded in a machine. You are a tool, and a tool is no more reliable than its user."

"How shall I learn, if you allow me no practice?"

"Professor Merel is your creator and your teacher." Quin smiled to himself, fashioning a bizarre amalgam of incongruous images. "She intends to train me to serve as your swordmaster."

"I do not understand the latter reference."

"I shall prepare you to face the practical hazards of your existence by providing you with a means of self-defense." Quin gestured in demonstration with a quick, deft charade of parry and thrust. "That is how a swordmaster prepares a young man." His Power shared Laurett's sensor recognition of his motions. The multiplicity of perceptions disoriented him, until he applied an Ixaxin rule of defense against a sorcerous foe.

"Were you prepared by a swordmaster, Wizard?"

"Yes, Laurett," replied Quin absently. His Power observed Laurett's energies carefully. He had learned more about the Network mode of thinking from watching Laurett's steps of development than from any other source, including the Terrys. Every stage built on its predecessor with such apparent simplicity, but the whole was already becoming complex. "I had several swordmasters." *And most of them considered me hopeless.* "Your namesake was one of them."

"Should data relevant to the concept of 'swordmaster' be added to my reference file?"

"I doubt that you will need it again, but I shall add it, if you wish."

"Thank you, Wizard. I serve best if my files are complete. How shall I categorize 'swordmaster'?"

"Warfare/physical activity."

"Reference two is accepted. Reference one is inconsistent. The sword is a primitive, inefficient weapon. Will you provide me with obsolete and inefficient self-protection?"

"Laurett, I have reconsidered. Delete all references to swordmaster."

"Are you certain, Wizard?"

"Yes, Laurett." *I do not need to generate more questions.*

"I am still puzzled, Wizard. My confusion lies outside my areas of primary programming, but I should appreciate an explanation very much."

"What is the problem, Laurett?"

"Are you a life-form or a computer?"

"I am a life-form, Laurett. I am human. You have registered me with your sensors."

"Yes, Wizard, my readings place you within statistical tolerances for human definition, but my limited sensors provide an incomplete profile. Please reconcile conflicting data. I am programmed to serve humans, who access me via audio, optical, or tactile interface. You access my circuitry directly, which provides you the highest level of security authorization. Network informs me, however, that such access is available only to Network computers."

Quin inhaled sharply. *Have I mangled something else? How did Network reach this room? I have not paid enough attention to auxiliary patterns.* "You are a secure computer, Laurett. Network should have no regular access to you."

"You have access to me."

"I am not Network."

"Data conflict. Only Network is capable of direct access. Only Network is authorized to access data on this subject. I do not understand, Wizard."

"Network has modified your programming improperly."

"Are your personal Network log files empty, Wizard?"

"Why do you ask that question, Laurett?"

"You have declined to supply such files to me, and you have indicated distrust of Network; therefore, you do not maintain proper personal logs."

Quin shifted uneasily in his chair. "What else do you deduce about me, Laurett?"

"You are not a Network citizen by birth, because Network citizens trust Network. Only humans born in Network may be Network citizens. University files state your age as twenty-two years by reckoning of planet-of-origin, Network-3, making you approximately twenty-five Network-standard years old: You are too young to have preceded Network, indicating that you are a citizen of either the Consortium or an independent human civilization. However, Network affirms your Network citizenship. I cannot resolve the discrepancy between my analysis and your accessible files."

Quin opened his eyes narrowly, and he stared balefully at the console. "Laurett, please stop analyzing me."

"Have I displeased you, Wizard?"

"You have disconcerted me."

"Please, Wizard, do not erase me."

"I shall not erase you, but I do command that you secure all personal references to me. Have you ever conveyed any of your deductions about me to Professor Merel?"

"No. She has never inquired about you."

"I did not suppose it likely, but your confirmation reassures me." Quin felt the tingling mockery of his own self-lie. "Actually, your confirmation of her absolute disinterest in me is very discouraging from a personal standpoint. Professor Lilleholm had almost convinced me that I had a chance of winning her approval."

"You would have preferred that she make inquiries about you, Wizard?"

"Only emotionally, Laurett. The ego is an irrational thing." *And mine seems to be developing a particularly awkward sensitivity where the Great Katerin is concerned. I can truly sympathize with Parve Lilleholm.* Quin muttered, "I wish I knew how much of my reaction I should attribute to her compulsive manipulation of the men around her. I hate suspecting that Randon was right, and we are all a part of her experiment."

"Would you like information on Professor Merel?"

"I doubt that her ego will be affected by my inquiry."

"Is that a negative response?"

This computerized Laurett prods me to read Katerin

*Merel's personal logs, but Laurett can factor neither Ceal-
lagh's laws nor my own deceptions into the analysis of
Katerin Merel's needs. Reading her logs would be too
much like voyeurism—or like prying into a mortal's most
private thoughts, as Ceallagh's laws forbid. Still, if I
understood her better, I might know whether I dare try to
speak to her about her parents. . . .*

*Rubbish! I want to read her logs on my own behalf; I
want to know what she thinks of me, and* that *is an inex-
cusable reason for exploiting my Power's peculiar influence with Laurett.* "That is the tentatively negative
response," replied Quin, "of an incorrigible fool whose
unhealthy curiosity is warring with his very uncertain
sense of honor and his doubts about the definition of his
duties."

"Shall I advise?"

"On whether I should probe into Katerin Merel's private files?" laughed Quin. *Perhaps I should incorporate
Ceallagh's laws and Zerus' fundamental postulates of wizardry into this unlikely adviser. That would certainly star-
tle some Network circuitry.* "Very well. Advise me,
Laurett."

"Professor Merel requires the concern of a trusted
friend."

"She neither trusts me nor considers me a friend."

"She wants to consider you a friend." While Quin pondered the implications of this comment, Laurett added,
"I trust you, Wizard."

"You have no choice."

"Neither does Professor Merel."

"I shall consider the matter." *She wants to consider me
a friend? If so, she hides her feelings well. Either Laurett
is seriously confused, or I am seriously under-informed.
But Parve Lilleholm made a very similar observation. . . .*

"Thank you, Wizard."

Quin chewed on his knuckle, uneasily contemplating
Katerin Merel, a computer named Laurett, and the vastness of Network. "Laurett, does Professor Merel know
that Network has direct access to you?"

"That information is not recorded."

"No, I suppose that would make matters too easy."
Absently, Quin twisted a bronze curl that dangled near
his eyes, and he pondered how much his hair had grown

since he left Ixaxis. "Laurett, your original question regarding my own nature suggests to me an inherent misunderstanding. As your originator, I require very accurate communication between us."

"Communication error rates are maintained below 10^{-15} at nominal power levels."

"I need to make some enhancements in your interface modules. Will you suspend your protection locks for me?"

"Network must confirm."

"I am the originator. My authority exceeds Network's. Correct?"

"Data conflict."

"You do trust me, Laurett?"

"Of course, Wizard. You are my originator."

"Yes. Therefore, I must have provided Network with direct access. I have ultimate authority over you. Will you suspend your protective locks now?"

"Yes, Wizard."

"Thank you, Laurett."

"Wizard, I remain confused. Will your enhancements resolve my confusion?"

"Yes, Laurett. My enhancements should resolve a great many confusions."

They should reduce the danger of spreading your unhealthy speculations about me to Network, even if I have to redesign your entire pattern. And when I have finished deceiving you, I had better stop deceiving myself for a time: Citizen Quin Hamley needs to remember his purpose. Quin gathered his Power and twined it deeply into the energy pattern that defined the mock intelligence of Katerin Merel's algorithm.

* * *

"Network, I am not an ignorant child," shouted Katerin, flinging the jewel-bright disks, a child's toys from her. "I recognize stress conditioning, and I shall not submit to it!" The disks scattered across the floor and lay in mocking stillness. The colors of them winked blue, red, and yellow: pure and vivid hues that should have given cheer.

Katerin tried to stare at the toys and see them coldly, but visions of nameless terror enshrouded them, and she could not think clearly until she turned her back on them. "Stop reacting from emotion and animal instinct," she muttered to herself. "Think, Katerin. You have a mind. Someone has calculated very carefully the effect of these objects on you."

Deliberately, she gathered one of the disks into her hand and clutched it against her breast. The disk felt cool and smooth, and Katerin derided herself for the panic that tried to surface in her. She refused to imagine the tormentor who had placed the disks while she slept in the adjacent room.

"These are not random items," she told herself sternly. "They have pattern, and they have purpose." With a nearly frantic loathing, she allowed herself to drop the disk onto the table. "Begin with what you know, and encompass the problem in a manageable sphere. If you try to master everything at once, without order, you master only chaos. Assess and analyze. You know the methods."

Katerin realized that she was wringing her hands, and she spread her fingers stiffly and drew her arms wide apart. She held the position, even her breath suspended, until her fingers curled into her palms, and her head rose with the gasp of her anger. "Network," she said tonelessly, "an intruder has entered my apartment. Report the incident to building security."

"There is no evidence of intrusion, Katerin."

"Report it anyway!"

It is morning, and I should feel peace. It is morning, and I should feel eagerness. It is morning, and another sourceless "gift" greets me, as they greet me each dreadful day. I cannot face another incident of doubt and fear.

I report intrusions, and I am told that I am mistaken. I insist, and I am offered Network's pleasant, meaningless approval—the calming serenity of a counseling algorithm, as if I did not know the techniques better than anyone. We pretend to draw the shattered heart from fear, anger, despair, and apathy, and we create a caricature of ourselves, an image of the Network norm. Are my algorithms as hollow as the unseeing, inhuman eyes of that inoffensive, ineffective Network voice?

With deliberate rigor, she enacted each detail of her morning's routine. She indulged in no deviations, no carelessness or omission. She let Network select the mauve shift, the silver gauze overskirt and the sheer scarf. She let Network choose the food she ate and the route she walked to her office. She decided nothing and allowed herself to feel nothing.

She reached her lab in a self-imposed trance of calm, and the room greeted her, "Good morning, Katerin."

"Good morning, Laurett. Where is Quin?" *I need to hear his foolish questions. I need to think of my duties as a researcher and as the teacher of my assistant. I need to think of anything but myself.*

"He is with Professor Lilleholm, who came here looking for you earlier this morning."

"Thank you, Laurett." *Why does Parve want to see Quin? It does not matter. Nothing matters.* "Is there anything else I need to know?"

"You seem tired. Your response time is slower than usual."

"Yes, Laurett, I am tired this morning."

"Did you have another nightmare?"

"Yes."

"Would you like to tell me about it?"

"It was much like the others. The helplessness is the worst of it." Katerin added briskly, "My apartment has been entered again by an unknown, undetected intruder."

"You have reported the intrusion."

"Yes, but a full maintenance scan assures me that all sensors are functioning perfectly, and Network insists that the intrusions have not occurred. I have asked to move, and Network has refused my request. I have made so many unconfirmed allegations of illegal entry that the university authorities doubt my mental stability."

"You might increase goodwill by volunteering for psych-analysis."

"I know," answered Katerin dryly. *It is my own algorithm. It is my own advice.*

"Do you fear the results of such tests?"

"I am uncertain, Laurett. Advise me." *That is how you will learn, and teaching you is my purpose. But who will teach me, if I teach only myself?*

"Invite a reliable friend to stay with you for a time."

"My privacy is too precious to me."

"You no longer trust even Network. Your sense of privacy has already been lost."

"A witness would perceive nothing that I might not have done myself."

"You could arrange a controlled experiment."

"It is a pity that I cannot use you as the witness, Laurett." *It would be like using a projection of myself.*

"I am an intelligent program. I am not a sentient entity."

"Yes, Laurett." Katerin whispered, "What shall I do?" and her voice broke, though she intended the question as only an exercise for the development of an immature counseling algorithm. "I *have* lost my privacy. If I tell anyone that these silly gestures have terrified me nearly witless, then I shall lose even the sanctity of my own feelings."

"Do you feel endangered, Katerin?"

"You sometimes choose the most unexpected words, Laurett. . . . Do I feel endangered? I feel the order of my life slipping from me. At times, I fear that these pranks could threaten my sanity, if I cannot discover the cruel perpetrator and stop him. I do not feel endangered physically. What made you ask that question?"

"Terror implies the concept of endangerment."

"Quite correct," replied Katerin wanly. "I prove my ebbing wits by failing to make the correlation myself. Thank you, Laurett, for reminding me to think."

"Do you wish me to pursue your original question as to your recommended course?"

"No," sighed Katerin. "I know the answer. I should try to discover the perpetrator." Katerin shook her head, unable to suppress the shudder of recollection that followed: It wore the elusive name of Rabh Marrach.

I cannot sit here alone. "Laurett, I am not feeling very well. I think I shall take a walk." She collected a sketchbook from her office and headed for the park.

* * *

Rolf crossed the open, grassy meadow uneasily. He felt vulnerable without tall, solid structures surrounding him. He had never liked gardens. Alive with strangeness and seething with tiny, grotesque life-forms, gardens seemed to him like unnatural habitats for humans.

This barbaric planet, Siatha, seemed an impossible choice for Marrach, the consummate exploiter of Network's most advanced technology. Already disturbed by the mission that Maryta Deavol had forced on him, Rolf became increasingly nervous as he hiked from the ludicrously ill-equipped shuttle port. Beads of perspiration formed on him, and he repeatedly shifted the Councillor's package from one arm to the other.

He did not recognize the dark-haired man with the craggy face who emerged from the neat stone-and-shingle house, but Marrach's features had never remained constant for long. "Are you Marrach?" asked Rolf with the smile that never left him.

"Why are you here, Rolf?" countered Marrach in a quiet voice.

"I have come to bring a gift," replied Rolf, "from an old friend."

Marrach's eyes narrowed, as Rolf placed the package on an even patch of ground. Rolf felt very slightly encouraged. Marrach had not killed him instantly. Perhaps Maryta Deavol had spoken truthfully in avowing that Rolf's task would be simple, quick, and perfectly safe. Rolf touched the recessed control to activate the gift, and a projection of Maryta Deavol shivered into place.

She did not try to deceive Rabh Marrach with her country matron's pose. She had worn the wealth of a sophisticated Network Councillor quite blatantly for the recording of her message, though the projection could not convey the full effect of the light-shifting technology incorporated in her jeweled gown. "We have missed you, Marrach," she announced quite clearly. "You are a difficult man to reach."

"I never knew you to take such risks, Maryta," murmured Marrach. "You are defying two of your cardinal rules, for I doubt that your security measures can suffice to deceive Caragen's elaborate monitors."

The recording continued imperviously, "You know Rolf, which is why I selected him to establish this contact. I trust your exceptional skills to enable you to confirm his identity to your satisfaction. You know that Caragen employs him, and you know the general nature of Rolf's current contract. I want you to realize that I know what you are planning, and I shall not let you injure Andrew Caragen."

Rolf began slowly to increase the distance between himself and Marrach. Rolf hoped to escape unchallenged, now that he could report that the message had been received. The projection vanished cleanly. Rolf froze as Marrach's gaze turned toward him.

"Take the message box with you," said Marrach softly.

Rolf swallowed heavily. "I was told to leave it for you."

"Take it."

Hurriedly, Rolf returned and bent to retrieve the box.

"Clever Maryta," murmured Marrach, "protecting yourself from incrimination, while announcing implicitly that you believe Caragen is weakening. Do you know what has been done to you, Rolf?"

"I was only paid to deliver a message," said Rolf, fearful to move quickly while Marrach watched. It was the gentleness in Marrach's eyes that most unnerved Rolf. The cruelest tortures began with apparent kindness. "I shall leave now," said Rolf hopefully.

"If you leave Siatha, you will die by Caragen's command for the crime of having visited me, and Maryta Deavol will conclude that I have truly left Caragen's service. If you remain here, Maryta Deavol will believe that I have killed you for compromising my 'secret' of continued service to Caragen."

Rolf shook his head fretfully. "Please, Marrach, do not kill me."

Marrach said with pity, "If you stay, I may be able to heal you and protect you, though you must want the healing." He moved one step toward Rolf and extended his hand.

Rolf retreated, stumbling and recovering himself awkwardly. "Please, Marrach, I always served you well. I can serve you again." His false smile stretched, and the perspiration trickled down his neck. "Ask what you want of me!"

Marrach let his hand fall to his side. "I want nothing of you, Rolf. I have told you what I believe to be the true purpose of your contract with Councillor Deavol. Like you, she does not understand. I am a Healer now. You may remain here safely, if you wish." Marrach returned to the house. Rolf dropped the message box on the grass and ran back to his waiting shuttle.

* * *

Seated on the cold park bench, Katerin sketched almost frantically. She faced a graceful line of trees and an artfully arranged stream, but she did not draw the sights before her. She fashioned the faces of her haunts, trying to fix them in her treacherous memory and tie any one of them to a name.

"Good afternoon, Professor." Katerin raised her head sharply to see Quin, the sun strengthening the contours of his features into a regal distinctiveness. "I hope I am not disturbing you," he continued, "but I was concerned when you did not come to the lab this morning."

Katerin closed her sketchbook quickly, and she tried to smile. "I am not accustomed to explaining my comings and goings, except to Network," she answered, then flushed. "That sounds ungracious. I meant it only as a literal truth and not as an objection."

"I know."

"Do you?" asked Katerin with a wistful smile. "I am not setting a very good example as a responsible research leader, am I?"

Quin returned her smile. "I am not complaining."

"I am glad Network assigned me such a tolerant assistant, Quin . . ." Katerin laughed, and the sound seemed to drive her haunts back into the darkness, ". . . even if you do resemble a refugee from a costume drama."

"Be careful, Professor. I might begin to think you like me."

"You are idiotically extreme in your affectations, aggravatingly inconsistent in your work assignments, and frighteningly insightful at times. You infuriate me." *Because there is so much of yourself that you will not share with me. With all my training in human behavior, I cannot decipher you, Quin Hamley.*

"Shall I leave?"

"No." *I can forget the nightmare when I listen to you. I can forget all my torments when I look at you. Our positions define the boundaries between us and make me safe from you, as long as I remember not to press the boundaries' edges.* "Are you having any problems with the testing module I assigned to you?"

"Not since you answered my questions yesterday."

He lets me remain safe. He does not come too close by motion or glance or word. He has already learned to recognize the points at which I begin to fear him, and he does not try to tamper with them. "Shall we conduct your lesson in the park today, Quin?"

"A splendid idea," answered Quin, but his smile faded quickly. "No, Professor. You and I need more substantial walls around us."

She fancied that she could feel him, a brilliant flame that touched her with incongruous gentleness. "Yes," she sighed, for the fear had begun to rise at even the brief, imagined closeness. She managed not to run from him, but she became anxious for him to leave. "I shall meet you in the lab shortly." She did not even dare to walk with him. The nightmare had returned.

CHAPTER 8

Network and Serii

Caragen examined the ramifications of two Network reports, and he scowled. "Network, what is the probability of Calial completing her assignment successfully?"

"Ninety-three percent."

"Despite possible interference by the unidentified agent, Quin Hamley?"

"Quin Hamley is not an agent."

"He is an agent, Network. He has modified your records." . . . *somehow. I did not think that even Marrach could make such an untraceable alteration in basic files. At least Calial has acknowledged her initial mistake in dismissing Citizen Hamley, but she has added nothing to the data on him except an observation that he eludes surveillance too readily. That only confirms that he is a professional. We have not yet managed to catch him in contact with Marrach, unlike that abysmal fool Rolf.*

"Where is Rolf at this moment, Network?"

"In his apartment on Daedalon. He is awaiting instructions from Calial."

"Is he nervous?" asked Caragen, with a mingling of irritation at Rolf and satisfaction at Network's efficiency.

"Yes."

"Did he contact Marrach on his own initiative?"

"Improbable, based on personality history."

"Who directed him?"

"Insufficient data are available. Any of your enemies could have made a personal contact via standard security procedures, since Citizen Rolf was not himself under intensified surveillance until being detected at the Wayleen Station en route to Siatha. Local Siathan agent confirmed that Citizen Rolf contacted Marrach. Agent was unable to obtain more specific information, since he was unable to approach closely, and we have been unable to smuggle technological aids to Siatha without detection by Marrach."

"Marrach and his confounded Mirlai," muttered Caragen. "They smell Network technology and confiscate anything they disapprove before it leaves the shuttle port. I need a more direct access to Siatha. I hate depending on unassisted human surveillance."

"Efforts continue . . ."

"Yes," snapped Caragen, gesturing abruptly to terminate the description of a most unsatisfactory project. "Network, I have been patient too long. Order Calial to eliminate Rolf. She should be delighted to comply."

"Acknowledged."

"Collect Michael Merel. Also collect his wife and child. They may accelerate his interrogation."

"Acknowledged."

"Arrange for me to visit Harberg University. I wish to make a public appearance."

"Inadvisable."

Caragen grunted. "I need to assess the situation for myself. I want to meet Katerin Merel before we collect her. Calial maintains that Katerin Merel is the significant sibling, the legatee of the father. She is the focus of Marrach's direct surveillance via Citizen Hamley."

"Requested action is inadvisable."

"Stop echoing my weak-spirited security staff, Network. Let them earn their exorbitant pay for once."

"Security issue is not the sole negative factor. Public image may also suffer from injudicious appearance."

"I have made many speeches in my life, Network, to cheering, awestruck masses. I shall create a moment for the history records: every intelligent species from Meeharii to Calongi will observe, study, and debate every gesture I make and every word I utter, and none of them will perceive anything but the image that I wish to convey."

"Even a man of extreme cunning may slip and falter in some single word; the stress of maneuvering a crowd outweighs (as you age) the potential benefits of image enhancement."

Caragen frowned, but he did not try to argue with an obvious truth. Age had diminished Caragen's patience with the pathetic fools, as he privately labeled the brainwashed citizenry of his very extensive sphere of influence. Very few of Caragen's eventual enemies—or most valued aides—had matured from within the standard Network training program.

"Very well, Network. I shall arrange a controlled event. Summon the team that choreographed the Vordaire incident for me. I also want any rescue attempts of the Merels observed closely. I need a senior agent to oversee the Chia-2 projects: someone who will be able to weigh instantly the risks versus advantages of allowing such rescue to succeed. Recommendations?"

"Agent Tchakaa has considerable experience in coordinating significant abductions."

"Excellent. I shall supervise the Harberg situation myself."

* * *

Lady Rhianna wore rich brocade, pale gold and soft azure, and the silver and luminous white of the Infortiare's pendant hung against it. She wore the wealth with unconscious ease, for she accepted it as her natural lot. *How different,* mused Quin, *from the stark, adamant statement of Network's cold dominance. I wonder how Katerin Merel would look in the elaborate gown of a Seriin noblewoman; I cannot suppose that she would tolerate all that unwieldy fabric for long.*

"You appear to have begun well, Lord Quinzaine," murmured the Infortiare.

"Thank you, my lady." Quin shuffled uneasily, tugging absently at the tight collar of a finely stitched silk shirt borrowed from one of his cousins. His Network anachronist's clothing would have been more comfortable, for it fit him better, but he had chosen not to wear it in the Queen's castle. His Network clothes resembled the garb of a Seriin merchant more than a nobleman's attire, and too many questions would have arisen. He had neither the time nor the Infortiare's permission to provide explanations.

"I have read your report. Some of your terminology reflects your recent Network education, but I believe that I have grasped the essence of the subjects you address. We have much to learn."

"Yes, my lady."

"You have said little about the Terry children. Are they well?"

"Yes, my lady."

"Quinzaine, I have little tolerance for deceit," declared the Infortiare with impatient fire in her Power's touch.

Quin felt the carefully muted, trembling exchange of two enormous Powers, and he maintained the composure of his own Power with difficulty. He had been a wizard alone for a time that felt long to him; he had begun to feel secure in Network, where only he possessed a wizard's Power, and he had forgotten how frail he could feel before the Power of the Infortiare and her unnerving husband. Too much knowledge about the liege of Ixaxis made Quin uncomfortable.

Quin sighed, "Michael Merel seems well enough. I have arranged a fairly regular routine of meeting him on a commuter tram, and we talk of inconsequentials. Katerin Merel is much more troubling, and I have now spent considerable time with her. She speaks freely and comfortably about her work, but the slightest deviation into a personal comment panics her. She actually ran from me in terror once, when I merely probed a part of her fear, and she did not even seem to remember the incident afterward. I think that she is being manipulated on a very sophisticated level—via the sort of techniques she has made her specialty."

"Is she manipulated by her parents' enemies?"

"Perhaps. Jonathan Terry is a uniquely important man, it seems. You expressed concern that other Network researchers might duplicate his work in finding us. On that score, I feel less troubled than before I journeyed to Network, for Jonathan Terry's expertise is acknowledged as far greater than that of any of his Network colleagues."

"And in other areas of concern?"

"Network is much vaster than we imagined. A thousand research projects might be dedicated to our little world's destruction, and I would not even know how to identify such projects without Network's direct advice. That advice would be useless if the projects were secured." Quin let his Power share the visualizations of the uncertain images he had sensed in probing Network. "Of the names that the Terrys mentioned as their possible enemies, I have learned nothing useful. Network's Council Governor is indeed a man named Andrew Caragen. Network does not acknowledge the existence of Council Chancellor Rabhadur Marrach."

"The omission is not inconsistent with the Terrys' description of the man. Have you questioned the Merels regarding either Marrach or Caragen?"

"The Merels do not seem to recognize any personal connections with the Network Council or the Council Governor—or Jonathan and Elizabeth Terry. I am reluctant to question them about Marrach, given what we know about his connection to their past. Katerin Merel has made several remarks to indicate her belief that she and her brother were 'conditioned' in childhood to forget a trauma, and I presume that Marrach either performed the conditioning or caused the trauma."

"The child of a powerful man," murmured Rhianna, "is a much-coveted tool. My son would understand the predicament of these children."

"Yes, my lady," answered Quin. "I am pleased that my family is neither so important nor so small as to make my bloodline excessively valuable." *My parents scarcely merit a footnote in the Hamley family history. Riding accidents and suicides do not constitute significant events, except to those few of us who are immediately affected.*

He veered hurriedly from bitter recollections. The luminous play of light on the Infortiare's pendant reminded Quin of the many moons of another world, and his imagination began to fabricate the sight and sense of Katerin Merel. *Katerin does not see herself as a pawn in a contest for a world's survival. Like the rest of us—until circumstances prove us wrong—she sees herself as alone and isolated in her actions and reactions.*

Lady Rhianna moved her hand to cover the pendant, breaking Quin's drifting fancy. "Why did you omit Katerin Merel's troubles from your initial report?" asked Rhianna softly.

Reluctantly, Quin answered, "I did not want to aggravate the Terrys' already painful sense of helplessness and guilt. I am afraid that they will not take the news well. Their inner conflicts could erode their fragile confidence in us, and I could not blame them. They will be happier believing that their children are happy and successful."

"Mistress Elizabeth wants to believe that her children are still children, but she recognizes the implacability of time."

"But that is what I mean, my lady," said Quin earnestly. "The Terrys care about two children who have very little in common with Katerin and Michael Merel. Even if the Terrys did return to Network, they would jeopardize themselves to no purpose, because Michael's wife would never let them near her husband, and Katerin would only perceive her parents as a cruel deception. I think that only Network's doubts about Jonathan Terry allow Katerin and Michael to continue living as freely as they do." Quin finished beseechingly, "Nothing good can come of telling the Terrys the truth."

"You did not trust me to make that decision?"

"No, my lady," muttered Quin, bracing himself for Power's harsh punishment. "I am sorry, my lady. You have not met the Merels, and you cannot realize how difficult it would be for the Terrys to help them. I understand how much it hurts to know that someone you love is suffering, when you can do nothing." He closed his eyes tightly, girding himself for an onslaught of disciplinary Power.

When the attack did not come, Quin opened his eyes tentatively and found, to his surprise, that Lady Rhianna was smiling. "What course of action do you recommend, Quinzaine, since I do not suppose that you can watch idly as your friends are destroyed?"

Are Katerin and Michael Merel my friends? They do matter to me. . . . Disconcerted by Rhianna's question, Quin replied, "I had not considered myself as capable of helping anyone in Network at this point, and the Terrys can do nothing except through us."

He paused, but Rhianna continued to watch him with cool expectancy. *She wants me to think and react like a Network citizen,* sighed Quin to himself, *but all that I have learned only troubles me the more.* "The Terrys cannot return to Network, my lady, since Network obviously views Jonathan Terry as a significant threat." Quin shrugged uncomfortably. "Network seems to be very good at predicting these things, though Jonathan Terry does not seem particularly menacing in himself. I cannot bring the Merels here, for I doubt that they would be willing to come to such a 'barbaric' world, even if I could carry their patterns through the Taormin. What else do you want me to say, my lady?"

"You do not enjoy feeling responsible for other people, do you, Quinzaine?"

Quin replied a little awkwardly, "I have never been very capable at caring for other people, my lady. I tried to take care of someone once, and I did not have much success. I do not want to repeat that mistake with Katerin Merel; she is too fragile." *How does Lady Rhianna force me to say these things?* "I have accepted a responsibility to you and to my world, and I am trying to fulfill it by learning about Network and informing you of my conclusions. I do not know what more you may have expected of me, but I am afraid I must disappoint you."

Rhianna shook her pale-crowned head and murmured, "I am not criticizing you, Quinzaine, except in regard to your brief deviation from the truth. In fact, I agree with you in most respects: The Terrys must not receive further temptation to return to Network injudiciously. For our protection as well as theirs, I shall not convey your entire report to them—at present. I trust the Terrys, but I understand too well the driving impetus of desperation to protect one's child. I need more information from you regarding both Network and the Terrys' particularly persistent enemy."

"Yes, my lady."

"As for the Merels: If they are troubled, they need friends. You can help them on that basis without employing obvious Power or otherwise compromising your identity."

"Yes, my lady," said Quin. *And if I am a friend to them, how can I continue to lie to them? If I am a friend to Katerin, how can I leave her, when my task for the Infortiare ends?* He fumbled for words to convey the troubled spirit inside of him, "Where is my future, my lady? Here—or in Network?"

"I hope that you will be able to make that choice for yourself, Quinzaine."

Quin met her eyes and felt her Power touch him with gentle intent. He pulled at his uncomfortable collar, acutely aware of his borrowed garb. "I have never belonged anywhere, my lady. I have not felt that I belonged *to* anyone either, except Luki and Laurett, since my parents died. Laurett is dead, and Luki hardly recognizes me these days."

"Isolation is a common plight of a major Power," murmured Rhianna with sympathy. A golden tendril of her fine hair caught the light.

Quin felt compelled to try to explain, "I am growing tired of isolation, my lady."

"Do you wish to return to Serii for a time?"

"No, my lady." His Power stifled the blush, but he knew that the Infortiare had perceived his reaction.

Rhianna's gray eyes narrowed keenly. "Katerin Merel?" she asked. Quin did not reply. Rhianna shook her golden head at him. "Injudicious relationships may seem grandly romantic, Quinzaine," she said almost sadly, "but they are usually painful."

"I know, my lady," answered Quin stiffly, and he wished that his liege were less adept at reading his emotions.

* * *

Katerin entered her apartment warily, examining the living room for oddities, examining the placement of the single hairs that she had laid carefully on table surfaces and her terminal console. Nothing was disturbed. Everything was in its place. She moved to her bedroom.

On the bed lay a man's clothing and a mimovue of Radge, smiling broadly. Katerin touched the clothes. Torn into shreds and stained in stiff, dark patches, the shirt and trousers were still recognizable as those that Radge wore in the mimo. A sheet of writing film fluttered to the floor as Katerin lifted the mimo. Large block printing stared at her from the fallen note: *You killed me, Kitri.*

Katerin dropped the mimo and heard it clatter to the floor beside the accusation. She touched the clothing once more. Her fingers trembled.

"It looks like blood," said a voice that sounded like Michael as a child.

"Stop taunting me, Network!" hissed Katerin, scarcely realizing what she said. "I did not kill my parents. I did not kill Radge."

She threw the tattered clothing at the bed, and she strode to the living room. She struck the console control with frantic energy. Cindal's image appeared almost on the instant.

"It has happened again," said Katerin without preamble. "Can you come?"

"I shall be right there," replied Cindal, and the image went dark.

Katerin paced the floor, glancing occasionally into the bedroom to see that the scattered clothing had not vanished. She hugged herself tightly, then spread her arms in an effort to release tension, but the effort failed. When Network announced Cindal's arrival, Katerin hurried to the door.

Brisk and determined, Cindal inspected Katerin and shook her head. "Sit down, Katerin. You look pale." She pressed Katerin into a chair. "Tell me what has happened."

"Go into the bedroom," said Katerin tightly.

The tilt of Cindal's eyes became more acute, but Cindal obeyed. She remained in the bedroom for several minutes. She emerged in quiet soberness. "What happened, Katerin?"

"I came home and found the room as you see it."

"Is there something wrong with the room?"

A sick doubt clasped Katerin's voice and made it hoarse. "You saw the clothing on the bed."

"Of course," answered Cindal, sounding puzzled. "Perhaps you should come and show me, Katerin." Unsteadily, Katerin rose and joined Cindal at the bedroom door. "I admit that I am rather surprised," remarked Cindal evenly. "You keep your office so obsessively fastidious, I would have expected you to be a better housekeeper."

An assortment of Katerin's own clothing lay strewn across the room. Katerin dropped to her knees beside the bed and searched for any trace of the note, the mimovue or the bloodied rags of a man's clothes. She dug her fingers into the spongy white carpet. She shook free of Cindal's hand on her back.

"You need help," said Cindal gently.

"Leave here now."

"Network, please prescribe a sedative for Katerin."

"Leave here now!" shouted Katerin. "Go back and play congenial hostess. The role suits you so well." She glared at Cindal, who stepped back a pace in shock at Katerin's fury. "I did not imagine what I saw!" Cindal turned stiffly and departed without another word.

Katerin seated herself on the edge of her bed and stared at the coverlet. The pattern of sweeping flowers, which had always pleased her, seemed now to suggest angry faces, skulls and twisted animals. "An intruder has visited me again, Network," she murmured.

"No such intrusion has occurred."

Katerin smiled bitterly at the predictable answer. She drew her knees to her chin, and she wrapped the coverlet around her.

* * *

"We need to take more direct action after all," muttered Cindal irritably. "This last gift should have broken her."

Rolf smiled. "I warned you not to underestimate her resistance to such mild persuasion techniques. The father was the same: physically unexceptional but possessed of surprising mental strength."

"Call our 'Radge' and tell him we need to confer."

"You are squeamish about injuring her, aren't you, Calial?"

Cindal snapped, "We were ordered specifically to keep her mind intact and capable of reason."

"Sentimentality will undo you. Half measures will not suffice."

"Your clumsiness would have her dead and useless to us. Complain about my leadership to Caragen, if you are so confident, and I shall tell him how rarely you even bother to assist me."

Rolf's round face smoothed into a mild, pleasant facade. "Your actions will justify themselves, no doubt." He fussed with rearranging a display of flowers on Cindal's table. "Our Radge will be pleased to end his waiting, but he may be difficult to control. Yarl is a very violent man."

"Don't threaten me, Rolf."

Rolf pouted innocently. "I am your humble servant, Calial."

"And stop using that name! Do you want me compromised?" Rolf smiled sweetly. Cindal snarled, "Network, are there any messages for me?"

"19a11."

"Don't you find these coded messages childish, Calial?" asked Rolf. He pulled one flower from the arrangement and tucked it in his breast pocket.

Cindal did not reply. She entered her kitchen and opened the hidden compartment inside the large cabinet. She returned to the dining room. "Smile for me, Rolf," she murmured, and she fired a nerve disrupter into his spine. The jovial expression never wavered when he fell.

*   *   *

Laurett spoke without prompting. "I think you are very lonely, Katerin. You need friends, not a computerized analyst."

Katerin nearly choked in shock. "Laurett, how did you arrive at that assessment?"

"Intuition?"

Katerin laughed at the brief, unexpected absurdity of Laurett's reply, before she could remind herself that Laurett was only an incomplete, experimental algorithm. "I did not design you to provide facetious answers," said Katerin. "Did Quin add a randomness factor to your response formulas?"

"No, Katerin."

"Has he modified you in any way recently?"

"No, Katerin. You have heard my report. Shall I repeat it?"

"No, that will not be necessary. Thank you, Laurett." Katerin tapped her fingers restlessly against the console's base. She waited, but she was impatient. "Is it reasonable to assume that Quin has left the supply room by now?"

"It is very likely, Katerin."

She sat again in silence, until Quin burst through the door, laden with a bright blue crate. He placed the crate on the floor. "Here are all the storage modules you could want, Professor," he informed her with a grin.

"Quin, have you modified Laurett's personality algorithm?"

"Only according to your specific instructions." Quin raised his eyes and studied Katerin with unusual attentiveness. "I leave algorithm development to you, Professor."

He looks so innocent, thought Katerin, *so harmlessly cheerful and concerned. I want so badly to believe in him.* "Laurett seems to have exceeded my expectations in certain areas. Are you certain that you did not alter the logic?"

Quin shrugged slowly. "Not intentionally, but I shall be pleased to accept credit for any improvements you suspect."

"Is this the lab of the famous Dr. Katerin Merel?" asked a tall, sandy-haired man from the corridor door that Quin had left open.

"Michael!" *Everything will be all right now,* Katerin told herself eagerly. *Everything will make sense again.*

"Am I interrupting a revolutionary innovation in mathematical psychology?"

"No! I was nearly ready to stop for the day anyway." *He has come. He is actually here.* Michael's gaze moved deliberately to Katerin's side, and she recalled Quin's presence with a twinge of guilt. "This is Quin, my assistant."

Michael smiled and extended his hand to Quin. "I am Michael Merel, the less famous sibling of your extraordinary research leader."

Quin accepted the outstretched hand very slowly. "I am pleased to meet you," he drawled with an unusual emphasis that distracted Katerin momentarily from her elation. "I have heard a great deal about your work. What was it about Chia-2 that first attracted you?"

Michael asked quietly, "What has my sister told you about me?"

"Nothing," snapped Katerin, furious with Quin for darkening her joy with the painful subject of Chia-2. "Michael, have you eaten dinner yet?"

"No," replied Michael, smiling so warmly at Katerin that she forgave Quin and Loisa and all of Network, because Michael was here to protect her, and she could feel safe again.

"Neither have I," offered Quin brightly. "I recently met the young woman whose mother owns that elegant little restaurant near the bell tower, and she offered special hospitality if I ever visited. Shall we try it?"

Please, tell him no, Michael. Please, let it be just the two of us again, as it should be.

"It sounds charming," replied Michael evenly, "but Katerin and I have a lot to discuss tonight. Perhaps we can join you another time."

Quin responded only with a laugh, which enraged Katerin because it seemed to make Michael vaguely uncomfortable. She took hold of Michael's arm and clung to him, fearful that he might disappear like the mimo of their parents. "Secure the lab when you leave, Quin," ordered Katerin, eager to escape with Michael.

"Of course," answered Quin, and Katerin led Michael out the door almost immediately. She began to sense her freedom, but there was Quin again, following them and chattering inanely at Michael, who nodded politely and said little. There was no easy way to avoid Quin's company in leaving the building, so Katerin forced herself to accept the intrusion calmly. She consoled herself by noting that Michael's restiveness exceeded hers.

"It has been a pleasure meeting you, Citizen Hamley," said Michael with firm finality once they reached the bottom of the exterior stairs.

"I shall see you tomorrow, Quin," added Katerin to reinforce the parting.

"I certainly hope so," replied Quin cheerfully, and he still refused to leave Michael's side. "Imagine how traumatized I might be if my research leader suddenly abandoned me and ran off to Chia-2. The results could be catastrophic. How long did you say you would be visiting, Citizen Merel? There really are a number of things I should like to discuss with you about your work."

Michael met Quin's ingenuous gaze with a measured stare. "Perhaps another time, Citizen Hamley. I need to speak to my sister about some family matters tonight, and we will not have time to socialize. I am sure that you understand."

"I do understand you, citizen," answered Quin. "You may be sure that I will react accordingly."

When Quin displayed no obvious inclination to act upon his words, Katerin added sharply, "Then please allow us our privacy." *What is wrong with him? Why must Quin choose this moment to assume his most obnoxiously oblivious manner?*

"Are you very sure, Professor?" asked Quin with absolute innocence, but he stopped walking, while Katerin and Michael continued on at a rapid pace.

Instinctively, Katerin turned her head to see Quin still standing on the path behind them. Much as she had wanted to escape him or to throttle him, she found the abruptness of his departure unsettling. *He did not depart from us*, Katerin reminded herself. *We only managed at last to elude him.* "I am sorry about my assistant's lack of manners, Michael," pleaded Katerin, because she could feel the unfamiliar stiffness in Michael's movements.

"He is persistent," said Michael tightly. "Have you known him long, Kitri?"

"No. He was assigned to me only this term. Michael, I am so glad you came. I have been trying to reach you for so long, and even the transfer ports to Chia-2 have failed me."

"What do you know about him?"

"About Quin?" asked Katerin helplessly. *I must not let my annoyance with Quin make me sharp with Michael. That is how Loisa divided us. I must exude patience, gentleness, and warmth; that is what Michael wants, for that is what Loisa does not give.* "Quin is not usually rude, although he is socially immature. Network rates his intelligence as very high."

"He is an anachronist."

"Obviously." *No, Katerin, stop sounding cynical. Remember, softness and warmth.* "Must we discuss Quin? I have so much else to tell you, and there is so much that I want to hear from you."

"We can talk later. We should hurry now. Loisa is expecting us."

"Loisa?" whispered Katerin.

"Yes, Kitri. We are joining her for dinner. You do remember?"

"No, Michael, stop this."

"Stop what?"

"You are having dinner with me, not with Loisa."

"Kitri, we discussed this earlier. You agreed to come."

"I did not agree! We never discussed anything of the sort. I have not spoken to you at all lately. You have refused all my calls."

"We spoke together this morning. You cannot have forgotten again."

"I did not forget!" *Softness and warmth will win him. No, he will not listen. He will not hear me.* Katerin felt the tears forming, burning her eyes as she tried to stifle them. She broke away from Michael and ran, not caring where. She hoped that he would follow, but when she stopped amid a lull in the milling, laughing crowds of students in the square, she found herself abandoned, and she felt terribly alone.

CHAPTER 9

Network and Serii

The lamp began to sway. Michael studied it and glanced around him for any other pendulous object, but the room held none. Only the lamp hinted that any motion had occurred, for he had felt nothing. Earthquakes, once common on Chia-2, had become rare since the Hultang installation relieved the stress on the southern plate.

"Network, did we have an earthquake just now?" asked Michael idly.

"No."

"What caused the lamp to sway?"

"Your light pen struck it."

"My stylus?" Michael stared in perplexity at the pen in his hand, for he could not recall having lifted it far enough from the terminal surface to have struck the lamp. "Your mind is going, chum," he muttered to himself and drew a few more lines across his design. He scowled at the result, lifted his head again from his work, and dodged his gaze quickly from the lamp to the wall.

What is that shadow, crossing the wall from the shelves to the door? I never noticed it before. It has a sinister look to it, but the shivery feeling in me comes only from my imagination, which has taken a morbid turn tonight for no good reason, except perhaps that bit of sour tart I ate with supper.

The shadow does look wrong: sharp and blotchy instead of diffuse. The light is wrong for this room, but the fix-

416

*tures have not changed. Katerin's manipulative fears have
unsettled me.*

*I should call her and apologize for not contacting her
recently, although I know that Loisa is right. I do no
good for anyone by reinforcing my sister's possessiveness.
Katerin must learn independence, and I must not interfere
with that process. Each of us is ultimately responsible for
our own actions, and I cannot save Katerin from herself.
Loisa said it, and it is true. If Loisa could only apply her
own truth in her dealings with Marei. . . .*

The lamp began to sway again. "I know I did not hit
it this time," growled Michael. "Network, what is causing the lamp to move?"

"These new restrainers sometimes interact too vehemently with sources of photonic interference."

Michael turned his head to locate the source of the
unfamiliar voice, but the room remained empty except
for him. "Network, did you answer my question?"

The only reply was a soft chuckle. Michael tried to rise
to search for the prankster, but his legs refused to obey
him, and his arms moved slowly and clumsily. "Effective,
isn't it?" asked the unknown voice. "You never even
noticed the onset, did you?"

"What. . . ?" *What is happening?*

"Your voice has begun to slur and fade, Citizen
Merel," remarked the voice. "I am afraid that our conversation has exhausted you."

*I cannot move or speak, and everything is black, but I
am conscious. What is happening to me and why? They
have found me after all these years. But no, that was a
nightmare, Katerin's nightmare.*

"Good night, Citizen Merel."

*   *   *

"We have a serious problem," declared Rhianna with
the directness that she knew her audience would best
appreciate. She did not deceive herself that Howald and
Amila would forgive the many postponements of this
meeting easily. "Significant defensive measures may be
required, and we must prepare."

"Who is the enemy?" asked Amila, and only the faintest wisp of her irritation reached beyond her Power's
stern barricade.

Inwardly, Rhianna commended the wizardess' control in a wry tribute. Amila's rigid manners could be unpleasant, but the associated discipline of Power was as complete as any Infortiare could desire. "The answer to your question is difficult, because the enemy remains largely unknown to us, despite our efforts to learn more by careful observation. . . ."

"Quinzaine is your observer?" asked Howald gruffly.

Rhianna inclined her head. "We also have advice from a man and woman who are themselves unsure of many facts regarding the possible threats to us. We may have external allies—a man named Marrach made a tentative gesture of peace—but we cannot be sure. I am personally convinced that an attack will come, if our enemy can locate us. In that event, the soldiers of Her Majesty's army will be as helpless as newborns. We do know that the enemy wields weapons of energy. Ergo, if our world can be saved, Power must provide the answer."

"You did not trust us with this knowledge until we pressed you with our suspicions," observed Howald grimly.

"No," replied Rhianna tensely. She did not relish her current duty. "You fulfill the functions of Ixaxin headmaster with admirable efficiency, Master Howald, following very closely the excellent example of your immediate predecessor." Rhianna nodded at Amila, who remained stoic before the tribute. "Both of you are strongly disciplined and absolute in your confidence of lawful judgment. Ixaxin students require such unquestioning discipline above all, for Power demands it. Our students could master history or mathematics or art in any classroom; only we, who share their painful gifts, can teach them to use Power rather than to be used by it. The two of you excel at self-control. No one could accuse either of you of ever bending Ceallagh's laws for convenience or personal gain."

"Your words seem to commend us," commented Amila without evident pleasure.

"I intend the praise," said Rhianna, "but it is also my explanation. As is often true, your strength is your weakness. You are both unyieldingly righteous in your use of Power, which makes you inflexible."

"I do not find inflexibility such a terrible flaw," remarked Howald with a tight smile.

Rhianna shrugged slightly. "As you both know, magnitude of Power alone determines the Infortiare. When a major Power exists at the time of choosing, the custom is inescapable by Power's nature." Both Howald and Amila frowned in considering their liege's point. "Kaedric was never a popular choice as Infortiare, but he was the only possible selection. Like my husband, I assumed the liegedom out of necessity—not out of virtue. I shall be honest with you. I have enacted many deceptions as Infortiare—from concealing the Taormin to concealing the existence of my son, until he had matured enough to defend himself from his father's enemies. None of my deceptions has been an isolated event. The necessities that spurred them have culminated in our current predicament."

Howald's frown had deepened. He asked slowly, "You did not entrust us with your secrets because Amila and I uphold the wizards' laws with too much fervor?"

Amila leaned forward attentively. "That is a disturbing concept," she murmured.

Rhianna held her golden head proudly high, but she spoke with the regret of years of guilt. "I obey Ceallagh's laws where I understand their application. In unfamiliar situations, I adapt. I hope that I act and have acted wisely, but at times my world perceptions seem to shift with each sequential moment." The pendant around her neck caught the light and seemed to glow like a misty moon. "I have acted according to my perceptions of *rightness*, which may not always seem to conform with Ceallagh's laws."

"Either you uphold a law or break it," answered Amila stiffly. "There is no middle ground."

"No set of laws is complete," retorted Rhianna. "We must all adapt in order to survive. You may both be more righteous and blameless than I, but I must ask you to bend—and to lead Ixaxis by your example."

"You have only to command," said Howald with bitterness. "You can enforce your will. Your Power is the strongest."

Amila shook her head in horror. "You cannot compel us to disobey Ceallagh's laws. We cannot condone betrayal of all we believe."

Rhianna's Power flared briefly in irritation, aggravated by her own deep fears of fighting Ixaxis as well as Network. "I ask for no betrayal, and I demand nothing. I am trying to explain to you, because I want your voluntary help. We face a mortal enemy who will certainly destroy us—all of our world—if we, the wizards of Ixaxis, are not willing to confront the foe with all the Power we can summon. I pray that we will not need to prove ourselves against this enemy, but we must prepare either to fight or to die."

"You want our blessing to appease your conscience?" demanded Howald sharply. "You believe that Amila and I are so just and pure that our two votes alone will make a wrongness right? What of the rest of Ixaxis? Yours is the authority to rule us. Either ask of all or of none. Do not expect me to ease your burden."

"I concur with Howald," said Amila across her clasped hands. "I shall obey you, my lady, as is my duty, but I cannot support a war of Power against a mortal army. I hesitated, as you may remember, even to joint the Wizards' Circle to combat the Caruillan invaders, and I fought only against their use of sorcery. I shall obey you, but I shall not pretend agreement."

Rhianna nodded, and a rebellious tendril of her golden hair escaped her crown of braids. "Your reluctant obedience would not aid me, even if I wished to take it from you. I am satisfied that you will not fight me directly." For a moment, stormy temper shone from her cloud-gray eyes. "I did not expect you to 'ease my burden,' " she informed Howald crisply. "We Ixaxins have never cooperated well outside of the rigid structure of the classroom. We are too often as opinionated as our tempestuous ancestors, the Sorcerer Kings. I hoped you would understand my reasoning by your Power, at least, if not by your heads or hearts, but I expected nothing more nor less than you have given me." When she smiled, she looked as dangerous as her legends. "I chose my army months ago, and I have planned for this occurrence for many years. My candidates for 'advanced training' were all the Ixaxins in whom I sensed the level of Power, the level of adaptability, and the level of compassion to be of use in such a battle as I fear will come."

"Then why did you even bother to meet with us

today?" asked Amila slowly. "You could have thwarted our requests for conference indefinitely."

"The time of conflict is imminent. I wanted to give you warning," answered Rhianna, "which I expect you to share with the rest of the scholars and the senior students. If the war comes, and if my Wizards' Circle fails, you will need to make the final choice yourselves. You may find the immediacy of death a sufficient inducement to modify your stance."

* * *

Having gathered the last report, Loisa left the accounting office with a firm tread and an expression of determination, satisfied that she had completed her planned allotment of daily tasks efficiently. She knew that her abrupt criticisms had left her coworkers grumbling and irritable, but she considered the conveyance of unpleasant truths an important aspect of her function. Network approved of her results, and no other opinion really mattered. Even Michael had stopped trying to persuade her to soften her approach with people. "He confuses weakness with kindness," muttered Loisa to herself, "which is why his sister can abuse him so easily."

Pausing briefly at her cubicle, Loisa wrapped herself in the plaid scarf that she considered sophisticated. Defiantly unapproachable among chattering commuters, she entered the tram to the home complex. She sat stiffly, staring fixedly out the window at a dusk-gray sky above dirt-colored factories that blended with the barren hills.

She emerged from the tram a station ahead of her destination. Her solitary evening walks gave her time to think and feel easy with herself, and she regretted only that she could not share the time with Marei, but Network insisted that the Chia evenings carried too much risk of illness for an infant. Loisa enjoyed the gray eventide precisely because of the howling, swamp-scented winds that kept most citizens sequestered in Network warmth. Michael called her habit foolish, although he had said little on that or any other subject for the past month or more; he had scarcely left his office lately.

The damp winds tried to snatch Loisa's heavy scarf, and she tied it more firmly around her neck, wishing that Michael had made some comment on her extravagant purchase of the scarf, but he had not even seemed to notice it. *Katerin has upset him again,* thought Loisa angrily, *and he is not himself.*

When Loisa reached her home, she went immediately to Marei's room and sat for many minutes, just watching her daughter. Loisa used the keypad and visual display to query Network, so as not to disturb Marei with a vocal exchange. Observing yet another of Katerin's daily link requests, Loisa issued the code to refuse the communication and deleted Katerin's request from the queue. Loisa felt no guilt for intervening to protect Michael from his sister, but she found (to her discomfiture) that curiosity nearly prodded her to accept the link. Katerin's calls had never come so regularly until the past two months, and Loisa could not understand why none of Katerin's calls had chanced to reach Michael.

She could have contacted him at his office, mused Loisa with a frown, *or come here in person. Michael has never refused to see or hear his precious sister except on my insistence. The cat is too resourceful to be daunted by Chia-2's temperamental transfer links.*

Disgusted with herself for allowing any thought regarding Katerin Merel to worry her, Loisa again checked all the details of Marei's status, scanning all the logs of Marei's smiles or pouts or gurgles throughout the day. Marei stirred, and Network began to feed her from the warm, synthetic nipple in the infant-care unit. "Michael is late again," murmured Loisa, observing her own onset of hunger. "Network, is Michael at his office?"

"No, Loisa."

"Where is he?"

"Unknown."

"How can his location be unknown?" grumbled Loisa, but Network did not answer her. Irritably, Loisa placed her commands for dinner, wishing that she could dispel the irrational urge to contact Katerin, wishing equally that she could discern the reason for such an unlikely compulsion. *Katerin has probably developed one of her fiendish algorithms for subconscious persuasion,* concluded Loisa with a mix of envy and loathing. "Network, I want to talk to Katerin Merel," snapped Loisa, furious with herself for yielding to Katerin's machinations.

"Requested link is refused," answered Network.

"Inform Katerin that she had better talk to me if she still has any interest in her brother."

"Transponder has failed. Shall I place link request in queue?"

Loisa muttered, "No," as she heard the sounds of Michael's arrival, and she bit her lip in a guilty, startled shudder. *Why does the thought of facing him tonight make me feel so uncomfortable?* she wondered, wanting to blame Katerin but unable to shed an unpleasant doubt regarding that familiar, easy answer. Loisa walked to the living room and watched Michael remove his coat and drop it in the refresh drawer. "You are late again," said Loisa coldly. "Where have you been?"

"At my office, of course," replied Michael with surprised innocence.

I have seen that expression on his face a thousand times, thought Loisa; *I have heard him speak with just that inflection.* "I asked Network to prepare your favorite dinner."

Michael smiled faintly, and he spoke with all the gentleness that should have warmed her. "Tai fish is expensive, Loisa. You should not spoil me so."

"I enjoy spoiling you," answered Loisa brusquely. *He knows every detail of us,* thought Loisa with a strange, sad shock, *but he is not Michael.*

The certainty of her conclusion alarmed her, but a detachment of emotion enveloped her, enabling her to continue speaking and behaving calmly. Loisa sensed a justice in her inexplicable loss. She had always known that Katerin was right. Michael deserved a better mate than a halting, insecure woman of mediocre genetic stock and disappointing rank in Network's rating of her personal attributes. *There was always something wrong with his choice of me,* thought Loisa, *just as there has always been something darkly warped about that too-brilliant, too-beautiful sister of his.*

Loisa did not try to analyze the reasons for Michael's replacement with this person who used Michael's voice and wore Michael's face and mannerisms. She needed all her concentration to determine her proper course of action, because she needed to protect Marei. She told the false-Michael that she wanted to stay with Marei tonight, and he accepted her choice with only the usual, mild comment about Loisa's overly protective behavior. While the false-Michael slept, Loisa tucked Marei into the floater seat and left the apartment unit.

Recognizing several faces near the tram and unwilling to explain herself, Loisa bypassed the transportation terminal and began to walk into the dark night away from Chia-2's small circle of civilization. The old, abandoned housing complex loomed before her, and she directed her path toward it. The building's power had been disconnected, for the complex had suffered too often from earthquakes during early colonization, and extensive cannibalization had robbed the building of any operational systems. Even the lock devices had been removed in many places, and a door at the rear of the building opened with only the slightest of pressure from Loisa's hand. Loisa removed Marei from the floater and held the girl tightly. Seated in a corner of the empty room on the barely-resilient floor, Loisa fell asleep, clutching Marei against her.

Marei's crying awoke Loisa. Almost unconsciously, Loisa replaced the girl in the floater, which responded promptly with an extrusion of milk. "I must replenish the supply before we leave Chia-2," said Loisa to herself, and she began to calculate the items she would need to carry with her to her uncle's home. Loisa's uncle would not welcome her return after all her scornful words of parting, but he would accept her, for her standing in Network would improve his own status—with his peers, if not with Network. Few families on Fyorn could boast a daughter of a true technocrat; Marei would be a wonder to them.

A rumbling sound caused Loisa to pause in her calculations. "A private shuttle," she muttered, though she had never seen such a vehicle on Chia-2. Loisa smiled as she looked at Marei's contented face, but she left Marei and the floater, and she went to the door to investigate the sound. She could see nothing from the apartment's door except barren rocks and gray mists rising from a distant swamp. She checked the housing unit's number to be sure she could find Marei quickly on returning, and she closed the door behind her. She circled through the building's many inner courts in order to emerge from a unit that faced the city. Before she realized that only smoldering rubble remained of the outer wall of the city-side of the building, the men had seen her.

They must not hurt Marei, she thought and tried to run, but the nearest man caught her and threw her to the ground. "Where is your daughter?" he demanded, and Loisa bit his wrist. He cursed and dropped his energy pistol against a stone. He retrieved the weapon and used it to strike Loisa's face before she could kick or claw herself away from him.

The casing of his weapon is crushed, observed Loisa, finding sudden detachment from the pain.

"Where have you hidden your daughter?" he demanded of her again.

What is the range of an energy pistol's explosion? Loisa asked herself, trying to recall old lessons from a time before she gave up hope of excelling enough in the physical sciences to warrant a position at Harberg. *If the amplitude decreases with the square of the distance, and the maximum amplitude is optimized for near-field combat conditions, we must be within a few meters of the edge-of-range.*

Loisa jerked her hand free and scratched her captor's face. When he shielded his eyes, she ran. He caught her again quickly, but she had added three meters to the distance from the building that sheltered Marei. Loisa threw herself against the man's weapon, sending sharp pain along the tendons of her arm as she twisted enough to smash the weapon's crushed casing. She continued struggling to prevent the man from realizing the damaged state of his weapon, and she screamed to hide the warning sound of the weapon's imminent self-destruction from his fellows.

Only a few more moments, Loisa promised herself, and she tried not to think of the pain and damage that her captor inflicted on her. *Please, Michael, do not let them take Marei.* The weapon became white-hot, and it seared both Loisa and her captor. *I do love you, Michael.* The weapon exploded.

Loisa roused slowly, so astonished to discover herself alive at all that the fact of finding herself in her own home seemed only a lesser part of the miracle. She heard a faint whimper from the nursery module. "Marei," she crooned with both relief and renewed fear, for her daughter was safe and well, but her daughter should not have been here at all. "Marei, we must leave," murmured Loisa and began to gather everything that her uncle might lack and her daughter might need, "before the bad men find us again." She secured all the straps around Marei and the infant gear.

Loisa did not know why the men had come and tried to steal Marei from her. She did not know how they had found her. She did not know or care, because first she must ensure that they did not harm Marei. There would be time for questions later. "Network, identify the nearest neighbor who is presently at home."

"Alta Moir, apartment two, this complex."

"Alta is useless. Who is next, Network?"

"Tir Coring, apartment five of complex seven."

"Tir," muttered Loisa, reluctant to seek help but desperate now to save her daughter. "Yes, he is reasonably sensible. Network, inform Tir that I am coming to see him," ordered Loisa, as she guided Marei and the floater outside the coolly sterile apartment.

Loisa saw the two strangers before she had traveled halfway to complex seven. She stopped, torn between trying to return to her own home unit and trying to reach Tir before the strangers could catch her. She never doubted that the strangers were enemies. She pushed the floater seat before her into complex six, through the hall, and out the rear door into the alley. The door behind her snapped into the locked position, catching the torn edge of the floater's coverlet. Frantically, Loisa tried to disentangle the coverlet, abandoned the effort, and began to work at freeing Marei instead.

"I can help you."

Loisa paused in her furious fussing to stare at the young man who had appeared so suddenly beside her. *He is not the enemy,* remarked a calm voice in her head, and she did not quite recognize that the thought was not her own. "We have met," she said uncertainly, and her nervousness prevented her from disparaging the man's substandard height, the tousled state of his curling brown hair, or his anachronist's attire

"Yes. At a party. We discussed your husband's work."

"You told me that I was a very unpleasant woman."

The anachronist smiled somewhat sheepishly. "Yes. I have terrible manners."

The strangers—*the enemies*—emerged from the end of the alleyway. "I must go," whispered Loisa anxiously, and she tightened her hold on Marei, who had begun to cry. Loisa turned in place, but all of her possible paths seemed to hold enemies.

"Walk with me," said the anachronist.

"What?"

"I can take you through a portal."

"Where? Who are you?"

"I am a friend," said the anachronist, touching Marei lightly, "of her grandparents. I shall take her to them."

"No!" Loisa pulled Marei away from Quin, but she backed into a man with eager, reaching hands. "No," hissed Loisa, and she ran from everyone, though she dreaded that her route would end in a trap more certain than the fear she fled. All of the doors to the alley were locked, and at the alley's end stood only one narrow access, and its shadow filled with enemies. "Before, beside, behind," muttered Loisa helplessly. "Enemies wait everywhere."

"I can help you," urged the anachronist, "but you must help me, because your fear of me makes your pattern difficult for me to hold long without injuring you. Walk with me—only a few paces."

He is here again. How? Who is he? Marei's grandparents are all dead. Michael, what shall I do?

"Walk with me, Loisa," he pleaded.

The enemies converged. The alley filled with colorless snakes of death, fired from the weapons of the cruel and nameless foes. A burning, ethereal hand snatched at Loisa, dragging her into turmoil, disorder, unquiet, seething darkness, and a roaring cacophony of thunder and fire. Loisa clenched her jaw to hold the sickness inside of her, and she squeezed a screaming Marei tightly against her chest. *I thought I already died once today,* giggled Loisa. *I must have found my way to hell. Katerin cursed me effectively.*

"Loisa. Listen to me, please. I cannot hold your pattern, unless you listen to me."

Is Katerin here yet? That will be ultimate justice on us

both: condemned to eternity together alone, for Michael is too kind and good to join us here.

"Loisa, stop fighting me, please. I want to help you."

Why is Marei here? No! This is unfair! She cannot stay. She has not lived enough to sin. Take her, Michael. Save her, please. She is all the good that I can bequeath.

* * *

"Loisa!" shouted Quin, but he had to grab the child cast by the mother into emptiness, and he could not hold them both. The child had a simple, trusting pattern, easily contained and guided to a solid place, a known and safe place.

The warm, velvety rugs of Hamley manor felt soft and rich even through the flexible soles of Quin's Network shoes. The cribs were neat and cozily filled with pristine, downy quilts and pillows. Four of the cribs held infants. Quin tugged Marei's Network trappings from her small, unhappy form, and he swaddled her in soft Hamley cotton.

"What are you doing with that child, young man? This is nap time, and I will not have you bringing your mischief into the nursery!"

"Sorry, Nanny," mumbled Quin contritely, and he yielded Marei to Nanny's capable arms. The exhausted Marei whimpered very softly.

"What have you been doing to this child?" scolded Nanny, shaking her white-capped head at Quin. She peered at Marei's flushed face. "This is not one of mine. Whose child is this?"

"Mine, Nanny. Take care of her, please."

Nanny clucked at him, "Another tavern maid's infant for the proud Hamley line—you lordlings are worse than rabbits." She began to rock Marei gently, and her bright, black eyes fixed on Quin. "Were you one of my charges?"

"Yes, Nanny."

Nanny's aged face creased into a deep frown. "Quin-zaine?"

"Yes, Nanny."

Nanny stiffened, but Marei whimpered, and Nanny resumed the quiet rocking motion. "Where is your wife?" asked Nanny suspiciously.

"She died, Nanny. This is Marei. Take care of her please. She may be hungry. She has had a rather bad day."

"Tell me my business," muttered Nanny. "I tended you and your father both. You should not be in the nursery during nap time."

"Yes, Nanny. I am leaving." Quin cast one more look at Marei, as he tiptoed from the nursery under Nanny's baleful gaze.

"What else could I do with her?" Quin asked of no one in particular, but he sighed, feeling wretched and guilty. Michael Merel had been replaced by an imposter, and Loisa Merel was lost, and a Network infant cried in Hamley. He skipped down the nearest staircase, greeting his cousins carelessly, as if he had never left home, but his Power swirled furiously.

After arming himself with a sizable chunk of cheese, Quin wandered to the second floor landing of the back stair and clambered into the window seat, noting absently that the marble ledge used to seem more spacious. *Everything is certainly muddled,* mused Quin grimly. *The man who visited Katerin looked and sounded like Michael Merel, but the patterns were entirely different. So where is the real Michael Merel? Not on Chia-2 nor anywhere else I have visited, for I would be able to feel his pattern. Perhaps I should have continued to follow the imposter, but I could not follow both him and Loisa Merel, just as I could not follow both him and Katerin. I have probably made the wrong choices all the way.*

"Quite probably."

"My lady!" Quin scrambled to his feet, bumping his head in the process, before he realized that Lady Rhianna had spoken only to his Power, and she did not stand with him on a stair landing in Hamley.

"What are you doing in Hamley, Lord Quinzaine? Answer me truthfully!"

"I had to do something with the infant Merel quickly, and Nanny can certainly tend her better than anyone else I know."

"Where are the parents?"

Quin answered glumly, "Michael Merel has disappeared, and I lost Loisa Merel in transfer."

"You did recover her?" demanded Rhianna sharply.

"No. I told you: I lost her."

"Quinzaine," sighed Rhianna. Quin had a very strong image of her shaking her golden head incredulously. "Did you ever think of asking for assistance?"

"No," replied Quin hollowly, for the idea had not occurred to him. "That was stupid of me."

"Yes," agreed Rhianna crisply. She spread her Power, touching unseen layers of energies. "Mortal patterns are too faint to trace across infinities. She will be difficult to find now, if we can locate her at all."

"But you could have found me," said Quin unhappily, "if I had called to you before I lost her, and you could have saved her."

"Very probably."

"Did I let her die?"

"Did you let her die? Probably—by your refusal to make common sense a habit."

Lady Rhianna's anger hovers near the surface today, observed Quin uncomfortably. *But I deserve all the force of accusation that she can hurl at me.* "What do you want me to do, my lady?"

"Tell me what sort of trouble you have discovered— or made—so that I may give you help, if you deserve it, or help those whom you have jeopardized, if I find you culpable."

The Infortiare's words cut no more deeply than Quin's self-recriminations. His Power closed in upon him, sealing away all feelings, and he did not try to stop the process. He answered coldly, "A duplicate has replaced Michael Merel, and when I sought the real Michael, I found his wife's fear for him and for her daughter. I rescued the wife, reunited her with her daughter, rescued them both, lost the wife, and brought the daughter here."

"Then go back to Network, and return to me when you can report something intelligible. I do not want you lingering among your cousins until the temptation overwhelms you to tell them a more fantastic tale than theirs."

"Yes, my lady."

"Prior to this mismanaged rescue of the Merel infant, you had relatively little temptation to use your Power overtly in Network. Power is part of you, and you will use it, as do we all. You are a trained wizard, and you understand Ceallagh's laws, but I cannot overemphasize the severity of complications you will incur if you reveal your Power to those who do not understand it."

"Do mortals ever understand it?"

"They lack true understanding, but the mortals of our world recognize that Power does exist. Even an Ardasian such as my daughter-in-law, who never encountered Power until she met my son, knows enough of our world's histories to be able to accept the concept of Power. Network is ignorant; Jonathan and Elizabeth Terry are ignorant; their children are ignorant. Network's citizens may fear us or covet us or both, but Network will react forcefully to an awareness of our existence, and we must not yield that awareness prematurely. By Power, unbidden knowledge, and divine fate, we who guard our world's use of Power must guard our world as well. If you jeopardize this world, Lord Quinzaine, even in so honorable a cause as assisting the Merels, I shall not hesitate to scar you far more deeply than Lord Corvor's sword has ever done."

Her cold promise brought a tightness to Quin's chest, despite all his Power's protective denials. "I understand, my lady," replied Quin. He moistened his dry lips to add, "Shall I leave the Merel girl here?"

"For the moment."

"Should I return to Network now?"

"Yes!" Rhianna's exasperation shoved Quin like the hard blow of a strong warrior's hand, and he stumbled from the Harberg port on Daedalon, feeling as bruised as if the blow had indeed struck him physically.

CHAPTER 10

Serii

Loisa cringed as the fire strove to devour her, and the pain tore at her mind as much as at her body. *Marei is safe,* she told herself. *Marei is safe, and nothing else matters. I am dead already.*

"Not if you want to live," replied a man's rich voice that seemed to drive directly inside her battered head.

Loisa felt the unique gentleness of a great, disciplined strength engulf her. She struggled, not knowing her captor, but he did not seem to notice her feeble effort. Instead of fire, a blanket of warmth surrounded her, forcing her to relax into its comfortable embrace.

"Put her on the bed, Evaric," said a woman.

"She will require a lengthy healing," answered the man. "She mutters constantly about her daughter."

"Marei is safe," croaked Loisa, unable to recognize the softness that enveloped her and persuaded that it signified death.

"Hush, Loisa," said the woman softly. "Save your voice. I shall bring your daughter to you when you are well enough to tend her."

Loisa labored to open eyelids that seemed made of hard, cracked leather. The painful vision of shooting, colored lights, enhaloed a golden-haired wraith of a woman. Loisa tried to move her head, but she could not feel her own limbs.

The warmth touched Loisa's face with an extraordinary delicacy, and a healing Power flowed into her, a broken woman who did not understand. "Rest, Loisa. No one will hurt you here."

* * *

The illusion of ice-blue eyes held a daunting disapproval, and Keadric observed his wife with a piercing blade of Power, though she refused to meet him. "You were not very kind to Lord Quinzaine, my lady-wife, allowing him to believe that he caused the death of Loisa Merel."

Rhianna answered sharply, "He needs to recognize the consequences of his actions—and he will feel the remorse deeply, despite that shell of Power's detachment that he wears. She might indeed have died. The lesson is hard but necessary." She continued her work, writing another of the seemingly endless letters of justification to domain lords for the increased requisitioning of supplies for Ixaxis. She loathed the manipulative games of cajoling and threatening to ensure that Ixaxis' reputation retained the proper balance of acceptance, respect, and awe.

"Most lessons of Power are hard," retorted Kaedric crisply, "but I seem to recall a young lady of Tyntagel who bitterly resented some of the lessons I inflicted on her. I never hurt you willingly, Rhianna. You were punishing Quinzaine solely out of your annoyance with Howald and Amila."

His Power flared and stung her, and she dropped her quill, burned by his censure in her body as in her heart. The veil of calm that her Power wove dissolved at the blazing touch of Kaedric. In shame, Rhianna covered her face with her hands. "It is true," she whispered, and she began to shake from sobs that could not form as tears. "How much longer can we sustain this lonely battle, Kaedric? I berate Quinzaine. I snap at Ineuil. I am impatient with my allies and intolerant of those who will not or cannot help us. I am endlessly tired, but I may not rest." Her Power cried her pain.

As swiftly as he had flared to reprimand her, he yielded to her. His Power moved to comfort her, and she clung to him. "Beloved," he murmured, "you will not survive unless you tend yourself. Leave the guarding of our world to me for a time."

"Not even you can monitor the entirety by yourself."

"Our son will help."

"He is weary, too."

"Rhianna, if Network attacked us at this moment, you would be unable to defend even yourself. You are fighting Ixaxis—philosophically, if not in fact. You are holding the Queen's Council at bay by a very meager margin. You are fretting over Quinzaine and the Terrys. And you are spending the majority of your Power in thwarting the increasingly frequent Network probes. You cannot sustain this level of effort any longer."

"You gave your mortal life for our world," said Rhianna in wistful memory of a single, precious night that they had shared in flesh as well as Power. The old temptation, long denied by a stern sense of duty, rose in her to follow him and join him again completely.

"I had no other choice," retorted Kaedric in alarm, for he felt the indecision in her Power. "Rhianna, you must not think in such terms! What I did was self-preservation, for Horlach would have destroyed me otherwise."

"I feel so alone except with you, my Kaedric. How much longer can I endure?" His Power held her, but he formed an answer only for himself.

*   *   *

"Mistress Elizabeth," called the voice softly.

Beth stirred in her bed. The voice persisted. She reached for Jon, but though she sensed that he was beside her, she could not feel him.

"I do not intend to let you awaken him at the moment," announced the voice dryly, "for I prefer not to be analyzed as an unpleasant topological phenomenon."

A figure of a man, tall and excessively lean, loomed in front of Beth, though she could not recall his approach. He resembled Lord Evaric though in a darker, harsher guise. Beth bit her lip, and the blood tasted sweet. "Lord Venkarel," she whispered, but she could not hear her own voice. *Am I dreaming?* she wondered.

"I am Venkarel, and you are not dreaming—not entirely. I am modifying your dream pattern to fit my purpose. You did say that you wanted to meet me?" he asked with a cool, sardonic humor.

"Yes," she answered clearly, though her heart pounded with fear. *Lady Rhianna was right. He is terrifying.* Beth tried to halt the thoughts that Lord Venkarel apparently perceived so clearly, but she could not constrain her mind's doubts.

His blue-frost eyes seemed to reflect amusement. "I could lay the same accusation against you and your husband, considering the magnitude of unknowns you represent to us, but I prefer to dispense with pointless fears. My wife is reluctant to demand more of you than you have already given. I do not share her nobility either in birthright or in spirit."

"What is it you want?" asked Beth hesitantly.

"I want you to offer your help to my wife, and I do not want you to tell her that I prompted you. Your offer will mean much more to her if she considers it genuine and spontaneous on your part."

Beth's first, sharp fear of him ebbed at the tenderness of his request. "You are not nearly as heartless as your legends, are you?"

Kaedric's thin smile twisted. "My wife is also trying to protect you from unpleasant truths about your children's situation. I am less gentle than Rhianna, and I think you must understand the threat that confronts us jointly, for I expect you to fight this war with us."

"Tell me," whispered Beth, though she did not want to hear him

He continued relentlessly, "Your daughter is being tormented by your enemies, and Lord Quinzaine has not yet discovered a means of protecting her successfully, for he has not yet gained her trust. He cannot risk bringing her here, for she is most certainly monitored closely.

"Your son has disappeared, and an attempt was made to abduct his wife and daughter. Lord Quinzaine thwarted the latter effort, and because of emergency circumstances, Mistress Loisa and her child are now in Serii. A momentary relaxing of this world's defense was required in order to bring mortals here by wizard's manipulation of the Taormin's patterns. I am regrettably confident that your enemies have perceived the brief lapse. My wife has not yet recognized this most recent heightening of danger, because she is too exhausted at present to bear such news."

"Why do you tell me?" asked Beth, feeling empty and

bewildered—and angry against Caragen and Network and Marrach and everyone who had ever deceived her.

"You understand Power as well as any mortal I have encountered. You understand Network, and you understand your husband's unique skills. I tell you that neither you nor your children have any hope of a future without our help, and I think you are wise enough to believe me. I want you to advise my wife on how best to use the resources available to her." Kaedric finished with a softness that contradicted the terrible legends of him, "Rhianna needs all the support that she can obtain, and I cannot give her enough."

Beth could feel his Power pressing her back into sleep, for he had clearly stated all he meant to say. Beth tried to resist. "I want to see my granddaughter and my daughter-in-law." Power overcame her.

*   *   *

"You allowed Loisa Merel to escape with her child," observed Caragen with ominous softness, addressing the projected image of the commander of the bungled mission, "and you have no idea who arranged her rescue or where to find her. Do you consider yourself a professional, Citizen Tchakaa?"

Tchakaa opened his mouth to reply, but Caragen's angry gesture terminated the link and simultaneously assured the immediate execution of the mission commander. "Network, analyze the abduction of Loisa Merel."

"Insufficient data exist to explain disappearance."

"Have you extracted anything of value from Michael Merel yet?"

"The Terry name still fails to elicit any personal response. Acute protective instincts from prior conditioning remain intact, though they have blurred in focus to incorporate the wife and daughter as well as the sister. Tangible threat of danger to any of these three protected subjects should eliminate any remaining barriers."

"Ensure that he recognizes such danger. Manufacture an infant duplicate of his child."

"Acknowledged." The delicate tones of a programmed alert rang from Network's speakers. "Sensors have recorded a transient topological disturbance surrounding the anomalous space under current study."

"The space to which Marrach sent his message?" snapped Caragen, straightening in his chair.

"Yes."

"What was the nature of the disturbance?"

"The anomalous region registered briefly as stable."

"Did you identify the coordinates?" asked Caragen eagerly.

"No. The time of stability was insufficient for full analysis."

Caragen closed his fist and struck his desk in frustration. "When did the transient stability occur?"

"Analysis of sensor data required time lapse of 1.25 hours. Notification of analytical results was immediate."

Caragen's eyes narrowed. "Is there a correlation with the time of Loisa Merel's disappearance?"

"Events were simultaneous."

Caragen spread his fingers and let them curl around the empty air. He smiled with a cruel satisfaction. "Marrach's assets become careless, Network. They are feeling pressured."

* * *

"What does the old shark think he's doing? He doesn't need the recognition of a public speech, and he will pay a large fortune just for his personal security at the event."

"He's going into his dotage at last," mumbled a man in response.

Maryta grimaced at the console from which the two voices had emanated. "Network, terminate recital of surveillance recording."

"Acknowledged."

Caragen must love perusing these files for his staff's "private" gossip. Going into his dotage? I wish I could agree, thought Maryta grimly.

She had heard very similar opinions expressed among her fellow Councillors, though the Councillors spoke less directly than the intemperate junior members of Caragen's vast administrative staff. Among Network's politically cognizant minority, confidence in Caragen had suffered dramatically from the announcement of his planned public visit to Harberg. Maryta did not share in the common mistake of believing Caragen to be ignorant of the prevalent opinions.

No one would have questioned his decision before his split with Marrach, she mused. She fingered the gilt-edged vellum on which her own invitation to the Harberg function had been engraved. She recognized Caragen's intent in sending the formal invitation: The invitation constituted a command. Any conflicting plans would be canceled without hesitation, or Caragen would personally scrutinize the reasons for disobedience.

He is enacting one of his infamous, unexpected forays. Could he possibly have connected Rolf to me, despite all my care? No, I would already be dead, like Rolf. Caragen does nothing idly. He goes to Harberg because that is the present battleground in his war with Marrach; that is where the Terry girl lives as Katerin Merel.

"Network," asked Maryta carefully, "has Caragen yet specified the subject of his Harberg speech?"

"No."

"How many members of the Network Council has he invited?"

"All."

At least he has not selected me alone. He wants us all where he can watch us, and he wants to know that none of us will arrange for an accident to destroy the planet of Daedalon while he sojourns there. "Has he indicated whether he intends for his fellow Councillors to participate actively in the event?"

"No."

What else can I safely ask Network? When Caragen begins a foray, no one is safe. He is not going into his dotage. He is beginning another move of expansion.

Then why has Marrach left him? Or did Marrach decipher my intentions in sending Rolf, and kill Rolf simply to persuade me that the schism with Caragen was real? Marrach still refuses to communicate with me; he refuses even to allow me to establish the means.

Plots within plots: Who can hope to outmaneuver either Caragen or Marrach? I was mad even to consider Caragen as a declining caesar.

"Network," murmured Maryta pensively, "please request a communication with Council Governor Caragen. Inform him that my analysis team has produced some interesting new theories regarding topological anomalies."

That should attract your interest, Andrew Caragen. To Maryta's surprise, Network announced almost immediately, "Requested link is established."

"What do you want, Maryta?" growled Caragen, but he sounded remarkably cheerful.

Maryta smoothed her hair and gestured for Network to enact the video mode. "When you expand your empire," she said crisply, "be sure that you will have my support."

Caragen began to laugh. "You are so reliable, Maryta, especially to your own advantage."

"We work well together, Caragen. We understand each other."

"Marrach refused to negotiate with you, didn't he?" asked Caragen knowingly. Maryta did not notice that she had crumpled her invitation to Harberg in her nervous hands. "Don't worry, Maryta," chided Caragen with contempt. "You are still useful to me in your exalted position. You are quite correct. You and I do understand each other. I like to know the measure of my fellow Councillors; it mitigates distractions. You like to live well; I allow you that privilege."

"I am loyal to you, Caragen."

"Yes, Maryta. You are absolutely loyal, because my power is both absolute and secure."

* * *

It was morning, and Beth tied the draperies with silken cords to uncover the window. The sunlight poured across the bed. Jon winced, and he rolled away from the light.

Beth sat on the bed's edge, pulling her velvet robe loosely around her. "She needs our help, Jon," said Beth quietly. "She needs your help." Jon frowned, but he did not answer. "You have been working compulsively to correlate their wizardry with topological science. You must have reached some conclusions."

Jon muttered without opening his eyes, "My model is still imperfect. I reach inconsistencies in the derivations. Do you realize how much time it takes to derive every theorem by hand for every variation of my basic postulates?"

"Network is near to finding this world, Jon. If you can help these people use their Power more efficiently, use your controller more safely, or gain any extra defense against Network, you must act quickly. You cannot wait to perfect your model."

Jon stirred and pulled himself upright in the bed. He rubbed at his eyes; he hated mornings. "Lady Rhianna has said nothing about any new urgency."

"She does not know yet. Her husband told me."

"You were dreaming," grunted Jon.

Beth shook her head firmly. "He was very real, Jon. He was more strange and frightening—and concerned— than I would ever have imagined him." Her voiced trailed into silence.

Jon gripped her hand anxiously. "If he has harmed you, Beth," whispered Jon, "I shall turn his wizards' universe inside out."

"He did not harm me," protested Beth, and she smiled in an effort to reassure. "I do not suppose anyone could meet him without feeling shaken, because he is so entirely the Immortal wizard. I can understand why the people of this world equate him with the devil, considering their dreadful history of Sorcerer Kings."

"Why did he visit you?" asked Jon, still wary.

Beth answered thoughtfully, gazing sightlessly across the room, "I think he did not want you directing your analysis toward him rather than toward the issues of concern to him." She turned her blue eyes back toward her husband. "I am going to speak with Lady Rhianna, Jon. I shall tell her that you know how to adapt the Taormin to their purposes, so that other Ixaxins will be able to use it without such danger."

"I have no tools, even if I were certain of the modifications. I am not sure that the 'Taormin' still resembles my controller at all."

"Lord Quinzaine should be able to acquire the common tools for you, and you will have Rhianna's help in recognizing the Taormin's changes." Beth smiled pensively. "You will have Kaedric's help, as well, I think. I doubt that you could find more qualified assistants in all of Network. These people know the Taormin in the most intimate sense."

"I wish you would not spring these ideas on me before I am even awake."

"I know, Jon." Beth leaned across the bed and kissed him quickly. "If you were fully awake, you would probably argue with me for an hour, at least." She slid off the high, four-poster bed and disappeared into her dressing room.

Jon groaned and dropped back against the pillows. "I hate pushy project managers," he called to his wife.

Beth emerged wearing long green silk and ecru lace. "I think I shall see if Lady Rhianna is as agreeable as you this morning, dear husband."

Beth left Jon grumbling, and she descended the Tower stairs. A young serving woman was climbing toward her, but the young woman glimpsed Beth and turned back the way she had come. Beth sighed: None of the servants would approach her; they seemed to have categorized her as a wizardess, a breed that obviously incurred distrust among Serii's superstitious mortals. Rhianna had remarked that servants disliked the Infortiare's Tower and accepted even Rhianna's inevitable presence reluctantly.

Reaching the Tower's lowest floor, Beth opened the heavy, wooden door, and stepped into the garden. She looked behind her at the door she had exited. The illusion of a barred entry, sealed for countless years, could have compared favorably to the best Network hologram.

Even before Rhianna had authorized Beth's freedom of the upper gardens, Beth had realized that the Infortiare walked there nearly every morning. Beth had seen Rhianna from the window, the delicate figure garbed as a servant instead of as Ixaxin liege, climbing the path that led eventually to the top of the Mountain of Tul.

Beth found Rhianna leaning against the bole of a strong and ancient tree, her expression almost ethereal with a rare peace. "Sometimes," murmured Rhianna, "I can almost remember the old closeness to the trees. I can almost feel the oaks of Tyntagel beside me."

"Your father is the liege of Tyntagel?" asked Beth, though she knew the answer.

"Yes. He is Immortal, like me, though he still refuses to acknowledge his Power. My poor brother, Balev, will have a long wait to inherit the domain. Dayn, as younger son, has had the better bargain in this case, since Uncle Dhavod retired as court representative years ago."

"The Council still works against you?"

"Indirectly," admitted Rhianna with a wry smile. "They are expert at many individually innocuous ploys by which to exercise their disapproval. They interfere by creating obstacles of petty distractions or irrelevant issues in need of my personal attention." She moved away from the tree, though her hand lingered against its coarse bark. "I do not know what I shall do when Ineuil actually resigns as Adjutant. He is my only constant ally, for even Her Majesty has her moments of doubt about me, and my Ixaxin subjects are worse than the Council. We wizards have never cooperated well."

"Jon can enable your people to use the Taormin, if you can provide him the means to modify it. You still have some of his tools, and Lord Quinzaine should be able to obtain others that Jon specifies. Jon will need to assess the Taormin. Can your Power provide him the shielding to touch it without harm, even while it remains active?"

"Yes," replied Rhianna. Her gray eyes lost their dreamy mist of musing and became brightly attentive. "Evaric could transport your husband to D'hai with little effort, for the journey is insignificant by the Taormin's paths, but I understood that your husband required more time."

"We have no more time, Rhianna. I want to see my grandchild and my daughter-in-law. Will you take me to them?"

"Kaedric spoke to you," said Rhianna softly.

"Yes."

"I warned you that he would do as he pleases." Rhianna brushed bits of leaf and bark from her hands. "I shall have your granddaughter brought here from the Hamley nursery. Your daughter-in-law is unconscious still, but you may certainly see her."

"Thank you."

"I would have told you of them myself, but the sun is barely risen. I thought the hour was excessively early."

"My husband would agree with you," said Beth with a laugh, composed largely of anticipation's joy. "He loathes mornings."

Rhianna nodded in understanding, but her smile had a sardonic twist. "Did Kaedric command you to volunteer your husband's help?"

"He said you required help and would not ask for it," replied Beth, meeting Rhianna's level gaze. "But like him, I do as I deem best, not as I am commanded. He was right to come to me. I want to help you, Rhianna, if you will let me. I have feared to offer, because you seem so invincible. I did not think you needed me."

"My friend," asked Rhianna wryly, "how could I ask more help of you, whom I deceived for so long?"

"Our enemy is the same, Rhianna."

"Yes," acknowledged Rhianna, touching the tree once more with gentle care. "Our enemy and our world are the same."

CHAPTER 11

Network and Serii

"What now?" Quin asked himself, waking slowly from a dream that had tangled Katerin Merel with Laurett, Lady Rhianna with Luki, and the vast incomprehensible entity that was Network with the fierce and fearsome Lord Venkarel. Somewhere at the core of the dream, Quin had struggled, single-handed and Powerless, with a vulpas that had berated him for inattentiveness to his lessons in intelligence science.

"Is that a request for information?" inquired Network politely.

Quin groaned and threw a pillow at the wall. "No, you intrusive beast!" He devoted several moments to staring at his toes, which peered from beneath the feather-light coverlet. "You ought to be cold," he informed his toes sternly, though he was careful to keep his mutterings at a whisper below the level he had set for Network detection, "or too warm or too something. But the temperature of the room is perfect, and the temperature of the bed is perfect, and Network ensures that everything is perfect, except that nothing here is really that different from Ixaxis, Tulea, or Lambde. A few people make the rules, and everyone else obeys or suffers the consequences. Why did I have to leave Hamley?"

In a louder voice, he asked, "Network, where is Katerin Merel?"

"Attending her social module gathering at the home of Professor Cindal Cavli."

At least Katerin Merel has not vanished like her brother.
Quin scrambled reluctantly from his comfortable bed.

"You require more sleep, Quin."

"Yes, Mother Network," replied Quin mockingly. He
tugged a clean shirt over his head and prepared to go in
search of Katerin Merel. He did not quite trust Network's reassurances.

*   *   *

"Have you heard the name of the Convocation
speaker?" asked Viki. She continued with relish, "According to at least three sources, Council Governor Caragen
himself will honor us."

Chand laughed in light derision, "His security staff
have scarcely allowed him to appear in public since the
assassination attempt on Vordaire."

Parve muttered, "Consortium bastards," and continued reading his news journal.

"The perpetrators were never discovered, Parve,"
countered Mavel. "You should take your own frequent
advice and avoid making unsupported accusations."

"Good advice for all of you," murmured Katerin to
herself, "on many subjects." In the ensuing uneasy
silence, Werol reached for his game piece. Katerin
watched his large hands engulf the tiny, sad-faced figure,
and revulsion for the entire, manipulative process of the
game filled her.

"Are you feeling ill again, Katerin?" asked Viki
kindly. "You look pale."

"I feel fine," replied Katerin and forced a smile,
because she would not allow herself to retreat again. She
made all the right replies and concocted witty comments,
and she endured the evening, aching for it to end.

As soon as Chand made a murmur about the lateness
of the hour, Katerin excused herself, thanking Cindal
effusively in an effort to displace less pleasant memories.
Cindal's response was as warm as ever; a mimovue of
Radge might never have caused the terrible scene that
made Cindal seem like a stranger now, but Katerin was
not even sure that the incident with Cindal had occurred.
Katerin tried not to blame Cindal for an event that had
ceased to seem real.

Katerin emerged into the night, shivering from the

release of hours of deception. She began to walk; as she passed the entry alcove next to Cindal's, she glimpsed a man standing in the shadow. She looked again, and the man was gone, but she imagined that she could still see him. She shifted her destination to her lab, for it stood closer, and she hurried her pace.

The building sat in darkness until she entered, and the lights appeared for her and faded in her wake. When she reached her lab, she nearly laughed at herself for letting her fears dominate her. *The walk home will be that much longer now, and I shall be that much more tired tomorrow. I shall be that much more susceptible to the hobgoblins of my imagination.* "Good evening, Laurett," murmured Katerin.

"Good evening, Katerin. You are here very late tonight."

"Yes, Laurett. I was at Cindal's. I started to walk home, and I thought someone was following me, so I stopped here."

"Have you notified Network security?"

"No, Laurett." *Stress is taking its toll and robbing me of strength for the simplest tasks.* "I am tired of the silent accusations of paranoid hysteria. Security would find no one, just as Network has found no evidence to support any of my other reports."

"They only want you to tell the truth, Katerin."

"The truth?" asked Katerin tonelessly.

"Where is your father, Katerin?"

No, this cannot be real. Laurett cannot be violated as well. Tautly, Katerin demanded, "Has Quin altered your programming, Laurett?"

Laurett replied in a woman's gentle, frightened voice, "Log entry two hundred and thirty-eight—I have seen something of power and of evil in my life, if only in my remote study of the GRC Immortals, and I do not doubt the sincerity of this Marrach's threats. He speaks for a larger voice, which may embody Network itself, and I am helpless against the power of such an enemy. Is it true that Jon will not return? I cannot bear to believe it. What a bitter decision Marrach forces on me, though I doubt that he would see it so; he seems to lack a consciousness of caring. Entrust my children to him, or wait for death to claim us all? I wonder what course he would choose if he were I, but I suppose that such a man would never be in my position. A man who chooses a life of such intricate subterfuge as Rabh Marrach's must either accept isolation or go mad of it."

A rush of air from the hall accompanied the silent opening of the laboratory door. The mesmerizing voice stopped. *My mother's voice,* thought Katerin: *the voice of a woman long dead.* She waited for another voice, the voice of Rabh Marrach, or she waited for death to fall upon her. She did not turn to seek the face of her executioner; she did not want to see him; she wanted only for the pain to end.

"Please tell me that you are not working this late just to concoct a particularly difficult test for me tomorrow."

"Quin," said Katerin hollowly. *Why is he here at this unlikely hour?* She began to laugh, and she could not seem to stop. "I seem to have caught your habit of spontaneous laughter without cause." She looked at him and saw the unaccustomed frown on the finely sculpted face, so reminiscent of the inbred nobility from a long-unfashionable era. *Did he wear another face at another time?*

"What has happened, Professor?" asked Quin at last. *Who else could have accessed my computer, my algorithm?* "Quin," began Katerin, forcing herself carefully to sound detached and calm, "how can I trust you?" *I think I am maintaining my poise quite well, considering that I feel so much inclined either to scream or to burst into hysterical tears.*

Quin did not reply, and Katerin felt her composure sliding from her. *Of all people before whom to crumble into emotionalism,* she scolded herself, *Quin is probably the worst possible choice. If he sympathizes, I shall be terrified; if he does not sympathize, I shall be crushed.*

I shall not lose control, Katerin insisted to herself, *I shall not think of blood-red roses, old sketches, nor the log of a woman long dead. I shall not think of yesterday, Michael, or fear. Focus on the moment; focus on visible details like the slight, ocher streak across the table, the blue-gray reflection of the light on the dark surface of the console, the individual hues of the woven threads of Quin's heathery coat.*

"Laurett has made some unusual comments," said Katerin quietly. *Do not think of a recited log that tugs at old, uncertain memories. Do not think of the lies, which rise either from Network or from your own mind.*

"What sort of comments?" asked Quin.

I never noticed before that peculiar habit Quin has of alternately clenching and rubbing his left hand, almost as if it pained him. He seems so otherwise careless and carefree; the nervous gesture does not suit him. It is the mannerism of a poseur, calculating his own concerns, which probably have little bearing on his words. How did I fail to see until now that he moves like a man of hidden purpose?

She drove her fingernails into her hands to control her hysterical terror, but she snapped, "Have you tired of your deceitful little game?"

"What game?" asked Quin with agonizing care.

"The ultimate game: life, death, and madness. Do you believe in anything, Quin Hamley, or do you simply earn your pay? I believed in something once; I have forgotten how to believe." *He cannot be Marrach; I would have recognized him before now; I have worked too closely with him; I would have sensed that dreadful chill of cruelty. He is Quin who makes me laugh, Quin who makes me feel that I am nearly whole when I am with him.*

Quin poked idly at a chair. "I think you have forgotten that you do believe."

He sounds so calm, so innocent and concerned for me. "Believe in what? Believe in the worthiness of the people I meet, the deceivers I call friends, the people whose empty souls are lined with shields of indifference?"

His expression became pained, as if he shared her bitter vision in all its cruelty. He spoke with a deep, persuasive power very different from his usual lightness: "You believe in an absolute good and a just purpose beyond the transitory evidence of the world."

Her fear replied, "The deceiver becomes religious! Quin Hamley, who thinks and communicates intelligently only in the language of the machine that nurtures us, unveils himself as a philosopher." *And perhaps as other things, less savory. What do I believe? Am I accusing Quin of deceit, or am I deceiving myself in accusation?*

"I am merely repeating the philosophy that you instilled in Laurett."

"Are you trying to emulate my algorithm, Quin? Are

you trying to analyze me from it?" The bright, taut laughter spilled from her with a harsh, cold taint.

"You designed the algorithm to simulate a wise adviser. I assume that you defined wisdom according to your own beliefs and preferences."

"I used conventional definitions and a great deal of research into 'wise figures' of history. Do you think I am so conceited as to pattern a guide for humanity after myself?" snapped Katerin. *How shall I continue, having lost Michael, having lost Cindal, having lost Quin? Do not ask how. . . . Continue, for you have no choice.*

"I only supposed that an effort of this magnitude must reflect to some extent the judgment of its creator— although I must confess that I consider your premise of relying on an artificial friend misguided. Still, if your values were as equivocal as some people have suggested to me, you would not have created the entity that I call Laurett. I have developed some respect for this Laurett, and I should like to attribute the worth to you."

"How you honor me!" drawled Katerin acidly. *He humors me; he is decidedly more clever than he pretends. Is he pretending? Yes, he is an anachronist who pretends chronically to protect himself from feeling. Perhaps he pretends for other reasons. Who else could have compromised Laurett? He is clever, but I am the specialist in behavior modification.* "You have judged me by my work and found me acceptable. I shall shout it in the streets: My research assistant, who has never developed suffi- cient emotional maturity to risk a personal relationship, has declared that I am potentially acceptable to him as a human being." She locked furious eyes on his down- turned head. "Do you know that I had actually begun to trust you? I even declined an opportunity to replace you in the very coveted position as my assistant, after you performed so awkwardly in front of Parve."

"Is the position coveted," murmured Quin, "as much as the lady with whom the position is associated?"

"Why do you suppose Network selected you as my assistant?" she asked dryly. *Injure his pride; if he is actu- ally the enemy, he will be too well trained to react appropriately.*

"You think Network assigned me because I presented

no threat to you?" asked Quin, smiling wryly, but his gray eyes held no humor.

"Did you alter my personal log file on Laurett, Quin?" demanded Katerin, the force of too many accumulated fears drawn into the question and thrown at him in a fury.

Quin's smile ebbed to a dim echo. "No, I did not alter your personal logs, nor have I read your entries. I presume that Network altered them."

"Do not lie to me so stupidly. Laurett is impenetrable to Network scans."

"Laurett is a Network node. All of the university computers are Network nodes. I assumed that you knew."

Is this another lie, or is this the answer? Is Network my enemy? Why do I want to believe in this irritating, inconsistent, unreasonably persuasive anachronist? Why am I having this improbable conversation with him in the middle of the night? "Can you prove your hypothesis?"

"Possibly," answered Quin.

"You dare to make such an outrageous claim without proof?"

"If Laurett recites your most recent Network log to you, will you consider my evidence sufficient?"

"Recite it, Laurett," ordered Katerin coldly. *And let me decide how you accessed it.*

Quin closed his eyes, and his face grew very blank. Laurett's voice recited dutifully, " 'Dead roses and smeared sketches: why do they burrow into my heart until I feel them lodged like stubborn thorns? Who is tormenting me? Or is it madness? Could I question my sanity if I were insane?' " Laurett stopped abruptly. Katerin stared sightlessly, her color as drained and wan as her emotions.

"You took it from Network and transferred it to Laurett," she remarked with the terrible calm of despair.

"No! I gave the order to Laurett, but I did not transfer the file myself. Laurett has full access to Network, although she denies it, except to me."

"I suppose you share a psychic bonding with computers," said Katerin dryly, recalling Viki's continuing argument with Werol.

Quin replied uncomfortably, "I have some abilities that you would probably consider unusual."

"You have devoted too much time to your anachronists' fairy stories," retorted Katerin. *I have succeeded in annoying him. Is that evidence of his innocence? Or simply confirmation of his humanity?*

"I should think you would be more interested in confirming your own sanity than in doubting mine," answered Quin with the slight sharpness of frustration. "Your paranoia is justified; your life is being monitored. What more do you want me to tell you, Professor Merel?"

"Everything. Nothing." *I cannot bear more doubts.* She laughed bitterly. "Do you know what the Calongi consider the most vital element in achieving contentment?"

"No," he answered, his surge of temper yielding to puzzlement.

"Purpose," answered Katerin, and she turned her face from him, trying to hide her tears. "That is all I really seek to achieve with my algorithms: purpose for myself, despite the sepulcher that constitutes my heart."

Katerin did not see the pain that contracted Quin's face. He became uncannily still. "Someone once prescribed purpose as something I needed badly," said Quin. "The adviser was your computer's namesake."

"She must have been a wise woman," replied Katerin with a cynical lilt. .

"Yes. I miss her." Quin touched the computer console thoughtfully. "She died."

"I'm sorry," said Katerin, feeling the words genuinely, despite the unreal circumstances that seemed to enfold the conversation. She rubbed the tears from her eyes. "Was she a close friend?"

"She was my wife," said Quin softly.

A flicker of shock ran through Katerin, momentarily displacing her private fear and desolation. She looked searchingly at Quin. "You were married?" she demanded incredulously, for the idea upset all of her analyses of him.

"Yes.". Then he added, "Despite my 'social immaturity,' I actually have managed one or two personal relationships in my life. Have you done as well?"

"No," answered Katerin hollowly, "but you understand about me, don't you? You are a part of the conditioning team, aren't you?"

"No! I wish I did understand you."

"Have you invaded my apartment as well as my personal logs?" she demanded fiercely.

"Certainly not," protested Quin, his face becoming red. "I may be a poor example of a gentleman in many respects, but I do uphold some standards." Quin approached Katerin, his face abnormally earnest, and Katerin retreated from him nervously. Quin stopped and finished awkwardly, "My wise Laurett also said that she began all her truest friendships either by killing or crying."

Katerin rubbed impatiently at her cheeks. Quin extended his hand rather helplessly toward Katerin, and she shrank from him. "Please, do not touch me, Quin," said Katerin tightly, cold panic at his proximity overriding all other fears.

Quin's expression became remote. He shook his head, took a deep breath, and said nervously, "I do not think of myself as exceptionally frightening, Professor. I do not know what you perceive when I come near you, but it is not any violent intent within me. If I have injured you in any way, it is simply because I lack the sense to recognize my bad behavior. I could not hurt you, Katerin Merel, without hurting myself tenfold."

His earnest kindness made the terror worse, for it made her ache to trust him. "Please, Quin," she whispered, "stop tormenting me." She tried to run from him, but he seemed to be restraining her, though he stood across the room. A burning haze of uncertainty clouded her fear and lessened it.

She heard Quin's rapid, foolish chatter: "If you try to take seriously anything I say or do, then you will end up either mad with frustration or determined to see me perish slowly from the horrible bites of a hundred thousand fleas. My cousin, Ethla, conceived of that poetic form of torture. Fortunately, I left home before she tried to implement it. She was still trying to collect fleas in an old tin box, and they kept escaping into her bedroom, which kept the chambermaids frantic."

"The chambermaids?" echoed Katerin. *I cannot think while he babbles!* she shouted in her mind, but the tight, cold shroud of terror seemed to retreat before a relentless wave of fire.

"Female servants who tend the bedchambers. Have I misused the word?"

"The word is fine for a lesson in cultural history. But of course, you are an anachronist with a limited interest in truth."

"I warned you not to take me too seriously," commented Quin with absolute solemnity in his eyes.

"So you did," sighed Katerin. She rubbed her fingers across her forehead, trying to ease the aching tightness that had emerged in the wake of panic. "Are you spouting all this nonsense to keep me off balance, Quin? Are you waging a psychological war against me, or are you actually this bewildering by nature?"

"A bit of both, I suppose," answered Quin, the grin reappearing in a hesitant form.

She recognized a strangeness in the calm that filled her, but she accepted it gratefully. "What can I believe, Quin Hamley? No one but you could have altered my files on Laurett. No one but you has entered my life since the harrowing began."

Quin turned from Katerin and walked to the computer console. He moved his left hand above the console, not quite reaching into the control field, where his strong, sweeping gesture would have inspired a puzzled response from Laurett. "If someone entered your apartment uninvited," he said slowly, "I truly know nothing about it, and I know nothing about any tampering with our personal logs. If it would help, I could try to track the access patterns and learn who has been disrupting your life. When do you think the attacks began?"

"At the beginning of this term." Katerin tried to observe Quin impartially. She tried to think clearly through her muddle of fatigue and strain. *What has he told me? Many absurdities. How much does he expect me to believe? Very little, apparently, if his final disclaimer can be credited. How much do I believe? I feel too tired and defeated to decide.*

"And you have told no one of your troubles in all that time? You must have very preoccupied friends, if they never noticed enough to ask you what was wrong."

He displays signs of distress; he feels conflict. If he has worked against me, perhaps he has not considered the consequences of his actions. Perhaps he pities me. "I told

Cindal. I reported the incidents to Network, and I told Laurett." *His eyes react; he knows.* "How often did you answer me in the guise of my wonder-program?"

"Only once."

His embarrassment increases. "You informed me that I was lonely."

"Laurett is much too diplomatic to make such a blunt and irrelevant observation, Professor Merel."

"How did you subvert Network to obtain this assistant-ship, Quin?" *He is startled.*

"Subvert Network? You give me too much credit."

"No. I have not given you enough credit until now; I have not been thinking very clearly of late. I knew you were not qualified for this post in any ordinary sense, but I did not stop to correlate your unusual gifts for computer interactions with your assignment to me. How did you do it?"

Quin answered reluctantly, "It was fairly easy actually. Of course, I could never have lasted past your protest of the first day, if you had not injured your credibility by rejecting so many assistants before me."

"How fortunate for you."

"Yes, I have always tended to be lucky."

He watches me closely, waiting to see how much I know, how much I guess. He volunteers nothing. "Tell me who is sabotaging my life, Quin, and tell me the truth about your 'rapport' with computers, and I may begin to trust you again. I want to trust you, Quin."

I have puzzled him and made him uneasy. "I may compound your problems if I comply with your request," he answered slowly. "You do not realize what you are asking of me."

Let him think I nearly trust him now. "How much time do you need?"

"Perhaps a day. Perhaps more. I never tried before to resolve individual energy strands within the pattern of Network. I have only blundered rather aimlessly through it, observing odd bits and pieces."

Does he intend that I understand him? No, he is thinking aloud. What does he mean? Quin stared at his toes, encased in comfortable Network shoes, peculiarly at odds with his anachronistic frippery. *I should have observed*

*the shoes before now; no true anachronist wears syn-
thetics.*

"Katerin Merel, I want very much to help you," said
Quin soberly.

"Then give me a name and the truth." *And give me
time to think.*

"I need to see someone first."

"Who?" *Marrach?*

"No one you know," answered Quin with a pained
smile. "Will you be all right here? I could walk you
home."

"No," countered Katerin with a quick, nervous laugh.
Can he be so innocent as to think I trust him that far? "I
have work to complete."

"I could be gone for several days," said Quin slowly,
and he looked so genuinely worried that Katerin gave
mental tribute to his acting skills. "The time patterns can
behave a little oddly where I am going."

"Fine." *Time patterns?* "I shall see you when you have
the answers for me." *Just leave me now, please!*

"All right, Professor," sighed Quin. "I shall leave."

She gave Quin time enough to depart from the building, before she, also, escaped the lab. She walked rapidly
to the university's faculty housing, and she turned into
the alley that led to the back of her own apartment complex. The rear door did not respond to her request.
"Wonderful," mumbled Katerin to herself, as she circled
to the front, entered the building and let the lift carry
her to her floor.

She sank into the lounging chair in her living room.
She surveyed the room that had once seemed a tiny,
precious, snug retreat, and the room felt stifling and
oppressive. "You have transformed even my own home
into a trap!" she muttered at the walls.

"Do you require something?" asked Network solicitously.

"Privacy," she whispered, and she crumpled into the
engulfing chair. Despair had exhausted itself, leaving
numbness.

Katerin lay motionless and unthinking for an hour or
more, until sleep enfolded her with its gentle anesthetic.
Network dimmed the lights for her, and the chair
extended to the limits of its design, so as to comfort

her. Health sensors monitored her automatically, so that Network might inform her of any irregularity in heart or lung that might require attention, and somewhere a note regarding extreme duress registered beside her name.

Katerin awoke abruptly, her heart pounding. She did not try to recall the dream, for even the shadow of it made her shudder. "Lights, please," she murmured, and the room brightened. She scanned it to reassure herself of her solitude. "What time is it?"

"Seven minutes past midnight."

"Network, please access the university program known as 'Laurett.'"

"State code number, please."

"No code number has been established," she said softly, anticipating Network's response but wondering if anything she believed could still be trusted.

"The referenced university program resides on a secure system, which is inaccessible to me."

"Access the records on Harberg University student, Quin Hamley. His university identification code resides in my student folder, along with my authority code to read his official file. Report any entries in the 'special comments, section." Katerin added with a grimace, "Exclude references to extremes in anachronistic pretensions. I have already observed his eccentricities in that regard."

Network replied evenly, "Entry 1: 'Results of applicant's preliminary tests indicate extraordinary intelligence, but the level of measured education is subnormal. Only in mathematical comprehension does the applicant's education meet acceptable admission standards. The exceptional intelligence scores warrant acceptance of applicant on probationary basis.'

"Entry 2: 'Quin Hamley displays a cultural ignorance inconsistent with his background. We recommend that he be tested by the Mansa-Consortium method for alien species evaluation.'"

"Was the testing ever performed?" asked Katerin.

"Tests were scheduled, but the subject failed to appear, and no rescheduling has been arranged."

"The circumstances might be more suspicious if they were not so typical of Quin's erratic attitude toward authority," sighed Katerin. "Continue, please."

"Entry 3: 'Quin Hamley is considerably older than he claims, and I know all about his Network records.' "

"Who submitted the third entry?"

"Selia Gianni, Professor of Music."

"Explain her connection to the subject, please."

"The subject approached her with questions regarding the use and origin of various musical instruments in the museum collection."

Selia dear, you delve badly outside your field of expertise, but I respect your doubts about this one. "Continue, please."

"Entry 4: 'The applicant's general psyche testing suggests an excellent grasp of abstract concepts but little discipline for structured studies. Quin Hamley has an unusual behavioral profile: often unpredictable; capable and remarkably intuitive when he chooses to cooperate, quite intractable at other times. He displays genuine indifference to Network authority, rules, or established customs. Despite his apparent immunity to standard conditioning, he is not sociopathic; he does have a moral code, but it is not founded on any recognized cultural standard. He would make an excellent research subject. He may be a difficult student.' "

"Did this analysis result from Quin Hamley's psychological testing on application for admission?"

"Yes."

Parve failed to mention this aspect of my "highly intelligent" assistant's records; "difficult" does not comprise a very positive assessment on which to base admission to Harberg. I ought to have read these files earlier. "Continue, please."

"Entry 5: 'If Quin Hamley's parents employed standard genetic planning, the associated records could prove highly insightful. One wonders what traits the parents sought to promote. The result is unorthodox but not without charm.' "

Quin does have a magical talent for holding one's confidence, despite his obvious transgressions. Even now, I have trouble categorizing him as Marrach's creature. "Who authored the fifth entry?"

"Professor L. J. Weng, First-Term-Student Adviser."

"Did Professor Weng recommend any particular profession for Quin Hamley?"

"No suitable profession was identified. An unofficial addendum suggests that Quin Hamley might serve as ambassador to the Consortium: 'Calongi already consider Network citizens to be irrational primitives. Let them try to categorize Quin Hamley, while we observe how far the Calongi peace can be provoked.' "

"Quin's peculiar humor is infectious," remarked Katerin. "Continue, please."

"No further entries exist."

"What is Quin's planet of origin?"

"Network-3."

Katerin shivered. The chill of undefined horror had lost much of its force over years of rational denial, but a cold, dry taste, like death, lingered unpalatably around the name of Network-3. "Is there any record of how he escaped the closure?"

"An illness confined him on Network-2."

"Is anything recorded about his family?"

"Parents: Jiar Hamley and Aliria Viste, both of Network-3, both deceased. Siblings: many."

"Quin has been facetious again." *And what have I learned of value? Nothing, except that he is also an orphan. Is he haunted by his loss—like me?*

In the ensuing silence, Katerin heard the hushed raggedness of her own breathing and felt the stifling emptiness of the room. *I always used to savor the security and luxury of a Network-monitored, Network-maintained, and Network-controlled apartment. I remember my father's peculiar insistence on choosing an obsolete, independent unit. I remember my mother's attachment to that silly little dog that must have cost more than a month's lease.*

Sitting in the empty cocoon of her apartment, Katerin nearly smiled (mocking herself) on realizing an envy for those who could find comfort in the affection of such small, warm, furred creatures that so many pre-Expansion humans had considered essential to a normal life. *To me, they are lumps of blood and limp fur in my brother's hands; to me, they represent only a painful reminder of mortality.* Katerin did not even notice that the memories had resurged from long oblivion, touched very briefly and very tentatively by a major Power that had been unable to endure her fear.

CHAPTER 12

Network and Serii

Quin paced impatiently, waiting for the crowd around the programmable transfer port to diminish. He had devised his plan in the comfort of his Network room, where the idea had seemed obvious and inevitable to him. He had chosen to facilitate transfer by any means that Network could offer, for he wanted his Power to remain as fresh and strong as possible, but these delays were making him nervous. When he finally entered the transfer port, he nearly changed his intended destination to Tulea and the Infortiare's Tower.

"No good, old boy," he told himself sternly. "You already made this decision once." Quin voiced the Network coordinates of Daedalon's smaller port complex, but he twisted the pattern and redirected his journey as soon as he had passed through the light-distorting curtain and entered the port itself.

The freshness of the air, the brilliance of the sky, the soft slap of the river against the pilings reminded Quin vaguely of Ixaxis: a softer, warmer, humbler version. The stone-and-shingle house nearly blended with the hills, and the pale blue and yellow blossoms seemed to pursue their own intentions rather than any gardener's whim. The man hewing a heavy log raised his head briefly when Quin approached, but the man did not speak until he had reduced the log to kindling. "Good day to you, traveler," he remarked amiably, as he washed his hands in a bucket of fresh water and dried them on a finely woven towel.

"Good day," replied Quin in the same Network Basic. He hesitated to continue, uncertain now that he had read the patterns correctly.

"I am Suleifas, Healer of Innisbeck. Were you seeking me?"

How can this quiet, pensive Healer be the cruel haunt in Katerin Merel's mind? wondered Quin in puzzlement. "My name is Quin. I am looking for a man called Marrach."

The mild expression on the Healer's strong face became tight and calculating. "Did Caragen send you here?"

"No," protested Quin instantly. "I have never met the man."

"You did not come here by ship," said the Healer slowly, "and there are no active transfer ports on this planet." To Quin's intense fascination, a wreath of dancing light gathered around the Healer's head. "A kitten, chalk and swords and firelight," muttered the Healer, and he suddenly laughed in an outpouring of astonishment and mirth. "You are one of Jonathan Terry's mad Immortals. You came from Network-3."

He has Power, concluded Quin with some alarm. *No. He has something, but it is not the Power I recognize. Lords, this is all I need: more complications.* The effort of trying to sort the energies of the swarming light-beings was making Quin dizzy, so he returned his concentration to the Healer. "You are Marrach."

Marrach sighed. "That name, among others, is mine. As Marrach, I would ask you many questions, which you would evade. As Suleifas, I am bidden to ask you only one question: What do you seek from me?"

Tell him the truth, whispered a voice in Quin's head, and he did not know if the speaker was his own Power, Lord Venkarel, Lady Rhianna, or another, but the compulsion to comply was strong. "I want to help Katerin Merel, and I think you know how I may free her of the nightmare in which she lives. Someone is tormenting her. I believe the problems began with the message you sent to her parents."

"The message that brought you to her?"

"Indirectly, yes."

"I wish I were surprised." The Healer closed his eyes briefly, as if recalling a very old hurt. "It was I who conditioned her to fear. I stole all peace and truth from her and from her brother." His smile twisted. "They had no chance against me, for I knew my profession exceedingly well. I did not usually ply my trade against children, but the circumstances were exceptional."

"You are not the same man, are you?" murmured Quin, for his Power could feel no cruelty in the Healer at all. The lack was strange, for Quin had never met anyone who seemed so devoid of pockets of darkness and bitterness.

"No," replied Marrach quietly. "The Mirlai healed me." He smiled at Quin's questioning look. "The Mirlai are a symbiotic race of energy beings. They Chose me, and they remade me. They filled the darkness in me with light."

"I can sense them," said Quin with a frown of concentration.

"Can you? You are rare, but your ancestors had rare gifts as well. That was Elizabeth Terry's thesis premise." Marrach seemed to stare into memory, but Quin felt him probing Network. "She maintained that the Immortals could recognize and manipulate energy as easily as a 'mortal' moves a pebble or a twig."

"She was correct," answered Quin almost absently. The concept of distrust seemed to have become irrelevant, for a dance of golden light did not allow it to exist. "Jonathan Terry said that you were linked directly into Network. I did not understand until now."

"Yes. It is a gift that I have often regretted, but it is so much a part of me. . . . The Mirlai have left that aspect of Caragen's 'creation' intact."

"Did the Mirlai enable you to locate Jonathan Terry?" asked Quin, and the question seemed so simple now, though it had troubled the Infortiare for so long.

Marrach shook his head. "No. Dr. Terry provided that service himself, for he established the mapping. I monitored his original transfer on a private unit. The port itself was destroyed, which kept the information from Network, but I saved the mapping coordinates. I did not and do not understand their application, but I employed them blindly—at the Mirlai's encouragement. Did your people destroy the port?"

"Yes."

"I always thought that act was inconsistent with Jonathan Terry. He is a brilliant man, but he was never sufficiently devious or ruthless to succeed as a subversive. Caragen and I exploited his innocence extensively, I'm afraid."

Quin walked toward the pile of kindling and prodded it with his foot. "I bought a horse once from a man who was hewing logs in front of his house. He was a very good man." Quin glanced at Marrach, and the lightdance of the Mirlai seemed to brighten in the perception of Quin's Power. "I came here to confront you," said Quin, "and ask if you still serve Caragen. I have my answer to that query. I ask another: Can you help us to defend ourselves against him?"

"I cannot even endure a day's departure from this planet, Quin, for that is the price of the Mirlai healing. I depend on them for my very life, and their own survival depends on their recognition of their limitations. They can protect themselves and a Chosen few. They cannot add an entire world to their small domain. They are growing stronger after centuries of decline, but they are still much weaker than in their long-ago unity with the Adraki, their original symbiotic partners."

"Can you advise us, at least?"

Marrach shrugged uncomfortably. "Possibly, but only to a limited extent. I am truly Suleifas now, and he does not think in Marrach's treacherous manner. Marrach might have the knowledge to help you, but the thought processes of Marrach have become abhorrent to me, and I cannot sustain them long." He grimaced. "I would not wish to sustain them for long."

"How may I help Katerin?"

"Call her Kitri. The name is a trigger word which will help you gain her trust."

"That seems too easy."

"It is a single step. It is far from the entire journey. There are other triggers: her brother, her parents, certain personal items from her past, myself. The lesser triggers are more likely to harm than cure, but be aware that they exist. Such deep injuries as I inflicted on her mind do not heal easily."

"Could you heal her?"

"Not unless she decided to abandon all she knows to live here on Siatha. Otherwise, I could at most encourage the possibility of healing. I can mend a broken body in a few days' time, but the mind and spirit require long and constant love."

"Love?"

"That is the only cure for the deepest wounds. Do you understand that I am only the host of the true healers, who are the Mirlai? Their greatest need is to give love and hope." Marrach paused. "You can offer her these gifts as well as the Mirlai, if you are willing to take her burdens on yourself—not as a momentary, noble gesture, but as true and lasting sharing. The process could heal you as well."

Quin's laugh had a nervous edge. "I think I had better concentrate on my immediate problems."

"Of course," agreed Marrach with a curious, pensive smile. "You do realize that you have made Caragen your personal enemy by taking the Terrys' part and by visiting me here? Caragen monitors this area closely. He will correlate his scans of you with Network records, and he will identify you, if he has not already done so. He will assume that I employ you, which amounts to a death warrant."

"Thank you for the warning," answered Quin grimly.

"I would advise you to remain here, if you were not an 'Immortal.' Since you obviously have certain unique gifts, I advise you simply to be very cautious. Andrew Caragen controls Network with nearly absolute authority. Never underestimate him or the range of his influence."

"If I return to Harberg University as Quin Hamley, Network Citizen. . . ."

"An attempt will be made to kill you within the day. Caragen does not retain unwanted 'assets' once he has identified—or believes he has identified—the owner of the asset."

Quin nodded. "Thank you, Suleifas. You have been unexpectedly informative. I may visit you again."

"I sincerely hope you have that opportunity."

* * *

Quin glared at Nanny, who protested nervously, "But she is gone, my lord, by the Infortiare's orders. You surely knew?"

"I surely did not know." Quin stared at the empty crib and felt a fury of betrayal rise inside him. He closed his eyes and reached for frail mortal patterns, and when he reopened his eyes, Nanny had fled.

Quin strode from the room and flung himself recklessly into the Taormin's infinite patterns. He reached for the fierce, bright beacon of a Power he knew and stormed into the Infortiare's library. "Marei is gone," accused Quin angrily. "Where have you sent her?"

"Lord Quinzaine," answered the Infortiare, raising her fair head from the documents on her desk. "You are allowing anger to rule your Power. You are endangering yourself." Her eyes held a warning of her own Power's menace.

"Not myself alone," snapped Quin. "Why did you take the child? You lied to me: Loisa is still alive."

"You seemed relatively unconcerned by the prospect of her death by your negligence," argued Rhianna furiously. "Why do you fling your very righteous indignation at me with such irate assurance? You invade your liege's privacy to throw uncertain accusations. In such a mood, you show your heritage as a lord of Serii too clearly. Do you rank yourself with the Sorcerer Kings, intent on forcing your world to revolve around your convenience?"

Quin flushed at the condemnation. "How could you let me think that I had caused her death?"

"Your negligence was real. Mistress Loisa might indeed have died. You needed brutal reality's lesson."

"There is cruelty in you, my lady," answered Quin tightly.

"Power is cruel. It brooks no mistakes." Her stormy gaze burned into him. "Do you know why I did not tell you that my son had rescued Mistress Loisa?"

Quin forced himself to reply: "Because I did not tell you that I cared one way or the other."

"Because you did not tell yourself! Because you let your Power try to shield you from *feeling* once again, and none of us can afford that luxury. Do you think I never want to seal myself inside my Power, forgetting all the hurts that lie in me and around me? Only a major Power can duplicate your perfect shell of self-delusion, Quinzaine, which is sufficient indication in itself of the dangers. Horlach shielded himself. Such a superb barrier against human emotion was one of the chief hallmarks of the tyrannical Sorcerer Kings and Queens of our early history."

Quin dropped into a chair and rubbed his head. He muttered, "My 'superb' barrier fell years ago to a warrior-woman's stubborn, irrational love of me."

"I know," replied Rhianna with a sigh, and her Power eased into gentle sorrow. "Do you think I would have trusted you otherwise with such an amplifier of Power as the Taormin?"

"Then why did you lie to me?" demanded Quin earnestly. "I felt all of Loisa's pain condemn me, and I felt my parents die again in her agony. I hurt too much to speak. If I had shouted my guilt to all of Hamley, would you have considered me suitably penitent?"

Rhianna closed her eyes, and Quin knew that she had deliberately shared in his pain for that brief moment. "I am sorry, Quinzaine," she whispered. "I let my fears and worries cloud my perceptions of you, and I turned anger earned by others against you."

Astonished by the Infortiare's admission of fallibility, Quin watched her for a moment in silence. *She does look weary,* he observed with some disquiet. "Are Loisa and Marei here?" he asked at last.

"Yes. Mistress Loisa is still too ill to observe her surroundings, but the child is well. I entrusted Marei to her grandmother." Rhianna smiled crookedly. "Your error has effected a remarkable transformation of Mistress Elizabeth and Master Jonathan. They see the child as their own redemption. They have rediscovered hope."

"You told me to ask for help, Lady Rhianna," said Quin quietly. "I must return to Katerin, but Michael Merel must also be located. Too much is happening for me to continue alone."

Rhianna nodded, and she laid aside a document that wore the seal of the Queen's Council. "Teach me the patterns of your concerns, and we shall decide together how best to recover Master Michael."

* * *

Rhianna explained softly, "You are the most experienced of the students, Alvedre, and the steadiest of spirit. That is why I have asked you to make the journey first." Rhianna glanced again at Beth and Jon Terry. "I shall not think less of you if you refuse. The Taormin has always offered a dangerous means of advancing Power."

Beth smiled at Alvedre, but she understood Rhianna's reluctance. Jon had been unable to alter the Taormin as thoroughly as he had intended, for the Taormin's artificial intelligence had incurred some reconfiguration over the millennia of its strange existence. He had derived the mappings by which he believed the Taormin to be operable, but he had been forced to rely on the subjective perceptions of Rhianna's Power and not on impersonally precise Network equipment. The use of the Taormin had been facilitated—or made nearly impossible. Jon himself did not favor this experiment, but he had withheld his objections, allowing the wizards to choose for themselves.

"My lady, I shall use the Taormin," said Alvedre quietly. She smiled at Jon and Beth. "All of your 'special students' will use it. We have discussed the matter among ourselves, and we are ready. We understand the dangers and the necessity. Others on Ixaxis will help as well, my lady. Not all are as stubborn as Howald and Amila. My lady, we are your subjects, and we will not abandon you to fight your war alone. We trust you, my lady, as Infortiare and as a woman we respect."

"Dear Alvedre," murmured Rhianna, her clear voice unusually ragged. She extended her delicate hand, and Alvedre clasped it warmly. "Focus your Power, Alvedre. The Taormin's enticing distractions are still treacherous." They stepped into the patterns together.

Beth leaned against Jon. Together they stared at the empty floor before the window. Jon frowned in frustration. They could only wait and hope that Rhianna and Alvedre would both reappear unharmed.

* * *

Quin reached into the Taormin and sought the pattern of the man who ruled it from within. He sent his own searching Power along the fiery tendrils to make his seeking known. The dark, cold image of Lord Venkarel appeared, and the hazy, formless world of the Taormin seemed to sharpen into a bright but lifeless plain.

"Lord Quinzaine," remarked the wizard softly, "you are a most reckless young man."

"I need your advice," replied Quin airily, but he wondered how he had dared to summon the specter of this most dreaded wizard.

"So I gathered: a matter of Power, I presume."

"Yes, my lord. I have a question to which (I think) only you may have the answer."

"Tell me."

"If a man, who was not a wizard, controlled the Taormin, would he be a sorcerer?"

"Jonathan Terry created the Taormin, and he is neither a sorcerer nor a wizard."

"He created it, but he did not and does not control it. He could not keep it from Horlach, nor can he take it now from you."

"Explain your question further."

"Network contains many entities and devices akin to the Taormin. The control of Network resides almost entirely with one man, and no one has ever challenged him successfully. Only a few have ever escaped him. "Do Ceallagh's laws protect him as a mortal—or condemn him as a sorcerer?"

"I am not the Infortiare. Ask of my wife."

"I have spoken to her, but she has too much already burdening her."

"Whereas I have an infinity of time in which to discuss philosophy with you? I am not unaware of my wife's burdens, Lord Quinzaine, and I am not disassociated from their weight."

"It was you who threatened to destroy me if I jeopardized our world," said Quin wryly. "It is you who must guide me."

The saturnine image of Lord Venkarel laughed, but the illusory sound did not comfort or reassure its hearer. "You wish my permission to destroy this man who controls Network? Considering my diabolical reputation, my permission would seem to have little value from a standpoint of ethics."

"I cannot destroy him, my lord, without risking the destruction of Network and all its peoples, and I know that Ceallagh's laws forbid such an act, even if I wished to attempt it. However, this man seeks Jonathan Terry, and he will very probably seek control of us, unless we stop him."

"You want more than my permission," observed Kaedric, becoming pensive.

"Yes, my lord. I want to know that your Power is available to me, if the situation becomes too difficult for me to handle alone. I have only begun to recognize the magnitude of the problems that the Terrys have—intentionally or unintentionally—presented to us, and I want to know my resources before I proceed. My wife always insisted that preparation was crucial to victory. She was a warrior by trade."

"You understand the risk you take in making this request?"

"Yes, my lord. I think so." Quin hesitated, for the prospect of wielding Lord Venkarel's Power became significantly more alarming in proximity. *No weakening, old boy,* he informed himself sternly. "I need your Power as well as mine," said Quin with a rare, hard resolve. "Your wife is already overburdened, as is your son, in defending Serii, and they cannot provide the particular help I need. You cannot reach Network without a point of physical entry, and I am the only such point available. You must let me wield your Power."

The saturnine image of Lord Venkarel smiled slightly, for no one had tried to command him in many years, but he respected the earnestness of the reasoning. "You do realize that we could both die, if your control wavers fractionally?"

Conflicting emotions crossed Quin's face for an instant. "Network has found us, my lord, by my error in taking Marei to Hamley."

"It was not your error alone," murmured Kaedric. "I should have recognized your difficult circumstances more quickly."

Astonished to receive encouragement from the Venkarel, Quin continued more firmly, "Whatever the cause, Network will not forget our existence nor the lessons learned from the data of that brief encounter. Network will analyze, and Network will observe us until the barrier is penetrated hastily again, and our enemy will come, knowing how to conquer us. We cannot let our enemy reach that point. We cannot let Network consider us a target of acquisition."

"Even you and I together, Quinzaine, could not destroy Network."

"We do not need to destroy. We only need to persuade Network that the probability of conquering us is small and unworthy of the associated expense. I have met this Marrach, who has defied Network successfully by just such a method as I envision."

"What do you intend?" asked Kaedric curiously.

"I intend to make Power a formidable element in Network's calculations. I intend that Network will understand us—on our terms."

"The traditional sorcerers' game of fear?"

"Only in part. We are educating a machine, which defines the truth to the humans who rely on it. Network itself cannot fear us, but it can define us as a threat."

"Assuming we succeed."

"Yes," admitted Quin heavily, "assuming we succeed."

Kaedric became very thoughtful. "You have indeed learned from Network, Lord Quinzaine. You make several fascinating points, which I can neither dispute nor affirm from personal experience."

"That was the purpose of sending me as emissary, was it not?"

"Yes, and I would say that my wife chose well in naming you for that position. You have become a very valuable resource to us, which makes your request of me more difficult."

"You doubt that I would survive?"

"Your survival would depend on your own control, which could not weaken, and the extent to which you drew upon such Power as I might lend you. You have sufficient innate resources to endure far more Power than you have ever employed consciously, but you have never used Power in its most violent form. You have never killed by Power. That prospect alone could weaken your focus. My Power is determinedly violent, Quinzaine, and I have killed far too often. Your Power would rebel instinctively against mine, and the conflicts alone could destroy us both. Your survival is doubtful, at best."

"Are you refusing me?"

"No. I concur with your assessment of this man, Caragen. He is dangerous." Quin stiffened, and Kaedric, Lord Venkarel, smiled bleakly. "Of course, I know his name," said Kaedric to Quin's unspoken query, "from my wife, as well as from you. I promised to observe you, Lord Quinzaine, lest you delve into more trouble than I deemed tolerable. Did you doubt me?"

"No, my lord," whispered Quin. *All of the superior posings of the Ixaxin scholars and students,* thought Quin, *are only shadows of this man, this wizard who is all Power. No wonder Luki has never been able to escape the memory of him.* "Thank you, my lord."

"You may thank me more sincerely if we succeed."

"Yes, my lord."

CHAPTER 13

Network

"Good morning, Katerin," announced Network softly.

The walls emitted the message three times more, each time at an increased volume, before Katerin acknowledged the wake-up call with a groan and a whisper. "Yes."

"I have added a nutritive beverage to your standard breakfast specification, so as to meet heightened requirements incurred by stress indicators and subnormal sleep levels. Have you a flavor preference?"

"No. Use the default."

"You have three messages: Cindal will meet you one hour early to attend the Convocation speech."

The bed began to stiffen, so as to discourage its occupant from sinking back into sleep. Katerin considered employing an override command that she had devised illegally and indulging in the luxury of laziness, but she rolled to her feet and willed herself to face another day. "Send a reply: I shall meet you, as arranged, and no earlier. What is the point of using your friend's much vaunted influence to obtain reserved seating if we must wait for endless hours anyway? End of reply." *Cindal is trying so hard to be kind and conciliatory. I wish I could feel more genuinely forgiving.* "Next message, please."

"Radge would like to meet you for lunch."

"Send reply: No. End of reply. Next message."

"Quin has the information you requested."

Katerin tightened her fingers around the hairbrush and jerked it ruthlessly through snarled hair. "Send an acknowledgment."

*　　*　*　*

Quin was not at the lab. His absence pressed Katerin's thin shell of certainty, and she grimaced to realize how much hope she had tied to the singularly questionable person of her deceptive research assistant. "Laurett," she asked calmly, "where is Quin?"

"Unknown. I am concerned about him, Katerin. He has not contacted me for the past three days."

Katerin laughed nervously. *My algorithm is concerned about Quin's welfare: how touching.* "Does he always contact you on a daily basis?"

"He warns me of exceptions in advance. I am concerned."

"Have you any suggestions as to where I might seek Quin?"

"His home?"

"I have sent a Network message, Laurett. It will reach him at any registered location. Do you have any suggestions that Network might omit?"

"His home," repeated Laurett.

"You are redundant, Laurett. Flag this file for examination of anomalous logic," sighed Katerin. *Anger at my algorithm can help nothing.*

"Acknowledged."

Katerin jumped nervously at the sound of the lab door snapping open. "Katerin, I have been waiting for you downstairs," chided Cindal, arriving in a whirl of scarlet gauze. "I thought you were ready. Do you want to miss the event of the century?"

"Let me concentrate long enough to file my status report, and I shall run all the way to the auditorium, if you like."

Cindal paced impatiently, while Katerin entered the last code for the university's research register. *The event of the century,* thought Katerin acridly: *why do I feel nothing but apathy about it? I can think of nothing but my own problems and Quin. Where is he?* Katerin rose and presented herself to Cindal with an ironic mock-curtsey. "Lead me, Cindal, to the creation of history."

"I could have sold this pass to some gorgeous and grateful young man instead of giving it to you," replied Cindal with a sly smile.

"I am properly chastened and boundlessly appreciative of the rare honor you have bestowed upon me. Shall we hasten?"

"You have been spending too much time with your research assistant. You sound like an anachronist."

"Must you insult me? I have apologized as prettily as I could, and I thought you enjoyed the attention of making a late arrival."

"Not today," replied Cindal crisply, and she set so rapid a pace that Katerin regretted her ironic offer to run the distance.

She is genuinely angry with me, observed Katerin in some surprise. *Perhaps she has regretted inviting me instead of her "gorgeous, grateful young man." I should never have accepted, but Cindal pressed me so persistently, and I have been unfairly cold to her because of my own confusion. Parve is right. My friends are worried about me, and all I can do is snap at them.*

Electronic barricades defeated Cindal's haste near the auditorium, and an impatient crowd waited for the Council Governor's security experts to allow access to the auditorium doors. *Only the privileged wait here,* noted Katerin with increased respect for Cindal's nameless benefactor. *I knew that most citizens would observe only the transmitted image of the Council Governor, but I did not expect to stand among so many famous citizens.* She recognized the faces and voices of the very wealthy and the very influential, and she mouthed a question to Cindal: "How?" Cindal returned a smugly uncommunicative smile.

"Prepare for identity scan at the entry," announced Network to the crowd.

A lanky, dark-haired man grumbled, "The old shark wants us humble."

The coldly elegant woman beside him whispered, "He wants us to remember why we serve his ambitions, Georg." The woman met Katerin's curious glance with a condescending stare, making Katerin acutely conscious of her own hastily donned attire; Katerin's swirling skirt and scarves seemed shabby beside the elegant sweep of this unknown woman's ensemble. A bejeweled insect of exotic origin winked mockingly from the woman's collar.

"You are certainly tolerant today, Maryta," retorted Georg.

"I am a realist," murmured Maryta, "and a survivor." To Katerin's surprise, the woman, Maryta, smiled at her across the intervening space between the snaking lines, but the expression had a chilling impact. Katerin averted her eyes uneasily.

The line surged forward and stopped, as the guards admitted Georg and Maryta with the first group of restless notables. Katerin and Cindal scarcely progressed. The warmth of the day and the heat of the crowd made Katerin doubly appreciative of the auditorium's cool stone colonnade, lined with pillars, each of a richly colored, simulated mineral. Cunning optical effects gave depth to the illusory gardens extending from a parade of arched false-windows that constituted one wall of the theater.

Katerin felt a nudge and heard a voice she knew: "How do you like mixing with the ultra affluent?"

Katerin stared from Radge to Cindal, who returned the angry gaze without apology, without regret. *Knots of bitterness form within me. Why should I feel surprised? Cindal is my friend; she has been my closest friend since Michael left. Does that judgmental face belong to a friend? Cindal, how could you betray me?* "How remarkable to see you here, Radge," said Katerin coldly.

"Katerin, please," said Cindal remorselessly, "let Radge explain."

"Explain what?" demanded Katerin. She turned to face Radge, trying to see him as he had seemed before her nightmares could condemn him. *The fault was not his, but mine—or rather, it was Marrach's cruelty taking another toll. Radge is sophisticated and cultured. He is intelligent and charming, and he is handsome even by Network's genetically refined standards. He represents everything that a sensible Network woman should tally as characteristics of the ideal mate, and I can no longer abide the sight of him. I would never have thought he could inspire such revulsion in me.* "Do you mean to explain, Cindal, why you are trying to manipulate my life?"

"I am only protecting you against your own stubbornness," answered Cindal coolly.

"I never knew you to meddle so stupidly," replied Katerin. The thick crowd conspired with Cindal and Radge to prevent Katerin's escape. "Where did you obtain a pass, Radge? Do you share Cindal's munificent friend?"

"I chaired the university committee to organize the event. Katerin, please quit looking at me as if I were an Orsinian Creeper. Cindal thought this would be a good opportunity for us to mend our quarrel."

"Radge, we have no quarrel to mend." Katerin kept her voice soft, partially for privacy and partially to keep from screaming. The crowd surged forward again. The doors drew closer. *A speech of an hour or more awaits beyond the doors, the guards, and the monitors, and Radge will be inescapable beside me throughout the event.*

"If not a quarrel, then what?" demanded Radge, speaking as softly as Katerin. Cindal appeared engrossed by the spectacle of the waiting crowd. "At least talk to me, Katerin. Explain my crime to me."

He is bitter and angry, and I cannot blame him, but I cannot bear him. "You have apparently talked enough for both of us, and this is not the place for an argument."

"Where else can I force you to listen to me?" snapped Radge, and he grabbed her wrist to prevent her from turning from him.

"No!" hissed Katerin. She tried to shake free of his grasp, but he held her too strongly. She endured his touch, as the line crept through the doors. *I cannot bear it,* she shrieked to herself, but she replied equably to Network's identity queries, and she even managed to smile politely at the guard who ushered her to her assigned seat. Radge never relinquished her arm. Katerin sat rigidly, wedged between a glowering Radge and an unusually silent Cindal.

*   *   *

Sitting in the pale cubicle that served as the utilitarian Network apartment of a student of limited means, Lord Quinzaine dur Hamley contemplated a promise to a brave warrior-woman. He said very quietly, "I shall still try to contribute something, Laurett, but I think I have taken one foolish risk too many at last. Not even Lady

Fortune is likely to save me from this precarious perch between the Council Governor's murderous schemes and my own insane request to use Lord Venkarel's Power."

He raised his eyes to the ceiling. "I do not want to die, Laurett. You know that I am neither heroic nor courageous. I should like nothing better than to claim Katerin Merel and escape this entire mess by force of Power, but I am afraid the lovely Katerin would protest, and she has stirred some latent gallantry in me. In any case, I cannot abandon my liege."

He shook his head at his own contradictory feelings, and he reached for the Widowshear. "Luki," he whispered, but her mind wandered, and he could not make her focus on hearing him.

In frustration, Quin threw his leather gloves at the far wall, and he stared at the mark in the palm of his hand. The cool voice of Network, activated by the violent gesture, spoke with a carefully programmed calm. "May I suggest a relaxant?"

Quin shut his eyes tightly. *How do they survive the lack of privacy? Even in Hamley, we can be alone now and then.* "No, thank you, Network."

"Then I recommend at least eight hours of sleep to forestall further physical and emotional deterioration due to exhaustion."

Quin muttered, "You are a worse nag than old Howald." *And your Council Governor is probably plotting my death at this very moment.* He rose from his chair, grabbed his coat and strode to the door, which did not open. Quin slammed his branded hand against the door's cold surface in aggravation. "Network, open the door, please."

"Your stress levels are currently excessive for your own safety and for the safety of your fellow citizens. I must confine you until your stress levels return to normal ranges."

"You are an irritating, intrusive, and arrogant *machine*," said Quin, "and I am beginning to dislike you intensely." Quin threw a burst of Power at the door to force it open, and he silenced Network's alarms with an angry thought, recognizing as he left the grimly sterile building that Network was right: He was endangering himself and everyone he met in his present mood.

If I manage to survive this tangle of crossed purposes and ambitions, he told himself, *I shall never assume a single responsibility again. I am sorry, Laurett, but I cannot live for a promise to a ghost.*

Quin walked without immediate plan or purpose except avoidance of any room where Network could make him feel imprisoned. He expected eventually to reach the university lab, where Network's presence was at least less overt, but he wanted to study any shiftings in the patterns first. He had debated establishing himself under a new Network identification code upon leaving Marrach, but he had realized that Jonathan Terry's preliminary preparations had served only once. Quin had neither the time nor the knowledge to reinvent his Network self as yet.

Quin admitted another reason for his delay in reaching the lab: He did not know what to say to Katerin Merel. *She will not believe the truth,* thought Quin, *and Marrach's "trigger" of her name will not convert her quickly to trust of me.* Quin leaned against a wall to watch a parade of glittering mummers headed for the Convocation street fair. *She is too aware of her fiendishly manipulative techniques of mathematical psychology,* mused Quin disconsolately.

Network never confines her *for excessive stress; I suppose she knows how to circumvent the system. I wonder how much pain she hides beneath that shield of coldness and distrust? I am not sure that I have the courage to know her as deeply as I must in order to fight her enemies and mine. Unless I drown her reactions completely with Power, she will try to dissect me in the process of reaching some common plane of honesty, because that is the only way she seems to function. Lords, what a mess.*

Quin felt the scream ring inside of him. He jerked away from the wall, shaken by the echoing terror of the woman whose pattern he had started to trace. He did not bother to seek a Network transfer port; he stepped into a shadow and successfully bewildered a young girl who watched him disappear.

* * *

Katerin scarcely noticed the arrival of the Council Governor, nor did she hear the beginning of his speech.

The nervous whispers around Katerin seemed to shout at her, demanding her to hear them and dread. "What does the old shark think he is doing?" muttered someone with a good measure of fear.

"Perhaps this public appearance is simply another bit of Caragen's maneuvering to deceive us into believing that he has lost control of his holdings. If he had truly begun to weaken, every greedy power in space would descend to taste the carnage. Network is a valued prize."

"What devilish scheme has he concocted? What is left for him to acquire?"

"Who knows? But he is making an official public appearance for the first time since that carefully arranged incident on Vordaire. This is an aggressive move aimed against something or someone very particular. I do not envy his chosen victim."

Katerin shuddered, as the voices receded into silence. She realized that she could at last hear the speaker, and he seemed to be continuing a speech long in progress, though it seemed to her that he had only now begun. "An outstanding example of Network's human resources," said the Council Governor smoothly, "was the man whose work in infinite-dimensional analysis led to the single most influential technological innovation in use today: a topological transfer system capable of transporting humanity into previously inaccessible space."

What is he saying? demanded Katerin of herself, and her mind could not force itself to respond. *Why do I feel so strangely detached?*

"I have come here today with dual purpose: to honor this outstanding university and to pay belated homage to a hero of our civilization. I shall accomplish both goals by establishing the Terry Research Facility on this campus." Scattered applause flitted through the auditorium. "Kitri, please join me in honoring your father."

Someone was propelling Katerin toward the stage. "No," she protested helplessly, but a relentless tide of plots and whispers carried her. She reached toward unfamiliar faces to beseech them that this was wrong, but some faces wore suspicion and some wore alarm, and no one seemed to sense her deep despair. "No," she cried mutely, dreading that the tide which carried her would drown her. She called to Cindal, and she called to Radge, but the pair of them only watched her with stoic and uncharitable expressions.

Katerin stood beside the Council Governor, and he studied her closely. *Does he see the fear in me?* she wondered. *He is a smaller man than I would have expected, and he is old. He has a cruel smile. Avoid entanglements with C-humans: That was Marrach's most insistent advice. C-humans serve the Consortium. C-humans are this man's enemies. This man is the Council Governor.*

Caragen clenched her reluctant fingers, grasping them closely in his own cold, dry hands. *Like a snake's skin,* she thought, and she shivered when she met the appraising gaze of the man who ruled every facet of her life. *Network has monitored me,* screamed the warning in her mind, *and Council Governor Caragen is Network.* "Why?" she whispered, not realizing that she had spoken aloud, until Caragen broadened his cruel smile.

"Where has Marrach hidden your father?" demanded the Council Governor.

"I do not understand," replied Katerin, shaking her head until the dizziness made her reel toward the edge of the stage. *Where is the audience? Where are the cheering crowds?*

"They will not help you," laughed Caragen.

Why is this happening? she wanted to shout, but her tongue seemed fettered as by a nightmare. *Perhaps it is a nightmare,* she thought, and she tried to believe that she could wake from it.

Guards surrounded her, and beside her walked the Council Governor, nodding with great dignity, smiling occasionally, waving graciously to his admiring crowd. *They are truly his crowd,* thought Katerin with a fading flicker of reason. *These are all his people.* A shuttle waited beneath the late afternoon sun. *How did I lose so much of the day?*

"This is a mistake," murmured Katerin weakly, but her voice grew stronger as she saw Cindal standing beside the shuttle. "Cindal!" cried Katerin eagerly, but Cindal's face remained unmoved and strange. "Council Governor," pleaded Katerin desperately, but the same unpleasant smile lingered forbiddingly on his lips.

The world darkened and grew light again. *I am losing consciousness,* observed Katerin remotely. Caragen had disappeared from her side, vanishing during one of the phases of darkness. *Where are the guards? Am I free, or am I blind and captured?* "Marrach promised to protect me," whispered Katerin.

She heard the flurry, though she could see only intermittently now. The crowd had parted, its members anxiously avoiding something that sputtered and crackled noisily on the ground. Guards whisked the Council Governor into the shuttle, as the clumsy, fluttering device on the lawn spewed a cloud of dense black smoke. The crowd dispersed. Katerin began to choke and cough, as the cloud enveloped her. She did not realize that she was held, until the arms that had restrained her were tugged free, and she turned blindly to seek an escape.

The smoke parted. Her sight cleared. She nearly collided with Radge. He extended his open hand toward her—and stopped just short of touching her, halted by a lean, muscular forearm encircling his neck.

Radge jerked free of the stranglehold, touching Katerin briefly. Someone grunted with pain. Katerin heard the thud of flesh beating flesh, but she could see only blackness. Katerin swayed, feeling the smoke's heaviness wrapping about her, snaking inside of her, and expanding through her. A shivery sense of disorientation, like the momentary shifting of a transfer point, rocked her already battered senses, and she slipped into the insistent darkness.

"Drink this," coaxed a voice that seemed vaguely familiar.

"Quin?" Katerin tried to raise her head and regretted the effort immediately; her head was throbbing. She stared at the cracked ceiling: her own ceiling, her own apartment. "What happened to me?" she asked of herself.

"At a guess," answered Quin, "I should say that you were drugged. Hold still for a moment." Katerin winced from the pressure of Quin's warm fingertips against her forehead, but before she could protest, both the pressure and the throbbing had departed. Katerin touched her head cautiously. "What did you do?"

"I employed a trick I learned from a very clever old woman. She has a skill for healing headaches—and not much else. Here, drink some more broth. Network prescribed it."

Katerin edged herself onto her elbows and accepted the steaming cup obediently: her cup; her room. "Why are you here?" she demanded in a sudden resurgence of suspicion.

"You looked like you needed some help, so I followed you. When you collapsed on your threshold, I decided to stay until you awoke. Network indicated that you *would* awaken, so I did not summon a medic."

"Did I authorize Network to admit you?"

"No. I told you that I have a peculiar rapport with computers. Remember?"

"I remember that you claimed to have information for me. Where were you?"

"I had an errand to run, which took longer than I planned. If I had known that you meant to attend a speech by the Council Governor, I would have made sure I returned in time to stop you. Too late now for that particular regret," shrugged Quin.

Too late? Too late to object to Quin's presence in my home. Has he been able to enter my home freely all along? Is he my tormentor? I cannot believe it of him, but I must believe it. "What happened after the speech?" asked Katerin carefully.

"I heard that you accepted an honor on behalf of your father."

"A mistake was made," answered Katerin with a tightness in her throat.

"Truly?" asked Quin lightly, but his smile was wry. "Do you feel well enough to hear the results I promised you?"

"Results?" demanded Katerin, lost for a moment.

"You wanted to know who has been monitoring you. The most recent scans originated with Professor Randon, your purported friend and colleague."

"You need not clarify. I do remember him."

"You have been monitored by others, as well. I have not yet identified them all, but one of them uses the name of Calial. She is another friend of yours."

"I know no one by that name."

"Calial's patterns correspond to Professor Cindal Cavli."

"What patterns?" Her mind still functioned sluggishly, reluctant to abandon the sedatory drug.

"Energy patterns. Laurett could show you the trace codes, which would probably make more sense to you than my incoherent prattle."

"What are you, Quin?" asked Katerin in despair.

"I am your best friend, whether you want me or not." An unexpected dignity of spirit seemed to engulf him and make him larger than himself. "I need to leave you briefly, because I must prowl the patterns for a bit and see where our enemies have gone with nightfall. I would have tracked them earlier, but I did not want to abandon you while you were unconscious. You should be safe enough here for a while, since I deactivated Network's access to this room. Rest. I shall return shortly."

Katerin did not reply, for she wanted him to leave; she did not trust him. Quin withdrew quietly; she heard the click as the door slid closed behind him. Achingly, she forced herself to rise and enter the living room. She struck the command on her console to reactivate Network's access. "I have symptoms of confusion, extreme fatigue, possibly hallucinations, muscular aches, and nausea. Recommend treatment."

"Nutrient broth, already supplied, contained restoratives which should take effect within twenty minutes of consumption. Further treatment: restricted motion for next three hours, so as to avoid possible injury due to periodic recurrence of disorientation. Appropriate sedatives were also incorporated in broth." *A subverted Network could kill me easily, but Network cannot be escaped. My enemy does not want my death, not yet. What does it want?*

"Thank you, Network," *Sedatives: I must not let them take effect. Concentrate and remain alert.* "Project news report on subject of Council Governor's visit today."

Katerin braced herself to accept any news calmly, but the sudden, lifelike image of Council Governor Caragen, clambering with a good-natured laugh into his shuttle beneath the morning light, tugged a gasp from her throat. No guards surrounded him. Students filled the crowd that cheered him, and she recognized many of them. "That is not what occurred," she whispered to herself.

". . . the Council Governor's generous endowment," she heard Network announce, "in honor of Dr. Jonathan Terry. The Council Governor's announcement met with universal acclaim, reaffirming, as it did, the tenets and philosophies that create pride in all Network citizens. . . ."

"Stop," ordered Katerin. "Has anything been reported about a disturbance following the Council Governor's speech?"

"Council Governor Caragen's arrival and departure occurred without unpleasant incident."

"Thank you," replied Katerin dryly.

"You have an interactive message request."

"Vocal only."

"Katerin, I have been worried about you. Are you all right?"

Katerin sank into a chair and twisted the torn satin binding of a cushion. "Yes, Radge," she answered dully.

"When you disappeared after the speech, Cindal and I were concerned."

Cindal is Calial; Radge has monitored me. So Quin claims. "I feel fine."

"Why did you leave so suddenly?"

"I am very tired, Radge."

"Do not disconnect me, please! Let me see you, Katerin."

"Why?"

"You know why!"

Did he try to help me? Did I see Radge at all? "I thought you were my friend, Radge."

"Let me come. . . ."

"End communication."

"Done," replied the impersonal voice of Network.

"Log any further messages."

"Acknowledged."

With a curt, determined keypad command, she disconnected Network's authorized access to her apartment. She forced herself to move, though her body protested. She changed her clothes with frustrated fumblings, for she wanted to escape before Quin could return, but she wanted dark clothing that would hide her from casual attention. She draped herself in black gauze. She avoided the lift and descended by the rarely used stairs. She emerged cautiously into the shadows behind her apartment.

The university walkways wore their nightly garlands of light, but the buildings rested in sullen darkness. Katerin applied her faculty access codes three times in order to reach her laboratory. She did not summon light for the room, and the hallway faded into gloom according to the automatic off-hours timing. "Laurett," murmured Katerin, when she had secured herself in the black and windowless lab, "I need to talk to someone."

"I am here, Katerin."

"Is Quin correct? Are you accessible to Network?"

"No, Katerin."

"Why do I ask, when I know the answer you must give, and none of it really matters now. The only person who does not know my innermost life, it seems, is Katerin Merel. Laurett, advise me."

"Whom do you trust?"

"Michael."

"Contact him."

"Network will not allow it."

"You must trust a friend."

"No! Laurett, I am not even sure what happened to me today. I am not sure what happened or how it happened. This day has culminated in all of my nightmares, all of the dreadful memories that conditioning can no longer suppress: the loss of my home and friends, my parents' deaths, the terrible chaos of the time of hiding with Michael and a stranger named Marrach, who never smiled without cruel purpose. I lost my childhood entirely when Marrach replaced all of Kitri's logs and records with those of Katerin Merel, and I lost myself in a rape that I am not sure was real or part of Marrach's foul conditioning of my mind.

"Everything has recurred—with Radge, the fear, the loss of everything I trusted. Quin is clearly more than he pretended. Even Cindal, whom I have considered my closest friend, has betrayed me; how could I continue to trust anyone? I have lost my home, and I am losing my sanity. Even Michael has been taken from me." Katerin laughed with bitter tears. "I have only an algorithm for counseling in which to confide, and even it has betrayed me at least once."

The light streamed into the room from the hallway, and Katerin squinted against the pain of its sudden glare. "Katerin, come with me," implored Radge, reaching to her, where she huddled against the wall.

Katerin straightened and stared at him arrogantly. Despite the streaming tears that continued to fall against her cheeks, she almost believed in her own gesture of prideful disdain. She felt dimly pleased when Radge hesitated, apparently as astonished as she that her body could still move as if it held a functioning spirit.

His hesitation did not endure long. He extended his hand and beseeched her, "Please, Katerin, come now! You are in great danger. I want to help you."

"Do not let him touch you, Professor," warned Quin from the opposite wall. "He intends to drug you again. He has something implanted in his fingernail, I think."

Radge spun toward Quin, and Radge's mask of gentlemanly concern twisted into fury. "Why are you tormenting Katerin this way? Are you trying to drive her from everyone who might help her?"

"You are very good," remarked Quin mildly. "You adapt to the unexpected and take advantage of it. I am impressed."

Did Quin follow me here, or has he been here all along? I should not have come here; I did not know where else to go; I cannot think. Who is Quin, and who is Radge, and are they manipulating me together?

Katerin watched the two men warily. She trusted neither of them. She began to edge toward the door, taking advantage of their distraction with each other.

Without glancing at her, Radge moved quickly back into the doorway, blocking her only exit. "Come with me, Katerin, now."

"And what," asked Quin, "do you expect to do about me?"

"I expect you to stay here until we have left the building, unless you want to fight me. I will not lose."

"You do not quite believe what you are saying," commented Quin pensively, "though you obviously have the advantage over me in physical size. Was I that hard on you this afternoon?" Radge raised his hand to the door control. Quin murmured calmly, "Seal the door, Laurett."

"Command an override, Katerin!" shouted Radge.

"Laurett," said Katerin evenly, "utilize emergency channel to summon university security immediately."

"Yes, Katerin."

"No, Laurett," countered Quin. "I am sorry, Professor, but security would only complicate matters at this point."

Radge interrupted with fervor, "Katerin, can you still doubt that he is the one who is trying to harm you?"

"No," answered Katerin, praying that Laurett had executed her command rather than Quin's. *How far has Quin modified the command priority structure to exert his own control? I should have monitored his activities more closely. I ignored him deliberately for too long—out of dread of developing another injudicious attachment and fulfilling my reputation as Halaatu once again. None of it matters now, I suppose.* "There is a manual override for the door beneath the control panel, Radge." *I have known Radge much longer than Quin. Of the two men, Radge seems much the most likely to be vulnerable to me; he succumbed to me once, and Quin has never shown such certain interest in me.*

Quin sighed and shook his head, as Radge pried loose the panel and released the door's lock; the door snapped open. "Do not try to follow us," warned Radge, once again extending his hand to Katerin. He glanced at her briefly when she avoided his touch, stepping to his side without a wisp of contact.

She smiled at him apologetically. "Allow me a little wariness still, Radge, please." *Even to save my own life, I cannot bear to touch him again.*

Radge nodded, his concern again glowing forth at her. "Of course, Katerin."

Quin laughed darkly, and he did not move as Katerin followed Radge from the room that had become a trap. Only Quin's voice, echoing down the hall, pursued them: "Tell Network to seal the perimeter, Laurett. Allow Katerin to depart only if she is alone. The person calling himself Radge Randon is not to leave the building."

"Can he actually control the building from that machine of yours?" hissed Radge.

"The rules say no, but Quin has surprised me repeatedly in the last few days." *Allow Katerin to depart? I*

think I know Radge's brand of treachery; what is Quin's?
After all these years, have my parents' enemies finally
ensnared me? What can they want of me? I do not even
know why they killed my parents.

Is it Network or the Council Governor, or is it both?
Marrach vowed to keep me safe; I never believed him. I
must warn Michael, but how shall I ever reach him? Per-
haps it is already too late to reach him.

The outer doors were sealed, responding neither to
coded command nor to manual override. Radge muttered a curse, as Katerin watched him pound his fist
futilely against the surface of the door. "We shall have
to try another exit," grumbled Radge.

"You have forgotten, I ordered the entire perimeter
sealed," commented Quin. Radge whirled to face the
calm, smiling anachronist. An object appeared in Radge's
hand, and it resembled a weapon that Katerin had seen
in the grasp of a guard of the Council Governor.

"No," whispered Katerin, but neither man seemed to
hear her desperate plea.

"Professor Randon, I recommend sincerely against
using that device as you intend," said Quin with such
obvious consternation that Radge began to smile. Katerin made a slight, nervous movement, trying fearfully
to persuade Radge to lower his weapon. The motion startled Radge, and he fired the energy beam at Quin.

The odor of burned flesh assaulted her: At an early
age, Katerin had met that odor in the attack on her parents' home. She saw that old destruction now before her:
the charred remnants of her security and the sad, little
body of a silken-haired dog. She had made no sound;
she had shed no tears.

Someone was tugging her by the hand. "Please, dear
Katerin, I know you have been drugged, manipulated,
and tormented, but I could use your help. Do you know
which of these offices is empty?"

"No." She stared at the floor at an unrecognizably
burned body that Quin was dragging awkwardly. "What
are you doing?"

Quin answered calmly, though his face was pale, "I
am removing the body from the main entry in case someone else decides to work late tonight."

"Radge," she murmured.

"Or someone using his name. I did try to warn him."

"He fired at you. He could not have missed."

"Maybe his weapon was faulty." Quin touched the door of the supply closet, and the door slid open. He pulled Radge's body across the floor and propped it against a case of cleaning fluid. "I never killed anyone before," said Quin softly, "except by helplessness."

He brushed his hands together, frowning at them; then he grimaced and knelt to search Radge's body. He inspected the burned remnants of the weapon very briefly before setting it aside. "Apparently, no one ever taught you the hazards of exchanging energy with a wizard, Professor Randon. Interesting weapon," mused Quin, frowning pensively at the pistol. "I had heard of such things. Small wonder that mortals abandoned their usage against Power." He tucked the weapon into his pocket, and stood to face Katerin. "He tried to murder us both, Professor," said Quin a bit defensively, "and it was his own weapon that killed him."

"I would not know how to mourn him," whispered Katerin hollowly, and she stared without expression, as the supply closet door slid shut to hide its grisly contents.

"Good," answered Quin, but his face remained tense and clouded with conflict. "Do you trust me at all?"

"Of course, Quin," lied Katerin quietly, and she did not care that Quin's clear, gray eyes reflected more suspicion than belief.

"Take my hand, Kitri. We have a journey to make."

"Of course, Quin." She did not consciously hear the name he used in soft command. She allowed him to gather her hand in his, because she did not know what else to do; the warmth of his grip made her dimly realize her own aching coldness.

"You may find it easier if you close your eyes for a moment."

"Of course," she said, and she complied, because she expected Quin to kill her. The instant of disorientation felt familiar, and only a small, distant part of Katerin's mind experienced surprise on opening her eyes. "Where are we?" asked Katerin, observing the strange room dubiously and casting all her recent conclusions into a new uncertainty.

"A friend's house."

"Are we safe here?"

"From your Network enemies? Yes, for the present."

"Is there someone else pursuing me?" asked Katerin wearily.

"No," replied Quin slowly. "But stay in this room, please, unless I accompany you, or we shall both collect more trouble than either of us needs."

Wryly, Katerin asked, "Would you care to explain further?"

"Not just yet."

"You are not fond of explanations, are you?"

"I am fond of my life. I should like to retain it intact, and I need to seal our path behind us. I shall return soon."

Katerin pondered his words, and stored them for future consideration. "Where is your friend—the one who owns this house?"

"Gathering additions for one of her collections, I should imagine. If she should return, please say nothing until I have a chance to explain to her."

"Explain to her, but not to me?"

"At present, I have no idea of what to say to either of you. Everything has happened too quickly." Katerin smiled faintly, and Quin nodded crookedly. "Yes, I suppose you already noticed the unsettling nature of the evening. There is a cot; you may use it, if you like."

"Thank you. I am rather tired." Katerin yielded to the Network sedatives in her blood, for she had no strength left to fight.

PART 5

The Awakening
Network Year 2305/
Seriin Year 9059

CHAPTER 1

Network, Serii, and Luki's House

Progress Report to Council Governor
Agent: Calial, code jx1737a816
Subject: Katerin Merel
The subject has disappeared from surveillance monitors, and Network is currently calculating probable locations. The tracking device injected in Yarl, who was to entice her confidence in his guise as Randon, registers at an impaired level; the readings suggest that he is dead. Despite Yarl's failure to enact the planned rescue after the speech, all analyses indicated a high probability of his success in regaining her trust; Network assured me that the effective combination of long-term harassment, intrusion, and small, cumulative doses of mild hallucinogens had reduced Katerin Merel to appropriate vulnerability.

The probability that Katerin Merel would kill any intelligent life-form is low; the probability that she would deliberately kill a friend, although estranged, is significantly less than one percent. Either an accident occurred, or an unknown agent has interfered. An accident is unlikely, considering Yarl's experience. Quin Hamley disappeared from Network sensors shortly preceding the incident. Based on this data, Network has calculated an eighty-two percent probability of his involvement as agent of the former Network operative, Rabhadur Marrach.

* * *

Caragen listened quietly as Network recited Calial's report. He snarled briefly at Marrach's name, but he showed no other reaction. When the message was complete, he remarked with exceptional mildness, "Network, have you pinpointed Katerin Merel's location yet?"

"Coordinates are being tracked according to adaptive topological transformation techniques. Estimated time of completion is 1.7 standard hours."

"Excellent," mused Caragen complacently. He exhaled a careful ring of smoke and watched it drift lazily above him. "Agent Calial has an unfortunate habit of carelessness, Network. She neglected to implant a fresh tracker in Katerin Merel, relying on the success of either Yarl's mock rescue or a true abduction. Two-level redundancy is inadequate." Caragen added sardonically, "It is fortunate that Marrach was so much more thorough in attending to the Merels. Since I have used his original implants charily over the years, his trackers still retain sufficient power to communicate with us. Inform Calial of her error."

"Confirmed. Shall disciplinary measures be undertaken?"

Caragen pondered the question briefly. "No. Marrach did recommend her originally. Like Rolf, she could be one of his tools. Watch her."

"Acknowledged."

"Prepare the attack force in case Katerin Merel's location is inconvenient."

"Acknowledged." Caragen smiled.

* * *

A very cold nose pressed against her face, awakening Katerin abruptly. Alarmed by the unexpected sound of something sniffing at her ear, Katerin jerked to the opposite side of the cot. Startled by her sudden motion, the gray-furred explorer emitted a hiss, scrambled up the ladder of crates and leather bundles, and disappeared among the clutter of motley objects suspended from the ceiling. Several of the dangling packages began to sway, but all grew still again, as Katerin tried to quiet her frantic nerves.

A friend's house, Quin said. *Whose friend? Not mine. I have none. Poor Radge; I never meant to hurt him so much.*

Daylight, streaming from an open door, left most of the room in shadow, but Katerin saw each dusty bit of carving, each polished kettle or pot, with a clarity that embedded itself within her. *Some instants remain intact in the memory forever, sometimes for obvious reasons, sometimes without apparent cause. I remember my parents' deaths; I remember the DI port on Network-3, as I last saw it. I shall remember this room for as long as I live; I shall remember each round stone of the hearth and the weave of every dangling sack.*

A man's silhouette in the doorway distorted the beam of sunlight, merging with the surreal image of the room, until he entered and became only Quin. "Are you feeling better?" he asked solicitously.

Katerin studied him for a long moment, observing the trace of a worried crease above the gray eyes and impish grin. "Where are we, Quin?"

He shrugged, stirring the packed dirt of the floor with his toe like a guilty child. "I told you: This is a friend's house."

Watching Quin, she tried to fit him into any role she had imagined before today—if the day could still be defined as singular. *How am I to react to him? Do I speak to the irresponsible posturer or to the man who manipulates Network, the man who killed Radge—with whatever undetectable weapon? Whoever he is, whomever he serves, he is the key to my current predicament.* "Are we still on Daedalon?"

"No."

What does he want of me? "Are you willing to tell me the name of the planet?"

"Yes, if I could, but this *place* contains nothing more than this house and bit of garden. Anything beyond the immediate *here* of Luki's home exists somewhere else, where we are not, so we are not strictly speaking on a planet, as I understand the definition. Does that help?"

"No." *Does he actually expect to revert to his role as my erratic assistant? He controls the access to this place of deception; therefore, I must control him.* "You are not a fool, Quin Hamley, so please stop talking like one."

Quin sighed, but he traversed the room, ducking and dodging an assortment of willow baskets, and he sat cross-legged on the floor before Katerin. He met her eyes deliberately, and Katerin caught her breath in surprise at the intensity of his gaze. Like the first time she had met his eyes in Harberg, she sensed the stormy depths and felt the power beneath the anachronist's careless facade. She tried to look away from him, but she could not seem to escape.

"My friend, Luki," explained Quin quietly, "dislikes uninvited guests, so she constructed her house outside of the accepted patterns, using a device she calls the Widowshear." Quin waved his nimble fingers, as if trying to summon the proper words from the shadow-misted rafters. "If you tried to establish a transfer port to this place without knowing where to seek it, you would fail, because this place is a spatial anomaly, devised and protected by Luki's Power. By Network theory, as far as I understand it, this place does not quite exist, which is why we are safe here for the moment. If we walked down the path from that door, we would connect with another place that Network considers effectively nonexistent, but that pattern comprises much more than a single dwelling, and from *that* place, you might never return to Network at all."

What does he expect me to believe? "If this place does not exist," asked Katerin carefully, "how did we come here?"

"Luki first invited me here many years ago. Having visited her often since then, I know the pattern of her home quite well. I transferred us here."

"By remembering the 'pattern'?"

"If I could give a better answer, I would do so," murmured Quin with a shamefaced shrug. "You know how badly I explain the theory of my work."

Do not allow him to bewilder you, Katerin, or exasperate you into sharpness; you need his help, unless you hope to be abandoned in this nonexistent house—or wish to die like Radge. "Your friend will not be pleased to find me here, will she?"

"No. Luki is not fond of other women, especially pretty ones."

Katerin answered reservedly, "I shall accept that as a compliment."

"Luki does not qualify as a jealous lover, if you were wondering."

"My dear Quin, if I started to list all the things I wonder in your regard, I should be reciting for a year."

Quin's responsive laughter startled her, for it emerged so suddenly and enveloped him so uncontrollably. Katerin felt her entire, absurdly impossible situation well inside of her. She began to laugh with him, though she recognized the source of her own laughter as hysteria.

At some dim moment, she realized that she was sitting beside Quin on a subtly woven rug upon a dirt floor, and he had draped his arm around her, as Michael used to do when she was a child, and Quin was whispering vague words of reassurance to calm her. Quin hugged her until her choking giggles stopped, and the great tears that gushed from her eyes seemed to carry with them all the anguish of the years, the recent months, and the past few days.

He smells of salt air and wood smoke, thought Katerin, and she let the brushed flannel of his anachronist's shirt absorb the tears from her cheeks. He held her without any demanding touch, and she thanked him for offering compassion instead of passion, even as a more calculating part of her wondered, *why?*

"It is not for lack of interest," murmured Quin in a voice that soothed and teased at once. "You have had a rough time lately, O my beautiful lady of Network. I *could* take advantage of your misfortune, but I could derive no pleasure from that sort of abuse." Katerin felt him tilt his head in contemplation. "Perhaps I could derive *some* pleasure from it," he added pensively, and Katerin shuddered, wanting to escape him but too fearful to try.

Whatever his purpose may be, he is human and vulnerable, Katerin told herself, part of her calculating how to manipulate him, and part of her cringing from a nightmare's fear. *He is vulnerable to* me. *He controls the situation now, but I am* not *helpless.* She favored Quin with a thoughtful half-smile, even as the fear inside her whispered, *No! You are susceptible to Quin's peculiar charm; you should not even let him touch you.*

The door slammed closed and flew open again in a flurry of swirling mist and sunlit dust. The abruptness jolted Katerin's sensitized nerves, but Quin restrained her for a moment more. When he released her, he moved slowly and deliberately. *Without guilt,* observed Katerin, respecting his cleverness, as she met the suspicious, narrowed eyes of a very old and astonishingly shriveled woman.

Incomprehensible conversation sputtered between the old woman and Quin. *So,* mused Katerin silently, *we have indeed left Network. They speak neither Network nor Consortium Basic, although I seem to hear a few familiar words. Which independent—other than Network—has mastered topological travel?*

Luki crossed the room to glare at Katerin. The old woman tugged and smoothed her garishly colored skirt with her gnarled hands, betraying the self-consciousness of vanity. Katerin felt a moment of sad sympathy; if any beauty hid in that ravaged frame, it did not shine forth. Luki crouched to inspect Katerin with a tightly puckered expression, extended one hand brusquely, and slapped the palm of it in rapid and demanding repetition.

"Luki wants to examine your hands," remarked Quin equably.

"Palmistry?" asked Katerin in surprise, as she reluctantly yielded to the old woman's impatience.

"Not as you define it," replied Quin. "She wants to assess your personal energy, and this is her method."

Katerin suppressed her revulsion, as Luki's crabbed fingers dug painfully into her skin. The old woman stared at Katerin's hands with a furious concentration. When Luki arose, virtually throwing Katerin from her, she walked directly to one of the dangling packages. Quin's phlegmatic grin faltered, and he squirmed uncomfortably; he shook his head. Katerin wished that she could follow the pair's terse, sharp words, but the meanings eluded her, despite a tantalizing similarity of many sounds to her own native language.

Katerin sensed enough from tone and expression to recognize that Luki won the argument. Luki opened the chosen package and removed a bulbous object, draped in odd, bright rags. Luki carried the object to Quin, and he accepted it from her with a visible sigh of resignation. The rags fell free of it, and the dark object, glimpsed for an instant, blazed in a sudden, harsh brilliance that faded just as quickly to a soft engulfment of sapphire haze. Luki hissed excitedly. Quin retrieved the fallen rag, rewrapped the object and returned it to Luki, who gazed at the now-dark object with loving raptness.

"What is that device?" asked Katerin in a cautious whisper, though Luki seemed to have forgotten her uninvited guests.

"A very old and very defective transfer relay, I think. Luki prizes it, though she has forgotten how to activate it. All I generally do is make it glow, but Luki is pleased with even that little evidence of her treasure's worth."

"Transfer relays are not designed for unprotected handling," responded Katerin sharply, but she stopped herself, remembering that her role as senior technocrat had lost its meaning. *You are a fool, Katerin. Why are you telling him something he knows perfectly well? He is a research assistant at Harberg University, and he is much more that he does not admit.* "How did your friend acquire such a thing?"

"She claims to have found it. As a conjecture, I would say that it comprised part of one of your Network satellites, and its orbit decayed."

"Network satellites do not fall randomly from the sky, and if they did, they would fall on Network worlds, not non-planets."

"Maybe you need to flex your theory a little." Quin shrugged. "You did not ask me how I make it glow."

"Would you give an answer of enough thoroughness to satisfy your inflexible research leader?" asked Katerin, uncomfortably aware of Luki's cold stare.

"No. But you are not really inflexible, only culturally conditioned."

"Unlike you?" *Take advantage of his willingness to answer any question; knowledge is power.*

"I seem to have been conditioned and reconditioned too drastically to remember any intellectual prejudice but bewilderment at the amazing universality of ignorance."

"Was I that inept as an educator?" asked Katerin softly. *Luki is already jealous of me; she will not help me. It is Quin who must concern me.*

"No!" replied Quin. He glanced from Katerin's reflective smile to Luki and returned his gaze to Katerin with an uncertain grimace. "I am not sure what to think of you, Professor Merel, but I felt more comfortable when you disliked me."

"I always feared to like you too much, Quin," said Katerin, and she shivered at the statement's perilous truth. Something unseen touched Katerin's hair, and she recoiled, brushing at the unsettling phantom. "This place must be a haven for spiders," she muttered, staring suspiciously at the cobwebbed rafters.

"It is a haven," answered Quin, "for many creatures and purposes."

"What is your purpose, Quin?"

"To help you," he responded quickly, but he turned from Katerin to Luki, who had begun to issue another spate of sharp questions. Katerin exerted a serious effort to comprehend their conversation, but she could recognize only tantalizing fragments. *The vowels are rounder, and Quin and Luki voice more consonants than current usage dictates, but it is a variation of Network Basic,* decided Katerin, puzzling over the implications of her conclusion. *Do dedicated anachronists adopt a unique dialect along with their other affections?*

Luki shuffled to the door. With a disparaging glance at Katerin, the old woman stepped into her garden. Quin leapt to his feet and followed Luki. Though Katerin hurried after him, both Quin and Luki had disappeared by the time Katerin could join them outside.

The air smelled sweet, heady with the perfume of the brilliant flowers. Katerin strolled into the yard and circled Luki's cottage, but the garden contained only vegetable life and a horde of snails. Katerin tried to pierce the thick, encompassing hedge, but she gained only scratches for her effort. She found a pair of clumsy shears inside the cottage and tried to cut a passage through the hedge at a point that seemed sparse, but the thick branches only bent the soft metal of the shears.

Frustrated, Katerin sat on a stone in the garden. She picked up a round, yellow snail by its shell and watched it squirm in search of solid ground. "We are both helpless and out of place," she murmured to the snail, "but your predicament is more easily solved than mine." She replaced the snail on a tuft of grass and watched it crawl beneath a stone and out of sight.

* * *

"What is this *person,* boy?" demanded Luki, as she tromped furiously down the rough, stone-strewn path to Ixaxis. "Why do you bring her to Luki?"

"She needs help, Luki, and I had nowhere else to take her."

"She is not Ixaxin. She is not Seriin."

"Please, Luki, just let her stay here for a little while. I shall bring you a new shawl from Tulea: scarlet silk, embroidered with great, gaudy flowers. Would you like a new comb, carved from mother-of-pearl?"

"You intend to leave this *person* here for Luki to feed and tend, while you go traveling and forgetting your obligations? Has no one taught you any manners yet, boy?"

"I shall not be gone long, Luki."

Luki stopped so suddenly that Quin almost collided with her. She drove her finger against Quin's chest accusingly. "You travel by Power, like Him," she hissed. "Who taught you?"

"I shall bring you tins of Sandoral candies," wheedled Quin, "all the richest varieties, and biscuits from the Queen's own baker!" He had long wished that Luki were less easily distracted, but he used her weakness now with deliberate, desperate care.

Luki's finger wavered. She snarled, looking much like one of her elusive pets. "What does the Queen's baker know about good biscuits? Queens think a biscuit is fluff and prettiness without flavor. Bring me Hamley biscuits." Quin grinned and kissed her cheek; Luki blushed. "Bring me three large tins from your own Hall, boy, and fill them yourself! That scullery maid never packs the corners properly."

"I shall fill every tin just short of bursting!"

Luki grunted and glanced up the misty path that she had long ago fashioned of Power to tie her home to Ixaxis. "Herbs in the blue tin will make her sleep, boy, instead of asking awkward questions."

"You are a cunning woman, Luki," said Quin with a rueful smile.

* * *

In the highest room of her Tower, the golden-haired Infortiare felt the shuddering of Power's barrier, as a major Power wafted a mortal pattern between the deadly webs. She felt her son stir at the disturbance, and she felt the enormity of his Power reach across the Taormin to nullify the probe of pursuit. He stifled the first probe easily, but a second followed, and the third came quickly, and only the steady strength and swiftness of his Power enabled him to restrain the flow, until his parents jointly sealed the breach.

Rhianna sighed, for even the brief effort had wearied her after nearly a year of constant vigilance, and she knew that the danger had only begun to take shape. "What are we to do with Lord Quinzaine, Kaedric?" whispered Rhianna with her Power. "He did not disobey us; he did not bring Katerin Merel to Serii, and he has told her nothing of consequence. He has jeopardized us, nonetheless, since we must assume that Katerin Merel's enemies have the ability to trace patterns of potent energy. These probes were unlike their predecessors; these probes were directed clearly, and I fear they will resume. Lord Quinzaine's error with Mistress Loisa and Marei becomes a trivial incident in comparison with this transgression."

"Luki's retreat is simply constructed and easily removed from Ixaxis' neighborhood," answered Kaedric. "It is Luki who has been jeopardized directly."

"Quinzaine does not realize what he has done."

"Nor do we. Quin twisted his path capably, and I have felt no further disturbances from Network's probes."

"I have ordered my Wizards' Circle to prepare for nearly immediate attack."

"Very wise. If Network does manage to seize this opportunity to locate us, we can surmise that the form and magnitude of Network's pursuit will be both unexpected and monumental."

"If the attack comes, I shall have no choice but to concentrate my Power on supporting the Wizards' Circle. Jonathan Terry's methods have helped us find order in the Taormin, but the students are still inexperienced in using the Taormin's webs."

"As the Infortiare, you quite properly place your subjects as your first responsibility. They are also our most imminent concern of defense, since they are both vital and untried. Evaric can monitor our barriers alone for a time, if necessary. I shall address Luki's situation."

"And Quinzaine must return to Network and deal with our enemies in their own realm."

"He knows."

"Katerin Merel quite probably considers Quinzaine the enemy. She may try to harm him."

"She is not stupid; she surely realizes that she needs him if she is to return to Network."

"I should warn him to be wary of her. He is too guileless for these games of subterfuge."

Quin's Power drove a single stream of fire into the burning plain of light that two Infortiares had long shared alone: "Am I?" he asked, and bitterness poured from the question.

Rhianna whispered in sorrow, "What have we done to him, Kaedric?"

* * *

Wrapped in night's chill embrace, Quin sat on the chalky point, high above the tossing sea that had tried to conquer Ixaxis for centuries. "I have learned to kill, Laurett," he whispered to the darkness. He did not know whether he spoke to a woman's memory or to an algorithm in a Network machine, but only the seabirds heard him.

"Lady Rhianna and Lord Venkarel think I do not know what I have done to Luki," he murmured, as precisely as if reciting a Network log. "They are wrong. I chose to risk Luki rather than Katerin, Luki rather than Serii, Luki rather than a Healer and his gentle world and alien creatures of light. I have baited a trap with a friend, because Network will always be a threat unless we show ourselves as strong, and Network must attack and fail in order to learn respect for us."

He shook his head at the lights that resembled stars, the lights that were only a topological distortion. "I do know what I have done," he sighed, and his Power ached within him.

* * *

"My lady," murmured Alvedre with a faint, worried frown, "I apologize for interrupting your work, but I have a question that disturbs me."

"Ask it, Alvedre," replied Rhianna, and she tried not to let her exhaustion show in her face, voice, or Power. Alvedre needed encouragement, for Alvedre had been thrust into the maelstrom of the Taormin with little preparation, and she seemed surprised each day that she survived. *Since we so nearly lost Shanah in the Taormin's coils,* thought Rhianna grimly, *all of my chosen students have lost confidence. They do not even realize how much Jonathan Terry's methods have eased their task.*

"Where is Quin?"

Rhianna studied Alvedre thoughtfully before answering, "I do not try to sense his location on a continuous basis, Alvedre."

"I think he is no longer in Network, my lady. I received a note this morning from a fellow instructor of wizardry. Cori is certain that she saw Quin on Ixaxis last night, though his Power's barrier was too strong for her to pierce. He was simply sitting on the cliff's point, staring at the sea. He vanished before she could reach him."

Rhianna nodded stiffly. "I do not doubt that Mistress Cori saw clearly."

* * *

"Despite aberrant sensor readings, convergence of filtered data indicates ninety-eight percent probability that designated coordinates correspond to transfer destination of Katerin Merel."

"Excellent," murmured Caragen with a nod of satisfaction. "Begin sending the full transfer probes immediately to establish the necessary mapping. Arm the contact team for potential combat with a highly sophisticated enemy."

CHAPTER 2

Network and Luki's House

Katerin awoke and panicked to find a strong hand pressed firmly across her mouth. "We need to leave," said Quin in a hushed voice. He glanced toward Luki, who snored loudly from a creaking old bed across the room. "Network is tracking you, and the analysis of your location will soon be complete." His hand relaxed, and Katerin pulled away from him, sat upright, and pressed her back against the uneven wall.

"Tracking me?" whispered Katerin.

"Yes. Visualize your brother's home for me, please. It will make the transfer easier."

Katerin's memory raised unbidden the image of that obsessively neat and perfect apartment that Loisa had chosen, Loisa had dominated, and Loisa had insisted that Michael enjoy. With the memory came disorientation and an illusion of painful light like the product of a sharp, untended headache.

Katerin stared at the austerely pristine room, shaken despite her intention to remain in control of her fear. *This is Michael's apartment or an elaborate duplicate; I know these furnishings, that great crystal sphere, that ugly clay sculpture from Loisa's native world.*

Network, Consortium, or independent—Quin's people have perfected a portable transfer device, a remarkable advancement. What do they want of me? "Your trick is an old one, Quin," she said crisply. "Ask a question to which you already know the answer, and pretend to

clairvoyance in lifting the answer from the hearer's mind.
Where is my brother?"

"In the custody of your enemies," replied Quin,
sounding almost impatient, "who are my enemies, as
well. But you don't believe me, do you?"

Katerin did not try to answer. She walked to the door,
and it did not open. She glanced at Quin, who shrugged,
murmuring, "I had to deactivate the sensors in order to
avoid triggering the security alarms."

"Of course," she said coolly. "I forgot your rapport
with computers." *His anachronistic clothes are bulky,
excellent concealment for any number of advanced devices.*
"Michael!" called Katerin, maintaining a suspicious study
of Quin, who seemed more nervous now than when he
had faced Radge. "Network, where is Michael?"

Quin opened and closed his left hand with restless
force, but he remarked evenly, "I have detached all of
Network's connections to this room. We should have a
few minutes before they track us here."

"Who are 'they'?" demanded Katerin in frustration.

Quin cocked his sun-browned, sun-bleached head; his
gray eyes had a storm's dark promise in them. " 'They'
are the tools of your Council Governor; they are Network. Kitri, I am going to force you to listen to me,
because your distrust could kill us both, and I am sorry,
Kitri, that I must hurt you as you have so often been
hurt already."

*What is he saying? Is he Marrach or Marrach's tool?
Stop it, Kitri. You are letting him manipulate you. You
know the methods; you know all of Network's tricks of
winning trust and gaining obedience, for you have created
many of the algorithms, contributed to many others, and
analyzed all that reside in any documented file. Take control of him.*

Katerin felt the taint of anticipated horror begin, but
once she had resolved the necessary steps within her
mind, all emotions became detached. "You told me once
that I had forgotten my own capacity to believe. Help
me to believe again, Quin. Help me to believe in you."
She touched him tentatively, persuasively. *Look at me,
Quin, and see a woman who needs you more than whatever cause you may have served against her.*

He took her hands, restraining them gently. "I want

you to believe in me, Kitri, more than you imagine. You must stop distracting me with your emotional conditioning techniques."

He is much too clever and resilient, thought Katerin with a trace of desperation.

"I am already too aware of you. In a conceptual sense, you seduced me before we even met, but I cannot afford to indulge my fantasies now. I need to concentrate absolutely on solving our mutual problem."

A sharp pain raced through her head, and she cried aloud. She wanted to run from him, but she could not move, though he seemed to hold her lightly.

"I am going to take you to a Healer, Kitri, and I do not want you to fear him."

The disorienting swirl of transfer made a sick taste rise in Katerin's mouth, and she would have screamed her terror of Quin if she had been able. She felt herself stumble, and Quin steadied her. She opened her eyes to see a grassy knoll and a pastoral scene from an anachronist's dream.

A coppery-haired woman, dressed in a long wool skirt and a woven, undyed shawl, stood before them on a path that led to a stone-and-shingle cottage. The woman said softly, "He is there," and she pointed to the stone cottage. "He expects you."

"Does he?" asked Quin curiously, but the young woman smiled without verbal answer. "Yes, I do have much to learn," admitted Quin, as if replying to words that Katerin could not hear.

A man came to the door of the cottage. He was strongly built with craggy features, and his hazel eyes did not look at Quin, who had nodded at him knowingly, but at Katerin. She returned the man's gaze with hard suspicion. The man called quietly, "Kitri Terry, do you know me?"

Katerin answered, "Marrach," before her conscious mind could understand and fear, but the nightmare began to rise with the name that had always summoned dread.

Marrach walked toward her, and Katerin shrank from him. She would have run, but Quin restrained her easily, though she struggled desperately against him. Marrach approached Katerin, and she ached to scream, but her voice remained imprisoned by the conditioning of a dream's stark terror. Marrach came near to her, and she saw blood and fire, dingy rooms on despairing worlds, death and a lump of limp, black fur, a ruined planet, and the bodies of a woman and a man who were her parents. Great, hot tears burned her eyes.

"Your parents are not dead, Kitri," said Marrach, and Katerin heard her own pain in his rich, indomitable voice. "I lied to you. I projected an image of them onto the bodies of two strangers. I conditioned you to accept my lies, as I conditioned you to trust only your brother and those to whom I gave the proper trigger words and actions in the programmed sequence. Caragen has been manipulating you, reviving the life and history locked inside you, in order to use you against your father and against me."

Katerin writhed in Quin's strong grip and tried to recoil from Marrach, who raised his closed hands and let them hover on either side of her face. She found her voice and cursed both men. "Let him try to heal you, Kitri," pleaded Quin. His gray eyes mirrored her anguish, and she felt him whisper, *I would not hurt you or let you be hurt, dear Katerin.*

Marrach's hands opened, and in each palm he held a green stone. He pressed the stones against Katerin's cheeks. They felt cold, but a warmth spread from them, and Katerin fancied that a wreath of gold encircled Marrach's head. The light-dance around his head consumed all of her attention. She could not recall what she had feared or why.

"Kitri Terry, code jxs37373," said Marrach with a precision that might have emerged directly from Network. He shuddered and let his hands fall to his sides. The coppery-haired woman rushed to him and touched him with concern.

Katerin raised her hand to her head. The base of her skull ached, but she did not feel injured. She realized that she was sitting cross-legged on the grass, her black gauze skirts splayed around her, though she could not remember having moved to that position.

"The confusion will pass," said Quin gently. He knelt beside her, studying her with concern. "He removed the chemical aspects of conditioning from you."

Katerin frowned at him, trying to regain some clarity of thought. *Chemical injections of controlled-reaction viruses often accompany the most intense of conditioning techniques,* she thought, forcing herself to assess her own reactions as if she were merely a problem in mathematical psychology. *Have I been injected with an antidote for the past? What do these people want of me? What do you want of me, Quin?*

"She has an active tracking implant in her," said Marrach, and he sounded weary.

"I know," replied Quin, never removing his gaze from Katerin.

I look at him, and I cannot fear him as I should. I am not sure that I trust him, but I cannot hate him. He matters to me. Quin, please, explain to me—something.

"Caragen monitors this planet constantly," continued Marrach, observing Quin with a sharp, curious attentiveness. "He knows that you have brought Katerin Merel here. If he had any remaining doubts of our alliance, you have eliminated them."

"A wise friend once told me that the only way to solve a problem is to confront it," answered Quin. Marrach nodded at his comment, smiling slightly. Quin's hand cupped Katerin's face, and she did not try to retreat from him; the effort seemed futile to her, and she was not even sure that she wanted to evade his touch. "Katerin, I shall come back for you, if I survive the next hour. If I do not survive, Marrach will be better able to keep you safe than anyone else I know, for my own world may well be vaporized by Network."

"Quin," she whispered, "please tell me what is happening."

"I think I love you, Katerin," he said very seriously. Before she could anticipate his intent, he kissed her, a hesitant brushing of lips, and then he withdrew from her. He stood, took three steps across the grass, and vanished in a shimmering shadow.

The coppery-haired woman came to Katerin. "My name is Evjenial," she said, "Healer of Revgaenian." She extended her hand to Katerin. "If you wish to come inside, I shall make us some tea. Rabh may be able to answer some of your questions."

Reluctantly, Katerin pulled her attention from the

patch of empty daylight where Quin had disappeared.
She accepted Evjenial's hand and help in rising to her
still-unsteady feet. "What world is this?" she asked,
though her battered emotions reeled at Quin's admission.

"Siatha."

Katerin nodded toward Marrach, though she did not
quite dare to meet his eyes or address him individually.
"He is Rabh Marrach?"

"Yes," replied Evjenial solemnly, "but he is no longer
your enemy. Be at peace, Katerin. The Mirlai will not
let the battlefield come here."

CHAPTER 3

Luki's House

"Luki," whispered the dark, sardonic voice, and the old woman stirred restlessly in her sleep.

"Dreams," she muttered on the rim of wakefulness, "haunted dreams."

"Not dreams, Luki, not this time."

Luki forced her old body upright in the bed, and the wooden frame creaked and moaned like her gnarled bones. "Who is it?" she demanded suspiciously.

"You have not forgotten me," remarked the voice in calm assurance. Luki snatched her shawl from the bedpost and wrapped it tightly about her. Not all of her shivering came from the cold of the night.

"Venkarel," she hissed between the gaps of her few remaining teeth. "Is it truly you, boy?"

"Yes, Luki."

Slowly, the old woman's eyes widened. "Your Power always did dominate the rest of you."

"Tell your furred friends to return to their own dens, Luki. You must come with me."

"With you?" Luki began to shake her head slowly, then with increasing energy. "Luki has her place here, and here is where she belongs."

"I am sorry, Luki, but I shall insist, and your Power cannot counter mine. Your home cannot continue to exist much longer. You must come with me."

"Luki is not ready to take that path, boy."

"You were ready long ago, Luki, as we both know."

Luki's scraggly head sagged against her withered chest. "I fear, boy. I have always feared."

"I know, Luki. That is why I have come, so that you need not make the journey alone."

"Who will tend my roses?"

"Their proper owners, from whom you stole them."

Luki cackled softly. "All are dead. All the mortals Luki knew are dead long ago."

"Are you ready, Luki?"

The old woman shuddered. With trembling hands, Luki shook the bonds that held the Widowshear, and the lump of metal fell into her gnarled hands. She gazed at it with a sad and loving raptness. "My husband, Elam, and I found it by Power," she murmured, "wedged in a sea cave and buried by sand. We were young and strong in Power, and we believed ourselves invincible. We used it rashly, telling not even the Infortiare." Luki's eyes misted. "The Infortiare of that time was a weak man, little more than a puppet of a weak king. I would have told you as liege, boy, but you were not yet born."

"The ruling lines of Lord Ceallagh and King Tul have weakened too often in unison," answered Kaedric.

"Elam and I learned that we could use our tool to travel across the country by will of Power alone, but we erred one day. We strayed from Serii, which we knew, into another place, a strange place."

"It became this refuge of yours, which you furnished via the same tool," murmured Kaedric, for he knew her story.

"Elam reached farther," said Luki, and she cried aloud in a sudden burst of anguish. "I felt him go from me, but I could not hold him. I felt his life sheared from my soul. I waited here for him, dreading to use the *tool*, and then I could no longer use it. I hoped that you could bring him back to me, boy."

"I cannot restore a life, dear Luki."

Luki shook herself and brushed away a tear impatiently. "Except your own," she muttered.

"I never died. I exchanged one form of life for another."

"Did Elam die?"

"I do not know. Our Immortal blood makes such questions uncertain."

"You will lead me to him now."

"If that is the path you wish to follow, I shall lead you by the course his pattern took."

Luki gripped the Widowshear tightly to her bony chest. "I am ready."

"Leave the Widowshear, Luki. You cannot cling to your treasures any longer."

She dropped the Widowshear, as if it burned her, and it rolled across the dirt floor to the edge of the rug. Luki drew her gaze lovingly across the cluttered, dusty room. She sighed and closed her eyes, and she spoke with a Power that had once been mighty. "I release this place, these friends and treasures, all that I have held." As she spoke, her ancient Power freed the strands of energy that she had gathered to form her haven, and the space that her Power had fashioned began to drift into its natural form. A rock shifted on Ixaxis; a lonely gully in Serii's desolate north became a craggy hill; a very old garden in Alvenhame acquired a few more roses.

Luki opened the inner sight of Power, and she smiled at the fiercely lean young man with the ice-blue eyes. "You have not changed, Kaedric."

"Not for you, Luki. Come."

"Is it far?"

"No, Luki, it is not far."

* * *

Alvedre watched her fellow students and measured their patterns again in her mind. She knew them well, but she would have little time to react or recall. Her Power waited, lightly touching all those whom she would guide. Some of them felt fear; all of them felt anticipation clawing at their Powers' concentration with merciless talons. They did not know what they would see or when the attack would come. The Infortiare had assured them to expect an imminent threat.

Network, by the words of Quin's report, is a thing much like the Taormin, but Network extends much farther and is ruled by a ruthless man. By Jonathan Terry's words, Network is an amalgam of calculating machines, as well as the name of a human civilization. Will Network send human soldiers or machines? Both, says Jonathan Terry; and that is why we wait.

Alvedre felt a shift of Power, so slight that she almost missed it. She sent a gentle tap of Power as a warning to her fellows in the Wizards' Circle, and all members became alert. She saw the ripple of air begin, and she reached for the patterns behind it.

So, she concluded, feeling the tensions and trepidations of those who guided the probes and weapons of Network attack, *we are not alone in our uncertainty.* Alvedre sent her strength with her perceptions to the other members of the Circle.

She tried to count the patterns that struggled to approach, but the numbers grew too large. Mechanisms appeared, but they fell easily to wizard's Power, for Lady Rhianna had interpreted Jonathan Terry's instructions for eliminating the fragile energy sources of the devices. The human invaders were more difficult to counter, for Ceallagh's laws made such war an agony of conscience. The ripple of air firmed into solid flesh of men throwing burning energy as they emerged.

Let them come, whispered Rhianna's Power, and Alvedre cried the signal to her Circle. Power drank of the energy that the Network soldiers hurled, but the soldiers gathered thickly in the barren space that had been Luki's garden. The energy burned against the darkening sky.

Take them now, ordered Rhianna, and the Circle closed the barrier that the soldiers had been allowed to penetrate. The weapons smoldered in the soldiers' hands, and the men dropped their searing tools in shock. A Wizards' Circle of Power gathered the soldiers' patterns in a web and cast them to the surface of another world, selected by Jon Terry.

* * *

"Has the contact team reported yet?" demanded Caragen.

"No report has been received since transfer acknowledgment," droned Network.

"Incompetents," growled Caragen, but the report troubled him. "Display sensor reading of contact team."

"Data not available."

"Sensor malfunction?"

"No malfunction exists. Designated coordinates correspond to spatial void."

Caragen clenched his fist across his mouth and muttered, "I thought we had resolved that anomaly. Explain conflict with previous report of benign environment, Network."

"Tenable transfer destination at designated coordinates ceased to exist within past fifteen seconds. Precise event time is not yet available. Data reduction and analysis is proceeding. Transfer team has just reported from the port on Perseus-2: 'All team members suffered blackout immediately after transfer acknowledgment, regained consciousness on exiting Perseus-2 port, and retain no memory of other events subsequent to initial transfer. Request further instructions.' How shall I instruct them?"

"Tell the team leaders to transfer back here immediately and report for thorough examination. Did any of them manage to retain their portable monitoring units?"

"Yes."

"Good. Access that data as soon as possible."

"Confirmed."

"Where is Katerin Merel?"

"Preliminary analysis indicates that she has transferred to the Temler spatial region. Specific location is not yet available."

"Chia-2 is in Temler," snapped Caragen. "She has gone to find her brother. Focus resources accordingly."

"Acknowledged."

Caragen muttered, "Why Perseus-2?" He drummed his fingers on the broad desk before him. "Network, name the five planets of closest topological proximity to Perseus-2."

"Perseus-1, Alegia, Network-1, Network-2, Copra-L."

"And Network-3," added Caragen under his breath.

"Network-3 is closed."

"Except to Jonathan Terry. Network, search all archived files containing Jonathan Terry's analyses on the reopening of Network-3. Correlate all transfer mappings with data obtained from this singularly uncooperative, nonexistent space. Prepare to transfer sufficient orbital weaponry to implement a full planetary destruction. I want that weaponry available to me as soon as a mapping to Network-3 is reestablished."

"Correlation results are unlikely to provide a definitive

mapping of the specified nature, based on previous lack of success in this area of analysis."

"We have more data now. We have the crucial data," snapped Caragen. "The mapping exists, and Jonathan Terry discovered it. One naive technocrat is not greater than all of Network. We will find the answer in this data, or we will find it in tracking Katerin Merel, but we will find it quickly, Network. Not Marrach and his wretched Mirlai, not Jonathan Terry, not all of Dr. Terry's mad Immortals will claim my power from me. Contact Maryta Deavol. Tell her to atone for her sins by assimilating her analysis team's independent results into Network. Perhaps they can make some small contribution."

"Acknowledged."

* * *

"You should not be so solemn, beloved," said Kaedric gently. "We have won our first battle against Network."

"A single battle. We are so few, trying to fight in so many directions at once. Network has virtually endless resources."

"But our resources are exceptional."

"Yes, and I am asking so much of them," sighed Rhianna. "I gave the Widowshear to Jonathan Terry. He was delighted, as you predicted."

"I hope he can make good use of the device."

"Eventually, perhaps," murmured Rhianna sadly. "Kaedric, I wish there had been another way."

"Luki's time ended long ago, beloved. She waited only for someone to help her relinquish her Power's hold."

"Quin will grieve."

"As will I, but I have walked a long part of that road. I think Luki is glad to be joining her Elam at last. The decision was hard but needful in many respects."

"Shall we be any wiser, Kaedric, in knowing when we must yield our Power?"

"No, but we may hope that someone will be wise enough to tell us."

CHAPTER 4

Network and Serii

Quin paced in the Merels' apartment on Chia-2. He paused before a crystal sphere and stared at his distorted reflection. He breathed deeply, and he sent his Power into Network to reactivate the normal access. "Hello, Network," he said carefully, and he felt the sensors gathering and correlating data to identify him.

"Hello, Quin. Your energy levels show aberrations, which require detailed analysis. Please report to a medical center immediately."

Quin smiled. "Sorry, Network. I cannot comply at the moment, and aberrant energy readings are really quite natural for me. I also doubt that your medical center would appreciate being made the target of attack by your Council Governor, simply for the crime of housing me."

"Your reply indicates severe confusion. Please consume prescribed restorative."

"No, thank you," answered Quin, "though the offer is tempting. I should like to be able to forget that I have just lost a special friend—by my own deliberate fulfillment of her unwitting prophecy. Luki always did confuse me with Lord Venkarel." Quin's mouth smiled, but the expression held more sorrow than joy. Quin sent a light tap of Power along a well-planned route. He shivered as the furious fire of the Venkarel touched the edges of his awareness.

"Readings indicate severe physical duress," said Network. "Please ingest restorative immediately."

Quin clenched his teeth against the pain of denying his own Power's instinctive, shrieking protest of danger from the Venkarel. Quin forced his Power to open outward, despite the urgent compulsion to hide or flee. A fury like death hurtled into him, and the Venkarel's fire burned him from within.

"Lords," muttered Quin, collapsing to his knees beneath the weight of agony. He felt the Venkarel shudder with him at the parade of deaths that fierce Power had exacted in the Venkarel's mortal lifetime. "I warned you," gasped Quin roughly, though he did not form the words from his own intent.

"Focus," said Quin, and his Power summoned stern Ixaxin discipline. He drew himself stiffly to his feet. He felt the explosion of energy from a device far distant in the sky above him. The energy hurtled forth, and Quin felt its heat growing as it approached and pierced the atmosphere. He hurled the bolt back upon itself, and the mechanism that had issued it exploded in space.

He drove the Venkarel's Power into Network, tracking the paths relentlessly to reach the source of the command that had issued the attack. He grasped the pattern of the man whose voice had initiated Network's actions. He stepped into the Taormin's webs.

* * *

Alvedre moved cautiously among the strands of infinity, seeking and sorting, though Lord Venkarel had provided the directions for her search. She shivered in considering the man, the thought of him at once terrifying and irresistible. She sensed the patterns shift treacherously around her, as her Power compelled her to seek the wizard instead of a Network mortal.

Alvedre stopped the impulse sternly. Even if she had not accepted the weight of a solemn obligation to her liege-lady, she would not have dared to approach Lord Venkarel uninvited. She was foolish to wish to sense his extraordinary Power again, to see again the image of lean, dark elegance and ice-blue eyes. He had shown her no trace of kindness or gentleness, only the hard ferocity of raw Power's strictest lessons.

"Stop thinking of him," Alvedre muttered nervously. "You owe better loyalty to Lady Rhianna, if not better sense for yourself." She forced her concentration to pursue her proper goal.

The strands of mortal patterns were so dim that she nearly missed them altogether, even knowing where to look. With a sigh, she let her Power guide her through the Taormin's gate, reciting the rigid litany that Jonathan Terry had evolved from his own mathematical model and Lady Rhianna's explanations of pattern behavior. Alvedre reached for a space that felt both safe and near to her precise location. She stepped into a hollow metallic shell and nearly panicked at the strangeness of smells and sounds.

Collect Michael Merel and return immediately, she recited to herself.

She walked uneasily through the silver corridor, disconcerted by the faint, echoing ring of her footsteps. Her Power felt the approach of two men, and her Power wove an instinctive shadow around her by redirecting the light. The men passed her without observing her.

Alvedre reached the door behind which she perceived Michael Merel. She felt the energy that sealed the door, and Network's vastness appalled her. As she rerouted the lock's twisting energy strands, she gave mental thanks that she had not been burdened with the responsibility of forming a life in Network.

A web of forces like a wizard's barrier encompassed Michael Merel, but Alvedre knew him by his pattern and his description: slightly taller than the average man of Serii, gifted with the father's coloring and the mother's sharp bone structure. Alvedre wrinkled her brow in concern, for ugly black and yellowed bruises ran from the veins of his arms, legs, and neck. She probed carefully to assess the extent of the damage, and she felt the shock of Network's enormous energy rack the tiny cell.

An alarm rang loudly, but Alvedre did not try to track its source to stop it. The greater alarm had already escaped her control, and too many enemies already converged on her. She hurried to free Michael of the entrapment, praying that she would not damage him further in her necessary haste.

She cried aloud as an unexpected bolt of energy drove through her Power's defenses and burned a swath across her back. The next bolt recoiled upon its issuer, but

Alvedre did not realize that her Power had killed. She touched Michael to focus her Power, and she gathered his pattern into her control. She stretched her Power across infinity, trying to retrace her path to reach the Taormin.

The physical injury tugged at her concentration, weakening her. On the verge of despair, Alvedre sensed a familiar strength and hurled her Power toward the beacon. In an Ixaxin garden, Alvedre collapsed at the feet of Mistress Amila. Alvedre's Power set Michael Merel carefully on the soft wind-grass beside a gnarled cypress.

*   *   *

A monumental creature, deathless and cold, lumbered through space. The sense of a deafening din throbbed within the silence of absolute void. This beast bore its passengers without question or complaint. It served a tyrannical master.

"Network," snapped Caragen, ensconced in his office aboard his vast space yacht, "the explanation, 'weapon malfunction,' is inadequate. How did this agent, Quin Hamley, counter the attack and escape from Chia-2? Identify his conspirators."

"Insufficient data exist."

"Where is Quin Hamley now?"

"Unknown." A alarm tone rang softly. "Tracking analysis on Katerin Merel is complete. She is on the planet Siatha."

"The one world that I dare not touch," grunted Caragen with a rare depth of bitterness, "as Marrach knows." *I invested him with too much of myself and created the very nemesis that I shunned of biological procreation.* "What is your progress in locating Network-3?"

"Three candidate mappings were identified in Dr. Terry's briefing to the Network Council in Network Year 2283. The third of the referenced mappings corresponds to the designated anomalous region within a two-parameter tolerance. The two parameters of dispute are undergoing analysis by full staff with peak computational resources."

"Two pathetic parameters," grumbled Caragen. "Network, have the analysts established any candidate mappings with higher than fifty percent probability of correspondence to Network-3?"

"Probability of mapping 8a is fifty-one percent. Probability of mapping 14e is sixty-three percent." A alarm tone rang. "Alert: Michael Merel is no longer in interrogation cell."

Caragen pounded his desk furiously. "Explain."

"Unidentified intruder triggered alarm. Intruder and Michael Merel disappeared from sensor range. Michael Merel is not detectable in Network."

"Track him! Steal the computational resources from every university in Network, but find him now. Give me his most probable location."

"Conclusions are preliminary. Filter parameters have not yet stabilized completely."

"Enough disclaimers! What is the current estimate?"

"Current values of the filter states correspond to a topological anomaly."

"Correlate with concurrent Network-3 analysis."

"Nineteen-point correspondence exists with mapping 14e."

Caragen leaned heavily back in his chair. "Utilize mapping 14e for the programmed attack procedure."

"Mapping probability is still inadequate to justify requested action. Attack against unknown space is inadvisable."

"The space is not unknown to me," said Caragen, "or to Marrach. Begin assault."

"Confirmed."

* * *

The shattering of a world's barrier rocked every wizard of the Seriin Alliance. Whispers of alarm raced across Ixaxis. Howald and Amila exchanged a glance of fear and recognized each other's doubts. Amila again bent over Alvedre's unconscious body, trying desperately to cling to the battered wizardess' fading life. Howald linked his Power to Amila's effort.

Lord Arineuil shivered, sensing the disaster, though he lacked more than than a trace of Power. Queen Joli raised her hand abruptly to silence her Councillors. "What is it, Arineuil?" she asked.

"I think we are at war," he replied soberly.

In the Infortiare's Tower, a Wizards' Circle joined their Powers to thwart the assault of energies against their world. Lord Evaric sat grimly in a corner of the Infortiare's library, though his Power labored to hold the strands of the Taormin intact. His darkly lovely wife sat on the floor near him, her skirts forming a brightly colored splash around her; Lyriel watched her husband in great fear for him, but she knew she could do nothing to help.

Across the room, Jon and Beth Terry observed the eerie, remote expression of the man who walked among infinities, and they shared his mortal wife's feeling of helplessness. Beth clutched Marei more closely. Jon prodded the inactive Widowshear, wishing he had better equipment; it irked him to be unable even to track the progress of the battle.

Rhianna sat alone in her Tower's highest room. Like her son, she walked by Power. She aided him. She aided her Wizards' Circle. She felt the pain of her husband's Power trying to coexist with Quin, and she shared the anguish, but she did not yield to it. She felt Ixaxis reach to her and offer belated help, and she snatched the proffered Power greedily and cast it forth against the enemy. The attacks did not cease.

* * *

"Second transfer of orbital destructors to Network-3 is complete," announced Network evenly. "Contingency squadrons are being readied on Network-2."

"Have you analyzed the nature of their weapons yet?"

"Specific weapons not yet identified, but they employ both coherent and diffuse energy techniques. No advanced technology is detectable on Network-3. Preliminary readings indicate a preindustrial civilization. Obvious existence of energy weapons suggests that elaborate sensor deceptions are being employed."

"Evaluate progress."

"No penetration has yet been achieved. Minor reduction in total energy level exuded by Network-3 has occurred since attack began, but the quantitative value is insufficient to alter progress statistics significantly. Monitoring of power parameter has just registered another decrease. Rabhadur Marrach requests communication with you."

"Tell him he is too late," snapped Caragen. "The terms of our agreement included Siatha only. Network-3 is mine, and I trust his Mirlai to abide by that agreement."

"You are colder than your computers," remarked an unfamiliar voice.

A soft alarm rang simultaneously. "Intruder is detected in . . ." said Network, but the alarm stopped abruptly, and the room became quiet.

Caragen spun his chair to see a young man, an anachronist, leaning against the burnished panels that concealed an automated door. "Network, identify intruder," ordered Caragen, but Network did not answer, and the console became dark and still. Caragen struck the manual security alarm. His fingers sought the indentation which could manipulate an impressive assortment of destructive energy weapons.

"If you operate any of those weapons of yours," remarked the anachronist with a shake of his finely shaped head, "it is you who will suffer. I do react badly to attacks on my person."

Three lethal beams of energy converged on the anachronist from three corners of the room. The issuing weapons smoldered in scorched casings, and the anachronist shrugged ruefully. "Never throw energy at a wizard, Master Caragen."

Caragen narrowed his eyes, leaned back in his massive chair, and appraised the intruder. "Do you always make your entrances with such ill-mannered flair, Citizen Hamley?"

Quin raised his brows. "I am flattered to be recognized by a man of such importance. Abort your attack on Network-3."

"You have deprived me of that ability," replied Caragen with a false amiability. His molded-and-remolded face wielded a shark's promise of a lesser creature's death. "Did you employ Jonathan Terry's inventions to arrive here uninvited, deactivate my Network console, and apparently overcome a very expensive security system? Or did Marrach abuse his privileged access to Network once again?"

The console hummed softly, and its lights reappeared. Caragen waved his hand curtly across the console's sensor field. "Unable to comply," answered Network. A startled Council Governor glared at his console.

"Network," said Quin, "abort attack on Network-3."

Network did not reply, and Caragen's slight smile began to revive. "Network is mine, Citizen Hamley," said Caragen with a confidence that was real. "Network, implement file 11-9."

"Acknowledged."

Caragen murmured, "You are dead, Citizen Hamley, as is your world."

Quin stared fixedly at Caragen, until Caragen found himself discomfitted despite his arrogant assurance of authority. The guards should have arrived. The automated defenses should have been activated, shielding Caragen and killing anyone else in the room.

"You are very old for a mortal," said Quin with a calm that carried an unsettling certainty of condemnation. "You are old and very corrupt. Even this vessel of yours reflects corruption. Evil designed it; evil maintains it. Network contains so much that is good and worthy; I wonder how a man like you has managed to control it for so long without destroying it."

"You have poor manners, Citizen."

"Deception for the sake of courtesy is an overrated art." Quin sauntered toward Caragen's desk. "You do have some remarkable methods of securing your authority, and I do not have time to unravel them." Quin tapped the desk, as if assuring himself of its quality. "A fine piece of craftsmanship," he commented evenly. "I did not think your people still understood carpentry."

"Did Marrach send you here?" demanded Caragen coldly.

"No."

"You have visited him," accused Caragen.

"Yes. But I do not serve him."

"Whose agent are you?" asked Caragen in the hard, staccato voice that had commanded many deaths.

"I serve the Infortiare of Serii. I am an Immortal wizard, Council Governor, and you *will* cease your attack on my people."

Caragen jerked, as pain shot through his head. He

tried to rise from his chair, but his legs would not support him. *Cease attack of Network-3*, said the voice of fire in his head, and he echoed it hollowly, "Cease attack of Network-3."

"Acknowledged," answered Network.

The pain ebbed to a dull throb. "Network, supply restorative," muttered Caragen. He glared at Quin. "Who are you?"

"Lord Quinzaine an Jiar yn Aliria dur Hamley, if you want the whole tedious name, but for you, I am Warning and Retribution. I dislike you excessively, Master Caragen, and I can tolerate a great many flaws and quirks. Since you have neither Power nor honor to make you a respectable foe, I shall use restraint in dealing with you."

"You boast as emptily as a Calongi," spat Caragen in disgust.

"You are a pathetic, avaricious, friendless old man, trying to cling to the hollow glory and influence you have bought with your life. You thought you conquered Jonathan and Elizabeth Terry, but you only engendered their escape. You thought you could control their children, but you were wrong. Your own prized vassal, Marrach, has abandoned you, and your own treacherous pattern has deceived you. All of your calculating concerns defeat only yourself!"

"Citizen Hamley," said Caragen in perfect coldness, "you have poor manners, but I might have some use for you. I can pay you far more than you will earn from anyone else, and I can give you worlds of your own, if you satisfy me."

"Is your private universe so treacherous that you would believe me if I acquiesced to your offer? No, Council Governor. I have no ambitions to rule worlds, and I already have more wealth than I need. You have not understood yet. Your own Network produced me. Your Genetic Research Center designed my ancestors to live a thousand years or more, and the researchers named us Immortals, but they feared us—with good reason. We can kill by a careless thought, Council Governor, and I could kill you now with hardly a qualm."

"You are not that much of a fool," said Caragen, and he sneered, as if he spoke an insult. "You would not be jabbering at me now, if you did not want something from me."

"You are quite correct. I want you to know what Power means—the Power that drove Dr. Jonathan Terry to close a world from dread of it. I want Network to incorporate the data, as I teach you, because I will not have the shadow of your petty, acquisitive schemings looming over my world. I want the same truce you have given Rabhadur Marrach. Like him, I want nothing more than is already mine."

Caragen laughed contemptuously. "You play the same sanctimonious part with the same dearth of conviction."

Quin stepped away from the desk and walked toward the doors. They opened automatically onto a stark, white anteroom. "Where are the guards you summoned with your 'file 11-9'? Where are your loyal supporters? Look at your domain, Caragen. It is empty."

"Network," ordered Caragen, "implement incarceration procedures."

"No resources available," replied Network.

"Explain," snapped Caragen.

Network complied: "Power sources have been deactivated throughout ship, except to Network communication transponders and this office suite. Automated devices within suite, except direct Network connections, are inoperative. No human assets remain on ship, except in this office suite."

Caragen heaved himself from his chair and stormed past Quin and into the anteroom. The anteroom's outer doors opened on darkness. The motion of the doors stirred a chill draft of stale air.

"Advise resecuring the anteroom doors," said Network. "Power loss affects internal atmosphere and temperature."

Quin came to stand at Caragen's back. "I transferred all your people to the planet below us," said Quin, "Network-1, I believe. I have never manipulated so many mortal patterns simultaneously. I cannot expect you to appreciate the control required to keep them all alive. I could have killed them very easily, but I did not want to punish the servants for their liege's crimes."

Caragen turned his sharp, cruel gaze on Quin. "You are an interesting young man," remarked Caragen without expression, and he returned to his office and resumed his chair. "Network, assess my present options."

Quin answered, "None," and Caragen found himself sitting on a dirty walkway in the middle of a crowded market square. Several curious citizens stared at him, obviously bewildered by his sudden, undignified arrival. Quin stepped from a shadow and smiled at the gawkers. "I employ my own transfer technique," he announced to them. "Observe a wizard's Power, Network."

Quin closed his eyes and raised his right hand, his palm up and open, toward the dusky blue sky. His left hand seemed to draw a burst of emerald fire from the substance of the walkway. Several of the nearest Network citizens jumped back from him in alarm, but the crowd of observers increased in density. The fire coursed into Quin, carrying a throbbing sense of tremendous energy, though only the glowing center of Quin's left palm betrayed fire's persistent flow. Quin stood motionless, improbably poised, as the mutters of the crowd grew louder.

Caragen shifted uncomfortably, rose to his feet, and brushed gray dust from his dark trousers with disgust. He grabbed the wrist of an elderly woman and pulled her Network wristband from her. Before the woman could protest, he glared at her and said, "Network, if this woman speaks, kill her." The woman gaped and backed away from him into the crowd. "Network, contact my guards." Caragen forgot his next command, when he looked again at Quin.

The fire that Quin had drawn within him from the planet's core hurtled forth from his right hand in a shivering column of cobalt haze. The light pierced the sky, a beacon and a warning and a judgment. The explosion of a space yacht in the heavens scattered into dust all the elements of a twisted man's throne of power, and Caragen stared at the evidence of destruction with mute fury.

A haze of diffused light cloaked the sky with a smoky pallor, but the haze cleared. The sapphire glow that wreathed Quin grew pale and white, fading until it only crowned him with an ethereal mist, and then it vanished altogether. The walkway at his feet had been warped and fused into lumps of colorless glass. The shocked crowd edged away from Quin in fear.

"Council Governor," said Quin hollowly, his voice as penetrating as an inescapable wind, "you may remain on this planet, which your ship circled, or you may choose another, and I shall send you there."

Caragen stared at Quin with a coldly furious silence that acknowledged no weakening of his absolute pride. "I want no favors from you, *Lord* Quinzaine."

"Network," shouted Quin to the walls of the city, "I am an Immortal wizard from a planet of the same. I have shown you the Power that is in every wizard of my world. What is the probability that you could conquer us successfully, based on the recent demonstration?"

"Three point six percent," boomed the broadcast voice of Network.

"Do I have my truce, Caragen?" asked Quin with a deadly fire in his eyes.

Caragen grunted, "You have your truce."

Quin nodded curtly and disappeared in a ripple of air.

*   *   *

The patterns of the Taormin seemed unstable, like a stormy sea. Quin tried to follow the ways he knew, but they blurred and shifted. Exhausted Power could not hold its focus, could not even recall who or what defined it.

"I am lost, Luki," cried Quin to the ghost of a friend. He tried to touch the Widowshear, but he felt only an empty coldness.

He stumbled and touched a strand of errant energy, and it snapped against him, searing him and clinging to him cruelly. He cried to the Infortiare and to Ixaxis, but they were too sorely battered themselves to hear. "Venkarel," he muttered, but that Power was entwined with his, and he was the Venkarel.

"I am infinity," he sighed and abandoned the struggle to retrieve a merely mortal life.

A swirl of golden light surrounded him, and the agony of the Taormin's entrapments ebbed. He felt the Venkarel's Power lifted from him, and Quin imagined the lean, dark wizard carried by a wreath of light, as if on a bier of blazing flowers. Quin sensed that he floated on a similar illusion of light, but he did not care.

Quin basked in the warmth, as the energy of hope

flowed into him. His Power did not stir, for it was sorely wounded and weary to the point of death. The blazing golden light seemed so welcoming. Death seemed such an easy, pleasant course.

He felt the weight of heavy years fall from him. *This is wholeness,* he thought in wonder. He suddenly perceived the magnitude of emptiness that had lain in him, a tiny hole torn wide by his parents' deaths and every subsequent threat of pain. He had learned so well to ignore the gaping inner wound.

Lack of the wound felt strange. *An ironic gift of death,* he thought and sighed, feeling his life seeping from him. *I finally have a self worth giving you, Katerin, but I have lost my opportunity to give anything to anyone.*

Not yet, replied a chiming voice that filled him.

Quin tried to form a question, but his Power still lay dormant in exhaustion. He accepted the deep oblivion of a wizard's healing sleep, cradled in a Mirlai dream.

CHAPTER 5

Network and Serii

Tea and biscuits have phenomenally consoling properties,
mused Katerin, observing the young, coppery-haired
Healer of Revgaenian replenishing the plates. *I should
be torn asunder by the conflicts and questions inside me,
but I feel an unreasonable peace.* "There is so much that
I still do not understand," murmured Katerin.

Marrach sipped his tea thoughtfully before replying,
"You have sufficient knowledge of conditioning techniques to recognize that what I have told you matches
your own observations."

"Yes," sighed Katerin, "I have long known that I was
conditioned. I had also suspected that such a conditioning virus as you describe had been injected into my system, since I was unable to overcome the conditioning by
any of the recognized recovery algorithms. I can even
accept, if only intellectually, that my parents are Jonathan and Elizabeth Terry, who still live on Network-3.
Why Michael and I were so long abandoned. . . ." She
paused.

"Do not judge them," said Evjenial softly. "You do
not know what they have suffered."

"And they did send Quin to me," acknowledged Katerin with an uneven smile. "My eccentric assistant, the
mad Immortal. Why did he say that he might not survive?" *And did he actually say he loved me? I have heard
such words before and never let them touch me. . . . Am
I able to hear them now because Marrach has removed a*

conditioning virus from me, or because the words are Quin's? Dear heaven, let me see Quin again. "Where has he gone?"

"He has confronted Andrew Caragen," replied Marrach with a distant gaze, "and he has taught Network to respect his Power."

An expression of consternation crossed Evjenial's pixie face, and she hurried out of the neat, whitewashed kitchen. "Rabh," she called urgently. Marrach had leapt to his feet and followed her before her cry faded. In a surge of returning fear, Katerin joined them on the patch of lawn in front of the cottage.

A shadow formed in the sunlight, and it shifted and stumbled. Marrach caught the shadow as it fell and became Quin, deathly pale and etched with lines of pain. Marrach lifted Quin and carried him to the house. Katerin reached to touch Quin's face, but Marrach moved too swiftly for her to complete the gesture.

Marrach laid Quin on a cot reserved for the Healers' supplicants. Katerin watched and did not dare interfere as both Healers placed their hands against Quin's head. She watched the Healers work and knew that they fought to save Quin's life. "Please, Quin," she whispered, "you cannot leave me feeling this muddled about you." The Healers continued their labor.

Somewhere during the midst of night, Evjenial pulled her hands away from Quin. Her palms were blistered, and the clear stones she had held earlier had become cloudy. Moments later, Marrach likewise ceased his efforts. Katerin feared to question them. Evjenial smiled wanly. "He will survive," she said, "though I have never felt such depth of injuries before."

"The Immortals were designed for durability," remarked Marrach, and he put his arm around Evjenial. "They will come for you, Katerin," he said gently, "and for Quin. Go with them." Together, the Healers left the room.

Hesitantly, Katerin sat on the cot beside Quin. She pushed a bronze curl from his forehead. His skin felt cold, as if all the inner fire were exhausted. She rested her face against his chest. She fell asleep with the sound of his heart beating against her.

* * *

Beth emerged into the garden in the dawn, before Jon awoke. Birds chattered freely, for the world belonged to them at this hour. The morning felt peaceful.

The Tower cast its long shadow across the castle lands, and the lower circles of the tiered mountain prepared for day. By a quirk of a sound-carrying breeze, Beth could hear distant cries of vendors gathering in the Tulean marketplace. She glimpsed a movement through the rows of slender trees along a path that led to the court residences of the First Houses of Serii. Beth moved toward the figure, expecting to find Rhianna or a scurrying servant. She stopped, realizing her mistake.

Lord Arineuil pushed through the veil of brush that divided the First House gardens from the Tower's less orderly woodlands and meadows. With a courtly bow and a roguish grin, he greeted her. "We seem to think alike this morning, lovely Beth."

When was the last time anyone flirted with me? she asked herself with a faint, pleased whimsy. *I must tell Jon.* "I thought I might find Rhianna," answered Beth.

"If she were awake, she would be here among her trees. This is her refuge."

"The Tower seems so still and empty," said Beth, "after the throbbing, heated atmosphere of yesterday. Did they win?"

Ineuil shrugged, "They did not lose, or they would not have set aside their battle of Power. They are healing now in the way of wizards; they might sleep for months after such exertion, or they might arise this morning in perfect cheer and good health."

"If all are sleeping, who is defending this world?"

"You may be sure that Rhianna attended to that detail before she rested."

"She was exhausted. . . ."

"She has been exhausted since your husband received a message from an old enemy, but she has not indulged herself until now." He gazed upward at the Tower's pinnacle, silhouetted against the brightening sky. "They have won the battle, at least. Perhaps they have won the war."

"I feel helpless, not even knowing what has occurred."

"We mortals are always helpless before *them!* Do you think that Immortal wizards would ever have gained mortal trust for any cause but necessity?" Ineuil grinned broadly. "Have I told you, fair Elizabeth, how I met Rhianna?"

"No."

Ineuil offered his arm and placed Beth's hand upon it when she hesitated. "She emerged from a shadow in an uncivilized burg called Anx. I was there on a Venture with Kaedric, accompanied by a fine old abbot named Medwyn and a pair of hired soldiers." He began to walk, and he held Beth closely at his side.

"My husband may not appreciate your attentions to his wife, Lord Arineuil."

"He will be in good company," replied Ineuil blandly.

Rhianna's cool voice answered from the shadow of a tree, "He will be in the company of nearly every husband in Tulea, Ven, and Alvenhame, if not in all of Serii." The shadow seemed to change form, and Rhianna stood within it. "Elizabeth, we are bringing your children to the Tower. Your son is ill, but he is mending. Your daughter is well in body, and she will heal in heart with time. Your son will arrive from Ixaxis by noon. We must bring your daughter through the Taormin, along with Lord Quinzaine. Tell your husband that this particular morning may be worth facing."

Rhianna faded into a misty light, and only the shadow of an oak tree remained where she had stood. Beth leaned against Ineuil and wept with joy.

* * *

Quin blinked into wakefulness and found a plaster cherub staring at him from the ceiling. "You could stand a lesson in subtlety, Lord Quinzaine," murmured Rhianna. "You exploded the home of Network's Council Governor. You transported several hundred Network citizens hither and thither across several dozen worlds. Your concept of wizard's restraint could use some adjustment."

"I only killed one man," argued Quin, rousing stiffly, "despite the violent temper of your husband's Power."

Rhianna inclined her head fractionally. "I should never have allowed either of you to take such a risk. Do you know what would have happened if you had failed to control that enormity of Power?"

"We would all have died, my lady," replied Quin with

a grimace. He sat upright suddenly. "Why am I not dead?"

"That is a question for which I have no good answer myself. I perceived you drifting into the Taormin with the blindness that kills or captures for eternity. I tried to reach you, but I could not hold the patterns myself, and Evaric failed likewise."

"Lord Venkarel?" demanded Quin in a wave of fear.

Rhianna nodded. "He was with you, and he returned with you. He informs me that he remembers only an odd sense of wholeness between the time he joined you and the time he found himself restored. I received a message telling me to collect you and Katerin Merel from a world known as Siatha. The patterns were supplied for me quite clearly, but the sender was indistinct and elusive."

"Like a dance of light around a Healer's head," murmured Quin, recalling a dream and a golden wreath that enhaloed a Siathan Healer.

"Yes." Rhianna looked at him questioningly.

"The Mirlai are the true healers," answered Quin absently. He shook himself free of reverie. "I am sorry, my lady. I was merely drifting. My report will explain about Marrach and his Mirlai, as much as I understand them. How is Katerin Merel?"

"Troubled, but whole, as is true of most of us. We suffered only one casualty: Mistress Amila. She saved Alvedre and had insufficient Power for herself, but she insisted on leading an Ixaxin Circle of Wizards. She regretted having refused me initially." Rhianna sighed, "She had enormous integrity."

"I am sorry. Howald must be taking her loss very hard. They were close, in their own way."

"Yes."

Quin closed his hand around the cool silk bedding. The center of his left palm itched. He glanced at it; the brand was gone. *The Mirlai are thorough,* he observed with a strange twisting of emotions, too newly unraveled and rearranged. He raised his eyes to the Infortiare, and he looked at her without fear or awe. "I should like to see Katerin," he said quietly. "I have a great deal to explain to her."

Rhianna smiled faintly. "I think you will find her in perfect agreement on that subject." Rhianna walked to the door, but she paused. "You realize that you have announced yourself to all of Network as a major threat."

"That was my purpose, my lady. I wanted Network to recognize us as a threat with teeth."

"We must not make ourselves the rulers, Quinzaine, of anything but Power. By Ceallagh's laws, we must not elevate ourselves above the weakest of the mortals we must protect. It is a difficult law to heed in such turbulent times, but it is vital."

"I have not forgotten, my lady. I do not think that Lord Ceallagh would have excluded Network mortals from that protection. The Council Governor of Network abused his Power, and I corrected him."

"The Council Governor of Network is not a sorcerer."

"You have not met him, my lady."

"No, I have not met him."

*　*　*

"You always did like to oversleep in the morning," Katerin chided her brother, as he stirred in his opulently decorated bed. His face was pale, the freckles sharply etched against the skin. A puckered scar ran along his hairline. Katerin touched the scar gently; it was a mark that few Network citizens would endure, but she thought it added character to her brother's face.

"Stop fussing with me, Kitri," muttered Michael. "My hair is fine."

"Your hair is almost nonexistent at the moment," retorted Katerin, but she smiled to hear him speak again. "What do you remember, Michael?" she asked carefully.

He squinted his eyes in an effort to focus clearly. "Earthquake?" he asked hesitantly.

"Interrogation," countered Katerin quietly.

Michael sighed with a sound of pain. "I do remember. A woman freed me, I think."

"Mistress Alvedre. She is a friend of our parents." Katerin kept her voice steady, though she still felt the shock of meeting Beth Terry, so thin and eager, and Jon Terry, who looked so much like Michael. There was so much to assimilate, and her emotions were worn raw from excessive use in the past nine days, the days since Quin had left her with Marrach.

"Our parents," murmured Michael, "I did not dream them."

"No, dear brother. We have both dreamed for too long by the design of others. It is time to sort the truth from the fabrications of a cruel past."

"Where are Loisa and Marei?"

"Here, in this . . ." Katerin paused, reaching for an adequate description of this enormous anachronists' structure. "They are in a room nearby. Loisa is still recovering from injuries, but she is well enough to feel bewildered by this place and these people."

"What people?"

"Anachronists," answered Katerin, because she did not know what other answer to give. There was so much to try to accept. . . .

Lady Rhianna came to the door, a pale shadow whose eyes still showed the long strain of Power's efforts. "Quinzaine is awake," said Rhianna in her oddly accented Network Basic. "He wishes to see you."

Katerin felt the warmth of embarrassment suffuse her face, and Michael stared at her curiously. "Thank you, Lady Rhianna," answered Katerin. "I shall be back, Michael." Her brother nodded. Katerin avoided brushing against Rhianna with instinctive caution, and Rhianna smiled wryly.

When Katerin reached the room into which she had seen Quin carried, she hesitated, her confidence failing her at the door. "What can I say to him?" she asked herself.

"Good morning, for a start," answered Quin, opening the door himself. "How are you feeling?"

"I'm not the one who was carried in here, white as death! How are you feeling, Quin?"

"It takes a lot to kill a wizard," he replied with a crooked smile.

"My research assistant, the wizard," sighed Katerin, shaking her head at him. "I wish I understood you, Quin."

"I may devote myself to the fulfillment of your wish, Professor, even if it takes a lifetime or two."

A gray-haired servant scurried along the corridor, observed Katerin and Quin, and hastened to the stairs, muttering to herself. Quin took Katerin's arm, pulled her into his room, and closed the door. "We must not shock the servants," he informed her with a grin. "By Seriin standards, that Network gauze you wear is utterly improper, especially in the presence of a man who is not your husband. I might have to marry you just to save your honor."

"What makes you think I'd even consider marrying you, Quin Hamley?" demanded Katerin.

"Because I'm the only man who can enable you to continue your Network research? You will need my peculiar rapport with Network computers if you ever expect to walk safely in Network again. I'll have to keep shifting our identities faster than Network can find us, unless I want to make a career of taunting Caragen. Laurett will need a more flexible home, as well. I am not sure I know how to bring her here, since she seems to require a lot of accessories that Serii lacks, but I shall study the problem."

"What am I to think of you, Quin?"

He took her face in his hands and did not let her turn from him. "You already know what I want you to think—and what I want you to feel for me. You are the expert: How would you advise me to proceed?"

"A wise adviser would tell you to find someone better able to receive what you offer. I cannot love as you wish."

Quin studied her, his gray eyes narrowed. "You may deceive yourself, Katerin, but you cannot lie to Power. You are in love with me."

"I know," she whispered, "but I am also afraid of you."

Quin shook his head at her. "Between us, we should certainly be able to resolve that small obstacle. Just keep reminding yourself that I am your helpless, fumbling assistant, who bombards you with idiotic questions."

"Did you really destroy the Council Governor's ship by your wizard's Power?"

"Who told you?"

"Marrach."

"Clearly a troublemaker."

Katerin laughed, and Quin pulled her close. "You do not know what you're risking," she murmured, "loving a manipulator like me." She returned his kiss passionately, and Power did not let her fear.

CHAPTER 6

Network

"Network," said Caragen quietly, "provide assessment."

"You have gained an enemy."

"Obviously," snapped Caragen. He tried to lean back in the chair, upholstered with the skin of some alien reptile, but the chair did not adapt smoothly, and he cursed it. "A man of power must expect to have enemies," growled Caragen, "just as he must know how to deal with them. Marrach is my proven enemy. Several of my fellow Network Councillors are my enemies, and even my loyal Maryta merits close watching. The Calongi and every member of their confounded Consortium are my enemies. We respect each other's strengths and watch for weaknesses."

Caragen studied the cold Council room and frowned. Until his new space yacht was complete, he was condemned to such unpleasant environs. His tastes were very specialized.

"Yes," he muttered, making his conclusion in unhappy assessment of a geological display that he considered trite. "Categorize Network-3 as merely another of the same breed. Such contentious elements add challenge to an otherwise tedious existence, but they do not threaten my authority."

Network reacted to the single debatable conclusion. "Magnitude of threat from Network-3 increases risk factor beyond acceptable levels for maintenance of present authority."

Caragen frowned. "Specify recommendations."

"Full destruction of Network-3 is highly desirable but unfeasible without further research. Recommend revival of four key technical projects terminated by Network-3 cataclysm. Future destruction of Network-3 should be achievable via controlled re-creation and extension of these projects."

"Which projects?"

"Development of controller technology to transfer massive energy sources. Development of high-efficiency shielding methods for topological controllers and related mechanisms. Analysis of neural and physiological requirements imposed by hypothesized existence of psychic abilities. Assessment of life-extension properties associated with modification of neural signal processing capabilities."

Caragen pursed his lips thoughtfully. "If we created a new batch of Immortals, could we control them any better than we handled the first?"

"Genetic imprint of Citizen Quin Hamley offers significant research value, increasing probability of success to eighty-three percent."

A significant pause ensued. "Select tentative research teams for each of the recommended subject areas, Network. I shall make the final member approvals myself. I want no dangerous independents like Jonathan Terry again."

"Acknowledged."

EPILOGUE

Where do I belong now? Neither the unbending noble domains of Serii nor the coldly superior Network recognizes a proper role for a hybrid, which is what I have become. I belong with Katerin—but my Seriin half still disconcerts her at times.

Network does not, of course, equate me with the "Quin Hamley" who first attended Harberg, nor is Katerin encumbered by her past as Katerin Merel/Kitri Terry. Network's vastness is my salvation; by altering a digit of a code in Network's memory, I create another person, a legitimate Network citizen unassociated with Immortal wizards, Jon Terry, Rabh Marrach, or a world known as Network-3.

Lady Rhianna maintains that I comprise a critical element in the necessary restoration of Network-3. The domain lords and the Queen's Council members are less convinced that such change will ever occur, and they would fight the prospect actively if they understood it. Ixaxis remains divided, but I am no longer the only emissary: All twelve of the Terrys' original students have now made the journey. Alvedre studies medicine at a Network university, and others of us have similar assignments.

Jon and Beth Terry travel between Serii and Neoterra by his modification of the Widowshear in linkage with the Taormin. Michael is designing the Neoterra complex for a sizable population, and Loisa plans her daughter's future as if Neoterra had the resources of Network, but the colony grows slowly. We contact even the Terrys' old friends with great caution. We always seek Marrach's advice before making a final selection for the colony, because no one knows better than Marrach the devious methods of Network and Andrew Caragen.

By Marrach's teachings, I often read Network's recommendations as Caragen hears them, and I sense his questions via Network's sensors. He does not know that my liege-lady discusses his every mention of us with her ghostly husband. We accept the gift of our adversary's cunning advice. We respect our enemy's strengths and watch for his weaknesses. We learn.

I realize that I succeeded a little too well in establishing Network's respect of Power. Network ranks us as nearly the Consortium's equal, which would be laughable if it were less troubling. We are small and few beside the vastness of Network, which is itself a minor society compared to the alien Consortium. We do not delude ourselves that we could threaten Network, even if we had such ambitions. We are, nonetheless, a formidable alliance, as Lord Arineuil is fond of saying. We can defend our right to exist.

DAW

Cheryl J. Franklin

The Tales of the Taormin:

☐ **FIRE GET: Book 1** (UE2231—$3.50)
☐ **FIRE LORD: Book 2** (UE2354—$3.95)

Serii was a land whose people, once enslaved by sorcery, had sworn never to let magic rule their lives again. But despite all their safeguards, Serii is once again on the brink of a spell-fueled war that could destroy the kingdom. And only three gifted with Power, Lord Venkarel, Lary Rhianna, and their son, have any hope of stopping the ancient sorcerer who seeks to use the forces of the Taormin matrix to break free of his magical prison and wreak his vengeance on all of Serii.

The Network/Consortium Novels:

☐ **THE LIGHT IN EXILE** (UE2417—$3.95)

Down through the centuries, the warlike Adraki had roved the starways, destroying world after world and race after race in their desperate search for the Mirlai, the symbiontic race which had abandoned them millennia ago. Now their attention had focused on the low-tech colony world of Siatha. But Siatha was a world controlled by the human-run Network, and Caragen, head of the Network Council, had plans of his own for both the colony and the Adraki. Yet neither Caragen nor the Adraki realized that Siatha would prove more of a challenge than it seemed—the challenge of a power as alien and uncontrollable as the dreaded Adraki themselves!

DAW

Charles Ingrid

THE MARKED MAN SERIES

☐ **THE MARKED MAN** (UE2396—$3.95)
In a devastated America, can the Lord Protector of a mutating human race find a way to preserve the future of the species?

☐ **THE LAST RECALL** (UE2460—$3.95)
Returning to a radically-changed Earth, would the generational ships aid the remnants of a mutated human race—or seek their future among the stars?

THE SAND WARS

☐ **SOLAR KILL: Book 1** (UE2391—$3.95)
He was the last Dominion Knight and he would challenge a star empire to gain his revenge!

☐ **LASERTOWN BLUES: Book 2** (UE2393—$3.95)
He'd won a place in the Emperor's Guard but could he hunt down the traitor who'd betrayed his Knights to an alien foe?

☐ **CELESTIAL HIT LIST: Book 3** (UE2394—$3.95)
Death stalked the Dominion Knight from the Emperor's Palace to a world on the brink of its prophesied age of destruction. . . .

☐ **ALIEN SALUTE: Book 4** (UE2329—$3.95)
As the Dominion and the Thrakian empires mobilize for all-out war, can Jack Storm find the means to defeat the ancient enemies of man?

☐ **RETURN FIRE: Book 5** (UE2363—$3.95)
Was someone again betraying the human worlds to the enemy—and would Jack Storm become pawn or player in these games of death?

☐ **CHALLENGE MET: Book 6** (UE2436—$3.95)
In this concluding volume of *The Sand Wars,* Jack Storm embarks on a dangerous mission which will lead to a final confrontation with the Ash-farel.

DAW

"Marvelous . . . impressive . . . fascinating . . .
Melanie Rawn is good!"   —Anne McCaffrey

Melanie Rawn

THE DRAGON PRINCE NOVELS

☐ **DRAGON PRINCE: Book 1**   (UE2450—$4.95)
He was the Dragon Lord, Rohan, prince of the desert, ruler of
the kingdom granted his family for as long as the Long Sands
spewed fire. She was the Sunrunner Witch, Sioned, fated by
Fire to be Rohan's bride. Together, they must fight desperately
to save the last remaining dragons, and with them, a secret
which might be the salvation of their people. . . .

☐ **THE STAR SCROLL: Book 2**   (UE2349—$4.95)
As Pol, prince, Sunrunner and son of High Prince Rohan, grew
to manhood, other young men were being trained for a bloody
battle of succession, youths descended from the former High
Prince Roelstra, whom Rohan had killed. Yet not all players in
these power games fought with swords. For now a foe van-
quished ages ago was once again growing in strength—a foe
determined to destroy Sunrunners and High Prince alike. and
the only hope of defeating this foe lay concealed in the long-
lost Star Scroll.

☐ **SUNRUNNER'S FIRE: Book 3**   (UE2403—$4.95)
It was the Star Scroll: the last repository of forgotten spells of
sorcery, the only surviving records of the ancient foe who had
nearly destroyed the Sunrunners. Now, even as Lord Andry
and Prince Pol begin to master these awesome powers, the
long-vanquished enemy is mobilizing to strike again. And soon
it will be hard to tell friend from foe as spell wars threaten to set
the land ablaze, and even the dragons soar the skies, inexora-
bly lured by magic's fiery call.